MISTER TOUCH

Also by Malcolm Bosse

STRANGER AT THE GATE
CAPTIVES OF TIME
FIRE IN HEAVEN
THE WARLORD
INCIDENT AT NAHA
THE MAN WHO LOVED ZOOS
THE JOURNEY OF TAO KIM NAM

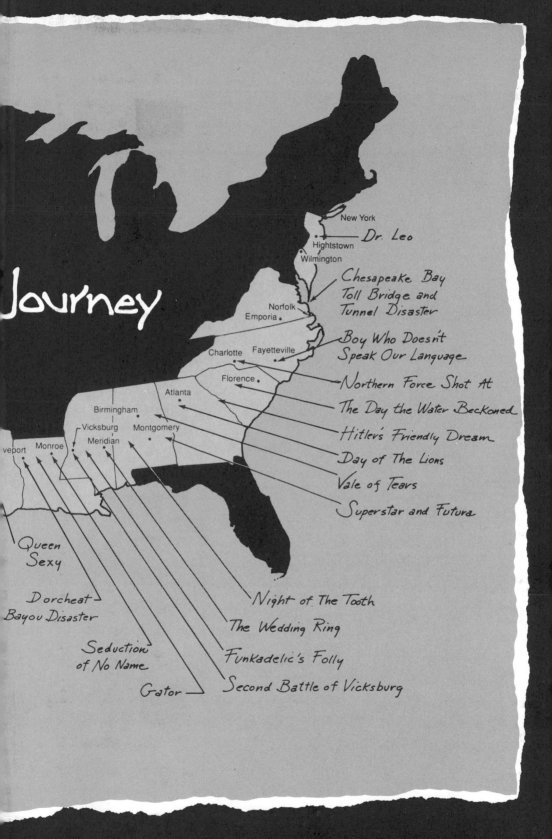

Journey

New York
Hightstown — Dr. Leo
Wilmington

Norfolk — Chesapeake Bay
Emporia — Toll Bridge and
Tunnel Disaster

Charlotte — Fayetteville — Boy Who Doesn't
Speak Our Language

Florence — Northern Force Shot At

Atlanta — The Day the Water Beckoned

Birmingham — Hitler's Friendly Dream

Vicksburg — Montgomery — Day of The Lions
Meridian — Vale of Tears

veport Monroe — Superstar and Futura

Queen
Sexy

Dorcheat — Night of The Tooth
Bayou Disaster

The Wedding Ring

Seduction — Funkadelic's Folly
of No Name

Gator — Second Battle of Vicksburg

MISTER TOUCH

MALCOLM BOSSE

TICKNOR & FIELDS
NEW YORK
1991

For information about permission to reproduce selections from this book, write to Permissions, Ticknor & Fields, Houghton Mifflin Company, 2 Park Street, Boston, Massachusetts 02108.

Library of Congress Cataloging-in-Publication Data

Bosse, Malcolm J. (Malcolm Joseph)
 Mister Touch / Malcolm Bosse.
  p.   cm.
 ISBN 0-89919-965-8
 I. Title.
PS 3552.077M5   1991   90-46780
813'.54 — dc20   CIP

Printed in the United States of America

AGM 10 9 8 7 6 5 4 3 2 1

Haiku by Matsuo Basho from *Japanese Literature*, Donald Keene, trans.; reprinted by permission of Grove Weidenfeld. Copyright © 1955 by Grove Press, Inc. "And Death Shall Have No Dominion," by Dylan Thomas, from *Poems by Dylan Thomas*. Copyright 1943 by New Directions Publishing Corporation. Reprinted by permission of New Directions Publishing Corporation.

Every effort has been made to obtain permission for use of copyrighted material. Any errors or omissions are unintentional, and corrections will be made in future printings if necessary.

Endpaper map by George Ward

For Lori and Fender with love

Though they go mad they shall be sane,
Though they sink through the sea they shall rise again;
Though lovers be lost love shall not;
And death shall have no dominion.

— DYLAN THOMAS

CONTENTS

ONE

THE SKULLS

1

ABOUT SIXTY PEOPLE have left an apartment building east of Washington Square Park in New York City.

They go by twos in a wobbly procession along the weed-choked sidewalk. Half a dozen Blindies are led by squinting companions. The caravan halts often to let Wheezers get their breath. Most of the marchers are young, about a dozen are middle-aged, a few have white hair. Most of the males carry rifles slung over their shoulders. Almost half of them carry portable spittoons — tincans dangling from their necks.

For protection against the autumn chill the men wear herringbone pea jackets, sheepskin coats with mottled lambskin collars, and nutria blazers. They shuffle forward in calfskins soled with lush crepe, in Bally shoes with tassels. Their mouths send out plumes of rapid breath; the exertion has many of them panting.

The females wear a spectacular array of jewelry that sparkles in the midday glare: ruby brooches, sapphire earrings, silver bracelets. Many hands are a dazzle of diamonds. The women and girls have draped themselves in mink, marten, in seal stoles, in fuzzy capes of houndstooth check. They sport a variety of headgear: floppy bonnets, plaid tams, Victorian sunhats, black bowlers, schoolboy caps, and purple sou'westers.

This procession of chaotic splendor reaches the edge of the park. Buildings on the Square have translated the autumn sunlight into their own varied hues, sending the luster of brick and metal back to the sky. Hawthorn and maple trees have not yet changed color. Dominating them is the elegant old arch with its two niched statues of George Washington — soldier and statesman who gave his name to this park — now given dirty white mantles of pigeon droppings. Pigeons are everywhere. They strut under the flagpole from which the Stars and Stripes yet hangs, stirred by a faint breeze into sluggish motion.

The pigeons peck at the limestone chess tables, heedless of a sign in block letters:

TABLES RESERVED FOR CHESS
AND CHECKER PLAYERS ONLY

Above them soars a squadron of gulls, having come from the Atlantic across the silent monoliths of Wall Street, across a jungle of smokeless chimneys, across deserted schoolyards and empty streets. Tumultuous in air, sparrows are skimming the weeds that encroach on every sidewalk. Birds tilt gracefully on the edge of another sign:

NO BONGO
& STEEL DRUM
PLAYING ALLOWED

Under the arch a large pack of dogs is gathering. They have smelled, then seen, the procession. An Irish setter leaves the growling melee and stares up Fifth Avenue, as if he can look beyond the miles of silence for a sign from his departed trainer that will tell him what to do. A poodle lifts his leg against a lamppost that hasn't felt the vibration of electricity in more than two years. Abruptly, as gulls flow overhead in ivory curves, the dogs turn toward the procession. Ears are up. A German shepherd growls deep in her throat, a sound copied by others until a hundred dogs are snarling, teeth bared, their scruffy bodies tense from the hunting lust. A Doberman barks. The whole pack leaps forward.

They congregate at an invisible barrier perhaps a dozen yards from the marchers where they circle and pace, working up courage to attack. A few maddened animals turn to nip their neighbors in a frenzy of predatory need.

A score of the men unsling their rifles, take casual aim, and fire. Half a dozen dogs are killed. A dozen others lie yelping and kicking, while the remainder of the pack spring away with tails curled under their pumping haunches.

One of the young men — he is black, as the majority are — mutters, "When they ever gonna learn?"

"When you learn they ain't ever gonna learn," says another, "is when somebody learn something."

Regrouping near the arch, the dogs are limp-eared and tame as they watch the procession worm its way through a sea of gray pigeons.

*　　*　　*

Having crossed the park, the faltering marchers approach an apartment building with a metal canopy, double doors — high rent for real. A young black wearing Perry Ellis corduroy pants, an Adolfo shirt, a cowboy hat, and huge sunglasses is guiding a blind white man, his prominent chin covered by a thick red beard, his tall frame spiffy in designer jeans, a pink sweater, an Alexander Julian herringbone jacket. The white Blindie is about thirty, somewhat older than the black dude leading him.

"Hoss, are we here?" the Blindie asks.

The black pushes back his cowboy hat, squints, and halts in front of the double doors. "We're here."

"We're waiting, Timbales," declares the Blindie, focusing his sightless eyes above the crowd.

A small teenage Latino shuffles forward when someone in the crowd gives him a push. His lips tremble in a narrow face. He has a scraggly goatee, slim hips, watery eyes.

Some of the people have raised their binoculars to observe him enter the building. But he doesn't go in, and says to the blind man, "You got it wrong. I don't have no cold, I got runny nose. Only like that."

While he is convincing no one that he hasn't got a cold — he has a beaut for real — two white guys are hauling into the dark foyer a wagon (a red wagon they found in a toy store and use for this purpose) filled with canned goods and a pile of blankets, a lot of tapes, two Walkmen, extra batteries, a rifle, medicine, and a flashlight. One of them says, "Here's your stuff, Timbales."

Timbales ignores the wagon. "Prez, how 'bout it, are you listening?" he says to the blind man. "I got no cold no shit. People lying. I got sniffles. Yeah, right, I got 'em, eso sí, I don't do no lying to you, honest. I got sniffles, only like that."

"Timbales, you got no behavior!" someone shouts in an Island accent.

People start chanting, "Go in, Timbales, *go in!* Go in, Timbales, *go in!*"

This only frightens him more. He hugs his hands in his armpits.

"Go in, Timbales, *go in!*"

Sniffling, he wipes his nose on his sleeve, keeping his hands hidden.

Someone yells, "Go in, man, we all got to go in sometime!"

Timbales searches the crowd to locate that voice. "Fuck you!"

he shouts. "Basta ya! Don't go laying a cold on me when I never had one and you lying!"

"Go in, Timbales, *go in!* Go in, Timbales, *go in!*" The loud chanting ends for many of them in breathlessness.

Reaching out as if to touch Timbales, the blind man says firmly, "Go in, guy."

It is a gentle enough command, but reduces the boy to tears. He squats childishly in front of the double doors, hands snug in his armpits.

Some of the spectators, embarrassed and frightened by his fear, turn away, but others call out angrily, "Go in, Timbales, you hard-on, GO IN!"

Two middle-aged women wince at the obscenity and extricate themselves from the yelling crowd. They stand on the perimeter, both wearing beige suits with brass buttons and white-trimmed pockets, each carrying quilted leather handbags. Unlike their younger companions they share a pulled-together look. They establish for themselves a power look. They have often told each other you can be just right with nothing more than collarless cardigan-style jackets and brass buttons; you can look dressed. But today, forced to join the procession that brings Timbales across the park, the slimmer woman (though they are both plump) can't take satisfaction from anything, not even clothes. "Every day I ask myself is this real? Am I dreaming? Why should I give one thought to what I wear?"

"No good will come of that attitude," says her heavier companion. "It's important to keep up appearances."

"As to that, I can't concentrate."

"Why not?" asks the heavier. "We always have. I was thinking only this morning I'm no longer comfortable with Chanel. That is, I don't take it verbatim anymore."

The slimmer woman turns to the crowd shouting at the reluctant Latino. A Bad Looker, she sees them at twenty yards away as dusky shapes in blurred motion.

"You can mix Chanel," suggests her companion, "with other things like Sonia Rykiel knits and Patrick Kelly."

The slimmer woman leans slightly forward to squint at a black girl nearby who is wearing a fur coat. "Look at that coat," the woman says, shaking her head. "Even I can see it is *perilously* expensive, but the girl hasn't a clue to its value. Some years ago I was talked into seeing that trashy film *The Road Warrior*, and I remember thinking at the time, what a terrible way to live! I remember saying you can tell these people are maniacs from the way they dress. And here we are, living that film."

"Not really. It's not a fair comparison," argues her companion. "Admittedly, some of us have poor taste. But we're still civilized, we still have our dignity. We aren't animals." She added thoughtfully, "Some of these young people have a flair for clothes."

The slimmer woman stares from her bad-looking eyes at the black girl in a cream beige Rovalia mink by Giorgio Sant'Angelo with pleated shoulders and a rolled wing collar. "Not that she can't afford mink or diamonds or anything else she wants in the world we live in. She merely needs a hammer to break a store window so she can climb through and take whatever catches her eye. I'm sorry, but I can't get used to it."

"Used to her wearing something so pricey or used to the world we live in?"

This question receives no answer, as the slimmer woman turns toward the wailing sounds of the Latino begging not to go in.

Hatless, the woman smoothes her hair back with both hands, then with a sigh of resignation drops them from her face, knocking against the tincan that hangs around her neck along with two gold chains. "I like pulling my hair back," she says, "with a black gros-grain bow."

"Your hair looks good that way," her companion says politely.

"I like to take off small earrings for evening and put on big gold ones. Of course, sling-back pumps like these" — she extends one foot to admire the black patent toe — "are a statement both day and night. I thought that way before V 70 Struck and I still do. Some things don't change."

"You see? Keeping up appearances is what we must do." The heavier woman turns to regard the gaudily dressed crowd, then smiles. "What we all must do. However we choose to do it."

The slimmer frowns. "Sometimes I get the peculiar feeling you enjoy this sort of life. I don't see how that's possible, and it's certainly nothing I would want to discuss because it would merely upset me, but the truth is you seem happy at times. I find that remarkable."

At the apartment house entrance, rocking back and forth, Timbales whimpers that he is scared shitless of going in there and staying like that by his own self and if he can only hang out awhile in his room or en el peor de los casos maybe on a higher floor away from everybody else but like still in the building, and he won't leave his room nunca till the thing, the fucking cold, the mierda sniffle go away —

Timbales is still stammering promises when a couple of muscular young men lift and carry him inside the building. It's a long time before they emerge again, panting.

"We got him up on the third floor, Mister Touch," one says to the blind whitey who has been stroking his red beard anxiously.

The whole crowd squints up at an open window on the third floor. Presently the young Latino leans from it, tearfully screaming that he can't like stand it alone by his own self for two weeks in this lonely place, not two *days*, man, not for no mierda cold that is nothing no shit but sniffle, only like that, no tiene sentido, and if they could put him somewhere out of the way, he promise on his mother grave, on the holy grave of his mother, until the cold go away he won't put no foot from the room. He is still yelling at the procession when it re-forms and shuffles past the park fountain on the way home.

"Hear him, bro?" says a boy in a wool tam and billowy Miami Vice pants. "Swearing on his mother's grave? Only she don't have no grave. Do your mother?"

"No," says the one he's leading by the elbow past the line of snarling dogs.

"See what I'm saying? Mine never have none either. I never even seen where she was when she kicked off and nobody was going to get her to a grave less it was one they be sharing, right? I bet you never seen yours dead neither or least you never seen anything done about burying her."

"Yeah, sure. Me and millions never saw nothing done. So what else is new."

"I bet most Skulls don't have mothers with graves."

"What else is new."

"Timbales just wanting sympathy. Swearing on his mother's grave when she don't have none."

"Timbales be plain yellow. He know when you get a cold you go across and stay till it dry up."

"Yeah, but some don't see a reason to go like that."

"Where do they get off complaining like that? IRT figured it out. So we do it."

"You got it, bro. We don't need colds in our lungs. IRT used to say that. Nobody better go around arguing about what IRT he said."

"I hear Sister Love coming down with something worser than cold."

"I heard too."

"Could be V 70 coming back."

"Nah."

"Could be."

"Don't fucking yell it out, man. Get your ass in bad shit talking low."

"Who we kidding? Taki sick too. So is Bobby Loves It. They be on the way out."

"Hey, man, have the bug come back on us?"

"Who could say one way or other."

They trudge awhile in silence. Finally in a burst of compassion one of them says, "Ah, the poor miserable fuck —"

The other nods solemnly, as they both imagine the poor miserable Hispanic turkey up there all alone in a dark building, sniffling and popping antihistamines and ramming steroid nose sprays up his nostrils and blowing his nose by candlelight, all there by his own self alone, sitting knees-up and whimpering in a corner because he fears ghosts and getting ready to bawl like a baby, going to make as much noise as he can get out of his lungs because loneliness is worser than anything you can have, bien puede usted de cirlo, worser than anything, worser than pistol whip or burn with cigarettes, but do the world care what he be facing, no it don't care, the injustice and plain shit of it and the bad luck, just like those dogs lying gutshot in the park, waiting for their buddies to get hungry enough to come eat them.

MISTER TOUCH was main man of the Skulls, the prez, even though he was a Blindie and a whitey at that. His red beard had not brought him to this eminence, nor had his six feet five inches catapulted him so high. He had been appointed main man by the former main man, IRT, now deceased. Mister Touch's detractors claimed that he had won IRT's respect by having committed white-collar crimes on Wall Street before V 70 Struck. Then there were advocates who maintained that the whitey got the job by proving to IRT he was not only criminally clever but also a survivor for real.

When the Skulls returned to the Club House from putting Timbales in isolation across the park, Mister Touch sat in his room and fumbled for his battery-operated cassette player. Seated at his desk, he leaned back and listened to the strange twitterings and disjointed melodic line of Scriabin's tenth sonata for piano. In recent months he had worked through early Mozart string quartets, symphonies from Haydn's late period, and all thirty-two Beethoven piano sonatas. After Scriabin he was going to backtrack and take on the Bach cantatas. One unexpected windfall from V 70: the dread of obsessing about it had encouraged him to put his mind elsewhere by pursuing a hobby.

But today he couldn't listen to music. Quarantining the little Hispanic had deafened him to everything but an interior voice which kept warning him that the Skulls were in deep trouble.

He imagined his face must look tense and frowning. He hadn't seen it now for about half a year. The last time his failing eyes had squinted into a mirror he'd seemed more like twenty-five than thirty-five. Today he must look a lot older. He *felt* a lot older. Three people were seriously ill of unknown causes, so it was just possible that V 70 or some version of it had returned to finish the job.

Turning off the music, the Skull leader sat in silence. He tried to picture himself a few years ago in Shep Miller suspenders, a blue worsted suit, gold tiepin, chunky cufflinks: the Wall Street image of a young man not on his way up but already there looking down. Until recently this image used to sadden him with its how-are-the-mighty-fallen message, but nowadays he felt well rid of the past. He was one of the fortunate few who had benefited from absolute catastrophe. After all, when V 70 Struck, it had kept him from going to jail.

The truth was he felt scared and depressed. Without Scriabin or Bach or Haydn filling the room with sound, he was forced to listen to the apocalyptic voice within. It was like a drum warning the village of an attack on one of those Saturday morning TV shows he had watched as a kid. Ever since taking over from IRT, he had managed to make leadership a low-key job, in part because he feared competing with IRT's memory and in part because life for the Skulls, if not exactly paradisal, had gone rather smoothly during last spring and summer. He had relaxed like a club-house politician who jollies his constituency while raking in the dough. He also saw himself in a more positive way, as someone who knew when to let well enough alone. But the truth for real surged back on him. He had watched the Skulls come reeling out of the catastrophe like stunned boxers, with IRT there to maneuver around them like a wily trainer, keeping them in the fight. Now there was no more IRT, and Mister Touch didn't know what to do.

In the silence of his room he listened to the interior voice (deep baritone with black accents) admonishing him more bluntly. "Get up, goddammit, bro, and get at it!" the voice of IRT declared. "Don't matter what you do so long as it done! Get up and do something right the fucking *now*!"

Urged by this bellowing voice, Mister Touch obeyed a sudden impulse to do something he hadn't thought through. He felt wildly around in the desk drawer until locating a cassette tape. Inserting it in the player, he said out loud to the voice of IRT within his head, "All right! Let me alone! I'm doing something!" He waited, and when the voice didn't protest his decision, Mister Touch hit the RECORD button.

"Are you . . . out there?" he asked in a shrill, tentative voice. "Whoever you are? Hello! Hello there, Whoever you are!" He paused, feeling calmer. "Whoever you are, you should listen to me because I'm a survivor. That's what I am, a survivor, and who knows, what I tell you might come in handy someday. What I survived you may or may not know about. But apparently I am going to tell you about it anyway." He paused briefly, giving IRT a chance to stop him. Silence encouraged him to go on. "Whoever you are, *if* you are, you can call me Mister Touch. I lead a hundred and fifty people who call themselves the Skulls in emulation of a New York street gang that used to spray their names on subway cars back when the world was ignorant of V 70. This is what I'm saying. We live in the empty canyons of New York along with a bunch of pets turned scavengers and more pigeons than this former city of ten million people had ever seen."

He felt he wasn't expressing himself logically but went on anyway, fired by relating the Skulls' history. "Some of us are getting sick and winter is coming and that's scary and people are feeling so damn lonely some of them are losing it and —"

Hearing a dull thudding sound repeated three times, he paused the recording. "Come in," he said.

"It's Coco, Mister Touch."

"How are you feeling?"

"Getting scared."

He couldn't blame her for that: a Poor Breather almost nine months pregnant. "You shouldn't be scared," he assured her. "Jesus Mary will be there when you go into labor."

"Yeah," Coco said cheerlessly.

"Are you doing exercises?"

"Can't do much. Jesus Mary say I got to go easy."

"Then do what she says."

"I don't want that natural childbirth stuff. I wanna be knocked out."

"What does Jesus Mary say?"

"She say I can't be knocked out. My heart could quit."

"She'll give you some kind of painkiller. You'll be fine, Coco."

There was a long silence. In the half year since Mister Touch passed over from Bad Looker to Blindie, he had convinced himself that his hearing had become preternaturally sharp so that he could hear Neat Breathers breathing their quiet breaths with the loud clear definition of a grandfather clock ticking. Of course, his new-found compensatory skill could be an illusion. What he heard now in the silence might not be Coco's erratic breathing at all, but the sound of his own pessimism about the future.

"I been thinking about Snooky," the girl declared.

Snooky's baby, born dead a month ago, had its umbilical cord wrapped around its neck.

"What happened to Snooky's baby," said Mister Touch, "had nothing to do with V 70. It was an accident. It could have happened before V 70 Struck."

"I don't know nothing about that. All I know is her baby born dead."

He extended his hands across the desk, keeping them there until she gripped them in hers. "We're all counting on you, Coco. You're our hope."

He heard her sigh. "Seem like I needed a talk. I thank you."

Letting go of her hands, he heard her slow footsteps move across the room and the door open, shut. What he had just done would not have been possible for him a few years ago when he concentrated on selecting a cigar cutter and stared through the plate glass of his Wall Street office across the water to the Statue of Liberty with a young man's pride of universal ownership. What had counted then was drinks at Harry's Bar and discussions of arbitrage with other arbs who also believed that the cosmos was nothing more than a giant trading house.

Just now he had soothed a frightened black girl with his touch. If V 70 hadn't Struck, he might never have soothed anyone with his touch except a good-looking fox in her bed or his after a steak dinner and a few tokes of a joint. V 70 had made a man of him, and maybe now, facing a doubtful future, it was going to make more than a man of him. He had an awakening sense of being tested. It reminded him of IRT about a year ago. Having just improvised a clever way of getting One Of The Lost Ones back among the Skulls and functioning for real, IRT had turned to him and said, "We gonna be new people, we gotta do it to it in a new way, man. Necessity is the great big mamma of invention."

Next morning the main man recorded one side of a ninety-minute tape without interruption. This time he lectured from a plan, assuming for this purpose a kind of jocular delivery, because Whoever You Are might be put off by an account emphasizing the sheer thudding horror of it.

Mister Touch began with the idea of a virus; after all, Whoever You Are might be ignorant of such earthly things. He explained that a virus could enter the human bloodstream like a thief in the night, steal away a few cells or possibly a whole life. It could give you the sniffles or the long good night. Before V 70 Struck, another dangerous virus for real, called the Human Immunodeficiency Virus, HIV, had spread from Africa throughout the world and caused terrible suffering.

Despite its destructiveness, however, it merely paved the way for V 70, which some scientists felt was an offshoot of the HIV AIDS virus. V 70 remained dormant and hidden in millions of bodies, as happy as a clam for months or maybe years. "Epidemiologists didn't have time to study its mechanism," Mister Touch pointed out dryly. Apparently the virus was waiting for something to trigger it.

And something finally did.

Each of these tiny killers, its internal alarm going off with commando precision, simultaneously converted a part of itself into a molecule within the body of every human being on earth. Upon viral command, lo! each cell produced more viruses and more and more until quadrillions of cells were infected, and there you were, explained Mister Touch to Whoever You Are, we had fucking had it. The immune system which had protected us for thousands of years simply failed. V 70, a brilliantly designed assassin, mutated at remarkable speed. It used immunological tricks to confuse and render senseless the T cells that were the last bastion of defense, Mister Touch said into the recorder. There was no vaccine available. Nothing could be done by virologists and toxologists because they were coming down sick like everyone else.

Mister Touch wiped the sweat from his forehead. He trembled from describing an event that had finished off most of humankind in a matter of weeks — ghastly proof that the species had no more protection against these tiny bugs than a fly has against a sledgehammer.

"When V 70 Struck," he went on, "I was living in Greenwich Village. Perhaps that means nothing to you, but I haven't time to explain. Maybe I haven't time for much of anything." He detected in his voice the self-pity that every Skull was pledged to guard against. "Well, enough of that," he said more forcefully. "At the time I had just bought a three-hundred-thousand-dollar condo. I was on top of the world financially. Then the day of the first news broadcast about V 70 I also heard I could go to jail because of an insider-trading deal. Next morning all hell broke loose. I mean, throughout the world. V 70 Struck in Rome, Cairo, Beijing, Iowa

City — various kinds of flu and pneumonia, new strains of yellow fever and polio and a virulent chicken pox and measles and a malignant gastroenteritis and a fatal mononucleosis and rampant new things causing blindness and emphysema and heart failure and cancers unlike any previous malignancies — fulminating illnesses that could waste a human system in weeks, even days. And it was happening everywhere. And there was no help. Hospitals? Forget it. Most people decided to die at home.

"I was hit late. I had symptoms associated with one of the new diseases called Jakarta flu. I might last for quite a while, so on my last legs I got some food in. The fridge worked. I had light, although it hurt my eyes. I lay in darkness and listened to gunfire, some of it from cops rousting out looters who could still get around, but most of the firing came from suicides. It was obvious to everyone that the end was near. Once, running a high fever, I got up to urinate and discovered there were no lights in the building anymore and the toilet didn't flush. When I got sicker and couldn't swallow easily, I was afraid of strangling so I found my biggest kitchen knife and put it on the bedside table. That night it was dark and silent except for screams and gunfire. I felt a heaviness in my chest, my throat constricting, and I reached for the knife many times, but drew back for fear the blade wouldn't go in right. I despised myself for lacking the foresight to buy a gun. And while I kept thinking about the gun I didn't have and the knife I couldn't trust I also began to feel hungry. Then sweat poured from me when the fever broke. What the hell, I just might live a while longer."

Mister Touch turned off the recorder.

This was hard work. Like the majority of Skulls he functioned pretty well most of the time, excluding the time of nightmare, of course, when the deep bugaboo descended on minds made vulnerable by drowsiness so that old memories sat between their eyes like demons and forced them to remember. They had a rule never to talk about the days just before and the days just after V 70 Struck, and although the rule was often and even openly broken, a head-on collision with life as it had once been lived was too painful for most Skulls to endure. Recording their history was also illegal according to IRT's policy of ignoring "the old people" and avoiding the past. Providing a Skull history was Mister Touch's first independent act of leadership since becoming prez. And without IRT's exhortation *to do something* (even if coming from the world of the dead) Mister Touch might never have found in himself what IRT had suspected was always there — the guts to do something.

Someone was knocking on the door again.

"Come in."

"It's Hoss."

Mister Touch had strong visual recall of some people, blurred memory of others, and none at all of those who had joined the Skulls after his eyesight failed. He had a vivid memory of Hoss: a well-built handsome young black man with wraparound shades and a cowboy hat that belied his former career as vice president of an ad agency. Mister Touch could still picture the graceful walk, the ironic smile, the hip presence that Hoss must have used to good advantage on Madison Avenue.

"Sister Love is worse," Hoss said.

"Does it look like V 70?"

"Jesus Mary says no. But she could be wrong or lying. She argues that V 70 wouldn't behave this way. More of us would already be sick. This lingering sort of thing doesn't fit the pattern. That's her story." After a pause Hoss added, "Let's face it, it could be a version of V 70. At any rate, she doesn't think Sister Love will make it."

"The other two?"

Hoss shook his head. When Mister Touch continued to wait for an answer, Hoss remembered a headshake didn't count with the prez. "She doesn't think they'll make it either."

"What a lovely day."

"We need medical supplies."

"Where's the nearest pharmacy now?"

"On Twelfth and University Place. I scheduled a team for the expedition: Cougar, Turok, Superstar, Web, and Shag."

"Is Web still gaining weight?"

"Web can't help gaining weight when he's in love."

"Does Flash like his boyfriends fat?"

"Not until Web came into his life. But Web wasn't fat then. He only became fat on love and candy bars. I understand Flash has tried to put him on a diet, but the more in love Web feels the more chocolate he stows away."

"I'm afraid it'll end badly. You put Shag on the list. Is that a good idea? I hear he complains about the Dope Rule — wants it suspended or something."

"Shall I cross him off?"

The prez thought about it. "No. Give him the benefit of the doubt. Let's see what he's made of."

"When they return, we'll search him for pills. If he's ever going to hold, that's when he'll do it."

"Am I wrong, Hoss? Wasn't there more tension than usual when we went across the park today?"

"Much more than usual."

"Why?"

"Maybe it's fear of winter coming. Then there's the dogs. More of them every day."

"There was no reason for shooting them in the park. Did anyone give the order?"

"No. It was just one of those extemporaneous things. You get some Looney Tunes together, they feel brave. One more thing. Cola Face has a complaint. It seems that Ace got her in a corner and demanded sex. Told her he has special privileges because he's a Neat Looker."

"Can't he get what he wants elsewhere?"

"He wants Cola Face because he thinks she's hard to get."

"Bring me Ace."

When Mister Touch heard the door shut, he hit the RECORD button again.

"When I felt hungry and started sweating, I wondered if there was a chance I might live. Getting up, I opened a can of beans that tasted so good I was sure I *wanted* to live. Testing responses, I jogged in place a minute, which had me panting. Even so, I learned my lung damage was not serious. I'd be a Steady Breather."

Although Mister Touch did not know it, the sun had slipped behind the steel canyon of New York, moving like a gently lobbed yellow ball across horizon after empty horizon toward the other coast.

Initially he had been able to see, Mister Touch explained to Whoever You Are. His eyesight had been greatly impaired, but when he leaned from the window of his condo and stared at the opposite building, his eyes discerned a network of gray smudges on a rectangular shape. It heartened him to see a brick wall.

In a few days he felt strong enough to leave the apartment.

There was no one on the street. Only a few people had been out before he got sick, and now there was no one. The silence felt as if it had weight; later he would understand that every survivor experienced this same sensation — the lack of sound as something heavy, like New York City on a humid day. He shuffled down the street until he noticed a thing sticking out of a parked car — getting closer he saw it was a head lolling through an open window. Bending down, squinting, he saw a young couple in the front seat. Flies were traveling in and out of the man's open mouth; a needle was still in the girl's arm. Jumping back from the scene, he felt something move against the calf of his right leg, causing him to cry out in fear. He lurched against the car and buried his head against the hood, expecting the worst whatever that might be. Then something moved against his ankle, rhythmically. It didn't hurt, so he turned and looked down.

A fluffy Angora.

For a moment he nearly kicked the cat, jealous of its genetics, but it was purring and swishing and doubling back, arching against his calf. He picked it up — soft, warm, a living thing that brought tears to his eyes. The finely tuned motor of its body hummed against his hands. He cried like a lost child.

Getting control of himself, still holding the cat, he walked slowly toward Washington Square Park, only a few blocks from his condo. As he walked he thought of people, even though it was the last thing in the world he wanted to do. He thought of his parents dead in their Des Moines bedroom in the early days of V 70, of his brother killed in a car crash years ago, of a girl and another girl, both of whom he had once loved, but where they had died he would never know, and he thought of college friends, of business associates, of neighborhood characters like the butcher who wore a straw hat. He thought of his great-aunt smoking cigars at ninety-two.

All gone.

And he stood in the middle of New York City gripping to his chest an uncombed Angora.

And then he heard the sound of a drum.

3

WHILE THE PREZ was talking history, in another part of the Club House two live ones came together for a rap.

"Guess where me and Cougar been," said the dude with a bandanna wrapped around his head, topped by a black bowler. He tossed his denim jacket on the bed. "Over to see Timbales."

The other dude sat in a chair with his long legs crossed over the side of a Chippendale settee. He was listening to hip-hop music on a beat box. "Yeah? You been over there?"

"Prez say go over and say hi to the poor miserable fuck."

"Timbales okay?"

"Complaining."

"Sure, that him."

"Telling us bodies was up there."

"Did he figure on living blondes?"

"Last time I had myself a cold and stayed over there, there was no bodies left on the low floors. We had cleared them out, remember?"

"Trying to forget."

"Timbales the dumb fuck go climbing to a high floor where sure he found bodies."

"You mean bones."

"So when we shout at him from the street he complaining about bodies."

"That be that bozo."

"Yeah, but don't lean on Timbales. Lonely over there."

"But we all done it. Anyone with a cold have. Nothing so special about that bozo he can't do it too." Dude tossed his bowler on the bed and stretched out beside it. "What you got playing right now? Why not put on some rap like Rakim, Kool Moe Dee."

"Don't you hear what's playing? You don't know nothing you don't move with Miami Sound Machine." Lustily he sang along with the tape: "Bad bad bad bad bad boy, you make me feel so good!"

Dude on the bed gave a fretful sigh. "Sister Love sick for real. Maybe we gonna conk out too. Know what I'm saying, homeboy?

What gonna happen do the Neat Lookers conk out? Like we can't read nothing, we can't get around. We gone then for sure. I be talking about King Super Kool and Tangy and Ace and Evil Eye. Do they conk out."

"They ain't everything. Mystique can read like them."

"Bullshit. Only with a magnifying glass she can."

"So can Funkadelic."

"Yeah? While he going round like a zombie?"

"Hitler can."

"Hitler ain't no Neat Looker for real."

"He can read big letters. So can Web."

"There you dead wrong. That big fat jive turkey just fronting. Web make something up and tell you he be reading it and you believe him."

"Yeah? He be going on expeditions just like you. He can see to shoot."

"So can I. Which is why they get me to go through a park full of wild dogs, just to keep a poor miserable fuck like Timbales from going nuts when he think some people dead a few years be sharing a building with him."

"You talk like you the onliest one who went across that park."

"Stuff it, homes."

"You saying you can shoot, but I wouldn't be standing near when *you* had a gun in your hand." Dude in the chair recrossed his legs on the arm of the settee, a vague gesture of triumph. "You wouldn't know man from building."

"Don't fuck with me, homes, I was raised hard."

The threat mounting in his voice was canceled by a new and terrible sound. A wail of pain curled up like smoke from the room below, followed by a scream coming through the floorboards with the crackle of a brush fire.

"Holy shit," muttered the dude in the chair. Pulling his long legs back, he set his feet solidly on the carpet and stared at its pattern.

The room below had been designated as the delivery room. "That be Coco down there. Bet she going in labor."

A cry licked up hotly at them.

Dude in the chair hit the PLAY button on his ghetto blaster so that Sheila E came rushing out at them from her *Sister Fate* album. But she wasn't loud enough to drown out the next yell.

"Got me one motherfucking headache," said the dude in the chair, staring gloomily at the carpet. "Sure could use some reefer now, just to take the edge off. Is Coco gonna make it? Or she gonna be like Snooky?"

"She got Jesus Mary by her."

"Don't mean she make it."

A shriek cleaved neatly through Sheila E's voice.

"Don't like the tune they playing down there. Pump up the volume. Listen to me, homes. If I be a fox, I would swallow me a whole box of birth control pills ever time I spread my legs. Good to be a man."

"Yeah. Snake he have the fun, now Coco down there paying for it. Do that baby live, Snake be the man of the hour. Only daddy for miles around, right?"

Another shriek.

Another.

"Wish we had water from a tap. Tired of hot Pepsi. Wish we could go to a tap and turn it on."

"Wishing don't make it so."

"Wish I could drink cold water from a fucking tap."

"Hey, you hear that?"

They both sat up straight.

"Wish I had me a jeep with one of them roll bars, so guys could hold on and we go rolling. Wish I had me a Whopper with lot of mustard on it."

"And fries."

"Wish I had me a ticket to the Mets."

Another shriek cut through the floorboards like a knife through butter.

"Holy shit."

"Yeah, I sure don't go for the tune she playing down there."

Dude on the bed, clutching his bowler, sat stiffly erect. "I could take my neighborhood any old way. Know what I'm saying? Guys got dusted, they got this narrow look in their eyes and you knew it be time to check out fast. I knew how to live with it. But the tune she playing down there, I can't listen to it no more. Pump up the volume, homes."

Send Em Back To Africa led the main man to the dispensary when Coco's labor began. It was long and difficult; Jesus Mary Save Souls was afraid to give her much meperidine because it might fatally depress her respiratory system.

While Mister Touch waited, someone came into the waiting room that had once been the living room and marital battleground of Joan and Jerry Glashow when he was cheating on her and she was going on retaliatory buying sprees at Bloomingdale's.

"It's me, Ace," a raspy voice announced at the main man's shoulder. "Want me for something?"

Mister Touch said, "Let's go where we can talk." He felt a bony hand on his arm as Ace guided him out of the dispensary. Mister Touch had never seen Ace, a newcomer, who from all accounts was a cranky twenty-year-old with red hair, acne, and bad teeth. "So why don't you tell me," the prez said when they halted down the hall, "all about you and Cola Face."

"What's to tell? Anyway, she's got a big mouth." Ace's voice came from far below the leader's chin. The kid was short.

"Did you tell Cola Face she had to sleep with you because you're a Neat Looker?"

"She told you that?" The kid blew his breath out in theatrical exasperation. "What I told her was she could show a little gratitude to a guy like me who was owed something."

"Owed what to whom?"

"Being I'm a Neat Looker I got to do the seeing for a lot of them around here."

"Good sight is a matter of luck, Ace."

"So is being white and having brains."

"Being white is no advantage anymore."

"Maybe if you wasn't blind you wouldn't say so. I guess color don't mean much to someone who can't see," said Ace.

That hurt. Mister Touch felt deeply vulnerable as his unseeing eyes swept the space below his chin, searching for the little shit who in the pre–V 70 world would have been a likely candidate for skinning his head and joining the New Reich. "Let's put it this way," said the prez. "If you don't like the way we do things, take your neat-looking eyes and go back where you came from."

"I don't do nothing wrong, but you got to come down on my case," the boy claimed, his voice furious.

"Leave Cola Face alone."

Silence.

"If a woman wants to sleep with you on her own volition, great, but if I hear of you telling her she has to because you've got a set of neat-looking eyes, I will kick your ass out of the Skulls —" He snapped his fingers. "Like that."

Silence.

"You hear me?"

Silence. But Mister Touch felt he was hearing something like a terrorist's bomb, a faint steady ticking of hatred and frustration in the kid's mind.

"So go on now. Get out —" The prez caught himself before saying "of my sight." Instead he added, "And remember you've been warned." There was a long moment of silence. Then he heard the heavy tread of Africa, followed by the lighter step of Ace hurrying away.

The kid wished him ill, the main man realized; if Africa hadn't been on the scene, something bad might have happened.

He hadn't wanted a bodyguard, but IRT had made him promise to have one. "Another thing," said IRT on his deathbed. "Don't worry do some of them dudes call you a tyrant. Called me one too and I never lost no sleep over it. Right now you gotta make it, a white boy who can't see but who got to keep this thing together. Show them power, bro." IRT had been breathing hard; it had taken him a long time to say these things, but he said them, hammered them into Mister Touch's mind like railroad spikes. "Don't forget, homes, people think they be steady but they sure as hell crazy without even knowing. Crazy for being here when everybody else dead. Crazy from thinking about still being alive. Don't trust them, homes. Hear what I'm saying? When I be gone and you take over, treat them tough, or they land you out on your ass and worst still they lose their last chance of making it."

"Africa," the main man called out. A heavy step, a heavy hand on his arm. "Back to the delivery room."

Hours later, when a dawn that Mister Touch couldn't see was starting to splatter a gold light against the glass windows of Manhattan the way ghetto kids used to spraypaint subway cars with the gang names now used by the Skulls, the lusty bawl of new life was heard.

Jesus Mary Save Souls came into the waiting room; the oil lamp she carried threw another kind of golden light upon the face of

Mister Touch, accentuating the jut of his jaw, the smoky look of his gray eyes.

A tall rangy woman in her midtwenties, Jesus Mary had curly auburn hair and ice-blue eyes and buck teeth. There was blood on her bare arms. She announced proudly that mother and baby boy were both doing fine.

"How's his breathing?" the prez asked.

"Like a normal child's."

Mister Touch slumped back on the couch. So V 70 was not transmitted genetically; that had been everyone's fear.

"Coco is really okay?"

"I wouldn't say so if I didn't mean it."

"What about Sister Love?"

"Sinking."

"Bobby Loves It? Taki?"

"They aren't far behind. I think V 70 weakened the lungs of some people until a bout of flu is too much for them. But it's not V 70."

He felt there was no gain in arguing against her optimism. Unwrapping a stick of gum, he popped it in his mouth and chewed vigorously. "The less said about their illness the better."

"You're telling me to keep my mouth shut?" Jesus Mary had an Irish temper.

"Yes," Mister Touch said.

"So I'll keep my mouth shut," she replied without rancor. "When people come around — and believe me they *do*, they're scared to death — I'll tell them to get out of my face. That's what blacks say and it's a good saying. Ah, here we are," said Jesus Mary, her voice buttery. "Mystique is bringing the little precious in."

"Let me," said the prez, stretching out his arms toward the sound of a newborn crying.

Later in the privacy of his room, Mister Touch again took up the secret history.

He had already described on side two of Tape One the Angora cat and then the sound of a drum coming from the direction of Washington Square Park. It was a familiar sound, reminding him of carefree New York summers when musicians used to entertain anyone who came into the park: university students, crack salesmen, out-of-town strollers, couples in love, kids with Frisbees, the homeless.

But then the drum was pounding a rhythm of fearful anticipation through his veins as he shambled forward with the fluffy cat held to his chest.

He walked toward the sound that came from somewhere near the park fountain. He could make out something huddled there. The rat-a-tat-tat abruptly ceased.

"Qué pasa, brother?" someone shouted.

Before Mister Touch could reply, the same voice, in a tone of command, called for him to come over. "Turn your pockets out, bro. We wanna see what you got."

Were they going to mug him? What did he have that they could possibly want? Fearful but resigned, by switching the cat from hand to hand he managed to turn his pockets inside out: a key chain hit the pavement, some Kleenexes fluttered down. Then he walked forward until he could see a half dozen people seated on the terraced steps of the dry fountain. Getting closer, he made out two white males, one holding a pistol; two black females; a black male holding a pistol; and a black male holding a conga drum between his legs.

Grinning, the drummer said, "Hey, brother, how you doing? Welcome to the only show in town. We got no attitude here, so we hope you don't come bringing one. Sit down."

Mister Touch sat down.

The drummer kept fingering the drum, eliciting skillful little rhythms from it; he could be a professional. On each finger he wore a ring: ruby, sapphire, you name it. Pinned to his leather jacket were more than a dozen diamond brooches. Perched on his head was a blue fedora with a long yellow feather jauntily stuck into it. He was tricked out for real.

"For me it went this way," he said with a broad smile. "Coming down from Amsterdam and One Hundred Thirty-six Street a few days ago, I had my eye out for loot. Never expected how much, though. Man, all these jewelry stores!" He rapped the drum for emphasis. "Coming this far downtown I tell myself you getting to the end of Manhattan Island pretty soon, so what you be doing then? Sit down, see what turn up. Think what you doing. Like my daddy used to say, 'When you find yourself up to your ass in alligators, it seem mighty hard to remember your goal be to drain the swamp.' Know what I'm saying? So I been sitting here doing a little bugaloo and waiting for what is gonna happen to happen and sure enough one of you show up and then another one and I keep playing and you keep coming." Another flourish on the drum; it sent a bunch of pigeons swirling into the air. "Now we got enough of us to see what we can do. So let's get at doing it to it." He got to his feet and so did the others. Mister Touch did too.

"My name is," Mister Touch began, but the black drummer interrupted him. "Don't wanna know *that*. Name you had don't mean nothing to me. Old names don't mean fuck. I been sitting and thinking about it. See what I'm saying? We gonna find a place to stay and then we gonna take new names and be *new* people. I am IRT from now on."

One of the white males said, "You mean, IRT like the subway?"

"You got it, bro." The drummer turned to Mister Touch. "Put the cat down."

Mister Touch looked at the Angora still in his arms. "No."

"Listen to what I'm saying. Get your own act together before moving with pets."

So the arbitrager, who had rarely taken orders from anyone, not even from the SEC, put the cat down and followed IRT into the future.

4

FUTURA STUDIED HERSELF in the sunlit mirror of her room.

What Futura saw with her good-looking eyes did not please her. What she saw never pleased her: the sallow cheeks, the receding chin, the eyes, no matter how good looking, watery and too close together. She dabbed rouge on her cheeks to give them color and combed out her long brown hair, which her mother used to say was her best feature. She swung her head to make the ruby earrings jiggle. "Just look at you," Futura said aloud, "wearing earrings worth thousands of dollars."

But it did no good. She was still terribly aware of being plain. Of course, she'd look better if she could discard the tincan around her neck. But like other Poor Breathers she had been left by V 70 with a perpetual residue of phlegm — something like postnasal drip — and so she was always hacking stuff up and needed to spit it somewhere. Spit it on the floor, they would throw you out of the Club House without a second thought.

Sighing, she fluffed her hair and stepped back to appraise her outfit: a tucked-in shirty top and a waist-cinching belt and stovepipe pants made of black cotton jersey with a bit of Lycra. Stretching to her ankles, these tube-legged pants with a little fullness at the hips and a high waistline gave someone like her, with chunky thighs and fat knees, a more chic and curvy silhouette. With these pants, though, she wouldn't wear heels the way some girls did; flats were classier . . . less suggestive.

She had never tried to impress men in a cheap way. Her mother had always claimed that a girl could look just terrific without enticing men. Futura had never surrendered to the Skull fad for promiscuous sex, which people justified by saying they didn't have other entertainment like the movies. Admittedly, she had done it once with Turok, who before V 70 Struck had come from Minnesota to study the martial arts in hopes of opening his own school one day. Turok had been only the second boy she had ever done it with, the first being a neighborhood friend almost as scared to do it as she had been when they went up to her bedroom and somehow got their clothes off and lay down and quickly did it. On the other hand, Turok wasn't scared. Just the opposite — he went at her hungrily like a guy after football practice dropping into McDonald's for a Big Mac. She had expected someone with such silky blond hair to be sort of romantic like a movie star, a Robert Redford, a Don Johnson, but this muscular boy from Minneapolis had just done it and was done before she had felt much of anything and then he got dressed — she would never forget the businesslike *zip* with which he zipped up his pants afterward. He had left with a cheery "See ya."

But then it was better to know the truth about a man right away. Her mother had always told her the handsome ones are fickle.

Futura dabbed more rouge on her sallow cheeks and was wetting her lips to see how she looked, when in the mirror a face appeared behind her right shoulder.

Futura screamed.

"Hey, mamma, chill out. Only me." Superstar stood there grinning.

With her good-looking eyes she was capable of appreciating the good looks of this youthful black man: tall, broad-shouldered, his teeth as white as a toothpaste ad, his features almost girlishly fine, his cropped hair glistening. She felt a warmth in her cheeks, not from anger but from a sudden yet unmistakable excitement, while harshly telling him it took a lot of nerve to barge in without being invited.

"Don't take nerve," he countered lazily and sat down on her bed, "if you like me being here."

"You came into my room without knocking. Who told you I wanted you in here? And don't call me mamma." As an officious afterthought she said, "I am not your mother."

Taking a chocolate bar from his jeans, Superstar removed the wrapper slowly. Futura stared, almost transfixed, at his long black fingers. The way he peeled back the paper was horribly erotic.

"Told myself this morning," began Superstar, "hey, man, why not go over and say hi to that good-looking mamma over there, Futura. Be like making a new friend. So I come by and the door wasn't locked so I just walk in to ask how you doing. Have some chocolate." Superstar extended the candy bar with one hand and patted the bed beside him with the other. "Sit right down. This chocolate taste like only yesterday."

Futura hesitated. Then with a fleeting backward glance at her mirrored rear in the tube-legged pants, she sat down gingerly — a mere handbreadth away from the handsome young man. She broke off a tiny piece of the stale candy that he offered her. "Thank you, kind sir," she said coyly.

After chewing and swallowing, the girl took a Kleenex from her shirty top and meticulously wiped her sticky fingers. She caught him staring at the shirt pocket, and it occurred to her with sudden pride that her breasts were almost as good as her hair. She tossed her head triumphantly, making the rubies swirl an inch below her ears. But when he edged over, closing the distance between them and slipping a warm hand around her belted waist, Futura muttered, "Stop that."

"Ah, come on, baby. I ain't doing nothing."

"You never knew I existed and here you're trying things and don't call me baby."

Throwing up his hands, he added to this show of bafflement a rolling of his eyes. "No one hitting on you, girl! I be just trying to get acquainted."

"Is that what you call it? I think you're a disloyal person."

"About what, pretty lady?"

"Never mind. And don't call me pretty lady."

"Want more chocolate?"

"No, I don't want more chocolate. Don't do that."

"Ain't doing nothing."

"You're starting up again." Futura edged away from the hand warming the skin above her waist-cinching belt. "What if one of my roommates was here instead of me? I bet you'd start up with her, with anyone who happened to be here." She recalled a cynical phrase from one of those pornographic novels she used to keep hidden from her mother. She said it now. "I suppose with you it's any port in a storm."

Superstar laughed softly; it was a sweet disarming kind of laugh that caught her off guard.

"Truth is," he said, "I been thinking of you."

Futura felt herself smiling, as if pleased in spite of herself by the compliment, while at the same time she lectured him. "You should be thinking of Sister Love, your girlfriend, who is desperately sick."

"Sure sorry about her being sick. But don't go calling that woman my girlfriend."

"People say she is."

"People full of shit like always. Sister Love and me have something going, but we broke it off a long time ago."

Futura knew that as well as she knew that Superstar had a reputation of invading a number of bedrooms. Abruptly she turned away, hacked, and genteelly spit into the tincan around her neck.

"You okay, mamma?" Superstar asked solicitously.

"As if you cared."

"Hey, don't come down so hard. What did I do?"

Had she gone too far? "I don't mean to be nasty," she murmured.

"Fact is, I never was tight with Sister Love. She always be on Valium for nerves. You be talking, she start nodding out." With his long black forefinger Superstar began tracing a small circle on Futura's knee which was covered by black cotton and a bit of Lycra.

Her skin felt like it was burning. A rush of warmth speeding upward from her knee toward her groin had her saying all kinds of crazy things. "Say, what do you think you're doing you're starting up you're you better stop well I like you more than it may seem a nice guy but no but really cute good-looking but hey we shouldn't you —"

She got no further.

Superstar moved one of those long black erotic hands of his in a soft downy circular motion from her knee along her cottoned inner thigh. "Come on, mamma," he whispered in her ear.

Her hand, trying to restrain his wormy fingers on their way up her thigh, was drained of strength, and she felt her own fingers start to glide on top of his, like all ten were traveling together upward.

"Mamma, I been crazy for you a long time. Need you, baby. Come on, pretty lady."

Hearing "pretty lady" again, she gripped his hand firmly, at last stopping its progress. Pulling back from him, her good-looking eyes met his. "You think I'm plain. I know you do. And I am." Futura knew if he could get past her fear of being plain, brush it aside like barbed wire on a battlefield, he'd win.

"You look real good to me, baby," he murmured against her throat.

She felt a warmth flowing through her, as if his fingers massaging her flesh sent out little tentacles of heat that wriggled into every crevice of her body until his hand reached where it wanted to get. She was lost and knew it and was glad of it.

Then briskly he got up.

She opened her eyes, in alarm suddenly aware they had been closed all this time. "Where are you going?"

"Just closing the door."

"You mean locking it." That was her last caustic remark. When he returned to the bed and started up again, she let him do whatever he wanted. With regal assurance and a delicate motion, Superstar removed the tincan from around her neck, an action so natural, so intimate, so loving that she sighed with intense pleasure and lay back before he even touched her again. She was open, ready, she didn't give a damn about anything but more of him touching her.

Later he rhapsodized, "Wowee, baby, you can sure do some doing." When he reached for her naked hip, she scuttled away and leaned over the bed, fumbling to retrieve the tincan. Rising on an elbow, he asked, "Okay, baby?"

Futura spit, put the tincan back on the floor, and rolled over heavily on the bed. "We shouldn't have done that." She turned to look reproachfully at him.

"Didn't do nothing wrong, baby."

"Your ex-girlfriend might be dying and you're here in my bed making love to me."

Raising himself and hovering above her like a big dark bird with folded wings, Superstar stared into her eyes not an inch away. "Told you and told you, mamma. I was on to your style a long time now. I like your hair and eyes and what you do with yourself with me. I like hanging out like this with you. And we both of us came like there was no tomorrow, right? So nothing wrong here at all."

She ought to have said, "I don't believe a word of it, and I don't like talking about coming and everything wrong's with you being here," but instead she just lay there and let him caress her body while she caressed his. She felt her mind go empty of everything except the sound of their breathing — hers more shallow — but for both of them each exhalation lasting longer than each intake.

Superstar made little circles with one finger against her forearm like a wooden spoon stirring cream. "White skin, brown — sure look good together."

She pulled slightly away so she could study him. "Well. Maybe so."

"Ever get it on with a black guy before?"

Futura disengaged herself from his touch and sat up, crossing her arms over her breasts. "Do you have to talk like that?"

"Come on, did you?"

"No, I never did."

"I look lighter than most of my family. Both my parents was real dark. They called me their coffee with milk in it."

"Hush. You're talking about the past."

"Rules don't apply after we just got it on, do they, baby? No better time for talking."

"You should know."

Ignoring her sarcasm, he said, "Yeah, you got some brown too. Look good too."

She felt herself blushing as he stared at her groin. Mother was back again, having come from Astoria, Queens, out of a rumpled bed where she had died from pneumonia soon after V 70 Struck. Mother was saying it was wrong for a nice girl to be lying naked in bed with a black womanizer and it was even worse for her to have enjoyed making love with him — to have enjoyed it more than anything in her entire life.

She must either throw the seducer out or grab her shirty top and tube-legged pants and get out herself, but under the lazily possessive gaze of this handsome black stud Futura could do nothing. "I know why IRT named you Superstar," she told him after a while. "You're sure of yourself, you're special."

"Guess that true," he acknowledged gravely. "I always be sure of myself since I remember. Always felt special."

"I admire self-confidence."

Encouraged by her remark, Superstar snuggled closer and began to caress her body, his fingers nimble.

Futura closed her eyes. She was letting herself go again, when suddenly his hand stopped.

He asked her for the time. Puzzled and hurt, she bent close to her watch and told him.

Briskly he got up and threw his clothes on. "Gotta go," he muttered.

"Oh. You have another date?" She heard the pain in her voice. "Is this hit and run?"

He turned to her with a gentle smile. "Baby, I dating one woman now and that be *you*. You hearing me? Reason I gotta go is the expedition. We got a team together going to a drugstore."

She watched his strong black fingers button his shirt and zip up his pants. For a while she had lost track of time, of where they were and why. She had been with this beautiful man somewhere else, somewhere far away from her mother and her own plain looks and the world after V 70 Struck. But now she was returning to it and felt a sudden but familiar fear. She thought of medical supplies, of Sister Love and the two other Skulls near death, of her own lungs always filling with phlegm.

Reaching out, she caught his hand and pulled it to her naked breasts. "What's going to happen? Is it getting cold? Can we make it through another winter?"

Superstar laughed uneasily, freed his hand from hers, knelt down and tied his Reeboks. "Got through last winter," he said, rising. "Get through this one too." Bending to kiss her tenderly, he said, "You and me, we gonna get through together. Don't you worry none, mamma. Listening to me? You be the Superstar's queen now."

5

WE SET UP HOUSEKEEPING in a swank high-rise not far from Washington Square Park," Mister Touch explained on Tape Two of the History of the Skulls. "I could have gone home to my condo, but the urge to join up with other survivors was irresistible. It was as if each of us validated our continued existence by maintaining contact with others.

"After we had cleared away the corpses from rooms we intended to use for our club house, drunk some warm beer, and eaten out of cans, IRT assumed leadership of the group without consultation. He just did it. His first official act was to christen us with names borrowed from graffiti sprayed across train cars in the early 1970s.

"Now, without protest, along with the other strays IRT had gathered around him in the park, I surrendered my identity and took up my new name. No one in those early days protested. Each of us was driven by a fear and a loneliness so strong they seemed to override other considerations. Here was someone who promised us a place to eat and sleep in the company of other human beings. IRT had the power — there is no question of that. It didn't matter if the new name fit our personalities. Sometimes it did, sometimes it certainly did not. In any case the new names reflected the wayward wisdom or mischievousness of our leader. We just went along with the power that had come out of Harlem with a feather in his cap, a drum, and a little hope.

"Each day we collected strays in the park by sitting around the fountain while IRT played drums. Each evening there was a christening of the newcomers. After brooding in a corner, IRT would come forward to tap the person's shoulder and say, 'I dub thee —' whatever name off the subway cars came to mind. 'I dub thee Shithead' or 'I dub thee Sister Love.' 'I saw them do it like that in a movie once' is how he explained the ritual of knighthood as he used it for baptism, that being the purpose of this ceremony. It was funny, it was serious — take your pick. Some people liked it, some hated it, some argued vehemently about giving up their names. A few even walked out rather than surrender their old identities to something that seemed whimsical and often downright idiotic. IRT made no exceptions whatsoever; either you got a new name or you got the hell out. Anyway, he kept us off balance with such antics. I think the names made us feel bold, a little defiant, maybe the way IRT felt when he and his friends sprayed subway cars with their nicknames so that passengers riding to Wall Street and Radio City would know they existed.

"While sitting around in the park, waiting for newcomers, we listened to him describe those spraycan days. We got to know the jargon. IRT and other writers boged their colors from paint stores, favoring Rustoleum over Red Devil Epoxy. He told us how they would bomb Yard Five at two in the morning. Wearing rubber gloves, they'd piece a train, do twenty-foot burners of naked chicks and Mickey Mouse cartoons. With tire irons they went after marauding slashers who liked to move in and waste masterpieces like the famous one written by Seen, king of the writers, in the Wild

Style with his tag, SEEN, and his girlfriend's tag, SWEET NUKEY, in unstraight letters that ended in fancy arrows. Waiting in the park for more survivors of V 70, we heard how the writers eluded police dogs. We came to fear and respect the transit cops Hurley and Janowski, the top blue in the city, who once held Seen over the third rail with a metal flashlight taped to his mouth. We learned how you sprayed on guidelines, worked on separate sections of a car, then hooked up the piece at the end. After guidelines came the fill-in and then your 3-D look and little doodads that made your piece special. We developed a disdain for toys, who wanted to be writers and go bombing but lacked the patience, the skill, the courage. Sitting around the park fountain, we put elbows on knees and hands on cheeks, imagining in the dead city what it must have been like in the dark tunnels with rats moving against your feet and the feel of tracks shifting when distant trains took a fast turn. I know that some of us, certainly myself, understood after a while what IRT meant when he tapped out a light rhythm on the conga and said something like 'You do bombing cause you be nothing but a small dude in the middle of high-power metal, and you come to live for it, dream about it, go along with it when your burner leave the yard and join the line and you go flying with your tag down the track through New York City like a bird.' Then he would tell us, with another drumbeat flourish, that we were doing the same thing, we were making our names known, we weren't just doing a throw-up design by sticking together, we were writing for real, we were bombing the whole known world.

"Another thing IRT did, he made us dance. When we slumped against the corridor walls, too stunned by depression to move, he'd move among us, disco blaring out of a huge sound box held in his broad hand, and he'd bend over, yelling out, 'Get up, mothafucker, and dance! Didn't none of you learn how to break? There's all types of footwork you could do: the Baby, the Turtle, the Head Spin, the Back Bridge, the Dead Freeze, the Headache, the Hump — sure as hell not one of you can't do the Hump if you be alive and know what I'm saying. Come on and dance, one minute, two minute. That's cool. Get off your ass, sister, and wiggle it. Tired of you cluttering the hall. Get up, brothers and sisters! We the best!'

"He'd do a breakdance spin that left him breathless, but

he'd still manage to yell something like 'Sock sockit rockit in the pocket!'

"We danced for fear he'd keep playing all night if we didn't and then he'd go beyond his endurance and die from breathlessness. So we humored him by dancing and maybe it kept us alive.

"He and he alone devised a few simple but effective rules for us to live by.

"One. No self-pitying indulgent nostalgic bullshit about the past. As new people we were to live in the here, the now.

"Two. To prevent contagion anyone with a cold had to leave the Club House until the symptoms were gone. In our weakened pulmonary condition even a common cold was dangerous.

"Three. No racist stuff. IRT said, 'We got enough bad shit to deal with without that too.'

"Four. Everyone who could work must work. No exceptions.

"Five. Sexual freedom. IRT said, 'We gotta keep doing it or wanting to do it or not wanting some other dude to do it with somebody we want to do it with or we be dead.' In spite of physical limitations, most of us accepted lovemaking as our main diversion. Lasting relationships were condoned but not necessarily encouraged. Getting pregnant was the goal of a few courageous girls who felt they had lungs enough to give birth and faith enough in life to raise a child in such a weird world.

"I have said Rule Four demanded that everyone work. There was plenty of work to do. Without plumbing, we had to create an alternative sanitation system or keep ransacking the neighborhood for toilets not yet used once. We located just the thing in a large hardware store uptown, where we sent a two-day expedition before the dogs got too troublesome. We found chemical toilets, called Porta Potties, that used two thirds water (we collected rain in garbage cans) and one third SteroKem. The chemical waste had to be dumped into plastic trash bags and carried out to the sidewalk. This sanitation job was called Misery Detail.

"There were other details as well, such as leading the blind, and expeditions weekly to supermarkets and monthly to pharmacies. There was also guard duty in the lobby, because IRT never lost his fear of intruders. He said, 'We be new on this earth, we got something going here. There could be mothafuckers who like to go backward fast and take us with them. Don't let nobody in here less we look him over good. With a gun, homes, in his fucking ear.'

"In winter, when it was cold and we didn't want to trek through snow, we made forays into higher floors where we chopped up furniture to burn in our fireplaces. Our apartments, assigned by IRT, were kept in perfect order so the Blindies wouldn't stumble over misplaced objects and break their bones. All the guarding and chopping and guiding and cleaning and dragging created the controlled turmoil of an anthill. The second and third floors of our building, those occupied by the Club House, were far busier than they had been in pre–V 70 days when people came home from work and shut out the world.

"Rule Six. No dope. I figured at some time in his life IRT had been on something, because his fear and hatred of drugs were so intense they suggested personal experience for real. He said, 'Dope get in here, we finished.' During the first year he found uppers and crack vials on two Skulls — tossed them both into the street in midwinter. I had sight enough then to see Santo and Alligator stumble through the snowy park, one good eye and two good lungs between them.

"No dope. No hard booze either. IRT rationed our beer and wine for meals and parties. We found room keys in the super's office and gave the key to our wine cellar to Wizard Brown, a virginal teetotaler who was not brown but pallid white. So we didn't snort or drink our blues away. For people who were depressed for real, we doled out Thorazine and Valium, but only under the direction of Jesus Mary Save Souls. It was everyone's responsibility, though, to look after OOTLO, who wandered into our protection from interior worlds of horror we couldn't imagine, even though, having lived through V 70, we could imagine a lot. If One Of The Lost Ones asked you for help, you better damn well respond or according to IRT, 'Your ass was outta here.'

"Rule Seven, our last one: No smoking. Most of us suffered from emphysema as one of the residues of V 70.

"So we survived, a gang of assorted people who had drifted into Washington Square Park in varying degrees of health. IRT rejected as many as he took in. He accepted the blind but refused emphysemics in terminal stages. He reasoned that the less we dealt with death the better. Even so, that first year we lost ten Skulls. During the next half year we lost only two, and all signs pointed to a stabilization of health in those who had survived V 70 for this length of time.

"But then the dogs became troublesome."

Mister Touch was interrupted by someone who came to his room with a complaint. Cancer Two was a brawny young blond with a big shapeless nose, tiny blue eyes, and ears flat to his round head. He was the Chief Cook. He was complaining about supplies. Ten men couldn't bring in enough food for a week because the weight of cans and the long haul had them going back and forth like Westchester commuters and a lot of them were scared because of the dogs. He wanted to use a pickup truck.

The prez was afraid of setting a precedent; use a truck and you'd raise a clamor for stretch limos and sports cars. Given their poor eyesight, the Skulls could expect a lot of crackups, even without traffic. Moreover, expeditions on foot gave people something to do, a goal of some difficulty to pursue. IRT used to say, "Don't need comfort, need something going on. Keep their mind moving."

So Mister Touch turned down the cook's request.

After Cancer Two left, Stay High came in. He was a young Jew of French ancestry who had been an anthropology student at — Mister Touch tried to suppress his knowledge of the facts, because even the prez should honor Rule One.

Although a Bad Looker on the inevitable path to Blindie (but a Breather For Real), Stay High wore glasses from habit. He adjusted them now on the bridge of his nose and gave Mister Touch a progress report.

His job was to solve a poem written by The Dream Queen before she died. The Dream Queen had been a tall rawboned woman with a long fierce nose and lank brown hair that hung around her skinny throat like a dirty mop. Ph.D. in biochemistry. Taught at — Mister Touch always had trouble with ridding his mind of such facts. After her acceptance into the Skulls, she engaged in spirited debates with IRT, accusing him of tyranny. But it soon became clear that people who disliked IRT didn't like her, and when she came along the hallways Skulls scattered like chickens in the path of a dray horse. To everyone's surprise she became IRT's devoted admirer and when she died The Dream Queen wanted no one else in the room but him. It was to him that she gave a poem entitled "The Mystery of the Universe."

IRT had read it, scratched his head, and told Mister Touch, "Don't know nothing about poems. You do something about it."

Ever since becoming prez, Mister Touch had vowed to do something about it, especially because IRT seemed to have had a mystical faith in its unknown message. "That woman," IRT said, "had me come up close when she was dying. She whisper, 'It's all there,' and slipped me this poem. What we gotta do is find out what the hell *is* all there."

Mister Touch's own response to the poem had been disappointing. He saw in it a jumbled statement of anarchy and hedonism, put into indifferent verse by someone on her way out who had never been a poet in the first place. Unable to do more, Mister Touch had turned it over to Stay High, the resident intellectual. After initial study, Stay High saw in the poem a meditative exercise, much like a Zen koan, a vehicle of insight into the nature of life, a cryptic means of seeking enlightenment. He had been excited by the prospect of unlocking its mystery, so much so that the prospect of losing his eyesight had been diminished by his search for the meaning of the universe.

Today he was eager to describe his latest findings and waved a copy of the poem around in the air.

"Read it to me again," said Mister Touch, ashamed of having let the verses slide from memory like so many other things — the names of colleagues, his last address, the color of Linda's hair, his mother's birthplace.

Stay High read it in a thin nasal voice.

> *"When the moon is nu [he paused to spell "nu"]*
> *Tides running in the gat*
> *Act freaky as a cat*
> *And do what you want to*
> *Says Cleo*
> *Fly to Rio*
> *Or jump on a nag*
> *Play tag*
> *Where others plod*
> *Or dice with God*

> *Or rob a bank*
> *Or walk the plank*
> *Or make a base hit*
> *When they least expect it*
> *Be mad as a Danish hatter*
> *Hitch up your trousers with string*
> *And have a last fling*
> *In the world of dark matter*
>
> *Thus do go about, about*
> *As if you had a universal goal*
> *Until the charm's wound up*
> *Then drop like Alice down the hole*
> *On a blood-red unseen beam*
> *Into truth too deep too rude*
> *Or curl forever nude*
> *Inside the singular dream*
> *At the setting of the sun*
> *When the hubble-bubble's done*
>
> *Mea Kalpa [he paused to spell "Kalpa"]*
> *Et cetera"*

Stay High adjusted his glasses in preparation for delivering a commentary. First, he dealt with "nu." In context he felt it meant "new," but with an echo of "mu," a mantric word used by Japanese Buddhists for "eternity." Or even more ambiguously it appeared in koans designed for meditation, such as "What is Mu on the day you die?"

Mister Touch was not touched by the pedantry. He only went after the poem's meaning because of IRT's faith in it. For himself the thirty singsong lines did little more than conjure in memory the horse face of The Dream Queen, which in turn reminded him of his great-aunt, an eccentric if there ever was one, who smoked cigars in emulation of her idol, Amy Lowell, who kept a dog pack not unlike those now roaming the empty canyons of New York. The Dream Queen had been irascible arrogant sulky melancholy spiritless disconsolate defeatist gloomy unsociable vaporish aloof crestfallen as hell, and intellectually brilliant or not, Mister Touch had found her to be insufferable even though, next to himself, IRT had been closer to this woman than to anyone.

Today Stay High had a few other discoveries to report. "In the second line, 'Tides running in the gat,' I take 'gat' to mean channel. But why didn't she use the simpler word 'channel'? Merely because it rhymed with 'cat'?"

"Well, after all, she was a scientist by trade, not a poet." This gave Mister Touch the chance to say what he really thought. "So we mustn't read too much into the thing."

Stay High ignored the comment, pointing out that "gat" came from the Scandinavian for a ship's channel, with linguistic kinship to the Old English "geat" or "gate."

When the scholar paused, Mister Touch asked an obvious question. "So what does it mean?"

"A ship's journey, a gate, or a pistol carried primarily by gangsters. Can I go on? Some of the lines refer to *Macbeth*," he said triumphantly and pointed out that "Thus do go about, about" was a direct quote from Act I Scene 3 and "Until the charm's wound up" was a slight corruption of the next speech. Stay High noted with satisfaction that they were the only two lines of "Mystery" that didn't rhyme, the reason being that they came from *Macbeth*'s text. He held up his finger for professional silence, although it would have no effect on the blind man. "There's more."

"More?"

"Line twenty-eight reads, 'When the hubble-bubble's done.' Actually it should read 'hurly-burly' — 'When the hurly-burly's done.' "

"So?"

"It could be that the poet — I'm talking about The Dream Queen, not Shakespeare — wanted to make a play on words. Of some kind not altogether clear." Stay High paused thoughtfully. "Or she did a piece of sloppy quoting."

"Something a nonpoet, especially a dying one, might do?"

"Exactly."

"Thank you very much, Stay High. I am beginning to see this poem in a new light, thank you, and keep me posted every step of the way."

When he heard the door shut, Mister Touch sighed. Had he not promised IRT "to do something with it," he would have dropped the project long ago.

At least the search for a universal mystery kept Stay High high. Perhaps that was sufficient. The main man's job was to keep people from becoming OOTLO. And there was a weird outside chance that IRT's intuition about the poem was justified. After all, insufferable though she was, The Dream Queen had been one smart cookie and perhaps into those thirty rhymed lines (excluding the unrhymed two from *Macbeth*, don't forget), she had precipitated all of her knowledge like a compound in a beaker and in a burst of dying vision had left clues behind about the future of the world. Such apocalyptic thinking, the main man recognized, was commonplace among the Skulls, whose wildest theories were mild compared to the biology that had destroyed their world.

"Dogs," Mister Touch said to Whoever You Are in the regained silence and privacy of his room. "They started appearing in packs. After the first year we saw more and more and more of them on the streets, the majority half grown or puppies. Then suddenly their population exploded, as we humans had often feared our own would. Dogs became a new threat to our health."

While reciting Skull history, the main man had begun composing his sentences carefully, sometimes artfully, in response to his sense of their potential importance. His initial desire to please IRT by doing something, such as creating a spoken narrative of the catastrophe and its aftermath, had become a conviction that this record might someday have meaning for other survivors, perhaps even for cosmic visitors. So he brought to his new daily task a messianic rhetoric.

"Not having succumbed to V 70, healthy canines took dominion of New York City. Human kindness had contrived to make them a menace: when V 70 Struck, many pet fanciers had freed their animals so the poor things wouldn't starve to death in stuffy rooms. 'Go Rex, Go Herman, Go Blacky — enjoy your short-lived freedom as you will.' But it wasn't short-lived; it was long, tumultuous, and wild. Poodles, terriers, boxers, Dobermans, shepherds, and all the other breeds that could have showed at Madison Square Garden and the mongrels so beloved in mythic wisdom as 'the smartest of dogs,' all of man's best friends, who had once ambled along peacefully on leashes and had squatted docilely in the gutter to do their duty while master or mistress waited with a scooper or a few sheets of the *Daily News*, now funneled through the streets and mixed together like water in water, copulating without shame in the middle of Madison Avenue and dropping litters all over Central Park and fighting savagely among themselves in front of City Hall and prowling like yellow-eyed beasts of prey through a jungle of parked cars and garbage cans, ready for anything.

"We have already lost three brothers to their rapaciousness, although lucky for us the cats and rats in abundance too have provided them with their main source of food. All last summer we heard them. Washington Square Park was like an African veldt teeming with hunters who still wore nameplates screwed to studded collars. Compared to this scruffy and uncontrollable mob the roaming dogs in Robert Altman's movie *Quintet* were pussycats. In fear of the burgeoning dog packs, we started to carry guns everywhere: half-blind men with automatic weapons.

"We lost JoJo that way." Mister Touch paused. "Well, I suppose I must say it. It was a dreamlike fiasco. JoJo wandered into the line of fire of some homeboys who couldn't see well enough to tie their shoelaces. It shook us so much that we erased JoJo's name from the list of club members. As One Of The Hip Immortals wrote, 'Calumnies are answered best with silence.' "

6

THE TEAM of Web, Cougar, Superstar, Turok, King Super Kool, and Shag returned from their pharmaceutical expedition without incident.

Except for the following.

Because the druggist had locked the store before going home to die, Turok of the blond tresses had to shoot the door off its hinges with a blast from his 12-gauge. Resting awhile before going inside — the ten-minute walk had bushed King Super Kool, a skinny Wheezer with neat-looking eyes — they discussed rules they hated, such as the rule that you had to spit into a spittoon (because at times you didn't have your tincan and when you hacked up stuff you had to swallow it or hold it in your throat until you got your can), and they cursed Timbales for being a wimp, and gave a vote of confidence to Coco's baby that was breathing so good it just might live, and talked about girls, who was and who wasn't putting out.

Web wished for electricity, so they could plug in refrigerators to preserve food and make ice. Remembering in the roots of their teeth the chill taste of ice cream, they spitefully threatened to tell Flash that his boyfriend, Web, was pining after frozen TV dinners. "I can read every sign, no matter how small," bragged Web in response and peered into the two-year-old window display: "*Head And Shoulders Shampoo Twenty Cents Off. Right Guard —*"

Shag, a delicately made Latino, muttered, "Chiugate."

"Same to you," said Web.

"Fat mariquita."

"Same to you." Turning to the others, Web said, "What did he say?"

"Fuck you, fat faggot," someone translated and they all followed a rested King Super Kool into the pharmacy where alone, behind the counters, he used his neat-looking eyes to find the needed medicines.

Superstar, thinking of his new queen, reminded him to get birth control pills.

In a breathy whisper King Super Kool read out the labels. "Butisol . . . Thorazine . . . Histapan . . . Valium," after which Cougar swept the bottles into a plastic bag.

Shag joined the little Wheezer behind one of the counters. "See any red?" he whispered. "Hey, don't give me that police look. I ain't no dirtball looking for blow. Ain't asking for splim or ram. Don't need no twenty-minute joyride to hell. Just some red."

Later, having filled one toy wagon with loot from the drugstore and deposited an exhausted King Super Kool in another wagon that Web and Superstar would pull, they set out for home. Dogs showed up. Cougar and Turok shot at them; a cloud of darting sparrows set up a racketing din all along the street.

From the corner of his eye Cougar got a glimpse of something other than four-legged growlers. "Hey! See that dude around the corner there? See him? He be looking at us!"

But the others saw no one. So they went home with a rumor, although for the Skulls, who had seen a crazy whopper of a rumor about a worldwide epidemic come true, rumors were just as good as facts. Someone might could be on their turf, maybe like more than one lone blood, maybe a whole gang of them ready to come down.

So the expedition was not without incident.

Six and a half feet of coal-black barrel-chested Africa led the way in his cable-knit sweater with a twenty-thousand-dollar ruby pendant around his thick neck. Although nearly as tall, Mister Touch had such a slim frame that he almost seemed dwarfed by his bodyguard when they went to the dispensary.

Neighborhood doctors' offices had supplied more medical equipment than the Skulls could ever use. Jesus Mary Save Souls had taken such things as roentgenoscopes and sphygmomanometers and microwave diathermy machines, their operation a mystery to her, and shoved them into a storeroom for show like the junk of a proprietary recluse.

Mister Touch sat in the living room waiting room, while Sweet Thing, a nurse who was not sweet, went to get permission from Jesus Mary so he could see Coco and the baby. This icy gray-haired Poor Breather explained carefully to the prez, "If I let you in without her permission, Jesus Mary will skin me alive — you know how she is about keeping control of *everything*." Control of the dispensary, Mister Touch knew, was precisely what Sweet Thing wanted for herself.

Coming into the room.

His head raised like a dog sniffing, Mister Touch called out softly, "Is that you? Mystique?"

"It sure is, you bastard. I haven't seen you in seventy-two or is it seventy-three hours."

Ignoring her complaint, he worked on recalling the exact shade of her hair. That honey-colored hair, which he had smelled and touched and swathed his face in three nights ago, was compensation for Mystique's possessive nature.

"I know you're not here to see me," she said. "The baby's fine and so is Coco."

"How about tonight?"

"Now that you've asked, frankly I'd rather not tonight. I'm exhausted from being up with Sister Love. She's worse."

He felt Mystique's hand take his, her warm fingers as knowledgeable in leading him as they were in stroking his body. She led him to the maternity ward, a back bedroom furnished by Joan Glashow in the Danish Modern her husband Jerry had hated, which is why she had chosen Danish Modern. Mystique guided the main man to a crib and lowered his hand to the baby's smooth flesh.

Touching the tiny chest with his fingertips, he felt the rhythmic in-and-out. Satisfied, indeed ecstatic, he asked to see Coco. Led into the next room, he let Mystique guide his hand to the new mother's shoulder. Touching her helped him recall Coco's dreadlocks and her broad smile from which two front teeth were missing. He told Coco he was proud of her.

"It were hard," Coco murmured. "You seen him?"

"I certainly have. Twice now. What a strong boy!" He felt her grip his arm and pull him down toward her.

She whispered, "They say he be fine, but they just be *saying* it?"

He assured her it was true. "I put my fingers on his chest. Motor like a Cadillac."

"Gospel truth?"

"Gospel truth."

Letting go of his arm, Coco sighed. "Do he have Snake's eyes? They say he do."

"I'm told he has your eyes," Mister Touch said gallantly.

"Go on."

"And with his lungs, he'll be a singer like his mamma."

Coco laughed. She was the best singer among the Skulls when she had breath for it.

Back in the waiting room, he said to Mystique, "Has Snake come to see her?"

"Once."

"Get him here today and every day. I want him *here*."

"It won't be easy prying him loose from Patch. I suppose you know Patch is his new girl."

"I want him *here*. I want him to hold Coco's hand and tell her he's proud of her and their son."

Mystique guffawed. "Have you any idea how old-fashioned

you sound? But it's nice to know of your concern for a woman's feelings."

"Okay, what have I done now?"

"It's what you haven't done. You neglect me and I'm not accustomed to it. Whether you know it or not, I'm a beautiful, desirable, intelligent, and giving woman."

"And spoiled and sometimes abusive."

Again she laughed. Because Mystique was tall, the sound came to Mister Touch from nearly face level.

Then there was coming into the room. "So here you are," a voice said brusquely. It was Jesus Mary Save Souls. After telling Mystique to take the baby to Coco for feeding, the Medical Director of the Skulls led the main man into another part of the dispensary where he spoke to Bobby Loves It, a teenage black who took air in in rapid gusts, and then to Taki, whose raling breath had an alarmingly metallic sound to it, and finally to Sister Love, whose breathing sounded faint and ragged like an old wagon heading into a motion picture sunset.

In her office Jesus Mary said, "I don't really know, but I think all three have pneumonia. I have no idea if V 70 is involved. Sister Love was in bad shape when she came to us, so it's a wonder she got this far. She's twenty-two, but her body's a lot older."

Jesus Mary didn't know that Mister Touch was privy to her secret: she had been a student nurse in geriatrics when V 70 struck. The Skulls believed that Jesus Mary Save Souls was an experienced emergency-room nurse who could handle just about anything. It was a misconception that Mister Touch fostered — as had IRT, from whom he had learned the truth. For the main man it was a bitter irony that Jesus Mary's expertise, what there was of it, focused on old age, something most of the Skulls could hardly expect to reach. He was trying to remember her auburn hair and light blue eyes and buck teeth in a freckled Irish face, when suddenly he heard her declare briskly, "Don't go taking it all on yourself."

"What are you talking about?"

"V 70 could be returning. What sets you apart is your need to take the blame if it happens."

"Am I really that foolish?"

"I have a sneaking suspicion you really are. So don't do it."

"Thank you," said Mister Touch gravely, "I won't."

"I was thinking only an hour ago, just imagine this funny little ball called Earth sailing through space without human beings on it. Who would be around to know the universe existed?" She added quickly, as if caught in heresy during catechism class, "Except, of course, God."

No sooner had the main man returned to his room than Hoss arrived with a report on the pharmaceutical expedition. It had gone without incident except for two things: Cougar might have seen someone spying on them, and Shag was caught holding reds.

"Didn't even try to hide the fact he was holding," Hoss added.

The main man told him to bring Shag here pronto. When Shag, who had been waiting under guard outside the room, came in and stood at the desk, Mister Touch searched his mind to find something to visualize about the young Hispanic whom he had never seen except as a faint blur.

Then he remembered. The tie. Shag was famous for wearing those belly-warming wide ties — four-inchers like those Ralph Lauren used to sell out of his car in the '60s before becoming famous. Following his feverish Latino imagination, Shag had made a decision to go wide. "Shag, are you wearing a tie?"

"Huh?"

"Are you wearing a tie?"

"Qué más da?"

Mister Touch had just enough Spanish to reply, "It makes no difference, but I want to know."

"Cómo no? Sí."

Good. The prez could now imagine a young man with a wide tie standing in front of him. His voice grew taut with authority, as he asked Shag why he had betrayed the Skulls by slipping reds into his pocket.

There was such a long silence that Mister Touch wondered if the kid was going to reply. Then suddenly, like a dam breaking, the words came tumbling out of Shag. "Like every day doing nothing getting me down, so I say, Shag, this ain't making sense what we doing, so why not fuck it, get a few reds. Not like I go for big stuff, just something to put in my memory what it was like in the old days when guys do Roxanne and MDMA and Angel Dust, but none of us banged horse in a serious way. Eso es. Know what I mean? What I do was nose candy. Simpler than freebasing with ether and smoking it. Used to be us guys hung out at bodega and in back we hollow out El Productos and fill them with chiba chiba." He chuckled at the memory. "That be reefer that zoot you out. I telling you, amigo, when we rock it was like taking your head off, like taking enamel off your teeth, man, por lo menos. What I was saying?"

Mister Touch pictured him standing in a soft rain of memory, and for a moment the prez nearly succumbed to the temptation to tell Shag, what the hell, go take your pills and recapture the rapturous sensation of having the enamel taken off your teeth. Instead, he told the young Hispanic to shape up or ship out. Another urge had him wanting to sound optimistic, to point out that the Skulls were surviving against odds, that Coco's baby represented a hope for the future — things like that to encourage and comfort the kid, but it would have sounded too much like one of those politicians who had promised Shag's East Harlem family the world every election and had never delivered so much as hot water for a freezing apartment. Yet something must be said to give Shag a reason for no more boosting of drugs from pharmacies, for snooking to relieve the kind of pervasive anxiety the whole Club House was experiencing.

"It won't always be like this," he told Shag before sending him away. What could he say when the kid was still listening to the sound of falling rain?

Hearing the door close that left him once again in silence, Mister Touch opened the drawer and got out his recorder stashed under some papers that had been lying there ever since the apartment owner had shoved them into the drawer one week before his death, hoping that his wife — somewhere in Europe — would survive and return to America and find two hundred shares of this, three hundred of that, and his Last Will and Testament, which left everything he possessed on this earth to her.

Mister Touch said into the recorder, "So in those early days IRT was everywhere, striding through the halls in a flowing cape and wearing a naval officer's cap studded with ruby brooches. He'd deck himself out in knee-high white boots, red velvet pants, polka-dot silk shirts, and often he fancied an ivory-headed cane. One Of The Hip Immortals wrote, 'He is great who is what he is from nature, and who never reminds us of others.' Even so, in such os-tentatious getups our leader resembled those dictators who sprouted like mushrooms after the colonial powers lost Africa.

"There was, of course, criticism of IRT's appearance and be-havior, but I maintain that whatever he did was to get us through. He had a gift for spotting the early signs of depression and turning it out on view before it burrowed too deep and produced OOTLO. And he never seemed at a loss for solutions. Sometimes he'd say, 'Let it ride and we see.' At other times he'd get up and shout, 'We gotta handle this one before another minute go by or it be doing us harm!'

"He was still functioning as our leader when his lungs got bad for real. Near the end he told me I was next in line. I argued. After all, by that time I was blind, scarcely able to manage myself much less anyone else. But IRT laughed at me. 'You gonna take over. That be that and don't ask why.' Then on one of his last days, he told me to sit by his bed and listen, because there were things that had to go down and being that I was going to take over real soon, I better know what they were. He said I must memorize a list of names for use in future christenings. He had written them down in large childish print from the memory of his days spraying tags on trains in Yard Five. He said, 'Don't let them think who they was but who they gonna be.' He said, 'Protect Jesus Mary Save Souls like she was a kilo of uncut heroin, worth killing for, because she be a treasure, one of them angels of mercy you hear about.' He said, 'Trust Hoss. Don't hold it against him he was house nigger for a white ad agency. One smart dude. And nobody gonna stand by you like him.' He said, 'Keep Send Em Back To Africa close as a tree and you standing under it. Anytime he fall asleep, you be in dan-ger.' He said, 'Let 'em have music. More the better.' He said, 'Keep 'em moving.' Almost with his last gasp he said, 'Gotta keep 'em moving.'

"It was that same day that he revealed his reason for appoint-ing me prez. 'What you got,' he said, 'is what we always look for where I come from — survivor luck. You was going to jail, you being on the take down on Wall Street. They was gonna nail you when V 70 come along and gave you a second chance. Being out for yourself gave you smarts. Now you gonna use them to get our people through. Do that, bro. Get them through, because getting through be what the Skulls was made for.'

"We cremated him in the park. We could no longer bury our dead because dogs would dig up the corpses before we got out of earshot of their howling. When IRT went up in flames, I cried like a baby. He had come looting all the way down from Harlem and saved our lives. Into my lap, though, he had dumped the future, and it was hard for me to believe in the last thing he told me: the blind see clearly because when looking for the truth they never lose sight of their goal."

7

COLA FACE ATTENDED the bridge game held every Tuesday and Thursday by The Ladies — older Skull white women who were drawn together by memories of a world predicated on wealth and education rather than the ability to breathe steadily and see across the room.

Cola Face didn't play bridge, but she liked the aura of sophistication created by The Ladies at their game. As a child she had dimly envisioned for herself the luxury they had known for real. Later, as a hairdresser in Manhattan, she had been fueled by the hope of someday living the good life, manifested primarily by a rich husband who belonged to the best clubs and who owned a mansion with a three-car garage in Westchester. Living with two roommates, likewise hopeful hairdressers, in a small apartment in the dating area of Yorkville on the Upper East Side, she often imagined herself going to lunch at Lutèce with her shoulders smothered in a black mink stole. Cola Face had such a mink now, casually lifted from an exclusive Fifth Avenue shop through a broken window; she rarely wore it, though, for fear of looking ostentatious in the eyes of The Ladies.

Her discretion about clothes was complemented by her secrecy about the past. Although many Skulls dealt cavalierly with the rule forbidding discussions of personal history, Cola Face obeyed it rigorously in order not to divulge the fact that she had been a hairdresser — and in a unisex hairstyling shop whose lesbian owner had sexually harassed her.

For her, as for Mister Touch, V 70 had created a world in which she could find herself a new identity.

As Cola Face hurried down the corridor toward the bridge room, she felt lust oozing from each doorway like animated jelly. It came from boys with their hands ready in an instant to yank down their zipper and pull the thing out. She had read from OOTHI, "I long to talk with some old lover's ghost, who died before the god of love was born." She didn't understand it really, but it seemed to mean that no one understood what love was even though nothing stopped it from happening. Not that the Skull men would know that love had happened to them. All they knew about love was unzipping that zipper. And now this pimply-faced Ace came around every day, panting like a dog, saying the nastiest things.

When she entered the bridge room, the players looked up with a welcoming smile (even Melody, whose eyes stared vacantly above the cards she held). Cola Face was glad that Pretty Puss wasn't hanging around. Cola Face hated Pretty Puss, who bragged about summering in the Hamptons and doing Bloomingdale's and about her friends at the Dalton School and her poodle Socrates. The teenage snip used words like "fresh" and "awesome" and her fake English accent made Cola Face terribly conscious of her own Bronx *a*'s.

In a corner sat Diamond Doll, a fat woman with legs bowed like a chicken's wishbone. Diamond Doll, an awful bore, was telling the bridge players what she had told them countless times already. "I got heart problems, I got kidneys, I got arthritis you couldn't believe. My doctor said people should know what I suffer. When this thing happened, I was getting ready to go to my sister. Her husband bought in Fort Lauderdale a big condo. Every day the beach."

The players ignored her as always, settled back to the cards and their conversation, the chief and perennial topic being the nightmare of their lives — the silly names, the indecent language, the outrageous clothes, although Fire, a book editor, sometimes winced when this latest objection was made, because V 70 had given her license to indulge a secret fantasy, which was to experiment with outrageous clothes, such as the orange jumpsuit, purple turban, and pixie shoes she was wearing today.

Snow, a heavyset woman in classic Chanel, and Sag, white-haired and sallow-faced, led the criticism of Mister Touch, who, as the black drummer's successor, was the object of their scorn for allowing delinquents to run wild.

"Not exactly wild," corrected Fire. "At least he's kept the lid on. And what's the alternative to him?"

Snow agreed. "Remove him and we might find ourselves in the hands of people 'with foreheads villainous low,' " she quoted from OOTHI.

Sag snorted in dissent. "That *crook*" was her eternal judgment of Mister Touch.

So persuasive was Sag that the others dropped the subject altogether. Fire bid no trump, while Golden Girl, a frail little girl whose main function was to read blind Melody's cards for her, suddenly blurted out the latest news. "They're having a party tonight!"

The players froze.

"What are they celebrating this time?" Sag sneered.

The little girl didn't know.

"Well, it gives them something to do," reasoned Fire, who spent her evenings with the complete works of Trollope, having failed in two marriages and lost a lover to V 70.

Down the hall Boo Bang and Dee Box and E.Z. and Pearl and Patch and Spat and T.T. all crowded into Black Pixie's room to model the dresses they'd wear to the party in celebration of the birth of Coco's son.

Designers, though dead, were still alive among the Skulls: Armani, Norman Hilton, Ralph Lauren were represented by their creations, to say nothing of Chanel and Givenchy and Yves Saint Laurent and Oscar de la Renta and Carolina Herrera and Josephine Sasso and Victor Costa. In the room were Swakara lamb jackets and rope-soled cotton espadrilles, frou-frou blouses and ghillie flats with ruby-red piping.

Black Pixie presided, a huge lampblack woman who helped in the Skull kitchen and always wore stockings and wide-brimmed hats and eye-turning crimson dresses, just waiting, she maintained, "for that big black buck to come along who is gonna take me out of this mess, girl."

As a pre-party warmup, she served Chivas Regal (hard stuff was against the rule, but like all the other rules it was sometimes broken) in crystal glasses taken from the breakfront where Sylvia de Broglie had put them before retiring to her bed from which she never moved until a Skull Removal Squad gathered her bones up gently and placed them with others on the building's utility cart.

Half a dozen girls were peering, with varying degrees of acuity, into a large mirror framed in Empire style.

Boo Bang, a streaked-blond countergirl at McDonald's in the old days, snapped open a Spanish fan and moved it rapidly, squinting at her freckled face above a stretch bra in French nude. From a forest of cosmetics on the table, others were selecting eye shadow and wrinkle sticks and blusher.

Big-butted finger-snapping T.T., who people suspected had been named after Tina Turner, was imitating one of The Ladies. "Like, honey, I only feel comfortable when I be in Chanel." Actually she was wearing one of Donna Karan's cotton poplin off-the-shoulder bodysuits with a notched collar.

Dee Box said, "Yeah, me too, honey. Wanna impress men, you gotta wear Chanel. I wears it to bed."

T.T. leaned forward. "Yeah? What do your men say?"

"Who could care what they say? Don't like Chanel, don't get nothing from me. I hold my ass back from men don't like Chanel."

A squeal of laughter. They were kicking back not with weed or coke but with generous emotion. A couple of girls lit into a few dance steps, hips swaying and breasts shaking, that might have brought back IRT from the grave had he not been cremated, so he could get down with those sweet mammas and boogie again.

Like a cold eye the unblinking moon stared down on the dogs gathering under Washington Square Arch. They surged restlessly away from it, then returned. Lost to the moon's gaze for swirling moments beneath the monument, they finally freed themselves from the park. In the moon-washed street they kept milling around until a large white dog separated himself out. Giving a yip of impatience he went in pursuit of whatever might be alive out there, the pack at his heels, a sea of motion among the parked cars.

With the dogs gone, Timbales could hear music clearly. A strum of electric guitars soared across the motionless autumn leaves, across empty benches, across the wings of sleeping pigeons.

It was coming from a battery-operated stereo on the second floor of the Club House, and although from where he was, in the building across the park, Timbales couldn't see lamplight in the Club House, he did get a woeful earful of rhythms surging like dogs across the silence.

"Una fiesta," he muttered.

In a large fifth-floor apartment, where he figured ghosts were less likely to hang out, Timbales was nursing his cold. He had inhalers, nose drops, jars of Vicks ranged around him in the candlelit room like an army of toy soldiers. He had a sore throat, a headache, and an earache in both ears that didn't prevent him from hearing them partying over there while he was here with a leaky nose, watery eyes, and no real cold but like sniffle.

Timbales opened a warm beer. Suds overflowed onto his bony hands. When he drank, the foam whitened a pencil-thin mustache that he had meticulously trimmed. He was nineteen years old and so lonely he couldn't stand it. As a boy he had shared a bed with two brothers and a sister, all of them snuggling together like puppies. Later, when he wasn't supermarket bagging, he hung out on summer afternoons with guys on stoops or like they did some vamping of fruit from trucks or toked reefer or stood around on the garbage-strewn streets near a copping corner to laugh at petros coming along with eyes bugging out and jaws working, so high and going to die. Even though there were bombings and shootouts, his neighborhood was a good place to be because when you were in the middle of it you weren't lonely. In his entire life Timbales had never been alone, but here he was at this very moment sitting in a five-room apartment big enough for five East Harlem families put together.

Getting up and going to the window, he listened for the dogs, but they must have gone far away, leaving the moonlit park solely to the sound of partying from the Club House. The fun was going on without him.

"Estoy perdiendo el seso," he told himself aloud. But if he went back over there, he wouldn't lose his mind. He told himself in English, "Go over there!" His angry and determined voice was booming in the cavernous room. It made him feel brave. "Go over there," he told himself again. "Estan por allá. Me, I go over there and party too!"

8

It had been a ritual with the main man and Mystique that when she came to his apartment and announced "Guess who!" they would shed their clothes without another word and make love wordlessly (that is not to say soundlessly) before succumbing to civilization's insistence on language.

Tonight, after Mister Touch had had a glass of wine at the celebration for Coco's baby, he returned to his apartment, dismissed Africa, and waited in the darkness. When Mystique came into the room, she used her flashlight to find the candle on the desk, lit it without looking at the man sitting nearby on a couch, and ignored the ritual. Instead of coyly announcing "Guess who!" she yelled out "Damn death damn death damn death!" while pacing fully clothed back and forth in the candlelight.

She told him Sister Love was dying for real, and the other two showed signs of being on their way out too.

When he offered the consolation that Coco had given birth to a normal child, she ignored him and continued to pace. Listening to the click click click of her heels on the uncarpeted floor, Mister Touch asked Mystique Of The Honey Hair to come sit on the couch beside him. But the clicking intensified. "I have always valued myself. I am an intelligent, attractive, accomplished woman, and here I am in this haunted house watching people die and having to beg for a little attention from someone who cares nothing for me."

Mister Touch told her how happy he was that she had come to him this evening. He really meant it, yet was aware that his voice sounded formal and unconvincing, even to himself, as if it knew something he did not.

Clicking across the room, she muttered how unreal it all was, a cosmic joke; they were living inside a comic book and every minute of the day was dangerous because it was like all the dead out there were a force, something heavy and hard and mean-spirited, that could emerge from the shadows at any time and squeeze the life out of everyone in this haunted house. The clicking stopped. In a voice of sudden comprehension, she told him that they really could die in this place. This was no joke, this was serious.

Mister Touch waited, listening to the thick breathing become softer and slower after a while. Then the sound of a zipper. A silken swish.

"Let's do it," Mystique whispered breathlessly. "I don't care what's going on in this damn haunted house. Make me forget everything."

He felt a hand roughly grip his and pull his face against warm skin scented with perfume.

Later they lay side by side, hips touching while disco from the party vibrated against the wall. Reflective in the aftermath of love, he considered love. He had once read that the human male is erotically dominated by sight: See her, want her. Maybe that had once been true of him, but of course it couldn't be now. Nevertheless, through his other senses he became aroused faster and the ensuing passion lasted longer. His other four senses vibrated to the slightest change in scent, temperature, and pressure, to nuances of taste and sound that he had never fully experienced as a man with vision, as if erections flourished in the dark soil of his blindness.

He had made it with a few other Skull women, Nando most prominently among them. Locked in visual memory was Nando's face, her high cheekbones like polished ivory and her hair cropped boyishly short; Nando, whose Asian eagerness to please him had been wonderfully exciting, but after a while oddly choreographed and much too chaste and ultimately false, and he realized that the Chinese girl's interest in him came from the pity he aroused in her because he was going blind. They had drifted apart — he descending from Bad Looker to Blindie, Nando moving back up the trail to assist another transient on the downward path from Poor Breather to Wheezer.

But Mystique, ardent and generous, if also combative and opinionated, was the best of lovers. Sometimes the touch of her skin reduced him in fantasy (vision might have spoiled it) to the size of a tiny sightless infant clutching the endless flesh of the world, a maternal landscape of soft belly and breast. He told her about it — how lack of sight somehow encouraged in him a return to babyhood. Mystique seemed to understand, even enjoy her role as the mother in this fantasy.

Yet something was missing between them. Blindness kept Mister Touch honest in his emotions. He couldn't cheat by finding more in smiles and gestures than was actually there. In the blackness of his mind he always sought Mystique during their lovemaking while she was whispering endearments from an unbreachable distance. He never could locate whoever held together that body pulsing against his own. He wandered through the dark country of their mutual need and heard her call but without ever finding her. It had taken blindness for him to understand that the binding element of love was nameless and invisible, hovering above lovers like a halo of grace. Not even mutual respect or goodwill or satisfaction could breach the gap between two people. He did not love her.

Playfully tweaking his nose, Mystique asked, "Feel good?"

"Can't feel better."

"Now that I have you in such a good mood, I'm going to take advantage of it. You never have told me about your love life. I don't mean what you've done here."

"What do you mean, here?"

"Come on. You're no Hoss, laying everything in your path, but you're no ascetic either. I wouldn't be surprised to hear you've hit on poor Cola Face."

"That wouldn't surprise you?"

"Well, every other male has. Poor Cola Face — beautiful enough to fascinate men without being fascinated by them."

"I never knew that."

"No, but every Skull woman does. Anyway, we were talking about you. I happen to know you had at least a half dozen of the women around here before you got to me. But don't tell me about it. I'm talking about the love life that counted — before V 70 Struck." When he said nothing, she pleaded, "Come on. To celebrate Coco's baby. Who did you love and who loved you?"

"To celebrate Coco's baby?"

"Unbend. Tell me."

"Okay." But all he told her was that before V 70 Struck, he'd had two serious love affairs. One he ended, the other she ended.

"Tell me about the one she ended."

"She wanted it all and she said I only gave eighty percent. You see, she saw life in terms of percentages. She was an accountant."

"But she was right about you. I understand her. She must have loved you a lot to think that way — that she wanted all of you and not just eighty percent. That's the way I am. I want all of you, one hundred and one percent."

"Even if it's not all available?"

"Then nobody else will have it."

Wishing he could see her expression, Mister Touch touched her face to let his fingers tell him whether or not she was serious for real. They told him serious. To change the mood, he said, "Listen to them party." From beyond the bedroom wall came the thumping rhythms of Yellowman, an albino deejay who had once been king of the reggae dance halls and who had left the decimated world a legacy of three albums. "Listen," the main man urged Mystique. He could imagine the Skulls, fifty or sixty of them, drinking beer and wishing they had toilets that flushed, heat from radiators, vanilla ice cream. They were probably arguing about the musical selections — whether to play Fat Boys or Mad Whip Thunder or Janet Jackson. Or maybe they were calling out names, fearing someone might not be there who had promised to come: "Wiggy? Sphinx? Said they was coming. Where's Blue Magic? Salt Noody? Salt Noody, you here? She supposed to be here."

Mystique touched his arm. "What are you thinking about?"

"About them partying. I hope they have fun."

"I hope they grow up."

He turned toward the disdainful sound of her voice. "You think they aren't grown up?"

"Most certainly aren't. How can they be? Think of the names they call one another. The weird way they dress. The promiscuity and the encouragement of it. Everything about the Skulls is designed to keep them from growing up."

"They seem to be doing fine the way they are. I mean, given the circumstances."

"I know you go for IRT's adolescent philosophy. I certainly don't, and I'm not alone."

Again he fell silent, allowing his ears to hear someone roaring over the thumping music. It was a slogan they often shouted from OOTHI: " 'While you live, drink! For once dead, you never shall return.' " Good for them, partying with gusto like that.

Mystique said, "Corks popping. They're into the champagne."

Good, he thought. The Skulls had better celebrate tonight,

because things might get worse. Only this afternoon, upon their return to the Club House, a food-gathering party reported hearing gunfire from the west, and the Eighth Street supermarket, when they got there, had been stripped clean. It must have taken a lot of live bodies to cart away so many supplies.

New people in the neighborhood meant trouble. Nomads or perhaps immigrants from uptown, they'd have to be armed to the teeth because of dogs — or maybe because of other humans?

He was pondering the danger when Mystique stirred next to him, turned suddenly, and stroked his cheek. "I shouldn't have said IRT was adolescent. I know how much you cared for him. But I don't see how you believe in all the craziness."

"Craziness?"

"The silly names, the rules, the idea of Skulls. I used to think you were pretending, maybe to keep some of the young hoods in line, but I know now you go for it."

"Yes, I believe in the craziness. It's our salvation to believe."

"Spare me a lecture, okay? Just forget what I said."

"I already have."

"You say that to be polite, but it makes me angry. I wish I could make you angry. I wish I could break through." Putting her arms around him, she murmured against his cheek, "Tell me your name."

"That wouldn't be a good idea."

"Breaking a silly rule? At least in bed we ought to be free."

"I thought in bed we have been."

"Don't condescend. I mean, do *not* be condescending with me. Save that for other women."

"I'm not seeing" — he kept on in spite of the irony — "other women."

"You aren't hitting on Cola Face?"

"I am not hitting on Cola Face," he said wearily.

"Do I bore you? I don't care about the others, not even Nando. I know my worth. Once upon a time when a man showed me a single moment of indifference, he got his walking papers. One day without a phone call? Forget it. But the truth is at heart I'm a one-man woman. There was one man like that for me in the past. Now there's you and you only. I know I can make you happy, even in this weird world. If you cared about me, you'd tell me your name."

"One doesn't depend on the other."

"You don't think so? If you loved me, you'd know better, but you don't, so you're blind to the truth. You don't even want to know *my* name. Mine is —"

He clamped his hand over her mouth, gently but firmly. "Don't," he warned, then let her go.

"See?" Mystique crowed in triumph. "You don't love me! But I don't care, I love you, and that's that. So what are we waiting for, more breath? Let's just do it again." Her hand began rooting around at his groin, so that soon he was squirming and his left hand lifted to her nipple — thumb and forefinger closing around it like the petals of a flytrap.

"Oh God," she breathed, "that's it. Let's do it, damn you. Let's forget everything. I love you, I always will, I won't let anyone else have you, I love you!"

9

IN THE PARTY ROOM there were raucous toasts to the baby and to Snake and Coco who made him. There were wishes and requests and body checks while the beat box blasted out Billy Idol Billy Joel Billy Ocean Echo and the Bunnymen Dead Milkmen Cyndi Lauper The Push Twangers Passion Fodder and enough reggae to sink a battleship.

"Here's to Coco!" "To the baby!" "To Snake who made him!" "Where's King Rat tonight? Said he be coming." "Where's Sugar Head? Zap?" "Where is Hoss tonight?" "Getting it on with somebody shall be nameless." "Wish we had lettuce and tomato. Wish we had meat." "Go kill a dog and eat it. Or let it eat you." "Here's to Coco! Here's to the baby! He gonna see good and breathe right and make us all rich!"

In a corner people were gassing about Shag, who was caught holding when they shook him down after the drugstore expedition.

Sitting nearby, alone, The Fierce Rabbit guffawed scornfully. "All Shag want was a taste."

The Fierce Rabbit had a sharp face the color of dark bitter chocolate and surrounding it, like a halo from hell, an enormous afro. It was so spiky (someone who shall be nameless once said) you'd think he was being jolted by bolts of electricity coming through his hair.

"Rule is a rule," declared Patch, who was ready for argument, having had an inconclusive one earlier with Snake after he'd spent the afternoon in the dispensary with Coco, his ex-woman and the mother of his normal child.

"No rule ever made couldn't be broke," said The Fierce Rabbit.

"Rule is a rule. No drug in this place."

"Where do you get off, pussy, saying what is what? Why get on Shag's case? For holding red? Pussy talk! Where I lived was this shooting gallery where dudes be coming to blow a little scag and wig out. I seen it since I was old enough to piss in a toilet. Don't mean nothing to me do people get high. Body drugs never interest me. You wanna take stuff and croak, do it."

"Rule is a rule. And you talking about the past. Rule against that too."

"Pussy, you telling me what I do?" Fingering the gold loop in his left ear, The Fierce Rabbit said, "Another thing. Nobody stop me using my real name do I want."

Heads turned in his direction.

"Yeah," he said, glaring. "What so bad in the past we got it better now? Run that past me, you pussies. Scared of what was? Don't give me rules to go against what I know. I know my own name. Yeah, I do. Marvin Johnson!"

"Cool it! Cool it!" people chanted at him.

"No sense denying who we be!" he yelled back. "I be born on One Hundred Twenty Street and Amsterdam Avenue! Marvin Johnson!" Drawing his long legs up to his chin like a spider contracting into its web, The Fierce Rabbit glared at people who had turned to see who was showing an attitude. "Yeah," he told them, "even with my own eyes I see black, white, Latin, chinks too, with names don't fit."

"Who say?" someone called out.

"Me. *I* do! *I* say! Marvin Johnson! And don't go telling me Mister Touch won't like me saying my name, because IRT didn't have no regard for brothers by putting the wrong man in like that. Don't like what I'm saying, tell it to my face. Wanna be dead meat, give me trouble." The Fierce Rabbit leaned forward, his coal-black face expressionless like a piece of iron.

After studying that face, the blood who had challenged him muttered, "Huh," like a cough only it meant that the Rabbit could chill his anger out in the icy stream of a stare-down victory.

Once more The Fierce Rabbit declared, "I be Marvin Johnson and proud of it," before lapsing back into his secret world of rabbitry, which was characterized by silent watchfulness and the introspective twitching of a black goatee, and the thoughtful rubbing of one big thumb against the loop of gold he wore in his ear. He would remain within the dark hideaway of his somber mind, from which he could imagine acts of such fierceness that they would someday shake the Skull world above his rabbit hutch like an earthquake.

The celebration lasted a while longer, then singly or more likely as couples the Skulls left the party room.

One of the resident deejays, Sony Boy, remained with a few stragglers. Sony Boy was a Poor Looker who wore his two-ounce headphones even when he slept and whose greatest fear was that batteries would somehow fail to operate his Walkman (a fear that one day would have a terrible basis in fact). All night he had been explaining his setup for the party — a Realistic stereo cassette deck with Dolby B Noise Reduction and a three-band equalizer for adjusting frequency response, with both AM and FM, which were no longer relevant but definitely there, and two-way speakers with four-inch Woofer and Piezo-Tweeter for full-range sound. This he described at meticulous length to anyone who made the mistake of standing too close to him. It was a mistake on two counts: one, he could bore your socks off, and two, he was the least hygienic of the Skulls, meaning that he smelled to high heaven, and periodically had to be held kicking and screaming in the massive hands of Send Em Back To Africa, while other hands scrubbed him raw.

Now he sat in the party room and calmly informed the remaining Skulls that the most important change in their lives since V 70 Struck was going to occur.

He put a new tape in the setup. He told them the change was going to be zouk. Zouk was going to take the Club House by storm. "That's right," he claimed, pointing to the large ghetto blaster. "In there is zouk."

"Some kind of animal?" someone asked sleepily.

"No," someone else said. "Some kind of monkey music."

Sony Boy told them imperiously that zouk was nothing but its own self. He had been holding it back until there was a special occasion, like the birth of Coco's baby, for introducing it to the Skulls. He hadn't played it earlier for fear people wouldn't listen. So only the privileged few who remained would be introduced tonight to zouk. When someone interrupted to say, "I know zouk," Sony Boy waved him off disdainfully. "Zoukers be from Cameroon, Martinique, places like that. They be playing electric guitars, Jap moogs, digital tape decks. They do midtempo gwo ka beat and the Saint Jean beat from Guadeloupe Carnival." He took a deep Poor Breather's breath. "You can hear soca from Trinidad in the grooves and soukous and West Africa high life, and throw in some Haitian pop, some funk, whatever. It all be there." After a few more breaths, he continued the lecture. "Zoukers do revved-up dance tune and knocked-out riff. They get high, they dream on their instruments. I predict it going to take over." Sony Boy's breathless prediction was heard, however, only by himself. Before his discourse on zouk music had ended, the final listeners had drifted away, leaving him alone with "Kassav" in the beat box and a room littered with champagne bottles but without a single cigarette butt, a room smelling of unpronounceable perfume and Calvin Klein Fragrances for Men.

All of The Ladies, along with ten-year-old Golden Girl and ambitious Cola Face, had closed their doors tonight at the first jaunty strains of Donna Summer's "Bad Girls."

Other doors had remained closed during the party. Having completed her daily stint in the dispensary, Sweet Thing locked her door so she could illegally smoke her nightly Winston in daily defiance of a world that had brought her so low that she was the lowly assistant of a freckle-faced Irish girl who probably had never been an emergency-room nurse in the first place. Sweet Thing sat cross-legged like an orange-robed bonze in one of those filthy

Buddhist temples she had seen in Asia on the only trip out of America she had ever made, a trip confirming her opinion that Americans were better than other people although all people were bad. Rebellious smoke rose over her head and her bad lungs sucked her defiance into themselves.

Stay High had put cotton in his ears to block out the noisy party. He lay in bed with "The Mystery of the Universe" and its thirty lines of broken iambic and anapestic meters beside him. It had been written by a scientist for whom Stay High had blind reverence, just as the proverbial Mexican peasant used to have for the Blessed Virgin when he brought his last chicken to the priest for a Christmas offering. Stay High never doubted that The Dream Queen had left in this poem a significant legacy to the world, the key to which it was his destiny to find and its mystery to reveal. What kept him wildly awake now was his growing conviction that these were the two *essential* lines:

> *And do what you want to*
> *Says Cleo*

Plainly the erotic and willful Egyptian queen who stood for rampant hedonism was telling everyone to live in anarchy during these catastrophic times. The Dream Queen had combined Cleopatra and a cat into a metaphor symbolic of an independent woman who does exactly as she pleases, bets on horses and plays tag like a child and travels around willy-nilly, taking upon herself the feminist role of a baseball player who bats against one of those Latino pitchers — that's where "Rio" comes in — even to the point of making fun of theological questions. But why walk the plank? That seemed masochistic.

Moreover, he was deeply perplexed by the use of the three witches in *Macbeth* and of *Alice in Wonderland*, and his theory of hedonism was contradicted by "Mea Kalpa," the misspelled Latin for "I am to blame," which would suggest that the poet was to blame for V 70 (although taking the blame for V 70 was commonplace among the Skulls, who had lost sonsdaughtersfathersmothersloversfriendsetcetera). Was guilt for all that death the rationale for making "Et cetera" the final line?

Other Skulls who hadn't attended the party were asleep, and

the sound of their ragged breathing could be heard in the hallways, but there was still plenty of activity in the Club House during the wee hours.

Returning alone to her room, Dee Box found Wiggy Of Everywhere in the midst of a nightmare, and the black girl comforted the white girl, who had been dreaming of dying in a blast of smoke and light, a dream that would unfortunately come true.

People walking past Bambu's apartment heard something from inside that sounded like "O Honey O Honey" and then "O Riot Honey O Honey O Riot Honey that feel good!" And they giggled, recalling how Riot had sat through the party with his tattooed white arm draped possessively around the long slim elegant neck of black Bambu, who had been an apprentice hairdresser before V 70 Struck (no one knew they had the real thing in Cola Face) and who now served as the Official Skull Barber.

Snake, who rarely spoke except to ask women to sleep with him, was still assimilating the idea of being a hero for real if Coco's boy continued to live. He had already forgotten The Fierce Rabbit's debunking of his reputation tonight: "Snake don't mean nothing," in a voice loud enough to catch the attention of a dance floor full of heavy breathing. "All Snake know how to do is wave his schlong at dumb pussies like Coco and Patch."

Now Snake was alone, having messed up his chances for togetherness by arguing with Patch about seeing the mother of a child who was making him famous. Patch had hoped for a little romancing in her power suit by Armani and red Reeboks with lateral and medial support straps. One of the girls had given her some French perfume with an unpronounceable name and she had liberally doused it between her heavy breasts that for the last month Snake had been calling his sweet melons from San Juan. But all he did was praise Coco's brat. Outraged, Patch had picked up her black sapphire mink jacket with a wing collar standing up for a tailored look and had gone home.

Shaken by the possibility of going to bed alone, Snake knocked on Patch's door for maybe fifteen seconds before she admitted him and they fought and frisked and frolicked and fucked until breath ran out of them just about the time the alarm was sounded at midday.

Boo Bang, giggling drunkenly, was thoughtfully helped to her room by Ace, flushed by his success as the supermarket expedition second-in-command. Slipping into bed beside her, hoping she wouldn't pass out before they could do it, Ace had in his mind an image of Cola Face asleep down the hall, dreaming her ladylike dreams of a tea party in white gloves.

"Let copulation thrive," said OOTHI. And so did Mister Touch whisper in Mystique's ear as they heard in the dark air around them certain unmistakable cries.

Elsewhere in the building people rasped out their breath in a humid autumnal night, tossing fitfully in sleep.

Baby Jane awoke suddenly, driven into consciousness by memory. Once upon a time she had been a bookkeeper. Then one day, for a lark, she had given a dollar to her nephew, who bought a winning Lotto ticket and put Baby Jane and her hubby on Easy Street. But the memory of good fortune was turning her into OOTLO. The bill with Washington on it changed shape, twisted and folded into a roiling lump, a thick oppressive object of dread that somehow eased out tentacles from itself, and these tentacles traveled through her veins into her head where they hung on and squeezed the life out of her, until her skull contained nothing but a single memory. This memory got bigger and bigger, expanding like a big damp balloon until it filled every space of the world. She could think only of handing over that dollar. Nothing but that. She did it a thousand, a million times. It was the sort of thing OOTLO were known for — the reliving of a single event from the pre–V 70 era. In the grip of this memory, she'd sit with hands folded into a single motionless block and smile smile smile although deep within her consciousness the lump was sending these terrible tentacles along her blood vessels and they were squeezing out everything except the thought of handing over that dollar. When memory was upon Baby Jane, it was like someone had shoved her inside a room too small for standing lying sitting, so that she was scrunched up like Alice after eating the cake, and she heard the key turn in the lock, imprisoning her forever, and panic set in and she kept her hands folded for fear if she didn't the room would get smaller, not actually crush her — that would be a relief — but press her into unimaginable positions, leg arm neck head, into an eternity of mind-bending contortions.

Right now, however, the memory of the dollar faded like a

dream, leaving her mind free for a few blessed minutes. In the darkness of silence Baby Jane had respite from being OOTLO.

On the floor below her, in the dispensary, the new mother slept as soundly as the baby in the crib nearby.

Downstairs, on guard duty in the lobby, Turok nodded over his automatic rifle, absorbed in a dream of combat.

Outside, the dogs were returning from an uneventful expedition. Trotting around a corner, they halted in stupefied surprise at the sumptuous prospect before them — a living man. Easing forward in a crouch, every ear taut, every tail up, they were upon Timbales before he knew they were there, before he had time to stagger drunkenly back into the building that he had just summoned up courage enough to leave, before he could even bring the gun into position, much less before he could find its trigger. He fell like an axed tree, a scream frozen in his throat, beneath a kinetic whirl of teeth and fur and claws, being eaten while he was still alive.

10

G o on, cry. It'll make you feel better."

"I don't cry," sobbed Superstar. "But I should of went and seen her last night." He shrugged off Futura's comforting hand. "I never even say goodbye."

"You really cared for Sister Love. I'm glad you did," said Futura, putting her arm around him again. "Here, take this."

"Ain't right what's happening." He did not protest when she put a Thorazine between his lips. "Call this living? Not a good set of lungs or eyes in the place."

"I know. But we have each other," Futura assured him.

"Catch a cold, they send you to jail. Get so lonely you come back, dogs waiting for you."

"I know."

"Ate so much of Timbales you could of put the rest in a shopping bag. Guys found him when they was going over to bring him a bottle of party champagne. Know how they know him? He wore this little bottle round his neck with something inside. Got it from Maria Luisa, the voodoo lady for La Bruja in his barrio. Keep trouble away. Dogs chewed the leather string off, but the bottle be there with the stuff inside."

She stroked his hair.

"Living without electricity like cave people. Eating canned food. Hauling our own shit."

"I know."

"No radio, no TV, no nothing but holing up in this building, scared of pets. Call that living?"

"Sure I do." Futura snuggled up to him. "It's better than being dead."

Closing his eyes, Superstar sighed. "Yeah, life is good when I be with you."

"You mean that?"

"You make me feel good, girl."

"I never met a man like you." She was stroking his close-cropped hair. "Men never found me pretty. At least they didn't treat me nice. But you do."

"Sure you be pretty."

"You just say that."

He opened his eyes and smiled at her. "You be the queen of my life."

When he heard the bad news — expected about Sister Love but unexpected about Timbales — the main man felt scared and depressed, somewhat like he had felt when an older partner in the investment house came to his desk one day, placed a paternal hand on his shoulder, and said, "A little bad news. Seems like the surveillance division of the SEC is interested in you. They think you've been taking unfair advantage of price movements."

He felt worse now; then it had been between him and the computer terminal: war fought on an abstract battlefield with junk bonds and mutual funds and greenmail. He had never thought of corporate raids and takeovers in human terms; that had been purely a matter of manipulating numbers. But now he was the leader of a hundred and fifty people suffering in varying degrees from eye and lung damage and depression and God knows what else.

Thinking of Timbales also brought on a spasm of guilt. The sniffling kid must have weighed crossing the park against his loneliness and had decided the dogs were less of a threat than silence.

He should have broken the rule for Timbales and brought him back over. Timbales could have remained in quarantine on a higher floor. It was an action Mister Touch had considered, yet his lack of confidence had prevented him from scrapping an old rule and following the path of good sense. He had feared the contempt of people who had already crossed the park and confronted their own fear.

To avoid such gloomy thoughts he felt around in his desk for the recorder.

"At the outset we were a ragged, half-crazy bunch of survivors. Ghetto kids, who learned the tricks of surviving soon after they were born, adjusted more rapidly than the middle-class whites who had more to lose when V 70 Struck. The gap in education between the two groups caused misunderstanding and resentment. The social chasm encouraged stereotypic thinking — sort of like night soil fostering the growth of worms. IRT put his mind to closing the distance between Harlem and Madison Avenue. He decided books would help. I suspect there have been few modern societies less disposed to reading than ours, but read we all did. Even OOTLO were brought into the reading room to listen.

"First, however, he banned books of history because they paid attention to the past. And he didn't want books of technology, either, because 'we get our own thing back together before messing again with machines and chemicals.' Good-looking Skulls took turns reading Dickens and Twain and James Fenimore Cooper (very popular in some circles). Poetry worked well, maybe because texts were shorter. 'The Rime of the Ancient Mariner' was a favorite, and in the corridors you could hear taglines from it that would have rattled the poet's wits more than the opium he used in order to write it: 'Water, water everywhere and not a fucking drop to drink.'

"Innovations, however, didn't work. A dramatic reading of

Hamlet was a disaster. Queen Gertrude, out of exasperation with Elizabethan language, threw down her script and yelled, 'Baby, I am *done* with this weird shit!'

"After the failure of Shakespeare, there was resistance to public readings until loneliness and the remorseless prodding of IRT brought people back for more. They got hooked by *The Lord of the Flies*. The few poor-looking Skulls who wanted Proust or Dante read to them had to pay for it by cleaning a good-looking reader's room. This gave the Skulls a rare opportunity for barter.

"We became aware of something strange happening — our memories were improving. With nostalgic conversations forbidden and many events of the past too painful to recall, the desire to exercise memory was relieved by the memorization of literature. The results were spewed out all day, a chaotic scattering of what The Hip Immortals had left to the world. Any quote from One Of The Hip Immortals was generally ascribed to OOTHI, the universal intelligence who filled our hours just as the lingering residue of V 70 must have filled our veins.

"So kids who could hardly write their name were reciting Shelley and Tennyson and Milton — well, maybe not Milton. This did not, however, make IRT happy. It was his theory that a better memory could be a plus only if put to work for real; a minus if we didn't know what that work should be, because then we'd go back to using it on stuff from the old world that no longer counted. He was trying to figure out what that work should be when he died. What should our work be? What should the Skulls do? Those were his questions that have now become mine. Except that right now —"

A loud insistent knock on the door interrupted him.

Putting the recorder away, he called out, "Come in."

When no one spoke, he said sharply, "Who is it?"

"That's what I am here to discuss — who I am."

He recognized Sag from her voice: measured syllables spoken in a low tremolo. She had joined the Skulls while Mister Touch was still a Poor Looker, so he retained a fuzzy image of a white-haired white woman in a severe black suit. For Sag and others of her age, he fully understood, life with the Skulls was a trying experience. They were a minority. Their skills and values had been shaped for another world, and their memories had deeper, more tenacious roots. Sag could talk in a knowledgeable manner on a number of topics — among them outdoor gardening, needlepoint, theater — but she had lost her husband and three grown children to V 70 and her summer cottage and her duplex on Fifth and her diploma from Sarah Lawrence and the photos accumulated during a decent life. In their place were beans that she ate barracks-style and a tin-can around her neck and a weird cluster of young people for companions, many of whom used language which to her was hopelessly obscene and illiterate.

Now she came with a request: she wanted her name changed.

"I walk down the hall and some of these creatures whisper, 'Here come old Sag.' Old Sag. How would you like that?"

"I'm sorry," Mister Touch said.

"Sorry won't do. I want my name changed."

"If I change yours, I must change others."

"Then change them. Maybe we should be who we really are."

"We are who we really are. We just can't be who we were."

His wordplay did not deter Sag. Her self-control, something Cola Face admired, deserted the white-haired matron from Fifth Avenue. Leaning over the main man's desk, she told him how she had despised the little black drummer who had given her such a despicable name and still irrevocably despised the Club House, the clothes, the language. With increasing anger she accused the former prez of insulting her because she was a white woman of good family and education. She hated the way things were run. There was too much catering to black interests. People didn't have enough say. Her stomach turned at the sight of vulgar young women running around in diamonds and rubies. She found the entire atmosphere revolting.

Listening, Mister Touch wondered in fact why IRT had given her such a name. He suspected it had little to do with sagging breasts and plenty to do with sagging spirits. The main man figured, as IRT must have too, that she was suffering from depression and instead of making her OOTLO it had turned her into a scold. He couldn't let her bully him into a decision that might harden into policy and bring malcontents down on him, demanding their own changes. He refused to change her name.

"You are Sag and as long as you're with us you'll remain Sag," he insisted.

"I know you," she said in a tone of voice that had him imagin-

ing her shaking her finger along with the words. "I saw your picture in the Business Section of the *New York Times*. You were being
indicted for something. If V 70 hadn't come along, you'd have
gone to jail. It was all there. I remember reading it and saying to
my husband, 'Look at the world today, a young man like that with
a good education and a family background and he's going to jail
for some kind of shenanigans.' "

"For insider-trading speculations," Mister Touch coolly corrected her.

"The fact is I know. I know who you are and who I am. I know
the world is a horror, I know what I have to endure, but I don't
have to be humiliated by crooks."

"You have your pride."

"You don't think I know sarcasm when I hear it? But you're
right, I *do* have my pride."

"And you have the name IRT christened you with."

From the doorway in fury, she called, "You'll regret this!"

Gone were the days, the main man thought grimly, when anything the leader said was law. People had stumbled into the Club
House then like frightened children, willing to conform for protection and solace. When people like Sag chose to risk their security in
an effort to recapture their past, "they be going through changes,"
IRT would have said, "so better watch out. Going through changes
mean having a need."

From what the main man was told, at the party The Fierce
Rabbit insisted on calling himself Marvin Johnson. If two people
were willing to make a public issue of their names, surely there
must be others grumbling in the background. Perhaps it wasn't
enough that they were surviving and doing a pretty good job of it.
Perhaps the Skulls were suffering from the leisure to demand
more. Perhaps the Skulls were having an identity crisis, a need to
define themselves so they could get on with getting it on.

Mister Touch was reaching into the drawer for the recorder so
he could continue the Skull history when someone else banged
hard on the door.

"Hoss here!"

Rushing into the room.

"Four dudes in the park. Armed. When our guys saw them,
they took off."

"Which direction?"

"West."

Here was a need more urgent than talking into a machine. He heard IRT shouting at him, "Get off your dead ass and do something!"

Thrilled by this call to action, the main man rose from his chair. "It's time we find out who these people are."

11

IN LEATHER JACKETS and crash helmets Riot and Cougar stood next to the bike that they had parked in the lobby. Curious Skulls stood around, looking at the Honda. One of them said disapprovingly, "If you guys ride out on that thing, you're looking for trouble. I'd tell the main man to shove it."

"Yeah?" Riot stroked the handlebar mustache that his O Honey O Honey Bambu loved to wax for him. "Who died and made you boss?"

Since they were going on a special mission, Riot and Cougar were authorized to use a vehicle that they didn't have to push or pull. That made some people jealous.

With a spit can and a pair of binoculars dangling from his neck, Riot was the driver. Cougar, tall and black and a Breather For Real, sat on the rear seat, an automatic rifle across his lap. Revving up, Riot yelled gaily to the crowd, "Have a nice day!" He drove off in a metallic roar, the rear wheel fairly scooting out from under the bike. There would have been a quick accident had Cougar not steadied them by shoving a big foot hard against the ground.

The afternoon was autumn windy with roiling black clouds overhead. The bike turned westward, because Hoss and Mister Touch figured the newcomers might have settled somewhere over there. Riot went up Sixth Avenue, flying along at breakneck speed.

A bevy of strutting pigeons scattered. Unaccustomed to anything but dogs moving so rapidly, they rose in a blue-white swirl, and a fluttering wing brushed against Cougar's jacket as the bike swept forward, leaving a single feather in the crook of his arm. Blank windows sped by, blind glass and empty doorways: Eighth Street, Ninth, Tenth, Eleventh.

"Stop!" yelled Cougar.

Riot brought the bike to a halt.

"Hear that?"

Revving up the engine, Riot cocked his head. "Hear what?"

"*Idle* the fucking thing!"

Along with the sound of a westerly wind sliding across brick and cement they heard the faint yipping of dogs, a crackle of gunfire.

"Let's go," said Cougar.

They set out in the direction of the noise, but this time at a cautious speed. Eleventh Street and Seventh Avenue, Hudson, Washington Street, and abruptly a view of the Hudson River where a Greek liner had been rusting at dockside for two years.

Cougar tapped the driver again.

Riot put on the brakes and again they heard the dogs, louder now, although the sound had changed from barking to a nervous whine.

"Some must of got shot," Cougar judged. "Park it. We make noise, they gonna hear."

Riot cut the engine. They got off and walked the bike up against a wall. Then Riot climbed on Cougar's back, because the effort of driving had tired the Poor Breather as much as making love to Bambu.

Cougar held both Riot and gun as he slogged forward in the direction of the canine whining, south on Washington Street. He went a block, then halted when Riot touched his shoulder. The Poor Breather slid down and fumbled for the binoculars. Cougar waited while the Good Looker looked.

"What happening?" Cougar finally asked.

"Dogs milling around," Riot told him. "I see people standing — some sitting — outside this apartment house next to a warehouse."

"What they doing?"

"Can't see. Let's go closer."

"Dogs gonna see us first?"

"They're watching the people."

"How many dogs?"

"Couple dozen. Well, maybe fifty. But they're scared. Two lay-ing in the street."

"People got guns pointing at them?"

Riot didn't reply but edged forward on his own power. A block later, Riot halted and they both crouched, half hidden behind a set of cement steps. This time when Riot looked through the binocs, he saw with the clarity of a Good Looker a guy sitting on a brown-stone stoop with a carbine in his lap. Other guys were lounging nearby, against walls, against parked cars, just hanging out like guys used to do when they were out of work, out of cash, out of luck. Unlike the Skulls, they dressed in ordinary clothes, jeans and sweaters they might have taken from a cheap store in the neighbor-hood. No jewelry or fancy hats. And there was something funny about them. They looked like they were nodding out. They looked stoned.

When he told Cougar, the big black nodded. "That why they out there with dogs and don't give a fuck."

"You're right, they don't. As long as the dogs don't bite them." Riot chuckled contemptuously. Then he saw through his binocs half a dozen women emerge from the building. They moved like sleepwalkers, leaning forward, as if ready to topple over. They didn't notice the dogs either, although the fifty animals had been joined by at least twenty more, all of them working up courage for another try. A couple of the girls wore only T-shirts and shorts, despite a cool wind.

"Chicks don't mind the cold," Riot said.

"Not when they got a rolling buzz they don't."

Riot noticed that piles of tincans littered the street and plastic garbage bags, untied, spilled refuse on the sidewalk beside the building.

When Riot told him, Cougar nodded again. "Toss their shit out the door like in the old days." He shook his head in disgust. "Living like trash. They black?"

"Mixed. But mostly white." Riot gave him a grin. "That gives you a kick?"

"Yeah. Used to be you people figured dopers was all black."

"Yeah? I never figured that." Riot raised the glasses. "Dogs are really getting worked up. Guy with the gun is nodding out. Those dogs are going to get one of them."

"They high. Don't give a fuck."

"More coming outside."

"They the same way?"

"Sure are. Now someone's taking the gun from the guy nodding out."

A short burst of gunfire boomed through the brick corridor of Washington Street. A following howl of animal anguish. A flow of pigeons around the corner.

"Shot two more," Riot announced.

Cougar was chuckling now, a low belittling sound. "Sitting around high, shooting dogs when the spirit move them. Bunch of torn-up pill poppers."

"More coming out."

"How many?"

"Oh, ten, a dozen. Must be plenty of them in the building. Wait —" Riot leaned forward, peering hard. "Dogs — I think . . . they spotted us! Jesus Christ, they're turning this way!"

Cougar stood up.

Riot said, "I'll run out of breath sooner than you will even if I'm on your back." Letting go of the binoculars, he climbed on — like a man wounded in one of those war pictures that used to feature courage and heroics. "Move!"

Cougar needed no urging, but rumbled along as fast as his burden permitted. Both arms around the muscular black neck, Riot glanced back to see the dogs standing there absolutely motionless, as if startled by what they saw.

A bullet whistled past Riot's head.

"Who," Cougar panted, "they shooting at?"

"At us, man, move!"

The shot unnerved the dogs for a moment, even though it wasn't meant for them. Then, barking wildly, they started down the street.

Riot tapped Cougar's shoulder. "Hand me the gun!"

Cougar swung it up and Riot took it with one hand, turned awkwardly, and pointed the rifle at dogs approaching fast with ears flat, fangs bared, tongues lolling in frenzy. Pulling the trigger, Riot swung the gun in a wide arc, spraying the street and nearly losing his grip on Cougar's neck.

Two dogs collapsed, their legs crumbling beneath them as they fell. Others kept coming, however, and after another short burst of fire, a third dog lay kicking in the street. Halting, the pack yapped angrily, faked another charge, and started milling again.

Cougar reached the bike. Slipping off his back, Riot turned to face the dogs. "Get on! Get the fuck *on!*" Riot yelled, seeing the dogs pacing in ever tighter circles.

"Can't," panted Cougar. He was slumped over, eyes bugged.

More shots from the apartment house. One chipped some brick from the wall just above Riot's head. "Get the fuck on the fucking bike!"

"Can't," panted Cougar.

Riot began shooting again. This time he emptied the clip and killed or wounded half a dozen more dogs. But a shooter was returning fire from the apartment building, as if protecting the dogs, who were scooting for cover with tails against their bellies.

"Get on! Get on!" screamed Riot. What scared him was the thought of someone with a clear head and good eyes getting hold of that gun across the way.

Cougar straightened up and managed to throw one leg over the bike seat. Riot had already got into the driver's seat and started the motor. A bullet dug into the cement in back of them, scattering fragments against the bike's chrome. Riot revved up and roared away, leaving the gun in the street, feeling Cougar's hot sweaty head pressed against his shoulder. From the corner of his eye Riot saw two dogs coming out of the shadows, dashing lean and low for the bike.

"Kick 'em!" he shouted and swerved, zigzagging crazily in an effort to retrieve the bike's balance. "Kick 'em!"

But Cougar didn't have the strength. A sleek Doberman seized his leg just above the ankle and held on, chewing furiously, while the bike leaned left and right. Cougar howled with pain, feeling the skin rip and shred and the bone crack. He would have fallen off had not the Doberman lost purchase and with it its grip and rolled free, crashing against a parked car.

"Hold on!" cried Riot, glancing back at his companion, who was moaning in shock and pain.

"Yeah . . . I holding . . ."

"Hold on!"

"Yeah . . . I . . ."

"Hold on, man, hold on!"

A cloudburst broke around them, washing Washington Street in a chill rain. Slanting raindrops pounded against the speeding bike, the leather jackets, the crash helmets, as Riot kept pleading for Cougar to hold on and Cougar kept muttering, "Yeah . . ." while blood poured from the wound into the rainy avenue, where there were no pedestrians to turn and gape in amazement at this peculiar sight: a young white man with a tincan and binoculars dangling around his neck who was driving with reckless abandon down the middle of the street while a big black clung to him, trailing blood from tatters of expensively tailored tweed pants of a stone beige hue, with side pockets, zip closure, and slightly tapered leg.

12

MISTER TOUCH had finished another tape that afternoon. His history was going in two directions at once. One group of tapes recorded past events, including a personal description of each Skull as well as he could render it. The other group kept up with quotidian events from the day, two weeks ago, when he had feared that the existence of the Skulls might go unnoticed for all time. He continued, however, to maintain secrecy about these recordings, not even telling Hoss, with whom he shared most of his thoughts.

But at the moment he was sharing them. "Hoss," he said, "I'm worried for real."

Ticking off his worries, he cited Ace demanding sex as payment for use of his eyes; Shag blatantly holding reds; Timbales eaten by dogs; Sister Love dying of an unknown cause, with two others not far behind; The Fierce Rabbit yelling his old name in public; Sag demanding a change of her new one; Riot and Cougar being shot at by a bunch of hopheads and Cougar sustaining a serious wound from a Doberman who used to be somebody's sweetums pet; and then a fight erupting over *Madame Bovary*.

There had been a reading of the novel this morning by Flash, the Neatest Looker of all. He was the sort of person who used his eyes for the common good long after his poor lungs said stop. Committed to finishing the book today, Flash read in a thin but determined voice the passage where Charles Bovary has just discovered letters written to his dead wife by her lover. " 'Spanish flies buzzed around the lilies in bloom, and Charles was suffocating like a youth beneath the vague love that filled his aching heart.' " Gasping for air, Flash continued. " 'At seven o'clock little Berthe, who had not seen him all the afternoon, went to fetch him for dinner. "Come along, papa," she said. And thinking he wanted to play, she pushed him gently. He fell to the ground. He was dead.' "

Flash paused, trying to get air into his famished lungs. Aware he couldn't go on, he lowered the book, done for the day.

"Spanish fly," someone said with a giggle. "Ain't that to get it on with?"

"Sure is. Charlie Bovary use a little Spanish fly on Emma, maybe she would have stopped fooling with other dudes."

The Skulls were sitting in chairs or on the floor of a living room with walls covered by half a million dollars' worth of contemporary paintings, though they didn't know it. What they saw were the dope dreams of wigged-out writers who must have moved in from subway cars to do pieces on walls.

"It don't make sense," someone observed. "A guy conk out because his dead wife was balling another dude?"

"What do 'fetch' mean anyway?" someone else asked. "Kid had went to 'fetch' him?"

At all the reading sessions Stay High was in attendance to answer such questions. It was his official duty. One of the few Skulls who dressed plainly, he went around in a baggy intellectual sweater and slacks, just as he had done while earning a doctorate in archeology at Columbia. Adjusting his glasses, he explained that "fetch" means "to get." He said further, "His daughter went to get him. Or I suppose in this context to bring him in to dinner."

"Why don't Charlie say so then?"

"Wasn't Charlie wrote it," someone objected. "Flobert did."

"Flaubert," Stay High said.

"Don't care who wrote it, he don't know nothing. Nobody gonna lay down and die being some chick be balling another dude."

"OOTHI said something about this," began Boo Bang, but because of her unwarranted reputation for stupidity, no one listened to her.

"Oughta shoot Emma and the dude both," said someone. "I don't mean Flobert shoot them. I am saying Charlie ought to."

"How do he do that, dummy? She already dead."

"At least shoot the dude."

After a silence someone commented further. "What do Charlie care about some love letter being Emma not breathing when he read it?"

"Yeah," someone agreed.

Someone said, "It wasn't one letter only, it was like a lot, which prove she been carrying on a long time."

"Kill himself for a dead chick? No way."

"Like I dig it. I dig *Madame Bovary*."

"Yeah? What you got here is one wiggy chick and a damn fool."

"Charlie, he really love Emma. What in fuck is wrong with that?"

"Nothing wrong. But Flobert don't tell it like it is."

"Which is what?"

"True to life. Charlie be a doctor, right? Get himself a new woman with no sweat, so it don't add up."

"You got no heart."

"You got no sense. I don't like this kind of story. I want something which tell it like it is. Flobert don't know shit. Tell me something. How do Charlie kill himself? No mention of a gun or knife or like that. Die from thinking? Phony baloney."

"Phony baloney to you."

"If he had went after the guy or cut Emma good with a blade, I believe that. No way do I believe he gonna sit down and think about his dead woman till he dead too."

"But he did. He die from a broken heart."

"Yeah? You got a broken ass."

"You mean as they come."

"Ah, let him be," said someone from the corner. "He got no heart."

"Who said that?" demanded Dragon, who had voiced the major objection to *Madame Bovary*. He was a heavyset black with a broad flat nose and hair shaven close to a round skull.

"Me." Lil Joint got to his feet. Not much over five feet, he was a slightly built Hispanic who moved with whippet-like grace. He had first joined the reading sessions when the book had been *Don Quixote*, whose hero he had come to love because his own brother had been a heroic fool too. Lil Joint had protested vehemently when by general agreement Cervantes' masterwork had been dropped because group interest waned around page 300. After pouting awhile, Lil Joint had returned to the sessions. Now he put his hands in his pockets and gazed from heavy-lidded eyes at Dragon.

"Go on and say what you said," challenged Dragon.

"You got no heart."

"Yeah?" Dragon smirked at others in the room, as if conspiring with them, before looking at Lil Joint again. "I give you the chance so you can get out of here before I do something."

Lil Joint said calmly, "Chiugate." To make himself perfectly clear, he translated. "Fuck you." And he added with withering contempt, "You nothing but a jealous toy."

Dragon's eyes bulged. "Nobody sound on me. Want to settle some shit, you?"

Lil Joint smiled.

"Call me a jealous toy?" Dragon said aloud but mostly to himself, as if he couldn't believe what was happening. One thing he did believe though: this greaser Lil Joint was rocking on the wrong turf by sounding on him. He was in the right, definitely. "*You* be the jealous toy," he declared. "I be slap fighting with razors before you could wipe your ass. No greaseball gonna sound on me. Watch out, little man, or I am gonna *do* you." He turned to the others seated around the room and grinned in pure triumph. "We be into reading and this greaser starts rocking like that when he don't know nothing about Flobert or nothing else but picking his spic nose." Before Stay High or panting Flash or a dozen others could stop him, Dragon had crossed the room and grabbed at the small Latino's throat.

With a single movement Lil Joint not only avoided the attack but whipped his right hand from his pocket and slashed at Dragon with a knife that seemed to open of its own accord.

Dragon staggered back, too surprised even to yell, clapping his hand to his face. In the ensuing confusion, Lil Joint crept discreetly from the room, leaving Dragon surrounded by dumbfounded Skulls.

Bent over, eyes startled and wide, Dragon slowly withdrew his bloody fingers, exposing to view a deep gash running from left nostril to left ear. Staring at the blood on his open palm, he muttered in disbelief at an injury as much spiritual as physical. "See what he done? What the crazy sonsabitching little greaser done? Cut me? Cut me like that?"

"Hey, I have the answer!" someone exclaimed so loudly that everyone turned to look.

It was Boo Bang again. Boo Bang, who rejected Superstar when he was bored by Sister Love and before he had become aware of Futura. Boo Bang, who had been called by the vengeful stud, whose feelings had been hurt, "so dumb that like if you told her this was a nightmare she would stay up all night waiting for it to end." Boo Bang, who actually had one of the better memories in the Skulls, which had helped her immeasurably as a countergirl at McDonald's because she never once got an order wrong. Boo Bang now ran her hand triumphantly through her streaked blond hair. "This is what OOTHI said about love and death," she told them. " 'Men have died from time to time, and worms have eaten them, but not for love.' "

"Yeah," mumbled Dragon, hand clamped to his cheek. "I be saying that all along."

Having heard this account from a witness who shall be nameless, Hoss had relayed it to the main man, who observed that even a French novelist was no longer safe from the rumblings of discontent within the Skull ranks. Of course, Lil Joint would be given a dressing-down for defending his aesthetics in a manner no doctoral candidate would have dared to do. Admirable or not, Lil Joint's passion was a measure of Skull unrest.

"Tell me, Hoss, are we losing it?" the prez asked bluntly.

"I ask myself the same question. It used to be cooperate or die," said Hoss. "Remember carrying handkerchiefs soaked in perfume when the wind changed? Blowing death our way?"

"I seem to recall something like that," Mister Touch replied tartly. "We were all punch-drunk then. And therefore easily managed. I remember the long afternoons, when IRT wasn't looking, how we used to sit around wondering if we were in a kind of purgatory, waiting to see if we were headed up or down. Weren't we religious in those days?" Or maybe the survivors in those days, he thought, had been less like philosophy majors than like snorkelers, moving in a dark landscape of wayward currents, floating among sea channels as ambiguous as death. And some years ago there had been that weekend in the islands with Jill — or was it Wendy — swimming languidly on the surface with their foggy masks pointed at what was below: fish sliding from sight into forests of brain coral and moray eels pulsing inside a bony reef like big thick veins and crabs in patches of white sand lifting their skinny legs in the tentative high-stepping way of dusted cokeheads crossing the street — an under-the-surface world of silence and viscous motion and unsettling mystery that reminded him of post–V 70. Murky, sluggish, undersea people; they, he thought, had been the Skulls in the early days.

But recently many of them showed signs of awaking from dreams of death. If so, they needed things to do besides merely surviving. They could learn tai chi ch'uan from Nando (he remembered her practicing the Chinese exercise nude next to his bed), and take art classes from Sphinx, who used to be an art critic, and study languages from tapes or from Skulls of European and Asian origin. Some of The Ladies could teach sewing.

"We could begin math and science classes," Mister Touch told Hoss. "I can teach simple math, the sort that got me into trouble with the SEC. We'll canvass the Club House and find a few people we can pass off as science instructors."

"V 70 played a mean trick by giving us a lot of high school dropouts but only one scientist — and that one dying and leaving behind a lousy poem no one understands."

"We can teach ourselves," the main man claimed enthusiastically. "We have all the classrooms and labs of NYU to draw from."

"Wait a minute," said Hoss. "Do you want to put test tubes and explosives in the hands of these Looney Tunes?"

"So we'll hold back on lab work awhile. Do you see what I'm saying, Hoss? We're coming out of the Grand Funk."

"At least you sound like you are."

"There's this, Hoss. In the months I've been prez I have done almost nothing."

"Well, now —"

"And people have accepted my doing nothing. Because without IRT to kick butt, we've all settled back and waited for something to happen. Now a lot has started to happen. Sister Love dying, others sick, Coco having the baby, armed druggies on our turf — we're being stirred out of a deep sleep."

"If you put it that way, I guess so."

"Know what I've thought about us secretly, Hoss? I've thought every one of us has lost an edge since V 70 Struck. We aren't as fast as people used to be. We think slower. At least that's been true of me. I mean, after V 70 Struck, when an idea came at me out of the shadows, I got scared. I didn't want to face it. An original idea was like the ghost of one of those dead millions. Know what I mean? I wanted to get rid of it, have some peace and quiet. I'd just walk away."

"True of me too," Hoss admitted.

"That was until lately. Now when an idea comes along, I manage to plant my feet and look at it."

"Stare it down. Yes, me too."

"I think it's happening to a lot of us. We're starting to think again. I mean, as fast as we used to, as boldly. And if I'm right about that, then people are going to be more critical and aggressive in their demands. Winter's coming. Some will be getting sick. Others will want something done about the new kids on the block. Skulls are going to get bitter, then angry, and then — who knows? Maybe IRT's concept of communal living won't survive. There could be revolts, splitting off, all sorts of turmoil. It's possible we can't live together anymore. Maybe we'll roam around in nasty little packs until we fade away."

"Like old soldiers," Hoss added grimly. "You know how bad it sounds? It sounds like —"

But he didn't have time to complete his negative comment, because someone was banging on the door and yelling, "Two strangers downstairs! From the West Side!"

13

THE BIG BLOND guy from Minnesota, Turok, had his automatic rifle pointed at them. A crowd of Skulls had gathered round.

"No jiving," said the tall black male wearing leather and a chain belt. "We" — he thrust a thumb in the direction of the woman beside him — "we wanna stay."

Sugar Head, wearing orange headphones, pushed through the crowd as if he had authority. It was something he had always dreamed of having. Blinking haughtily at the couple, he put his hands on his hips.

"You," he said. "Turkey," he said, looking up at the tall man. He paused to tell his audience, "Voy a decirle cuántas son cinco." He said about the same thing to the stranger. "I'm gonna tell you what is what. Skulls don't front. So when I ask question you give one quick answer, turkey." People said a better name for the tiny fellow would have been Mean Rooster because despite a lack of breath he was always spoiling for a fight. "So tell me," he demanded belligerently.

The tall black looked down on him in mild amusement as if watching a little dog kicking its back legs out in a gesture of proprietorship after pissing on the wheel of a big car. "Sure," the stranger said. "Ask me anything you want, I tell you what you want. Why not?"

Sugar Head glanced at the crowd and singled out Cougar. "You seen him before, turkey?" Sugar Head asked the stranger.

The stranger squinted at Cougar on crutches. "No, man, I never seen him before."

"You fuckers fuck him over."

"Meaning?"

Glancing at his audience, Sugar Head smiled and said of the stranger, "Le gusta exagerar," although if anyone liked to talk big, it was Sugar Head. "Hear I telling you cuántas son cinco, turkey," he said. "You fuckers over there took potshot at him and dogs tore his leg off por poco."

"Don't have nothing to do with dogs either."

"You turkeys work them up, they go after our guy here. Look at him."

"I'm looking but I don't know nothing," said the man, cocking a thumb at his companion again. "Me and her just wanna stay is all. We come in peace."

"Listen, turkey," said Sugar Head with heat, "you get to stay, which is promise no way, you better know what is going down."

"Sure," the stranger said. "Give me a for-instance."

"We don't talk about some thing. Es una regla inflexible."

"Somebody tell me what he saying," said the stranger.

"It be the rule for real," somebody told him.

"Okay. So?"

Turok, who felt as Club House Guard he must do more than just keep a gun on the strangers, put in his own two cents. "We don't talk about what happened before V 70 Struck."

"No naming name, turkey," explained Sugar Head. "No naming our ownself old name neither."

"I don't get that," the stranger admitted, wrinkling up his broad forehead of the color and sheen of a polished black Cadillac.

"Get it quick!" shouted Sugar Head, jabbing his finger in the air. The orange earphones gave him the look of an angry bee with huge faceted eyes. "*Your* name, por ejemplo. Don't tell us about it! We don't wanna know!"

"If you stay," added Turok, "you get new names."

"Who do we gotta see for that?" asked the man.

"*We* ask, not you," Sugar Head told him.

"Mister Touch gives the name," put in Zap. White, tall, good-looking, but a Bad Looker, Zap was tying knots in a piece of string that he could hardly see, but that unbeknownst to Zap had plenty to do with the universe.

"Mister Touch?" The man laughed. "What kind of name is that?"

"Se llama Mister Touch. Don't mess with him," Sugar Head declared.

The man put up his open hands in mock fear. "I just wanna stay clear of the dogs and that is that."

"Deje las cosas como son," warned Sugar Head.

"Somebody tell me what he saying."

"Let sleeping dogs lie," somebody told him.

"Cool it," added Sugar Head's only friend, Zap. With a single motion he made all the knots that he had tied in the string disappear.

"What we doing, man, is cooling it," said the stranger with a grin. "Ain't we?" he said to his female companion.

The woman looked at Sugar Head and the spacey head-phones, then at good-looking bad-looking Zap, who had begun to make more knots in the string, then at Turok with the gun. Apparently she chose the man with the gun to be the most significant spokesman here. "Is Mister Touch in charge?" she asked Turok.

"Bet your ass," Sugar Head told her. "Es un pez gordo."

"Can he see best?"

"Flash the best Neat Looker."

"Neat Looker?"

"Never mind that," Sugar Head snapped.

"If he isn't best, why is Mister Touch your leader?"

"He got the okay from IRT."

"I don't get it," said the male stranger. To the woman he said, "Do you?"

"So get it," grumbled Sugar Head. "We do asking, not you! Es imposible!"

Suddenly the crowd parted and Send Em Back To Africa approached, towering over them all. He took a firm grip on the male stranger's arm.

"Hey, what you doing?" the man asked fearfully.

Africa guided him toward the stairway and the woman, prodded by Sugar Head, followed.

The two strangers stood in front of the main man's desk.

"You say you were thrown out?"

"God's truth," the man told Mister Touch. "We come over here hoping for some luck."

"Your people over there, do they have a name?"

"Dragons."

"How did you get here?"

"Walked."

"From the West Side?"

"Not that far."

"What about the dogs?"

"We was plain lucky. Didn't meet none. I had a piece though."

"Where is it?"

"Throwed it away before getting here. Afraid you guys wouldn't like me bringing a piece inside."

"You have that right. Why did you come here?"

"Guys told us about you. They come from here."

"Who?" When Mister Touch didn't recognize the names of two men who claimed to have been Skulls, he asked for their description. Apparently they were Santo and Alligator, both having been kicked out of the Skulls for holding.

"They join up with us about six months ago," explained the stranger. "When we was living in the Twenties."

"And today you came from?"

"Washington Street. Over there."

"Did you see our people the other day? Two on a Honda? After you people shot at them did you see one of them get bit by a dog?"

"Don't know nothing."

"So Santo and Alligator told you about us. Did you know about us before you moved into the neighborhood?"

"They use their real names now. So do everybody." He sounded proud of it.

"I asked, did you know about us before?"

"No, we didn't know about you here before. It was when they told us we knew about you being here."

"When was that?"

"Don't exactly know."

"Well, months ago? Yesterday?"

A long silence. "Maybe some days ago."

"Before or after our people on the Honda were shot at?"

"Man, I don't know that. I don't know nothing about shooting at somebody. God's truth. I don't front."

Mister Touch doubted that. "Why did they shoot at our people?"

"Oh, some maybe got high and did it for kicks. Like throwing us out for kicks."

"So you Dragons use drugs?"

"Not me and her."

Mister Touch did not believe that. Although the stranger's voice had a brassy careless tone, the hesitant thoughtful way he spoke suggested fronting. "Do your people often get high and throw someone out for kicks?"

"Look, man, I don't front you. Some got high and we complain like if they go on like that we gonna get too messed up even to get supplies and stuff. But they don't go for it. So they toss us out like that. God's truth, man."

"Call me Mister Touch."

"Yeah, sure. Anything you want. Mister Touch, sure."

The prez was troubled by the blatant servility. "How many in the Dragons?"

A long silence. "Don't exactly know."

"Give me a ballpark figure."

"Oh, hundred, I don't know."

"You sound like a Good Breather."

"I breathe pretty good. Yeah." He sounded proud.

Mister Touch estimated from no sound of breathlessness that the stranger was probably a Breather For Real and as such a potential asset. "What about your sight?"

"Not bad, I guess. Same as hers."

The prez turned slightly in the direction of the woman, whose soft voice he had heard only once so far. "Do you see well?" he asked.

"Nothing to brag about, I'm afraid," the woman said.

"You sound like a Good Breather."

"Yes, well, I'm okay."

"Good enough to get you here." Mister Touch paused and thought. "I don't understand why they let you go — people in excellent condition."

"Dragons don't need us. Doing all right, considering. Till lately."

"What has happened lately?"

"Some lungs going bad. You know how it is. You having the same run of luck?"

Ignoring the question, Mister Touch asked if the Dragons had a doctor.

"We had this medical student, we have this medical student."

Leaning forward with interest, the prez said, "Which is it? *Had* or *have*? Past or present?"

"We still have got him, only he down with flu, so he ain't been helping out lately. So I said we had one, but we have got one too, see? You sure trying to trip me up."

Mister Touch suspected that the West Side Dragons lacked someone with medical skill. He asked again how many Dragons there were.

"I told you. About a hundred. No fronting, man — Mister Touch. Nobody know for sure, I guess."

"Who's your main man? Santo? Alligator?" He guessed Alligator.

"Them and some other guys too."

"What is it, some kind of oligarchy?"

"Huh?"

The woman spoke up. "Things are discussed freely, so in that sense it's democratic. But there's hardly a government, if that's what you mean. People do what they want. Nobody is really in charge."

"People getting high," added the man with a guffaw, as if he couldn't suppress mirth at the memory.

"It sounds like chaos," Mister Touch observed.

"It *is* chaos," said the woman.

"Are you holding now?" the prez asked sharply in the direction of the man.

"Nah, like I told you. Neither of us be users."

"Hoss?"

Hoss, standing behind the couple, explained that they had been searched.

"Because dope here is out," Mister Touch told the man.

"No kidding?"

"No kidding."

"Okay. Fine with us, man. We just wanna join up."

"Why?"

"Got no place to go."

That made sense, but something held the prez back from inviting them in. "I still don't understand two things. Why they let people like you go and how you got past the dogs." He was wondering if the Dragons let them go because they were troublemakers. Or had the Dragons sent them over to spy? If so, the Dragons would have given them protection on the way over.

"Man, Mister Touch, I told you. We got lucky coming over. I had myself a piece but didn't use it."

"Awfully lucky."

"We really were lucky," put in the woman. "But the Dragons have a method for handling dogs and we were ready to use it. They take a dead dog or a few dead rats along when they travel and if the pack comes at them, they throw out the carcasses and it keeps the dogs busy. Then they can shoot them or get inside somewhere. They'd rather not shoot if they can help it."

"Why?"

"With dogs milling around and guns swinging around to follow them, people get shot instead of dogs."

"You were ready to use this method?"

"I had a shopping bag full of dead rats. We have a lot of them over there. We were lucky not to meet the dogs, but I think between the rats and our gun we could have handled them."

That too made sense.

"Mister Touch," the woman said in her soft voice, "if you throw us out now, it's getting dark and the dogs will be on us for sure. They're worse in the dark. I don't think there's a chance of our handling them at night."

That made complete sense. Her remark and their physical potential tipped the balance in their favor. Mister Touch said, "All right, you can stay."

"Hey, bro, terrific," said the man. "Can we get something to eat?"

"Hold on," Mister Touch said. "Before anything is done, I'm going to name you."

"Yeah, I heard about that," the man said with a giggle.

"Go into the other room and wait," Mister Touch told the woman. "I'll take you first," he told the man. He told Hoss, "You can go." For christening there had to be privacy.

"How old are you?" Mister Touch asked.

"Twenty-five."

"Where did you live before V 70 Struck?"

"Convent Avenue and One Hundred Twenty-six. I suppose to tell that? They say downstairs we not suppose to talk about that."

"Now, yes. Afterwards, no. Once you leave this room with a new name, the past is dead. You understand?"

"Yeah, sure. Why not?"

"What sort of work did you do when V 70 Struck?"

"I was between a job."

"Well, when you had one, what sort of work did you do?"

"Whatever come along."

Another drifter. Mister Touch couldn't get a clear impression of the man, so he pulled out one of the first names that came from the list IRT had put in his mind. "Lil Guy," he said. "That's your name."

"Lil Guy?" The man chuckled. "Being I six foot two, that is some joke."

"Lil Guy."

"Yeah, cool. Whatever you say, boss. You the power."

"Don't Uncle Tom me, fella."

"Whatever you say, Mister Touch. I'm cool."

"Get down on your knees."

"Hey, man, what?"

Mister Touch felt beside his desk and located IRT's old cane, the dubbing sword. He picked it up and worked his way around the desk, sensing the tall man still standing in front of him. "Get down on your knees. I am christening . . . knighting you." Mister Touch had always been confused about the process, perhaps because IRT had surely been. You gave a knight his vocation by dubbing him with a sword. You brought someone into the Church by sprinkling him with holy water. The IRT method at least recognized that both ceremonies had in common the giving of a new name. Women were dubbed as well as men. It was the way, and Mister Touch followed it.

"I said, get down on your knees."

"Yeah." The man got down on his knees. "Whatever you say, Mister Touch."

Reaching out with the cane, the prez located the man's shoulder. Raising the sword, he said in a measured voice, trying to imitate IRT's low resonant tone, "I dub thee Lil Guy in the name of the Father, the Son, and the Holy Ghost."

"This something Catholic?" asked Lil Guy, rigid as a board.

"This is survival," Mister Touch told him, while tapping each shoulder three times. "Rise, Lil Guy!"

Going back to the desk and sitting down, the prez said, "Send her in." When he heard nothing, Mister Touch said, "I told you, get up now."

Getting up.

"Wowee," said Lil Guy. "Ain't that something? That sure waxed me. Never knew anything like that before."

"Tell her to come in."

Going from the room, coming into the room.

The woman was twenty-six. She lived on the West Side, Eighty-second Street and Amsterdam, with two girlfriends now dead. Occupation: social worker.

His heart sank. No real help here. Altogether the Skulls had thirteen social workers. It seemed to him sometimes that all of New York City had been divided into social workers and welfare recipients, with a few secretaries and school dropouts thrown in to complete the demographics. But he was arrested by the thoughtful melodious cadences of the woman's voice. He began ticking off the memorized female names in his head, halting abruptly at Spirit In The Dark._____

14

IN A VOICE breathy from exercise, not from V 70, Mystique exclaimed, "That was wonderful."

"I've been poleaxed," admitted Mister Touch as he lay spread-eagled on the bed.

"You could be more romantic."

"Poleaxed is an accurate description. Besides, I never had a reputation for sounding romantic."

"You can be romantic," Mystique persisted, "when it comes to selecting names for newcomers."

"I get them from IRT."

"Out of all the choices for the new woman you selected Spirit In The Dark."

"It's a nice name, isn't it?"

"A romantic name. Better than Cola Face, for example."

"Or Sag."

"I remember when Cola Face joined up. She nearly left when he named her that."

"IRT said the name would fit her," he explained, "after a while." He recalled the blue-eyed blonde who might have stepped out of *Cosmo*. The prediction had come true. Her personality became dark, like Coca-Cola, her feelings remained bottled up in a glassy exterior, and her opinions stung the air like carbonated bubbles. Everyone knew she had grown into her name.

"I think Spirit In The Dark already fits the newcomer," continued Mystique.

"Why is that?"

"Well, she's dark-skinned, although on the light side. And she's spiritlike in the sense of being mysterious, having come here the way she did, although I don't think a pretty woman like that reminds anyone of spiritual things." Mystique paused, waiting for what Mister Touch knew should be a response. "Well," she went on when none came, "does it interest you that she's very very pretty?"

The question surprised him. To what depths did jealousy plunge Mystique! Why would he care if a woman whom he could never see was pretty? A better question, one that he would not put into Mystique's head, was how would that woman feel to his touch if he touched her? And what might happen if, after running the tips of his fingers over her cheeks and lips, he created in his mind an image of beauty for her to fill?

"No," he told Mystique, "it doesn't interest me in the least if she's pretty."

"I wonder why she came over here." Having an answer of her own, Mystique said, "She must have had a lover's quarrel with one of those druggies over there. I bet they had a terrible fight and she ran away. He must have threatened her with violence because she was unfaithful, so she ran for her life. He probably held a gun on her. 'If you so much as look at him again, I'll kill you!' "

Mystique's scenario was not too far off the mark, but the details were far less conventional then she supposed.

First of all, Spirit was no runaway. She was here on a mission.

At the outset she would have to acquaint herself with the Skull life-style. Wandering through the Club House, she liked what she saw and when Spirit In The Dark looked she really did see, because she was a Looker For Real. She had concealed the truth from the Skulls as she had concealed almost everything else, except the way Dragons sometimes handled dogs when they thought about it — when they weren't so high it didn't matter if they shot dogs or themselves. She certainly hadn't walked over here from the West Side. She and Eddie had been escorted over in a police car driven by a half blind dirtball cokehead at sixty miles an hour through the empty, but considering his condition, very dangerous streets of New York City, and she had judged herself awfully lucky to be alive when the blue-and-white skidded to a halt a few blocks from the Skull Club House.

Sitting beside her in the back seat, Marty had patted her hand before she left the car. Marty was, in her opinion, the meanest ex-lawyer on the planet. Cocaine had bored into his heart and rooted out whatever compassion had resided there before V 70 Struck. In its place was a wriggling mass of wormlike nasties such as malice and cruelty and ruthlessness that he brought out to view as easily as a proud father opens his wallet and displays photos of his kids. Marty was pasty-faced, but sensual when you looked only at his deepset eyes and not at his mouth, because his tongue undulated like the Snake in the Garden when bad thoughts were sending out tremors of pure evil.

Once again he patted her hand, paternally. In his drug-induced rages and inept sexual arousals he had not so much had her as he had made her have him.

"You're going to be a good girl?"

"Yes," she said.

"I hope you're convinced of that," he said in the pleasant voice that frightened her witless. "Did you say goodbye to the kid?"

"Yes."

"You told her not to worry?"

"I told her not to worry." But even a child knew enough to worry. She was ten years old but had lived a century or two during the last two months that she had been with the Dragons. The kid had wandered into camp one morning, tongue-tied and stuporous, evincing obvious symptoms of a common illness which all survivors of V 70 seemed to have contracted — the disease of unbearably painful loneliness, a symptom of which was sometimes the inability to communicate. Inside the Dragons' club house, the kid had recoiled from the casual sex, from the druggy walk and talk, the pervasive stench and squalor. Yet she had stayed on, because loneliness had clogged her bloodstream like V 70. In the last month Spirit had taken her on as she would have taken on the orphaned daughter of a sister or a close friend. After a few weeks, when some of the fear in the girl's huge eyes had disappeared — replaced by a simmering look of trust and sometimes even by a sparkle of hope — Spirit had sworn to protect this child with body and soul. She had already protected the kid once with her own body: a gone guy had grabbed the little girl and insisted on a headjob, but Spirit had talked him into accepting one from her instead. The girl was undernourished, only ten, but one of these days the sexual threat would be greater, and Spirit vowed to be there when it happened.

It would definitely happen. Men of decency had fallen prey in the post–V 70 world to constant depression leading to abject despair leading to booze and drugs leading to a pure enjoyment of violence. There was endless talk of a better life, followed by spasms of good will and compassion, and sometimes people swore off drugs for good, but the urge for an uplifting high returned, and those former solid citizens tumbled backward into a vortex of savage and uninhibited adolescence, leaving them finally to wander like abused children in a daze through a world of casual brutality.

Although Spirit had tried to keep secret an attachment that could make herself and the child vulnerable, Marty had learned of their friendship. His animal instinct, honed by chemical need, had given him an advantage in the Dragon world. He knew how to use an intelligent young woman for more than just sex.

She had hoped until the last moment that there might be a way out, but Marty's paternal pat on her hand convinced Spirit there was no escape.

"Do what you're supposed to do," he said softly. "Or your little friend is going to pay. We'll shoot her up —"

"No —"

He lifted his hand like a teacher demanding classroom silence.

"Shoot her up *hard* and let the dogs have her before she goes into shock. Understand what I'm saying?"

"I understand."

"Eddie isn't exactly a chaperone —"

She glanced from the car window at Eddie, pacing fretfully on the sidewalk.

"I'm telling you, if you make a wrong move, Eddie will take you out." Marty snapped his fingers. "Like that. Because that's Eddie. Understand what I'm saying?"

"I understand."

"Don't give the kid another thought. I'll tell her not to worry. You'll be back with her soon. Understand?" He waited for her to say "I understand" before pushing her out and closing the door and telling the driver to drive off — just like in a gangster movie, she thought — leaving her there with Eddie almost on the doorstep of the Skull Club House.

Now she was inside, walking through the halls as safely as you please. What amazed her was the restraint of Skull men. None had touched her so far, and she had been in their Club House for a whole day. From a doorway now and then someone cooed, "Hey, pretty mamma, let's get acquainted," but that was only an invitation, not a command. Where she came from, when someone said that to you, you went to him, humbly offering a condom and hoping it wouldn't be a gang rape this time. At least she hadn't gotten pregnant. A pretty woman rarely got pregnant because the men used condoms with her, not wanting to wreck a good body because some dude got careless and knocked her up. They didn't trust women to take birth control pills — and with good reason. Most women were too spaced to remember the pill, and even if they tried to be conscientious like Spirit there was always the problem of maintaining personal discipline in a building where people lived among litter like mice, howled and staggered through the day in a feckless search for good sensation. And there was always the daily forgetting of things — it could be merciful to forget filth, knifings, brawls; on the other hand, to forget birth control was terribly dangerous. Get yourself knocked up, you were shown the door. That's all. Out.

The Skulls seemed to treat women better — a lot better. She watched women her own age bedeck themselves in jewels and twirl around in mink, exclaiming, "Don't I look like something, though?" It gave her a twinge of unfamiliar joy to see a plain girl like Wiggy Of Everywhere wade through a sea of clothes, trailing a thick scent of too much cologne, wearing a floppy hat and ranch mink, her blue and nearly sightless eyes childishly wide with glee.

Were the Skulls really so together? She noticed a calendar pinned to the lobby wall with X's on it, so they knew the day. Some apartments served as latrines, and the air around them was charged with the brisk comforting smell of disinfectant. She watched in admiration those plastic bags being hauled out by people assigned to Misery Detail. On the West Side they started at the top of a building and worked down; when it was half full of shit, they moved to another building.

And then there was the dispensary.

Until six months ago the Dragons had had a sort of medical help. They had possessed a badly emphysematous young man who had been in his third year of medical school and who, in spite of bad lungs and depression, had managed to do some good. He came under Marty's protection, but not even Marty, whose need for power under the implosive energy of cocaine had spread out like a shock wave of nuclear fallout, was able to safeguard his property. The frail medical student was a whiner. One lazy afternoon after an April shower, a couple of guys high on something roughed him up for the fun of it. He stumbled off by himself and was found the next day after a dog pack dined. He had been heading north, probably trying to reach the safety of his medical school. Since his demise, there had been no one who knew medicine. As IRT had often claimed, a physician or nurse or even witch doctor would be a treasure of value beyond estimation.

To acquire someone like that was the purpose of the Dragon mission.

Spirit entered the dispensary. Someone was sitting at a desk on duty, like in a real hospital, and a stocky little Japanese Wheezer named Venus Girl was bent over a whisk broom, squinting at nonexistent dirt which she was sweeping into a dustpan. Nodding in a chair was Shithead, a broad-shouldered black guard for Jesus Mary, who rated as much protection as the main man. Spirit could see through a doorway the Irish Medical Director, reading a book with a magnifying glass.

"Can I see you?" Spirit asked.

"If you can see me, you can see me." It was the sort of remark that Jesus Mary Save Souls thought was funny.

Spirit went into the room. "I'd like to work here if I could to earn my way. I don't know medicine, but I *can* see."

"How well?"

Afraid of revealing the full extent of her gift, Spirit said, "I can read labels with a magnifying glass."

"Show me."

Taking the book and the glass from the Medical Director, Spirit read: "Coramine (nikethamide). Indications. To overcome central nervous system depression, respiratory depression, and circulatory failure. Contraindications. Hypersensitivity to nikethamide or related compounds. The safety of Coramine for use in pregnancy has not been established."

"Okay," said Jesus Mary. "You're hired." She extended her hand and shook Spirit's vigorously. "You're part of the team now."

No sooner had she said this than a yell rang out from another room. Rushing in, they found Sweet Thing bent over Bobby Loves It, who was gagging, his face purple.

"Elevate his head," Jesus Mary told them. She took an endotracheal catheter from a nearby cabinet and inserted it into the young man's mouth, trying to stimulate a cough. In a few moments he did cough, hacking up a fat volume of mucus. Holding the tube firmly in his mouth, she half turned and said to Spirit, "Get me aminophylline. In the bottle there," nodding to a Chippendale cabinet.

Peering rapidly down a line of bottles, Spirit found the aminophylline and shook out a tablet. Giving it to the director, she caught Sweet Thing glaring at her like a middle-aged schoolmarm, which she had once been.

Half an hour later, when Bobby Loves It was resting comfortably, Spirit again caught the woman staring at her.

Sweet Thing was smiling unsweetly. "That was quite a performance."

"What do you mean?"

"The way you found the bottle of aminophylline."

"I don't understand."

In the presence of this pretty young woman Sweet Thing

reached back self-consciously to touch her tight gray bun. "I heard you tell Jesus Mary you could read with a magnifying glass. But you found the bottle without it. A bottle with very small print."

"I must have been lucky."

"Awfully lucky," said Sweet Thing. "You read the label without a bit of trouble."

"Did I?"

"You certainly did. It was quite a performance."

"Maybe my eyes are better than I thought."

"Maybe they are." Then Sweet Thing added in one of the coldest voices Spirit had ever heard. "Or maybe they are not."

"Not what?"

"Better than you thought," Sweet Thing said with a smile.

Leaving the dispensary, Spirit carried Sweet Thing's terrible smile with her, and for a long hard minute she remembered intrigue in the world of social work. The poor, the maimed, the drugged, the destructive, and their dreadful problems were no harder to handle than were her own co-workers and their petty feuds, their pitiless struggles, their aggressive competition for something or other — say, for an office beyond the open cubicles, one with a door that by shutting would confer on its inmate the power of privacy.

About noon of her third day, Spirit climbed to the eighth floor, unused by the Skulls, where she looked around to make sure she hadn't been followed. Entering an apartment, she walked past two skeletons lying in bed together; they had the desiccated look of small dinosaurs embedded in fossilized mud. At the window she peered out at a blustery day with clouds streaking the sky like drawn-out wisps of cotton, giving it a smoky blue look, and for a moment she was possessed by one of those strikingly clear images from the past that plagued every survivor of V 70: this one came from her childhood, when her mamma took her in her white organdy dress to a classmate's birthday party at McDonald's.

Far below the window were clumps of trees in a park and a playground with large circular sandpiles. Beyond one sandpile was a tall red slide; visible beneath its metal curve was half of a standing man: face shoulder hip shoe. Spirit glanced around again, then took a white handkerchief from her jeans pocket. Holding it close to the window, she waved it slowly from left to right, once twice three times.

A hand holding a pistol appeared from the left side of the metal curve and waved back once.

Returning to the second floor, Spirit saw Eddie leaning against the wall: eyes darting, hands thrust deep into his pockets as if to keep them still. He beckoned with a crooked finger — a sexual command where Spirit came from.

Docilely she went to him.

"Hey, what's doing, mamma?" he said in a jocular tone, as someone passed. Waiting a moment, he added in a whisper, "When do you do it?"

"I just did it."

"Sure?"

"Sure I'm sure. Someone was there under the slide as he was supposed to be. I signaled, he signaled back. Once."

"Allll riiight," Lil Guy drawled. "So it's going down." Then his face twisted in pain. "Jesus." He swallowed hard. "I sure need a taste."

"Eddie, I really wonder," she began, and was going to finish, "if we should go through with it" when it occurred to her that he couldn't hear her. He was listening to the nerves screaming in his gut and behind his eyes. His body was begging for a taste of scag or lady snow or a downer upper or any damn thing that could send him off. He was nearly dancing from need.

"Better take a tranquilizer. I have —"

"Leave my case alone, bitch. Just be ready, hear?"

"I hear."

"Don't let on around these fuckers, hear?"

"Of course I hear. Don't you let on either. One good look at you, they'd see your need."

He wiped his forehead. "Sure could use a taste. Hey, split. A lot of them coming."

Spirit looked down the hall. Half a dozen Skulls were coming, led by Send Em Back To Africa with Mister Touch slightly behind him. The tall young man held his head high, chin jutting out in the searching posture of the blind. She wondered, as the procession went by and she flattened against the wall, what he looked like without the red beard. His sightless eyes were a smoky blue, reminding her of the sky she had seen from the eighth floor a few minutes ago. She watched the strong-looking fingers of his left hand brush against the belt of his black bodyguard. This faint contact guided him. In their discriminating touch his fingers seemed to have a life of their own. They fascinated her, and for a very odd moment Spirit wondered what they might feel like on her.

15

THE CORROSIVE NINTHS of Scriabin's "Black Mass" Sonata fitted the main man's angry mood. He turned up the volume and waited for the newcomer. She had lied about her eyes in the dispensary. Of course, all newcomers were paranoid; it took time before they believed the Skulls were for real. Sometimes even he wasn't sure, hearing them yell out their weird names in the corridors.

Knocking.

"Come in."

"It's Spirit In The Dark."

"You told Jesus Mary you needed a magnifying glass to read, yet without it you read the small print on a bottle. Is this true?"

"Yes. Sweet Thing told the truth."

"I will say this once. We take the difference between Good Looker and Neat Looker very seriously. We're a bunch of amateur ophthalmologists. I never met a V 70 survivor who didn't know exactly what he could and could not see. You knew all along your eyes were terrific."

No response.

He continued more gently. "I appreciate what you did. Bobby Loves It was strangling, so you forgot to conceal the truth in order to save his life."

"Where I come from you conceal what you can. If they know you see really well, they handcuff you to a bedpost."

"Why?"

"People have a way of coming and going, of not being there. So if you have what they need, they make sure you're around when they need you. After the job's done, like reading labels in a pharmacy, they let you go for a while."

"Do you just come and go when you feel like it?"

"I ran away many times."

"But loneliness brought you back."

"Of course."

Tall, he thought. From the direction of her voice beyond his desk he figured she must be five nine or ten. A mellifluous, bewitching voice.

The prez tried to steady his mental view of the newcomer in order to see what was really there. He saw someone who had to be straightened out. If she wished to stay with the Skulls, he explained to Spirit In The Dark, she had to use her eyes for the benefit of others. He would put out the word that she was a Neat Looker, and that meant she would be asked to thread a needle, find a cassette tape, help a Blindie with makeup. Within the limits of endurance she must meet these demands. And she would continue to work in the dispensary and take turns at reading sessions.

He could not anchor her down in his imagination. Spirit In The Dark remained a chaos of jumbled impressions, none of which focused long enough for him to find the woman who went with the voice. "I think we can trust you," he lied. "But remember, you're a Neat Looker and also, I suspect, a Breather For Real. As such you have responsibilities. So go back to Jesus Mary and tell her you're ready for work."

Lil Guy tiptoed down the corridor, feeling his way with fingertips. He counted five doors, halted at the sixth, and waited. When she didn't come out, he tried the door. Locked. Since Riot and Cougar's expedition, every door had been locked at night. He paced anxiously until the door opened and Spirit In The Dark emerged.

Grabbing her arm roughly, he snarled, "What in the fuck *wrong*, woman? You suppose to be here waiting."

"Eddie, listen."

"They out there by now. Must be."

"Listen —"

"*You* listen! Run it pass you one more time. I take a bunch of guys to that dispensary. You take other bunch to the blind dude. Kill the big motherfucker first. Try to get the blind dude for hostage but if you can't, you guys kill him too."

"No."

"What?"

"It's better here, Eddie. They'll let us stay if —"

He squeezed her arm hard, getting a groan out of her. "Marty hear you talk like that he gonna shoot up the kid and throw her to dogs."

"Eddie —"

"And you, I don't even *think* what Marty do to you. But worser sure than he do to the kid. This has gotta go down *right*."

"Listen a minute —"

"Shut *up*, woman! These people do you for being in or our people do you for *not* being in. Either way you dead, but it hurt more do our people do it. So help it go down *right*."

"If we say something now, maybe we can get them to help us free her, Eddie, and we'll stay here. At least it's a chance, it's —"

Clapping one hand over her mouth, he kicked her hard in the stomach. Leaning close and keeping her from buckling, he whispered, "I won't say nothing about what you just said. Or finish you here. You gonna do right?"

She managed to nod her head.

"We go down and fix the guard now. Ready?"

When she nodded again, he let her go.

Taking her hand, tall Lil Guy moved toward the stairway. They inched their way down to the ground floor. Ahead was the soft bronze light of an oil lamp burning in the lobby, where King Rat nodded in a chair, a carbine lying across his lap.

Crouching, pulling her down with him, Lil Guy whispered, "Go up to the dude there."

"What?"

"Go up to him, goddammit. Shake that ass in his face. Get him going."

"Listen —"

"No shit I *kill* you on the *spot*, woman! *Move!*"

Spirit forced a loud cough, which made the little Hispanic guard open his large childish eyes.

King Rat pointed the carbine. "What you doing?"

"I can't sleep."

"Never my problem." King Rat drew a thumb slowly across his mouth. Studying her a moment, he began to grin sleepily. "Qué se le ofrece? Play checkers? I got here. I see good enough for it."

"Sure. Only —" She turned slightly, aware of Lil Guy's presence beyond the lamplight. "How is it outside?"

"Dark," said King Rat.

Walking over to the front door, Spirit looked through its glass into the night. Did they really have the kid out there? Marty swore they would bring her along — with enough hits in a needle to overdose a gorilla.

King Rat was appraising Spirit's figure, his eyes wide and appreciative, a smile on his face in response to the sudden pop of an erotic thought within his dark little head, just as Lil Guy crossed the lobby at a loping run. Taking King Rat by the throat, he did it quickly. A head taller and seventy pounds heavier, with a Kung Fu black belt and better lungs, he turned the neck like sliding a bolt back and cracked the vertebrae. Even so, after releasing King Rat and letting the corpse slump to the floor, Lil Guy had to gasp for breath. He leaned against the wall, panting. He stammered, "See something?"

Spirit tried to look at the door instead of the dead boy. "Don't see anything."

"Must be out there now," he panted. "See something?"

She glanced again at the dead boy, whose beard was scraggly and who a moment ago had admired her with soft bovine eyes.

"You *looking?*"

"Yes. Nothing."

They waited, Lil Guy still breathing hard.

"I am going the fuck out and see." Lil Guy pushed his fist against his chest as if forcing air into his lungs. "Don't you *move*. You done good so far. Don't mess up."

"You're going outside?"

"If they ain't coming soon, we better split with him" — Lil Guy jerked his thumb at the dead boy — "like that. You stay here at the door. Hear something, like somebody coming downstairs, you whistle. Can you whistle?"

"Yes."

"Open the door, whistle, get your ass *moving*!"

"Where do I go?"

"Home, dumbhead."

"I hadn't thought of it as home."

Rummaging through King Rat's pockets, Lil Guy found the building key, picked up the carbine, and shouldered past Spirit. At the glass door he shoved the key into a huge padlock and the heavy chain circling the double knob clattered to the floor. Grimacing at the foolish noise he had made, Lil Guy slipped out.

Turning, Spirit stared at the dead boy near the oil lamp. She went back to the stairs and began climbing them, wondering what to do. As Eddie said, she was going to die, but she mustn't die a fool, although a fool is what she'd been so far.

"Give me another hit."

"You high enough, pendejo."

"Don't you call me sucker, sucker. We gonna bop tonight. We gonna do them mothafuckers. Be rocking on their turf."

"Shut up."

"I got three clips for this Beretta I got here and I am gonna use all three."

"Shut up. You be so high you turn that gun around and blow a hole in your own gut."

"Who's there?"

"Me. Eddie." Lil Guy was bumbling along the bushy path near the playground.

People rose from the bushes. "All set?"

"You tell *me*. I be waiting in there — you are fucking *late!*"

"I asked you," said a stocky young man who stood outside of the bushes with a .45 in his hand. "Is it all set?"

"Yeah. The nurse she got freckles. Red hair. That broad you sent with me, Marty —"

"What did she do?"

"She give me problems or I be here earlier."

"What problems?"

"Nothing I couldn't handle."

"If she's a problem, we'll see about her later." Marty turned. "Get ready."

An answering murmur from the bushes.

"Remember," Marty whispered, "don't touch a hair on that nurse and don't forget she's a freckle-faced redhead. You sure you know where she is, Eddie?"

"Sure do."

"Then Floyd and Barry and couple of others and me will go with you. What's it like in there?"

"Organized. But the leader nothing but a blind dude."

"Does the woman know where he is?"

"Sure."

"Al?"

"Yeah, here."

"You and your bunch go with the woman and get the leader."

"Watch out for a big black dude," Lil Guy warned them. "About six eight. Could of played nose guard. Better take him out first."

"So take him out first, Al," said Marty.

In the bushes there was murmuring. Someone said, "Get your exploder out."

"I do when we go in. What they got in there is bozoland. Gonna fuck them over good, so stop worrying."

"Shut up," Marty told them. They shut up.

"What about the mud kid?" someone said, coming out of the bushes and pushing ahead of him a skinny little girl handcuffed and gagged. He held a hypodermic needle. "Want me to hit her now?"

"I told you," said Marty. "When I say so, not before. What's wrong with you, can't you wait? Now, move."

A score of men moved forward at a crouch through the darkness. Marty slowed them down to prevent panting. At the entrance Lil Guy pushed the door open and stood at the switchboard. "That bitch," he grumbled, peering around the lamplit lobby.

"Where is she?" asked Marty.

"Supposed to be right here."

Marty stared briefly at King Rat. Marty's receding hairline emphasized the size of his large head. He still looked like someone able to plead a case in court. "Quiet," he told the men filing into the lobby.

"Wonder where she be," said Lil Guy. "Maybe the bitch hiding."

"Maybe she's up there warning them," said Marty, while studying the men assembling in two groups around him. "Forget about the leader, Al. Just get the nurse. So you give us cover."

They passed the dead man and turned on a single pencil-sized flashlight when moving out of lamp range.

Beyond the lobby at the foot of the stairs, Lil Guy murmured, "Don't like it."

Marty turned and pointed the .45 at him. "You don't like it, I don't like it. Get up the stairs and show me the nurse's door. Do one more thing wrong, I kill you."

"Did I do something wrong?"

"You left her here when you should have sent her out if she was kind of a problem. Why do you think I brought that mud kid along? One look at her the woman would have done anything we asked. But you, Eddie —" Grimacing from disgust, Marty pushed the tall black ahead of him up the stairs.

16

Reluctantly lil guy mounted, followed by twenty men dressed in black leather taken from a gay clothing store on Christopher Street. Their labored breathing accompanied them halfway up; there Marty halted them. After cocking his head and listening awhile, he said, "Sounds okay. I don't think she warned them. What do we do at the top of the stairs?" he asked Lil Guy.

"Turn left for dispensary."

"How far down?"

"Halfway down on the left. Got a sign on it."

"No lights," Marty told the others behind him, "unless someone comes out of a room. Then turn your lights on and shoot anything that doesn't have red hair." To Lil Guy he said, "Go first."

At the top of the stairs Marty waited until everyone was there. "Well, you're right, she must have hid," he whispered to Lil Guy. "Just get us that nurse and you're still in business."

They went single file down the hallway. They had nearly reached the midway point when suddenly behind them there was a click. Raiders at the rear swiveled flashlights around and caught in the glare the bandaged face of Dragon as he peered from an open doorway with a 12-gauge shotgun held waist high. It went off at the same time he was cut nearly in half by bursts from two 9mm HK5AD submachines.

"That bitch —" But Lil Guy wasn't able to finish his denunciation of the perfidious female who had betrayed them, because Marty shot him in the chest for being dumber than the dumbest law clerk. Lil Guy was slammed against the wall as if he'd been hit by a sledgehammer.

Dragon had dropped a Dragon with the shotgun blast. The other raiders rushed down the hall behind Marty, whose flashlight had picked out the red letters on a cardboard sign: DISPENSARY. Intermittent flashes illuminated the hallway, as other doors opened and Skulls fired weapons they had never fired at anything except dogs and maybe mean-spiritedly at a stray pigeon. Marty swung the light, ordering one of his men to get the dispensary door open. The raider, having suppressed a coughing spell from the outset, now felt able to cough as he emptied a full magazine into the door frame.

It blew inward and half a dozen Dragons poured inside, while the others, crouching or lying flat in the corridor, answered the Skulls' fire until the air of the Club House was filled with the acrid smoke of burned cordite.

In the dispensary a small black girl was sitting behind a desk in the dark. The swinging arcs of flashlights fixed on her nurse's uniform and her look of terror. A CAR 15 and an MP5A3S noise-suppressed submachine gun went off at the same time. The girl and half the desktop splintered into pieces.

"Don't shoot!" Marty told his men. "You might hit the redhead!"

"That weren't no redhead," someone observed, but Marty ignored him. There was a rolling roar of gunfire from the hall; a raider in the doorway, grunting, pitched forward dead.

Pointing to the closed door that led to the examination room, Marty yelled, "Open it! But for chrissake don't shoot! She might be behind it."

A big raider went up and with a heavy kick knocked it in. There was a scream from the other side. Marty entered with pistol in one hand, flashlight waving in the other.

Two women stood next to a bed occupied by a goateed young black so ill that his eyes never opened in the glare. Throwing his gun on the bed, Marty drew a hunting knife like one of those massive killer-blades Rambo used to wield for real in his true-to-life movies about heroism.

"Where is the nurse?" Marty asked the women. "The red-head!" He waved the knife at a light-colored girl with an afro.

"Gone," said Soda. "I swear it."

Marty walked up to the other woman, a small black with a crooked nose.

"She don't know nothing," Soda told him boldly. "She OOTLO. Just come in here for a pill to —"

Marty grabbed Snooky's arm hard and wrung it; for his pains he got nothing but a grin.

"Where's the redheaded nurse?" Marty demanded, poking the point of his knife against Snooky's stomach. "Tell me *where is the fucking redhead!*"

Soda yelled at him. "Leave her alone, you!" This from a girl who had once screamed so loudly on a midnight Bed-Stuy street that an attempted rape ended with the three guys running as fast as they could to get away from that voice.

With a short cry of impatience, Marty drove the knife into Snooky's stomach, twisted, and pulled it out gouted and bloody.

"What's in there?" he yelled at Soda, pointing with the blade to another door.

"No redhead in there, man. Gone before you come —"

Testing the knob, he turned it and flung the door back and charged through to find himself in full collision with a huge black body. They grappled while Marty's flashlight swung crazily. Pulling free, Shithead drove a surgical scalpel into Marty's chest. The other raiders had already rushed out of the dispensary for fear of being trapped, except one who before leaving shot Shithead in the face.

Marty felt the body fall across his. He still had strength enough to roll free. His mouth opened and shut like a fish. He made it to one knee, looking in disbelief at the steel handle protruding from his chest, and then he fell on it, driving it inside to the slanted end.

Outside, the raiders were trying to extricate themselves from bozoland. Fallen flashlights cast slanting rays against bodies all along the corridors. Moving like somnambulists, the exhausted raiders kept firing to keep the Skulls inside their apartments. Through the withering fire, someone was screaming, "Let them go! Give them a chance to get out of here!"

A Mexican standoff if everyone cooperated.

Lurching down the stairway the Dragon raiders sent up a last defiant barrage and disappeared. Silence came abruptly then, as if a gigantic hand had reached down and covered the building.

The silence didn't last long before the prez began feeling his way through the sulfurous smoke down the corridor. "Hoss!" he yelled above the sobbing and moaning. "Africa! Find me Hoss!" he called out while stumbling over something.

Ahead of him someone was crying hysterically. "Look! Look at that! An *arm* laying there!"

Hands out, moving along the corridor wall, Mister Touch breathed in the bitter smoke of burned gunpowder.

"Hey, Blood," someone said with a giggle, "this be a cold world. You ain't gonna like this."

"Who's there?" asked the main man, hearing an odd sound like air escaping a punctured tire. "Who's there!" he yelled.

Again the giggle. "Me. Fierce Rabbit."

"What's happening?"

The Fierce Rabbit guffawed. "Done happened! I cut the mothafucker's throat."

Backing against the wall, Mister Touch heard from down the corridor a war whoop. The main man walked his fingers along the wall, hearing screaming and choking from every direction.

Another war whoop.

"Who's there? Who did that?" the main man demanded.

"We sure messed them up good."

"Who said that?"

"Ace," a proud voice said from the smoke. "Wow, I can't believe it. Like in the movies."

Flattening his hands against the wall, Mister Touch wished for eyes that would let him see, because nothing could be worse than what he imagined. He panted for breath, overwhelmed by smoke, violence, the ripe odor of bleeding humanity.

Half a dozen Skulls stood at the glass doors irradiated by the first light of dawn. The men held automatic weapons. Sitting outside on the curbstone, like someone waiting for a rural bus, was Spirit In The Dark, who had been summarily ordered out of the Club House by the main man. Someone muttered, "Look at her there. Dogs gonna get her before noon."

"I take that bet. She gonna last maybe till late afternoon."

All of the corpses lay in the lobby, Dragons separated from Skulls.

"This sonofabitch," someone remarked, "is Santo. IRT threw him out for holding."

"He gonna be thrown out again," another Skull said. "Only this time he ain't gonna land on his feet."

The West Side Dragons had lost thirteen. There were no wounded. Who had not escaped had not survived, and it was clear that The Fierce Rabbit hadn't been the only Skull to finish off a wounded Dragon.

Skulls slumping against lobby walls cradled guns in their laps, having exhausted themselves by hauling the dead down here. They were silent, absorbing the fact of their own ferocity.

"We got the best of it," someone observed suddenly. But no one bothered to comment.

This was the casualty list:

King Rat. His spinal cord had been snapped in the lobby.
Dragon. Cut in half by gunfire.
Sugar. Shot behind the duty desk in the dispensary.
Snooky. Lived a few hours, then died of internal hemorrhag-
ing from a knife wound.
Shithead. Dead of a gunshot wound in the face.
Bambu the barber. Slain when she stuck her head out of a room
to see if her boyfriend Riot was safe.

OOTLO. Name lost. Shot through a door.

Critically wounded:

Spic. This handsome boy of German descent who loved no one
would die before nightfall from massive shock induced by
loss of an arm.

Wiggy Of Everywhere. Shot through the groin in front of her
beloved closet of pretty clothes. Her condition was extremely grave.

Eight others sustained wounds that were not life threatening.

Jesus Mary Save Souls worried about infection, although the
wounds had been flushed with isotonic saline and cleaned of super-
ficial bullet fragments. She couldn't probe to remove deeply
embedded particles because she lacked the skill as well as the vision
for such surgical work. She crossed herself and hoped.

Few people that she knew of had clung to their religion after
V 70 Struck — aside from those who stumbled into churches and
chose to die there in the pews — but she herself had never lost
faith. Suffering was a test, nothing more, and she believed in Judgment Day.

That's what she told herself while giving a shot of morphine to
Wiggy Of Everywhere. Looking down at the mangled girl whose
greatest sin had been to preen in front of a mirror, Jesus Mary
found it hard to accept what was happening as a trial of faith.
OOTHI said, "The bright day is done, and we are for the dark."
She couldn't get those words out of her head while going from
wounded to wounded.

Filled all day with a terrifying emptiness, she wondered if she
had been living her entire life in an ornate room without knowing
it was merely a stage set. That night she prayed for a renewal of
faith and for forgiveness.

17

AFTER THE PREZ had returned to his room, Hoss came with peculiar news. "The spy is sitting on the curb outside the Club House. That's not all —"

The prez interrupted angrily. "We took her in and look how she repays us. Go tell her to get out of here."

"That's not all," Hoss repeated. "She isn't alone. People are sitting with her in case the dogs come."

"What do you mean?"

"They're protecting her, even though they call her The Dragon Lady."

"Tell them to get back inside and leave her alone."

"I already did. They won't come inside unless she comes too."

"What is going on?"

Hoss explained that just prior to the raid she had gone to the dispensary, taken the Medical Director out of there and up a stairway to safety in a linen closet. Then she awakened people and calmly told them to get ready for an attack. She had saved Jesus Mary and alerted many Skulls. So they were ready to protect her as she had protected them, even though she was a spy.

"It's complicated," the main man admitted. "We'll have a meet in the lobby. In half an hour. Tell people to be there."

When Hoss was gone, the main man sat awhile in silence, waiting for the voice of IRT, which finally whispered in his ear, "Don't you forget, bro, you be the power. Without a take-charge guy leading them right now, they might could act stupid. You listening?"

Mister Touch replied to that inner voice, "I'm listening."

Fewer than half the Skulls were moving around the lobby or sitting against its walls. The remaining Skulls were either wounded or lying exhausted in bed or cringing in corners somewhere, because in spite of their odd lifestyle, many had slipped without knowing it into a kind of middle-class complacency, and only today had they fallen backward into the unconventional terror and despair they had known when V 70 Struck.

Shuffling toward the chair placed for him near the lobby door, not far from the rows of corpses, Mister Touch wondered if the nurturing of Skulls for almost two years had overnight come to nothing.

Sitting down, he declared in a firm voice, "Through the power invested in me by IRT, I open this emergency session of the Skulls."

"We're not all here," someone called out. "You giving out proxies to vote?"

Someone else yelled, "What in hell is proxies?"

Ignoring them, the prez said, "Bring the woman forward."

He heard someone coming through a loud corridor of confused muttering.

"The purpose of this meeting," he said to Spirit In The Dark, "is to decide if you return to the Dragons or stay with us. First, tell your story, and people will discuss it. As main man, I'll listen to the evidence, the pros and cons, and then decide what to do with you. If I think you're fronting, I'll declare this meeting closed and there won't be any discussion. You'll be out the door. And anyone who goes with you can forget about coming back."

There was silence, while everyone absorbed his threat.

Spirit In The Dark began to speak in the low but resonant voice that had earlier bewitched him but that sounded now like the seductive voice of a sly witch. She had guts, though, and spoke without pleading. Coolly she first explained the Dragons' plan. They had needed someone with medical knowledge. Marty, the Dragon leader, had wanted her to find out if someone with such knowledge was here. If so, the Dragons would conduct a kidnapping raid.

"Why were you chosen for the job?" asked Mister Touch.

"I could see and I wasn't a doper. Believe me, I didn't want the job. Not because I disliked spying on you but because I figured it was dangerous. Anyway, I meant to do what they wanted."

"Out of loyalty?"

"Loyalty?" Spirit In The Dark laughed. "No, they held a hostage."

"I see," said the blind man.

"I don't think you do. But Marty did. He was very smart and very bad and coke made him worse. Let me put it another way. I was with them long enough to lose pride, hope, everything but the will to live. I didn't know anyone there I wanted to help. Now and then I did a favor, but nothing big. There wasn't room for something big when you were holding on to each day's breath. There wasn't anyone I'd do more than an errand for. That was until the kid showed up — what they called a 'mud.' Latinos were called 'the mud people.' They got that from a skinhead who was a powerful Dragon. He wanted to take over the known world with his SS knife. Believe me. On the hilt he carved BLOOD AND HONOR. Lucky for everyone, he got into a quarrel about honor with one of the muds and the mud knifed him. It was that way over there . . . It was terrible over there . . . I'm afraid I'm not . . . I'm . . . I'm upset . . . What was I saying?"

He could tell from her voice that she was on the verge of revealing something terrible or of falling apart. "You mentioned a kid showing up," said the main man.

"Ten years old. She wandered into camp one day. At first she never said a word. But she started following me around and when I'd look back, she'd be there with her big round eyes. After a while she came along with me everywhere." Spirit In The Dark paused. "Terrific kid."

Mister Touch said, "Go on."

"So Marty found out about the friendship. He told me either I did the righteous thing, which was anything he told me to do, or the kid would suffer." Another pause, as if she were thinking through the implications of the threat all over again. This time the main man let her continue in her own good time. "Not much happened until Marty got the idea of stealing your doctor. Then he told me if I didn't do the righteous thing — come over here and check things out — the kid would get an overdose. That was one part. The other part was they'd throw her to the dogs before she lost consciousness, so she could feel that too."

"They would do that?"

The woman said in the quiet voice of logic, "You were going to do it to me. At least the dog part. And who knows, after this trial you might give me to the dogs, right? Sure they were going to do that."

"Go on."

"So like a fool I had the idea of saving her."

"Why like a fool?"

"Because I didn't see how things really were . . ." Once again she paused. It was like someone holding her breath underwater.

The main man waited, knowing this is what she had to say but couldn't. Finally he prodded her. "So how were things really?"

"Whatever I did, Marty would get rid of her."

"Why?"

"Because that was Marty."

The lobby was as silent as Grand Central Station.

The main man took a troubled breath. "Marty died. So maybe the Dragons would forget about her."

"No, I've seen it happen in my mind. The needle going in hard. The plunger pressed down hard. I see it. Till the shit's out of the tube and going through her arm . . ."

The main man waited, sensing she wasn't done.

"Well, so next," she said in the flat voice of finality, "the dogs got her. Before she went into shock. I've seen it in my mind all morning."

Now, the main man thought, she has said what was unsaid and we can get on with it. He was awed by the suffering she must have seen and endured; otherwise, she would have cried or at least sobbed. But her voice had the metallic hardness of someone practiced in grief and horror.

"Yes, well," the woman said, clearing her throat.

"Go on."

"Do you think I have more to say?"

"I hope so. Go on."

"What do you want me to say? Do you want me to talk about you people? Because I can. You may not believe me but when I got over here and saw people making sense of life, I knew I *really* wanted to live. There could be something to live for."

"If that's true, why didn't you throw in with us? We'd have taken you in." He added, "Maybe we could have got her over here too."

"I didn't think you had a chance against them."

"Describe your part in the raid."

Calmly, evenly, she explained signaling from the window and diverting the guard's attention so Eddie could silence him.

"Did you know Eddie was going to kill him?"

"No. But I didn't think about it one way or another. I only thought about it after it happened."

"Go on."

"When Eddie went outside, I went upstairs. I had the kid in mind and then you people and the kid and the poor dead guard and suddenly I knew Marty would kill her whatever I did, and I knew I'd been a fool and that's what made the difference. I couldn't save her anymore. So in a way I was free to do what I wanted. I think that's what I was thinking while climbing the stairs. First I got Jesus Mary out of the dispensary, because that's what they wanted."

"You mean, *who* they wanted."

"Yes. *Who*. I'm not used to thinking of people as people. If I had known what you were, I'd have taken the kid and slipped over here a few weeks ago and looked at the difference."

"Wait outside," said Mister Touch. "Someone stay with her in case the dogs come."

When she was gone, Mister Touch declared a short recess before discussing the case further. People started talking among themselves.

Someone said, "She weren't fronting."

"You believe what she say?"

"I do."

"I don't. Lie once, lie twice."

"Yeah, but this be different. Before she was with them, now she with us."

"Don't make no difference with a liar. Both ways she lying to look out for Number One."

"Who ain't looking out for that?"

The prez called for order and the official discussion began.

Sag spoke first. In her opinion the newcomer should be extirpated because her activities had a direct bearing on the deaths of seven (eight in another hour) people living in this building. That was a simple incontrovertible fact.

"What she trying to say?" someone whispered.

"Nothing worth saying."

Someone said he didn't care about legal stuff, but in this world it was dog eat dog (more than a metaphor these days) and what they better do they better teach those motherfuckers over there a lesson by putting a bullet between her eyes and dumping her on their doorstep.

A few approving cries of "Right on!"

Still others spoke, among them Adidas, who said, "Adidas argues against any action absolving an accused assassin." Taking a breath he asserted, "Adidas advocates arresting anyone additionally accountable."

"Hey, Adidas off again? Shut him up!"

"Anyone aged and alone and also annoying," Adidas added.

"Come out of it, Adidas!" people shouted, until the former butcher emerged from the letter A. "Kill the bitch! Cut her throat like a chicken! Give me a cleaver!" he yelled, remembering his former occupation, after which he plunged into the abyss of the alphabet and remained there with a pocket dictionary so long that people figured he was OOTLO for real.

Then Turok spoke. The muscular blond from Minnesota made a long rambling speech, mostly about his qualifications for military service now that he could no longer train in the martial arts and return to open a karate school in Duluth. But recovering the drift, he condemned speakers who showed callous disregard for a woman who had been fucked over for nearly two years and hardly knew which end was which. His speech was followed by claim and counterclaim. Voices rising.

One of The Ladies suggested that Turok's compassion was in direct proportion to the accused woman's attractiveness. He countercharged that her remark was prompted by envy.

Mister Touch restored order.

Then Eagle spoke, amazing everyone, because the little tailor in his threadbare yarmulke rarely spoke at all, but spent most of his time praying in a corner, rocking like a windup toy. People leaned forward to hear his timid voice. He started by quoting OOTHI: " 'We all have strength enough to endure the misfortunes of others.' So we are not thinking what has the woman gone through. We should suffer so much. She saved our nurse. She let people know so they could arm and prepare. What more to ask of someone who has suffered and saved us?"

More voices raised in controversy and anger. Once again the prez restored order, this time by beating his hand against the leg of his chair.

Someone yelled out, "Hey, main man, you gonna let us vote on it?"

Sag took up the suggestion instantly. "I demand we vote! We must all share in the decision. In any organization —"

But the main man's deep baritone drowned her out. "The woman is obviously a spy!" Mister Touch began. "But she's also a Neat Looker and probably a Breather For Real. Don't forget this. She has potential and God knows we need as much of that as we can get. She wanted to save a ten-year-old kid so she accepted the assignment and came over here. At first she didn't believe in us, so to save her skin she went along with the Dragons. That makes sense. After the murder of King Rat, she wanted out and she was willing to do something about it. Maybe, when all's said and done, she did save us. But the fact remains she was a spy, knowingly in on a raid designed to steal our most precious treasure, Jesus Mary. We have to balance one thing against another."

There was deep silence in the lobby. Someone finally yelled out, "So balance it, main man!"

"That's what I'm doing!" Mister Touch shot back. "I am putting Spirit In The Dark on probation! One false step, she's out for real. Someone go tell her." It was that simple. The Skulls bought his show of authority.

But even as someone ran to tell Spirit the good news, someone else was shouting, "When do we hit the bastards back!"

Whistling, screaming.

Shaken by the outburst, the main man leaned into the smoky air as if by stretching forward he might see their faces and learn from them what their voices didn't tell him. Were they boastfully pumping fists? From the noise they were making he figured they were half mad with the desire for vengeance. It was one of the most dismal moments he had ever known. Two crippled gangs were murdering each other over a student nurse in a dead city ruled by dogs and pigeons.

Raising his arms and holding them there until the noise subsided, he declared that the Skulls would not hit back. "We'll defend ourselves, but we won't go looking for trouble."

"That policy is militarily unsound," declared Satan, a white and wheezing former toy salesman who had been easing lately into OOTLO, his obsession being Heartbreak Ridge north of Yanguu where he'd lost a leg in the Korean War.

Nevertheless the main man held his ground. A full-scale war

with the Dragons would drain off energy they needed for facing a cold winter.

Riot shouted to be recognized.

Sweetheart of the dead barber, Bambu, he asked in a voice of keen sarcasm why they spent so much time saving a spy when they should spend it wasting the enemy. "Let's vote on declaring war!" Riot yelled. "It's our right!"

Mister Touch realized that he was on the verge of losing his authority. IRT, dying, had whispered to him, "They start on you about rights, don't listen or they mess themselves up for good. Keep the power, bro. Promise!" Mister Touch had promised.

This challenge brought him to his feet. What he said was coldly passionate. In a lifeboat, he told them, there was one person who held the gun and doled out precious water. If they wanted someone else taking charge of this lifeboat, so be it. But he would not budge one inch if it meant license for a hundred and fifty egos to go their individual ways.

He stopped abruptly.

Not a word, not a sound except for breathing. Then someone yelled, "You got it, main man!" A chorus of approval followed.

"But what do we do with Dragon bodies? Can't burn them with Skulls!" someone cried.

Others began to chant, "Let the dogs have them! Let the dogs have them!" A jubilant refrain, an outpouring of pent-up tension. "The dogs! The dogs! The dogs! The dogs! *The dogs!*"

Unwilling to risk further confrontation, the main man acquiesced: the Dragon raiders should not burn with the Skulls. "Riot," he called out. "You're in charge of disposing of Dragons. Tomorrow we take care of our own."

Hours later, extricating himself from Mystique's arms, the main man sat upright in bed. Mystique, rubbing her eyes, sat up too.

"What is that?" she asked sleepily.

"Barking."

A hurricane sound of terrific howling then swept across their bed, as if a dog pack had somehow leapt through the third-floor window.

Rushing to the window, the lovers looked down at the sandpile of a nearby playground into which, by Riot's order, the West Side

Dragon corpses had been dumped — a tangle of arms legs heads that might have recalled for older Skulls a film of bulldozers over-turning corpses in the concentration camps of World War II.

Soon, throughout the Club House, the volume on Walkmen would be pumped up high, in order to drown out the sound of dogs — famished for protein, smelling blood on the wind, they had come yowling and snapping.

"Can we wake up from this nightmare?" Mystique asked in horror, as they stared at the scene below: sand whirling along the flanks of New York pets unleashed from sidewalk civilization to tug at the bloody meat of Dragons. They looked, Mystique said, re-markably like wild dogs in a TV documentary. The main man could appreciate that. He had seen the same film — dogs groping into the torn gut of a wildebeest they had run down on the hot plain of the Serengeti.

18

Having pulled wagonloads of chopped wood to the park, weary Skulls climb over the parapet of the fountain area and sit on the steps under the watchful eyes of armed guards, whose guns are trained on a dog pack gathering beneath the Washington Square Arch. The wind is brisk. Clouds are scudding overhead along with pigeons, hundreds of them, which Harlem bird fanciers used to call homers and carriers and clinkers, white caps and blue splashes, beardeds and tipplers and flights, red Birminghams and saddlebacks, and what had once been rare — the black pigeon with red eyes — now dozens of them too, soon to be circling their way back to the windowsills and ledges where their ancestors had nested in the days of humanity. A Skull looks up in awe at the sight, wishing he might pull some of his friends by the scruff of the neck back into this life to watch this spectacle with him, as he used to watch with them their pigeons homing in on rooftop cages.

The park fountain, capped with a steel grate before V 70 Struck, looks like a sawed-off chimney, and the six smaller spouts arranged around it are fitted with bronze hoods. Previous funeral pyres are still visible as piles of charred wood, soggy ashes, cinders composed of bone and cloth and carbonized shoes.

The full procession begins at noon. Stereos carrying identical cassettes have been started simultaneously, and through the breezy autumn air a dozen sound boxes blare out the mighty chorus of "Cum Sancto Spiritu" from Bach's B Minor Mass, tape copies of which had been scrounged that morning from three neighborhood music stores on an expedition under Ace's command.

Wrapped in blankets, the bodies of the dead (along with Spic's severed arm) are removed from utility carts and carried with panting effort over the parapet to the fountain. They are placed on bed posters, chair legs, and tabletops lugged here and crisscrossed into a rickety wooden platform. A gray galaxy of sparrows spins closer to dip down and flit away like an idle thought.

Husky blond Turok lifts a five-gallon drum of kerosene and pours out the clear liquid until bodies and furniture are thoroughly soaked. He does the same with two more drums.

Then Hoss in a ten-gallon cowboy hat and studded boots and wraparound shades comes forward to strike a kitchen match. Lighting a yellowed newspaper with it, he throws the flaming torch against the pyre. Fire whooshes up with a sonic boom, frightening dogs beneath the arch, so that they skitter off.

Standing near the bonfire and lifting his head as if to sniff the burnt air, Mister Touch delivers a brief eulogy, then motions for Africa to lead him down the stone steps.

The pyre burns fiercely, and after a while something happens that the Skulls have grown accustomed to if not comfortable with: the cadavers cinch up when moisture leaves their tissues; they sit upright and look as if they are going to run away. This happens because unlike professional cremators at the burning ghats of Benares, the Skulls don't tie the bodies to logs with baling wire (a fact supplied by the Indian girl, Salt Noody). One by one the Skull dead rise, then curl up and go down again. The living Skulls breathe easier; some of them believe the dead have just said goodbye. A few dogs bark in the distance, but fire keeps them respectful.

When the flames dwindle, leaving embers in the waning afternoon, Hoss tells the main man it is time to go. Mister Touch rises and the others follow.

In the procession someone says to his neighbor, "That man sure make a good speech. Saying the names be remembered as long as one Skull live."

"Main man supposed to do that, homes. But it don't mean nothing. What mean something is going over there and wasting Dragons."

Someone else is gloomily quoting OOTHI: " 'We die only once, and for such a long time.' "

Last in the procession is Riot, his stocky Italian figure slouching and shuffling, his mind dragging him down, heavy with the memory of his sweetheart Bambu. Someday Mister Touch was going to pay for her death.

By the time the procession leaves the park, the Mass's concluding section, "Dona nobis pacem," roars into the sparrowful air.

In the following days many things happened. Coco's baby was christened in the lobby with the name Rattler in honor of father Snake, a handsome, bad-looking Steady Breather who sported a droopy mustache. He had heavy-lidded eyes some Skull women thought were sexy and a thin leering smile, and he displayed a bit of class by doing just enough work to maintain his membership in the Skulls, thereby assuring himself access to women, his only interest in life, his only reason for living. Snake didn't care if the world had been destroyed for all practical purposes nor did he worry about being half blind and he was none the worse for dogs howling below his window each night, hoping a miracle would drop him into their jaws, and it meant little to him if the underspicing of canned beans abused his Latin palette or if he was often placed on Misery Detail because certain people envied his sexual prowess or if a hard winter was coming on and he might be one of those who died from a bad cold. He cared for nothing but the warm lips of women who admired him.

Bobby Loves It died of a bronchial infection of unknown etiology.

He was cremated in the park fountain, and the ashes of Bobby Loves It then mingled with ashes he had secretly lusted after when they had been flesh, those of Spic, the misnamed silver-haired blue-eyed boy of German heritage who had never loved anyone but who had been coveted by the magnanimous Chief Reader of the Skulls, Flash, who displayed a streak of selfishness only when in love because he had used Web as a surrogate for Spic and had therefore never really loved the fat man, despite being the reason for Web's obesity, because Web had grown fat on candy bars of desire, his appetite for sweets increasing for no other reason than his love of Flash, who was crazy about the secret obsession of Bobby Loves It, Spic, the ashes of the delicate black boy and his Norse hero mingling erotically now in the park fountain — further proof of IRT's premise that love has a way of solving problems.

In the hallways of the Club House there were rumblings of discontent caused by another ravenous appetite, this one for revenge: Let's get those motherfucking West Side Dragons.

Moreover, there were tremors of fear from the dread of approaching winter, as though people had started shivering before the temperature had dropped out of the sixties.

Clumps of malcontents began forming among the candles and oil lamps of evening.

Sag was often in the middle of them. She was not happy with the probation of Spirit In The Dark, who should have been shown the door, dogs or no dogs. "That's one of many things wrong with this place — the sexual emphasis. I'm not against sex, I had a husband and children, but my goodness, nobody around here seems to think of anything else but going to bed. I am convinced this Spirit has won the sympathy of males because she's somewhat attractive in a cheap sort of way. I think it was her opportunistic eroticism, merely hinted at I admit but palpably there, that swung opinion in her favor."

Cola Face, who often accompanied Sag from apartment to apartment on these junkets of social criticism and political dissent, added, "He places too much confidence in Hoss, who is every bit as sleazy as Snake. Why does Mister Touch trust such a man? Because Hoss is black? I'm no racist, but the two of them bend backward to please the blacks. And it's the blacks who foster this sexual attitude."

Fire, maintaining an image of judiciousness, would argue that they had no alternative to Mister Touch but there ought to be a co-leader capable of promoting dissent. It was clear that the works of

Trollope were beginning to bore her, so she was looking around for something else to do — like stirring up trouble.

Snow also had her say over cups of tea among The Ladies, whose bridge sessions were turning into political forums. She feared an outbreak of total war between the rival Skulls and Dragons. Guns should be confiscated, rabble-rousers confined to quarters, black activists monitored.

Meanwhile, on the fifth floor, a group of Negative Blacks (so designated by Sag) created their own enclave of dissatisfaction in an apartment once occupied by Julia Maxwell, a dental technician who each year had starved herself for eleven and a half months to afford two weeks of exotic travel and who had painstakingly collected, at more expense than her friends believed reasonable, a buffalo mask from Senufo, a Benin bronze, and some ornamental wooden combs from the Congo.

The Fierce Rabbit sat in a big leather chair. He was saying, "Main man nothing but a dumb nigger. Dumber than him" — gesturing at young Wise Ass, whose perpetual grin grew wider from the attention. "Honkies got the man in their pocket, so they going for power. Tell me this. What do he do the other day? Took in the West Side pussy who snitched for the Dragons. Meanwhile we treated like slaves."

"When he took her in," Wise Ass said thoughtfully, "do he know she was snitching?"

The Rabbit glared, but Wise Ass couldn't hold back. "It wasn't like he showed the honkies favor. Spirit be black."

The Rabbit gave him a fierce look. "My granny come from Georgia would call her high yella, not black. Anyway, put a brother in charge, you see her go back to the Dragons in a box. By a brother in charge I don't mean Hoss either. Hoss nothing but a Tom."

"Put yourself in charge!" Wise Ass called out enthusiastically but for his loyal effort got a glance of withering scorn from The Fierce Rabbit.

Taki died of a bronchial infection of unknown etiology. Cremated in the fountain of Washington Square Park.

People were beginning to fear an epidemic for real. Sniffles were heard in the halls, even when they were desperately suppressed. People would soon have to go across the park. Hoss and the main man discussed the danger of separating out any Skulls from the main body. Holed up across the park, they might become prey for the vengeful Dragons.

So Mister Touch effected a new policy. People with colds would go to a higher floor of the Club House, perhaps as high as the sixteenth or seventeenth. Guards would be stationed at the stairways so people afflicted with sore throats and loneliness could not return to civilization for a few whispered germ-transferring moments with lovers and friends.

A good policy, well received, but it also made obvious the severely limited movement available to the Skulls.

Jesus Mary Save Souls reported there were mounting requests for tranquilizers. And indeed, the corridors began to resemble a 1960s sit-in: tangles of arms and legs out of which sullen faces loomed like apparitions from a B-grade horror movie as people rocked their anxieties to sleep with Thorazine.

Hoss, usually too clever to be repetitious, began his daily litany of ills with the OOTHI phrase "For the rain it raineth every day."

And Flash and Turok went on a reconnoitering mission from which they never returned. Last seen speeding bravely away in the direction of Third Avenue: Gallant Flash, generous Flash, gay in more ways than one, laughing and waving, bent over the handlebars of the Honda, pendant ruby earrings on his elflike ears; and Thor-like Turok of the long blond mane and massive arms sitting in back like a warrior astride a war pony. They vanished into the dead city like smoke: the Skulls' best fighter and best reader.

Web mourned the loss of his beloved Flash, even though Flash had loved Spic who had loved no one. Replacing chocolate bars with a brooding resentment against destiny, Web started to lose weight and regained some of his breath. People stopped laughing at him, falling silent in the presence of this thickset young man whose fat had the potential of becoming angry muscle.

Web was talking up vengeance in the halls and was soon joined by Riot and Ace. The three held a midnight meeting with The Fierce Rabbit and Cougar, whose mangled ankle communicated to him a daily rush of rebellious pain. They noted with solemn glee that among the five of them they possessed two Neat Lookers and one Good Looker — Riot, Ace, and The Rabbit respectively. That gave them a measure of power even before they had done anything except grumble. But it was an uneasy alliance: one Eyetalian, a punk whitey, and a mean black dude.

Wiggy Of Everywhere died of her wounds.

For the rain it raineth every day.

She was cremated in precious gems and in a lovely Rei Kawakubo layered organza and in high-heeled dress pumps with a choked-up silhouette that would be the last thing to burn and in a full-length Persian lamb coat that was pretty enough to knock your Calvin Klein socks off, as Wiggy would have wanted. The park fountain was now ankle deep in incinerated furniture, charred bones, ashes, and burned fragments of high-fashion accessories.

Sag and Snow openly called themselves Helen and Christine (although The Fierce Rabbit called Sag "the old white-haired old white bitch" and Snow "the other old white-haired old white bitch").

Futura and Superstar left the sixth floor where they had been living in isolation and climbed to the eighth, finding the atmosphere only two floors away from other people too close for lovers' comfort. Holding hands, they went up floor by floor, often halting for breath, for a comforting kiss, for a spit in the can that Futura wore for their mutual benefit (though Superstar spit not out of need, as she did, but out of tactful solicitude for his white queen's feelings).

Then Stay High came to see the main man with a gloomy assessment of "The Mystery of the Universe."

"It is extremely difficult to explicate," he confessed. "For example, these willfully obscure lines — 'Or curl forever nude / Inside the singular dream' — seem rather like an amateurish attempt at presenting rich poetic ambiguity. However, all is not lost."

"Good," said the prez.

"We already have the major theme, I think, although a scientist like The Dream Queen, even outside of her own medium of endeavor, poses formidable problems in a thematic way for the reader to solve or, as I like to think of myself in this context, for a researcher to examine in search of clues to something other than literary expression. Be that as it may, certain symbols seem to emerge clearly as controlling elements of the poem."

"Good," said the prez with a sigh.

"I am convinced The Dream Queen in her last days had lost control of her emotional life. I really believe this is true, however tragic it may sound. That's why her theme is so peculiar, why she advocates living a life of reckless abandon and hedonism."

"Good," said the prez patiently.

"What I am looking at now is the following: 'As if you had a universal goal / Then drop like Alice down the hole.' From my perspective Alice is what we must first deal with."

"Good," said the prez gloomily.

"Alice embraces fantasy by plunging down the rabbit hole. Quite a match, I dare say, for the earlier references to cats and Cleopatra, symbols of anarchy and disorder. Of course, 'As if you had a universal goal' is intriguing. Especially the 'as if.' "

"Good," said the prez. "Good, Stay High. I want you to keep working, keep thinking, keep going at it. I know you can do it." The truth was that Mister Touch didn't give a damn about "The Mystery of the Universe." The pursuit of meaning in The Dream Queen's odd little poem was nothing more than a race against time and circumstance for possession of the unworldly young scholar's mind. The prez figured if Stay High didn't exercise his overdeveloped brain, it would fold in on itself like collapsed muscle. The kid needed something to do.

When Stay High was gone, Mister Touch turned on his cassette player and played something by Haydn very loud in order to drown out a question that he did give a damn about, that battered his mind like a trip-hammer: "What do we do now? What do we do now? What do we do now?"

An hour later Mystique found him, head cradled in arms crossed on the desk, listening to silence because the tape had long since finished.

"What's the problem, lover?" she asked softly, bending down and snuggling her cheek against his.

He pulled away, his sightless eyes fixed on a spot a few inches above her head. "Would you like to go on a little journey of self-revelation with me?"

Mystique, happy to share more than just sex with him, pulled up a chair. "Let's go."

What he said was this: though he didn't believe in the cosmic significance of human survival, when he thought of Haydn and countless other people who had struggled in the heart's fire to forge some enduring memory of an odd experiment on a minor planet in an average galaxy, he was able to imagine that the Skulls were like the coda to a great symphonic movement.

"Meaning?" she asked impatiently.

"I think we're important. I realize I am secretly a romantic."

She perked up at that admission. "Really? Does your idea of romance bring us to me?"

"To the next stop on the confessional. OOTHI said, 'Of course God will forgive me; that's his business.' But I can't forgive myself. I can forgive everyone else almost anything, but I can't forgive myself. I suppose that's the plus of having a rotten past. You're humbled into compassion."

"Meaning?"

"I feel like the last man on the totem pole."

She was beginning to think it was better, after all, to share only sex with him. "I wish you wouldn't blame yourself for what happens in bozoland, lover. Because that's where we're living."

"Mystique."

When he added nothing, she got up, walked over to him, and mussed his hair. "Don't take it all on yourself. But there's a remedy for your illness." Taking him by the arm, she helped him to rise and guided him toward the bedroom.

She didn't realize that he hadn't finished the little trip through his consciousness, that the last leg of the journey represented his determination to forgive himself by doing something — whatever that was going to be.

19

DAMN DIRTY DOGS doing doo doo downwind, despite declarations denouncing dumping despicable dreck down declivities, drains doing dreadful damage, distressing disbanded denizens detached dispersed and dead."

"Adidas at it again. Only this time he doing D."

"Thought he be doing A, homes."

"Doing D now. Adidas go to D. Given A up for D."

"At the end I hear 'and.' Left over from A?"

"What you fuckups gassing about?"

"Hey, bro, don't sound on us. We be talking about Adidas. He doing again, only this time doing D. Ain't you, Adidas? Is that you there, old butcher boy?"

"Definitely. Don't deny description."

"Hear that? Old Adidas doing D. Exerting hisself. Living a little."

Hearing that Adidas had changed to D, the main man wondered if their luck might be changing too. After all, without other value systems to believe in, you learned to believe in omens signs auguries. The former butcher Adidas had been stuck obsessively on the letter A for months. Because he spoke only those words which begin with A, therefore speaking but seldom (there was of course the murderous outburst at the trial of Spirit, but that was an anomaly an abnormality an aberration after all), people had given him up as OOTLO. If he was ranging beyond A, perhaps there was hope that he wouldn't fall permanently into the deep ditch of his obsession and become OOTLO for real. Today he had talked about dogs, a subject of topical interest. Dogs who had once been followed around by their owners with pooper scoopers were now disturbing the dead by doing it wherever they pleased. Good for Adidas. He was acknowledging the world in his own alphabetical way. "Keep 'em moving," IRT had said. Adidas was in a sense moving. That meant hope. And hope was exactly what Mister Touch was hoping for.

That night he dreamed and in the dream he could see. He was hurrying down a crowded street looking for an address which he had forgotten and then in aching flashes felt he could remember if only it didn't get away from him at the last possible moment, just as it was easing into his mind. People shouldered him roughly as he kept looking for it. There were skyscrapers along a narrow street and a Greek-columned building that seemed vaguely familiar, but when he knocked at a huge door someone yelled from behind it, "No plea bargaining for you, motherfucker!" Then through the bustling crowd came a lovely woman in a long white robe. She was smiling but somehow featureless. With both hands she slowly parted the robe to expose beautiful breasts while speaking his name softly, "Mark," again "Mark," and again, which sounded like a dimly heard chorus from *Pelléas et Mélisande*. He was trying at the same time to remember the melody and the address. Then the crowd fell away and he was alone with her, lying in the grass of Washington Square Park, naked. He wanted her desperately, but something prevented him, even when she pulled him closer. "I have forgotten the address," he told her. He had to find the address before they could make love. Then he was running out of the park, which had begun to burn fiercely like a bonfire. Hearing the clatter of something metallic above him, he glanced up and saw a huge pigeon soaring through the sky, a pigeon that became a winged dog with bared fangs and wings creaking like the blades of a windmill as it swooped down to snap at him with iron jaws.

Mister Touch found himself sitting upright, soaked in sweat, his heart hammering. The dream remained with him while the fear subsided, but finally the beautiful woman faded along with the winged dog and what remained clearly was his desperate search for the address.

White, wheezing, former toy salesman and pretty much OOTLO, Satan was spending more and more of his time on Heartbreak Ridge in Korea. He was always climbing the hill, hearing the clatter of machine guns, the thump of mortars. He was forever climbing past craters bodies rocks bushes in eternal smoke until his left leg once again and again and again went numb, jerking out from under him, the bottom half of it flying loose like a snapped-off piece of uncooked spaghetti, presaging the metal parts that he would later travel on for the rest of his life, making him a more appropriate candidate for the Skull name Deadleg than Deadleg would ever be — another of IRT's christening errors or whimsies, take your pick.

In order to keep from becoming such a thoroughgoing OOTLO that he could do nothing except sit in a corner and climb Heartbreak Ridge, Satan decided to go on a military mission of his own choosing. He left the Club House one morning carrying a modified M16A2, determined to show those Dragons what a veteran of Korea could do.

Later that afternoon there was an angry screech of tires skidding in the street just opposite the Club House. Tangy was on guard duty. A big rawboned Swede who had taught aerobics in a health club, she had taken over Turok's post as Chief Guard of the Club House when he failed to come back from his mission. Running from the lobby, her rifle held with the confidence of a trained infantryman, she caught a fleeting glimpse of a motorbike speeding away which looked suspiciously like the Honda on which Flash and Turok had disappeared like heroes a few days ago.

The cyclist had flung something big into the street.

It was Satan's bullet-torn body. He had been stitched from buttocks to neck with enough slugs to have killed a dozen men. Worse, they had yanked off his prosthetic leg. The Dragons, so reasoned Skulls, must have jumped him while he was climbing Heartbreak Ridge and caught him in his own mind's ambush before he could get that modified M16A2 swiveled around into firing position.

That night Mister Touch dreamed again and in the morning called Hoss to him. "I saw miles of cacti. I saw a long river from the top of a high canyon. I saw hundreds of rabbits and a huge sun. We were all there, even Satan and Turok and Flash and Timbales and Bobby Loves It and Wiggy Of Everywhere. We were all breathing easily. I *saw* us breathing in and out without effort." Mister Touch paused. "How does it strike you?"

"It strikes me the dream took you a long way off."

That afternoon the main man called a meeting to which he invited four people: Stitch, Stay High, Jesus Mary Save Souls, and Hoss. It didn't require eloquence for him to persuade them of the Skulls' predicament. Illness, dogs, gang war, and winter could either finish them off or leave them so debilitated and fearful that life on such terms might be less attractive than joining the billions snoozing around them.

Turning to Jesus Mary, he asked what could improve the general standard of health among the Skulls, aside, of course, from a hospital and a full staff of doctors.

"Dry air."

Next he turned to Stitch, a gangly young black who used to work in a gas station.

"Stitch," said the main man, "assume we took a long trip. How would we go about it?"

"More than a few blocks?"

"More than a few miles."

"Then you gotta use cars."

"Why not buses? I'm talking about all the Skulls going."

"Well, your bus need plenty of gas. But you ain't gonna pump gas less you got electricity. Gotta use siphoning and that be easier with cars." He stopped a moment to think hard. "Plus you crack up one bus, a lotta people go."

"Hoss?"

"I agree. We don't have a helluva lot of twenty/twenty vision. If you're talking about a long trip, you could have crackups. Spread your odds better with cars. You mean a long trip?"

Ignoring that question, the prez asked Stitch, "What about a majority of cars and a few vans?"

"Just right."

"And of course if hostiles spotted us, we'd look more formidable if our caravan was long. Would it be hard to get the vehicles ready?"

"No sweat," declared Stitch with a snap of his fingers. He explained they could get the needed batteries and motor parts in auto supply stores. They could siphon gas from parked cars from which the gas in closed tanks hadn't totally evaporated.

"If you're going on a long trip," said Jesus Mary, "you'll need medical supplies and a place for the sick."

"A camper," suggested Hoss. "And a van for medical supplies. If you really mean it."

Mister Touch turned to Stay High, whose judgment he didn't trust but whose factual knowledge often turned up nooks and crannies of worlds that other people didn't know were there. "Would a long trip benefit us?"

"How long a trip?"

"I'm talking about a migration."

"Ah, in that case," said Stay High, "we better speak in an evolutionary sense."

"In any sense you want. Only give me an idea, philosophically or historically or sociologically or anthropologically or whatever, what a long trip might do for a hundred and fifty skittish and depressed people."

Stay High chose anthropologically by going back more than a

million years ago, when a ground-dwelling humanoid traveled from the African savanna along land bridges into Europe. Moving from the tropics forced him to cope with seasons and a variation in food supplies. He had to use fire for cooking and warmth. To protect himself against animals, he had to develop a complex social organization. In other words, migration into a new climatic zone made a man out of *Homo erectus*.

Before anyone could ask questions, Mister Touch ended the meeting. Warning them to keep mum about it, he returned to his room where he brooded over the address he couldn't find.

Then he sent Send Em Back To Africa to find his second-in-command.

When Hoss came into the room, the prez asked if he believed in obeying dreams.

"I never have," Hoss said, "but today anything's possible."

"Have you ever been to Arizona, Hoss?"

"Is that where we were in your dream?"

"Have you ever wanted to go?"

"Not really. Desert, heat, rabbits — that sort of thing never much appealed to me. I'm a city boy."

"But dry air, Hoss. That's what counts. Jesus Mary said so."

"You mean it? Arizona for real? Do we go by charter flight? Greyhound — Leave the driving to us? Or what?"

"We drive."

"I see. We drive to Arizona."

"Stitch can stitch together a motorcade." There followed a silence in which disapproval built like a thundercloud.

"All right, Hoss, out with it."

"I think you're wacky. You're talking about packing up dozens of Looney Tunes who never saw the west side of the Hudson River and getting them into cars that some of them can hardly see and driving thousands of miles through unknown territory." Hoss guffawed incredulously. "Like one of those wagon trains in the movies. Gabby Hayes yells Giddyup, the wheels creak into motion. The Skull Caravan."

"If going north made a man out of *Homo erectus*, as Stay High claims, then going west might make something out of us."

"I'll be damned," said Hoss.

"Which is probably what we'll be if we don't do something quick."

20

THE NEXT DAY at noon Mister Touch assembled the Skulls in the lobby. He began by pointing out the obvious: recent illness from unknown causes, winter coming on, the possibility of escalating gang war. Then he told them they were going to Arizona.

The prez was greeted by icy silence.

Once again he felt himself on the brink of failure, teetering on the edge of an abyss familiar to leaders throughout history. Facing this challenge, he dredged up from his deepest heart and put on public view a romantic notion he had not even shared with himself until now. He spoke of the Skulls being new people (with IRT nearby muttering *yeah!*) who needed to leave this old site of misery for a place where they could begin anew. It was time to move. It was time for them to seek their destiny because somehow time and space had decreed that they were important in the scheme of things, that what they did had a universal meaning, whatever that might be. So in pursuit of cosmic fate they must go where the air was dry, where the buildings were not stacked together like tall and massive gravestones in a cemetery of lost hope, where they could see to a far horizon and start toward it and discover why they still breathed on this planet. They weren't going to Arizona so much as they were going into the future to solve the riddle of their survival.

He had no idea how long he talked in this incantatory manner, as if wigged out on beads of base, but later he would imagine that he had experienced something like an internalized nodding high. At any rate, when he stopped talking, another pin dropped. In succeeding moments, from the lilting murmurs and little exclamations of delight he realized that the romantic idea of mission had gotten through to many of them.

Throughout the rest of the day nothing was heard in the corridors but varying analyses of the "Arizona Plan." The reaction to his visionary message, however, was not universally idealistic. There were Skulls who merely welcomed an escape from dismal corridors and a chance to travel. Others welcomed a different kind of freedom: "We get on the road, we don't have no more Misery Detail. We just stop anyplace and shit right there." An especially optimistic Skull quoted OOTHI: " 'Sweet are the uses of adversity, which, like the toad, ugly and venomous, wears yet a precious jewel in his head.' " But a pessimist, overhearing this, countered with lines of his own devising: "Only a toad like you be dumb enough to put his head in a noose" — a mixed metaphor but effective when delivered to a grumbling crowd of New Yorkers for real who didn't want to leave their hometown even if it was surrounded by fierce dogs and patrolled by machine gun–toting dopers. Loyally they threw up their hands in dismay, asking heaven where in the world could you live like human beings except here in the Big Apple?

Sag resented the decision being made without her input. And The Fierce Rabbit saw in it a racist plot: "They wanna get us off our own turf where we still got power." Sweeping his long sinewy arm across the vastness of America, he exclaimed, "Out there be honky land. Think on that awhile."

In the privacy of his room, convinced by the hodgepodge of reaction that he had done right to decree rather than discuss, the main man quoted OOTHI to Hoss: " 'I wish it, I command it. Let my will take the place of reason.' "

Preparations for departure began immediately, so there was no time for brooding. The first order of business, reasoned Mister Touch, was transportation.

Stitch had been no more than a skinny black kid from nowhere somewhere in Brooklyn, neglected and ignored, but as Chief Automotive Engineer of the Skulls he emerged from obscurity, soon commanding respect for his hustle, knowledge, and enthusiasm. But his passion for cars overwhelmed the main man, who heard in Stitch's explanations the sort of incomprehensible jargon used by Stay High in his lectures on tribal rites or metrical inconsistencies in The Dream Queen's poem.

"Gonna find us a Jaguar XJ-6," burbled Stitch. "A four-door rear-drive notchback which has got a new fuel-injected twin-cam 24-value 3.6-liter aluminum in-line 6-cylinder engine. Brakes is four-wheel discs with anti-lock control, man. It got leather and wood inside and heated door locks when it be cold."

"I hope," said Mister Touch patiently, "we never have to use those heated door locks."

"This Jag nearly good as Mercedes 560SEL. Now that got in-line 6-cylinder —"

"Stitch."

"Yeah, Mister Touch?"

"Get us some of those and some station wagons and about four vans, right? And a trailer for the galley and a truck for supplies."

"Trailer," repeated Stitch dreamily. "Find me one of them travel trailers with extra hitches, jacks and caster and tow bars and couplers and other gunning gear along with them dollies we gonna need. I say an RV with raised roof, heavy-duty cabinets, captain seats, partitions, ladder, and cargo racks. And it got a burglar alarm."

"Fine," said Mister Touch. "A must for going through crowded urban areas known for vehicular theft. If we stop for anything on the way and leave the trailer out of sight for a minute, we don't have to worry because we have our burglar alarm."

"Huh?"

"Take Superstar on your expedition. He has instincts I trust. Go wherever you need to go and get whatever you need to get and come back as soon as you can."

"Maybe we get us one of them Jeep Cherokees, a five-door wagon with Command-Trac. That be a part-time 4WD system with shift-on-the-fly."

"Stitch."

"Yeah, Mister Touch?"

"Go!"

He went. The expedition got a battery and installed it in a large moving van. They stockpiled generators, spark plugs, air filters, oil gauges, tires, and gas siphons in the truck. Back at the Club House they loaded two garbage cans filled with purified rain-water — for batteries and radiators. They cruised around from dealer to dealer seeking the right cars. Here Stitch revealed a hidden aesthetic capability, choosing them for beauty as well as performance: a Cadillac DeVille in prussian blue, an Olds 98 Regency with velour seats in stone beige, a Chrysler New Yorker in lipstick red. Over the next few days he managed to collect the travel trailers and four vans: a Dodge Raider, a Nissan Pathfinder XE, a Toyota 4Runner, and a sensible Datsun B210 Plus that could get fifty miles to the gallon. For the traveling dispensary he found a GMC Motorhome. Finally he picked up a Pontiac Safari with a four-speed overdrive automatic transmission to haul the Motorhome, after deciding against a Mitsubishi wagon. This decision came after a heated argument with adherents of the Mitsubishi. He told his opponents, "No fucking Mitsu wagon. It got good maneuverabilitiness but the front doors be located over front wheels and it make a long step up inside through that narrow opening. What about Blindies climbing in there? No way!"

Mister Touch couldn't have been more pleased with his Chief Automotive Engineer.

All kinds of expeditions set out from the Club House for uptown stores. They were driven in vans protected by machine guns set on tripods in the rear. They collected sleeping bags, tents, canteens with water purification filters, insect repellent (his knife having been taken from him after the argument over *Madame Bovary*, Lil Joint was designated Official Exterminator and from that moment on his skillful little hands were concerned with spraycans), sunglasses for those who could use them, blankets, towels, new weapons, and big wooden boxes of shells. The list was exhaustive, as Skull after Skull contributed ideas. Fifteen heavily armed raiders accompanied Jesus Mary to a large uptown pharmacy where they spent most of a day cleaning out shelves, until the family interior of the GMC Motorhome looked like the inside of New York Hospital.

Poor Breathers forgot to spit in their cans. Bad Lookers crashed into objects without complaint. Wheezers and Blindies sat against the lobby wall in awestruck admiration for the quick decisive tread of feet going and coming, and for the hum of motors outside the Club House door, and for the shouted orders and busy swearing, for the huff and puff of non-unionized labor.

Meanwhile, the main man was working on the Arizona Plan. What he felt now was familiar. It was like some days on the Street when you were working the phones and you looked at prices scrolling on the video screen and you knew that a hundred million dollars was going to pass through your hands. You felt it in your tingling fingers, in your dry mouth, in the faint headache which helped maintain your superalertness. It was like that for him now.

He and Hoss spent a lot of time poring over road maps. At last they settled on a southern route that would avoid the Appalachians and the Rockies. It would also take them through a warmer climate. They were not very keen on interstate highways. After all, they didn't need them. Back roads would bring them through towns where they could pick up supplies easily and find parked vehicles with gas tanks to siphon. Moreover, they wanted to stay as clear as possible of large cities, at least for overnight stops. Who knew how many gangs like the Dragons were running amok in the streets of America?

Then the leaders turned their attention to the structure of the caravan and its method of travel. They had assembled a dozen cars, four trucks, four station wagons, four vans, two travel trailers, and the Motorhome — enough space, comfortably, for a hundred and fifty people. The trip was approximately 2,500 miles. Considering the eyesight of the drivers, it must be negotiated at a very moderate speed, say, a maximum of twenty miles an hour. Realistically, the leaders could not predict the ETA in Arizona, but it might take a month or perhaps two or even longer if bouts of illness called for frequent and lengthy stops. They would leave no one behind. If they had to halt for a few weeks while someone got well enough to travel, then by God that's what they would do. Mister Touch would travel in the vanguard car, Hoss in the rear, with the Motorhome dispensary and the gallery trailer and the supply trucks in the middle of the column.

Next problem was to locate enough drivers who could not only see the road but drive on it. They had a bus driver in Bones, but he was a wheezing Blindie and as old as death. So Hoss canvassed the Club House.

Ace and Jive Turkey and Hitler and Web were reputedly capable drivers, if you took their word for it. King Super Kool offered to drive, although his poor breathing was a drawback. Wise Ass was also selected; he might be the dumbest nigger that The Fierce Rabbit had ever seen, but he could shift gears and put his foot down on the brake.

Stitch had established himself as such a brilliant star in the Skull firmament that he was entrusted with the precious Motorhome. Good-looking Tangy, built like a truck, was assigned a truck. Although still limping, Cougar was placed in charge of supplies. It was an important job, Supply Officer, and his mental health began to improve faster than his injured leg. He stopped hanging out with the Negative Blacks. He no longer joined Ace, Riot, Web, and The Fierce Rabbit in their ego-boosting rap about potential power. He became loyal to the present administration. Score one for Mister Touch.

One day Spirit In The Dark came to see the prez. Standing in front of his desk for a long time in silence, she finally made a star-tling revelation: she had paid for college by driving a hack. She was a New York cabby! She then vowed to do her best because she owed the Skulls for taking her in.

After consultation with Stitch and Hoss, the main man decided that a New York cab driver had the best credentials for leading the cavalcade. Anyone who had handled the traffic of Manhattan could handle the untraveled roads of America. She would drive Car One.

When people heard of this decision, they generally approved (although the SS — Sag and Snow — approved of nothing the main man did). In recent days it had been obvious that the new-comer Spirit was receding down a tunnel of her own memory, bumping against the dark walls of a remembered horror, descend-ing rapidly into guilt over the kid's death until people began whis-pering she was OOTLO for real. Now, having been marked for stardom as driver of Car Number One, she became an overnight celebrity. Spirit had saved herself by declaring to the world, "I can pay my way."

21

THEY COULD DO IT. The prez was startled by his faith in them. He talked his optimism into the taped History of the Skulls which he still kept secret. "Even when IRT was alive, there was, I think, an air of artificiality about us. How could existence be real for less than two hundred people when everyone else in the world was dead? But now we are real for real. The voices I hear in the hallways are those of people getting ready to travel."

Knock at the door. Coming into the room.

It was Cake. In the last year he had probably spoken no more than twice to Cake, probably because Cake hadn't spoken more than twice to anyone. He remembered her with the last of his eyesight: a short heavyset woman with gray hair, tottering along on swollen legs, her black face a wrinkled mass of stoic dignity. Now he knew her through her soft voice, which was relating certain basic facts. She had raised four children without a man around; two of them had graduated from college, one then earned a Ph.D. in some kind of science. "I saw five grandchildren," she told the prez. "I saw my youngest boy buried. That was before that V 70. Now I just plain tired. I gonna stay here."

After a few moments Mister Touch replied, "Very well, if you want to stay, you can stay."

"I wanna go home."

"Where is home?"

"I was living with my eldest on East Twenty-eight Street. Had a room to my own self. I wanna go there."

"Then we will take you there."

Cake had hardly left the room before a poor-breathing Blindie came in. Melody was middle-aged, but V 70 had wormed itself into her cells and had pretty much shut each of them down. In life before V 70 she had not been a whirlwind either. Methodical, going to work and coming home by the clock, buying three theater tickets per season, enjoying her nephews at Christmas and Easter only, reading four sections of the *New York Times* each Sunday, climbing into bed after the "Eleven O'Clock News" and sleeping without interruption, usually without dreams, a full eight hours on the left side of the otherwise empty bed, this middle-aged old woman Melody had been stalwart, forthright, unimaginative, and the most faithful of friends.

Now she came to inform the prez that she wasn't going on the trip either. It wasn't the journey itself that bothered her but the lack of privacy. She needed solitude (a rare Skull need). She could not envision a long car trip with all those noisy youngsters. On the road she would be prey to incessant confusion as the youngsters played their games and laughed and yelled and joked and teased one another and used the sort of language she had been raised to abhor and otherwise did all of the things they could not help but do because they were young. Moreover, she feared the surprises that come with travel and disliked the improvised schedule that a long journey necessitates. She wanted peace and quiet. She would literally give her life for them. She added, "And I'll have a chance to use my old name."

"There won't be anyone to hear it," the prez pointed out softly.

"I will hear it. I will say it out loud."

"Melody, I'm saying the obvious, of course, but like me you're blind. If you go it alone — you mean to stay here in the Club House?"

"Yes. In my own room."

"You won't be able to get supplies for yourself."

"Perhaps I'll find a way," she declared stiffly.

Going from the room.

And if this wasn't enough for one morning, Mystique came to see him about the driver of Car One.

"First you let her stay, you give her a lovely name, you take her back even after she's responsible for so many deaths. Now you give her the honor of driving the car *you* will ride in. What's going on?"

"Spirit's a cabby," Mister Touch said in a kind of telescoped explanation. "Here's someone with a skill we need. And she went through hell with the Dragons. People say she might become OOTLO. So giving her a job might prevent it."

"Why prevent it?"

"So we won't have another OOTLO." Perhaps it was a shaky defense of his judgment. Mystique thought so, stomping out of the room and leaving him humbled at his desk, the leader of men but no prophet of a woman's heart.

During the preparations for departure there were rumblings of discontent among the Skulls that marked the passage of their distorted time.

Sky Hook, for example, felt a grave mistake had been made in the selection of vehicles for the cavalcade. Scarcely five feet tall, he was a Los Angeles Lakers basketball fan, though he came from the Bushwick district of Brooklyn and had never seen the Lakers except on television. Since joining the Skulls last year, he had stayed in the background, but now a sense of injustice brought him forward. He stood in the lobby with a pair of binoculars trained at a Chevy Corvette that had been parked across the street for two years without a parking ticket. To people passing through the lobby, he said, "We should of took that Corvette over there!" They didn't realize he was logically linking Chevrolet cars with basketball through the medium of television advertising. For Sky Hook it was eminently reasonable to take a Chevy if they were going to see America. The ads told you during timeouts to listen to the Heartbeat of America. He muttered to himself, holding the binocs up, "We should of took that Corvette or leastwise a Camaro a Caprice a Cavalier a Celebrity a Corsica a Monte Carlo a Nova a Spectrum a Sprint or a 510 Blazer High Country, because *that's the Heartbeat of America, today's Chevrolet!*"

Then three guys went on an expedition to Barnes & Noble from which they never returned. In fact, they drove that same Chevy Corvette up Fifth Avenue the wrong way and entered the bookstore through a window broken by the Skulls more than a year ago when, as Chief Librarian, Stay High had put in a large book request. The trio had gone this time to locate guidebooks. When they failed to return, Mister Touch did not send out a rescue team that might turn up missing too. This was war.

Preparations went forward. People were overworked and exhausted, but the prez drove them mercilessly, fearful of time running out on the Skulls. Only this morning five Dragons had been sighted at the edge of the park, carrying rifles through a sea of pigeons.

Loading was completed at last. The caravan was lined up in front of the Club House and guarded by two M60 machine guns on bipods and a half dozen SAWs with 200-round magazines.

On the seventh day the Skulls rested.

That afternoon Star Two disappeared without saying a word to anyone. Named in honor of Star, who had died a year ago of pneumonia, Star Two was a quiet Polish kid who used to daydream about eating fresh ham. It was suggested by Skulls who knew him well that Star Two had probably trekked uptown where he could break into one of those East Side pork stores and die among the hanging sausages so prized by his ancestors.

That last night, their exhaustion notwithstanding, the Skulls celebrated. Nobody sounded on nobody and they drank some champagne, although it was rationed carefully because tomorrow was a big day of travel.

Deejays played punk disco like "Big Lizard in My Backyard"

and Brazilian fusion and some reggae, but when Sony Boy took over, he unleashed on the unsuspecting dancers the socko rhythms of "Kaka Mulema" — zouk! His prediction came true; the Club House was zouking. The punch sounds of zoukery boomed de-fiantly across the untraveled miles of America, soon to rattle the dark windows of deserted towns, to screech through the empty canyons of Atlanta and Dallas, heralding the approach of the funk-iest gang ever assembled south of Harlem.

"Homes," said a zouker to his friend, "we probably the baddest dudes on this planet."

"Hope so. That way we got a chance to make it."

"Yeah? Like one in a hundred?"

"Good odds, considering."

TWO

ON THE ROAD

22

SHORTLY AFTER DAWN the halls of the Club House were astir with people hauling their Samsonite and American Tourister luggage down to the lobby. The sun hadn't climbed much higher before everything was loaded into cars, trucks, and trailers. Finally, the Skulls assembled in the lobby for a group photograph.

The main man wanted a visual record of the Skulls to go along with his secret taped history. He had designated Jive Turkey as the Official Skull Photographer, and the diligent Korean youth had set up tripod and camera at first light. The Skulls lined up in rows like a graduating class. They hadn't lost their flair for finery merely because their traveling clothes might get rumpled in a car.

This is what Jive Turkey saw through the lens of his camera. He saw pullovers, turtlenecks, leopard jackets, wool capes, ponchos, snuggle-collared raincoats. He saw suede suits, pinstripes, knickers, jodhpurs, chinos. He saw popsicle-colored blouses, slithery cerise skirts all languid and lux. He saw bowlers, felt hats, red tams, billed caps, and a few crash helmets worn by grumbling pessimists. He saw foxtail neckchains among the spit cans, ruby brooches, hand-hammered gold rings, beaten copper bracelets, and four Omega watches studded with precious stones on a single arm. Only OOTLO wore plain jeans and old sweaters. Their interest in clothes had ended when V 70 Struck.

Jive Turkey peered through the viewing lens, blinked at this grab bag of glitter, held his breath, what there was of it, and snapped the group portrait. He took a half dozen altogether. Doubtless the film had deteriorated, so its color would be poor when Jive Turkey had the chance to develop it, but snugged away in his Nikon F like sleeping kittens were the Skulls.

Hoss waved his ten-gallon hat and they began funneling out of the Club House into the cars. Seated behind the wheel of the lead car, Spirit In The Dark turned to the main man and said, "Say when."

"Now."

She honked three times, startling a bevy of pigeons, turned on the ignition, shifted gears, and put her foot on the accelerator.

She was off at an initial speed of five miles an hour, and the long cavalcade shuddered into motion behind her.

Someone down the line, paraphrasing OOTHI, yelled out, "Fair stood the wind for Arizona!"

They slowly circled the border of Washington Square Park which, for the moment, had been deserted by dogs but not by two armed boys who stood near the arch, awaiting the cavalcade.

"Why, they're hitchhiking," exclaimed Spirit. "One's got his thumb out and the other is . . ."

"Yes?" demanded the main man.

"Waving a leg. I mean, holding a leg and waving it."

"We'll stop for them," Mister Touch said. "I have a feeling it's Satan's prosthetic leg."

And so it was. The two teenage hitchhikers had found it in the park, a little the worse for fang marks, and figured it must belong to the gang in the cars. They called themselves the Okra Slime, a gang of two. The main man asked them if they wanted to come along. They did. Mister Touch called for Hoss.

"We're taking them along."

"Why? I don't like the looks of them. They smile like kids but they've got the eyes of twenty-year-olds going on sixty. They're not from the Dragons? I mean, they have Satan's leg."

"Spirit says no. She's never seen them before. They call themselves the Okra Slime," Mister Touch added with a laugh.

"It's not so funny. Do you know what the Okra Slime was in the old days? A Jamaican posse that dealt drugs all over the South."

"Well, these kids didn't belong to it. Anything wrong in keeping your courage up by giving yourself a tough name? If they don't obey, they're on their way, as IRT used to say. On this trip, Hoss, if we meet people who want to come with us, and on our own terms, so be it."

"So be it."

Starting off again, the caravan turned up Fifth Avenue and rolled silently on. Skulls who could see well enough gawked at the forest of buildings whose windows glinted in the morning light. Some of them had labored alongside friends in these buildings, and they craned their necks for a last glimpse of a certain window on a certain floor where they used to spend their time.

"Did you bring in strays when you were a kid?" Spirit asked the main man as they sped along at ten miles an hour. "I mean, there was me, and now those hitchhikers."

"My mother used to do that. Best dog we ever had was a stray. My father hated that tendency in her. He called her reckless. My father was a high school football coach, and one of his greatest disappointments in life, I think, was that I grew tall enough for sports without showing a talent for anything except Ping-Pong." He might have said more, but remembered that others were in the car, hearing him break the rule against talking of the past. He had fallen easily into the nostalgic mode with Spirit. Odd, but he had just told her more about his family than he had ever told Mystique and Nando combined.

At Fifty-ninth Street they turned past the waterless Plaza Fountain and crept alongside Central Park at a snail's pace. They hadn't gone one block before a pack of dogs came rushing from the autumnal woodland to set up a howling clamor around the slow-moving tires. Riders rolled up their windows; some of the larger animals began lunging with gnashing teeth. Saliva covered the glass. A few dogs in their heedless charge rolled under wheels and were killed. Looking back, the riders saw a number of smaller dogs stop to tear at the fallen bodies. The pack multiplied until three or four hundred were accompanying the caravan, snapping, lunging.

All the way up Broadway the dogs maintained their terrifying escort, but when the caravan turned onto the West Side Highway, they began to fall away. When the procession broke free of the steel enclosure of Manhattan and rumbled parallel to the Hudson River, the last of the dogs gave up altogether and returned to their cannibalism in the cement corridors of doggy memory and may even have returned to their old apartment buildings, whimpering and expectant, hoping that their owners might come to the lobby with a dish of Alpo and a word of endearment.

Ahead sparkled the empty span of the George Washington Bridge.

"Beautiful," murmured Spirit.

"What is?" asked the blind man sitting beside her.

"The bridge in sunlight."

"I can imagine."

"I'm sorry."

"Don't be sorry. Tell me things as we go along. I can see them in my mind." Reaching behind him, the main man gripped the thick biceps of Send Em Back To Africa. "Brother," he said jubilantly, "we're on our way!"

That's what Sister Fate was thinking too. In one of the rear cars she turned to look back at vanishing Manhattan with her good-looking eyes. She recalled her life there with affection, even that part of her life when New York was empty and there were no matinees, no luncheons at Lutèce, no evening glitter at the Waldorf.

Sister Fate was one of the oldest Skulls, though one of the youngest at heart. None of the Skulls were happier than Sister Fate when told a trip was in the offing, because none of them had traveled more extensively. She had been on the road since her early twenties, either with or without male companionship, husband or lover. She had strolled through an inordinately large number of streets in this world.

She had particularly loved Spain, favoring the Castilian countryside, its long lean hills, the red earth of their cropped and gentle slopes dotted by olive trees and lush vineyards. Loved flamenco, the tumultuous hand clapping, the arched backs, the incredible intensity of dancers' eyes, their look of pure willingness to die — to die as no one had died when V 70 Struck.

She had sat with un fino on the terrace of the Hotel Parador de San Francisco overlooking the gorges of Granada and the tidy gardens of the Generalife, then had eaten in the hotel dining room (melon with ham, a cold Andalusian gazpacho, brochette de langostinos a las finas hierbas) seated near a Swedish industrialist with his white-haired children at attention; comfortably detached, she had watched him cast sly lustful glances at intellectual Frenchwomen with their summer boy- or girlfriends; and in the mornings she had made yet another tour of the Alhambra in the midst of a school tour and camera wielders from Munich from Yokohama from Minneapolis — all dead now, gone, and the wind blowing hollowly across the plains of La Mancha, with neither young nor old people gathered in the evenings at the town square of Toledo, but only the swallows still curving and lunging through the narrow cobbled streets. Ah, the swallows, the unforgettable swallows of Toledo! They might look today like silver balls racing through the alleys of a pinball machine — one rusting somewhere, perhaps in a coffee shop. Perhaps rusting in a coffee shop like the one she remembered in the midwestern town where she had spent her girlhood. She used to watch her happy-go-lucky father, heir to a fortune, play some pinball while she stood beside him, yearning to travel.

"Are you all right?" Someone touched her arm.

"Of course."

"Well, you have tears in your eyes."

"It's the dust," Sister Fate said. "We're on the road, aren't we? I couldn't be happier."

23

THAT FIRST NIGHT they bivouacked in a motel outside of Trenton, New Jersey.

The Skulls had breathed through their first day on the road without seeing more than a few stray dogs on this side of the Hudson and a single hawk wheeling silently overhead. They had gawked at huge jetliners dead on the vast acreage of Newark Airport and had squinted at power cables crisscrossing the highway like spiderwebs, no longer humming with electricity.

Beginning the day with the excitement of fresh travelers, the Skulls ended it with their expectations unrealized. The bitter truth was that most of them had secretly hoped to find men and women living as people had lived before V 70 Struck. It was as if they believed the catastrophe had been limited to New York City — the rest of the world conspiring in a monumental hoax. Once out of New York City they'd find the planet taking care of business, having cut the city off awhile as punishment for urban arrogance. An infantile idea, baseless beyond reason, and yet even their leader had hoped for something amazing, for a revelation beyond their wildest dream, and therefore like them the prez had ended his own day with a vague sense of disappointment.

That night the Skulls were too weary to cook, so they dined on tins of tuna and stale soda crackers. Some who still had breath for it took a stroll on the highway, staring haplessly down its moon-washed ribbon of emptiness. They heard nothing but wind that no longer brought across the swampy countryside a pungent smell of heavy petroleum from the oil refineries of Elizabeth, New Jersey. What the wind carried now was the sweet but breathless sound of Coco humming "Precious Lord, Take My Hand" to baby Rattler while she gave the Skull tot her breast. The sadly odorless breeze carried her faint sonorities along the deserted strand of cement backward toward the island of Manhattan, opposite from which, on rocky ledges of the Palisades, a few roosting ospreys blinked like fat-cat landlords, fixing their satisfied gaze on the tall parallel sheets of black glass across the Hudson River, the steel canyons of West Side New York, up which that morning the Skulls had sculled through an angry river of dogs. It had been a long, long day.

That's what the main man told Spirit In The Dark when he asked her to walk with him after dinner. He found it difficult to say good night to someone who all day long had supplied him with verbal images of the drive. He couldn't let her go just yet, his dark mind still entwined in her words, but he couldn't ask her back to his motel room for a glass of wine, because Mystique, after her stint in the Motorhome dispensary, would go straight there, open a bottle of wine (obtained from Supply Officer Cougar and signed for), remove her clothes, and wait impatiently for her date to show up.

So together the main man and the lead driver strolled down the middle of the highway, with his hand lightly touching her arm. He told her that she had done New York cabbies proud today. She had led them out of the city into a new world, at a prudent speed, the ride smooth enough to warrant a nice tip.

Spirit replied as thoughtfully as she had driven the lead car, "I'm sorry to leave the city. It's all I ever knew outside of a few trips to Boston and Atlantic City. I think New York is beautiful — was, is, maybe will be when it's nothing more than ruins. A lot of times I left the Dragons and took long walks through the streets. I'm talking about before the dogs multiplied and got mean. Shops, restaurants, but most of all the streets lined with cars, not a sound but the wind blowing scraps of paper around — the new New York, silent, empty, but beautiful. The cement, the glass, the sunlight. That was what got me most . . . sunlight hitting against windows, windows of buildings, windows of buses no one was traveling in. Plate glass filled with this sunlight, and only myself to see it. It scared me — elated me too. I felt powerful for having it all to myself and sad for having it all to myself, and sometimes I'd sit down in the middle of Madison Avenue and look northward between the parked cars at the shops with mannequins wearing fur coats and with antiques in the windows and I'd expect something to happen, a door to open maybe, people to rush out yelling, 'Surprise! Surprise!' But nothing ever happened, no one ever came out, and I'd sit there doubled over and I'd cry until it was dark and I had to find my way back through the silence to that place."

They walked awhile. Halting, Mister Touch took his fingertips from her arm and raised his outstretched hand toward her face. "May I touch you?" But even as he asked, the main man felt a kind of turbulence, faint but unmistakable, just beyond the fingertips that did his seeing for him. "You don't want me to touch you," he said, pulling his hand back. "You don't want me to touch you," he said again.

"No, I don't want it."

"Is it because of what happened over there?"

"Yes."

"Touching is my way of seeing."

"I understand that."

"But you don't want me to touch you anyway." He added, "Even for seeing."

"You can if you want," she said coldly. "You're the boss."

"You forget I'm a Skull, not a Dragon."

"I shouldn't have said that. I'm sorry. I was thinking like a Dragon woman. You only want the truth from me. The truth is I don't want you to touch me. Except on the arm when we're walking. I just don't want it. Not now."

"If I try again sometime to touch you, tell me honestly if you want it or not."

"I have. I will."

Walking back to the motel, she led him to his room and briskly said good night after putting his hand to the doorknob. Opening the door, he heard Mystique call out cheerily, "If only you could see me now!"

Next morning the Skulls slept late and didn't get under way until the sun was edging toward the center line of the turnpike. To make time, the prez decided they would drive awhile before stopping for breakfast. It was how his parents had traveled back in Iowa. Getting up at dawn to beat the traffic, they drove until midmorning, when they had bacon and eggs in a diner. He would always sit on his mother's side of the booth, listening to her rollicking stories of a mischievous girlhood while the worry lines deepened on his father's brow.

Before leaving the motel, Mister Touch named (without actual dubbing) the two gang members of Okra Slime. Henceforth they were Wishbone and Yo Boy. The first name came to Mister Touch when he ran IRT's list through his mind from Z backward. He got the second name from Yo Boy himself who yelled out "Yo!" when the main man summoned him. It was the first time Mister Touch had ever departed from the given list.

All aboard! (Sister Fate had been seated in her car long before anyone else appeared; this would be her practice every day — to be ready for more travel, to be so mad for it that she got to her seat while most of the Skulls were still sleeping.) Twenty-seven vehicles rolled slowly forward. "Where them dogs?" people asked, almost hopefully. Then from a clump of red maples flapped a crowd of brown hawks in migration. "Be dead here. Least in the city we have dogs hassling us and Dragons. Here nothing but birds." They squinted at mallards silhouetted in arrow flight against high shreds of cirrus, having had a pleasant nonpolluted time of it flying over smokeless Philly.

At midmorning the caravan pulled off the turnpike at a large motel whose blue and orange gaiety seemed forlorn, but it did have a restaurant. They broke in. An hour later they were eating two-year-old provisions, reamed out of cans and plastic and cooked up with a handful of paprika by Cancer Two and his staff on kerosene braziers brought in from the supply truck. Suddenly a stranger walked through the shattered restaurant door and doffed his fedora.

Middle-aged, pale, and hawkfaced, he wore a gray business suit and a rumpled white shirt with a striped tie impeccably knotted under the frayed collar.

He seemed completely at ease among the Skulls, who stared at him bug-eyed. As if the practice of social amenities were part of his daily life, he explained that he lived across the highway and had seen the caravan pull up. Usually he saw no more than a couple of solitary cars every month or so, although once he had seen three big motorcycles barreling down the turnpike. They had been driven by young men in leather with young women on the rear seats. But he had never seen anything like this caravan. He guffawed to underscore how high he rated it and accepted a plate of beans.

By the time everyone had finished eating, the newcomer expressed the desire to join them. Grandly he declared, "I have walked up and down this road the last year looking for my destiny. Now I have found it."

The prez took him into the motel lobby and had a quiet chat with him. With effortless candor the man told his story. When the Skull rules were explained, he readily agreed to abide by them. Told of the necessity of taking a new name, the man seemed to think Mister Touch was doing him a favor by ridding him of his old one. "Wonderful!" he declared.

Mister Touch decided to use IRT's list again. Scanning it on the scroll of his memory, he stopped at "Doctor Leo."

"Doctor," the man said with a happy smile and straightened his tie proudly. "I like that." He added suddenly, "A doctor in the science of chemistry."

Swiftly he merged with the communal rhythm of the Skulls. He so lost his identity that no one expected anything of him. It was therefore a rude shock to everyone when he went mad outside of Hightstown, New Jersey.

He was riding in Car Nine when two other passengers, Sugar Head and Zap, got into one of their interminable arguments, this one about driving.

Sugar Head said, "You got no sense, man. We never get all the way there. We ain't got drivers could pass the driver test."

"No one is giving or taking tests these days," Zap argued, making another knot in the string that never left his hands.

"Soda here can't pass no test but she driving."

"Don't lean on Soda, man. She's a dope driver. Just fine. She hasn't run off the road once," Zap affirmed. "I bet she drives better now than you used to with eyes. And she damn well breathes better. So use your breath for something besides mouthing off." Tying another knot, Zap added, "Don't lean on Soda or you might wind up DOA."

"Huh?"

"DOA. Dead On Arrival."

Leaning forward, Doctor Leo repeated, "DOA?" In a high thin voice of extreme excitement he said, "You have it wrong, friend! It is not Dead On Arrival! It is Deoxyribose Nucleic Acid! DNA!"

Zap turned slowly from the front seat where he sat next to Soda, the small black girl in whose grip the steering wheel looked as big as the Wheel of Fortune at seven-thirty, Channel Two. Making a new knot in the string for emphasis, Zap said, "I mean DOA. Dead On Arrival."

Doctor Leo nervously adjusted his tie. "Sorry, friend, but it is DNA. D ... N ... A ... DNA!"

"DNA, TWA, BMT, NFL." Zap undid the knots with a flick of his hand. "What's the dif? None of them are operating anymore."

"DNA is operating," retorted Doctor Leo, his voice rising. "It surely *is* operating! DNA is operating in everything that lives!" He paused thoughtfully. "And so, of course, is RNA."

"What getting to you, man?" asked Sugar Head innocently.

But by then Doctor Leo was incapable of answering his question. He was gesticulating so wildly that the others were afraid he might cause Soda to run off the road. They yelled at him to chill out, but the appeal had no effect on the man in the gray flannel suit.

He was furiously deep into a description of two purines which occur in nucleic acid.

Soda honked the horn frantically.

The caravan halted. Doctor Leo was forcibly carried from the car and set babbling on the shoulder of the road. People gathered around curiously at high noon and listened to him expostulate learnedly on the genetic composition of cells which, as most of them knew, had a lot to do with their being here on this empty road half blind and breathless. If V 70 hadn't used an enzyme to convert its RNA into a DNA molecule, then, Doctor Leo yelled at the wide-eyed crowd, you would all be back where you were a couple of years ago! and this road would be jammed with traffic! and all those empty factories along the way would be filled with workers!

For almost two hours the newcomer sat on the roadside, hunched over and frequently drooling, while describing the chemistry of the four bases: adenine, guanine, cytosine, and thymine. "I am talking about the genetic code of life!" he screamed wildly. He had to be held down.

Both Sugar Head and Zap refused to ride again in the same car with the crazy fucker, a decision, little did they know, that would eventually cost them their lives.

Finally, a change came over Doctor Leo. Ruddy from excitement, his face regained its normal pallor. The tense mouth relaxed. The crabbed sentences lurched and staggered to a halt. Tears filled his eyes. His hands clasped and unclasped spasmodically and fell at last into a fisted clump. "It's not my fault if claims are made," he sobbed dejectedly. "It's not my fault, it's the fault of DNA."

With help he managed to get back into Car Nine, but Sugar Head and Zap did not. Their decision appeared to be justified. Doctor Leo had periodic intellectual seizures, set off usually by no more than a random word which precipitated out as a chemical concept in his mind. For example, someone mentioned a *bass* player with a jazz band (Sunoco was guilty) and Doctor Leo filtrated the musical instrument, combined it with a catalytic memory, and the smoking residue was a lecture on pyrimidine, a nitrogenous *base*. His face glowed. Arms flailed. Words came gushing forth.

Soon the Skulls learned that instead of halting the caravan until the storm of chemistry abated, they could control Doctor Leo by shoving a few tranquilizers into his mouth.

Stay High was not impressed by the newcomer. In his opinion Doctor Leo was a specious spellbinder without a college degree. "I venture to suggest," Stay High sniffed, "the man sold shoes and read science fiction."

Stay High was right about his being a salesman, although he sold life insurance, not shoes. He had flunked out of college because of poor marks in chemistry and physics. He had never been

well balanced, having inherited a capacity for madness from his
mother, who ended her life in a mental hospital after two decades
of impeccable service as a lab assistant in the endocrinology department of a well-known university. Even with more than a measure
of quirkiness, Doctor Leo had managed to hold himself together
until V 70 Struck. Then he fell apart. He kneaded in his cramped
mind the notion that the insurance company he worked for would
be forced to pay out countless claims on policies which he himself
had sold to people who died of V 70. The result? He would fail
catastrophically just like his father had predicted. Only later, when
he enjoyed the solitary leisure to evolve a more comfortable view
of the worldwide catastrophe, did he transfer the guilt from himself to the DNA of V 70 and place the blame for billions of deaths
on shoulders other than his own.

For six months he had lived in a Camden library, alone among
the dusty stacks, absorbing what he could from books on biochemistry. He put a bedroll on the second floor and slept near the appropriate shelves, defecating in the chief librarian's office from
spite because intellectuals had never recognized his genius, and
wiping himself with pages from books on physics, a subject he
hated. Finally, he had taken to the road, brooding like a prophet
on the evil of DNA.

Once his outbursts began, Doctor Leo found it hard to make
friends among the Skulls. Only one of them sought his company,
and that was Stifle, who lived in a world of outbursts too but also in
a world of absolute silences. Every so often Stifle would surface
from silence to talk of politics, basket weaving, and music. He knew
more about violin concertos and piano sonatas than Mister Touch
did. But mostly he talked, when he talked at all, about stationery:
paper clips, thumbtacks, typewriter correction film, bank case files,
diskettes, and copiers. Then he would fall back into a stony abyss
from which he never called out for days or weeks.

Now, however, to everyone's bewilderment, he began to follow
Doctor Leo around like a dog, wagging his invisible tail, sitting
when Doctor Leo sat, heeling when Doctor Leo walked. They were
fed, led, and bedded down like mystics whose bizarre actions entitled them to generous care, although Stay High maliciously nicknamed them "our crazies."

At present, the young archeologist from Columbia was savoring a secret discovery. Four three-letter words in "The Mystery of the Universe" were composed of A, C, G, T: Act, Cat, Gat, Tag. A and T were used four times, G and C twice, adding up to twelve altogether. There was a mysterious reason for this, Stay High was certain. It accounted for their peculiar use:

A tide running in the GAT
ACT freaky as a CAT
Play TAG

Surely no accident. Stay High would have staked his intellectual reputation on it, which was like saying he would have staked his life.

24

O N THE ROAD, as Spirit described it to Mister Touch, there were car dumps and water towers everywhere. In nearly every village the white-goateed colonel leered at them from Kentucky Fried Chicken, and a great many rabbits halted to watch the passing caravan, having escaped from a hutch somewhere and multiplied like viruses. As the caravan motored southwestward, it became clear that outside of the concentrated environs of Manhattan dogs were capable of living in solitary independence off the Land of the Free, sharing with muskrats and skunks the tiny morsels of wildlife that trembled in the blue shadows of marshes, under alder and black oak.

Nevertheless, when the motorcade halted, guards surrounded Jesus Mary Save Souls like ants protecting their queen. In one town a mangy-looking mutt showed up around a corner, wagging its tail in the great joy of seeing such a multitude of potential masters. Bang bang bang bang. One burst from an Uzi tore it to shreds.

Fearing that unbridled hostility toward dogs would get somebody accidentally killed, Mister Touch ordered firing withheld unless a situation was threatening.

He called frequent halts, asking Spirit to stop where there were little stands of trees, picnic areas, parks, so that the Skulls, many of them so urbanized they didn't know a hornet from a horsefly, could adjust themselves to a world of earth.

On a noon halt outside of Masonville, New Jersey, in a park brilliant with the fall colors of hickory and maple, the prez asked Spirit to walk him into the woods. Under many Skull feet, as travelers moved away from the parked caravan, leaves crunched like Wheaties (a staple if stale Skull food, swallowed down with water).

Spirit led him down a meandering path to a park bench with a view that he couldn't appreciate: distant hills where horned owls awaited nightfall and weasels sniffed out the tempting existence of newborn spaniels.

As they sat on the bench, saying little in the midday air, Mister Touch was slightly horrified to find himself succumbing to the sudden urge to tell the former cabby how his career on Wall Street had come to a bad end.

Like so many midwesterners he had come east to seek fame and fortune, settling for fortune. What he lacked in Ivy League credentials he made up for in daring and ambition. Armed with his mother's adventurous spirit he got into high-risk corporate dealing, and driven by the example of his father's unrealized aspirations to become a college football coach he shouldered his way into the high-tech world of buyouts, funding raids, megabuck mergers, where something beyond the dollar was of greatest value — the excitement of outsmarting outguessing outmaneuvering an opponent. He became a highroller in the gambling arenas of blue-chip law firms and investment houses.

"We used to say knowledge was power and power was money and money was excitement and excitement was everything. So in arbitrage I had everything. Once I greased a takeover or two I had the feel for what excitement can be. I worked twenty-hour days on three phones at once. I was at risk twenty-four. I looked for the hook that gave me an edge. You did it right, you made sums you didn't have time to spend. Above all, you felt a sense of tremendous power, like being connected by electric cable to God's heartbeat. That's not my phrase. That's the phrase we used."

"What happened?"

"I fell into playing poker with a marked deck. Without going into the grisly details, three of us assembled stock for a takeover we'd targeted and in pricing it we got a wee bit of inside help, a definite no-no. The SEC and the London Stock Exchange got on our tail. We had but days to live, in a manner of speaking — and then V 70 Struck. I'm one of the few given a second chance when the world as we knew it ended." Then he paused. "My name is Mark."

"Mark."

It was the first time Mister Touch had heard that name spoken since waking up alive in his apartment and going downstairs to find an Angora cat.

"I won't tell you my name," Spirit said. "I left it behind when I walked into the Dragon Club House."

"You're like IRT. Good. I thought I was too — ready to leave the past behind. I don't know why I wanted you to know who I was."

"What you've told me isn't very flattering."

"At least it's out of the way. We're on a long drive together. Now you know who's sitting beside you."

They sat in silence until Spirit told him the break was nearly over.

Rising, Mister Touch reached out while she placed his finger-tips on her arm.

As they stepped through the brittle leaves, Spirit said, "I'm glad you told me."

They would be entering Delaware the next morning, and this evening the prospect of crossing state lines made some of the inexperienced travelers anxious. Many went to bed early in their motel rooms outside of Auburn. They pulled the sheets up to their noses, trying to rid themselves of a fear of flying across America at ten miles an hour.

But Mystique was far from sleep. She took a long walk alone and then joined a group of young Skulls who were listening raptly to Sister Fate's account of a boat trip down the Rajang River in Borneo. The inveterate world traveler was becoming a star in the Skull firmament, but her newfound popularity annoyed Mystique, who had little patience with youngsters crowding around to hear about exotic lands when most of them scarcely knew there was a place called Wilmington, Delaware, that they'd drive through tomorrow. Fretfully, the honey blonde paced up and down the moonlit highway until the motel grew quiet. Then, resolutely blowing her breath out, Mystique headed for the main man's room. She did not bother knocking, but pushed the door open, rushed in with her flashlight ablaze, and raked its light across the room to see who was there. Finding no one but Mister Touch in jockey shorts lying on his rumpled bed, Mystique sighed. "Well," she said. "I'm surprised."

Sleepily, Mister Touch rubbed his sightless eyes. "I thought you told me you had duty tonight."

"No, I didn't," Mystique claimed, although she had told him earlier today of her night duty in the Motorhome dispensary. Mystique had wanted to show up unexpectedly and catch him at something. Last night she had treated him to wild sex in a determined effort to rid his mind of The Dragon Lady. But today she had seen him walk into the woods with the spying slut. It had taken all of her willpower not to follow them. Instead of doing that, however, she had devised a plan of attack. Part of it was to surprise him in bed with The Dragon Lady. Since that hadn't happened, she was not only surprised but relieved, if ashamed of miscalculating.

"What's so surprising?" he asked.

"That you're alone."

"Why? You said you were on duty tonight."

"What do you take me for?" Mystique turned off the flashlight, changing nothing for him but leaving herself swallowed up in the blackness of anger. "The other night you go on a stroll with her down the highway. I heard about it. And today I saw you walk into the woods with her."

"You mean Spirit?"

"The Dragon Lady."

"You're making something of nothing."

"Men have always told me I am a beautiful woman, but here a new face, pretty in a cheap sort of way, comes along and you go for it like that."

"A face I can't see. Are you as blind as I am?"

"You've told me you want me, but you've never told me you love me."

"Look, she's driving the lead car, that's all."

"As to that," said Mystique, "why didn't you ask me to drive the lead car?"

"One, you told me once you didn't drive. Two, she's the most experienced driver we have."

"How convenient for you. Did you ever get into a cab and hope to God you'd get where you were going alive? *Anybody* used to drive a cab. You didn't even have to speak English, let alone know where streets were. As for The Dragon Lady, she's a terrible driver. Zigzags all over."

"Zigzags? I haven't felt it."

"Because you're feeling other things. I'm telling you she can't drive! She's giving you more lies." Mystique paused, then set out in a new direction. "You mentioned my giving a first aid course. I'd like that. I think I could start it on the trip."

"Great idea."

She heard the relief in his voice; it made her furious to think of him getting off so easily from charges of infidelity, justified or not. But Mystique had a plan she was determined to carry out. "Will you discuss it with me? If you can tear yourself away from the New York cabby, perhaps one of these days you can drive part of the way in the dispensary and I'll tell you what I have in mind."

He agreed, then patted the bed, inviting her.

"Not tonight," she said, triumphant in this chance to refuse him. Leaving the room without another word, Mystique went in search of ways to set her plan in motion.

All Ace had ever been in life was a mailroom clerk, and he had always thought of himself as a victim.

At least until V 70 Struck. Afterward he saw himself as a superior being, doubly so because he was white and had good eyesight. What did it matter in this half-blind world if he had flaming red hair and a face full of pimples? Now that Flash was gone, he had the best eyesight of all the Skulls. He could read every billboard, every used-car ad, every placard in a tavern window, let alone all the traffic signs. Behind him were ten cars, four vans, four station wagons and four small trucks, two trailers, and a Motorhome, all depending on his superior eyes to find the way.

And yet people didn't give him respect. Here he was at the

wheel of Car Two — *second* in the line of march — but no one had slapped him on the back and said, "Ace, buddy, you're great." Not one. Not even Zap and Sugar Head, who had begged to ride in his car because they were scared of riding with that loony Doctor Leo. Not even old Mister Lucky who used to ride in his car. He had come along as Cola Face's chaperone. She had insisted on having one after learning she would ride with Ace, who had insisted she ride with him if he agreed to drive. Old Mister Lucky had then begged to ride elsewhere when Sugar Head and Zap had come aboard with their incessant arguments.

But for all of Ace's importance in the scheme of things, whoever told him, "I appreciate what you're doing for all of us"? Nobody.

That is, nobody until Mystique.

Along with Riot and The Fierce Rabbit he had been sitting one autumn evening around a bonfire made of motel office furniture. They were boasting of their superior talents when the tall good-looking Good Looker came along. Squinting at Mystique, they fell as silent as three conspirators planning the downfall of Republican Rome.

Ace was astonished to see Mystique crook her finger, beckoning him out of the triumvirate. Smirking at his companions, Ace went with her across the highway to stand under an icy gibbous moon while she told him he wasn't appreciated enough.

"*You* should be the lead driver," Mystique exclaimed, "not the spy. After all, your eyes are the best we got."

"You're right there."

"You led an expedition too. You have a warrior's heart."

He liked that. "Yeah," he said. "I gotta admit."

"I also think she doesn't appreciate you."

"What?"

"Cola Face. She's stuck up like girls are sometimes. They don't know who is good for them."

"Yeah, she needs a comedown."

"She needs to look at you in a different way."

"Yeah? Like what?"

"Like the leader you really are."

Ace stared through the milky moonlight at the tall attractive woman. It was like she read his mind. He stood there trapped in her eloquence as she described a new life for him: he would advance quickly, overtake Hoss, supplant Mister Touch, let everyone know what was what, and have any woman he desired, including Cola Face.

"How do I start?" he asked eagerly.

"By making a fool of the spy. By letting everyone see you're a better driver." Drawing him into the shadows of roadside trees, Mystique told him what to do.

25

A_s THE CARAVAN motored slowly through the towns of Delaware, each carload established its own mood. People were quiet in some, talkative in others. In some cars the occupants developed the kind of ominous silence that could lead to OOTLO.

The real cutups were in Car Seven, even though it was driven by still-grieving Riot. He recited to himself words from OOTHI, arduously learned, that he used to whisper in Bambu's ear:

> *To men a man is but a mind. Who cares*
> *What face he carries or what form he wears?*
> *But woman's body is the woman. O*
> *Stay thou, my sweetheart, and do never go.*

But the other occupants of Car Seven were into riddles.

"If a man should give one son fifteen cents and another ten cents, what time is it?"

"A quarter to two."

"When is it a good thing to lose your temper?"

"When it's a bad one."

"Why is death like a boy breaking your window?"

"Because it puts an end to your pains."

That sort of thing. Because of Hitler's persistent dream in which he rode a man-sized stick of dynamite into the sky, straddling it like a broom, the following riddle was their favorite and went the rounds of the whole cavalcade.

"Why did the moron eat dynamite?"

"He wanted his hair to grow out in bangs."

While the lead car rumbled through Delaware at a speed you would get a ticket for only in a hospital zone, Mister Touch realized that everyone had been silent a long time. Aside from himself, they were all Lookers. The passing landscape must seem peculiar to them.

One weekend he and a girlfriend had driven down from New York through this same region. He remembered the land going by and people alive on it: women hanging laundry in yards cluttered with auto parts; children sucking their thumbs in the doorways of mobile homes; weathered old men sunning in front of roadside fruit stands; and a special old geezer, grizzled and lean, sitting ramrod straight in the sunlight, puffing a curved pipe, in front of a shakily painted sign spelling PEECH with baskets of peaches collected around the old fellow's feet. The memory could be false, of course. He had probably made up the old man, but the PEECH sign had been real and so had the baskets of fruit.

Surely it was better not to see the new world passing by. His companions must be watching gas stations and churches recede like so many movie sets long abandoned by film crews, while he continued to see what was there in memory: RC Cola signs, piles of rotting tires, rusted boilers in fields choked by weeds, and shopping malls. He recalled the water towers of this land, how dramatic they had looked, rising above clumps of woodland. He remembered all that and more, but he remembered everything in the context of *living people*. That was the appalling difference between what he remembered and what his fellow travelers were now seeing.

His four remaining senses limited Mister Touch to sensations that were pleasant. Smell, for example — that of loblolly pine and earth rich in oxides. But his companions were looking at land that lacked human hands to make sense of the funny-looking artifacts of civilization: the wheels, pipes, wires, the fantastical shapes unknown to nature. Stretching ahead, the main man knew, was the intimidating expanse of a great country. The imaginations of people able to see it would not be able to resist it, as America unrolled mile after mile like a remorseless carpet.

Mister Touch fumbled for his cassette player and slipped in Janáček's *Missa Glagolitica*. Spirit asked him what it was. He wondered if they would explore together the vast territory lying between Monteverdi and Martinu.

"Music was always background for me," Spirit said. "I was always too busy to listen."

"So was I," admitted the prez. "One thing we have on the road is time."

But the rolling rhythms of Janáček did not appeal to others in the car, who put on headphones and tuned in their own private worlds as the dead world rolled past them.

When the caravan stopped, Mystique stared down the line to Car Two. Seeing Ace get out, Mystique walked forward and raised one hand in secret communication.

He nodded sharply.

With a deep breath of decision, Mystique walked back to one of the supply trucks. She talked briefly to the driver. Then she went to the front of the caravan, hearing the jaunty strains of Bach issuing from the open window of Car One. Going up to it, Mystique looked down at the red-bearded prez sitting alone in the car and said quietly, "Can I see you?"

"I suppose you're doing that right now."

"Funny." She was glancing around to see where The Dragon Lady had gone. Nowhere in sight. Odd, but wonderful. "About the first aid course. Can we talk it over now?"

Mystique opened the door and led him out. She was relieved that the main man left Africa at the lead car with instructions to signal "go" in fifteen minutes.

"Don't you have to tell your cab driver you're riding somewhere else?"

"She knows I might shift around."

"Not because you're bored riding with her but because you're obligated to see how everyone else is doing. Right? How commendable."

When he didn't respond to the sarcasm, Mystique figured she'd better stick to the scenario.

Taking his hand, she led Mister Touch down the line to the

supply truck. "I thought we'd ride in here instead of the dispensary. I don't want Sweet Thing eavesdropping."

She helped him into the back of the supply truck, lined head-high with cartons of canned food, soft drinks, coffee tins, jars of peanut butter, and boxes of stale biscuits. There were plastic bags of ramen, the dried Japanese noodles loved by the Skulls because only hot water was needed to make them ichiban good.

Shutting the truck door and settling with him against a dark wall of boxes, Mystique assumed a businesslike voice as she detailed a syllabus for the first aid course. Her mind, however, was elsewhere — zeroed in on the intentions of the redhead who would be driving Car Two when the caravan set out again.

They were approaching the Chesapeake Bay toll bridge and tunnel. On the right was the bay, on the left the ocean. Peering from their windows, Skulls could see something weird out there — a sailboat on the bay, its white sails snapping in a fresh breeze, as if a well-heeled Maryland family was taking a weekend cruise.

The caravan threaded its way down a narrow road between the two bodies of sparkling water.

Beneath Car Two (a Mercedes of a lavender color which Ace thought was sissy) the road disappeared slowly into the blue mist like thread winding off a spool. At the rate they were going, thought Ace bitterly, they wouldn't get through the tunnel until sunset. The idea of creeping along for hours, coupled with his mounting sense of indignation, was bringing him closer to the moment of truth. His hands were sweating as they gripped the wheel when they should be gripping those luscious tits of the stuck-up beauty Cola Face, who sat next to him, staring straight ahead, as if she were being driven to the airport in a limo by a nameless jerk from Brooklyn.

He looked out at the water. The sailboat had vanished in the roiling haze. There was nothing for him to fix his wonderful gaze on except the gunmetal gray surface of the bay. Car One was plodding along ahead of him like an eighteen-wheel crane-truck going up a steep grade. All the other vehicles following like sheep. Well, *he* was no sheep . . .

Back in Supply Truck F the main man continued to listen while Mystique outlined procedures for splinting bones. He smelled

cardboard and heard cans rattling. Then he felt her take his hand
and lead it . . . to a place very familiar to him. There was just space
enough for them side by side on the floor of the truck. The first aid
course was forgotten.

What Ace had not forgotten was the way Cola Face had ignored his every attempt at conversation through Exmore,
Nassawadox, Birdsnest, Kendall Grove, and Cape Charles, turning
away with a petulant shrug every time he claimed that it was a nice
day or suggested that she look at the ocean or noted that they were
moving quite slow — if instead he had growled "Fuck you, lady!"
she would probably have given him the same indifferent shrug, because she wouldn't have heard that either, she had never heard one
word he said. Turning from the road to Cola Face, his eyes confirmed what he already knew: she was gorgeous. Why didn't she
ever look at him? Maybe because the cheek facing her had seven
pimples on it — a new one today, Oh my God, yellow with pus!

Gripping the wheel tightly, he knew that Mystique was right.
He had to take matters into his own hands, had to prove that the
caravan needed a new lead driver. Mystique had told him what to
do and in spite of its being a woman telling him what to do he was
going to do it. He found himself veering out of the column, as if
his hands on the wheel and his foot on the accelerator possessed
independent lives of their own. In a moment he had zoomed
around Car One and was out in front. Then he braked so fast that
his back bumper hit the cabby's front one. Giving it the gas, he
braked again, but this time the former cabby eluded his attempt at
another playful collision. Slowing, he came alongside Car One,
yelling at the black chick behind the wheel, "Chicken!" With that
he swerved toward her, but she swerved too, away from him, only
a tire's breadth between her car and the retaining barrier. Her skill
infuriated Ace. He put his foot down hard, ignoring Cola Face,
who was yelling at him. He experienced the joy of snubbing her as
she had always snubbed him.

Hunching forward, Ace focused his wonderful eyes on a road
unreeling in front of the windshield like a VCR on Fast Forward.
All the passengers were screaming at him, while his neat-looking
eyes glanced at the speedometer as it swung from fifty through seventy eighty ninety — he'd show them! Wind coming through the
open windows shrieked like an inmate of a booby hatch; it tossed

Ace's long red hair to and fro and swept across his cheeks where a new zit had popped out that morning, humiliating him further in front of the blond bitch, because the pimple glowed like a death's-head on the side of his face presented to her view if ever she had the decency to look at him at all. His superior eyes squinted in the rush of air. The center line wiggled like a worm, as he gaily zig-zagged the car at a hundred miles an hour between bay and ocean.

A hand reaching from the back seat clutched his shoulder.

He swiveled his head around and declared in the flush of mad ecstasy, "Stop that! *I* am driving this car!" In the time it took him to make this imperial announcement, his seven last words, the car scooted off the road through the retaining barricade, and sailed across the slick pale uninteresting surface of Chesapeake Bay like a lavender boat without sails before plummeting into the water with an impact that shattered glass and crushed metal.

Ace of the red hair sank through the bay and with him forever sank pretty Cola Face, the true cause of the accident. All he had wanted to do was impress her with his daring and win her love.

Others accompanying Ace were Tito, whose neck snapped while he was in the midst of acute indigestion, because in the last twelve hours he had consumed, among other things, a five-pound box of chocolate, a half dozen party-sized bags of pretzels, an economy-sized jar of kosher dills, three cans of Spam, four tins of Norwegian brislings, and seven jars of Gerber's baby food; and those two inseparable companions, Zap and Sugar Head, who by changing cars to avoid one madman had encountered another.

The car settled into the deep muck of Chesapeake Bay, with the toll fare unpaid, and a driver at the wheel whose license had long since expired. Five Skulls had been lost, one of them a valuable Neat Looker.

The caravan halted and people got out to look. The surface of the bay once again appeared slick, pale, and uninteresting. "I knowed something like it would happen, sooner or later," someone declared.

Someone down the line was grimly quoting OOTHI: " 'There's a divinity that shapes our ends, rough-hew them how we will,' " without, of course, realizing that divinity in this instance had been present in the nubile shape of a hairdresser from the Bronx who had wanted three cars in a Westchester garage but who now had to settle for a single Mercedes at the muddy bottom of a bay where perhaps for eternity (who knows) she might have to fend off the advances of the sort of boy she had gone to school with and hated for being part of her life and had sworn to avoid, once she moved into Manhattan, if it was the last thing she ever did.

When the hubbub began beyond the supply truck, its driver had braked so violently that Mister Touch, inside the truck, was pushed even farther inside Mystique, if that were possible. Just as the truck lurched to a halt, so did he, orgasmically. Mister Touch had hardly buttoned up before people outside of the truck were yelling.

"Get me out there!" he called to Mystique, who answered as if far away in a disconcertingly calm and musical voice, "I guess something must have happened."

After sorting out Ace's wild ride and Spirit's skillful escape, the main man resolved never to leave Car One again. If the ship went down, metaphorically speaking, he would go down with it.

Mystique nimbly avoided any guilt she might have felt. After all, she hadn't told Ace to hurtle into the bay at a hundred miles an hour. She had merely asked him to drive circles around the spying slut. Ace had failed to do what he said he would do, which was to expose The Dragon Lady's ineptitude behind the wheel. As things turned out, he had merely confirmed the main man's belief in the cabby's skill. Rather than feeling guilt for aiding and abetting Ace's mad dash for recognition, Mystique blamed herself for enlisting a damn fool in her fight against a foe who was beginning to look formidable.

Later, after the Skulls walked slowly back to their vehicles and the caravan staggered through the final light of afternoon with the tunnel ahead and beyond it the state of Virginia, silence was broken in one of the cars at last.

Someone said in a voice of forced nonchalance, "Anyone here remember they had 'Soul Train' on Saturday?"

"Channel Eleven."

"You got it. Channel Eleven. Thirty minutes they danced disco."

"I remember."

"They put the train on before ads. It was animated, that train."

"Forgot that part, homes."

"Remember Don Cornelius? Emcee? Before the last ad, to get you back looking the next time, he always say, 'It's gonna be a stone gas.' Remember that?"

"When you tell it I remember."

"They had little rubber-butt mammas could really dance. They put it in drive, man."

"I sure ain't forgetting that. Sweet mammas dancing."

They grinned at each other in shared nostalgic joy.

26

Having slept alongside the road outside of Norfolk, the Skulls got up early the next morning. Mister Touch almost beat Sister Fate to the cars. Africa seated him in Number One, then went for a cupful of coffee which was brewing in four twenty-quart stockpots set in the middle of the road.

The door on the driver's side opened and someone got in.

"Spirit?"

"Yes. I saw Africa bringing you here, so I thought maybe you'd like to talk. If not, I'll leave."

"Stay. I have something to talk about. We lost five people but no one knows why. Does V 70 leave a residue that makes some of us go wild? What was Ace thinking of? What's the next thing? How can I prevent what I can't imagine?"

"You're taking too much on yourself."

"I suppose so. Can I hold your hand?" He felt her warm fingers slide against his, and for a moment he held her hand tightly, then let it go. "I don't feel guilty," he said.

"You shouldn't."

"But I do."

They sat in silence awhile. "Can I suggest something?" Spirit asked finally.

"Go on. I'm out of ideas."

"Why not split up?" Spirit paused. "If we went in two groups we'd have more chance. I mean, if something happened, there wouldn't be a total wipeout."

"Playing the percentages," said the former Wall Streeter.

"Like parents who had money enough to travel by air. They took different flights, so if a plane went down, the kids would still have a parent."

"You think like a survivor," he said admiringly. Later in the day, during a roadside break, the main man had Hoss take him for a stroll. They discussed splitting the caravan into two groups. Hoss liked the idea. They could reunite down the road.

On that basis they hastily developed a plan. Hoss had always loved maps. He had one in his back pocket, took it out, and focused a small magnifying glass on the crisscrossed lines. One group could go through Charlotte, distance 422 miles from Norfolk. The other could travel through Fayetteville and Columbia, distance 491 miles. They could meet at Atlanta. Depending on the weather and other unpredictable circumstances, they figured the trip might take about ten days. Whoever arrived first would camp on the capitol steps and wait for as long as a week for the other group to show up. If the second group didn't reach Atlanta in time, the next rendezvous would be Meridian, Mississippi. After another week there, if a reunion failed to occur, the surviving force — a military term they used — would continue alone to the Arizona state line.

That evening Mister Touch explained the plan to the Skulls gathered around big iron pots of ramen. A hue and cry went up. He could not suppress a smile. Such a lively reaction was like a Bach fugue to his ears. Yesterday, after the disaster, he had heard few sounds, a terrible thing for someone blind, and what he had heard had been like the shuffling of old men. Now voices were raised in anger and anxiety. Friends didn't want to be separated, not even for a day. Those destined for the northern route suddenly wanted to take the southern, and vice versa. People grumbled and squabbled and bargained with one another to exchange seats.

Since Fire had been in publishing, she was in charge of the

Caravan Roster. What connection her former profession had with keeping a list of who sat where in which vehicle was a well-kept secret, but the ex-editor never turned down a challenge. Fire met this one, though she needed the eyes of little Golden Girl to read her the list. Her own, ruined by Trollope as much as by V 70, could barely read labels with a magnifying glass anymore and were destined for worse unless somewhere in America there was still a practicing optometrist who could correct her glasses. People gathered around, shouting, complaining, as Golden Girl piped out names. Next morning, two hours were consumed by the process of shifting people from here to there.

The Fierce Rabbit popped out of his hutch and went to Fire with a request so fierce that she acquiesced to it without a murmur. It didn't matter to him whether he went north or south, just so long as three people went with him: Evil Eye, Wishbone, and Yo Boy.

As Mister Touch had hoped when they joined the Skulls under the arch at Washington Square, the two hitchhikers were unusually cooperative and quiet. Ominously so, Hoss would have thought had he given them any thought. Almost immediately, they had gravitated to The Fierce Rabbit, as if he were the Strong Force that binds proton and neutron inside an atomic nucleus. The truth was, they had credentials that impressed The Rabbit, who had never been part of a real-life gang. Wishbone, however, had ascended from a wannabe to gang member in South Brooklyn before V 70 Struck. Yo Boy had the curious distinction of coming from Los Angeles where his brother had been murdered in a gang war and he himself had been a peewee on the verge of becoming a cholo in the Quatro Flats because he was tight partners with people who were in. Yo Boy knew things that fascinated The Fierce Rabbit — like rolling cartridges in garlic. If you killed a guy with a garlic bullet he wouldn't just die, he'd go straight to hell.

As for Evil Eye, she was contemptuous of gangs and macho pretensions. That was one reason why The Fierce Rabbit was showing interest in her — she rejected his beliefs and rejected him. Evil Eye was a sloe-eyed chocolate-colored five feet two inches of wisecracks and indifference to men. She was attracted to The Rabbit, however, and enjoyed fluttering her lashes at him, giving him a full-busted profile and then drawling out "Down, homeboy, *down*" when he started hitting on her.

The SS was also grumbling up and down the line of cars. Sag did most of their talking. In her opinion the main man and his lackey Hoss were splitting up the caravan to nullify a growing political opposition. Snow would punctuate her friend's pronouncement by nodding her white-haired head and murmuring, "This is *definitely* so."

They managed to attract the attention of Riot. Once Ace left the triumvirate, Riot fell out with The Fierce Rabbit, both racists to the core. Now Riot nursed his pain and anger in solitude. What attracted the Eyetalian kid to the SS was their clean-cut-all-American-mom-look which reminded him of his mothergrandmother-greatgrandmother, all of whom used to give him kisses and osso bucco when he was depressed.

While people were exercising their fears and frustrations about the split, Mister Touch said to Hoss, "We have a problem with the dispensary. We can't divvy that up the way we have the vans and trucks and cars.

"Toss a coin?"

"Do you have a better idea?"

But they didn't have a coin. And when the call went up and down the line of vehicles, people searched their pockets but without success. So they waited until they got to Franklin, Virginia, where they smashed the window of a supermarket, broke open the rusty register at Checkout, and extracted a nickel.

Heads the Motorhome went with Hoss, tails with Mister Touch. Tails.

The rest of that day was consumed in transferring equipment equally from supply trucks and some of the vans and providing the Northern Force with sufficient medicines from the Motorhome to last a couple of weeks.

They needed two nurses for Hoss's group. Jesus Mary Save Souls designated Sweet Thing in a move to get the scheming woman out of her red Irish hair. Mystique volunteered as the second nurse.

Her decision was one more in a long line of strategies designed to vanquish Mister Touch utterly. Mystique's brand of militarism came to the Skulls from the Upper East Side where, until a year ago, she had been one third of a ménage à trois as hectic and destructive as any love triangle she had known of before V 70 Struck.

Having escaped Ellen and Bob, she had drifted southward, stumbling finally into Washington Square Park where the Skulls found her cowering in the dry fountain. She fell instantly in love with the tall red-bearded second-in-command to the outrageous black drummer. In those days Mister Touch had enough sight left to appreciate her honey-haired beauty. At the time he was involved with Nando, but Mystique waited patiently, secure in her skill at prewar maneuvers. She smiled at him in the halls, played up to his interest in music by inventing one of her own, bumped into him in the right places as if she, not he, had failing eyesight. Finally when he disengaged from Nando, leaving himself unprotected in the middle of No Man's Land, Mystique marshaled her forces for a full-scale assault.

Initially she unleashed an arsenal of seductive weaponry that had conquered numerous men in the old days. When the siege failed to carry all before it, Mystique merely felt that the old adage was true about losing the battle but winning the war. She struck again, this time a commando raid at midnight, knocking boldly on his door — with nothing on beneath her raincoat. Although the attack gained a momentary objective, it did not succeed in winning his full capitulation. So she tried to overwhelm him by an aggressive, continuous, and fearlessly executed campaign which had for its target his admission that he loved her. When this too failed, her concept of war was modified by an image from plumbing: she ran hot and cold — one night fucking him and the next day waving perfunctorily from a distance. This last tactic had occupied recent months, again without unconditional surrender. The man seemed content to accept with unsettling equanimity either her body or her indifference, whichever came first. Even so, Mystique clung to her belief that women had to convince men they were in love or else the bozos would never figure it out for themselves.

Now, with the caravan splitting up this way, she had the chance to test another hypothesis, namely that absence makes the heart grow fonder.

Moreover, when she raised the veil of jealousy and stared in the clear light of objectivity at Mister Touch and The Dragon Lady, she saw no telltale signs of intimacy for real, only a kind of mutual regard. That might be all there was to it: a budding friendship shaped by her distorting passion into the sort of imagined romance she herself desperately wanted to have. Mystique prided herself on an ability to see things as they really were. She had therefore a sense of her own propensity to overreact when it came to men. So perhaps she could leave him with Spirit for a while without doing her own cause harm. And perhaps her absence would work on Mister Touch like a virus, burrowing into his mind and multiplying there until thoughts of other women withered like diseased cells. It was a high-risk decision, but Mystique decided it was her best strategy. If it failed, then nothing would work except removing The Dragon Lady from his presence altogether.

Next morning the Northern and Southern forces separated at Emporia, Virginia. The group with the Motorhome turned south on Route 95 and the other group continued west to meet 85. As the caravan split, arms appeared from open windows, waving goodbye. There were tears. A few people crossed themselves.

"See you mothafuckers in Adlanna!" someone yelled gaily.

And the columns moved away from each other into the yellow-leached soil and forests of the Carolinas.

In a van traveling south, an elegant elderly woman quoted OOTHI: " 'Why stay we on this earth except to grow?' "

In the Northern Force someone remarked with a sigh, "That Mercedes flying through the air and disappearing in a wink. Think of it. The five of them down there in a lavender car forever."

"Cola Face won't like it," another Skull said.

27

Fayetteville, north carolina, had been burned out. The town they motored through on a drizzly morning lay in gray soggy ruin. The bank building, the police station, stores, and many houses in residential areas had been gutted by numerous fires.

In the lead car Spirit cried out, "Look! A boy!"

He ran across the street in front of the cavalcade like a kid in the old days rushing home to announce the circus was in town or like a frightened child hightailing it like a rabbit: Skulls who could see him took their pick.

The prez ordered a halt. People saw the kid run into a stationery shop through a shattered doorway. "Africa," said the prez, "go get him."

Along with half a dozen men the huge bodyguard crossed the street and entered the store, ready to rummage through rubber bands and paper clips for a living body. The travelers sat a long time in the drizzle before Africa finally returned, he and the others puffing hard, with the boy tucked under his arm like a rolled newspaper.

A photo shop nearby also had a shattered doorway. Mister Touch had Africa take the boy inside. A dozen Skulls stood around gawking at the long brown hair, freckles, torn T-shirt, jeans held up by a piece of rope, and tattered sneakers.

Sitting in an office chair under the blowup of a Kodak bathing beauty, Mister Touch told Africa to set the boy on the counter. Speaking calmly, the main man questioned the child. What had happened here? Were there other people? How had he survived?

To every question the boy glared from under thick eyebrows. Now and then, turning a little, he glanced warily at the oddly dressed people around him.

"Would you like to come with us?" Mister Touch asked gently. "We won't hurt you. We're on a trip and we'd like you to come." He added into the silence, "Better than staying here, don't you think?"

"Maybe he can't talk," someone suggested.

Someone else said, "Douse him with perfume. He stinks like a shithouse."

Spirit came up and knelt beside the boy. "Will you come with us?"
The boy said, "Edzu hoto moo."

"What he saying?" someone whispered and someone replied, "You heard him."

"Ahgee tee toe," the boy continued, staring dejectedly at the floor.

"Let me talk to him," declared Stay High, and pushed through the crowd. For another ten minutes he tried in vain to elicit anything comprehensible from the boy. "Interesting," said the Skull scholar. "I think the boy has created his own language."

Someone whispered, "Hey, what's Stay High saying?"

"Same bullshit he always saying."

"I think," Stay High added, now beaming, "the trauma of V 70 and living alone all this time have turned the boy into a linguistic amnesiac. He forgot English, and in order to talk to himself he has developed a new language."

At Stay High's urgent request, the prez turned the newcomer over to him.

They stayed in Fayetteville most of the morning, taking care of chores. Under the command of Automotive Engineer Stitch they siphoned gas from parked cars, an arduous task because most of the tanks were only about a third full, the rest having evaporated. Gas was poured into drums brought from New York, which were then loaded by hydraulic lift, worked by the running engine of a truck, into the truck's freight area.

Meanwhile, an armed and wary expedition went into a supermarket for canned goods and bottled water. The water was stored along with cases of soda and beer in a van called "The Watering Trough."

Skulls like really into clothes scoured the local shops for more clothing. When one of The Ladies sniffed at them and called them "Road Warriors," they bristled. Those uncool bikers in the movie dressed like savages, whereas Skulls were big-city slicks who wore wild threads only to get off in a world without television, discos, and subway trains rattling into a station where muggers lurked. As someone said in a Fayetteville department store, while studying the incomprehensible label on Creative Fragrances' "Phantom Pour Homme," "Good to smell good when you don't have no electricity, no fridges, washing machine, and phones, man."

Mister Touch had remained in the photo shop, staring blankly at a wall of photos featuring all-American boys and girls.

Suddenly, words came rushing at him out of the darkness of his world: "Things are going forward!"

He was developing a feel for individual voices. This one was high, the tone clipped, the words rapid. "Stay High?"

Nodding, as if that meant anything to the prez, Stay High said, "I am applying transformational grammar to the boy's speech. I am trying to get him to use kernel sentences."

"I don't understand a thing you are saying."

Undeterred, the scholar went on to say that he wanted to establish two levels for the boy's speech: one, a deep structure representing the sense of it; and two, a surface structure representing its sound. He pointed out that when a surface structure relates to more than one deep structure, ambiguity will most likely result.

"I don't understand a thing you're saying," Mister Touch repeated.

"For example, if I say 'John painted the car in the garage,' I have made a statement with two possible deep structures: when John painted the car, he did so in the garage; or, the car that John painted was the car in the garage."

"Okay, I understand that. But are you saying this has something to do with the boy?"

"Everything!" Patiently the scholar explained that the native speaker of a language can detect such ambiguities as well as produce, theoretically, an infinite number of sentences.

"You're saying the boy is a native speaker of the language he created?"

"That is one thing I am saying."

"And he can detect ambiguities and make a whole lot of sentences? Well, okay. But is he trying to *tell* us something?"

There was a long pause. Then Stay High said sheepishly, "I don't know."

"Can't you tell?"

"So far I can't relate to his phrase-structuring rules. For example, when I point to a car, he says 'ziti' one time and 'ogu' the next. In fact, each time I point to a car the word changes. I have heard 'ziti,' 'ogu,' 'tella,' and 'boo' so far for a moving vehicle."

"Every word ends in a vowel."

Stay High snapped his fingers — Mister Touch heard the sound. "Why didn't I think of that!"

"It helps to be blind. Has it occurred to you he might not want to communicate and that's why he talks this way?"

"No."

"Considering we found him half dead in a town put to the torch, don't you think it's possible? God knows what happened to the poor kid."

During the ensuing lull in their conversation, Mister Touch assumed that the scholar was wondering just what it was God knew about the poor kid, but when Stay High finally broke the silence, it was to admit that along with unlocking the key to "The Mystery of the Universe," he wanted to discover the strings the boy used.

"Strings?" said Mister Touch. For an instant he remembered during his time of seeing things how Zap, asleep now forever in a lavender-colored car, used to tie knots in a string and untie them with one swift motion.

Mister Touch tried to follow the scholar's explanation of a different sort of string. "The sequence of grammatical symbols and words representing the underlying form of a sentence," Stay High explained.

"Okay, look for his strings if you want to, but tell me this. Does this boy *respond* when you talk to him?"

"If you mean, respond in the sense of display 'affect,' psychologically speaking, why, I would say yes. But that's not the issue."

"I think it is. I think you'd better concentrate on his responses, Stay High, instead of his strings."

There was a silence that told Mister Touch his admonition had fallen on deaf ears. "At any rate," he said with a sigh, "I've decided to name him The Boy Who Doesn't Speak Our Language."

"I think it's remarkable how you discovered his use of vowels. That was very observant of you. I'll look there for his morphophonemic rules."

"Good," said Mister Touch. "Go look." He reached to his side and pulled out a couple of blades of grass and held them to his nose, smelling reality.

A boy perhaps too frightened of reality to make himself understood and an intellectual so wounded by reality that he avoided further contact with it: those two traveling together into the future.

*   *   *

The rest of the day they drove past lines of long-leaf pines, with glimpses of small lakes, once almost fished out, but now only a year away from brimming with blue gill and crappie. The travelers squinted at the smokeless smokestacks of paper factories. When dusk fell, they camped in downtown Florence, South Carolina. Parking at the corner of Evans and South Irby, they set up a dozen cooking fires in the middle of a tree-lined cul-de-sac which, with its European boutiques and milk-white streetlamps, had once been the showpiece of town.

Cancer Two supervised the preparation of baked beans, canned tacos, which tasted awful, and a variety of veggies — hoping to please at least some appetites by a liberal use of spices, particularly his favorite: paprika.

It was another balmy and moonlit evening, so many of the Skulls took a walking tour of town after dinner. When the main man asked Spirit if she would go for a stroll, he felt her hand reach out, take his, and lead it to her arm. They set out under the moon he couldn't see, its ghostly glow enshrouding the John L. McMillan Federal Building. When they turned the corner, Spirit noticed something move in the shadows across the way. She gave a little cry and clutched his arm at the same time someone else gave a little cry from over there. Two people, carrying bedrolls, stepped into the moonlight. One of them called out anxiously, "Hey, you over there, who's there?"

The blind prez recognized Superstar's voice, a rich chocolaty baritone. "Superstar?"

"And Futura too," Spirit said.

"Of course Futura too."

Hand in hand the lovers crossed the street.

"Going for a stroll?" the main man asked.

"From the bedrolls, I'd say," said Spirit with a laugh, "they're looking for privacy."

"You got it," said Superstar.

The main man heard him and his girlfriend giggle and walk on.

"Where are they going?" he asked Spirit when he could no longer hear their footsteps.

"Into a vacant lot. They're spreading the bedrolls against a cyclone fence."

"I guess Florence is too crowded for lovers."

They were silent, allowing the cool air to bring to them the sound of more giggling from the parking lot where three cars were parked forever and two living humans were going to make love while crickets bleeped under engine hoods.

"It just goes to show," said the main man, "people in love never get enough. I mean, of privacy."

After walking awhile beneath the stars of quiet Florence, the main man stopped and turned toward Spirit. "Tell me about it," he said. "What it's like to see this world? I mean, town after empty town?"

For a while Spirit In The Dark was silent. Then she told him that sometimes she wanted to stop the car, walk into a house, dial a phone number, and wait until someone answered. While driving past an ice cream parlor, she wanted to rush inside and pull one of the spigots to make sure no soft ice cream would spiral out into a mildewed cone, a bluish green color now after a couple of dozen months, but a cone just the same. She was tempted to wait for traffic lights and had to resist an urge to look both right and left before driving through four-way intersections. Now and then she could almost swear that a neon sign had blinked at her. More than once, out of the corner of her eye, she had seen something in human form scampering away — or maybe the only thing that had been there was the fear of something being there.

"In New York I never had a sense of something weird happening," Spirit said, "because I knew the city. It may have been filled with muggers, but I always felt safe because the dangers were predictable. And after V 70 Struck, the city itself was still there. It would be there the next day. All that cement and steel. But moving from town to town the way we're doing, I get a feeling that things aren't solid, aren't anchored down. It's as if things are shifting under the ground from one place to another."

"I don't like the idea of seeing that."

"That's not all. Things might be happening just out of sight. It's hard to explain, but there could be a lot more secret activity going on here than in New York. I keep wondering if just around a corner, maybe around the next bend in the road or down an alley in a little town, I'm going to catch a glimpse of something horrible."

"Horrible?"

"Something . . . I don't know what. But horrible. Maybe people doing something indescribable, something new and incredibly vicious because out here there's no longer any law."

"I don't remember any law in New York either. Not lately."

"I know. But there the tall buildings seemed to be watching. It was a kind of deterrent. Do you know what I mean? Windows looked down like cops. Do you know what I mean?"

"No."

"Anyway, I keep looking for something to happen out here in America, something people wouldn't have thought of doing before V 70 Struck."

"Something horrible."

"Yes. Of course, I know it's paranoid."

"And possibly rooted in reality."

They were silent again. Spirit took his arm to lead him on, but he stood in the middle of the moon-washed street as if something weighty kept him there.

"Spirit?"

"Yes?"

"I'm asking again." He was deliberately vague. He wanted to see if she could find her way into his thoughts.

"Yes," she said after a long pause, "you can touch me."

He put his fingers against her neck, feeling her shiver. His mother had once picked up an abused stray. For weeks that dog would shiver when you touched it. Even a gentle stroking along its mangy flank would bring on a spasm of shivers.

He dropped his hand.

"No, it's all right," Spirit told him and lifted his hand to her face.

His fingers skimmed each feature. "Is it all right?"

"Yes."

A fingertip brushed the edge of her eye, an eyelash.

She gave a short nervous laugh. His hand continued, lightly touching her hair, moving over it like wind across wheat. Her hair, pulled back into a bun, was thick and scented.

"Do you know what I look like now?" she asked.

"Only what you feel like."

"Well, how do I feel?"

Pulling his hand back, he said as casually as possible, "You feel good." Indeed, he had placed her features in solid space: wide cheekbones, a broad forehead, full lips, large eyes and long lashes, a delicate chin, all of which added up to an image he created for her. Her mouth, perhaps, was slightly too large, her nose too wide — that gave to her created beauty the blemish of reality.

"Yes," he said and repeated it. "You feel good."

"Then I'm glad." Taking his arm, she led them back toward the encampment in the middle of downtown Florence.

28

COUNTRY ROADS. Power poles, shacks, gas stations. Red-whiteblue little flags rippling gaily on wires strung above used-car lots no longer used.

As Spirit drove, the main man dozed. He hadn't slept well last night in Florence. First, he woke from a nightmare and then lay awake with his mind filled with images Spirit had mentioned as part of her paranoia. Visions must be passing through Skull skulls like bolts of electricity, banging away at sanity moment by moment.

That's what he had spoken this morning into his tape recorder during a stop in a trailer park where the silent bulky vehicles, crouching among trees these last two years, looked to Skulls like tired old dinosaurs. Demanding some moments of privacy, the main man was led into the RV of Danny and Ethel Kelvin, where he sat alone at their dusty table and described The Chesapeake Bay Toll Bridge And Tunnel Disaster. He wondered aloud if last night other Skulls had also dreamed of the lavender Mercedes hurtling into the bay. In his own nightmare the action had suddenly reversed so that the water was sucked up on impact as if into a funnel that led to an automobile arcing away into the sky. "So the five remain forever in their car," Mister Touch had told Whoever You Are. "IRT once said we didn't need bone pots to put people in and remember them by. Dead Skulls live with us always."

Now as they drove along, he dozed and was still dozing when

the lead car, failing to signal a halt, halted anyway. Sitting up and rubbing his eyes (it didn't help him to see better), the main man asked what was wrong.

Spirit hesitated. "I'm not sure."

He heard a bubbling sound. "What's that?"

"It's a little river. We're on a bridge. I stopped on the bridge to . . . I had to look at the water."

"Had to?"

"Do you mind my stopping?"

"I guess not." He did not add, But it's strange.

She did. "It's strange."

"That water," said T.T. from the back seat, "sure look good." She stopped her fingersnapping to Walkman music.

Mister Touch heard the window roll down. "People are getting out of their cars," said Spirit.

"Why?" asked the Skull leader.

"Water real beautiful," said T.T.

"Looks like . . . ," began Spirit. "They're starting down the embankment. Everyone."

Mister Touch heard the rear door open. "Blindies too?" he asked.

"Everyone," said Spirit.

"Well, parking on a bridge isn't usually done," the main man said with a rueful laugh, "but I guess just this once we can get away with it. Let's go." He reached for the door handle and was soon being led down a pebbly incline by Spirit.

"Everyone's going down to the riverbank. Someone is . . . A lot are jumping in."

"Is it deep?"

"No more . . . than waist high, it seems. Some are already out in the middle."

"Is the current strong? Good God, are they going to be drowned?"

"Almost no current. It's . . . I think it's safe. They're splashing around . . . clothes and all." Her voice lifted over the noise of laughter. "Splashing, ducking one another."

As they slowly descended the embankment, he felt tiny stones under his shoes, weeds brushing against his legs, and from nearby, to his right, came the deep gravelly sound of Diamond Doll talking. He could remember her clearly: a short fat old woman with wobbly bowed legs. She was talking to someone who was helping her down the embankment too.

"My sister and her husband had a condo in a classy neighborhood in Fort Lauderdale. Every day the beach. Thank you, dear, for helping me down. You remind me of my niece, a go-getter, straight-A Columbia. She was in the morphology of Arachnida. That's spiders, dear. Watch the rocks. If I fall here, let me tell you, I won't get up. I got heart problems, I got prediabetes, I got kidneys, I got arthritis my doctor says you can't believe. You can't believe what they give them for studying spiders. My niece got grants and scholarships worth money. Traveled places you wouldn't want to go. Watch so I don't slide, dear. She —"

In a roar of laughter and splashing, the main man lost the rest of Diamond Doll's discourse on the arachnidologist. Spirit had brought him down to the riverbank. He heard her squeal suddenly like a child. Then he felt his hand yanked and found himself knee-deep in tepid water and in memory, hearing with seven-year-old ears the shouts of children on the Florida beach in front of his rich uncle's house. Along with new friends he had jumped up and down in the rolling breakers, shoving his chest out to meet the sizzling spume, screaming at the top of his lungs for Howie or Jimmy or Sarah or Becky to join him in running away from the approaching surf — the panic the terror the ecstasy — then turning just in time to meet head-on the next full charge of white water.

Up to his waist in the placid stream, the prez slid under, feeling bubbles lift his hair, thrum against his eyes. He emerged sputtering and was ducked emphatically by Spirit. Then her arms went around him, her cool wet cheek against his. He was so startled that he froze as if someone had rammed him down into an ice floe. Then she broke free and laughed merrily. In his mind's eye he saw Skulls, their skins parched these last two years save for niggardly sponge baths with rainwater collected in garbage cans, cavorting now in the cool stream like otters, the water they must be tossing into the air as brilliant as crystal in the refracting sunlight. He put his hands on Spirit's shoulders, pushed her roughly beneath the water. She came up gasping but laughing, and embraced him again for a few wonderful moments, while around them the voices of Skulls receded deeper and deeper into separate childhoods.

*   *   *

Not everyone went into the water. The Oldies and The Ladies didn't and neither did the virgin Pretty Puss, who had taken over Cola Face's position as a younger spokesperson for the SS in their opposition to Mister Touch. She was appropriately uptight and pompous, watching from the riverbank the horseplay that was getting both rough and erotic. She disapproved of Golden Girl, who was just as intact as herself and at ten years old almost as old as Pretty Puss at seventeen because Golden Girl's mind was growing old among the old minds of The Ladies. Unable to resist the lure of water, Golden Girl was among those Skulls who cavorted the most.

The afternoon seemed timeless. Everyone said so afterward and someone found the right words from OOTHI to go with it: " 'They came into a land in which it seemed always afternoon.' " Some people trudged wearily back to the cars for towels and dry clothes, hoping they hadn't caught colds. A few Wheezers had nearly drowned in the shallow water. But most people, stimulated by the first real bath they'd enjoyed since V 70 Struck, got out of the river exulting like born-again Christians. Vanishing into the piney woods, some of them were doing it almost before removing their wet clothes, because the afternoon woods and river seemed to function like an aphrodisiac.

Two woodchucks, emulating the first humans they had encountered in a coon's age, grunted sinfully in the undergrowth near sinning Skulls who shall be nameless.

Teenage Pretty Puss slunk along the increasingly X-rated riverbank and crept through the woods and listened to the sounds of love until her ears burned. Finally she stole away, terrified that the bushes might part of their own accord or with her help and she might witness what her ears told her was something a girl her age should avoid — a peculiar resolve that had lent her career at the Dalton School its only distinction.

A profound love affair began that day in the land of afternoon between Web and Boo Bang. The streaked blonde who had been a terrific countergirl at McDonald's began by splashing water on the young man who, mourning the death of his lover Flash, had shed pounds faster than any Weight Watcher in advertising history. Losing weight, he had also lost interest in men. Splashing water on his broad chest and bulging biceps, Boo Bang had told herself, Go for him, girl, you have got to have him. Leading him out of the water and taking his hand, she had walked him into the deepest part of the woods where they shed their clothes solemnly with motions slow and ritualistic.

The Fierce Rabbit was one of those who held back from the river — not on principle: he was afraid of water. He sat on the bank transfixed with lust by the sight of Evil Eye's coppery skin. When she came out dripping from the river, he caught her arm. "How about you and me having a talk," he said with a grin that told Evil Eye everything she needed to know.

Sex to Evil Eye had always meant pills pleasure power, not necessarily in that order, and after her last brief affair with a Skull who shall be nameless, she was ready for someone a little rough and a little weird and a little frightening like The Rabbit. So she followed him up the bank into the woods. He was rap boasting all the way. "We gotta stir up honkies so they don't know what they doing. Like that old white-haired old white bitch Sag and the other one. You just watch me con them and Tom them till they don't know which is which. Hey, I say, you be the power, and they just stand there not knowing what, just taking it in." He draped one arm around her. "You listening, sweet lady? Stick with me you be fine. Don't worry about nothing if you got Marvin Johnson looking after you."

Evil Eye gave him a cool-eyed appraisal. Once they were deep into the woods, she decided on a spot. Then she halted, briskly stripped, and waited for him to do the same. Then they went to work. Not that she liked or trusted him. She had learned by changing money in the token booths of subway stations not to trust or like humanity; to jar her memory of this profound truth she kept her fingernails clipped short because in the booths you couldn't change money fast with long ones. So when she came in The Rabbit's arms, her raking him with both hands across his back left him with no physical reminder that he had done his job well.

Then there were Spirit and Mister Touch.

She had led him far into the woods so that the distant splashing and laughter from the river were heard only faintly. They sat down with backs against a tree trunk, arms touching.

Remembering their brief embraces in the magical river, he said, "I want to touch you again."

"I know."

"I don't mean touching you to know who you are."

"Yes, I know. I want you to understand. There was a time when I thought I'd never want a man to touch me again. Then a few days ago while driving, I kept turning to look at you. I looked at your hands. They were lying in your lap, and suddenly I wanted them on me, and then I knew if you really touched me I'd want all of you on me —" Turning toward him, Spirit took his hands and held them together, then let them go.

"Touch me," she said.

Back at the riverbank Salsa Sal was sitting there, watching the Swedish wonderwoman Tangy swim up and down and up and down like the aerobic instructor she had once been. Salsa Sal, utterly misnamed, was a small wizened Chinese woman who had come recently from Hong Kong and whose English was so poor that people thought she should be put in the same car with The Boy Who Doesn't Speak Our Language, the idea being that the two of them could teach each other each other's language (Stay High, sensing malicious intent in this suggestion, saw to it the two never traveled together). Before V 70 Struck, about all that the little Hong Kongese had learned in America was to chew gum. She chewed it all day (some said all night), slowly, methodically, like a cow chewing its cud. With her gray hair pulled back into a bun, wearing the blue jacket and black trousers of a Cantonese peasant, Salsa Sal was apparently indifferent to the universe except in her passion for chewing gum. No one was ever more grateful than Salsa Sal when someone returned from an expedition to a supermarket and dumped into her open hands a few dozen packs of Dentyne.

When Tangy finally ended her swim and slogged out of the water, she found the tiny Chinese woman waiting for her, a stick of gum in hand, Salsa Sal's idea of a reward for a job well done.

By the time everyone had returned to the caravan, it was late but still afternoon, and they went a few more weary miles before bedding down in a roadside burg. Few people were still awake when the last streak of light faded in the west, shutting down the eternal afternoon forever.

Next time the prez talked secretly into his tape recorder, the interlude of the river went down in the History of the Skulls as The Day The Water Beckoned. He also recorded the fact that he had fallen in love for real.

29

THE EFFECT of that timeless afternoon remained with the Southern Force during succeeding days on the road. For some of the Skulls it then wore off, but for others it stayed with them for the rest of their lives.

Boo Bang and Web became steadfast, faithful lovers. So did The Fierce Rabbit and Evil Eye, although that relationship depended strictly upon Evil Eye's whim because she tended to change lovers with the rapidity with which she had changed money for tokens in the subway booths.

As for Mister Touch and Spirit, The Day The Water Beckoned marked the beginning of a love affair challenged for intensity only by that between Futura and Superstar.

Whenever the caravan stopped for a rest, the main man and his Spirit would slip away and enter another world in which, they claimed, identical counterparts of themselves had been living in secret since birth. In his Spirit's arms he sometimes had a flashing vision of the children their surrogates had been: giggling, naughty, always together. The odd fantasy befuddled him until he realized it was merely a way of explaining to himself what was beyond understanding: love as destiny. So he gave up analysis altogether and enjoyed his good fortune. He could not get enough of Spirit: he whimpered deep in his throat when he touched her.

For her own part, she loved the long lean body that could wring from her such passion. Fate had been kind for sending a lover who couldn't see in her eyes the fading but still visible reminders of sexual horror. When his hands reached out and touched her, she felt her eyes growing wide and wild as those of a frightened horse. And she felt too a sense of relief because he couldn't look into her eyes and see in them the reflection of pain and fury and frustration as she remembered the use made of her by men whose bodies were shaped like his but whose hearts lay in slimy sewers of befouled humanity. So she had time to bring emotions under control if, at his first touch, they began fluttering at the outer verge of panic. And if she felt the muscles of her face twisting at the prompting of bad memory, at least she was spared the need to apologize for it. She had the luxury of allowing those muscles to speak for the past, until her present love for this man took dominion of her mind and heart.

But it was the fate of the Skulls to find few placid moments in their lives. No sooner had the Southern Force received a terrific boost in morale from the ineffable mystery of love than they were shaken by an unforeseen event.

In a small Georgia town they lost Hitler.

He was a good-looking rather ugly Steady Breather, a slightly built boy of nineteen who wore a mustache that looked like Charlie Chaplin's in *The Great Dictator*. Chaplin's mustache had served as the model for the mustache worn by Hitler's father, who had also been slightly built, a self-effacing accountant for Maybelline Cosmetics for which Hitler, under another name, had been a shipping clerk.

Hitler had never seemed self-conscious about his name, although many people felt it was the worst handle bestowed on any Skull. Others argued it was the mustache to which IRT had reacted, so the kid got what he deserved. Surely Hitler did not emulate his namesake by ambitiously plotting to rule and destroy the world, although perhaps in imitation of his role model he was a little mad.

That day when the caravan entered the outskirts of the little town, Hitler saw with his good-looking eyes a sign belonging to a mining company: WARNING — BLAST AREA.

That night, when the Skulls had bedded down in the town square, Hitler slipped away with gun and flashlight and returned to the company buildings that stood back a few hundred yards from the road. He shot the lock off a storage shed and found dynamite inside, capped but not fused. Undeterred, this shy, inoffensive young man found the fuses and drove one into the cap of a dynamite stick. Everyone had been saying that his recurrent dream had finally driven him around the bend. He knew what they said: "Why did the moron eat dynamite?" "He wanted his hair to grow out in bangs." But good-naturedly Hitler defended his dream of dynamite, calling it basically a friendly dream.

In this dream he lit a dynamite stick which, instead of blowing him up, elongated into a witch's broom and shot him like a rocket into the air from which he could serenely view the entire earth, the rivers and valleys and mountains in a cool bright silence.

Originally in the dream the dynamite broom had finally descended, throwing him into the ocean and thereby waking him up. Since the trip had begun, however, he had never once been flung into the water, but continued to drift across the globe until one of his Skull companions managed to wake him.

But here, in this Georgia town, he was confronting the real thing at last: in his hand he held a dynamite stick for real, which in real life he had just fused. He held a real match in his hand. He believed in the reality of his dream and trusted it to raise him far above this world for real, where he could fly endlessly through the cloudless empyrean and gaze down serenely on all those myriad rivers and mountains and fertile but uncultivated fields that his timid father and his bold mother (she had deserted him before he could walk) were not alive now to see.

The idea of seeing what was denied to the dead gave Hitler a sudden rush, a terrific sense of power. He felt it shake him for the first time in his life, a towering ambition that overwhelmed considerations of safety and sanity, so that he felt an earthquake of desire for more power, for absolute power appropriate to his namesake, roar and rumble through every fiber of his body, perhaps in the way V 70 must have rammed through the tissues of almost everyone alive, and he lit the match.

He lit the dynamite stick and held it between his legs like a broom or whatever. Then the dream treacherously deceived him. The dynamite blew him up and left the Skulls with one less good-looking Steady Breather.

In the schoolyard of another Georgia town, during an R & R stop, Stay High gave The Boy Who Doesn't Speak Our Language an English lesson by reciting haiku to him. The idea was to give The Boy something short and evocative that would pique his curiosity. As they sat in swings, the scholar from Columbia recited a famous poem by Matsuo Basho:

> *"Such stillness —*
> *The cries of the cicadas*
> *Sink into the rocks."*

Getting no reaction, he tried another:

> *"The ancient pond*
> *A frog leaps in*
> *The sound of the water."*

While Stay High was reciting poetry, someone came along and began propelling a third swing into the air. Its rusty chains creaked like doors in a horror movie.

A disdainful glance told Stay High that the oscillating figure was loony Doctor Leo. Turning back to The Boy, he said, "These poems are calculated to make connections in the reader's mind through unconnected associations. They do not feature strings. Remember strings? The sequence of grammatical symbols and words representing the underlying form of a sentence? Well, you don't find them in haiku. Haiku uses seventeen syllables in Japanese to establish a complex verbal signal out of disparate elements that ultimately coalesce into a kind of spiritual unity. Maybe someday in your language you can create a haiku for me. Do you think someday you can do that?"

Glaring at him, The Boy mumbled something.

"What was that?"

Defiantly The Boy said in a loud voice, "Go!"

"Did you say 'go'? Did you mean 'leave'?" Stay High asked excitedly.

"Blu lu."

In disappointment Stay High started up his own swing until his feet no longer touched the ground. The Boy sat hunched over, motionless, while to his side the loony genius was flying madly through the air in his gray flannel suit.

Swinging faster, Stay High began to recite "The Mystery of the Universe." It gave him solace even though recently he had reached the grim conclusion that the poem was not only rampantly hedonistic but pessimistic as well. He had come to the realization by studying the single phrase, "As if you had a universal goal." He assumed that "universal" referred to "universe," so that an exegesis of the phrase would be something as follows: *Act as if there were purpose in the universe,* an existential statement if there ever was one, with a hypothetical force so commanding that it meant there is no purpose in the universe.

Stay High became more and more depressed. By the time he reached the poem's "Et cetera," the swing had slowed almost to a halt. It took him a few moments to shake off this funk before he could fully understand what the madly swinging loony was saying.

"That poem contains a mystery I have solved," said Doctor Leo, his voice getting louder and softer in the sonic arc he made through the air.

"Really?" scoffed Stay High.

"The essence of it," claimed the life insurance salesman, "is Nucleotide. Along with all those meaningless words you said 'nu' and 'cleo' and 'tide.' Nu . . . cleo . . . tide. Now nucleotides are any of several phosphate esters coming from nucleosides, which consist of a purine or pyrimidine base linked to a carbohydrate. The key here is 'base.' *Base! You* even said it. BASE! What, in fact, you are talking about is *the genetic code of life,* because nucleotides dictate the code for twenty-four amino acids. It all" — he swung furiously to and fro, so that Stay High was getting dizzy glaring at him — "adds up to DNA. Your poem is about *DNA!*"

In a huff Stay High turned to The Boy, who sat motionless in the swing like a plaster sculpture of a dejected child. The scholar recited loudly, to drown out the squeaking chains of the madly gyrating swing, a linked verse of fourteen syllables created by Basho's disciple Kikaku. This made a tanka of Basho's "pond" poem. " 'On the young shoots of the reeds,' " Stay High shouted, " 'A spider's web suspended'! "

But later in Car Eleven, when the caravan had started again, the Skull scholar turned over in his mind what Doctor Leo had said. "When the moon is *nu.*" "Says *Cleo.*" "A *tide* running in the gat." *Nucleotide.* "Or get a *base* hit." *Base.* Doctor Leo's favorite word. Stay High could scarcely contain his excitement. There was something here beyond a reasonable doubt. The biochemist The Dream Queen had placed these clues deliberately carefully fiendishly obscurely, and it had taken a loony genius to pick them out of the air. Stay High never sneered at Doctor Leo again, but to everyone's surprise treated him with the deference a scholar like Stay High might be expected to give only to Nobel Laureates.

And behind Car Eleven in Truck One:

"Fairies fornicating fiercely far from familiar forests fart frequently for fun."

"Why do they do that, Adidas? Why do fairies do that way?"

"Freedom feels fabulous. Fuck frugality, fellow fool."

"That Adidas opening his trap again? He take a bath in that river like some did and come out flaky?"

"Flaky, freaky? Fortunately faithful, philistine!"

"See? He on F now. He gone from D to F and foul mouth too. What we got now be the F sound to get used to. Fuck, fart, fill-something, things like that."

"Don't matter. Take days for Adidas to come up with enough words to say something else. Which be why he always got his nose in that dictionary he won't go without. Keep him from being OOTLO all the way, I suppose. Good he using it."

"Good for you, Adidas. Keep going, old butcher boy."

"Forever fast forward."

And down the way in another car, Sister Fate was telling rapt listeners of a journey she had once taken through Burma. First by Irrawaddy steamer from Mandalay across three rapids to Bhamo, then by train to the northern city of Myitkyina in the foothills of the Himalayas. She saw the Ledo Road that had been built by American engineers to link India with Burma during World War II. When she had seen it the road was overgrown with weeds, but hundreds of men had lost their lives to Japanese snipers and disease and accidents while each mile was hacked out of jungle, blasted by dynamite through mountain ridges. It had been called the man-a-mile road.

"Dynamite," someone said, interrupting her hypnotic account of travel through a magical country few of the Skulls could locate on a map. "Hitler would of liked it there."

They had halted along the roadside for yet another rest, which meant a lot of moving around that sometimes left them more tired from resting than from driving. Even so, the frequent stops kept the mass mind occupied — stopping and getting out and peeing and snacking and looking around and getting back in and going on. At night, because of the good weather, they camped out under the Georgia stars.

Lovers went off alone and wrapped themselves tightly together in desire. Spirit and the main man found themselves one night in the back yard of Mister Willard Teller's house. They made love. Then he asked her to take him into the house and leave him there until he called for her.

"Secrets?" she asked.

"Yes. In my briefcase." He had kept it with him constantly from the moment the caravan had left Washington Square. "Do you want to know what's in there?"

"Do you want to tell me?"

"No."

"Then I don't want to know."

She took him to the house, which was conveniently unlocked, since Mister Willard Teller decided on his deathbed that at the last moment they'd find a cure for this damn thing and go around the world administering the antidote. Eternal optimist that he was, Mister Willard Teller had left the door open so the doctors wouldn't waste time getting in.

Seated in a room that smelled of mattress ticking, Mister Touch took his tape recorder from the briefcase and began. "We lost Hitler to his dream. It's a wonder we all don't topple over into madness. But most of us don't. That is a fantastic thing: we keep our sanity. All my life I've heard of human endurance, which sounded just fine, but I was never sure of believing in it. Tonight I do. It's remarkable we've made it this far on the way to Arizona, no matter what happens tomorrow. Whoever You Are, I hope you understand two things: the instinct for survival and the power of love, how they enhance and transform. Otherwise you won't understand the mood I'm in — one of imperishable hope."

30

INTO THE FOOTHILLS of the Blue Ridge Mountains through the land of papershell pecans and Jimmy Carter's peanuts and antebellum mansions and Stuckey's Candies, into the southern metropolis where on a churchyard tombstone were the graven words FREE AT LAST FREE AT LAST THANK GOD ALMIGHTY I'M FREE AT LAST, drove the southern column of the Skulls.

From the expressway they saw a tall blue-metal column with its outside elevator: the Plaza Hotel. Then at Exit 93 the lead car turned off for the state capitol and ascended a hill where it parked beneath the shimmering cupola layered with gold leaf. The Skulls debarked and strolled under the trees, squinting in sunlight at girdered acres of construction that never would be completed between the state buildings and downtown Atlanta. The shining facades of Peachtree Center looked empty; indeed, they were as empty as banks and stores on a table-sized architect's model.

Hours passed. The waiting Skulls ate stale potato chips and drank warm Cola-Cola in the home of Coca-Cola and listened to the wind. Hours passed. More Coke. The day grew hotter. Frequent climbs up the capitol steps to gaze anxiously at the empty expressway. Where was the other column? Where were those airheads? Come on, homeboys!

Night came on. Some slept in bedrolls in the privacy of the state capitol. Others curled up in vans, still others sought out cafes and electronic stores where they could sleep out old fantasies about fancy food and twenty-thousand-dollar sound systems.

"Take me for a walk," the main man said to his Spirit. "This night's made for it."

On Peachtree Street he stopped suddenly, stood her gently against the wall of a store and made love to her in the middle of downtown Atlanta. Spirit leaned her head against his shoulder and told him it seemed incomprehensible that they had been lovers for only a week. It wasn't true that when you were happy things went faster; when you were really happy, things moved in slow motion, because events were so heavy, so crowded together, you were living sixty thick seconds of each minute.

The next day followed the pattern of the preceding day. Hours passed. Warm Coke in the warm sunlight. Heels clicking on the capitol steps. Nighttime in the state capitol.

Once again the main man was led by his Spirit through Atlanta, where once again, this time on the sales mattress of a furniture store, they made love. Afterward, as they headed back to the caravan, Spirit said, "Coco's not strong. She could use a hand with Rattler."

"Are you volunteering?"

"Yes. I've been pregnant. When I see her with the baby, I remember."

Mister Touch didn't press Spirit for details, and she offered none. The fact of her pregnancy fell into the deep well of secret memories that lies somewhere in every land of love.

Next day the Southern Force continued to wait. Accompanied by Evil Eye, The Fierce Rabbit held cranky court for Negative Blacks (Sag's name had stuck) some distance from the capitol steps, under a tree where a sign said NO WALKING ON GRASS. Rhetorically he asked his listeners if the loss of the Northern Force had racist significance. Damn right it did! he thundered. There were more blacks in that force than in their own. Therefore, the northern route had to be the more dangerous. Touch and his honky friends had deliberately sent blacks on the worser road. On his fingers The Rabbit counted off the names of brothers and sisters in the doomed Northern Force, while his young henchmen, Wishbone and Yo Boy, surveyed the crowd for signs of opposition. Both wore wraparound shades, giving them the half-smiling inscrutable look of bodyguards for a Latin dictator.

Meanwhile, under the capitol's portico, Sag was criticizing the executive decision that had authorized a split into two groups. She blamed this poor judgment on their blind leader. From a whimsical desire to exercise power, Sag claimed, Mister Touch had jeopardized their collective security. She ranted on, waving her hands, her voice rising until the object of her scorn, Mister Touch, might have heard it from where he sat on a curb between parked cars (if he had not had his mind completely on his Spirit).

Sag was on the verge of calling for the formation of an ad hoc committee to conduct an investigation of his presidential conduct,

when abruptly a covey of settled robins, placid after dominating
this square for two years, had their avian peace disturbed by the
yammering of engines. Coming into hazy view after thirteen days
of separation was the Northern Force, which had been lost only in
the imaginations of those who might gain from that loss.

Arms waved gaily from open car windows. "Hey, mothafuckers! We gotta put up with *you* again?"

The waiting Skulls cheered and clamored down the steps.

It looked like people meeting in an airline terminal after the
release of hostages from a hijacked plane. Going from place to
place, the middle-aged butcher Adidas was saying, "Greetings,
gadfly gypsies. Groups gambling gratuitously get gloomy. Generous God grants genuine grace." Anticipating good news, he had
worked it up from G, a new letter for him, in only one day.

Everyone sat around the capitol steps and talked. Mister Touch
introduced The Boy Who Doesn't Speak Our Language. The Boy
glared at the newcomers, while Stay High put a protective arm
around his scrawny shoulders.

The main man described the land of afternoon, where many of
them had been drawn into a Carolina stream. He finished by re-
porting the loss of Hitler, who had been drawn irresistibly into a
dream of flying from which he never emerged.

Then it was Hoss's turn. He stood on the steps like an Oklahoma politician in his cowboy hat and explained how the Northern
Force had been shot at in Charlotte. It was only a single shot, possibly a warning for them to get the hell out of there, so they did.

A few miles out of Gaffney, South Carolina, someone in Car
Eight had noticed that Bones was dead. He hadn't been shot by that
stray bullet in Charlotte, but like an old soldier had just faded
away. He sat upright in the back seat, his blind eyes turned to the
window as if trying to see the radioactive waste dumps out there.
Hoss digressed. He noted that the dumps no longer had humans
to kick around. Instead, their toxic mush, leaking from the soil, was
leaching into gullies and swampland on the lookout for new victims, no longer hunting for human babies to kick around but easing on down the yellow brick road in search of the throbbing little
hearts of ducks and weasels, cats and hummingbirds. Hoss took a
deep breath, pleased with the sort of spontaneous eloquence that
had been wasted in advertising.

When the Northern Force stopped to cremate Bones by the side of the road, they had been astonished by his age. He had always seemed old, but in death he was ancient. He looked like so many pieces of dried fruit: his face a white raisin with Adam's apple sticking out like a withered plum; his eyes little seedless prunes; his lips two shriveled strips of lemon peel; and so on. For the last two years he had lived so much like a vegetable that he died looking like something rooted in deep soil, picked long after ripening, left to dry in the sun. In the smoke of kerosene-soaked brush, his pollen-light body vanished almost instantly and ashy parts of him stuck to the clothing of his comrades.

That was not all.

According to Hoss, the town of Anderson, home of fifteen textile mills, was a very strange place. They had gone there to find whiskey for Deadleg, who demanded it and who, they feared, might drop dead from fury if he didn't get it. While looking for a package liquor store in Anderson, they noticed a number of skeletons lying in the street — not unusual in itself, but the sight was complicated by signs of violence. During the final days of V 70 some of the townspeople, berserk in the act of dying, must have staggered from their beds to settle old scores by fighting a pitched battle downtown. Maybe they had all been related somehow, with generations of family hatred boiling in their veins. Shotguns, rifles, boxes of cartridges, and hunting knives lay mixed with the bones and rotting clothes of at least twoscore people — both men and women.

A few miles out of Anderson, the caravan had stopped again. Deadleg wanted out. The only friends he had made among the Skulls had been Cake, ensconced now in her own room in her eldest son's apartment on Twenty-eighth Street, and Bones, now dead. He knew Mister Lucky, of course, but didn't like him. Mister Lucky's ill-fitting dentures made a ceaseless racket that got on his nerves. Having no one to rely on anymore, Deadleg resisted pleas for him to stay.

From Hoss's description, the Southern Skulls tried to imagine Deadleg sitting on the side of the road, clutching a few bottles of Old Bushmill's Irish whiskey to his shrunken chest. Even so, they would never know that his mind had been fixed not on the caravan's departure but on his own. He scarcely waved goodbye.

Instead he muttered under his breath something from OOTHI:
" 'Good-bye, proud world! I'm going home; thou art not my friend
and I'm not thine. Good-bye.' " He opened a bottle, got the small
of his back comfortable against the tree trunk, and began to think
of his youth among the cornfields of Iowa. Grasshoppers whirled
up like miniature airplanes at each remembered step he took
through the waist-high husks. He recalled his schooldays when
mean-spirited Miss Galileo used to rap his knuckles with a ruler for
his having dipped a girl's pigtails in the inkwell on his desk — what
was the girl's name? Her brown hair bound in pigtails had trailed
down near the inkwell so temptingly . . . Maybe he was kidding
himself but Deadleg felt he could still see every strand of that hair,
held with loops of a rubber band. He moved his mind next into
college where he learned to drink and read financial statements
that led to an executive job with a New York export firm. He
thought of his wife (her flesh startling white when shed of the
chrysalis of the wedding dress) and of his two children, the classic
boy and girl, great kids, no problem until they left loneliness behind them when they left home, who — far from him when V 70
Struck and far from their mother, who died in his arms — were
doubtless dead today in Los Angeles and Munich respectively.

He remembered the years going by like a landscape glimpsed
from a swiftly moving train — certainly not from a Skull car.
Deadleg had retired almost a decade ago from the company bearing his name for real, E. F. Edwards & Co. He had possessed a
good stock portfolio at the time, a five-room co-op on Fifth Avenue, a summer home on the Cape. But everything was gone now,
the family and the possessions, all swept away in a tide of bad eyesight and corrupt lungs. He sat under the shady tree, pulling at his
second bottle of Old Bushmill's as evening drew near. When the
sun slipped behind a clump of hickories, his mind was thoroughly
befuddled by alcohol and memory. Before falling into a stupor, he
suspected that the last two years had been nothing more than a
long wicked nightmare from which in the morning he would
awaken in his own bed — hearing bacon sizzling in the kitchen and
his bride of a month mildly scolding him for drinking too much the
night before.

Tales were exchanged in Peachtree Center. Coming together after
two weeks of separation, people felt both celebratory and pensive.

Off to themselves, the main man was asking Hoss what he thought about splitting up again.

"I think it's a good idea. Better get some through than none."

"Better one than none."

"Now that we're talking about survival," Hoss said, "there's yours to consider."

"I don't get it."

"You and Spirit In The Dark. The word's out."

"I figured it would be."

"Which means Mystique knows."

"I figured that."

"Half an hour ago she told me if we split up again, she wants to go with your group."

"I figured that too."

"I imagine she wants to be in your group as a kind of chaperone for Spirit. What do they call them in Spanish? Duenna?"

"You aren't funny, Hoss. Why not send her over here and I'll talk to her."

"Before you two meet, give me a head start so I can take cover."

"Funny."

The main man waited — far more anxiously than he would have admitted, although knowing Hoss and his complicated love life, he supposed the former adman understood how anxious he felt. He heard the steady snap of Mystique's footsteps.

"I hear," Mystique said without prelude, "you're making beautiful music with the New York cabby. How convenient for you I went with the other group. Did you plan to get me out of the way?"

"It just happened."

Her laughing response was harshly theatrical. "Ha ha ha! That's rich. It just happened! Pardon me, but that's the oldest line in the world. So what am I supposed to do?"

"Go on with your life. I never lied to you. We liked each other, that's how I took the relationship."

"I never lied to you! *Second* oldest line in the world. How about a little originality, you asshole. I saw it coming. First when you gave The Dragon Lady such a romantic name — Spirit In The Dark. My God, it makes me want to barf. And when I walked up there and heard music coming from Car One, I told myself, it's going to happen through music because that's how he got me. But I told myself, all right, let him make love to her a couple of times, then see how he feels, because I don't believe in possessiveness, I believe in freedom, I believe two people should hold each other through love and nothing else, I believe marriage is bogus, I believe a person should have enough rope to hang himself with, I believe —" Mystique ceased speaking as if she had just smacked into a wall. Her breath was coming in furious little gusts. "You'll regret this," she said in a voice of steel. "The time is going to come when you'll want me back. And you know what? You bastard, you sonofabitch, I'll come back at the snap of your fingers, because you're the only man in the world for me, I'll fight for you, I'll wait as long as I have to, I'll do anything, I won't ever let you go!"

After these whirlwind declarations, Mystique moved on like a passing tornado, leaving in her wake a vacuum of silence. Mister Touch slumped forward, resting elbows on knees. He felt relieved the confrontation was over. He regarded her threats as a temporary expression of hurt feelings, nothing more, and he deluded himself into imagining for Mystique a new life with someone else who would love her as she deserved.

31

THE NEXT MORNING, when Skulls staggered from their sleeping bags and vans, three black boys a couple of blocks away were hunched together at a corner, one of them studying the parked caravan through binoculars.

People called out to them in a friendly way, but it was Funkadelic's bland greeting of unruffled good cheer — "Hey, brothers, what's happening?" — that apparently encouraged them to come closer.

They crossed the open square and halted as solemnly as bishops at an altar. The oldest black boy carried a snub-nosed .32 and had a three-foot machete strapped rakishly to his side. He was their spokesman. He was also their eyes; the other two, Bad Lookers at best, clung to a six-foot length of rope tied to his belt.

At the gentle prompting of Hoss, who in his shades and cowboy hat had apparently won their confidence, the trio's spokesman described their lives after V 70 Struck. His tale took a long time to tell and for many Skulls required translation, since the spokesman was unaccustomed to public speaking. Three brothers from Birmingham, Alabama, they had been visiting their grandparents here in Atlanta when V 70 Struck. For a while they had run with a group of fifty or so survivors who were always arguing about God and government. One faction awaited the Last Judgment, while the other backed candidates for elected office. From what the Skulls gathered, these people had concluded that the issue of separation of church and state was vitally important in the post–V 70 world. When the religious group was outvoted on its proposition — henceforth the capital of Georgia must be a theocracy with dietary laws, curfew, and sexual regulations in preparation for Christ's second coming — there was an angry exchange with the governmentalists, who wanted a new mayor. The theologians split. Democrats and Republicans stood screaming at them in the middle of Lenox Square, while dogwood was in bloom. So the three boys split, too, and since then they had seen no one.

Mister Touch asked if they would like to come along.

The eldest glanced around doubtfully. "Where yawl going?"

"We're bound for Arizona."

"Yawl going through Birmingham?"

It was explained to him that half were going through Birmingham and half through Montgomery and they would join up again in Meridian, Mississippi.

"Oke with me, can't speak for them, they got their own mind," said the boy. "We might kin go with those heading for Birmingham. Ain't been home in two years."

"Is that all right with you?" Mister Touch asked the two younger boys.

They nodded as one. One said, "Oke with me." The other said, "Oke with me."

Mister Touch named them on the spot, figuring they might change their minds and join the Skulls for real. He called both of the younger boys Rerun, not needing to distinguish one from the other because adversity had molded them into a single survivor; and their older brother he named Brother Love. They were all Steady Breathers.

Before departing, the main man made another decision. He called Pretty Puss to him and offered her the job of Skull Hair-stylist, because people had told him no one took better care of her hair than Pretty Puss did. T.T. had been given a try, but those chocolate-colored hands proved to be less skillful at working scissors than at pushing the buttons of a Walkman. People grumbled about her laid-back who-gives-a-shit approach. "That girl got an attitude," someone said. "Stand there fingersnapping and grinning and hips going round like they greased and T.T. looking good and don't know nothing and don't care she don't know nothing and someone like her is gonna cut my hair right?"

"You want *me* to take that job?" Pretty Puss asked the main man. "I wouldn't want to be called a barber," the girl said loftily in her private-school accent.

Bambu hadn't minded the name of barber, but the prez didn't say so to Pretty Puss. "You are our Hairstylist," he assured the girl.

"I have never cut hair in my life," she declared.

"You will learn."

The simplicity of that remark was foreign to a teenager who had been coddled and corrupted by a well-meaning family, to say nothing of teachers in a school that lived on contributions from satisfied parents, to say nothing of Skull Ladies who wanted young blood around them and knew how flattery could keep a spoiled kid near. Pretty Puss didn't know how to argue against the flat-out simplicity of "You will learn," much less how to say no to homespun candor when the main man added in a burst of parental impatience, "You haven't done a damn thing since joining us, so here's a chance to contribute something by cutting our hair." Without more hesitation, she took over both from dead Bambu and, in a certain ethical sense, from the hairdresser for real, dead Cola Face.

At the second parting of the caravans, there was even more grumbling than at the first, but no one had the guts yet to challenge The Powers That Be. So Hoss led his people west on Route 20 and Mister Touch turned south on Route 85.

The Southerners passed the Atlanta Airport where huge commercial jets stood rusting in hangars and on runways. A few miles beyond the terminal someone in a van yelled out, "I saw a monkey!"

"Like hell you did."

"Saw a monkey!"

"Bullshit."

"In a tree . . . well, it's back of us now, but I saw a monkey sitting on a branch, scratching its ass."

"You coming to be a Bad Looker. Ain't no monkey you saw. This be Georgia."

"I saw a monkey scratching its ass."

"Yeah? And I saw Martin Luther King sitting on the front porch of a house back there."

The caravan broke free of the metropolitan area and motored into open countryside. At a pace of fifteen miles an hour (having increased speed to conform with an increase in confidence), the Southerners went down the center line of a tree-bordered highway.

In the lead car Spirit saw something ahead that made her ease up on the accelerator. "My God . . ."

"What is it?" the main man asked. He heard Send Em Back To Africa grunt loudly from the back seat, which for that big guy was like a thundering exclamation of extreme surprise. "What is it?" Mister Touch demanded.

"Lions," said Spirit In The Dark.

"Lions?"

"Lions," repeated Spirit.

"Lions," said T.T. from the back seat, whistling low.

They stood in the middle of the highway, gazing indifferently at the approaching caravan. The pride consisted of a thick-maned male and four females. They did not look like they were going to move, so Spirit put on the brakes, slowly, carefully, fearful of giving the beasts a signal of hostile intent.

At least ten feet long from the end of his tufted tail to his shiny black nose, the male flexed the muscles beneath his yellowish hide and yawned.

"Stop," the prez ordered, although Spirit was already stopping, and the caravan behind her too. They were not ten yards away from five African lions who weren't going to budge one paw from where they stood.

Leaning from car windows, the Skulls squinted for a better look.

"I don't believe I be seeing what I seeing but I be seeing it," someone murmured from a van.

Squinting around his shoulder, another Skull asked, "What you seeing?"

"Lions."

"Ain't *lions*."

"Am too, homes. Don't *you* tell me what I be seeing when you be seeing nothing but what you can reach out and touch."

"Ain't *lions*."

"Then tell me what them things be ahead if they ain't lions."

"Yeah, something out there. I see shapes. But they ain't *lions*."

"Yeah? Great big yellow cats and one has got like this real funky mane? Tell me what that is, then."

"Ain't lions for *real*."

"Real enough so I ain't getting out to go up and pet 'em."

"Real lions live in Africa."

"Look like real lions live in Georgia too."

A young lioness padded softly toward the lead car, her massive head cocked in curiosity. Send Em Back To Africa pulled his .45 out of its holster. Hearing the sliding sound of it, Mister Touch ordered Africa not to fire. Shoot one and the others might charge, and with a lot more power than the dogs of New York City. And anyway, what was the good (in a Platonic sense) of shooting a lion on Route 85 out of Atlanta? Just keep the windows rolled up and wait, he commanded, rolling his own down for a moment to shout back at the others to keep their windows rolled up and wait.

They had barely rolled theirs up when the female reached Car One. Her tongue flicked the air like a boy putting his foot in the water to test it. After a moment of thoughtful calculation, she leapt onto the hood, her paws spreading across the warm metal like a cat's on a New York apartment radiator cover. The lioness stared at the stunned travelers inside, then lay down leisurely, preparing for a snooze in the sunshine, having come from a nocturnal hunt that had filled her belly with thirty pounds of Georgian cow.

The caravan remained parked on the highway, the engines off to prevent overheating. Each vehicle grew hot because of the closed windows. The male lion had long since stretched out in front of Car One's wheels, his hide shivering off the bluebottle flies

that hovered around his bloated gut. The other four lionesses, figuring their sister had a good idea, loped past the first car, leapt
onto other hoods, and spread themselves across the warm metal.
They closed their eyes in contentment.

Rising from the left side of the road, the sun worked itself directly over the caravan. Inside the hot interiors, Skulls sweated and
waited out the feline siesta.

Some passed the time wondering where the lions had come
from. In the last days of V 70 when radios still operated, guards of
zoo and circus animals had been ordered to shoot any beasts considered dangerous. Yet here in the middle of the highway were five
lions; and quite possibly that monkey scratching its backside had
been a monkey for real.

"It isn't all that strange, lions at this latitude," Stay High observed. "In prehistoric times the lion was distributed across the
greater part of Europe." He turned to The Boy Who Doesn't
Speak Our Language. "Understand what I'm saying?"

"Agoo."

"Stay High," a fellow passenger said, "you so smart, tell us
when lions was distributed across this state of Georgia until now?"

Loftily, he ignored the sarcasm.

Finally the first lioness lifted her massive head from crossed
paws and yawned. Blinking lazily at the sweating occupants of Car
One, she flexed her paws like a contented kitten and leapt from the
hood to the road. The other females followed her because (to mix
a metaphor) this lioness was obviously the queen bee.

The old male just lay there, covered by flies he had been too
lethargic to shake off.

Gathering around him, the females looked down at his fat
belly, his matted chest going gently in and out. Finally, the queen
gave a tremendous roar. Even then the bone-lazy male didn't get
up; he merely opened one eye to gaze listlessly at his impatient
women. He wasn't going to let broads tell him what to do. Nonchalantly he licked his paws, eyeing the queen with a slit-eyed stare of
independence. The females began pacing. They paid no more attention to the caravan than a cat would pay to an endive salad. Having asserted himself by doing nothing, the male at last got slowly
and unsteadily to his feet, like a patriarch who has presided with
dramatic self-indulgence at a family feast.

He sauntered after the brisker females into the roadside undergrowth just as he had followed them that afternoon two years
ago when they left Kingdom Three, a vast wildlife preserve about
twenty miles south of Atlanta (before a gentle guard could work up
the courage to shoot them) by jumping a metal fence from the top
of an abandoned park van. They had entered and left the preserve
at leisure, remaining around the periphery for more than a year to
dine on many of the thirteen hundred animals that touristic hordes
had once paid good money to see and hear (the ads promised the
fun sounds of SNARL HISS ROAR CHUGA-CHUGA BOING-BOING
YAHOO and SPLASH) from their slow-moving automobiles with the
windows rolled up and with their pet dogs and cats safely ensconced in the park kennel, all between the hours of 9:00 A.M. and
5:30 P.M. from Memorial to Labor Day — other hours the rest of
the year.

When the pride had gone their haughty way, the caravan
geared up and continued down the highway. Little was said. For
many of the Skulls little would be remembered of this day, like a
dream recalled at noon.

It would go down secretly in the main man's History as The
Day Of The Lions and might provide people with a story for Coco's
Rattler, if the Skull tot got old enough to appreciate a real-life
counterpart to his wildest boyhood imaginings.

32

THEY WERE RUMBLING along Route 85, past cottonless cotton farms and tobacco fields that Reynolds Tobacco Company
wouldn't make a cent from and not because of the Surgeon General's warnings either, and peach orchards where possums nested
now in complacent safety, when a small object appeared on the
horizon.

It was something coming toward them.

A car.

It looked forlorn or scary, depending on the eyes of each Neat Looker.

Then Good Lookers were able to see that it was an ivory-colored Chevy Impala, vintage 1959, with the antiquated tail fins that attracted movie directors to this model of car for Hollywood films made in the '80s about the '60s.

It kept coming unwaveringly on.

Close up, even Poor Lookers could see the driver, a white-haired woman wearing a pillbox hat with a bunch of plastic flowers attached gaily to it like she was going to a wedding or church. She never gave the caravan a single glance through her thick glasses, but continued to drive past the thirteen vehicles with admirable concentration on the road; here was a driver who wasn't going to crack up because of personal negligence.

Looking from the rear window of the last car, Evil Eye gave a low whistle of awe. "Don't believe what I just saw."

The Fierce Rabbit muttered a bland "Yeah?"

"Listen to me," Evil Eye said. "I am looking back, right? I see the old woman change lanes. I mean, she put on the *turn* signal. Swear it on the grave of my grandmother, the only person I lent money to in my life. That turn signal was flashing left, right, then left, like the driver was moving through traffic. Don't matter what you think, Marvin [in her excitement she used his old name, a rare loss of cool for Evil Eye]. Don't matter what I think either. That old woman is navigating in heavy traffic!"

The Rabbit merely grunted, having in recent days forsaken the mundane world around him for a deep burrowing into his mind of minds where everything was fierce and dangerous and where he was putting together a terrifying puzzle. Instead of smiling at Evil Eye, whom he felt he couldn't trust, he gave smiles to the boys in the front seat, Wishbone and Yo Boy, who had been introduced into his presence for the simple aim of allowing destiny to play itself remorselessly out.

When they stopped at night near a roadside stand of trees, Mystique went in search of Snake, getting to him before he had bedded down with anyone else. OOTHI once observed, "A woman always has her revenge ready," an axiom demonstrated by Mystique, who by dragging the Latino rogue into the woods that evening took her own brand of revenge on Mister Touch. She tore at Snake with savage impatience, calling herself by her old name (Lucy) at the moment of fierce climax. The violence of her orgasm so unsettled Snake that he could not achieve his own. He slunk away with what was left of his Romeo pride, while Mystique lay seeded with hatred of the man she loved for real. A plan was forming in her mind. Next day she would tell Snake that if he didn't help her remove The Dragon Lady from Car One she'd tell everyone the great Snake was a sexual worm.

And in another part of the woods, Mister Touch lay with his Spirit. "Is it a moonlit night?" he asked.

"Yes."

"I was sure it was. I know it can't be true, but I swear I feel the light weighing down on me. Like a substance. Like heat on a humid day."

"The moon is full."

"So with eyesight I'd see everything about you." When she didn't reply, he reached out to touch her cheek and lips. "A few minutes ago, when you lay on top of me, your voice came from low over my face, and I knew you were looking down on me, just inches away. You were looking like a woman in love looks who has just made love. And I knew what I was missing — the way you look. It seemed like the blackness behind my eyes got blacker. I had the feeling I could plunge straight through and drown in my own stupid blindness. It was like panic."

"You must have hated me."

"Hated you? Because I couldn't see?"

"Well, when you put it that way . . ."

"It wasn't hatred."

She placed her hand over his hand that was caressing her face.

"Then I felt the light like it was something heavy," he said. "I knew it was there, and the idea calmed me."

"I shouldn't have said you hated me. You loved me more."

After a long silence, he asked what was on her mind.

"A woman never feels sorry for her rival, so I won't lie and say I feel sorry for Mystique. But I wonder how I'd feel in her place. I think I'd be paralyzed. I'd be OOTLO."

"Mystique isn't that way. She'll go on with her life. Really, what I had with her wasn't love."

Events would confirm his belief that there was ample proof of Mystique's ability to move beyond their affair. But no matter what happened in the following days, Spirit was not so sure.

The neat-looking poor-breathing Chinese boy Blue Magic had lived on Mott Street all his life and worked in the family grocery store until V 70 Struck. Long before that, however, he had nearly died of envy of his cousin, an honor student at Bronx Science.

Having joined the Skulls about five months before they left New York, Blue Magic had put himself through an elementary electricity course, self-taught. He had drawn sparks from an old piece of newspaper, caused water to wiggle, built a leaf electroscope, a Leyden jar, an electrostatic palm tree, and he made beans jump. He had constructed a simple galvanoscope, a voltaic pile; got electricity from a lemon; built a fuse with a battery, two feet of insulated copper wire, and a small strand of steel wool, duplicating Edison's invention which was patented in 1880; created an electromagnet with a three-inch nail, ten feet of copper wire, a 1.5-volt dry cell, some paper clips and pins; and finally put together a lamp assembly which made a 6-volt bulb glow like Christmas was here.

"As long as you can do that," Mister Touch observed, "there's hope for lights going on again all over the world." The main man was counting on Blue Magic to become their electrician for real. But his optimism was premature.

During the trip Blue Magic discovered his watch was slowing down a few seconds, then minutes each day. Then one day it stopped. All of the Skull watches stopped, which only meant half a dozen, since most people stopped wearing them when they no longer had appointments to keep. The button batteries that drove the surviving watches no longer operated.

It was scary when things simultaneously went wrong — that was how V 70 had worked. The virus hidden in bodies throughout the world had emerged with clockwork precision in accordance with a schedule genetically programmed. And now button batteries were suffering the same fate. It seemed as if a corrosive capable of attacking the metallic structure of this particular kind of storage system had somehow evolved in the brilliantly timed way that V 70 had zeroed in on human cells.

There wasn't a single old windup watch among the Skulls. Not even ancient Mister Lucky carried one.

Mister Touch thought of breaking into a jewelry store and getting some old pocket watches. But almost all of them were twelve-hour timepieces, without a date function. IRT had resisted the idea of relying on watches anyway. He had argued that without appointments to keep, people would forget to care for timepieces. At IRT's insistence, they kept an old-fashioned calendar, ticking off the days with X's.

So Mister Touch said to Blue Magic, "We can break into a jewelry store somewhere and get some old pocket watches. But for dates we'll stick with the calendar, just the way IRT wanted it. Have you been marking off each day on the trip?"

"I have," Blue Magic declared proudly.

"Good then. See how we've settled time? Just keep making the X's."

Then came the matter of electric light. Blue Magic had continued to carry on elementary experiments in one of the trucks while the caravan rolled along, and late one afternoon he was doing a current control experiment with a pencil, a 6-volt lantern battery, four feet of insulated copper wire, and a flashlight bulb. He had succeeded the previous week, but this time the bulb did not light up. Neither did other bulbs. He repeated the experiment a dozen times until he finally got one to glow weakly.

Next day most of the flashlights carried by the Skulls failed to light. Maybe something had crept into the structure of tungsten — in the same insidious way that viral DNA had wormed into human DNA. When a flashlight did work, it was, like the Skulls, a survivor. In towns along the road a Survivor Squad was assigned to find flashlight bulbs that had outlasted the latest epidemic.

Blue Magic blamed himself because light bulbs were succumbing to disease the way his family had succumbed to V 70 in their apartment on Mott Street. The prez hid his own anxiety by reassuring Black Magic. "We have our own calendar," Mister Touch maintained, "so we know where we are in history. Someday we'll figure out another way of getting light."

33

PAYBACK WAS FIFTY-SEVEN, a former merchant seaman. Being a blind Wheezer kept his bellicose nature in check, but it didn't prevent him from using his mouth now and then. None of the Skulls, not even those trained in the worst streets of Harlem, could match the old sea dog's foul mouth.

He kept to himself, save when he needed help to move around; after getting it by screaming out profanities, he never offered thanks, just grunted. He rarely knew where he was. He didn't care. In his mind he lived at sea, aboard tankers and cargo ships bound for the Mediterranean or Panama. He tolerated his present situation in order to maintain the memories which were all he considered worth living for: recollections of ports of call, women, hurricanes. He contributed nothing to the life of the Skulls, not finding landlubbers fit companions for a salt who had spent most of the last forty years at sea. When V 70 Struck, he had been waiting at the union hiring hall for a ship and had therefore missed the chance to die aboard one. He had been wandering almost completely blind through the City of New York for a month before Skulls discovered him staggering around Washington Square Park, bloody and bruised from countless falls, his rugged frame shrunken by malnutrition.

He had a salt-and-pepper beard, a vile temper, and thirteen tattoos, which he grudgingly displayed for admiring young bloods, their favorite being a corpulent stripper whose navel corresponded to Payback's own. When the trip started, he was in terrible physical condition and grumpier than ever.

Then something happened that changed him. There had almost been an accident when someone in a truck near the middle of the column had to go badly. Honking a couple of desultory times, the driver had simply put on the brakes and the truck at his rear had bumped him. No big deal, but there could have been trouble for real and could be in the future when the two groups joined up again (if they ever did). That would give them twenty-five vehicles capable of piling up like you know what happened in the old days during the holidays — those freeway free-for-alls with trucks and trailers and automobiles jackknifed into a crinkly metal heap and the colored lights of patrol cars revolving luridly over a scene reminiscent of devastated Berlin a few hours before Hitler (not the Skull one but the other one) left his bunker for a barbecue.

Someone had once read Payback something that OOTHI had said, and on the spot he had repeated it until it was firmly in mind, because these words contained his entire philosophy: "The winds and waves are always on the side of the ablest navigators." He hadn't known who Edward Gibbon was, and all he knew about Rome was that it wasn't a port on the sea, but the fellow must have been one helluva sailor.

So overhearing the ruckus about lack of communication within the convoy, Payback repeated Captain Gibbon's words to himself and resolved at last to make his own contribution to the Skulls. He devised a honking system whereby the task force could maintain station without colliding during maneuvers.

Emergency (SOS) ···————···
Request Stop For Call Of Nature ·——· ···
Request Acknowledged (Roger) ·—·
Prepare To Put On Brakes (To Stop Engines) ·——· ·—· · ·——·
··· — ——— ·——·
Put On Brakes And Stop (Execute) · —·——
Turn On Ignition (Prepare To Cast Off) ·——· ·—· · ·——·
—·—· ·— ··· —
Shift Into Low Gear (Execute Cast Off) · —·—— —·—·
Drive Off (Get Under Way) ··— —··

And so on. It was, to be brief, the International Morse Code, with signals adapted by Payback for the Skull convoy.

The main man, when informed of the grungy old seaman's accomplishment, hesitated to install the system. After all, once they hit a city they could find walkie-talkies. But the code gave people something to do in the caravan besides jabber and sleep. IRT would have said, "Keep 'em awake figuring out which honk is which." Having consulted his mentor in absentia, Mister Touch put the Payback System into operation. Payback had finally joined the Skulls for real by providing them with Rules of the Road.

On this warm cloudless day, just across the Alabama border, the caravan was alerted by a signal from Car Five: ·——· ···, which stood for the letters P and S, Payback's impolite terminology for a Call of Nature.

Car One honked ·—· (Acknowledged) and a mile later pulled into Chewacla State Park, then signaled ·—· ·—· · ·—· ··· — ——— ·—·. After curving through the southern pines and coming into sight of picnic tables, Spirit gave a final short blast followed by one longshortlonglong. The convoy executed the maneuver and stopped. Clumsy though it might be, the Payback System worked.

People went into the underbrush for their P & S, while others strolled around the wooded park. The locale was so pleasant that the main man decided to camp here for the night. Some of the Skulls walked to the edge of the eighteen-acre lake in a valley as craggy and rugged as any below the Appalachians. Yellow-hammers darted in the trees, autumnal flowers dotted the pine-needle floor of the southern forest.

Like tourists immemorial, the Skulls lingered on the paths to admire the beauty. Some of the Good Lookers took snapshots with Polaroids, and Jive Turkey, Official Photographer of the expedition, worked assiduously to maintain a daily visual record of "what happening, bro."

Throughout the day's ride the two lovers Futura and Superstar had been sitting in a supply truck, isolated from the world, thighs touching, hands hotly busy with little messages of desire. Sometimes they did it in there; at other times they abstained merely to build up tension. In Chewacla State Park, they slipped away from the others in a mood of intense excitement, as if the truck motion had worked on them like an aphrodisiac.

Farther and farther into the woods they scrambled, panting from their exertion and impatient to get beyond carshot of their companions' voices. Superstar encircled Futura's waist with one arm and led her as rapidly along as her lungs permitted. She, in turn, warned him about small logs and hollows that he might not have eyes enough to see. The farther they went the farther they wanted to go, because they were searching for a place outside of this world where they could do it. And the farther they went the greater their anticipation. Finally they stopped for a rest, their smiling faces dripping with sweat.

They leaned against a tree and looked around at the tiny clearing in which they found themselves. They hadn't even kissed once during the hike, and didn't now either, but continued to wind themselves up as tight as springs.

Without looking at his white queen, Superstar described in a hesitant voice the secret fantasy that had pursued him through Harlem adolescence and early manhood. In this urban fantasy he had been transported suddenly into a deep forest (the only woods he had ever walked through for real had been in Central Park) with a girlfriend when suddenly, without warning, she hoisted her dress up, planted her hands against a tree trunk, and called to him over her shoulder, "Come and get it!"

"Never told nobody but you," he told Futura.

His confession was so guileless that Futura's initial reaction of disgust at such a sexist daydream quickly dissipated. It took a while longer, though, for her to rid herself of the implications of "a girl-friend" — not "my girlfriend" or the name of a girl or anything, just "a girlfriend" — because in the fantasy, any girl would do.

"Say something," he asked nervously.

Futura's mother wasn't around, thank God, to overhear what the girl answered. Without looking at her black Superstar, Futura murmured shyly, "Would you like to try that? I mean, your fantasy?"

"Wowee! Sure would," he exclaimed. "Never did have trees where I growed up. Girls around there would of just said, 'Don't you mind no trees, let's go in the alley.' "

"Don't."

"Don't what, mamma?" he asked innocently.

Turning to look directly at him, she saw the gentleness in his bad-looking eyes. "Never mind," she said, thinking she loved him beyond understanding. Futura took his hand. "Pretend we're just walking along," she said and guided him to the edge of the clearing, where she released his hand and sighed thoughtfully. Then skipping up to a hickory tree, Futura pulled down her panties justlikethat, briskly lifted her skirt, flipped it over her back, and planted both feet widely like a Chicago Bears tackle bracing for a goal-line stand. With both hands she gripped the rough bark of the tree trunk.

She wanted to contribute "Come and get it!" but that was just too much for a Queens secretary who had only given up her mother for real a month ago. So she just waited, feeling a soft breeze against her bare rump. It was the naughtiest sensation she had ever experienced in her life — that rush of cool air against the naked flesh of her buttocks with a man standing right behind her. She had enough vision to see clearly a trail of ants zigzagging across the hills and valleys of the hickory trunk and nearly mentioned it to Superstar, not because the ants bothered her but because in some way they were part of what was happening. She said nothing, however — having heard the metallic sound of his belt buckle loosening.

"Gonna be something," he mumbled excitedly, and she almost asked him please not to be crude.

A drop of sweat rolled down her nose, only an inch away from the reddish-brown column of ants. Futura had always made a point of using "perspire" instead of "sweat," but my God she was sweating now while presenting her posterior this way — as brazenly as a monkey — to a black boy in a steamy woods down in Alabama.

"I love you, mamma," he muttered huskily and moved into her timidly as if afraid of his fantasy coming true, but then with growing confidence Superstar thrust deeper. "Sweet goddamn Jesus!" he yelled.

She nearly told him not to swear, but the words caught in her throat just as her emotions were entangled in the bucolic bestiality of the moment. She was thoroughly taken from behind. Bracing herself bravely against the trunk of a hickory tree, Futura shamelessly wriggled her white rear against the black sword that was buried in her right up to the hilt.

Afterward they went still farther into the woods, lost in the magic of love, arriving finally at a winding creek edged with willows. Stripping, they entered the bubbling water. In slanting light their black and white skins glistened, as they held each other while the clear stream eddied around their waists. They heard a mockingbird, without knowing what it was. A squirrel skittered along an overreaching branch, making a sound like paper rustling, and halted to stare keenly down at them. The sun rolled lower, snatching its light back until the undergrowth was a dark green smudge along the bank. When the sunshine deserted their bodies altogether, they looked around as if wondering who had turned the

lights low. Climbing out, they lay in the grass until the late afternoon air, not so sultry now, dried them. Then they dressed and
looked around again, bewildered by the possibility soon to become
a probability that they had no idea where they were.

Neither of them knew anything about forests. Suddenly they
were enveloped in a strange world, which had been inviting when
a fit of passion had led them into it but which was now becoming
more and more ominous. Getting here, they hadn't followed a
path, had they? They couldn't remember, but clung to each other,
hearing new sounds in the undergrowth that seemed to creep toward them, an impenetrable wall of prophecy and threat. The hike
and the lovemaking had tired them more than they had realized.
Standing on the creek bank, not knowing where to go, they felt
riveted to the earth by fatigue. They set out anyway, stumbling
through the brush for half an hour, then sinking down, flat on the
pine needles which felt cool now in the sunless air.

Night was coming on; that obvious fact startled them. There
were new sounds in the trees and bushes, certain swishing noises
that caused them to cock their heads and wonder.

"Don't you worry," Superstar assured his queen. "We gonna be
okay."

"What are we going to do?"

"Stay here awhile, sweet thing. Get some rest. Gonna set out
early and find them in the morning."

"But if they've already left?"

"Find them before they get started," he claimed. "We gonna be
just fine. Set out early and find them where they be waiting for us."
His voice grew stronger with each word. "I promise it. Hear what
I'm saying? Listen to me."

"I do. I believe you."

But when the night fell, the chill of darkness descended too
and against a tree trunk they huddled and shivered. Owls startled
them with hooting. Things rustled nearby, causing them to sit upright. Their teeth chattered. They got up and worked their arms
like bellows to generate a little warmth. The moon appeared icy
through branches, owls hooted, and other things scampered and
squeaked. Then the moon disappeared like a snuffed candle
and their teeth began to chatter. But miraculously, when they
squinched up to the tree again, holding each other, they fell asleep
almost instantly.

When they awoke, drenched by dew, stiff in every joint, the day had already begun. An overcast sky gave them no sense of the hour, though. They felt they had slept a long time.

Futura suggested that they choose a direction and go for it. "Isn't there something about moss on a certain side of a tree . . . or something?"

"Don't know nothing about that," Superstar admitted sheepishly.

They were silent awhile in the sunless glade. Then Futura began sobbing. "They're gone."

"Hell no, they ain't gone. They be waiting. Looking for us right now."

"They're gone." But she looked at him hopefully.

"Not yet. Skulls don't act that way. I know them."

"Did you hear any honking?"

"Didn't hear nothing. See? That mean they ain't even up yet."

But for real there had been honking an hour ago, when Futura and Superstar were sleeping the sleep of fucked-out cats. There had been ·——· ·—· · ·——· —·—· ·— ··· —. Keys turned in ignitions, motors groaned into life, and at the signal · —·—— —·—· they shifted into low gear and at ··— —·· they got under way.

They would travel all day and stop at night and get up the following day and travel all of that day and stop at night and get up the next day and travel most of that day before someone would ask where Futura and Superstar were.

A search for them proved futile. What had happened? The main man sat disconsolately on a log and with his Spirit's help attempted to solve the mystery. For one thing, Futura and Superstar had ridden in the windowless rear of one of the supply trucks; they had preferred privacy to the passing landscape. So they wouldn't have been missed quickly.

"I wonder if there isn't another dimension to this as well," he told Spirit. The lovers may have been so lost in each other that they had ceased to exist for anyone else. Maybe their closeness had made them one, then less than one until they became invisible. "I like to think it," this man in love added.

"Well, if they had been more outgoing, someone would have missed them earlier."

There was no way of telling at which of countless P & S stops the lovers had slipped away. When the caravan heard the main man's decision to go on, a few people like The Fierce Rabbit and the SS grumbled, but only in an obligatory way.

Appalled and saddened, another weight of guilt resting on his shoulders, Mister Touch ordered a buddy check after each succeeding stop to make sure no one was left behind. Gloomily the convoy set sail for a hoped-for rendezvous in Meridian, Mississippi.

"Do you really think they're looking for us?" Futura asked, gazing into a directionless sky.

"Sure. We gonna go meet them."

"But where? Which direction should we take?"

"Don't know nothing about directions," Superstar confessed. "Except in the subway. But we gonna go."

Futura was sobbing.

"Hey, sweet thing, we gonna be fine. Hear me? I be taking care of you."

So they set out through the dense woods. In a couple of hours, thoroughly exhausted, they sat down on pine needles and Futura murmured sadly, "I was misnamed. I'm never going to see the future. I'm never going to be part of it."

Taking her hand in his, Superstar studied the white object in his black palm as if it were a wounded bird lying there. "When I first know you," he began softly, "I was coming on. Jiving."

"I know."

"But real soon I grow to love you. Sweet thing, I loves you," he said. "God's truth."

"I know."

"So come on, baby. Take my hand." He rose and helped her up. "We gonna walk through these woods like we own them!"

And walk boldly they did for another hour, coming abruptly into a clearing at the edge of which, next to a stream, stood an old cabin of clapboard and logs. Weeds had grown up around it like a spray of green water lapping the boards. Ragged tatters of cloth hung in the windows. A few roofing planks had warped and buckled, leaving gaping holes overhead. There was no door. Perhaps at the turn of the century it had been a small hunting lodge.

"I told you!" exclaimed Superstar, whacking his thigh for emphasis. "We got a place to stay now." He added quickly, "Till they find us."

Futura clung to his arm, her mouth working soundlessly.

"Told you," he told her, "we gonna make it."

They entered the cabin and found some broken beer bottles, crumpled yellowed pages from a twenty-year-old magazine, a broken knife blade, a shoestring, and a couple of used condoms which an enterprising spider had decorated with cobwebs, making them little houses of death in two ways. The furniture was a two-legged chair.

"Clean it up some, it ain't bad," Superstar observed with lips pursed judiciously.

Futura nodded, fighting back tears.

"Thing we gotta do," he said, "is get some things in."

"What things?"

"Oh, things we need."

"You mean, for a long time?"

"Well, for a while."

"How?"

"Well," he paused thoughtfully. "I be getting them tomorrow."

"Where?"

"Don't go worrying right now, mamma. Right now we gonna go get something to eat."

"Something to eat?"

Again his black face grew rigid in thought; he glanced around as if the answer were staring back at his bad-looking eyes. "Berries," he declared suddenly, "and stuff like that. Out there in the woods."

That night they slept better in the cabin, although their teeth still chattered and their stomachs rumbled from the half-digested berries. Next day Superstar washed his face in the chill stream and squinted at the sun. He was going to get what they needed. Like that.

After a breakfast of berries, he kissed his queen and stroked her hair and cupped her receding chin in his loving hand and told her how pretty she was. Then he set out through the woods.

For such an expedition he must pretend that he was a neat-looking Breather For Real rather than a bad-looking Steady Breather. After stumbling along for a couple of hours, he came to a road. Sitting down to rest awhile, he wondered if he would find the way back to the cabin on his return. So he remembered something in a movie and ripped some cloth from his shirtsleeve and tied it to a tree limb. He felt damn good about this.

But which way to take on the road? In another movie somebody had wet his finger, put it up to find where the wind coming from, and then this dude had went in that direction. Which is what Superstar did now. He turned left up the road according to the cool side of his index finger.

Superstar hadn't walked more than an hour before coming to a junction where an old country store, still intact, was awaiting its first customer in two years, maybe more. Even so, inside he discovered a large wheelbarrow and loaded it with bags of sugar and flour, with canned goods and soft drinks, with blankets and pans, with an ax and hammer, with matches and kerosene, with nails, a shotgun, a dozen boxes of shells, and a can opener. By the time he had finished making his selections and loading them in the wheelbarrow, Superstar was exhausted. He slept that night on the floor and early the next morning started back, panting every foot of the way over hillocks and down into hollows, stumbling on exposed roots, overturning the load twice, but at sunset he dumped the treasure at his white queen's feet.

In his absence — frightened out of her wits but not out of her belief in him — Futura had swept the cabin with a few strands of old broom and bravely propped the two-legged chair in a corner.

"We could move into that store," Superstar told her, "but it stand at a crossroad where people used to come through. I like it better back here where we be alone for real."

In the following week Superstar, who could not see well enough to shoot, taught her how (he had learned, sort of, by watching westerns on TV). And shoot she did, bagging three rabbits, four squirrels, and some kind of a bird on her first day out, because wildlife was proliferating at leaps and bounds without human interference so that even a conservationist would not have argued against Futura's hunting out of season.

Awkward but determined, Superstar eviscerated the game. Futura cooked it with comparable determination but just as awkwardly. They snuggled in front of their fire when the sun went down, smelling the good clean smell of pine burning in the old grate, hearing an owl screech.

While they caressed each other under the blankets, Futura quoted the last thing she had read by OOTHI: " 'Let us live then and be glad while young life is before us,' " without remembering it was from a song sung by medieval students.

Young enough and in love enough, far from the cement streets of home, from the sight of bustling crowds, and even from the memory of their Skull companions, the plain secretary from Queens and the high school dropout from Harlem might make it for real in the wilderness, because as she often so optimistically claimed, they were basically very together people. Besides, Futura had her name to fulfill, Superstar his to emulate.

34

SERVE HIM RIGHT, moving with honky pussy that way," was the valedictory for Superstar delivered by The Fierce Rabbit.

Sag delivered Futura's epitaph to The Ladies during a P & S stop. "When a woman loses her virtue, she loses her dignity, and when she loses her dignity, she loses her self, which is all a woman has of real value."

Sag and The Fierce Rabbit could not have shamed the lovers, now alone in an Alabama woodland. Without realizing it, Futura and Superstar had left the Skulls a long time ago, because there was nothing left in their lives for anyone but themselves — or so thought Mystique.

Mystique believed in a love so strong that two people could disappear into each other and drop from public sight for the rest of their lives. Although she had no more proof than her woman's intuition that this was true of Futura and Superstar, the possibility made her furious, because it meant injustice, because it was unjust that she herself was denied such bliss. Her fury was augmented by the daily sight of Mister Touch and Spirit together. They swung hands like two children in a playground. They smiled at each other in public as if they were playing bad games in bed. They could be seen out of earshot, their mouths moving ceaselessly, conveying secret messages that made them grin or frown or otherwise show signs of life for real. They made Mystique sick. She longed to get between them like a human crowbar and pry apart their hands genitals minds hearts souls and then brick herself up between them like a wall so they could never join again. To keep herself from going OOTLO, Mystique clung to the plan evolving out of her own mind like an irresistible virus. She looked to men for help. She had always sought men either to consummate her own private passion or to realize a secret goal that had nothing to do with them. Already, in the last couple of days, she had won through blackmail the everlasting loyalty of Snake. Either he did what she told him to do when she told him to do it or he was dead meat, an apt expression, considering it was precisely what Mystique threatened to tell every Skull female that he had been that time with her in the woods. What she was going to tell Snake to do, however, was not yet clear to her. But she had recruited him — locked him up and put the key in her pocket. Of one thing Mystique was certain: whatever the evolving plan would finally demand of Snake and other men certain to be drawn into it, the result would be something most unpleasant for The Dragon Lady, a.k.a. Spirit In The Dark.

Spirit In The Dark led her lover and his followers into Selma, Alabama, where the caravan halted for P & S. Instead of leaving the car for a relaxing stretch, Spirit remained there, upright, tense. Mister Touch, sensing in the air the turbulence of her emotions, stayed too. "Let me guess. You're thinking of the civil rights movement."

"Sweetheart, I don't imagine you'll find many black people coming through this town, even when it's empty, without thinking about it. An uncle came down here on a march and got his jaw busted. No solid food for a year. As a kid I remember him eating with a straw."

"I had an uncle we used to visit in Florida. He had a beachfront condo. I guess we can't share the past."

"For your own good as main man, you have to share mine. Do you know why so many Skulls come from the ghetto?"

"They're young, and the young survive."

"Because they learned survival at their mother's knee. Outside their apartment doors guys were pitching twenties of crack. Kids of ten were tempted to make some bread by running drugs. There were girls who got into high heels after their first period and went out to sell themselves. Or they boosted TV sets with their boyfriends. Then there were the assassins who hung out on the corner. They told admiring teenagers the only thing you had to do was keep shooting until you hit something. Every day was a struggle. My kid sister and some good friends just crawled inside the misery and died."

"I know what you're telling me."

"Sure, white people saw the news on TV and read the papers. They got the violence, the despair. What they didn't understand was how much strength and cunning it took to survive. There's something else for you to understand."

"I figure there is."

"Something a little subtle. It has to do with getting better before you get worse." Spirit laughed. "I can't help enjoying the look on your face. I admit I used to like the idea of confusing whites when they tried to understand us."

"So I'm confused. But I'm listening."

"And I love you for it. What we used to fear in social work was the time a delinquent began showing progress. He was getting better and that meant he was vulnerable. He might turn around suddenly and use his new strength in exactly the negative ways that had got him into trouble. We never knew if he'd go backward or forward. We might as well have tossed a coin."

"You're telling me our kids are at a crossroads?"

"When they joined the Skulls, they were scared, so they did what they were told. But now they think of themselves as seasoned travelers. They're crossing America. Some are boasting how great they are."

"That's bad?"

"That's a sign of being at the crossroads. When you've been down all your life and start to go up, you get the idea you can do anything you want, you have this terrific sense of freedom, and you think you're better than you are."

"What does that mean to us?"

"Some of these kids could attach themselves to a big mouth ready to do harm. A mouth that tells them they're fantastic, they can do anything they want to do. I'm thinking of The Fierce Rabbit."

"He'd be my choice for someone like that."

"He already has two disciples — Wishbone and Yo Boy."

Mister Touch sighed uneasily. "Hoss warned me not to pick up strays."

"Hoss was wrong. I picked up strays in my own work. If we don't pick up strays, we don't earn trust."

"But what about those two?"

"So far so good. I think. They're never out of line, they keep their mouths shut, they smile. But of course that can mean nothing. I've seen it. You walk down the streets and nothing is going on, but you feel something is very wrong. Of course, maybe everything is just fine. Or one day the whole neighborhood explodes. It's unpredictable. It's only predictable afterwards. 'Oh, Thomas was such a nice boy, good grades in school, but recently I saw him hanging out with a bad bunch.' That sort of second-guessing. I just don't know about those two or The Rabbit either. He's carrying twenty years of rage on his shoulders."

"So what are you telling me?"

"Be ready for anything."

"How do I prepare for that?"

"I can warn you, but it's all I can do. I think I've always lived in a world where the problem was obvious but not the solution." Looking through the windshield, she watched two young bloods sashaying across the highway. A sudden fear sent her hand shooting out to grip her lover's arm. But when he asked if anything was wrong, she put her hand in his and merely said, "I'm talking too much about the past."

"Many of us are. I hear them sometimes before they see me coming. The past seems more important than ever, maybe because the Skulls are getting farther away from home. But I don't think the past will stay that important. When we get to Arizona I'll officially lift the ban on talking about it."

"Why?"

"Because we'll be three thousand miles free of it for real. The past won't be a threat then. Maybe it'll become a kind of remembered dream, sometimes good, sometimes nightmarish, but only a dream. Until we get to Arizona, I'll just improvise and hold on to the status quo. Let people bitch about things — the SS and The Rabbit and guys like Web and Riot who blame me for the loss of their lovers. Only one thing counts and that's to keep moving. I have one rock-solid idea in my mind: to get where we're supposed to be."

After a while Spirit said, "Yes, I believe in that. Maybe because I believe in you. Isn't that corny? But it's the truth."

Mister Touch squeezed her hand. "I heard what you were saying about the kids. I listened to IRT, who told me some of the same things. I know I'm handicapped two ways: I can't see the look on faces and I haven't lived on the streets. But as long as I can listen, I'll learn a thing or two."

"And you have my eyes to use." She added with a little laugh, "And everything else I've got as well."

Ten miles out of Selma, where black and white hearts had ached in pre–V 70 days, poor Snow could no longer suppress her awareness of an aching tooth. She had tried bravely to imagine the pain was a figment of her imagination, but the truth of pain kept insinuating itself into her presence, so that she began to feel her imagination had betrayed her.

The pain ambushed her at an especially bad time. In Atlanta her friendship with Sag had come to an end because of Pretty Puss's acceptance of the post of Skull Barber — Snow used the term "Barber" instead of "Hairstylist" because she had always "called a spade a spade" (a thoughtless phrase which offended black Skulls).

Sag argued that the Dalton School teenager ought to take the job and thereby become a spy within the official hierarchy. But Snow believed The Powers That Be meant to disarm any potential opposition by offering them jobs in the administration. The longer the SS discussed the matter the angrier they got, until both were convinced that an important principle was at stake. To Snow Sag betrayed it; to Sag Snow misunderstood it. To Snow Sag was deceitful; to Sag Snow was dumb. Implicit in their confrontation was this question: was it better to dissemble in the cause of democracy or by remaining honest perpetuate tyranny? Snow of the snow-white hair had embraced the principle of revolution at the prompting of Pretty Puss, who had done so at the prompting of Sag. Can anything be worse than a conservative who succumbs to uncompromising radicalism only to have radicalism abandon her? A question something like this was raging through Snow's normally placid bloodstream. She wanted to be a rebel for real.

She had managed with considerable success to inure herself to disagreeable reality for nearly twenty years in her tenth-floor apartment on Fifth Avenue. After a conventional career in college and a conventional marriage which had ended in conventional divorce — her husband finding a younger woman — Christine Rebecca Mach Higgs had retired from much of active life on the interest of stocks inherited from her father ("No man ever matched him!" she declared, calling a spade a spade), surely not on the pittance received in a divorce settlement from that sniveling degenerate of a husband.

To her relief if not surprise, Christine adjusted quickly and completely to celibate life. She had a cat, she had her box seat at the Met, she had accounts at the best boutiques, she spent a fortnight yearly at an expensive health spa in Florida, she had a loving sister and a generous brother-in-law who invited her for the Christmas holidays at their Southampton estate. Holding the warm body of a purring cat, she used to stare down from her tenth-floor window at Central Park, at the seasonal change of trees, without seeing humans, except perhaps as antlike dots on a jogging path. Most of what she saw of people was across a counter or from a car window or safely inside lobbies or rooms where outsiders posed no threat.

This was the good life lived within the American dream as dreamed across America. Yet the truth was Christine Rebecca Mach Higgs had always doubted herself. Rankling behind a face kept immaculate by cosmetologists had been the suspicion that if push came to shove, she wouldn't be able to hack it. Maybe that wouldn't have bothered Christine if she had only herself to consider. But her failure would have bothered her father and ultimately that's what counted. He had had one son, a hideous failure, and two daughters, one who married early and brilliantly, and Christine, his favorite. Her father got up at five o'clock every day of his life until his final few weeks, took a cold shower, ate a spartan breakfast of corn flakes, and marched briskly into days of almost unvarying triumph.

What had she, as a grateful daughter, ever given him in exchange for participation in the American dream? She had answered that question by avoiding any action that might lead to failure (not counting a marriage that her father had not counted anyway). Her own success in life had been to escape from the possibility of defeat. And now she was living among weird creatures who had rarely known a moment of security or a day of success in their lives.

And now Sag had betrayed her by persuading Fire — who had also betrayed their principles by handling the Caravan Roster — to reassign them to different cars. "For a temporary change of scene," Sag assured Snow coolly, but had then told Fire who told Snow, "I can't stand long rides in the company of stupid people."

As a consequence, Sag and Pretty Puss rode together and Snow, although with four others, rode essentially alone. And now Snow was left with a toothache that she tried not to believe in, although memory kept forcing itself upon her: only days before V 70 Struck she had been warned by a Park Avenue dentist that her lower right cuspid needed a root canal. In fact, on the date of her first appointment for therapy, her loving sister and generous brother-in-law both died of V 70 in their Southampton estate — a coincidence of no exceptional importance until now, more than two years later, when she felt something happen in her mouth, a flashing twitch, a throbbing, a toothache which by association made her think of death.

Plodding now through the state of Alabama, a place she had never wished to visit, Snow began to suffer intractable agony. She resolved not to believe in such pain, but the pain, growing eloquent, finally convinced her. Whimpering, she cupped her jaw and pleaded for relief.

··· ——— ···

·—·

·——· ·—· · ·——·

· —·——

The caravan halted.
It didn't take Jesus Mary Save Souls long to diagnose the

woman's condition as serious. They put her in the Motorhome dispensary with Coco and the baby. Getting in too with her were Diamond Doll and Golden Girl; one sat on either side of Snow. The fat old woman with legs bowed like a chicken's wishbone took hold of Snow's right hand and the little old ten-year-old gripped her left. What were they doing? Snow wondered through her pain.

"I got trouble too you wouldn't believe," announced Diamond Doll, giving her hand a squeeze. "Heart, kidneys, prediabetes. My arthritis, you should know what I suffer. Did you have a good doctor? I had one, but not cheap. Cheap I don't need when it comes to health. I want results. Listen, dear, go ahead cry. Here, I got." She took out a wadded handkerchief and Snow was in too much pain to refuse it, but grabbed it up gratefully and thrust it against her throbbing cheek as if in some desperate way she was remembering how her Park Avenue dentist could make everything nice.

At her side, little old Golden Girl, her face haggard with adult worries, craned her neck toward Snow like a drinking bird, and recited shrilly from OOTHI:

> *"i can't go on . . .*
> *i really*
> *can't go on*
> *i swear*
> *i can't go on*
> *so*
> *i guess*
> *i'll get up*
> *and go on."*

Though in extreme pain, Snow turned to look at the girl. She recognized in Golden Girl's strident recitation an attempt to encourage the sort of courage expected of Judge Thomas Mach's daughter. Retreating to a tenth-floor room in her mind, Snow sat there a while and reflected on whether a living soul aside from her father (her mother had died when she was only five) had ever cared enough to recite a poem on her behalf. When she emerged from that imagined room, handkerchief clamped to her cheek, Snow had the answer and it was a resounding no. Snow melted under the warmth of such closeness and heard herself weeping tears of gratitude. But the pain took over again. She sat back and yelled while an old trembling hand and a young firm one gripped both of her own, helping her to hang on.

35

WHILE THE CARAVAN parked for a short rest before pushing on in search of a dental chair, the Skulls gloomily congregated in clumps of discontent and tried to think of something else besides the intermittent wail issuing from the Motorhome.

Sag, who had vengefully stayed clear of her old friend, was nevertheless prepared to demand better health services for the elderly. With what was left of The Ladies ranged around her, Sag winced at the decibels of pain rising from the mobile dispensary, as she bitterly maintained there ought to be periodic checkups for everyone, especially for people over fifty, without, however, designating who had the expertise to make such examinations.

Nearby, Sister Fate sat with a circle of young people who always congregated around her at P & S stops to hear her travel stories. She wore a plain cotton blouse, a pair of jeans, and hiking boots. Her blond hair laced with gray was tied back efficiently in a ponytail. She had a lean hawklike weathered face and unpainted lips and clear blue eyes. She looked ready for a hike into the Amazon jungle.

At the sound of more pain from the dispensary, Sister Fate nodded as if to reply to an unsaid question. "Yes, this is what happens when you travel," she told her audience. "You must expect hardships, all sorts of odd and sometimes terrible things to see or experience."

She told them about traveling through India.

There was the train ride through dacoit country south of Agra, where ravines were honeycombed with caves in which horse-riding bandits holed up. Her train, halted at midnight on a siding, was boarded by dacoits who tried to smash down the metal door of her sleeping compartment; after failing at that, they dragged an old merchant from the next one, which he had unluckily forgotten to lock, and took him out into a cold desert night from which he never returned.

There was the bus tour through Karnataka: no leg room, no drinkable water, no stops for soft drinks either, so that the tongue in your mouth felt like an old sock, and the constant horn blowing and the deep canine growl of the gears when shoved lustily to and fro — a rattling remorseless ride for forty-two hours with the dust pouring through open windows and a driver careening madly along roads crowded with children and cows.

Seated in a pedicab on a cold night in Ambritsar, she saw two men coming toward her through the fog. But the mist, billowing around their legs, deceived her into accepting an illusion. The men were walking in the opposite direction, so instead of reaching her, they disappeared.

And so the tales of travel in India went on, until a Skull yelled out, "You must have hated India!"

Sister Fate turned with a surprised smile and murmured, "Why no, I loved India."

By forced driving they reached Demopolis long before sunset. French aristocrats had colonized the land grants thereabouts in the early nineteenth century, but had failed miserably at the job of farming. Now they lay dead under the earth of Demopolis, just as their unaristocratic descendants were dead in curtained houses above them.

Here a dental office was found. By the light of oil lamps Jesus Mary Save Souls went shakily to work. A couple of Good Lookers took turns reading to her from books on extraction, but these were too technical and of little use. She found hypodermic needles in plastic bags, but they were of different sizes and she had no idea which was the right one. So she took a medium, like an aunt buying clothes for a niece growing up in a distant city. A Good Looker discovered a vial of novocaine.

Jesus Mary had never put a needle into a mouth before, but filled the hypo chamber anyway with novocaine, and held it above

Snow's snowy head where she sat moaning in the chair. The student geriatric nurse tried to recall her own experiences in a dental chair, but that wasn't much help either.

Jesus Mary took a deep breath, leaned forward, pried open Snow's mouth, which was rigid from agony, and heeding the anguished patient's finger, which pointed in the general direction of trouble, drove the needle in. Snow reared out of the chair as if someone had goosed her. Minutes later, remembering to ask Snow if the area around the tooth felt numb, Jesus Mary selected an extraction forceps from a dozen lying in a cabinet. Was this one appropriate for removing a lower cuspid? She felt the presence of anxious Skulls at her back, doubtless wondering what might happen to them if they got in the same fix.

With a sigh of decision, Jesus Mary parted Snow's lips, avoiding eye contact with the terrified patient, and got the steel clamps approximately where she estimated they should go. Saying a silent prayer, as she had learned to do in childhood at moments of crisis, Jesus Mary began to pull. And pull and pull.

Snow's head moved forward in response to the pressure, as if the freckled hand were a magnet that her mouth, by an inexorable law, must follow. Jesus Mary paused, sweat dripping down on her patient's sallow cheeks. Mustering a calm tone of voice, she ordered Cougar, who stood bug-eyed in the crowd, to hold the woman's head firmly.

Limping over, he clamped his big black hands on either side of the snowy head. This time Jesus Mary chose not to apply steady pressure. Once the forceps were placed around the base of the tooth, Jesus Mary muttered a Hail Mary and yanked desperately with an arcing motion, putting her Irish Catholic soul into it — and with dramatic results: out came a tooth followed by a remarkable fountain of blood, like a Texas oil well.

Regardless of Cougar's powerful grip, out of that dental chair came Snow as well, a great flailing white-maned beast, because the dismal truth was that the novocaine had numbed the adjoining tooth, only superficially deadening the right one. As long as Snow lived, she would periodically awaken at night, mouth askew, sweat exploding from her brow, and, in memory of the worst pain she had endured in her life, attempt to lunge from that dental chair.

It took Cougar, Africa, and Web — three of the strongest

Skulls — to get her back into the dreaded seat and to keep her there long enough for Jesus Mary to probe for pieces of detached bone and tooth fragments.

By the time the bleeding had been brought under control with gauze sponges, Snow had subsided into a pale withered semblance of herself. She muttered something. Little old Golden Girl, having stayed near throughout the operation, leaned forward to listen.

"She's saying," said Golden Girl with tears in her eyes, "this is the worst . . . the worst . . ."

Drawing a sleeve across her sweaty face, Jesus Mary compression-packed the gaping hole with gauze soaked in thrombin, because one of the books had mentioned thrombin and one of the Good Lookers had found thrombin in a drawer somewhere. Ice bags would help, but they couldn't use ice bags without ice, so Jesus Mary dosed Snow with phenobarbital. The freckled Irish nurse at last smiled and leaning toward Snow whispered something from OOTHI: " 'The worst is not, so long as we can say, This is the worst.' "

The exhausted Snow was carried from the dental office to the Motorhome dispensary, grandly, like Hamlet up the fogbound steps of the castle to his pyre in the final noble scene of Olivier's film.

That evening in Demopolis, hunched forward at the campfire, Jesus Mary Save Souls drank more whiskey than she had ever consumed since joining the Skulls. People turned discreetly away and let her get snot-flying falling-down-stairs drunk. They were relieved when their national treasure, in whose defense some Skulls had died and for whose continued safety this trip was in part being made, at last fell into a well-earned slumber, better known as passing out.

With infinite gentleness she was carried into the Motorhome and deposited on a bunk below Snow, whose smile the next morning no one would recognize: it would be gap-toothed and it would be warm.

On her feet again, the white-haired woman would give up self-serving politics, both conservative and revolutionary, and join the Skulls for real. She could usually be seen with one of the oldest Skulls, Diamond Doll, and certainly the youngest, Golden Girl, and when anyone was kind enough to listen, she would tell her story about losing a tooth and gaining her freedom, because she had discovered to her personal satisfaction that friendship was more important than success. That was her pitch, as some Skulls crudely called her revelation. At any rate, her father and his success faded into the background, replaced by a garrulous little woman on spindly legs and a mousy little ten-year-old who was old before her time.

On that Night Of The Tooth in Demopolis the main man lay awake alongside his Spirit in the musty bed of Ben Ames Hawking and his wife Emmy who had slept in it together thirty-eight years, four months, and seven days until deciding to end life together with two shots from a coon rifle behind the woodshed after learning that their last of six children had gone before them.

"Mark? You're awake, aren't you?"

"How did you know?"

"When you can't sleep, neither can I."

"So it's come to that already — I can't sleep either when you can't, but I haven't told you because I didn't want to sound soapy."

"I don't mind you sounding soapy."

"I never think of what you say as soapy," Mister Touch gallantly declared.

" 'Sweetheart, darling, dearest' — soapy."

"Yes. But terrific."

"Since you've told me your secret, I'll tell you mine."

"You have only one?"

"That I'll tell you now. We're zeros in the grand scheme of things, driving along deserted highways maybe to nowhere, but somehow we count and your leading us counts."

"If so, it's the only thing I ever did that counted. This and loving you."

"Ah, how nice to say."

"Soapy."

"Terrific."

"Put your cheek against mine, sweetheart," Mister Touch murmured. "We'll sleep then."

"There's the secret I haven't told you."

"I thought the secret was you believe we count."

"The secret is how I feel about dreaming. I have a recurrent nightmare and in it I'm with the Dragons . . . getting beaten and raped. It comes back disconnected, like if you took a horror movie and cut and spliced it together. Faces floating in front of mine like balloons — the strings tied together."

"God."

"I wake up heart pounding. But that's not surprising."

"No. Bad, not surprising."

"Then there's the other nightmare. *That* is surprising. In this one I'm in the world before V 70 Struck. I'm walking down crowded streets, then I'm seeing clients in welfare hotels. I go up and down dark stairs. I smell the urine, the dope. The dream always ends with me with my boyfriend."

"You never told me —"

"He worked in the mayor's office. In the dream we're at a disco."

"You love to dance."

"I love to dance, but in the dream I'm not happy doing it. I want to get out of there, but people hem me in, people I know."

"Former boyfriends?"

"Among others. My mother. I want out but the dance floor's too crowded. Then I start yelling I want to zouk."

Mister Touch laughed.

"That's right. I want to be back here zouking with the Skulls."

"A lot of Skulls would say you have it all wrong. The nightmare should be being here."

"I'm so desperate to get out of the disco I wake up with my heart pounding. Like I wake up from the Dragon nightmare. That's sure as hell surprising."

"I think it means you're happy where you are."

"The most surprising."

"Not to me. Come on, sweetheart, snuggle close and we'll fall asleep."

"If we hold each other, we'll fall asleep. A soapy idea."

"But terrific. Soapy and terrific and maybe even true."

Minutes later he murmured against her cheek, "I'm thinking about your boyfriends." He waited, knowing she was still awake. When she pretended to be asleep, he accepted her decision not to talk about them now. Kissing her lightly, he let the darkness beyond his own darkness ease him along with his Spirit into a world of dreams.

In another house Mystique lay in bed with Lil Joint. All day, while other Skulls had focused on an aching tooth, Mystique had been observing with mounting interest the Official Exterminator, who directed his flit gun at flies and mosquitoes with the same quick motion that had sent his switchblade across the cheek of Dragon (now but ashes lodged among crevices in a New York building). Mystique had witnessed that fight over *Madame Bovary*. It hadn't been the violence that fascinated her, but the tiny good-looking steady-breathing Latino's defense of a book which featured dim-witted men and deceitful men and fickle men, in other words, according to Mystique, all men.

She had Snake in her pocket, ready for use at any time, as if all she had to do was lift the lid of the basket and a full third of cobra would rise up and fan out its neck muscles into a hood. It was recruiting time again, she had decided while a crowd of Skulls were wincing along with Snow. Ignoring pain and suffering not her own, Mystique decided to go after the Official Exterminator, who had fought for the proposition that all men are dumbbells and cads.

So that night Mystique had walked up to him, his good-looking eyes level with her breasts, and murmured "Hi." She then hauled him into a house once occupied by Jake and Mamie Penrose, who had died of V 70–related flu and pneumonia respectively.

Having ground her hips fiercely against Lil Joint in a vengeful assault on Mister Touch, she lit a post-coitus cigarette without opening a window, so that the forbidden smoke coiled around their sweaty bodies like the memory of sin. In a voice of pride and defiance, she quoted OOTHI: " 'I gave what other women gave that stepped out of their clothes —' "

"Sí," panted Lil Joint.

" 'But when this soul, its body off, naked to naked goes, he it has found shall find therein what none other knows.' "

"Qué?"

Turning to him and blowing a smoke ring that made him cough, Mystique said, "Tell me about *Madame Bovary*."

"Qué hay de *Madame Bovary*?"

"You defended the book against Dragon. You said it told it like it is."

"Me? I say that?" He guffawed. "All I do I cut this mother-fucker."

Mystique persisted. She questioned him about the lovestruck but fickle Léon and the callous libertine Rodolphe and the vicious moneylender Lheureux and the opportunistic notary Guillaumin and last but not least that long-suffering dummy Charles — all scumbag males. Weren't they? she asked Lil Joint fervently. She implored him to agree and thus enter into conspiracy with her, as one woman might with another, against the cruel masculine world.

Lil Joint, more surprised by her incomprehensible talk than by her sexual adroitness, pulled back more and more until he was lying at the edge of the bed. "Hey, señora," he finally said, "Charlie and Emma and they don't mean nothing to me. Only one book — *Don Quixote*."

"What are you talking about?"

Lil Joint was out of bed, hastily drawing on his trousers. "You tooting on something, señora? You fucking loco? My brother be like Don Quixote — en paz descanse." He crossed himself rapidly. "You don't know Don Quixote?" he asked in disgust while slipping his bandanna over his head and shoving a black bowler on top of that. "La Bruja," he muttered. Having called her a witch, Lil Joint was out of there.

Drawing thoughtfully on the cigarette, Mystique told herself that you can't win them all. She would cross off Lil Joint as just another dissembling undependable male — like Rodolphe, who not only seduced Emma but coldly refused her a loan when she needed it most.

36

Like would it be great if this was a nightmare and we gonna wake up from it?"

"What you getting at, homes?"

"How people used to worry about life being unreal."

"I remember that, sure."

"Wanted life to be for real right now. But we don't, do we? Want it to be real right now?"

"Run that past me again, homes."

"We wanna think we be living a bad dream and someday wake up from it, right? So what we be doing we be dreaming. Real life waiting for us to wake up. Difference between then and now. They was into real life but call it unreal. They knowed better. We ain't sure what we into."

"Run that past me again, homes."

"What in hell you back there rapping about?"

"The truth."

"Don't need truth today, we just driving. Why not play cards? Why not take a nap? Why not get out your Walkman? Why not practice Morse Code? Why not count telephone poles going past that don't carry messages no more? Why not tell riddles?"

"Why not button your mouth?"

"Because it's damn hot in here since the AC went on the fritz and we can't fix it and Wizard Brown, he suffering from lack of breath and we don't want him running off the road because he can't get breath and has to waste what he got telling you to stop rapping that way so he can drive, which is what I be saying for him."

"You got breath to say all that, you should be driving."

"I would could I see."

Meridian, Mississippi, where the two groups were supposed to rendezvous.

Hoss's Northern Force arrived in late afternoon, their cavalcade parking in front of the ugly brick courthouse. Over the doorway, graven on the pediment, were the words WHATSOEVER A MAN SOWETH THAT SHALL HE ALSO REAP.

"What do that mean?"

"Mess up, you pay."

They shuffled over to squint at a red sign in the dusty window of a small shop: *Need Quick Cash? We Pay Up To $100 Per Month For Blood Plasma. Fast Safe Painless.*

Other Skulls ambled through the low-slung humid town over which, with a certain ironic majesty, rose the Greater Mississippi Life Insurance Building.

Hoss was strolling along with E.Z., whom he had started balling the last stage of the journey. They looked hip and together, like a couple on show along Lenox and 125th Street: Hoss in dark glasses, cowboy hat, tight jeans; E.Z. wearing a herringbone tweed head-wrap, tighter jeans than his, and six-inch platinum strands in her ears. At the windows of Lerner's Jewelers they halted to show interest in what no longer had value — the owner, dying, had ordered with defiant professional pride that his most precious gems be taken from the safe and placed in the store window for dying passersby to gawk at.

Hoss looked cool, with one hand in the back pocket of E.Z.'s jeans, but he was as worried as Mister Touch had been in Atlanta. What was taking those Southerners so long?

At twilight he gathered everyone in front of the Lauderdale County Courthouse where a fire had been built. He told them all to keep together and wait. And wait they did, long after darkness set in. When people complained of hunger, he ordered them to wait. So they sat in gut-rumbling silence. The Mississippi air hung over them like a blanket of wet wool. Wheezers had trouble. Three were put in a car with the motor running, so they could benefit from the AC. When the motor started to overheat, they changed cars. Mosquitoes appeared, at first dancing around the fire, then diving like kamikazes.

In the midst of swearing and slapping and buzzing and hissing there came the faint, then hardy sound of engines. Insects forgotten, everyone strained to hear the approaching caravan. Headlight beams fell against shops along the street — The Vogue, Floyd's Formals — as the Southern Force broke free of darkness into the firelit square of Meridian.

They exchanged stories right away.

Mister Touch told of Superstar and Futura, whose love had

rendered them invisible. He described The Night Of The Tooth.

After a brief silence, Hoss got to his feet and began his account with The Woman Whose Husband Had Indigestion.

She had come out of a ditch near Eastaboga, waving her arms wildly. When the caravan halted, she explained that her husband was took real bad and needed help and she'd be much obliged. So she climbed into the lead car and guided the Northerners down a muddy back road. Along the way she talked about her husband, how he had been a mite poorly some days now. It was his gut couldn't keep down fat no more the way it used to when he et hunks of lard on a spoon jist like it was corn mush. A good man. Hard bit though, since God Almighty had never seen fit to give him luck. No man ever planted beans with more fuss or bother or had more trouble in the bargain. On rainy nights he hunkered down in the bean patch and fretted till dawn jist so he could study what the rain done to it and he would pick over bean rows with fingers so tenderlike you could of swore he was caring for younguns. Father of five younguns, every one of them buried out by the bean patch. That ailment took them all, that scourge sent from the Good Lord to punish wrongdoers in this Vale of Tears. Not one of them five boys was the man their father was, though. Shiftless like their grandfather Hoyle on her side.

She kept talking until a small cabin came into view. Parking, the Skulls watched a few scrawny chickens puff across the dilapidated porch. The woman was not ready to go inside, but stood in front of the collapsed steps and told the travelers that only this morning her husband spoke of a bellyache and didn't have good color. He wouldn't take grits or even a swallow of corn liquor to settle hisself, and she was plain worried he had caught cold on his bowels last night. A God-fearing man. Never did get cranky less he hurt like sin. So she had been waiting by the road these three days now, not moving less it was for a necessary. She had jist et some berries and a bit of corn pone, hoping for a body to come along and study his ailment. "And here you be." She smiled a gap-toothed smile (more gap-toothed than Snow's).

Some of the Northerners idled around, glancing at the gutted wreck of an old Ford truck, a woodpile with an ax rusting in the chopping block, shucks of corn, a broken hoe handle. Others stepped gingerly on the broken steps and went into the cabin.

Stench nearly bowled them over, but clapping hands to their

noses, they bravely followed the woman through a ramshackle kitchen — a black kettle hanging over a cold fireplace — into a bedroom where her husband lay on an old four-poster. More than a dozen Skulls crowded into the musty room to stare at the contorted shape under a patched quilt.

Two hands were thrust back on the lumpy pillow, their fleshless fingers curved like talons. Projecting from a faded nightshirt was the neck and skull of a man, the dun-colored skin stretched tight over the bones, the eye sockets puckered and empty, the teeth flared from the lipless O like a horse neighing, a mottled cranium sprouting a crown of white hair.

The woman asked Hoss to study her husband and see what was ailing him. She would be much obliged.

So Hoss lifted an edge of the quilt and peered at what was beneath it. The man must have died a few months ago. In this sweltering heat the bacteria in his gut had turned liver and lights into a seething broth of cells. Gases from the process had swelled the abdominal cavity until the skin bag had burst open, pouring a grayish-green slime onto the bed. Bacteria from outside the body, waiting patiently to gain admission, had then percolated along every blood vessel, turning eyeball, penis, buttock, and tongue into a stinking liquid which had since then evaporated, leaving tags of fibrous tissue and gristle and a cavern of bones to mark the final passage of a man who had never been lucky in a bean patch.

A few Skulls giggled nervously. A few retched, not having seen a corpse in this condition for almost two years. Half of them got their asses out of that reeking deathroom as fast as their V 70 lungs would let them.

The old woman didn't seem to notice their rapid exit, but anxiously inquired of Hoss if her husband looked as poorly as she thought he did.

Hoss replied that her man did look a mite poorly, but if he laid off the spoonfuls of lard he would feel a lot better.

The woman squinted from her weak blue eyes, thoughtfully scratched a hairy mole on her cheek, and said, "I declare, I done told him that too. But he won't listen none. It's the Newton blood in him. Newton folk knowed for never taking advice was the Lord Hisself giving it."

Then Hoss and the remaining Skulls got out of there with the woman right behind them, asking their backs if her husband looked poorly, having already dismissed Hoss's diagnosis, still looking for help, still wanting confirmation that the lard was doing it.

The Northerners got into their cars and drove off with more alacrity than was safe, heading in a whirl of mud for the highway, sucking air into their lungs through the open windows, trying to rid themselves of the smell as well as the memory, knowing that the old woman would soon be trekking back to the main road where she would hold another vigil, waiting for help and wondering if her man on the sly would be spooning lard into his gut while she was gone, thereby giving her more trials to contend with in this Vale of Tears.

But that was not all. Next day the Northerners had entered Birmingham where they made a pit stop. Later they discovered that Brother Love and his two brothers, Rerun, had slipped away and doubtless were living now in the home of their parents. They had simply hitched a ride from Atlanta. The three black brothers needed no one but themselves, however — and a length of rope tied to Brother Love's belt, a gun, and a machete.

But that was not all. Two days later they learned that they had a pair of hunters in their midst: bad-looking steady-breathing Chico and sharp-eyed wheezing King Super Kool, who had given up driving recently because of a persistent cough.

The two had gone out one steaming morning before the other travelers were up and they had brought back a brace of partridge, two rabbits, and a coon. What they did was this: Chico carried King Super Kool on his shoulders with no more effort than if the little black Wheezer was a bag of laundry; when King Super Kool detected movement in the underbrush, he tapped the muscular Latino's arm and Chico handed him the M16A1 and after holding his breath so he wouldn't cough and without really taking aim, except at a half dozen bushes, King Super Kool pulled the trigger, spraying the area with 5.56mm rounds at a rate of 150 rpm — enough to fell an elephant.

In the next few days they made forays into the woods for game each time the caravan halted. They bagged plenty in a short time because many animals, having lost their fear of humans, came sniffing into view, eyes bright and curious.

After being skinned and gutted by a Skull who shall be nameless, who liked the look and feel of carnage, the bullet-riddled game went into a couple of large pots along with wild greens and berries picked along the roadside and some canned veggies and a lot of pepper and Worcestershire sauce and Butoni tomato paste and oregano and garlic powder and MSG (because it made things taste better if you weren't allergic to it) and enormous handfuls of paprika, mountainous handfuls of paprika, because Chief Chef Cancer Two had Hungarian blood in his veins. The steaming indescribable ragout would not have tempted a gourmet's palate before V 70 Struck, but for people who had not eaten fresh meat in two years it was indescribably delicious. They licked the spicy grease from their lips like children eating ice cream on a hot summer day. The only problem was the bullet fragments which had gone into the stew; they had to be removed from the meat like bones from a fish.

The Southerners were beside themselves with anticipation at the description of such food. So to celebrate the reunion Mister Touch officially designated the next day to be a Skull Feast Day. The entire caravan waited anxiously while the two hunters — guarding their role jealously, they let others do nothing but retrieve fallen game — stalked through the Mississippi undergrowth and proved their legendary mettle by bringing down enough coon, rabbit, squirrel, quail, and wild turkey for a tremendous feast that everyone thought was as tasty as any they had ever eaten. For as Lil Joint said, " 'There's no sauce in the world like hunger' " — quoting from OOTHI whose hero Don Quixote reminded him of his brother. The celebration ended in diarrhea and vomiting and the most ecstatic intestinal cramps the Skulls had experienced during the last two years of canned food. Belching grinning panting, their hands flat on distended bellies, they sat around ogling one another blissfully from heavy-lidded eyes, yawning like the lions must have yawned after consuming half a ton of domestic cow somewhere along Route 85 south of Atlanta.

37

THE MAIN MAN and his Spirit did not overeat, however, because they were eager to satisfy another appetite. After the dinner Spirit led her man down the street, looking for the right place. She stopped in front of the ugly brick courthouse with its stern prophecy above the entrance. " 'Whatsoever a man soweth that shall he also reap,' " she said out loud. "I want to go in there. I want to do it in a government office."

Mister Touch laughed. "All right. Let's try the door."

"It's open."

As they strolled through the warm fusty halls, Spirit described each office. "Here's one with an American flag next to the desk, pictures of politicians on the walls, a swivel chair —"

He interrupted her. "A swivel chair? Take me inside." Then he told Spirit of a fantasy he had in college when he dreamed of corporate success. (It was not unlike Superstar's fantasy about making love against a tree trunk.) Mister Touch would sit in a swivel chair under a portrait of the President of the United States while the nubile object of his fancy undressed and sat on him, and they would twirl slowly around and around.

Spirit giggled, removing her clothes and helping him with his. "There's a framed photograph on the desk. A pretty blonde and three pretty blond children are looking right at us."

"Turn it on its face. We don't want kids watching an X-rated movie."

Leading him to the swivel chair, she watched him sit down. "What now?" she asked.

Unwittingly the main man used the same coarse invitation dreamed up by Superstar: "Come and get it!" Except his queen was black.

When they left the courthouse with its prophetic warning, Mister Touch asked Spirit to find a jewelry store. She found Lerner's with its window still intact, gems cobwebby on satin cushions only an arm's reach away.

"Is there a ring in there?" the main man asked, and when she said yes, he told her to find Chico and bring him here. She did.

"Have you got that M16 with you?" the main man asked, and when Chico said always, Mister Touch told him to blast the window in, and when Chico did, Mister Touch thanked him and then told his Spirit to reach in there and get that ring, and when she did, he told her to give it to him.

He turned it around in his fingers awhile, as if studying it for flaws. "Is it pretty?"

"Beautiful. A big diamond. I wouldn't even guess the weight."

"Do you like it?"

"Of course. Any woman would."

"Will you marry me?"

She laughed uneasily. "What are you trying to say?"

"What I said. I love you and I want to marry you."

"Now?"

"Do you love me?"

"Yes, I do, I love you."

"So will you marry me?"

Through another silence he strained in his darkness to imagine her standing there. He'd have given a year of his life for a thirty-second look at her face.

"Before V70 Struck," she said finally, "you wouldn't do a thing like this. You'd want to know more about me."

"Remember, I was a Wall Street high roller. I loved a gamble."

"Not that kind. Before V70, this never would have happened."

"I'd have married you then if I'd known you."

"Did you ever date a black woman?"

"No. But it wouldn't have made a difference between us."

"It would have made a difference."

"We're talking about now."

"So I'll tell you about me. I was a welfare kid. I did drugs at sixteen. I was in rehab at seventeen. I swore never to tell you."

"But you have. Will you marry me?"

"Yes."

"Are we going to get everybody together and have a big ceremony?"

"I wouldn't have wanted that before V70 Struck. I certainly don't want it now."

"Then —" Reaching out he gripped her left hand and slipped the ring on her finger, holding her hand firmly while saying, "With this ring I thee wed."

Mystique didn't know about the ring that evening, because she was busy with Riot. She had been busy with three other male Skulls that day, changing partners often in her recruiting zeal. She used the back of the supply truck she had shared with Mister Touch while Ace was racing toward death in Chesapeake Bay. Each time Mystique climbed into the truck, she wrested from a lover his promise to help her when she needed him most. Not that she altogether believed in the sanctity of a hasty promise made in the heat of the moment, so to speak, but Mystique had confidence in her ability to call in a marker when the time came.

It got out that the tall good-looking woman with the honey hair and limpid gray eyes like those of a fucked-out cat was putting out in a supply truck, aptly nicknamed The Bordello by one of the more literate Skulls, who shall be nameless. Sag stopped speaking to her. Other Ladies nodded grimly in passing. Young bloods snickered, rolled their eyes, and murmured, "Hey mamma, how you doing," when she walked by.

When Mister Touch heard of her promiscuity, he gave it a generous interpretation. It simply meant that Mystique had forgotten him and was searching for someone new. Spirit kept her own counsel, hoping that her man was right instead of naive. Had Spirit not been the cause of Mystique's degradation, she would have befriended her out of pity.

Mystique had just finished with Riot about two blocks down the street from the courthouse where the man she loved had betrayed her again with a spying slut whose degradation, according to Mystique's view, required nineteen adjectives to describe.

They were lying on the pulled-out sofa bed in Harry Milliken's law office where the good old boy had composed love poetry and briefs in defense of property rights.

Mystique turned and threw her arm across Riot's belly with a proprietary familiarity that belied the fact she had known the young Italian's body for less than an hour. "What are you thinking about?" she asked.

"Nothing."

"That's not true. You're thinking of her." Mystique knew she didn't have to name Bambu.

"I guess I am," admitted Riot.

"That's all right. I admire you for it. I like men who have passions, who love women, who are willing to die for them."

"Yeah, I guess I knew someone like that."

Mystique knew he was referring to Ace, the pimply-faced kid she had sent to his death. Riot had been one of the few people who could stomach him.

"When I saw him," continued Riot, "giving it the gas, showboating like that, I knew he was doing it to impress that snooty broad Cola Face. Nothing would stop him except death."

"I believe you're right."

"The Rabbit laughed when I told him that. He said no man who was a man would kill himself for a broad."

"The Fierce Rabbit doesn't know as much about love as you do. I admired Ace for what he did."

Riot turned to regard her. "*Admired* him? For dying like that?"

"Of course. A woman will do anything for a man who gives himself to love." Her eyes were smoldering. "I believe you're that kind of man. I've only given you a *taste* of my love. I'd give it all if you'd go all the way."

"What's all the way?"

She heard the edge of caution in his voice. No sense frightening him off, she thought, so Mystique replied vaguely. "All the way is protecting me."

"Oh," he said, relaxing.

But Mystique was no longer sure of keeping him on the roster. Riot was too thoughtful for her purposes, especially because her plan was still not clear to her. It lurked in her mind like a mugger in the shadows. Perhaps she ought to simplify things. Instead of marshaling a loyal squad of men and marching to the prez with demands, chief of which would be the ouster of that spying slut, she ought to junk them and rely on one man only. That would keep her firmly in control of events. Perhaps all she required was someone with good eyesight and nothing else but a driver's license.

38

O<small>N THE FOLLOWING DAY</small> both groups set out together, much happier that way because claustrophobic life in the Club House had made them dependent on one another, like a family of kids who have lost their parents. Moreover, drivers had acquired experience, so they could be trusted to avoid wholesale crackups, especially since the Payback System had given them a complex but challenging way of communicating. Rather than subject themselves to another bout of waiting like those endured in Atlanta and Meridian, Mister Touch decided they would continue en masse.

Setting out, they were happy that their prez and his lady were married, because it was probably the first marriage in the world since V 70 Struck.

But Mystique was not happy.

She heard about the ring called A Diamond As Big As The Ritz before ever seeing it on the slut's finger. One look and she almost vomited her lunch, yet Mystique had the presence of mind to walk right up and smile from ear to ear and wish Spirit In The Dark every happiness. Turning away, fearful of retching, she went back to recruiting with a vengeance. Now she was looking for only one man with the perfect combination.

First came Sluggo, the Dutch boy who served as the Skull Disk Jockey For Latin Music but who really worshiped the jazz-fusion group Azymuth and specifically their pianist, Jose Bertrami. Not only did Mystique have carnal knowledge of him beyond his European understanding but she went away playing Azymuth tapes on a Walkman, a grand and scary display of vengeance if there ever was one. In following days Mystique became horribly adept at forcing earphones on people to enjoy a particular passage of Bertrami on keyboards, so that when people saw her coming, even music aficionados like Sony Boy and Sunoco, they ran for their lives. Sluggo, however, confessed finally that he couldn't drive a car, so Mystique scratched him from consideration for Plan A and relegated him along with Riot and others to Plan B.

Next she dragged Sky Hook into the back of the supply truck. Mystique was at first hopeful that the mild-mannered little black basketball fiend who worshiped the Los Angeles Lakers was going to be her man. Before working him over, she got acquainted. She asked Sky Hook about his shoes and was rewarded with a description of Air Jordan Nikes with a foot frame of high-density polyurethane. It was soon clear that he had no basic skills, so-so eyesight, and nothing going for him except arcane memories of a dreary sport. So rather callously she did nothing with him at all and at the next stop let the crestfallen boy out with nothing to show for his ride in The Bordello.

Before the caravan got under way again, she had loaded Funkadelic aboard the supply truck. It would prove to be a marriage made in heaven, sort of. Although he had been given a groovy name by IRT and wore one earring, a leather jacket, and silver chains like a black stud, at heart he was a downright wimp who easily surrendered to Mystique's vengeful passion. She placed him on the floor, stripped him, and gyrated wildly against his ordinary body in a fierce assault on Mister Touch's conscience. Later, panting beside the befuddled young black, Mystique hauled out her cigarettes, lit one, blew smoke into his good eyes, and murmured, " '— O remember in your narrowing dark hours that more things move than blood in the heart.' Now listen to me."

"Yes, ma'am," Funkadelic said.

While that was going on, Shy Guy slipped completely from Poor Looker to Blindie. The truth was, the tongue-tied kid with the shelf haircut had been stone-blind for days but would not admit it because he was afraid that on some level unknown to him it might offend people.

He stumbled, crashed, gazed blankly into the air, but if anyone gently inquired about the state of his vision, Shy Guy stammered pitifully and a few times in frustration he even struck out at the abstract sky with the heavy gnarled hand of a powerful youngster who had once navigated long metal racks loaded with hundreds of dresses through noontime traffic in the garment district of New York City. He walked now with his hands out, swearing on his mother's grave (which she didn't have) that he could still see. At last, falling, he had broken his nose during a P & S stop.

While treating it, Jesus Mary passed her hand across his sightless eyes like they used to do in the movies when someone went blind but wouldn't admit it. "You," she said harshly. "Quit it right now! You are *blind!* You are a *Blindie!* So start acting like one."

"Ac . . . ac . . . acting like wuh . . . wuh . . . one?"

"Be what you are for real. Maybe then you'll pull your weight."

The sudden brutality was like a blessing from heaven. From that moment on Shy Guy started pulling his weight and then some. Although barely five feet, he possessed tremendous upper-body strength like the famous little Turk who won an Olympic weight-lifting title in 1988. Now, whenever something had to be lifted or held or pulled, Shy Guy would be led up to it like Samson to the pillars. He would stand motionlessly, a reliable little Prudential Rock of Gibraltar, gripping what had to be gripped, lifting what others could not budge, his sightless eyes open, his bunched biceps rippling like the muscles of a lion, his broad back as rigid as a plank. Shy Guy, a gift from the gods, a pint-sized Atlas.

And while Mystique was interviewing Funkadelic in the supply truck, in the following car some comments were made about love and women, subjects of considerable import now that the main man had got himself married and Hoss had found a new main squeeze and Web was with Boo Bang and The Fierce Rabbit was hanging on by his fingertips to fickle Evil Eye.

"Heaven help Hoss. Her halters hiphuggers highheels having haunted him horrendously henceforth hammered him hard. He's had. Ha ha ha."

"He meaning E.Z. who have got Hoss now."

"Yeah? Hoss be moving on from Spat?"

"Adidas, how you get to know what's happening? Going round like you does, nose in a dictionary, looking for words — he on H now?"

"Sound like it. Right, Adidas?"

"Hellish hags, heartless honeys, hotheaded head-hunting horny harlots."

"Seem like Adidas changing his tune. Last I remember he talking foul mouth about fairies and fucking. Seem like he don't like girls no more. Maybe one done him in."

"Woman don't fool with a man with a nose in a dictionary."

"That be definitely true, homes. But never you mind, Adidas. Keep right in there. 'Fast forward forever' — ain't that what you go around saying?"

"When he was on F."

"Forget when he was on G. What was going on then?"

"Heterosexual homosexual homoerotic hermaphroditic hymeneal hijinks horrify higherups hunting harmony."

"If he meaning Hoss and Mister Touch by higherups and them not wanting all that sex this and sex that that he talking about, Adidas dead wrong."

"Ain't like you, Adidas, being square. What we gonna do with you, old butcher boy?"

"Half hitches have held hateful hooligans. Haul him here hobbled however heartrending his hollering."

"Who is *him* you talking about? We talking about what to do with *you*, Adidas."

"Hang him."

They were driving at a snail's pace this afternoon; cumulative fatigue had both drivers and riders panting for breath. The vehicles plodded like old dray horses past roadside cemeteries which, for lack of care, were beginning to resemble lots full of weeds and stones. The caravan motored through towns that were returning themselves to the natural landscape: weedy green tendrils pushed arrogantly up through sidewalks and streets, harbingering the day not so far off when a squirrel might skip from office roof to residential sapling without discerning any difference in the rough texture beneath his claws — a rugged carpet of greenery — when Main Street and town dump would equally provide homes for bees and when foxes could nest comfortably on the porch of the mayor's home.

The Skulls passed at least a dozen country churches which all looked the same, the steeples sharp as a pin. Around most of these churches were parked dozens of cars, for when V 70 Struck, many devout people had rushed to the Lord's House and now lay inside of it, bent over pews, stretched in aisles, the faithful asleep in their bones among cobwebs and prayerbooks.

The caravan stopped near such a church midway through Mississippi at noon for P & S and R & R. In recent days Stay High had been ruminating furiously about the meaning of "The Mystery of the Universe." Clearly, the poem was in part a blunt discourse on hedonism. The Dream Queen suggested that universal disaster ushers in a period of rampant nihilism and moral chaos. But beyond this opening meditation came an interesting line, perhaps the heart of the poem: "As if you had a universal goal." "*As if*" posed the existential need to live honorably no matter how absurd life had become.

Now then, he had discovered that four letters in various combinations had created four three-letter words in the poem: Act, cat, gat, and tag. Of perhaps greater significance, however, was the contribution of Doctor Leo that day on the schoolyard swings, when he pointed out that NU CLEO TIDE BASE appeared in unmediated form within the text. So, to summarize the analysis thus far: From a general societal observation about the consequences of global disaster upon a surviving population, the poet had then exhorted the reader to value good works above pleasure. But on another level the poem was alluding to the chemical basis of life itself. The symbolism was not yet clear —

Such things, at nearly every stop of the caravan, Stay High explained again and again to The Boy Who Doesn't Speak Our Language, as he was doing now in sight of a church which Stay High regarded as nothing more than a cultural artifact. The Boy sat glumly beside him, glaring at anyone who dared to look their way.

Suddenly, at a skipping gait, along came Doctor Leo in the gray flannel suit he wore even in sweltering heat. There was nothing friendly in his broad grin as he approached Stay High and The Boy. But the scholar from Columbia had formed too high an opinion of his loony intellect to deny Doctor Leo their company.

"Please sit down," Stay High said politely.

"Just as I suspected!" cried Doctor Leo, clapping his hands. "There's more in your poem than you know! But I won't tell you what it is!"

"Do as you please," Stay High told him quietly.

Leering, the insurance salesman said, "No, I am sorry, but I won't tell."

"Then I assume there's nothing to tell."

"On the contrary, Mister Knowitall. I know this life insurance policy backwards and forwards and if you don't understand it, that's your tough luck. I'm through kowtowing to people just to sell them something I understand but they rarely do, although they suspect I don't, and even if I do, they suspect I understand it only to bleed them dry so that when they finally kick off there won't be anything left, I mean in the bank, to pay their funeral expenses, because everything will have gone to pay their annual premiums — What was I saying?" Leaping to his feet, he danced around ecstatically. "I have proof of the poem's meaning! I know what's in the damn thing! But I won't tell you! I won't! I won't tell you!"

Stay High turned back to The Boy. "Pay no attention," the scholar said with a knowing grimace, but he was dying to find out what the loony knew.

"Gorgee kai," commented The Boy with extreme displeasure, although Skulls standing nearby could not tell at whom the displeasure was directed.

That day passed, that night passed, the next day began, and Mystique shared every second of every hour with Funkadelic. Plan A had emerged in all its terrifying potential. She had the right man to implement it, a fool who would do her bidding. She had easily enslaved Funkadelic, and he could drive a car. Moreover, she had convinced him it was all right to scare the new bride as a kind of wedding joke. As she explained, when people get married there are always rituals entailing fun and games. In the game she wanted Funkadelic to play, there would be a car, a bride, and an opportunity.

"Yes, ma'am," Funkadelic said.

"What you have to do," Mystique said, recalling her effectiveness with Ace, "is scare her." She hoped, of course, by accident he would do more. "Go straight for her and if you want to, at the last moment swerve."

"What they gonna do to me for doing that?"

"Do you love me?"

He stared at her hard. "Yes, ma'am."

"Since the world began, men have performed feats of valor to honor their ladies. You are a chivalrous knight in shining armor, did you know that?"

"Yeah?"

"And consider this when they ask you why you did that. You say one of two things. If you simply scare her, you say it was only a joke to commemorate the marriage. If on the other hand you manage to do more than scare her, you maintain you defended the Skulls from a spying slut who was just waiting for the chance to bring down disaster on our heads."

"Can't remember all that."

"Don't worry. I'll say it for you." Mystique meant it. She had the speech memorized already — each word set in the concrete of her righteous anger. Ladies and gentlemen of the Skulls, let me put Funkadelic's action in perspective. He has seen The Dragon Lady insinuate her poisonous self into your good graces, especially of our exalted leader who, although a man of intelligence and vision, knows very little about dissembling females like this wicked graceless infernal monstrous devilish plaguey unscrupulous foul unprincipled insidious diabolic blameworthy heinous demoniac furtive dishonest stealthy evasive conspiratorial slut. And so pro bono publico (she had looked it up in Adidas's dictionary to give her speech a kind of Ciceronian class) our friend and fellow Skull, Funkadelic, took justice into his own hands, aware of the precedent set by Martin Luther King (a crumb she would toss to blacks in the audience), who wrote, "Society must protect the robbed and punish the robber," which in our case applies to the probation of The Dragon Lady. In eliminating her from our midst, our public-spirited Funkadelic "is in reality expressing the highest respect for law," according to Dr. King.

If Funkadelic had heard this speech, it would have confused and frightened him. In truth he had never felt much conviction about anything except wearing dreadlocks and a leather jacket and an earring, man, in the hope of looking more like a stud than the wimp he really was. A Neat Looker but a confirmed illiterate, he took in only a smidgen of his honey-haired honey's explanations for what he must do. It did get through to him, however, that by playing a joke on the bride he might win people's attention, perhaps their respect. And if by accident he did run over the bride and if Mister Touch didn't order his execution, Mystique would keep her promise and let him live out his days in her white-hot arms.

So he was ready when she said ready and pointed up the barren street of a little Mississippi town where Spirit was standing with a knot of women, talking. "Go for it," Mystique whispered.

The muffled sound of her honey voice galvanized the overdressed dude. He jumped into the first car available, turned the key in the ignition, and with his neat-looking eyes fixed on the tall black woman in the middle of the street, slammed his foot down on the accelerator and whooooops, took off.

He had only about twenty yards to go. Barreling at her with wheels churning and motor roaring, Funkadelic was overtaken by destiny in the form of a winged insect that was sucked into the funnel of the open window and whirled around so that it smacked hard into the corner of his left eye, causing him to lift one hand off the steering wheel and swerve at the last moment. Instead of hitting Spirit In The Dark as Mystique had hoped he would do, Funkadelic missed her by no more than the length of Mister Touch's erect penis. Unable to brake fast enough, he slammed into a storefront, hurtling beyond the broken glass of a boutique window into a sea of lingerie — panties, bras, teddies, garter belts, and lace nighties.

As people rushed to take his lifeless body out of the crumpled car, Mystique vanished discreetly into the crowd. Spirit, visibly shaken, was leaning against her blind bridegroom, who turned his head wildly in this and that direction in a vain attempt to envision what was going on.

Let it be said that later, in secret, he would allude to this incident as Funkadelic's Folly. The main man would theorize that this bizarre event was the result of stress caused by more traveling than the young man could handle. Funkadelic may have imagined that he could drive right through buildings in a shortcut to Arizona, determined to get there first. Why except in the blindness of a delusion would poor Funkadelic have driven hell-bent down the street of a little Mississippi town? The horror of having almost lost his Spirit spread through the man's mind like a black sludge, leaving him spiritless for the rest of the day.

39

As the skulls moved deeper into the South, they might have watched for creatures from the Blue Lagoon watching them: narrow-mouthed toads, spring peepers, pig frogs, banjo frogs, green tree frogs raising a chorus of quonk quonk and gray tree frogs answering with brrill brrill. Or they might have heard woodpeckers drumming against tree trunks for bark beetles and combing through crevices for termites whose nests have been known to rise twenty feet, a distance comparable in human terms to a skyscraper over two miles high. So Stay High explained to The Boy Who Doesn't Speak Our Language: "Over a fifteen-year period the termite queen lays about thirty thousand eggs a day. Her mate requires fifteen seconds to walk the length of her swollen body."

Another passenger guffawed. "Reminds me of a joke. Midget in the circus marries the fat lady. Giant looks through the transom of their wedding suite. Tells the troupe what he sees. Midget's running back and forth over the naked body of the fat lady, clapping his hands and yelling, 'Acres and acres of ass and all mine!' "

"Coo," said The Boy with a glint in his eye.

In another car Evil Eye was taking care of Number One. She had had enough of The Fierce Rabbit, his vain boasting, his mean-spirited desire to bring down all whites, his tiresome dream of rising to main man, his low sex drive after a couple of dominating performances. As long as he brooded in his hutch he had been fun in a scary way — a sleeping giant always on the verge of waking — but when he came to the surface and peered out and began talking, especially to Yo Boy and Wishbone, those bright-eyed weasels who followed him around, The Fierce Rabbit seemed dangerous in a serious way. Convinced he was heading for trouble, she decided the wise thing to do was detach herself altogether. In recent days, therefore, she had begun to vanish like the smile of the Cheshire Cat. She became a pillar of blandness, so cold and smooth that her skin had the eerie look of a seal surfacing in an ice floe. She allowed her imagination to isolate her from her boyfriend and his companions, sending them away to wander in the back of her mind like lost little boys. She resolved to commit herself to nothing but her own wisdom.

When The Fierce Rabbit, impatient with her moodiness, finally yelled at her, "Baby, *you be one fucking drag!*" she laughed scornfully and said, "Baby, I've seen my share of afros and let me tell you something, they don't make a man out of a fool, so at the next stop I'm getting myself reassigned to another car because I am done with you, done with you, done with you *for real!*"

Having humiliated a man for whom a raised eyebrow constituted an insult, at the next stop Evil Eye sought out Fire, a divorcée who could relate to the idea of getting away from the wrong man. At Evil Eye's request Fire assigned her to a carload of white women.

In the back of the supply truck, Mystique was romancing another dummy, who shall be nameless. She wasn't living up to her well-earned reputation as one hot mamma, however, because ever since Funkadelic's death, Mystique had been depressed. Had he really believed she meant for him only to "come close"? Had he really been that dumb? Men often were. She thought of dim-witted Charles Bovary and the insensitive Latino Lil Joint who had defended him unwittingly. Mystique knew who she was — Lucy Rutherford — and could identify her immediate objective — revenge against The Dragon Lady — and understood precisely what she wanted in life — her man back. Yet her righteous desire for justice was now coupled to a foreboding of defeat. Never the one to lack confidence, Mystique had been shaken, nevertheless, by two failed attempts at punishing The Dragon Lady. She found herself plagued by odd fantasies in which everything went wrong. When she tried to push The Dragon Lady over a cliff, the bitch stepped aside and Mystique herself plunged over. When she tried to shoot her enemy, the gun misfired and, as she bent over to inspect it, went off and blew her own brains out. If she tried poison, somehow the cups got switched and she died in agony while the black slut soothingly wiped her feverish brow with a damp cloth. However much she schemed and sacrificed and labored, her revenge became The Dragon Lady's vindication for taking Mister Touch away from her.

Whenever she felt depressed, Mystique had noticed it helped to remember when V 70 Struck. Initially she had conceived of the virus as a mean-spirited idea in the mind of an evil god. Splitting into the form of tiny bugs, this satanic concept had come to earth for a joyride through the bloodstream of humanity. The notion had horrified her, but at the same time another more appealing conceit seized her imagination: since millions had died but she had lived, it must have been by design. Lucy Rutherford was special.

At the next stop, she climbed into the supply truck's cab and rode there chastely beside the driver instead of inside the window-less rear of the truck with a bozo pawing her. She sucked in the pure rushing air and watched the sweet gums red oaks short-leaf pines willow pepper grass and sour dock slide past the bug-stained windshield. With the wind funneling into the cab and rustling her honey hair and with wheels beneath her feet taking her somewhere new, even if it was at fifteen miles an hour, Mystique felt a newborn conviction growing in her gut, as remorselessly as Rosemary's baby, that when the storm of battle lifted, she would have her victory and the world would be hers.

It had been a glum drizzly ride past Bill's Dollar Stores and rural mailboxes with their red flags down and power cables transmogrifying from mineral into vegetable — creepers hiding more than half the wire. Now at its tardy pace the caravan entered the hamlet of Pelahatchie, which in fact was no more than a line of frail wooden houses along the highway, a monotonous series of broken porches and motionless swings and trailers on blocks and rainwater in footpaths leading to buckled screen doors. After such a long rainy afternoon of cheerless driving, the bedraggled village of Pelahatchie offered to the Skulls little consolation.

It was too wet to sleep out in bedrolls, so they decided to make use of the houses. That meant disturbing some of the thirteen hundred citizens of Pelahatchie, Mississippi.

The strongest stomachs could have been assigned to the dis-agreeable task, but at the outset of the journey Mister Touch had decided such a grim effort must be communal. Only blind Wheez-ers were exempt. Otherwise, it was up to the people who would sleep in a particular house to remove its former tenants. This was done by folding bedsheets around the bones, then dumping every-thing disposable into plastic garbage bags that were then lugged outside and unceremoniously tossed into a heap. Some of the

Skulls wouldn't sleep in a house until every corpse had been removed. Others, less fastidious, settled for getting rid of the dead in the room they themselves would occupy. They had all to varying degrees become insensitive to the sight, if not to the idea, and in two years the smell had vanished. In nearly all cases so had traces of mortal tissue — the corpses weren't as offensively human as the old woman's husband who had been eating lard by the spoonful only a few months ago. It was simply a tiresome, unpleasant task. But sometimes a Skull would awaken in a strange room and recall having dumped the remains of its former occupant on the front lawn for all the neighbors to see. This could lead to insomnia or nightmares, take your pick.

In Pelahatchie, when they started removing the bones at dusk, Eagle flew out of a little clapboard house as fast as a Poor Breather can, his threadbare yarmulke coming free of his bald head. What he had found in a back bedroom was no pile of bones in a matrix of rotting pajamas but something that moaned and moved. Stupefied, the middle-aged tailor dropped the flashlight, raced out, and stood in the twilight of Pelahatchie where he muttered Hebrew prayers and dipped back and forth like a windup doll and swore between pleas for salvation that he had just seen a dybbuk in the body of a living man.

A hastily organized expedition returned cautiously to the house, led by limping Cougar and massive Africa. They found a living man all right, just this side of dead, who had a high fever and was choking on his own phlegm. Jesus Mary was called in.

Sitting on the curb of Pelahatchie's main and only street, Mister Touch decided to wait until the man died or could travel; if he lived, they would put him in the Motorhome and take him along. So they stayed that night in Pelahatchie, but no one could sleep — there were rumors that Eagle had been correct: the town was haunted. So the main man decided that most of the Skulls would backtrack a few miles to the Bienville National Forest east of Raworth, where there was a camping area. A small group would remain in town with the sick man.

The decision aroused the usual controversy. What was surprising was its insipid and ephemeral nature.

Sag suggested that Mister Touch was jeopardizing the whole project merely to exercise power in the willful way of a man corrupted by power. They had precious little time left before disaster set in; their physical condition was deteriorating every hour that he delayed them. Her prophecy of invalidism startled people, making them realize the contrast between such a claim and the reality of their improving health. Since leaving New York City there had been only a few runny noses.

Even The Fierce Rabbit failed to stir up more than momentary dissatisfaction with how things were being handled. He argued that Mister Touch wanted to adopt whites along the way, even if they were dying, in order to beef up the numerical superiority of the honkies. But those who listened to him said nothing.

"Ignorant imbeciles inevitably interfere intellectually in imaginative ideas involving immensely important if imponderable implications."

"Right on, Adidas. He on the letter I now. Giving it to us, sound like, about something."

"About people talking about things they don't know about. Ain't that right, Adidas? Speak to us, brother."

"Ignore inane idiots."

"Harsh words, butcher boy. And trouble, be you speaking of the wrong people and they hear you. Don't you be coming down on homeboys. We just traveling and taking you along. Ain't that okay?"

"It is idiosyncratic."

"That mean crazy?"

"It is irregular inaccurate illusion."

"It is?"

"Inadequate illusion is irrational."

"It is, is it? Is it insane?"

"Careful, homes, *you* be going off with him! You saying plenty that start with I."

"Hey, old butcher boy, don't you fuck *me* over! Ain't you saying more?"

"No, he ain't. He run out of words awhile. Got to hit his dictionary for more. Then he tell us."

The caravan drove back to the campgrounds and spent the next three days resting, sunning, playing cards, eating copious stews, while in Pelahatchie, Jesus Mary nursed the sick man. Stitch repaired two of the cars. He worked on them in the local garage and slept there alone on the greasy floor. It would have been easy enough to find new cars and merely abandon these two, but Stitch felt a responsibility toward them. They were professionals, veterans, they were loyal soldiers you didn't leave behind when wounded. He'd rather slave over their engines for hours than cross the street and put batteries into new cars. No one had guts enough to scoff at his intrepid folly.

When Jesus Mary felt the invalid could travel, Riot drove back to the campgrounds and told Mister Touch, even though the sight of the blind leader always tied a knot in his stomach, while pounding in memory were the breathless words of his murdered Bambu, "O Honey, O Honey, O Riot Honey, O Honey!"

The caravan regrouped in Pelahatchie. Jesus Mary rode alone in the Motorhome with her patient. Next day she reported that he was well enough to talk, so for one stretch of the afternoon's drive Mister Touch resolved to break his rule never to ride anywhere save in Car One. He shifted to the Motorhome. The convalescent stranger lay wrapped in sheets, his bushy brown mustache neatly trimmed by Jesus Mary. The prez asked questions. He learned that the forty-year-old man was from Louisville, had driven south to spend the winter in warm New Orleans, but in Pelahatchie had been overtaken by fatigue, chest pain, and fever. He'd figured it was V 70 Striking late, found himself a bed to die in, and had just about accomplished it when a little man wearing a black skull cap blundered into the room.

What impressed and delighted Mister Touch was the man's line of work: he was a TV repairman who also knew something about plumbing. When the prez asked him to join, the man was way ahead of him. "I was just going to ask if I could come along."

After explaining the name rule, Mister Touch said, "You are now Dragon Two. That's in honor of Dragon One who died in New York."

"No, I'm not," the man declared. "I won't take none of your crazy names."

"Everyone has."

"I won't. Try and make me, I won't join. I mean it."

Without seeing the man, Mister Touch could see that he meant what he said.

"I want my own name. It was given me, it's mine, it's all I got left, it's the only one I mean to take to my grave." The man's voice was weak but firm.

Mister Touch faced a dilemma. He couldn't let this man get away with dictating terms publicly or his own power would be weakened. On the other hand, this man possessed skills that some-day might be of great value. After more discussion, they cut a deal: the TV repairman could have his old name but without revealing the fact that it *was* his old name. When people asked him, "Hey, is that your old name?" he would pretend his old name was some-thing else. So it was agreed that Harold would have his old name but call it his new one. Then they agreed on another secret: his skills would be revealed only when Mister Touch saw fit. They shook hands. The Skulls now had two national treasures: a nurse and an electronics expert.

That night after camping in a village, Mister Touch snuggled close to his Spirit and listened to a startling revelation: Jesus Mary had developed a feeling for the sick man beyond that of nurse for patient.

To match his wife's disclosure the main man told her the truth about Harold's name. "Harold really is Harold. But why would anyone cling to a name like that?"

"It doesn't say much to me."

"To keep 'Harold' he was willing to say goodbye to us and stay alone in a haunted town like Pelahatchie."

"And give up a woman who wanted him."

"I wonder if Stay High would have any theories about that?"

"Don't ask him."

"Don't worry. I've never been accused of masochism."

Next morning, when The Fierce Rabbit heard about the nam-ing of Harold, he wasn't fooled. "Dude's going with his old name," he maintained. "See what I'm saying?" he said to Wishbone and Yo Boy. "One rule for them, another for us. Mayors and governors and presidents never fool me. They got a long-winded rap game, tell lies to cop votes, then when they in they make up rules as they go along." He snorted contemptuously. "Had this party for the kid Rattler before you guys come along. Right there I say my real name right out. None of these scumbags around here say theirs too. Skulls be a bunch of yellowbelly motherfucking pussies." Squinting down the line of cars, he saw Evil Eye strolling along, hanging out with a couple of white broads. "Where I come from," he said bitterly, "no woman get away with acting smart-ass to a brother without his friends straightening her out good."

"Yo," said Yo Boy. "I hear you, El Viejo."

The Rabbit turned and looked at him.

"Because that be you," explained Yo Boy. "The top top, the old man, the reason."

"Yeah?" said The Fierce Rabbit proudly. "Someday I say go and we go. Hear what I'm saying?"

"Whatever you say," said Wishbone, "we hearing it."

40

I F ASKED, Stay High would probably not say he was happy, but then he had no clear notion of happiness. What he had always known was the satisfaction that comes from hard work. He could not remember a moment when he was not applying himself to an intellectual task.

In grade school he was already toiling long hours at his desk, righteously aware that his classmates were outside having fun. He slaved over Hebrew, memorized passages from the Talmud until he wondered if his head might split like an overripe melon. In college he applied himself to every academic task that came his way until he had four European languages at his disposal, the labor crowned by his mastery of Sumerian cuneiform script.

In spite of his accomplishments, however, in his heart of hearts Stay High doubted his abilities. Two older brothers had been casually brilliant, both becoming physicians with exotic specialties, and his younger sister — he couldn't think of *her* without wincing. She had revealed her mathematical genius at six and had raced right past him at every mental endeavor as if he were one of those goyishe athletes who never open a book.

He had to sweat for everything he learned. He worshiped the life of the mind, but sometimes in a library Stay High felt like a penniless boy who presses his nose against the windowpane of a deli, haplessly staring at lox and bagels and pickles so good even Diamond Doll wouldn't believe. He was humble enough to suspect that his intellectual flaws were significant. He recognized in himself a dangerous propensity for grasping facts without the meaning behind them. He concentrated on a detail until it burgeoned into the totality.

Once he had spent a student summer in southeast Turkey at the archeological dig at Catal Hüyük, one of the oldest cities in history, and had emerged from that experience with almost no recollection of the site, with no imagined sense of the people who had lived and loved and suffered there eight thousand years ago, but with a clear and accurate memory of a few objects which he himself had carefully extracted from the dig, among them a seven-inch-long clay goddess whose breasts, like his mother's, were enormous.

Now, finally, he had something of real importance to work on. There was the poem, of course, but its solution was probably so far in the future that he might not be alive to enjoy it. What truly energized him was the other problem, The Boy Who Doesn't Speak Our Language. Sometimes, studying him, Stay High wondered if his own bookish travail had been channeled by destiny for this single purpose — to analyze the private language of a twelve-year-old. Painstakingly, with the aid of a magnifying glass, he made dozens of branching tree diagrams of The Boy Who Doesn't Speak Our Language's language, so far without results. Nevertheless, Stay High was convinced that the kid was a linguistic genius who had created a verbal system of such brilliant complexity that other languages merely bored him; proof was his refusal to remember English. It was unthinkable to assume, as Mister Touch did, that the kid was making up random words.

Not that he disliked Mister Touch, even though sometimes the leader behaved like a philistine. To be fair to the main man, he had asked about the early development of civilization as if it had some relevance to the Skulls.

Asking him a question was more than Stay High's three brilliant siblings had done. So Stay High dredged up information about metalworking among the Urnfield people of Eastern Europe, lost-wax casting in the Andes, the significance of wild einkorn wheat for the emergence of agriculture. Stay High was proud of his knowledge, even when he suspected there was something not quite authentic about the way he used it. At least he was grateful to Mister Touch for letting him feed back information from books he had sweated over in gloomy rooms at midnight during those hopeful years when he had waited for a miracle to happen that would endow him with the intelligence of his two hatefully smart brothers and that impossibly gifted sister and two harshly critical parents, who snubbed him in a household that worshiped brains to the extent that his Ph.D. from Columbia meant little more to them than graduation from kindergarten.

So whether Stay High realized it or not, he had never been happier than he was now among the Skulls, who were producing in him the sense that he belonged. He was learning from them, especially from the Harlem kids, and this gave Stay High an anthropological high. Privately he derived happiness from a conviction that he was researching their myths and rituals. He regarded them as a neglected culture with its own folklore and taboos. He listened intently to their squabbles, boasts, and complaints, searching for behavioral patterns to incorporate into a Venn diagram of cultural dynamics. Someday he would do a monumental study based on the Skulls, suspecting that their syntactical transformations were as rich as the Kachin tongue of Burma or the Ulithian of Micronesia. It was indeed a heady thought, perhaps even a happy thought, that he stood on the verge of contributing to the store of human knowledge. But in truth he often forgot to study his comrades. He simply joined them in their activities, learning their styles of dancing for real and enunciating, just like they did, the noun "shit" with three syllables.

Stay High was happy without knowing it, yet something prevented him from reaching a new high. That something was sex or the lack of it or the lack of significant sex. Privately, he wondered if he was a sex maniac for real. He had enjoyed a few casual encounters with a couple of Skull girls, but what he really sought in the deepest recess of his mind-cum-loins was an intellectual woman who screwed. He sought in vain for such a one among the choices available. He would not be happy enough to know he was truly happy until such a woman came along (with enormous breasts, like the goddess of Çatal Hüyük, who reminded him of his mother) and in her powerfully loving way created in him a brilliant intelligence.

Slowly the caravan ascended the tall bluffs of Vicksburg, city of remembered violence, where the earthworks and trenches of Civil War battle had once brought in considerable profit from tourism. Having crossed the Yazoo and Big Black and Pearl, they were now awaiting a glimpse of the mother of all those rivers, the Mississippi, and when the cars reached the summit, there it was, lashing out of the wooded plain like a brown snake, sliding sinuously under stork-legged double bridges.

Hoss came up to Mister Touch, who faced the breathtaking sight without seeing it. Spirit had left him there while going for P & S.

"It's Hoss."

"We haven't talked lately. Can we now?"

Hoss looked around. "Sure. Everyone's on P & S or looking at the river."

"What do you think?"

"We seem to be making it."

"Any rumors?"

"Always," said Hoss. "And always bitching. People gather around, for example, and listen to Sag and The Fierce Rabbit. It's something to do."

"Meaning it's harmless?"

"I didn't say that."

"What's the rap?"

"Well, you're a nigger lover or a honky bigot. Take your pick. I am a Tom. We're both tyrants."

"I suppose it keeps people from getting bored."

Hoss laughed. "You're a piece of work, friend. I groove to nonchalance too." After a pause, he added thoughtfully, "But sometimes — I don't know."

"Walking through a peaceful neighborhood, you get the feeling something's wrong."

"I don't know where you got the analogy," said Hoss, "but it's exactly what I feel."

They stood quietly, listening to a faint rush of water ease along the riverbanks below.

Finally Mister Touch said, as if meeting an old friend after months of separation, "How are things going for you these days?"

"That's what I should be asking. You're the one who got married."

"I really did get married, didn't I."

"For real. You smashed in a jewelry store window, stole a fabulous diamond ring —"

"They tell me as big as the Ritz."

"As big as the Ritz and within earshot of about a dozen people you said, 'With this ring I thee wed.' I call that as married as you'd get with a bishop, a rabbi, a minister, a city clerk."

"And you? Who is it?"

"It's E.Z."

Mister Touch laughed. "I already knew. Even a blind man knows what goes on around here when it comes to love."

"OOTHI says, 'Woman would be more charming if one could fall into her arms without falling into her hands.' "

"So you're telling me she isn't so easy."

"Exactly. So long, pardner." This cowboy from the canyons of Madison Avenue touched the brim of his Stetson and slouched away like a hard-bitten wrangler.

While Stitch went along the line of vehicles, checking oil and looking under each hood, Skulls stood on the edge of the bluff, staring at the muddy water. Leaning against the Motorhome dispensary, Hoss wondered how much longer he could stay with E.Z., who was a shrew and a sex maniac no normal Steady Breather could hump for long without running out of breath. His brooding was interrupted by someone whispering at his elbow, "In that motel across the road a curtain moved."

Hoss turned slowly, removed his shades, and studied the broad Korean face of Jive Turkey. "What is that?"

Jive Turkey pointed at the Magnolia Motel, a red brick complex of single-story units. "In that last window on the left. Curtain moved."

Hoss went to Mister Touch, who was sitting on a curb listening to the Archduke Trio on his Walkman.

"Be careful," warned the prez.

Ten minutes later, six armed Skulls led by Hoss returned from the Magnolia Motel, prodding ahead of them a tall, powerfully built adolescent who wore jeans, a work shirt, no shoes, and no expression. Mister Touch switched off Beethoven as Spirit, who had gone for snacks in a local supermarket, came over to sit beside him. All six feet six of the husky boy towered over them. His breathing was as regular as a metronome.

Hoss explained that the squad had gone over to the motel, called out, and getting no answer had kicked the door down. The boy was lying in this filthy room on a filthy bed, with Twizzler wrappers and pretzel bags scattered over the rumpled sheets. The boy lay there, not looking scared or even curious. Just tired. He wasn't happy to have visitors, but he accepted them. He didn't try to run or resist being taken out, although he was as big as Africa and healthier than anybody seen since V 70 Struck. He might have kicked the shit out of all six Skulls, guns or no guns.

"I can't get over that room," Hoss said with a rueful grunt. "Nothing in it except garbage. I mean, I would make book that the dude has twenty/twenty vision, but there wasn't anything to read in the room. Not even an old *Playboy*. Just a filthy bed, garbage, and this big kid."

Mister Touch lifted his head to catch the warm sunrays on his face. "Sounds depressed."

"We didn't threaten him, but he looked up at us, two hundred pounds of pure health, and said, 'If you're gonna shoot, shoot.'"

Mister Touch called out to the boy, "How about you and me having a talk?" Extending his hand, he kept it there until the boy took it and helped him to his feet. With two fingers touching the youngster's hard bare arm, the prez asked him to lead them where they could talk.

They walked awhile. "Sit down here," the boy said.

The main man gingerly lowered himself to a curb. He heard the boy sit down beside him.

Skulls, watching from down the street, were satisfied that everything was fine. They turned then to gaze down at the river whose majestic passage was unblemished by barges and motorboats.

"Why didn't you run?" Mister Touch asked after a long silence. "Or prepare to defend yourself?"

"Tired of that."

"Why did you tell them to shoot?"

"Been in that room a long time. I don't know. When them friends of yours busted in, I figured my life weren't worth begging for. Reckoned they'd do what they wanted."

"Don't you figure your life is worth much?"

After another long silence, the boy said, "I been in that room so long I get to thinking nothing is. Depends, though. Sometimes my life seem like something."

"How old are you?"

"Last time I really knowed I was fifteen."

"Then you're probably seventeen or eighteen now. Are you from Vicksburg?"

"No sir."

Sir, thought Mister Touch; that's hopeful. "Are there other people around here?"

"Some was."

"Dead now?"

"Sure."

"Of natural causes?"

Silence.

"Look," said Mister Touch, "I'm just curious about what happened here." He added, "But it doesn't matter."

"People got to shooting people up. Dozen oncet had a shootout down the hill. Restaurant used to be down there. They fought right in front."

"You watched?"

"Sure. Used to go see what was doing when I heard shots." He paused. "Then I stopped going. But I went down there that time and seen two of them, the ones left, going round to ones on the ground, slitting throats to make sure."

"What was the fighting about?"

"Same old things. I don't know. When they was finished with throats, one turnt on the other one and laid his guts open with a knife. Then off he went. He was panting." The boy paused again, as if trying to recall precisely what it had been like. "He couldn't breathe good. Reckon he's dead somewheres. Or hiding."

Mister Touch cleared his throat. "The people I'm with are going to Arizona."

"Never been to a place like that."

"Would you like to come along?"

"Won't mix with liquored people with guns."

"We're not liquored."

"Around here they was. It's what got them murdering each other."

"We drink sometimes, but we don't get drunk. You see, we have someplace to get to. We're going to Arizona."

"Because I seen people getting liquored up and then what happened."

The prez could never remember having heard a voice like this. If the dead could talk, perhaps they'd pitch their voices to a similar flatness, with the same dull thudding cadence. Sonority of a graveyard. "You've had a very bad time," Mister Touch commented softly.

"Weren't too good for nobody."

"What happened to you, son?"

There was such a long silence that the main man didn't expect an answer, but it came at last, suddenly, in a torrent.

"Thing is, three men come into the house and kilt my mamma. She was blind and coughing, so they couldn't of been scared of nothing she might do to them for coming in to steal stuff. Not there was much to steal. This one, he walked up where she was laying on the couch and shot her in the head. I saw from the other room. I told my brother Jimmy not to run in there but he did, and one of them cut his throat. Jist turnt from stuffing my mamma's locket from Grandma Dyson into this sack he had and give Jimmy one swipe with the knife and went back to work. I run out the back. That was in Memphis," the boy said in his dead voice. "So I come down here to git away from things going on in Memphis. Met up with two coloreds. They and me stuck together a couple months and it was going pretty good till they got liquored and knifed each other. Laid there side to side and slashing away, too drunk to knowed they was dying. I met this gal maybe eighteen and said, 'Hey, you and me, let's stick together,' and she said it was okay with her, only when my back was turnt, she went and shot me in the leg. Bullet went in the calf one way, come out another. Got fever from it and I'm still some gimpy." Mister Touch couldn't see him shrug. "Met more people like her. No good come of it. Reckon I'm gonna tell you, sir, 'cause it don't matter what people know or don't." He paused.

"I'm waiting."

"Thing is, I don't like nobody no more and don't figure to."

"Will you come along with us?"

"I'd be obliged, but it don't mean I like you. I jist be moving on from Vicksburg."

"You've given up on people?"

"Yes sir. I have. I give up on them."

Across the road Stitch banged down the last hood on his vehicle inspection.

Mister Touch explained the rules to the boy. "And we don't use our old names. I'll give you a new one."

"Don't mind what you call me."

So the boy had survived another battle of Vicksburg, but at the sad cost of zest for life. Mister Touch couldn't think of a name to go with that cheerless, hopeless voice so devoid of emotion. At last, with a helpless wave of his hand, Mister Touch said, "I name you No Name."

41

NEXT MORNING, as the caravan was being loaded, three Skull women came rushing up to the lead car with bad news: Evil Eye was missing!

A womanhunt began the likes of which Vicksburg, Mississippi, had never seen: gaudily dressed whites and blacks searching high and low through a town of skeletons for a black girl who would never have left New York City for anything, except to save Number One's life.

Mister Touch asked for The Fierce Rabbit. When they met in

front of the Magnolia Motel, the main man said, "We haven't spoken much lately."

"You got that right," said The Rabbit.

"But I understand you know Evil Eye pretty well."

"Yeah?"

"Do you have any idea where she might have gone?"

"Don't ask me. Dumped her days ago. I be looking now for a woman who know how to treat a man right."

"It sounds as though you didn't part amicably."

"What?"

"She went away mad."

"Man, I don't know how she went away or what and I don't give one flying fuck neither."

After an entire day of calling her name and rummaging through empty rooms, the Skulls sat down disconsolately and contemplated the loss of still another club member. No one knew better than the prez how this sometimes worked. From the first days of the Skulls he had seen it happen: someone joined up and seemed happy and then out of the blue just wandered off, drawn away by memory and secret despair, pulled toward a final solitude and death by the powerful magnet of guilt for having survived. It was a way of being OOTLO. What made it so dangerous was the lack of symptoms; you couldn't get hold of such a person and say, "Here, we can handle this," because by that time the person was gone for real.

"You're doing it," Spirit said, putting her arm around his shoulder as they sat in deck chairs on the lawn of the Magnolia Motel. "You're taking it all on your shoulders. You can't help it if Evil Eye decided to give up on the Skulls."

"There was a time I ruined lives. I orchestrated takeovers that left people jobless, without dignity. I never lost a night's sleep. I was a player and proud of it. There wasn't room in the game for sentiment. But I won't sleep tonight, wondering where in the hell Evil Eye is. Don't get me wrong. I haven't become a hearts-and-flowers guy, and I never will. I'd never trust anyone who bragged about caring. But yes, I'm taking it all on my shoulders because IRT taught me how to do that, and I'm stuck with it."

"It hurts to see you low."

Someone who wasn't low was Yo Boy, who came whistling up to

The Fierce Rabbit in a Wild Bunch T-shirt, black Spandex tights, Reeboks, on his left wrist a Patek Philippe manual-wind watch with mesh bracelet band in 18-karat gold which sold for fourteen thousand dollars before tax and on his head an oversized fedora with a wide felt brim. A step behind him, whistling the same tune, was Wishbone in jeans and a cotton shirt, smelling tremendously of Prince Matchabelli's Hero.

"Like old times," declared Yo Boy, sitting beside The Fierce Rabbit on a sidewalk bench in downtown Vicksburg.

"What old times?"

"When tight partners get together and ponga le for a brother cholo."

"What in the hell you trying to say?"

Yo Boy smiled at The Old Man. "What El Viejo say do, we done it."

"Which was what?" asked The Rabbit impatiently.

"We done her, the smart-ass whore like you say. Do we ponga le, Wishbone, or do we?"

Wishbone grinned.

"She was looking in this store window," explained Yo Boy, pushing the fedora back. "I hold a blade behind her on the kidney, tip of it, a boss-move my brother taught me please-the-Blessed-Virgin-may-his-soul-rest-in-peace, and I push a little so she just feel it there, and I say, 'Come on, gran puta, party time.' She go where I tell her and we move her out over to this parking lot near some cliff and beat her good and then me and Wishbone both have her and then he cut her throat and we dump her over the cliff there so far down there nobody gonna find her body the next two hundred years."

The Fierce Rabbit scratched his head. "Let me run that one past me again. You two did *that?*" Having slit the throat of a dying Dragon during the Club House raid, he had a vivid personal memory of how it was done and what it felt like and what it looked like and the sound it made too. Wasn't no work for wannabes, he figured. Work for gangbusters. He stared at the two kids who came no higher than his armpits.

"You say ponga le," declared Wishbone proudly, "we do it."

"You being El Viejo," added Yo Boy.

The Fierce Rabbit turned and squared his body so he could study both boyish faces as closely as possible.

The Fierce Rabbit had never heard of Henry Fitz-Empress, King of England, or of Thomas Becket, Archbishop of Canterbury, nor did he know that the king, weary of the man of God's opposition to his ecclesiastical policies, had thoughtlessly uttered a curse against those false varlets who had failed to rid the kingdom of such an insolent fellow. And surely The Fierce Rabbit lacked knowledge of what happened next. Fired by what they took to be a royal command, four knights rode out from Bures and murdered Thomas Becket on the steps of the Canterbury altar. If parallels existed between the experience of Henry II and The Fierce Rabbit, there were also significant divergences. Told of the consequences of his thoughtless outcry against a former intimate, The Fierce Rabbit did not weep or beg forgiveness, as Henry had done in similar circumstances, or call for sackcloth strewn with ashes, nor did he walk barefoot over cobblestone or bare his back to penitential scourgings at the hands of indignant monks, no, not The Fierce Rabbit.

After thinking a while longer, he grinned. "Ain't saying I told you do it, but ain't saying you did wrong doing it. Serve the bitch right." The more he thought of the pure justice of it, the broader he grinned.

"You sure be cool dudes," he told his henchmen, who gave him the hard proud look of falcons home from the kill.

They were driving at a slow but steady pace when some Neat Lookers spotted a man fishing on the bank of one of those interminable Louisiana streams.

.——. .—. . .——.

. —.——

The caravan halted.

Without missing a cast, the tall skinny man in overalls waved pleasantly at them. Even when Skulls approached warily, the fisherman kept flipping the line across the water. A fly at its end settled on the surface like something tremulously alive. Gathering along the bank, Skulls watched silently until the water rippled, the line grew taut, and the limber nine-foot rod bent into a long shivering arc.

Not until he had landed the bronzed smallmouth bass did the fisherman turn to the crowd and proudly doff his ragged felt hat with brightly colored zonkers and hellgrammites and hard-bodied poppers stuck into it, ready for instant use on a line. He murmured, "How do."

Squatting on the bank, he talked easily. He wanted them to know how the fishing was. Told them he didn't care too much for the fishing hereabouts, although right here where he was casting there was a good current split. He pointed to a long linear ripple in the stream. That was the margin between fast water where bass got food and slack water where they rested. He made a few short casts — better than long ones that take time to be retrieved (as if he didn't have time) — on his 8-weight bug taper line with a Wooly Bugger fly. Spit a big wad of baccy and said, "That V 70 thing was good for something all right. Good for fish." He had a large Adam's apple that pumped up and down when he talked, which fascinated some of the bloods who were too awed by the old geezer to make fun of it. They stood quietly and listened. No more sludge, he said; it used to give fish sores and ruin their gills. But even after two years a lot of fish were still stunted from the chemicals them damn textile people had emptied into the streams round about. But catches were getting big. Caught 135 bass in one day last week. Kept two for eating, threw the others back. But it goes to show what letting a stream build itself up can do. He was mightily pleased to meet nice folks after all this time, he said graciously. Time was when he welcomed getting away from Doris, always nagging at him, and from the younguns, always pulling his shirttail for something, but they were all gone now, God give them peace, and so he had probably fished enough for a while. Been fishing for two solid years, he guessed, seven days a week.

One helluva vacation, he admitted with a grin. Asking where the Skulls were headed, he scratched his armpits and told the blind man it sounded pretty good to him. "Reckon I might could tag along?"

Mister Touch had no objection, surely to someone healthy enough and skillful enough to catch over a hundred fish in a day. There was no need to draw the man aside and ask about his life. Doubtless it was a history of fishing rods and well-stocked streams and favorite lures. In between had been menial work and the acquisition of a family that had prevented him from fishing all day every day — so nothing much to speak of there.

On the spot, seized by inspiration, Mister Touch named him Gator.

The fisherman nodded happily. "Gator. Hell's bells, better than the name I got. Used to trap gators with a wire snare looped on the end of a pole. Keep the snout shut with your shoe, tape it, then hogtie the legs. Meat from a ten-footer could fetch five hundred dollar. Yessiree, Gator's a good name."

Into Car Eleven he climbed smelling of bass, weeds, and his own unwashed body — fished the water, didn't bathe in it — and so without fuss the Skulls had acquired a fisherman.

Early morning.

Some of the Skulls began to stir in their bedrolls. They awoke alongside the road with dew on their noses, hearing around their urban cars the quonk of frogs, the chirp of crickets, the quack of wood ducks. A few Skulls went down to the edge of a pond, its surface the color of molten lead in the faint light, and they saw a great blue heron with one leg sculpturally poised over the scummed water. Above the hardwood trees they squinted at a glittering film of dust, glowing red from soil ladened with iron oxide. A flying squirrel startled them, leaping from sweet gum to shortleaf pine. They slogged through pepper grass, sour dock, milkweed. Someone said they were like in a Paul Newman movie where this convict from a chain gang gets loose and is cutting through swamp with police dogs baying in the distance. It was weird everywhere they looked. A burst of sunlight illuminated a dappled, half-sunken log on which a red-eared turtle sat like a gnarled knot, like one of Shy Guy's pint-sized Atlas hands. They returned to the cars, having been lost awhile in a primeval world reigned over by woodpeckers, coachwhip snakes, and mourning doves.

All of the Skulls were awake now, moping and grumbling in the hot moist morning, licking their lips, wishing as they had done for the last two years that a hot bagel, liberally buttered, would miraculously appear, a glass of chilled orange juice, maybe some crisp bacon, and how about a Dannon yogurt for health.

Over a few fires people like Swear To God and Black Pixie, those staunch and uncomplaining scullions, were boiling water for instant coffee. They'd travel on that this morning and some candy bars.

Then through the willows came tall Gator, face florid from weathering, his thin shanks shuffling in faded overalls. He was grinning from a mouth more gap-toothed than Snow's. Across his shoulder was slung a thick cord on which at least twoscore fish had been strung: bluegill, largemouth black bass, yellow perch, brown trout, lots of smallmouths, and three eels almost two feet long. In his bony hand he carried his tackle box and rod.

"Found myself a nice crick a ways back in there," he announced, throwing the catch on the ground.

Skulls stared at the silvery bodies that would be their breakfast.

"Got to have an eye fer water," Gator observed proudly. "Specially fer bottom water. Bottom fish is real good. Cat's a good bottom fish, so is speckled and brown trout. What I eat best is perch. What I fish best is black bass caught the way we caught them when we was kids. On a bamboo pole with a cork bobber." Pulling his rumpled hat with flies and spinners attached to it down over his forehead, he sat against a tree. And while the cooking fires were stoked, he played mumblety-peg with an old knife and told any Skull who came along, "For lures I was using Rebel crayfish plugs and Heddon Tiny Torpedoes and buzzbait spinners for the largemouths. Real nice crick back in there a ways."

They couldn't have been happier with their new acquisition. Someone raced back to the truck that carried Stay High's partial library and rummaged through old books until he found *The Compleat Angler* by Izaak Walton. He rummaged through it until finding what he had tried to remember: "God never did make a more calm, quiet, innocent recreation than angling." And he found, "As no man is born an artist, so no man is born an angler." That sure applied. And he found, "Time is but the stream I go a-fishing in."

Gator wasn't too impressed by OOTHI quotations. (Had he known of it, he would have subscribed to Emerson's "I hate quotations, tell me what you know.") But he liked attention. And when Pretty Puss, who had shown exceptional talent for barbering, gave him a haircut, Gator beamed with pleasure. His stringy gray hair was higher than his ears now, something Doris would have approved of.

And he had the first manicure of his entire life. Snow came down from her tenth-floor apartment on Fifth Avenue and gave it to him. Snow had become a gap-toothed manicurist, working for the people. Her boss was Pretty Puss, the Dalton School miss whom Snow had once castigated for betraying The Party of Opposition by becoming the Skull Barber — after all, Pretty Puss had persuaded her to eschew Republicanism for the big L; and until an abscessed tooth taught her otherwise (in this life you need help no matter what you believe), Snow had swung beyond Liberal to Radical and had come to believe that socialist principles were everything, even if they led to anarchy. Born again through removal of a tooth, Snow had swerved back to middle ground where, according to her own enthusiastic admission, she had discovered democracy and friendship. All those years of watching expert manicurists do her nails in the chic salons of Madison Avenue enabled Snow to teach herself manicuring; and after only a few mistakes (she practiced on old ten-year-old Golden Girl, who squeaked but thrice) she could do a set of hands without drawing blood.

Gator turned his own around in front of his eyes, staring at the immaculate nails as if they were newfangled spinners, and murmured, "I'll be goldern."

A new star named Gator might have risen in the Skull firmament had he not chosen to slip away two days later in Monroe. The thing was he had heard long ago that the fishing was pretty good a few miles north of there. Now that people had let the fish hereabouts breed up awhile there might could be some awful good holes. He couldn't leave this land of bayous and creeks, not even for companionship, because his true companion awaited him among the weeds under the banks of warm streams, impatient to judge how good his casting was for real, how lifelike he had fashioned his flies from peacock quills, cock hackles, and starling wing feathers, ready to reward him by taking the bait or to chastise him by swimming on.

In his haste Gator did not even say goodbye, but set out with rod and tackle box long before dawn, hoping to get north of Monroe in time to find himself good water, maybe even a current split, before the fish started to bite.

42

THE MAIN MAN, sitting in sunlight during a stop, heard coming.

"It's Helen," Sag said from above him. "Can I talk to you?"

He heard going as his Spirit left.

"Well," said Sag, "I got a good look this time. That diamond you gave her —"

"— As big as the Ritz."

"— Almost as big as that vulgar thing Richard Burton gave to Elizabeth Taylor although considering the jewelry store where you got yours it's probably fake or flawed. But I didn't come here to discuss your personal life. This new boy called No Name —"

"I know." He had already heard that the funereal boy never smiled, his forlorn face moving like a reminder of mortality through the Skull ranks.

"It was a mistake to bring him along," declared Sag.

"A worse mistake not to."

"You see, you accepted an obligation when you forced these people to take such an awful trip. Your duty is to them, not to strays you find along the way who add nothing, but take away our hope, like that boy does." She took a deep rasping breath that he could hear down to his toes. "People aren't happy. They want their own names. They want a say in what happens. That nice Italian boy, for example, is devastated. He's so unhappy —"

"You mean Riot?"

"Angelo."

"Riot's never got over losing his girlfriend."

"Because of that gang war that should have been avoided."

"How?"

"Through negotiation. You should see Angelo's face," Sag said. In her zeal she had no idea how malicious that sounded. "There are more OOTLO every day —"

"I didn't know that, I never heard that," he said, irked.

"Because you're isolated from the truth. Tyranny feeds on ignorance."

"What do you really want? My job?"

"A say. That's what we all want. That and our rightful names. Things that can give us a sense of life as it was."

"Life as it was? First we have to get through life as it is."

"In oppressive countries it was always wait for this, wait for that, then you'll have rights."

"Aren't you —" He was going to say "overreacting," but thought better of it and said nothing. While Sag was talking, he had been thinking, Ah, she's right, that's how it should be: everyone having a say. But IRT was leaning over his shoulder, whispering, "Go on and get that bunch to Arizona, then maybe do some thinking about civil rights and who scratching whose back, which is the politics of leisure time, bro."

So Mister Touch said, "Aren't you forgetting we have no police force, no goon squad? People who don't like the way things go around here can leave. Now. This instant. As apparently Evil Eye did."

Going.

And coming.

"It's me," said a woman's voice. "Sweet Thing."

Ah, yes, the misnamed medical technician who wanted Jesus Mary's job. A dulcet voice, a mean heart. He hadn't talked to her in weeks.

He didn't talk now either, but sat back and listened while she explained why Jesus Mary Save Souls should be removed from the field of medical care. Not that the young Irishwoman was incompetent, Sweet Thing said. She was simply so preoccupied with one patient, namely the newcomer named Harold, that there wasn't room in her day for anyone else. Considering the communal needs for competent health care, Sweet Thing believed it would be better for everyone, including the little Irishwoman and her favorite patient, if the Skull Medical Service were immediately reorganized.

Finally Mister Touch spoke. "Thank you for your input," he said.

"I didn't mean anything against her," Sweet Thing said sweetly.

"Of course not. Who among us knowing what she's done for us these last two years could possibly badmouth Jesus Mary? So thank you. If we all keep our cool, we'll get to Arizona."

Going.

Coming.

It was a complaint about that other newcomer who never smiled. "He getting me low."

"How does he do that?"

"Don't know how, but he do. I be getting out of OOTLO lately, but he putting me right back in."

Perhaps it was true: the cheerless wake left by No Name wherever he walked was drowning the Skulls in a lachrymose mood of new depression. Yet he was the healthiest male in the club, probably the strongest next to Africa. He had seen his family murdered in Memphis and in a grotesque replay of Civil War horror had spent the best part of his adolescence in Vicksburg under siege, hiding from armed drunks. Instead of enjoying the discoveries of a normal teenager, he had holed up in a motel room and functioned like a nursing home inmate who hangs on to life from habit. Through his Spirit and Hoss the main man let it be known that he'd welcome suggestions for helping their new brother get a smile back.

After the marriage of the main man and a New York cabby, Mystique magnanimously divided her need for revenge equally between them. Since it took two to tango or get married, the fault was as much the man's as the woman's. They both deserved to suffer, and yet Mystique failed to derive satisfaction from this reasonable conclusion. Unfortunately, she was also having a new nightmare in which Mister Touch, not the spying slut, managed to punish her. It also dealt with a runaway car — a measure of her obsession with her two past failures. In this nightmare she got into the lead car beside the only man she had ever truly loved. He called out "Spirit" on the assumption that the person now at the wheel was The Dragon Lady. Releasing the brake, Mystique allowed the car to start down a steep hill. Her idea was to jump out once it was going fast enough, but when she opened the door and scooted out from behind the wheel, a bracelet on her arm got caught on the stick shift or her foot got trapped under the accelerator, so that together they went roaring down the hill, heading for a cement wall. At the very last instant she saw from the corner of her eye that the unrepentant bridegroom had managed to get his own door free and was jumping to safety.

The fantasy of defeat notwithstanding, Mystique had no intention of giving up. She had put aside Plan B, which entailed some kind of vague rebellion involving the men who owed her their allegiance, and moved on to Plan C, which depended solely upon her own performance. To implement Plan C she had to befriend Spirit. Mystique had observed that the slut was fascinated by baby Rattler and sometimes diapered the kid for Coco. During a couple of stops, when the main man was elsewhere, Mystique had ambled up to The Dragon Lady to make conversation about the kid. "I understand Rattler has started to talk," Mystique began with a smile. "That is, he makes a sound like 'da' or 'ga,' which some people are calling the word 'father.' "

When The Dragon Lady smiled skeptically, Mystique said, "Soon the kid will be talking for real. We'll have to provide for his education," she said, emphasizing "we."

"What about Stay High?"

"Would you want that guy for a kindergarten teacher?"

When The Dragon Lady laughed, Mystique laughed too, conspiratorially. She was setting it up.

One night when the caravan stopped in a Louisiana town, the sort of opportunity that Mystique had hoped for came along: having consumed too much of Cancer Two's greasy paprika-ladened squirrel stew, Coco had an upset stomach and needed someone to care for the baby. That would get The Dragon Lady out of the way for a while. But Mystique's luck went further — crossing the motel lawn, she saw the slut with a couple of warm Cokes in her hand. Yelling out before the bride could get back to the bridal chamber, Mystique intercepted her. She explained Coco's plight. "The thing is," she lied, "I've been in the dispensary all day and I'm bushed. I wonder —"

"Of course I'll take care of the baby," said the slut with such good will that Mystique felt nauseated. "I'll just go tell him."

"You go on to the dispensary," Mystique took the Cokes from her. "I'll drop by your room and tell your husband."

Their eyes met, until The Dragon Lady averted hers in a doggy capitulation to superior strength — in Mystique's opinion.

But what The Dragon Lady said wasn't altogether the stuff of surrender. "I'm glad we're able to talk, but I know you don't like me. I know you can't like me. I can't really like you either. But we're traveling a long way, we need to get along."

"Exactly how I feel," claimed Mystique with a tight smile.

She turned and watched The Dragon Lady walk toward the mobile dispensary. The slut was no fool, Mystique decided gloomily, but she had just made a big mistake. Hadn't anyone taught her never to leave a man unprotected, even if he was a saint, which this tall lovable Blindie surely was not?

Walking rapidly to the motel room which was serving as the bridal chamber, Mystique turned the knob and boldly walked in.

The only man she had ever loved was lying, all seventy-seven inches of him, naked on a rumpled bed, staring at the ceiling with a silly smile on his face, one familiar to Mystique from her experience of sexually satisfied men.

"What you read me," he said, "I remember. John Donne must have been some kind of guy: 'Full nakedness! All joys are due to thee, as souls unbodied, bodies unclothed must be, to taste whole joys.' My naked Spirit!" The main man moved his hands sensually through the air, like playing an invisible piano. 'License my roving hands, and let them go before, behind, between, above, below.' "

By the end of this recitation Mystique had thrown off all her clothes and was climbing into bed beside him. She felt him move instantly down her body, his red beard faintly tickling her breasts belly the insides of her thighs, preparing to zero in. Mean-spiritedly she was appreciating the fact that he had never gone down on her so quickly, so enthusiastically, when the beard stopped tickling her, and he pulled back.

"Who is this? Mystique?"

"Look, before you say anything," Mystique said, managing to slip her arms around him and bury her head against his shoulder, "you're the man I can trust to make a difference —"

"Mystique," he said, pushing her away.

She came back at him, murmuring desperately against his cheek, "Lover, listen, forgive me for this, but I had to see you, I had to give you one more chance, I had to help you see what a fool you're making of yourself because the woman's no good" — Mystique was scooting her hand around at his groin, appalled to discover him as limp as underdone bacon — "because she's just using you to save herself — Please!"

But he had pulled free for real and was climbing out of the bed.

In his haste he smashed against the wall, stunning himself sufficiently to slump down.

Mystique, alarmed, went around to him.

When she touched his shoulder, Mister Touch said coldly, "No, go away, leave me alone."

Mystique straightened up and looked at his long white body like one of Gator's bass hanging from a line. That hanging image shot through her mind like a bullet of vengeance.

"Leave you alone? All right, I'll leave you alone. And you'll live to regret it, believe me. I meant what I said. I'll never let you go because I know in my heart we belong together and nothing on earth, certainly not a sluttish whoring spy, is going to change that, no matter what you say or believe. Leave you alone? I'll *never* leave you alone! *Never!*" By this time she had thrown her clothes back on. Stepping over to the stunned man, Mystique said, "You will live to regret this. I gave you another chance to see the light. Now it is *war!*"

And Mystique flounced out as if she had just righteously scorned the advances of one of her recruited dummies.

Late the next afternoon, while Steady Breathers were building a campfire in the town square of Ruston, Louisiana, Hoss came to Mister Touch with E.Z.

"E.Z. says the solution to No Name's problem is easy."

"Do you tire of people making fun of your name?" Mister Touch asked E.Z.

"Sure do. Don't know what got into IRT when he naming me."

"Well, let me hear what your solution is."

"What that boy need is a woman."

Spirit, sitting beside the main man, said, "That sounds reasonable."

"I knows the boy need that," continued E.Z. "I seen it in his eyes when he be looking at ladies and they don't know it. But I don't gotta see his face to know."

"I don't quite understand," said Mister Touch.

"I mostly tell what a man thinking from his walk. Like when he be thinking of ladies, he kind of gets his neck scrunched up and his feet turn out and he go along slow. I tell what a man want from his walking. That boy walking like he be in need."

Mister Touch thanked her for her input, taking it seriously, because E.Z. was experienced, if not altogether easy. "Who is going to volunteer pro bono publico?" he asked.

"Huh?"

"For the public good."

"Later," the pretty black girl said in goodbye.

In the morning E.Z. was knocking on the door of the Ernie and Enid Faraday two-story house on Main Street, her broad face gleaming like iron in the early light. Spirit came to the door, rubbing her eyes.

"Got a nice girl for the kid," E.Z. said proudly. "Standing right over there."

From the bed Mister Touch said, "Have you explained what's expected of her?"

"Leaving that to The Powers That Be."

As they dressed, Mister Touch asked his Spirit, "Who is it?"

Peering through the open window at someone across the street, his Spirit said, "Sweet Walk."

"What do you think?"

"Sweet Walk would be perfect."

"I think maybe you should talk to her."

Spirit laughed. "You'd never be a player."

"I think you mean pimp."

"That's what I mean." She went across the street to Sweet Walk.

After a while Spirit returned. "Sweet Walk says it's okay with her."

"Does she like him?"

"I asked her that. She seemed puzzled by the question."

"Pro bono publico. If she's willing, she's willing. Tell everyone," said Mister Touch, "we'll be staying here awhile. I'm not going to leave until No Name rises from the dead."

A few hours later, Mister Touch was rocking on the creaky porch of the general store with his Walkman on, playing Debussy, when he felt a tug at his sleeve.

"Here comes Black Pixie," his Spirit told him.

"Is she wearing stockings and a flowery hat and a red dress?"

"Because she's waiting for a big black buck to come along and take her out of this mess?" Spirit laughed. "Yes, she is."

Coming heavily up the porch steps.

"Me, Mister Touch. Black Pixie has got something to say."

"Is Cancer Two putting more paprika in the stew again?"

"Huh," she blew out her breath. "That man got Hungarian blood in him that cause him to do like that. When we not looking, he be shaking more of that stuff in. Swear To God saw him do it twicet yesterday."

"Yes, I tasted it."

"Something else I gotta tell you."

Coming to the rocker, Black Pixie leaned so close that Mister Touch could feel her breath on his face. She told him she had heard something weird while strolling at the edge of town. It was the putt-putt sound of a motorbike. It reminded her of the Honda that Turok and Flash rode one afternoon into enemy territory and never came back on. "Remember?" she asked the main man, who could never forget. It was the sound of an engine like that, she declared. When she had looked down this dirt road, a thing was moving like down another road behind a lumber yard, so she didn't have more than a second, but it was long enough for her to see a bike with someone on it. Wearing a crash helmet.

"Keep it to yourself," the main man told her.

"I do jist that." Then Black Pixie backed off and sauntered away like she had just announced dinner.

When she was gone, he reached out and instantly felt his Spirit's hand in his. "What do you think?" he asked.

"Maybe someone lives around here and has a bike."

"With a crash helmet? For a jaunt through a town like this? If you spit in any direction, it lands outside the village limits — that's what Hoss says. Someone's following us."

"Why?"

"That's the question. All we have worth stealing is Jesus Mary. But she doesn't go around in starched white and a winged cap, so who would know she's a nurse?"

"At least the rider rode off without killing someone."

He felt her hand tighten in his. "Wait, what's this?" she whispered. "It's Sweet Walk." Her voice held a touch of awe. "She's walking down the middle of the street."

"Is No Name around?"

"He's leaning against a wall." She added, "Looking dead."

"Does he see her?"

"Not yet. He's staring into space. But he will. He can't miss seeing her. Sweet Walk is seeing to it he'll see her." Spirit's voice turned merry. "He's looking in her direction. I suppose because everyone else is too. That gal is looking good. He sees her all right. His head's going back and forth like he's watching a tennis match."

"What do you mean?"

"He's watching her hips move."

Mister Touch tried to locate Sweet Walk in his memory. A steady-breathing good-looking Chinese girl, who wore jeans and chewed gum and had high school classmates who ran numbers for the Tong lords. Sweet Walk had an imagination limited to one plus one equals two. Before V 70 Struck she had taken accounting in the hope of becoming a bookkeeper and saving enough money for a sports car. She was as practical about sex as about money. She had erotic skills and a willingness to use them. When Sweet Walk walked, her slim body moved on invisible ball bearings, smooth, if metallic. As a dozen Skull males could attest, she gave and took pleasure like a cashier gives and takes money — no hangups, no regrets, no memories. Mister Touch carried with him a mental image of a pretty face and cold brown eyes.

"She's talking to him," whispered Spirit.

"Where are they?"

"In front of the hardware. He's still leaning against its wall. She's standing in front of him."

"What's she wearing?"

Spirit giggled. "Appropriate for the occasion. Hiphuggers. A shirt with the tails tied above the navel. Frankly I'm glad you can't see it. And no bra. Obviously."

"Good," said Mister Touch. In imagination he took the scene from there. What must the sight of her firm breasts and fruity expanse of belly be doing to a teenager who had been living like a hunted old man? She must be shifting from one foot to the other, causing flesh to ripple slightly below the tied shirt, a slight creasing of hip above the belt line. Good girl. She was probably meeting his gaze, but not boldly enough to frighten him off. She must be wetting her lips under his stunned regard to let him know what they promised. Go on, Mister Touch told her in imagination. Act out the universal fantasy of furtive masturbatory boys. She must be pushing him on greased wheels from curiosity to hope to anticipation of the wonderful act, each step of the way satisfying for her too, like adding a column of figures to bring credit and debit into balance. Would there be magic? Anything was possible.

"She's walking away," reported Spirit. "She's stopping and looking back. What a navel. And those jeans are so tight I can't believe she'll ever get out of them — even if he helps her. People are watching from the corner, from doorways, from windows along the street." After a pause, she added happily, "He's following her."

"Good!"

"He's . . . at her side."

And so with her melon breasts and mango buttocks, Sweet Walk walked the boy into an abandoned house (the main man had ordered any skeletons removed from there so as not to disturb them), and they remained inside for the day, that night, the next day, the next night, and emerged the following morning with their clasped hands swinging.

The patient Skulls, having been keenly and vociferously obscene throughout the long wait, were awed into respectful silence when the couple appeared. Not a crude word was yelled at them, but someone shyly asked, "Hey, how you doing?"

No Name merely replied, "Okay." But he smiled for the first time.

"Well?" asked Mister Touch anxiously.

Spirit took his hand. "He's smiling."

"Tell me how she looks too."

"Changed. Soft." Spirit added, "Very soft."

"You mean fucked out."

"I mean something more. She looks like a girl is supposed to look in the last paragraph of a Harlequin romance."

And so Sweet Walk had sweet-walked herself into No Name's life for real, where she strolled around leisurely with her hips rolling and her cute buttocks quivering succulently like (said a Skull who shall be nameless) lemon mousse being carried in on a dessert plate at the end of a long and satisfying meal. She might well perambulate erotically through his existence for as long as they both should live. That's what Spirit suggested.

It had really happened then, the main man thought in wonder. It had happened between a spiritless boy and a businesslike girl, as it had happened between a harassed blind man and an outcast woman. Magic. There was no accounting, he thought, for the sudden leap of energy across two bodies, and no stopping it, not even in a world of skeletons.

This event would go down in the History of the Skulls as The Seduction Of No Name, when Mister Touch could secretly record it on Tape Eleven. He said the seduction had made everyone happy.

But Mystique was not happy.

After considerable soul-searching, Mister Touch had also recorded The Night The Main Man Said No To Sex. He did this in the interest of providing a full and candid account of executive activities during his tenure as President of the Skulls. But what he was willing to report to Whoever You Are, he kept secret from his Spirit in the interest of maintaining peace on the journey.

43

THEN THERE WAS The Dorcheat Bayou Disaster.

The day began beautifully in northern Louisiana: fleets of cirrocumulus clouds sailing through a sky designated by Payback as 9 on a seaman's visibility scale.

But before reaching Minden, the sky did a number on them. Got gray, sullen, mean-spirited, and as rapidly as Doctor Jekyll into Mister Hyde the cirrocumulus flotilla transformed itself into cumulonimbus turrets and anvils, heavy-bottomed, muscular, in a hurry.

Just west of Minden, while the lead car was passing a yardful of ornate birdbaths for sale but not one sold these last few years, the storm broke. Thunder, lightning. Overhead wheeled a turkey buzzard, its crimson head thrust forward as its broad wings defiantly beat against the terrific current before surrendering to Mother

Nature, thundering down to vanish in the trees. Thunderhead after thunderhead had a chance at the moving column, dumping hogsheads of rain on the road ahead. Despite the steamy heat, which fogged the windshields, people rolled the windows up to keep rain from pouring in.

"Should I stop?" asked Spirit In The Dark.

The main man could not, of course, see how bad the storm was, but to be frank he could hear it: a ferocious clatter against roof and windshield, as if enormous sluice gates had been opened over their heads. "Go on," he told her. "Stop and we might skid into one another. Just drive through the damn thing. At least there's no oncoming traffic to worry about."

So now we come to Wizard Brown.

He was a Good Looker but a Poor Breather and had been coughing all day, while other occupants of Car Four were talking and laughing, all except Mystique, who had left the supply truck to ride just this one leg of the journey beside Wizard Brown. She eyed him thoughtfully; he seemed a viable candidate for Plan D because he could drive and do little else. He had a cough and insisted on describing it in such graphic terms that Mystique hoped she could win him over without doing more than sitting beside him in the car today. In a high scratchy voice Wizard Brown was saying he felt as if a furry little animal were stowed away in his chest, afraid to move, sitting there kind of puffed up and quivering.

Each time Wizard Brown coughed, the animal squeezed against the wall of its hiding place, escaping capture when he tried to dislodge it. The funny thing was, he was getting so used to it that if the cough went away now he'd feel as if he had lost a pet, like the kitten that had crept under a sofa at home to die dreadfully of cancer.

Wizard Brown was not brown but pale white. Frail, narrow-faced, with a long heavy nose and eyebrows so colorless they seemed hardly to be there, he had never been wizard enough to attract women. Not even his mother had told him he was special. He could fly a kite and he went to church three times a week and at Sunday school had taught the Authorized King James Version of the Bible. When he joined the Skulls, none of the girls started up with him, and since he didn't know how to start up with them, Wizard Brown had never made love. He would die a virgin, here in this hot sticky alien land of sluggish rivers and cottonmouth moccasins, because at a bridge spanning the Dorcheat Bayou, which ran dark and deep between bald cypress and flooded loblolly, he had a violent coughing fit. And in a split second some remembered words from OOTHI seemed to push up through his throat into his mouth, " 'O, I'll leap up to my God! Who pulls me down?' " as he began skidding. In reaction he jammed his foot down hard on the accelerator, rushing past the preceding car like a launched rocket (reminiscent of Ace's mad dash for a different reason into Chesapeake Bay).

He tore through a rotten guard rail at the approach to the bridge. The car plummeted over the embankment, ramming into the dark blue bayou with a deafening impact, and Wizard Brown sank slowly through the waters of his time; and the time of Mystique, who had changed vehicles to her disadvantage; and the time of Do It To It, who would no longer read recipes to Chief Chef Cancer Two; and the time of deejay Sunoco, who loved Bird and Trane and Miles although the ancient blood of China ran in his veins; and the time of Wise Ass, whom his idol The Fierce Rabbit had called "the dumbest nigger I ever seen."

Gone in a moment.

Caught in OOTHI'S "enchafed flood."

Two with broken necks — having been rolled around like raffle stubs in a tumbler — the others struggling with rolled-up windows.

The caravan had slowed to a halt, forgetting the Payback System, each vehicle for itself, skidding and sliding but not following Car Four into the bayou. Soon people were standing at the bridge rail, peering through what was becoming a misty drizzle at the muscular surface of a stream that seemed placid enough now, although moments earlier it had been roiled by a huge metal object hitting at it.

"Tell me, tell me," Mister Touch muttered, while the back seat of Car One emptied out, leaving him alone with his Spirit. He gripped her arm so hard she winced. "It's bad, isn't it? It's really bad?"

"A car ... just ... ," she stammered, ". . . disappeared."

"Where?"

"Into the water there. It's a small river. The car just ... swerved and went in."

"Gone?"

"Yes, gone."

"Which car?"

When she told him it was Car Four, he ticked off the occupants, unaware that today it had carried a fifth passenger.

"Wizard Brown, Do It To It, Wise Ass, Sunoco. I should have called for a halt until the rain stopped," he said morosely.

Leaning toward him, Spirit said in a low, rapid voice, "Listen to me. Are you listening?"

"Yes."

"You call yourself a survivor, but you don't sound like one. Know why? A survivor says no to guilt. But I guess you middle-class whites learn to feel guilty about anything. Want to lead these people?" When he didn't reply, she said, "I'm asking, do you want to lead these people?"

"Yes."

"Say no to guilt."

From beyond the car he heard the shouted exchanges of false hope among Skulls looking for a miracle. The way his Spirit had just spoken to him reminded Mister Touch of something. Of his mother speaking to his father. "Don't keep blaming yourself," she'd scold when his father's football team lost a game. His mother could shrug off failure and go to the next thing, but his father worried it like a dog worries a bone.

"Are you angry?" Spirit asked, putting her hand to his cheek.

He didn't tell Spirit her voice had merged with his mother's. But he felt the guilt leaving him — it whooshed out like air from a balloon. "Remember a TV ad where a guy gets slapped and he says, 'Thanks, I needed that'?"

"Sure. Are you telling me what I said was okay?"

"I needed that. I need you."

"It's what I always wanted — someone to love who needed me."

Their hands entwined, they heard Skulls murmuring through a steady drizzle, continuing the search.

"No sign of the car?" the main man asked after a few more minutes.

"It must be at the bottom of the mud."

"Look!" someone yelled.

Skulls were leaning over the opposite side of the bridge, under which the Acura Legend sedan with the 161-horsepower 2.7-liter

V-6 engine (described to onlookers in an elegiac voice by Stitch, who had kept the car in tiptop condition throughout the journey) had been dragged by the flooded bayou. Thrust up through the water, churned into gumbo by sediment and marsh plants, was a brown hand. It looked like something breaking ground in a plowed field. The hand that came alive to wave frantically must have been five yards past the bridge, then maybe another five before someone hurtled through the air — it was the Swedish aerobic instructor Tangy — fully clothed but barefoot, her blond hair fanned out like a ragged halo before she hit the water.

"Tell me! Tell me!" Mister Touch yelled at his wife.

"Tangy dove in — she's swimming . . . she's . . . got hold of . . . she's . . . it's somebody's arm . . . she's pulling . . . swimming . . . she's . . . almost . . . she's to the bank with . . . people are . . . it's . . . they're pulling someone out . . . it's . . . I . . . I think . . . it's . . . Mystique!"

When people gathered round, all Mystique could hear was their stupid murmuring: "We thought everyone was dead . . . gone . . . lost . . . drowned," which made her smile inwardly in triumph and vindication. Even while trying to spit the mud out of her mouth and to see through a haze of sediment, she knew the truth — it must have been what people call a miracle. Even before ridding herself of the lugubrious images of a bayou horror show, Mystique was thinking, Marked for death, I died. Destiny brought me back, she thought, because it had made a terrible mistake. I haven't yet had my revenge, brought about justice, got my man back, so I have been given another chance.

She heard herself telling a circle of awestruck Skulls how she lost consciousness, then saw something thready like weeds going past and smelled fish. Somehow her hands found the handle and began rolling down the window, and somehow she had wiggled out while water rushed in and somehow she had managed to fight to the surface though she couldn't swim.

"Miracle," someone murmured.

Mystique went along with the gag; in her opinion it was hardly a miracle, it was merely fate. Destiny had a plan for her because she was special. God Himself had opened that window and when she started to wiggle out had given her attractive derrière a push so she wouldn't get stuck and God had yelled in the Swede's ear, "Get your ass in that water, girl, and retrieve the agent of my revenge, who shall go down in history as The Woman Who Never Quit!" Then the car rolled sidelong into the mud, sealing the other occupants in.

A couple of swimmers for real, along with Tangy, dove into the murky bayou, hoping for more wonders, while onlookers paced anxiously along the marshy bank. After a while the divers gave up, accepting fate's offer of one miracle.

So four, not five, Skulls were left behind. They would wait together for the sluggish motion of water to ease them through metal seams, through vents and hoses, until free of their Acura coffin they would drift into the muddy stream and ooze toward spring. When in time they reached it, their potential would wet the black-cherry roots and contribute to sap and help azaleas bloom and at last they would rise through the sweet air in nectar borne homeward by honeybees.

But destiny had not erred in its mathematics. Five Skulls had been scheduled to go that day.

As the caravan pulled out with Tangy and Mystique still smelling of fetid swamp, someone noticed that Baby Jane, who usually sat smiling like OOTLO often did, was dead.

Jesus Mary figured it must have been a heart attack.

What the geriatric nurse didn't know was this. When Car Four sped off the bridge, Baby Jane was sitting alone in another car, unaware of what was going on because for the umpteenth time she was winning Lotto. Just when Mystique lost consciousness (or temporarily died), Baby Jane felt something shove her mind into a small room. She was pressed into a space too small for standing lying sitting, and a key turned in a lock so she couldn't get out, although she pounded and screamed in the worst panic of her life and screamed and pounded until the room, closing in, began to push her into unimaginable positions, one arm behind her neck, her torso twisted with one foot nudging her spine and a knee against her chest, so that every time she screamed it hurt terribly to breathe and it might have continued to hurt her throughout a long dull OOTLO life had not merciful fate stepped in to break down the walls, releasing her spirit into the same swampy air that awaited the dead denizens of the Dorcheat Bayou when they rose out of the water next spring, so that all five comrades would be together in the marshland of Louisiana *saecula saeculorum*.

The Skulls could not cremate Baby Jane's body that day because there was no dry wood around. So the next day, near a small village, they foraged for dry kindling, made a pyre for Baby Jane, and lit it with lighter fluid.

Ironically, Wizard Brown at the bottom of Dorcheat Bayou would have been the appropriate Christian, considering his Sunday school teaching experience, to say the right biblical words over Episcopalian Baby Jane's remains. But while Mister Touch was asking for someone to step forward with words, someone else who shall be nameless stepped forward and repeated words that had been splashed on the Club House wall: "In the name of the Most Merciful God: Praise be to God, the Lord of all Being, the Most Merciful, the Master of the Day of Judgment. Thee do we worship, and of Thee do we beg assistance" — words from the Koran.

Off by himself, out of earshot of the crackling tinder and splitting bone, rocking back and forth as if Someone with a key had wound up a spring inside him, the skullcap set upon his head as firmly as the helmet of a Christian soldier, Eagle was saying Hebrew prayers for the dead.

44

THEY SAY LIGHTNING doesn't strike twice in the same place, but apparently disasters do — that's what the main man was thinking as the caravan pulled into a motel parking lot. What he couldn't see was a sign looming high above the unlit neon corona of the Holiday Inn; on a long metal stalk the round globe that advertised GULF looked like a carnivorous insect searching for prey in the dry depths of the swimming pool.

The sky was clear in the blue glow of dusk, but a few rapid flashes of heat lightning added a sort of mournful coda to the loss of five Skulls in the last twenty-four hours. While everyone else got out of their vehicles to explore the grounds of their motel, the prez remained alone in Car One. He told Spirit that he'd just like to sit awhile; he detected in her answering silence the question, Why?

"I want to get the sound of motors out of my ears. I want to sit awhile in the silence."

Going. Spirit promised to come back for him later. He heard muffled voices without listening to them because his mind was seeing something: the rotted poles of a guardrail giving way, a car tearing through, and over a short embankment and into the placid bayou.

There was a knock against the rolled-up window. The prez leaned across the seat and rolled it down slightly.

"It's Hoss. Whew. Why are you sitting in this heat with the windows rolled up? They've got a sign in the lobby: 'All Guests Are Invited To Attend Our Employees Sunday School Class. Inquire At Front Desk.' I inquired, and I'm definitely attending. Are you all right?"

"Sure."

"Not blaming yourself?"

"Spirit straightened me out about guilt. What I'm feeling now isn't guilt. I think she verbally spanked the guilt out of me."

"She's the best thing ever happened to you." Going.

The main man rolled the window back up. Right now he felt a bit foolish — a blind Moses leading wheezing outcasts to the Promised Land. IRT had tricked him by bringing him to this precise moment, sulking in a parked car on a hot afternoon in Louisiana. It wasn't guilt he felt now, it was embarrassment. He had allowed the little black drummer to sell him a bill of goods — that there was some kind of meaning to the Skulls. And that would imply a cosmic plan, a divine support system, a god. But a god was out. No god worth mentioning would be so stupid and malicious as to destroy a complex experiment like humanity through such an unimaginative holocaust, engineered by revved-up bugs. And no god, not even one of the historical ones who had managed to exterminate untold millions throughout the centuries in the name of God, would have been so squalidly petty as to topple poor Wizard Brown and that carload of surviving innocents into an overgrown pond. It was meaningless, it was dumb, it was what you'd expect from a nasty little third-rate mind.

Coming. A knock on the window.

"It's Stay High."

Great, the main man thought; just what I need.

Stay High was merciful, however. He stayed only a few moments to give a progress report on his two projects. Research on the poem had snagged; he had a few leads but thus far they hadn't led to anything definitive. Work with The Boy Who Doesn't Speak Our Language continued assiduously, but thus far without positive results.

In other words, Stay High had nothing to report.

"Thank you," the prez told him, trying to put a little zest into his voice. "Keep up the good work."

Going.

The main man rolled the window back up; even so, he could hear the powerful voice of their big-chested Chief Chef giving orders. Cancer Two was telling someone to bring the stew pots and braziers over to the swimming pool. They had enough food for a feast tonight. Chico and King Super Kool had knocked off a bunch of squirrels, rabbits, and pheasants today during a long stop.

Mister Touch realized with surprise and dismay that he felt so low he couldn't get out of the car. He sat there paralyzed by The Dorcheat Bayou Disaster and probable disasters to come and the likely prospect of finding nothing out West any better than what they had left back East. He hunched down in the seat, wrapped in the stifling heat of leadership. Then he heard coming, a knock on the window.

"Who is it?"

"Sphinx."

He conjured up the image of a pretty woman in her late thirties with rumpled auburn hair and brilliant gray eyes. IRT had always said of the former art critic, "Keep her in mind when you be looking for sense."

"I have to talk," she said.

"Come in and sit down."

Door opening on driver's side, sound of the seat crinkling.

"My God, it's hot in here," she said.

"Yes, I suppose it is."

"I'm worried," Sphinx began. The plunge of Car Four, she said, seemed to have plunged everyone into a deep depression. As if each and every one of them had gone over the embankment and tumbled into black water. As if every head had knocked against glass and metal like so many beans shaken in a can. It was in the odd nature of a miracle that Mystique had survived; it was almost enough to make you believe in astrology and voodoo and God's will. Sphinx sighed resignedly. Poor people, they had died in water that wasn't even the Atlantic Ocean or Coney Island or Jones Beach, but in an alien soup full of alligators and soft-shell turtles, in a stinking pond strangled by weird-looking cypress roots. They looked awfully like the knobby knees of old men sitting on benches in a steam room — but she couldn't remember who had painted it.

Mister Touch sensed that her depression was as deep as his. He wanted his own fears confirmed, so he said, "Tell me exactly what you think."

This is what she told him. People were starting to believe they were marked for a bad end. They were losing the will to go on. They wanted to quit. Sag and The Fierce Rabbit were putting pressure on their followers. They argued that the caravan should halt right here in Shreveport, here at this motel, before anyone else drowned, because two carloads of Skulls had ended up in water just like lightning striking twice in the same place, and so it was time to call a halt, to give up, to brood, to sit without moving, to weep to yawn to go to sleep.

Mister Touch heard her gasping for breath. "But you don't agree with them," he said.

"No. Do you?"

"It's tempting, of course, but no."

"After dinner," Sphinx said, "let me talk to them."

"All right, fine. Talk to them."

"You sound — tired."

"Oh, a little," he admitted, although the prez knew that what he felt was helpless.

The leather crinkled, a door opened. Then Sphinx said, after a thoughtful pause, "Are you getting out?"

He stiffened, as if she had just asked him was he contemplating suicide.

"Not yet. Spirit will come for me."

At least he rolled down one of the windows. It was a concession to life. And through the open space this is what he heard without earphones on.

"Oh odious obnoxious obligatory ordained outrage!"

"What?"

"Adidas sitting over there. Old butcher boy with that dictionary of his. He on O now."

"Oh."

"You doing it too. Watch out!"

"What's his rap now?"

"Maybe about what happened. Lightning never strike twicet, but it do with us, and it got some low. Got old butcher boy low. Right, Adidas?"

"Originating outside of organizations, openhearted orations often overwhelm objectives or overcome objections."

"Just what in hell do you mean by that? Seem like a lot of O's is saying something."

"Don't know what that mean. But Adidas, he trying to tell it like it is."

"Only opinionated oafs offer otherwise."

Was it possible, Mister Touch wondered, that the demented butcher had overheard his talk with Sphinx and out of the jumble of O's memorized from a pocket dictionary had predicted the outcome of her talk in front of the Skulls tonight? Would this cool lady's speech goose the Skulls into a new orbit of enthusiasm? For Arizona? Or by unforeseen reaction would her words encourage them to quit? Anything was possible after V 70 Struck. In this case Adidas was already a prophet, because he allowed for two results: Sphinx would either help or hinder them in getting to Arizona.

It occurred to the main man that if he didn't leave the car this instant, he might never leave at all. Or he might leave it ignominiously. He might be hauled out of the car by Send Em Back To Africa and Cougar like a cranky old man in a nursing home, arms crossed, deaf to good words, petulant as a spoiled child. And his Spirit would see it all.

That did it.

Mister Touch scooted across the seat with the alacrity of a bad boy escaping punishment, and got the hell out of there.

*   *   *

In their motel room the main man said, "Let's dress for dinner. Sphinx is making a speech tonight. Let's make it an occasion."

So his Spirit put on an ice blue flaring skirt, a plain white cotton blouse, a deep cloche hat pulled firmly down with a purple silk scarf draped rakishly over one shoulder. She described what she was wearing, and after listening critically, her husband said, "You're looking good."

Then she dressed him from things picked up in a Birmingham men's shop: double-pleated white slacks, a burgundy sport shirt, cap-toe oxfords of hand-rubbed boot leather, and a flowery ascot.

"How do I look?" he asked when she had finished decking him out.

"Beautiful."

"Sure, but aside from beautiful?"

"Tall, slim, with good cheekbones, a forehead maybe too broad but that gives you a look of intelligence."

"The look of it is better than nothing."

"Wonderful lips. Straight, full, firm. Kissable."

"If I looked half as good as you say, I'd be just another pretty face. But I know the truth: a beard too red, worry wrinkles at the eyes, a twitch —"

"No twitch!"

"Maybe one's on the way. Who knows? Give me a kiss if I'm so kissable."

She did. This intimacy encouraged her to bring up a touchy subject: Mystique. She asked him what he'd felt when his former girlfriend had been rescued.

"Good. Of course, I felt good. And relieved. And surprised."

"Why surprised?"

"I had no idea she was riding in Car Four."

"Mystique gets around."

"Was she riding with a new boyfriend?" He tried to think of his former girlfriend with someone like Wizard Brown or Wise Ass, but they sure didn't seem to be her type.

"Mark," said Spirit, using his name for real to emphasize the seriousness of what she was saying. "Don't you get it? Mystique wants you back. No matter how many men she gets involved with, only one means anything to her."

"Oh, I doubt that," he scoffed.

"She's been nice to me lately," Spirit said. "It's called infiltration."

"Maybe she's just given up and means to be nice for real." To support his thesis Mister Touch told his Spirit about the night Mystique had come into the room and tried to embrace him. He was not altogether forthright. He merely said that Mystique had tried to embrace him, that he had turned her away.

"You're telling me nothing else happened?"

"I don't like the sound of your voice."

"You hear jealousy and disbelief in it?" Spirit laughed harshly.

"What I told you is true."

"All right," Spirit said, "it's true."

"I didn't know you were the jealous type."

"Mark, sweetheart, most of the women I have ever known were the jealous type. And most of the men never told a complete story to a woman about another woman."

"Shall we leave it at that?"

"Do you love me?"

"I love you. A girlfriend once told me I only gave eighty percent of myself. I think she gave me more credit than I deserved. It was more like sixty percent."

"And now?"

"One hundred percent." When she said nothing in reply, Mister Touch added, "Does that sound corny?"

"Of course it does, and terrific, and we'll leave it at that." She kissed him.

"So we'll leave it at that?"

"We'll leave it at loving each other. That should be enough for anyone." Again she kissed him and held him. He was shocked by the wetness of her cheek. She had been crying.

Pulling away from him, Spirit cleared her throat and said in a businesslike voice, "So what is Sphinx going to say this evening?"

"I don't know. But I hope it's not depressing."

"Anyway, what counts with me is you. And you're just fine."

"Am I?" he asked happily. "Thackeray said, ' 'Tis strange what a man may do, and a woman yet think him an angel.' "

"Did one of your girlfriends read that to you?"

"No," he said, but it had been Mystique who had read *Henry Esmond* to him in bed.

The Skulls ate their stew — heavy on the paprika — seated around the swimming pool. Oil lamps on iron pedestals had been taken from the locker room and were placed around the area, illuminating the diners seated under beach umbrellas at round tables. Adding to the festive atmosphere were real china plates brought from the motel kitchen. At the foot of the rock garden was a small pond in which three goldfish still lived. They had existed for two years without a single flake of TetraMin, living on flies and water beetles like fish for real and keeping properly wet through the generosity of rain clouds rather than the impersonal labor of electric pumps. Skulls stared with respect at the three survivors, because it takes one to know one.

Aside from the goldfish, however, nothing seemed to interest them. They had been brought to the nadir of hope, a black sludge of silence at the bottom of a bayou. They could hear themselves chewing mechanically, haplessly, while a quarter mile away some bullfrogs were bellowing in their bog with joy, an entire generation of them having been spared knowledge of gigantic two-legged creatures with nets.

At the end of the meal, Mister Touch rose and said, "Sphinx would like to tell us something."

Sitting down, he whispered to his Spirit, "How does she look?"

"Dressed for the occasion like us. She's pulled her hair back —"

"— auburn —"

"And tied it with a yellow ribbon. A pink dress, youthful-looking. She's looking good."

"What I'm going to tell you may seem strange," the former art critic began. Both hands nervously clutched a chair back as she stood in front of the pool, facing a crowd stuffed with stew. "But here is the truth," Sphinx declared. "IRT and I were lovers."

There was utter silence until someone yelled, "You was getting it on with *him?*"

"We were lovers. But we kept it secret."

"Whose idea was that?" someone asked.

"His. He had the idea you wouldn't follow him if he took a

white woman for his lover. Too complicated. He used to say, 'Right now we Skulls gotta keep things simple.' It was a contradiction, of course. Racist stuff was out, according to the rules, but according to life it was still in. We both knew it."

Leaning forward in the lamplight, people studied the auburn-haired woman closely. Henceforth, many of the males would see Sphinx as ravishing, desirable, a good ten years younger than she was, an unattainable fantasy.

"So he kept us secret. We had to meet like adulterers. But that's not what I want to tell you about. One afternoon we went up to the eleventh floor of the Club House. Up different stairways. You see, we'd found a nice apartment with a bedroom that had mirrors. Beautiful Victorian mirrors angled around the room so from the bed you could always see yourselves. Well, on this particular day, we were especially intimate. He told me details about his life which I don't intend to share with anyone. But there was one thing I want you to know.

"He described the neighborhood he grew up in. Burned-out buildings, vacant lots overflowing with garbage and broken needles. There was a kind of playground. Kids played basketball there when it wasn't used for other purposes. This particular day he hadn't been chosen for a team — too short — so he sat on a curb and watched some ants going in and out of a crack in the cement. He got more interested in them than in the game. He watched them hauling crumbs of food. They kept at it while the sun shifted across the path and left the sidewalk in shadow. They went in and out all day and he sat there watching long after the other boys had left the playground and the junkies had taken over."

For many, surely for Mister Touch, it was as if IRT was speaking, the syntax and diction and rhythm were his for real.

" 'Now ants. They don't know what they doing, they just be doing it. Go in and out this crack in the sidewalk. Don't mind what the sun doing, don't mind what we doing, don't care about pickup ball, don't care about fun city and taxes and crime and stars overhead. Ants just doing what they do. Now we be smarter — or supposed to be. We got hopes and dreams no ant have. But when you come down to it, we go by the same plan. We get hold of some kind of aim in life and go for it. That's what living supposed to be for any live thing. We go in and out all day long, we got our own crack to go in and out of, and do what we got to do. Don't mean nothing what reason we gives for it, we just do it. Being we lucky enough.' "

Sphinx said that she had asked him what he meant by lucky.

" 'Lucky enough to know we gotta do what we supposed to. Ever see ants not doing what they supposed to? No, cause they be organized. Smarter than us that way. We got a choice like we can say fuck it to going in and out like that. All there is to it. Way it come down is like this: you don't go in and out, you just might curl up then and there, because you be dead but don't know it yet. You figure you got faked out. Truth be you fake yourself out. You give yourself bad luck by not getting down there to some crack in the sidewalk like you supposed to. Like ants. Now I figure Skulls be that way. We been left here on our own. We can run around, get tired, curl up, quit. Or we can find our own sidewalk. Don't matter to the sun, don't matter to stars overhead. We can just lay down and die. But I don't see the kick in that. Best to find a crack somewheres and go in and out for all life long, no matter what, because we meant for doing that. Plus it be the way to have fun.' "

She sat down. There was a long silence. Then out of the sultry night came the swelling rhythms of "Estreito de Taruma" with Jose Bertramo at keyboards swinging as icy bright as the bright sparkle of Spirit's diamond ring. Sluggo pumped up the volume on his beat box.

Almost instantly people were on their feet, shuffling to Azymuth without tincans around their necks. Soon there was a hotshot New York disco Indian dance for real going on around the swimming pool, and funky jazz-fusion was booming across swampland, at first challenging and then silencing the arrogant frogs, making owls blink in righteous indignation, and sending woodcock scurrying for cover.

Next morning when they set out, the buzz words Go For It Get It On Just Do It were buzzing through the dark fields of the main man's mind. Skulls would get to the Promised Land come hell or high water. And then? And then? And then? That question came at him with mounting force like a brisk wind building into a storm.

45

STAY HIGH and The Boy Who Doesn't Speak Our Language always got up earlier than most of the Skulls (but never as early as the world traveler Sister Fate, who climbed into her car before most Skulls had finished their last dream). Staying in bed late made Stay High feel guilty; he had countless mornings behind him when he was at his desk studying while classmates were either sleeping off hangovers or reaching for a warm pound of flesh. As for The Boy, he was an incredibly light sleeper. One creak of a floorboard and he was sitting upright, ready to run like hell, as he had been ready each waking moment of every day for two years in gutted Fayetteville.

This morning they were strolling through an early-morning mist, watching it curl and balloon away from their dew-moist sandals. Cooks were already up, busy at fires and pots. Stay High halted at the sight of Sweet Walk bending over a kettle in her tight jeans. She was pouring boiled water into a canteen. The scholar understood that she was taking it to her seventeen-year-old lover, No Name, who must be waiting for her in a rumpled bed, and who smiled a lot these days even when other people were frowning because lightning had struck twice.

Stay High, bemused by the sight, murmured, "She walks." His eyes narrowing, he watched her move along on her invisible ball bearings. "Now that is a *walk*," he said, turning to The Boy.

The Boy smiled in response.

Was he smiling at the lovely sight or in response to unguarded words of desire? The curious researcher in Stay High got the upper hand. He pointed to the Chinese girl in tight jeans carrying a canteen of water. "She walks," he said. "Do you understand? *She walks*." He tried, if in vain, to simulate the pistonlike motion of Sweet Walk's hips. "Understand? She walks!"

Again The Boy smiled. "Ugu adsee," he said.

"Ugu adsee," Stay High repeated, waving his hand in the direction of Sweet Walk.

"Ugu adsee." It was one of the first times The Boy had said the same thing twice.

Whipping out a notebook, magnifying glass, and pencil, Stay High set busily to work, constructing a branching tree diagram of the phrase structure:

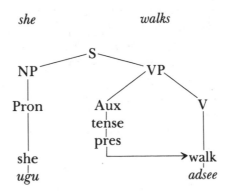

"She walks," Stay High announced in breathless triumph.

But The Boy replied glumly, "Aga ordo."

"She walks?" Stay High said, puzzled. "Aga ordo, she walks?"

"Aga ordo," repeated The Boy. "Ugu adsee."

"They mean the same thing?"

"Aga ordo ugu adsee."

"Damn," said the defeated Stay High, who never swore.

"Boo," said The Boy, the features of his thin suspicious face drawing close, pinching into inscrutability.

At just this moment Hoss came by. He had his wraparound shades on, although the light was still low. "Good morning," he said politely. "What's happening?"

"For a moment I thought I'd made a breakthrough," said the scholar. He turned from Hoss and appraised the sullen-looking boy as if the frail shoulders and long face were parts of an artifact just removed from a dig. "But no such luck."

Hoss stood a moment, hands on hips, studying The Boy too. "Do you think the treatment No Name got might also work on this kid? But I guess he's too young."

"He certainly is," Stay High said indignantly. Hoss shrugged and moseyed on. Sometimes the insensitivity of people appalled Stay High. The bitter truth was if anyone needed love it was he, not the linguistic amnesiac. But Stay High had always admired Hoss, a throwback to the free spirits of the '6os (Stay High had read all about them), a hipster for real. In Norwegian Hoss meant "good luck." Of course, IRT hadn't known that when naming him Hoss. IRT must have gotten it from street talk or subway graffiti or from a TV western. Anyway, it meant good luck, and that's what Hoss with his dark shades and cowboy hat brought with him when he moseyed up to women. The more Stay High thought about it the more he disliked Hoss; he decided to put a dent in the ex-adman's luck by joining the opposition.

His absorption in the way envy leads to political decisions prevented Stay High from being sure of what he just heard. Had The Boy cried, "Look over there"? Or had it been "Loo koo ovo aa ha"?

At any rate, The Boy was yanking his arm and pointing at the palisade fence that bordered the motel.

Stay High squinted. Was that a human shape flitting through the fog? But mists closed in, metallic and smooth, nothing beyond them. With a questioning look he turned to The Boy. "What did you say?"

The Boy shrugged and murmured, "Eeka."

Satisfied that a moment ago he hadn't heard The Boy speaking English, the scholar walked on, absorbed in thoughts of luck and political commitment, when suddenly he bumped into someone.

It was the loony genius Doctor Leo.

"Glad I bumped into you," he said with the hearty cheer of an insurance salesman. "That meaningless poem you like so much? If you don't read the small print, you'll make a big mistake." Looking straight up, he beamed as if releasing a balloon into the air. "Let me prove why mine's the best deal you can get."

"I don't understand," Stay High declared coldly.

"My friend, you will," Doctor Leo assured him and patted his shoulder, as if pitching a policy to someone a bit slow. With a touch of flattery, Doctor Leo began by commending Stay High for his discovery that four three-letter words appeared in the poem from combinations of four letters: Act, cat, gat, and tag. Of prime importance was the first letter of each word: A,C,G,T. They stood for bases. "*Bases!*" yelled the salesman, waking up Skulls still asleep in the motel. "Adenine, cytosine, guanine, thymine!" He panted a few moments before explaining that these four bases produce the twenty-four amino acids that account for proteins, which govern the structure of all organisms on earth. "We're talking about life!" he screamed, jumping up and down. "Your poem is about life insurance!"

To his credit, Stay High stayed low. He merely replied, "Really?" and strolled insouciantly away. But later he put all his powers of concentration on a new evaluation of "The Mystery of the Universe." Doctor Leo had revealed to him what he had intuitively guessed: science was hidden syntactically in the text. The Dream Queen had been saying, "Destruction will bring you a period of chaotic wandering and whimsical indulgence, but don't lose hope, because there really is a universal goal as long as nucleotide bases are lining up along DNA and producing life."

So in the final analysis, Stay High thought, the poem was simplistic and saccharine. He was dejected by such optimism. After all, he had worked assiduously to uncover a profound and complicated despair. Yet he was also optimistic about finding new aspects of the poem and within a few days would find himself continuing to search for other meanings.

In the middle of Louisiana he worked on an *explication de texte* (including Doctor Leo's contribution):

When the moon is nu	New/mu (eternity)/NUCLEOTIDE
Tides running in the gat	NUCLEOTIDE/GUANINE/gate/gun
Act freaky as a cat	ADENINE/CYTOSINE/anarchy
And do what you want to	Hedonism, post–V 70 era
Says Cleo	Willful Cleopatra/NUCLEOTIDE
Fly to Rio	Restlessness, post–V 70 era
Or jump on a nag	Diversion fantasy
Play tag	THYMINE/childish diversion
Where others plod	Adolescent contempt for values
Or dice with God	Bergman's *Seventh Seal*
Or rob a bank	Contempt for law
Or walk the plank	Masochism, post–V 70 era
Or make a base hit	Venezuela/genetic code
When they least expect it	Whimsical fate, post–V 70 era
Be mad as a Danish hatter	*Alice*: Mad Hatter/Danish ?
Hitch up your trousers with string	Awkward rhythm/determination

And have a last fling	Hedonism, post–V 70 era
In the world of dark matter	Earth
Thus do go about, about	Three Witches, *Macbeth*
As if you had a universal goal	As if: Existentialism
Until the charm's wound up	Three Witches, *Macbeth*
Then drop like Alice down the hole	*Alice*: The rabbit hole
On a blood-red unseen beam	?
Into truth too deep too rude	Poetic ambiguity
Or curl forever nude	Sexual implication?
Inside the singular dream	Poetic ambiguity
At the setting of the sun	Misquote *Macbeth*
When the hubble-bubble's done	Misspell "hurly-burly," *Macbeth*
Mea Kalpa	I am to blame/misspell "Culpa"
	Guilt for surviving V 70
Et cetera	To blame for death of everyone

Fortunately, the "Mea Kalpa" left him with hope that guilt might yet dominate the final meaning of the poem, just as he had been made to feel guilty for lacking the genius of his siblings. Anticipating a new discovery that would prophesy apocalypse, he succumbed to the critic's greatest temptation — creating the vision he was supposed to interpret.

Then that possibility of general cosmic ruin received a setback from an unexpected source.

Snow came to him during a P & S stop, her white hair brushed back immaculately, her ruddy face wreathed in a beatific smile. "I was giving this nice girl a manicure last night, when she confessed out of the blue to knowing something about your poem."

Stay High asked to see the girl immediately.

Once upon a time a dark-skinned lovely from South India spent enough time in Manhattan to see most of the tourist sights before V 70 Struck. It had been rumored that Salt Noody was one of Hoss's girlfriends, but it was a baseless (a word never used around Doctor Leo) and felonious charge. Salt Noody was just as intact as Pretty Puss and Golden Girl. This visitor from Madras was not going to surrender up her Indian virginity to Skull lust. She had been taught to believe her intactness was essential for making a sensible marriage and a sensible marriage was the point of being alive, at least for this go-round. She was a nice girl, true to her gentle nature, and rarely spoke unless spoken to. Now she was brought to Stay High in a multicolored sari, on her forehead the red tilaki dot she put there every day with paprika obtained from Cancer Two's spice rack.

In a quiet voice she explained to Stay High that she understood the meaning of "Kalpa."

"Yes, 'Culpa,' " he said impatiently. " 'Mea culpa' means 'I am to blame.' "

"I don't know anything about the 'Mea.' "

"It's Latin."

"But the 'Kalpa' —"

"Misspelling of 'Culpa.' Also Latin."

"I don't know anything about 'Culpa' either, but 'Kalpa' is important in Indian philosophy."

Appalled and ashamed by his own ignorance, Stay High sat back and stayed low during the Indian girl's explanation of the cyclical theory of creation.

There were four stages of yugas in cosmic time. In the fourth or Kali Yuga the world ends in a cosmic holocaust, after which the process of creation begins again. Each age lasts 4,320,000 years or a mahayuga. One thousand mahayugas represent one day in the life of Brahma, the Supreme Deity. This single day, along with its night, is one Kalpa, or eight and a half billion years. "We are now," she said, "in the Age of Strife, the Kali Yuga, when it is said the gods Shiva and Vishnu sleep and fail to hear our human supplications for mercy. We are coming to the end of the Kalpa. We are facing destruction."

"Ah," said Stay High, pleased.

"But another day will begin for Brahma, and His universe will emerge just like we do when the sun comes up."

Stay High wasn't pleased with this view of cosmic history. It meant the world went on forever. You could even conclude that there really was a universal goal and not just an existential one. So he decided not to believe one word of Salt Noody's faith in eternity. To be polite, however, he asked questions. "You're telling me the universe is destroyed after one day and one night pass in the life of Brahma? And that period lasts eight and a half billion years?"

"Yes, one Kalpa lasts that long."

"I'm no scientist," said Stay High, feeling higher, "but I remember reading our universe is now about twenty billion years old."

"I wouldn't know anything about that," Salt Noody confessed modestly.

He scribbled in the little notebook he carried everywhere. "That would mean we are starting Brahma's third day instead of ending his first night. I don't mean to denigrate Indian thought, but it hardly seems scientifically correct, does it."

"Oh, I wouldn't know anything about that," the girl admitted with an embarrassed smile. "But the world is born and dies and is born again and dies and is born again in the mind of Brahma, and the time intervals for these events are given in Kalpas. In the poem God is saying the universe is what I create and destroy and create again, time and space, everything, et cetera."

Apologizing for taking up his time, Salt Noody steepled her hands in a graceful namaste and left Stay High pondering a cosmos that was inimical to his analysis of "The Mystery of the Universe." This upstart from India was suggesting that the world was a place of infinite possibilities.

Sphinx had indeed energized the Skulls. It must have been difficult, reasoned the main man, for her to stand up in front of fancily dressed kids and admit to making love in front of mirrors. Why had she told them about something so personal? Clearly, to make them accept her story for real. And the gamble had worked. Instead of hooting at a white woman on the edge of middle age who got a bit kinky with a black guy who barely reached her shoulder, they had gone along with her public-spirited courage. Her account of IRT's belief in persistence had helped them regain their sense of purpose.

As Spirit was leading the prez back to their car after a pit stop, someone came up to report breathlessly that four or five people had seen a biker in a crash helmet peering through the bushes at them.

"*You* didn't see him, did you?" the Skull who shall be nameless asked the main man.

"No," said Mister Touch. "Perhaps I was looking the other way."

"Why do you suppose he is following us?" Spirit asked.

The prez shrugged. "I'm starting to believe in destiny. I don't think of it like a mantis hovering over a motel roof, looking down for prey. Nothing so ominous or sensational. But I wonder. Maybe destiny's the road itself."

"How does that work?" Spirit asked.

"It leads us where we have to go. We simply follow it."

"What if we decide to take another road? If we rebel?"

"Well, you might say fate provides the other road for the rebellion. It's rebellion in name only. We don't choose the roads we take, they choose us."

"Do you really love me?"

"With all my heart."

"Then whatever happens happens and I can handle it."

"As for the biker, let destiny handle him."

46

Destiny would handle that job sooner than expected, as if willfully deciding not to wait. But before handling the biker, destiny took care of business with Mystique.

Recently she'd learned that the only man she ever truly loved had revealed to the spying slut his old name. Someone had overheard the bitch purring against his shoulder, "Mark," so now everyone knew there was one rule for The Powers That Be and another — Sag and The Fierce Rabbit notwithstanding — for everyone else. Mister Touch's blatant disregard for the rules proved that nothing had changed, not even the corruption of politicians or the heartless betrayal of good women by bad men. Mystique privately recited speeches to her ex-lover — bound, gagged, and forced to listen. The gist was she would never let him go despite his deceitful ways. The speeches whirled through her mind like nuclear gas blown off the surface of a star — wheeling around the hard core of her resolve to get him back.

With renewed faith in justice and herself, Mystique decided to stop relying on wimps for help. She was looking for someone new, preferably tall, dark, and dangerous.

The Fierce Rabbit!

She blamed herself for failing to choose him earlier, but perhaps love of Mister Touch had blinded her to certain realities, among them the foolishness of counting on men who can do little else but drive. Her father used to tell her when you want action, go to the top. That could mean the tall black with an afro that fanned out a foot above his skull.

So she went to The Rabbit during a stop. He was lounging in the shade with his henchmen, Wishbone and Yo Boy, who flashed her such scary grins that she nearly turned and fled. Nevertheless, her desire for justice stiffened her determination, and she walked up to the frowning Rabbit, who had Walkman earphones on, and murmured sexily, "You remind me of a Zulu warrior."

"Yeah?" he scowled fiercely.

"You're looking good," Mystique said, trying to sound black.

"Good you got eyes to see that." The Rabbit hadn't removed the earphones. One hand, doing finger pops to the music, gave notice to Mystique that he wasn't about to give her his undivided attention.

"Are you as tough as you act?" Mystique asked boldly.

He stared at her.

"I've been thinking about you lately."

Fingers snapped briskly to the beat.

"I've been thinking we need someone else setting the pace."

"Instead of who?"

"Touch." She left off "Mister" in an act of contempt that brought The Rabbit's fingers to a respectful halt.

"Tell me about it," he said.

She told him people were restless, angry, confused. Her friend Riot also felt it was due to poor leadership.

"Don't tell me about Riot. I am done with that honky."

So she reminded him that Sag was heading another disgruntled group, although Mystique didn't point out that Sag's concern was not for another strong, charismatic leader but for freedom which would allow her to control things through a democratic vote.

"Yeah, Sag," he said with a grin. "That old white-haired old white bitch. Who could care what she say?"

"Some people do. They could all help."

"Don't need no help. I take care of Number One myself."

"When we think of changes, we think big, right?" Mystique persisted. "We have to plan, get our act together." She was trying wildly to think of appropriate black phrases. "Then we can get down."

"Woman, who in hell are you?"

"Lucy Rutherford. I'm thinking we can make things happen, you and me."

"Marvin Johnson be someone could make something happen."

"I hope you *want* something to happen."

The Rabbit grinned, a line of teeth appearing between his lips. "Name again?"

"Lucy."

"Lucy, you be smart as a whip. Plus sweet-looking."

The lust — or whatever it was — coming into his eyes frightened her a moment, but when he motioned her away from his watchful henchmen and into the bushes, she followed docilely and when he took her roughly into his arms, she raised her lips to his. And all the while she was thinking, If I can keep this loony but charismatic Rabbit under control, my first step toward complete victory will be to energize him right up to the black tips of his afro at just the right moment and propel the big oaf into a righteous act of vengeance. The idea of using him that way made what followed pleasurable.

The caravan was approaching the eastern end of a massive bridge that spanned the Red River. The last shreds of morning mist buffeted the horizon, obscuring the skyline of Shreveport. The hazy atmosphere gave its tall buildings the remote look of a Disney fairyland. Spirit In The Dark motored slowly through the fog. Just as she reached the summit of an upgrade, her neat-looking eyes caught a flicker of movement ahead — then it vanished on the downgrade. The bridge curved, dipped, and thrust upward again to give her a second look. This time she saw a motorbike plowing through the fog, heading for destiny.

When she told the main man he advised her to maintain speed. No sense in frightening the biker by trying to overtake him.

The bridge dipped again, and the biker was gone. Then Spirit had a fleeting glimpse of jeans, leather jacket, and crash helmet veering off an exit ramp, escaping into the Business District.

"A lone biker," Spirit said.

"Who hasn't killed anyone yet," added the prez.

Late that afternoon they halted in Marshall, Texas, a city of some twenty thousand dead souls, according to the last census, and cooked dinner on a main street, while an evening of ultramarine blue settled around their campfires. The main man was gulping down a fiery Cancer Two stew when a voice from out of his past whispered in his ear.

"I just saw someone," Nando whispered. "A woman was standing outside of the firelight. When I went over that way to get something from a car, I saw her. We stared at each other. Then —" Nando snapped her fingers.

"A woman?" said the main man. "You're sure?"

"A woman," insisted Nando. "And she carried a crash helmet."

"Sooner or later," said the leader, whose temporary belief in destiny had given him a laid-back air, "we'll meet up with her again."

It was sooner.

They bivouacked the next afternoon in the dusty village of Crow. Abruptly around a far corner of the street appeared a leather-jacketed woman on a Honda. Idling the engine, then revving it up as if to speed away, she throttled down again. Pushing up the visor of her crash helmet, she stared at the Skulls, most of whom were seated around campfires fed by tables and chairs from a nearby furniture store. Everyone who had eyes good enough was staring back (except Cancer Two, who was busy with bubbling pots of beef stew; they had shot a cow wandering across the highway at noon yesterday and butchered it right there, on the yellow dividing line).

Once again the woman gave the bike a spurt of gas and lifted one foot off the ground as if preparing to get out of there.

"She can't decide what to do," Spirit whispered to the main man.

"Ask her if she's hungry," he suggested, but someone else had already thought of that. "Hey, mamma! Come get some groovy stew! Be ready soon! Welcome to the Skulls!"

"She's taking off the helmet," Spirit whispered. "A blonde. Thirtyish. Looks like she works out. Hair's short, boyish. Wide-set eyes, thick brows. Getting off the bike. She's . . . a Breather For Real the way she walks. She's . . coming over here. She's . . ." Spirit stopped talking. A hush deepened until through it Mister Touch began to hear something — the tread of a steady footstep on the street.

The next voice he heard was low, throaty, but businesslike.

"I think you're the leader."

He knew she was speaking to him. Of course. Following them, she must have cased the operation. "Yes, I am."

"I'd like to talk to you."

"The feeling's mutual." He got up, felt a hand take his arm at the elbow to guide him. There was no nonsense in those fingers; they knew what to do.

"Where are we going?" the main man asked.

"I thought the barber shop across the street."

"Barber shop it is. Cougar!" he called out. "Open the door if it's closed."

Cougar limped over and blew the door away with a few blasts of an M16.

Holding his elbow firmly, the woman guided Mister Touch past the splintered frame. Behind them he heard the elephantine thud of Africa; it stopped at the shattered doorway. Soon the prez and the woman were seated in barber chairs, side by side.

She did the questioning. The main man had the unsettling impression of being on trial while he went about explaining the reasons for their trip westward. After a long silence, during which the woman must have judged the logic of his explanation, she then volunteered an account of her own life since V 70 Struck.

For six months she had lived with two married couples in Cleveland, her home. But the marrieds had squabbled as if the world hadn't changed and when the foursome began trading partners, she got fed up and left. She had managed rather well in a city of nearly one million dead until a number of tremendous explosions began taking place. They suggested that for someone V 70 hadn't been a disaster complete enough, that by leveling the metropolitan area a competitive human could show Mother Nature a thing or two about destruction. Then one day, someone took a potshot at her on Euclid. She had visions of Cleveland Browns football fans running amok during a long cold midwestern winter. She hadn't wanted to leave home — after all, her memories were there, anchoring her to a solid past — but the day she drove downtown and saw the blasted facade of the art museum was the day she left.

Her first stop was Nashville, where she might have stayed awhile had she not seen three carloads of armed men cruising down the street one morning, their faces as intent as chicken hawks, on the lookout for prey.

So she had gone farther south until one day in central Louisiana she had nearly blundered into the slow-moving caravan. For days now she'd been following the Skulls, weaving up and down the highway, speeding ahead, doubling back. Observing initially from afar, she had then crept near to their campfires, even crawled on her stomach within earshot of bedrolls, so she knew a little about their private lives as well as their public manners.

She could live alone, of course. She could get on her bike and leave right now. But so many people together had her longing for company again. Of course, if she misjudged them, she could lose her life or worse.

"Worse?" the main man asked curiously.

"There are worse things than losing your life," the woman said, as if fate were allowing her a glimpse into her future.

For the last few days she had studied the Skulls carefully and weighed her chances with them. She hadn't minded the odd clothes, but what put her off were the strange names. She had wondered if they were a psychotic hangover from V 70. On the other hand, the people bearing those names didn't fight among themselves and did seem to be headed toward a specific destination. When on the Shreveport Bridge they hadn't tried to overtake her bike — she'd deliberately tempted them with that possibility — she was impressed by their restraint and made the decision that had brought her to this moment.

"Are you asking," the main man said, "to come along with us?"

"I am. Yes."

During the interview, Mister Touch had been trying to grasp

the woman's character since he couldn't see her face. Her account suggested that she was a formidable, determined survivor. "One of our rules," he told her, "is never to discuss the past." He motioned toward the noisy people waiting for stew at the campfires. "You don't talk with them about the way it was before V 70 Struck."

"I don't do that. Okay."

"For my information, however, I want to know what you did before V 70 Struck."

"Corporate law."

"Corporate law. I hear that in your voice. But I also hear something else."

"What could that be?"

"You seem to like frankness."

"I do."

"Very well then. I hear a note of sensuality."

The woman laughed.

Then he explained the rule about names.

"So that's why they're strange — it's a kind of tradition," she said. "I like tradition."

"In the early days it was part of our survival."

"I like survival too."

Shuffling names through his memory, Mister Touch stopped at a name that, in spite of corporate law, seemed appropriate. "I name you Queen Sexy."

She guffawed.

"Are you offended?"

"Not at all. I'm rather flattered. I'd like some of my old friends to hear that. I wonder what they'd say."

He heard her rise from the crinkly leather of the barber chair. "I think the stew's ready," she told the main man.

"Do you like paprika?"

"What?"

"Like it or not, you're going to have it."

That night under the Texas stars, Spirit turned in a musty bed and told him she was pregnant. Having missed her last period, she had gone into a small-town drugstore yesterday and gotten an in-home pregnancy test kit. This morning the white stick turned blue.

Next day, throwing caution to the wind, he went around telling everyone his Spirit was pregnant. It was as if she had just given birth to a bouncing baby. Imaginary cigars were already in his hand. People laughed good-naturedly, at least some did.

But not Mystique. Next time the caravan stopped, she rifled through the clothes racks of a local boutique for something chic and trendy. During a P & S break, she strutted in front of the prez as if he could see the gorgeous woman he had stupidly discarded for a black woman soon to blow up as big as a house. She must have passed back and forth a half dozen times before realizing the thoughtful look on his face had nothing to do with her parade of beauty.

Her own blindness mortified her. That night in bed with The Rabbit, after ravaging him in a way that usually won commitments from her recruits, Mystique made a full disclosure of Plan B. She described an uprising in which she and The Rabbit led a score of rebels to confront Mister Touch and his scheming whore and demand a change of government. Then they would form a sort of oligarchy with a rotating presidency. As their first act of power they would turn out the bitch and warn the former main man that retention of his own citizenship depended on a new moral attitude characterized by loyalty and marital stability and a renunciation of the possible issue from that woman who was lying anyway and —

The Fierce Rabbit reached out to clamp his hand over her mouth. "What in hell got into you, woman? I don't get a word you babbling about."

Yanking his hand away, Mystique sat up naked in bed. "It's time to move, it's time to do something, it's time to stop what is happening from happening further!"

"Dumb broad," he muttered, getting out of bed.

Mystique was stunned. She had always felt it was her prerogative to call men dumb.

He was throwing on his clothes. "Don't go telling The Rabbit when to move," he declared. "Know what I do, woman? I go right to the bottom and stay down there awhile. I know how to look up from down there and see what be going on up top. I watch the motherfuckers fucking up, I study them, and when I be ready to do, I do, I go, I mean, I shoot on up there and go and they don't know what the fuck they got hit with, understand? That be Marvin

Johnson, his style. Now I got what I brought in here with me?" He was looking around the motel room.

"Not everything."

"Yeah?"

"You're leaving a little of yourself. Between my legs."

He grinned. "You gonna name it what, if it get born?"

She wanted to say Jungle Bunny, but imagined he might hit her for that, so instead she came out with Bugs Bunny.

Even that was risky — The Rabbit raised his fist to strike her, but then, showing his usual caution, dropped his hand. "Woman, stay out of my face," he said coldly. "Or I am gonna rearrange yours. Hear what I'm saying? You're dumb or plain nuts, I don't know which. But I sure the fuck know this: I don't need no honky goofball on my hands, telling me what to do."

After he was gone, Mystique lay there in the darkness, counting her breaths. It calmed her enough to think of the next step. Plan B had to be scrapped. If she couldn't get someone as angry as The Fierce Rabbit to lead a rebellion with her, then who could she count on? The plan was as harmless as any dreamed up by that old white-haired old white bitch, Sag.

With a determined sigh, Mystique decided to move on to Plan E — E for Eternity. She needed no help for Plan E. It depended upon no one but herself, and so late into the night she lay there and contemplated it — running violence through her mind again and again, like film through a projector.

47

SUCH SACRILEGE succinctly shows significant satanic sentiments."

"S now? Since when you got on S, old butcher boy?"

"Since Sunday. Sphinx's scandalous statements surely sound staggeringly sinful."

"Hey, he talking to us. Ain't talking to the air like he do usual. Looking at us, saying his S."

"Go to it, Adidas."

"Self-serving Skulls speaking so shamelessly shake sensitive souls seeking salvation."

"Seem like he doing religion now with S. Talking sin and salvation. Some day Adidas gonna go too far."

"Wait till he get to Z. That gonna fix him."

Adidas wasn't the only Skull still obsessed by Sphinx's confession, mirrors and all. Wherever she walked, people gave her a wide berth. But no one, not even Sphinx, could have predicted what happened next.

They had stopped in a windswept town a day's drive out of Dallas. As usual, they had a little target practice which enabled them to get into stores for a look-see. But today a peculiar communal mood seemed to descend, covering them like a binding fog. No one came out of a store with articles of clothing. They stood around restlessly kicking dust until someone who shall remain nameless walked up to a paint store, peered through the smudged window, and shattered the door with a burst from an Uzi.

Instantly a mob gathered around the entrance. They would all swear later that no one spoke a word, that they just knew what they were going to do. Funneling into the store, they carried out cans of paint and brushes and began sloshing color all over the caravan. On went wide swaths of chromium oxide green, rose madder, and cobalt blue, and all to a single purpose: the depiction of ants. In crude, less crude, and rather artful renditions, they covered the doors, the side paneling, the hoods, the back windows with sketches of formicidae in burnt sienna and vermilion red. They drew antennae, six jointed legs, bullet-shaped abdomens, square thoraxes, pear-shaped heads.

Mister Touch sat on the shaded porch of a country store and listened calmly to the chattering of mad myrmecologists who, when through with the vehicles, turned their artistic gifts and lack thereof on themselves, briskly marking their foreheads and cheeks with insects in Naples yellow and Mars violet. They went wild at their work and insisted that Sphinx supervise them. She did, with good humor and laughter, as more than a score of Skulls transformed themselves into a living ant colony of raucous color.

Stomping onto the porch, Sag stood with arms akimbo in front of the main man. "Do you know what they're doing? They're talking out there of the Ant God! In their twisted minds they're setting up the common ant as some kind of debased divine presence. Do you hear them, cackling like that, saying, 'The Father, The Son, The Holy Ant'? Do you *hear* me?"

Mister Touch looked up in the general direction of the angry voice. "I hear you," he said with a smile.

"Why are you *smiling* like that? You're encouraging their madness!" Sag exclaimed furiously. "I'm as broad-minded as the next person, but *really*, the joke has gone too far! Those people have drawn ants all over the caravan and now they say they're going to worship an ant god. It's vile!"

"Specifically why?"

There was an indignant pause; he could hear her drawing breath into a throat constricted by fury. "Specifically because they have accepted an insect as a sacred deity. But ants are merely robots. They don't think."

"Whereas we do?"

"I resent your sophomorically cynical remarks. Whoever heard of anyone worshiping insects? It's sick, destructive, corrupt, to say nothing of sacrilegious."

Mister Touch stroked his red beard. "Yes, ants are robotlike in behavior, but they're hard-working, unselfish, and they persist. Not bad qualities. If we need another kind of god later, we'll find one that's more independent."

"You're laughing at me."

"Yes, I'm laughing at you. But I'm also serious."

Going.

Through the yelling and the slapping of brushes on metal and flesh, he heard the creak of porch steps.

"Who is it?"

"Stay High."

"Come to report on your projects?"

Stay High adjusted his glasses and rubbed his sweaty face with a Kleenex. Ever since learning to dislike Hoss because of the hipster's good luck with women, Stay High had looked around for a

logical means of joining the opposition. At last he had found one
in the form of a formic god whom The Powers That Be had embraced in a mind-controlling effort to destroy the Skulls' common
sense. Lack of sex drove the scholar into a flat-footed stance of
righteous indignation not unlike that recently assumed by Sag.
He lectured his leader, noting that only priests had ever self-
consciously raised up gods and then only in the form of living rulers to celebrate significant reigns. The profoundest gods, those of
nature, had sprung up spontaneously within ancient cultures. It
was therefore a form of sacrilege — atheistic Stay High paused a
moment in surprise at the word he had just used — to consciously
set up a nature god. The logic was implacable. "I'm not speaking
for Jews and Christians," he said, "but in behalf of human dignity."

"Is human dignity at issue?"

"You're ignoring fundamental principles of society so you can
pursue psychological control of these people."

"I am? I'll be damned."

Stay High, readjusting his glasses, huffed off.

Meanwhile, the main man sat on the shaded porch and listened
to his people, who seemed to be having fun. It was hard for him
to feel anxious. His pregnant Spirit had mellowed him out. Go
for it . . . Get there . . . were humming through his head like bees
through a summer afternoon: persistent, hypnotic, a sound of
timeless certainty.

In succeeding days the paint would wear off skin but remain
on vehicles, and the caravan would proceed through Texas like a
gaily outfitted circus, featuring three-ring formic entertainment
and a new gospel of hard work and laughter.

"Know what happen in Dallas?"

"Any dope know. But I don't give a fuck."

"You talking about our president, Mister John H. Kennedy.
Main man said last night we be driving past the memorial where
they shot him."

At a sluggish pace matching the weather, they drove through
the seventh-largest dead city in America, serviced by nine railroads
and as many airlines. They came in from the east on Route 20 and
hit the Thornton Freeway, which took them to the State Fair Park
where they parked in a lot fronting museums no longer visited and

fountains no longer splashing and the Cotton Bowl, where rabid fans no longer outshouted one another at the Texas-Oklahoma football game.

As they got out and stretched, they noticed people lying around on the grass. Approaching, they realized that these people were blinded by more than V 70 — they were one hundred and one percent stoned.

Skulls strolled curiously among them. The sprawling people hardly looked up. They were ragged, dirty, with hair down their backs, beards to their navels, eyes sunken, mouths open in goofy grins, their shoeless feet splayed out like stiffs in a morgue.

Skulls murmured hi, staring at a veritable Garden of Eden for junkies. Lying in the grass, among the lounging bodies, were countless vials and needles and cooking cups and lengths of rubber hose and hookah pipes, all out in sunlight like the discarded toys of tired children.

Mister Touch asked to speak to their leader.

Plenty of giggles.

"You talk straighter than shit, blind man," someone slurred. "Want some PCP, some MDMA? A little base?"

Doctor Leo pushed forward eagerly. "Who's talking about bases? I heard chemicals mentioned."

"Get back, man," a Skull told him. "They talking Angel Dust and Ecstasy. They talking crack."

But the insurance salesman had to be restrained.

"Let me do the rap," offered Shag, who had been cool the whole trip, perhaps dreaming of the day when he'd meet up with his own kind. He established immediate rapport without even having a hit or a snort of anything. His comradeship glowed in his narrow face. He learned that these people had come from miles around soon after V 70 Struck. They had loosely organized themselves around the concept that V 70 had been God's justifiable retribution for ecological waste and brutal war and spiritual devastation. Most of them had only blown a little grass then — latter-day hippies — and through long rambling discussions had decided that survivors ought to seek a new lifestyle. Like that was the God route. Since there wasn't time to make amends for erring humanity, they couldn't get it together like buddhas contemplating their navels, man, they had to get it on fast, before additional punishment came down on them just for breathing. So they got the idea of breaking into medical centers and riffling through the drug supplies. Since then the group had dwindled from a couple of hundred to maybe fifty — is there about fifty of us around here? — because one way or another they just dropped out, wandered off and never returned because they were tripping with Shiva or like with some universal guru, so maybe they got over, they — what was it you wanted to know?

Shag glanced admiringly at the paraphernalia of paradise. "Wowee," he breathed. And to think at the Club House they'd hassled him for holding a bottle of reds! Not that he understood much of what these dudes here had to say. In his barrio back home they had talked attitude and what the high felt like and how much it cost, not this kind of weird bullshit. But he didn't mind hearing it if it led to something good. These people looked like they had la vida loca, the crazy life of trousers with a split cuff, a hairnet, a plastic hairbrush sticking from the back pocket, the herky-jerky walk, the PCP smoked in a ciggy, or a primo joint laced with coke. It was what Shag wanted, it was all he knew to want now that the world was crazy for real and there wasn't a dream any longer of leaving the barrio and working for campesino, the old-time values of Grandma, La Abuelita, who was next to the Virgin in purity.

"Find out what their plans are," the main man told Shag.

He found out that they had no plans, except to keep hitting the medical centers. Hospitals and pharmacies in Dallas would last longer than they would ever need before every last one of them reached Nirvana. And if they had a short go on coke or smack or some kind of pill you know, they could always send a space expedition down to Houston for more shit. They were happy.

"Do they look happy?" Mister Touch asked his Spirit.

"Well, yes they do, in that falling-forward way a junkie has of looking happy. Yes. I think they're happy."

"Then tell them, Shag, we wish them good luck."

Shag turned to the heavy-lidded spiritualist who had done most of the talking. "Hey, bro, okay."

The spiritualist grinned and made a feeble attempt at high-fiving with Shag, but his outstretched palm missed by a mile.

At this moment they all heard a motor gunned and one of the caravan cars, an Olds 98, shot out of the parking lot like it was being chased in one of those TV cop shows.

"What happened?" asked the main man.

His wife told him someone had stolen one of their cars.

Stitch, the Automotive Engineer, stepped up happily and assured the prez that he could get them a replacement in no time.

"But right now," said Mister Touch, "we're going to take that ride past the Kennedy Memorial."

For all their belief in discipline, the Skulls were often lax. They didn't take a buddy check before leaving the parking lot, and so they wouldn't know until nightfall that they had lost two Skulls.

One of them, Mystique, had stolen the Olds and was hightailing it two miles westward into the downtown area of Dallas in pursuit of Plan E. She was trembling from fear and excitement. She couldn't have felt higher if she had stayed at the State Fair Park and rammed herself into a chemical state of Nirvana. Because all day she had felt herself edging closer to destiny. Last night, when she heard that the main man intended to drive past the Kennedy Memorial, the final detail of Plan E fell into place with the inevitability of the square in the formula $E = mc^2$. Mystique knew that she was slightly askew, off the wall, edging into a different time zone. Had the world been different, she might have sought out a shrink and got her head straight. But there probably wasn't a psychiatrist alive in America, much less in the state of Texas. And there wasn't time. Time was squeezing out like the last toothpaste in her tube. And rushing into her mind to replace that lost time was a massive stinking load of despair, boiling and sputtering and rolling on like volcanic magma. All her efforts at defeating fate had been crushed. She had shown courage and persistence and commitment — of that she was sure. But when defeat finally came, it blew in with a rush and left the thriving places in her mind as barren and beaten as a landscape after a tornado. And so Plan E.

Having studied a city map of Dallas, which she found with all the other maps collected by Stay High for their mobile library, Mystique knew exactly where to go. Scared stiff but loose enough to turn a steering wheel, she drove toward the plaza bounded by Elm, Market, Commerce, and Record streets, on the west side of downtown. Parking on Elm at Dealey Plaza she looked up at the ugly building which had once been called the Texas Schoolbook Depository. She could go on up to Oswald's sixth floor, but Mystique disdained his old haunt; after all, it had become a tourist trap. She felt superior both to sentimentality and competition. Shooting the lock off the front door, she climbed slowly to the fifth floor, shot the lock off that door too, and entered a dusty warehouse filled with cartons. She took up her position at the southeast window from which she could look down on the thirty-foot white cenotaph designed by Philip Johnson for the Kennedy Memorial Plaza, two hundred yards from the spot where on November 22, 1963, the president had been killed.

Blocks away, years later, at five miles an hour, another cavalcade was approaching.

"Taking same route Kennedy done. How about that?"

"Dallas a bad place, man, don't like it. Not only he got shot here, the man shot him got shot."

"So keep that gun ready. No motherfucker gonna do our main man in."

"Do me in neither."

Back in the depository, Mystique waited with the M16 she had boosted from the Skull armory in Truck B. During the long minutes of waiting, she felt destiny leaning over her shoulder. Finally it spoke to her. "Lucy Rutherford, you're a bit of a dip right now, maybe close to being certifiable, but you're also honest, forthright, capable of seeing your life for what it has become — a personal disaster as complete and devastating as that of V 70. But let's face it, you never loved the guy for real. You never loved anyone for real, not even yourself. As OOTHI says, you were in love with loving. If you loved him for real, you'd stick around and wait it out or kill the bitch outright and finally get him. But you have lost it, dear, you have given up, you have abjectly surrendered. So if you're going down the drain, take a couple of bad people with you. Let justice reign!"

Then she saw the motorcade. She was surprised that it didn't correspond to her TV memory of an open blue Lincoln flying an American flag and with a presidential standard attached to the front fender. Oswald had insidiously spooked Mystique into reliving *his* thing, not living *hers*, and for a few dismaying moments, as the procession approached on Houston Street at ten miles an hour, she expected to see a man with ruffled brown hair and a woman in a rosebud pink suit with a pillbox hat on her dark pretty head. But with great effort — the distinguishing mark of someone special — Mystique managed to see what was there for real. Passing an oak tree and turning left was a closed BMW, not an open Lincoln. After a moment's hesitation, she began shooting at it. The effect reminded her of television history: once again pigeons whirled into motion over the sunny expanse of Dealey Plaza.

What happened next departed from the past. While Mystique held down the trigger, Skulls returned fire. Inspired by fear of what had happened here years ago, they followed this route with the vigilance of besieged warriors expecting ambush. Long before she could empty the magazine, they were firing at her. Mystique hardly had time to be surprised, because they flung her back from the window in unrecognizable condition. Her firm white skin turned mushy crimson, her honey hair lost its combed order, her pretty face shattered, her powerful heart flopped to its final rest, as a last thought streaked through her exploding brain: this is not justice.

And Lucy Rutherford, a.k.a. Mystique, died for real at last, a dupe of destiny. She would lie up here unrecognizable and unknown, a failure of purpose in this building, whereas on the floor above her another assassin had succeeded.

Not waiting to find out who was attacking them, the Skulls sped on at a fast clip — fifty wild miles an hour.

In her excitement Mystique's aim had been so terrible that only fragments of cement reached the caravan, the slugs digging into the street far short of the cars. Although untouched, Mister Touch felt a jab of pain travel through his groin, and had he known her fate, he might have felt that it was Mystique's spirit taking a final hit at him.

That night when the caravan halted, someone mentioned that Mystique was missing. People speculated that she might have drifted away on the soft tide of her musings, because lately she had been occupied by her thoughts to the exclusion of everything else except sex.

Others had different reactions. Sag claimed that Mystique's ruined reputation had finally overwhelmed her, leaving her desperate enough to wander off the way many people did when

V 70 Struck. They just got in their cars and drove into the sunset. It had been called the Drive Away Syndrome. Sag was positive that Mystique had fallen victim to it.

Some of Mystique's former lovers felt guilty, having deceived themselves into believing they had been important in her life. Had they treated her better, so they reasoned, she might have stayed.

Saddened but not guilty, Mister Touch considered a stopover in Dallas for a search, but decided there was no way to find her if she didn't want to be found. Ever since her abortive attempt to resurrect their relationship in a motel room, he had convinced himself that Mystique was looking for a new life. He believed that she had gone off in search of someone or something — a passionate heroine out of an epic movie, a recluse bound for mountains and meditation. When he described Mystique in such a romantic way, his Spirit smiled tightly and kept mum. She had a different interpretation of the disappearance. It was plain to her that Mystique had lost the war. Like any seasoned general, the defeated woman had led her troops in retreat, saving those left for the next encounter if such was available in the windswept empty battlefields of America.

Then there was The Rabbit. With his entourage around him, he had his own say about her disappearance. "Honky broad scared of me," he claimed proudly. "Rather take her chance out there in the unknown than mess with The Rabbit."

"I believe it," said Wishbone.

"Yo. El Viejo say something, we hearing it," said Yo Boy.

That same evening someone who shall be nameless went to the main man with another revelation. Shag had stayed at the State Fair Park. "Asked me not to say nothing till we was out of Dallas."

"I don't think we should go back for him," Hoss said to the main man.

"You're right. Sooner or later, he'd be caught holding. And we'd be forced to leave him in a tank town or the middle of nowhere. This way he's with his people."

"Of course, he won't last long."

"Well, that bunch has lasted this long. Spirit says they look happy. Let Shag share their fate — happiness or horror or both."

"He might even reach Nirvana," suggested Hoss.

"That's what I'm saying. We lost two today, but at least of their own volition and not violently."

But the day had not ended. Two characters wandered into camp, looking for a ride west. They swore they hadn't come from the fairgrounds, although both of them, white boys around twenty years old, had a spacey look, a faded-out stare like that of beach rats, surfer punks, skateboard stoners, motorgangs.

"They don't impress me," Hoss told the main man.

When they stood in front of Mister Touch, they swore they never took drugs. Like they were just hanging out in Dallas, waiting for something to happen, and today it had happened — a fleet of cars and trucks with insects painted all over them, heading west where they wanted to go.

"Spirit," said the main man. "What do you think?"

"I think you pick up strays."

He named them Snootchy Fingers and Daddy Rich, two of the few remaining names left from IRT's supply.

So two stayed in Dallas and two others signed on. Minus two and plus two equals zero.

48

As they strolled through a rodeo rink just outside a Texas town, Spirit turned suddenly to her lover. "I stopped taking the pill after the first time we made love. I told myself, this is the man, this is the time, even though the world is all wrong. I want this child. But I've been pregnant before. I've got to talk about that."

"You're sure? We can let the past go."

"I need to tell you. It's like moving into a new place. You clean it up."

"I warn you, sweetheart. If you open the past, I might react like we were back in it."

"I know that."

"I'm listening."

"When I was in rehab at seventeen, they forced me to look at the future. Either I went up or down. I already knew down, so I wanted to try up. It was that simple, that weird. I figured the best way to go was through education. That sounds simple enough, but for someone like me it was a harder go than a middle-class white can imagine. Harder than Hoss can imagine too. He came from a middle-class Harlem family — meaning the privileged few. Before I really went for it, education to me was graduating from high school. Education meant not dropping out, that's all. I didn't see beyond that idea. I had no father. My mother cashed welfare checks and went to the movies. So how did I manage to go for the up? I hooked on to slogans. Know what I'm saying? Dream The Impossible Dream. The Only Thing That Can Stop You Is You. Slogans drummed into me by counselors and I guess by my own hopes. I imagined I was somebody like Cicely Tyson, Aretha Franklin, Alice Walker. The slogans worked in the sense they got me through college — the slogans and working nights and getting state grants. By then I knew I wasn't going to be an actress or singer or writer, but I could do something worthwhile. I believed it. I had the idea of helping my people, I had confidence, I had dignity. Okay? All this was great. Then along came Daryll."

"Daryll."

They were sitting in bleachers, like earlycomers in seats that gave them the best view of a gate opening and a bull charging out, his horns prying up the air in front of him like a can opener.

"I see what you mean by reacting to the past," Spirit said. "The way you looked when I said Daryll. Do you want to hear more?"

Mister Touch laughed ruefully. "I've *got* to hear more."

"There had been guys, a couple of real affairs, but nothing like Daryll. I was starry-eyed, dopey. Growing up in mean streets didn't protect me from a dream of the good life with a handsome man on his way up, an aide to the mayor, no less — Harvard Law, charming. And one of my own."

"I get the idea," Mister Touch said acidly.

She put her arm around him. "I started it, sweetheart. I have to finish it now. Because you have to know how I feel about the other time I was pregnant."

"Was it an accident?"

"Definitely. Not like with you, although Daryll and I, I have to be honest, were very tight. I believed we'd work it out. He led me to believe we would."

"Were you living together?"

"He wanted us to keep separate places, and I went for it. Whatever he said, I believed. He said we had to go step by step, because that's what solidified a relationship. I said, Yes, Daryll. So when I got pregnant a kind of panic set in. We weren't moving off square one, and the clock was ticking. The fights started, then the inevitable — he got very very busy and couldn't see me. Panic turned to suspicion. I demanded a key to his apartment. He wouldn't give it to me. I was getting furious, depressed, scared. I couldn't get through to him at his office. Something happened to his home answering machine, so *he* claimed, and I couldn't leave messages. It's all so obvious now. Isn't it obvious?"

"Yes."

"So I waited for him this one evening across from his apartment. I felt nauseous, but I hung in there, even after vomiting in the gutter. Then here comes Daryll and hanging on to his arm is this zonked-out blonde. *Blonde!* I run across the street just as they're climbing the front steps, and I try to grab the keys out of Daryll's hand. I don't know. There was a lot of screaming. On my part. I remember the blonde cowering behind Daryll and Daryll trying to chill me out with some of his patented charm and then I was sitting on the steps crying and they were gone, they were up there in his apartment where that white skin must have been coming out of her clothes and Daryll must have been sitting there watching her performance from the bed with a self-satisfied smile on his face. Next day I made an appointment at the clinic for the end of the week. For two nights straight I dreamt of tadpoles. I kept a former rehab counselor of mine on the phone for half the night before my clinic appointment. The two of us tried to stop me from going in search of a cooking house."

She was crying. Mister Touch had long since put his arms around her. He was rocking her back and forth like a child.

"It's over now," he murmured.

After she cried a while longer, Spirit turned and said through her tears, "I think it is, I really do, I think it's over now. I know I want your child."

"Rattler is going to have a friend."

"Yes, yes. A friend for Rattler."

Another confession was being made in the opposite end of town, in a general store smelling of machine oil and chili powder and mice who were still dying from rat poison sprinkled in the corners more than two years ago.

Sag had drawn Snow into the back room for a talk, their heads an identical white, although Sag still wore her hair swept back, while in her newfound freedom as a woman of the people Snow wore hers loose and scraggly.

"I confess I'm appalled by your behavior," Sag declared. "We were friends." She sat down in the swivel chair behind the desk where Clifford Pauli had done his accounts for thirty-nine years. "Then something went wrong. Do you know what that was?"

Sitting on a straight-back chair, Snow popped a few stale jellybeans into her mouth.

"You're getting fat," Sag observed.

"I know, but I feel good. We're all feeling better, aren't we?"

"Are we?"

"I never meant to lose your friendship," Snow claimed with a smile. "What happened was my tooth."

"I know all about that," Sag said impatiently. "Having a tooth pulled is no reason to change everything in your life. One thing we both brought along on this trip is principle, a way of preserving a certain attitude. What if we survive? Do you want their" — she swept her hand at the front door — "vulgarity to be what the human race has to build on?"

"They have other things too. Alertness, feeling, courage."

Sag shook her head sadly. "A group of us are leaving and I want you to go with us."

"Why leave?"

"I firmly believe we're all sitting on a powder keg. Something terrible is going to happen. I don't know what it is, but the mix, the cultural gap, the inability to communicate —"

"We're healthier. Have you noticed that? Not so much wheezing, not so many mood swings."

"Christine, we're leaving to preserve something of the past. Values, principles. Please, come with us." Sag reached out as if to touch her old friend's hand.

Snow shook her snowy head. "I'm staying with the Skulls."

"Skulls! I detest the name."

"That's the difference between us."

Putting her hands on her knees and starting to rise, Sag declared, "The difference between civilization and barbarity. Ten of us opt for civilization."

"Where will you go, what will you do?"

"Find a small town somewhere, preferably in the Midwest, where traditional values were respected. We'll try to live Christian lives in an American way. Does that seem naive and foolish to you?"

"Yes," said Snow, "if you mean living in the old way. I don't think it can be done."

"The alternative?"

"We'll find it as we go."

Sag shook her head. "Delude yourself, go on. I pity you."

Snow laughed merrily as she watched her erstwhile friend stomp out of the room.

Out of Cisco they saw a girl in a Stetson and jeans standing in the middle of the highway. As the caravan approached, she stuck out her thumb like an experienced hitchhiker, flashing a smile that would have laid low the starting eleven of the Texas Longhorn football team. She had natural brown ringlets and sky blue eyes and cheeks childishly plump and a beaded edge of sweat above her full upper lip that caused those male Skulls who possessed the sight for it to eyeball her like prison inmates unaccustomed to seeing any women, much less a tall leggy beauty bronzed from the sun, her cowpuncher's shirt held together by a single button.

She waved like a cheerleader. And when the caravan eased to a stop, she called out "Hidy, padnahs!" before asking for a ride because her bike had run out of gas. Climbing into Car Seven, she accepted a proffered canteen of water, which she managed to empty before lowering. With a sigh she leaned back, hoisted up her long legs, and crossed her dusty boots over the seat top so that their bulldogging heels shot across the shoulder of — guess who — Sag, whose daughter had been presented at the Deb Ball and had never worn cowboy boots in her life.

The girl pulled the sweat-darkened brim of her Stetson down low and declared with a lazy East Texas drawl that it was mighty fine to meet friendly people on the road, because she'd been dogging it by herself a long time now. Had a boy of twelve with her about a year, but he got swept away by the Red River when they were up in North Texas. She hadn't seen one soul since, except a couple of old ladies setting on a porch somewhere, she forgot where, and a few Mexicans riding ponies through the main drag of San Antonio looking for trouble, and since then she had been up and down this old state of Texas more times than she reckoned she could count, either by foot or bike or by this real sweet palomino she managed to calm down long enough to get a saddle on and ride from Laredo up to Wichita Falls where a twister pulled him loose from the fence post she'd tied him to and sailed him halfway across town — went through the air just like one of Santa's reindeer, only he wasn't hitched to no sled full of toys — and came down in the middle of what used to be a mighty fine steakhouse, a two-pound hunk of sirloin for less than ten dollars. So she had to leave him right there in The Last Corral, which had a kitchen that never had cooked up any horse meat much less ever had a horse laying across its grill. And she'd kept dogging it from one place to another, so it sure was mighty fine to meet up with a lot of folks dressed to kill and neighborly enough to give a girl a ride.

She talked and talked like someone starved for talking until they stopped for the night in a place too small to appear on the map that lay in the glove compartment of Car One. Plastered all over the village was the state driving slogan, DRIVE FRIENDLY. Once they were comfortable, a roaring fire made, and kettles put on, Mister Touch drew the girl aside for a conversation, which went on interminably until she said yes to one question: Will you join us?

Finally, when she paused for breath, Mister Touch named her Do You Thing. For Do You Thing the thing was to talk.

And at the campfire that evening, listening to Do You Thing talking in her lazy voice, Stay High gawked and fidgeted and blushed and confided to The Boy Who Doesn't Speak Our Language, "That is the most intelligent-looking girl I have ever seen."

Next morning, before the caravan set out, Sag found the main man cleaning up a plate of breakfast beans beside his Spirit, whom the white-haired woman greeted with a stiff nod. Sag stood in front of him in a black Chanel suit which, though rumpled, looked elegant on her. She wore small gold earrings because it was before sunset, with a black grosgrain bow holding her silver hair back. Karl Lagerfeld would have approved of what Sag did for haute couture on a warm morning in a dusty Texas town, although the effect was wasted on Mister Touch.

She explained without fuss or stammering but in a_tone of triumph that a group of ten (later recalled by Adidas as the twirling turbinated tempestuous topsy-turvy riotous — in honor of Riot — Terrible Ten) had voted to leave this potentially dangerous caravan.

"Dangerous?" repeated Mister Touch, his gaze fixed a foot beyond one of the earrings.

Dangerous, yes, in Sag's opinion, because the trail of cars and trucks was in essence a powder keg — not because of the driving but because of the passengers. Thoughtfully, she modified the image to nitroglycerin: this motorcade reminded her of trucks in a French movie starring Jean Gabin, if memory served her, where they are carrying nitro across bumpy Central American roads and just everything happens.

She ticked off each of The Terrible Ten on hands unencumbered by jewelry — only the fourth finger of her left hand wore a ring. As she named the defectors, Mister Touch understood he had met his match. Sag had always been loyal to her past, and this powerful conviction was pulling others into the orbit of that memory. Disconsolate over the loss of his male lover, Web had blamed Mister Touch. The acquisition of a new lover, this one female, had not banked the fire of his righteous anger, and he was ready to defect out of principle. As for Boo Bang, Web held her like a spider holds a fly; she would stick to him wherever he went. As for Riot, to avenge the death of his beloved Bambu, he was willing to punish the Skulls by leaving them. As for Sweet Thing, power not love prompted her to join The Terrible Ten. Her campaign for overturning Jesus Mary Save Souls as Medical Director having failed, she wished to seek recognition elsewhere, and for that purpose was prepared to equip a small van with medical supplies under her exclusive control. As for the others, Putz and Shadow and two others who shall be nameless, essentially OOTLO, they were dragged along by Sag the way a park attendant drags a litter bag. Then there was Mister Lucky, an old man who became the tenth member of The Terrible Ten because someone would put him into the car as an afterthought the way you say "Oh, I forgot something" and shove a box of Kleenex under the rear seat before setting off on holiday.

"I won't argue," Mister Touch told Sag. "If you want to go, go. We'll help you get ready." He heard her start to go. "Wait," he said. "If you don't mind, we'll follow behind you on the same route."

Pursing her lips, Sag replied after some thought, "As long as you don't interfere, I suppose you can take the same route. It's a free country."

"Is that what you think you're proving?"

"You're different from the drummer. He was a tyrant. You're merely the head of a socialistic society."

He heard going and again he called out, "*Wages of Fear*. I saw it at a film festival. And it didn't star Jean Gabin. It starred Yves Montand and Charles Vanel!"

"I suppose you remember the director too," Sag called back sarcastically.

"Clouzot!"

Going fast over the ground.

He heard Spirit laughing. "You got her there," Spirit claimed. "Why do you want to follow them?"

"As long as they go westward, we'll be able to protect them."

"You're a mother hen," Spirit told him, while watching Sag gathering up her cohorts like a hen gathering chicks.

By the end of the morning The Terrible Ten were ensconced in two cars and had equipped a medical supply van with Jesus Mary's generous help — she wanted Sweet Thing out of the way — and were off.

As a cloud of dust whirled up around the departing vehicles, Snow stood in the middle of the road and watched her old friend recede into an America where The Terrible Ten might find more than they had voted for.

49

THE TERRIBLE TEN had stopped midway between Fort Worth and Abilene in a weathered little town set in the rolling grassland of the north central plains.

Wiping her forehead with a crumpled handkerchief, Sag studied a map. They could turn north at Abilene, go through Wichita Falls and Oklahoma City and get to Kansas City in the heartland of America (Sky Hook would approve), a place as steadfast and serious as the values that governed her life.

At Smith College Helen Detweiler had debated against radical classmates, one of whom had had the impertinence to pin a scowling portrait of Lenin above a dormitory bed. Helen had never forgotten her sense of outrage as an American, even though her own team won the debate. She had never voted anything but straight Republican. Her father would never have forgiven her. She had never forgiven the congressional district that had lavished a landslide vote on the knee-jerk liberal who defeated her father for state congressman.

She had lectured many of the Skulls during the journey — at roadside stops, around campfires, in motel rooms — that American citizens should not surrender to tyranny on the slim chance that they'd breathe better in a desert crawling with Gila monsters and rattlesnakes. Some had listened, especially when she deplored the use of names that made them seem like loonies. But not enough of them had been willing to make a difference. Sheeplike, they went along with every directive coming from Car One, which was driven by a sneaky inner-city woman who had shared the leader's bedroll long enough to get herself conveniently pregnant and so had illegitimately earned his confidence while chauffeuring him around the countryside like one of those medal-bedecked Latin American dictators.

Sheeplike people. It was utterly impossibly vile, incredibly depressing and disgusting. They even accepted as the emblem of their aspirations a crawly insect. Thumbing their collective nose at centuries of piety, they gaily adopted for their spiritual logo — an ant. Not satisfied with painting it on their cars and foreheads, some of them were doing a needlepoint tapestry (under the direction of that frump Sphinx, a misnamed courtesan if there ever was one, as if it were a secret that anything but pure ambition had driven her into the arms of the black drummer). In the center of the tapestry was an ugly-looking red ant. Perfectly awful, utterly impossibly, etc.

With absolute horror she had watched some of those sheeplike people ohing and ahing over an anthill, as if trundling in and out of it were Jesus Christ and the Twelve Apostles. Incredible. Incredible incredible incredible perfectly awful utterly impossibly vile incredibly depressing and disgusting.

But she wouldn't give in. Helen Detweiler never lost heart, her courage never failed. She meant to persist in the defense of democracy. By dint of willpower she had managed to herd together a small number of dissidents (whether or not they knew they were). The sad truth was that the only member of The Terrible Ten she had respect for was Riot. And even that regard was fast eroding. Lately Angelo had avoided her whenever she came around to discuss politics with him. Basically he was a rough Italian kid whose neat-looking eyes gave him more importance among these sorry people than he ever would have had on the streets of New York, back in Little Italy, selling restaurant equipment or making pizzas or playing cards in a neighborhood club with shrunken old Sicilians. All that brought him face to face with the ageless verities of social justice was personal injury. Whenever she used to speak of democracy, Angelo would shrug his shoulders, as if it were easy to locate, like a stolen car or goods ripped off a neighborhood vendor, and he would tell her with supreme confidence, "Yeah, well, forget about it. See, we gonna fix that bozo's clock." Often he alluded darkly to connections, perhaps forgetting that the Mafia had gone down the tubes with everyone else, including Colombian crack rollers and Afghan rebels and Sudanese refugees and the entire Congress of the United States.

Sag had feared that her streetwise associate might turn his energies elsewhere. Once the memory of his dead lover began to fade, so might his ardor for justice. It was not easy arousing in him a desire for democracy while nubile girls like Sweet Walk and Do You Thing and Dee Box were arousing in him a desire for something more immediately obtainable. She saw how they looked at him, craved him, wanted to devour him, because the awful truth was that Angelo had the physique and bearing of a god. Lately she had noticed that he was slicking his hair down with some kind of awful-smelling oil. It gave him the greasy, ominous, utterly exciting look of one of those stereotypic mobsters in movies that Italian associations complained were giving innocent people a bad name. What could this sudden interest in personal appearance mean? Had a girl caught his eye? One of those detestable creatures just burning to sweep him off and away? Lately Sag had felt gusts of anxiety beat upon her heart. She mustn't lose the boy. He was courageous and maybe in the old days his family had had good connections instead of illegal ones. When he nonchalantly told her "Forget about it," she forgot about whatever it was he ordered her to forget. She went to bed at peace instead of tossing all night the way she usually did, harassed by tarantulas of foreboding. The unfortunate truth was that she needed him. Her recent anxiety about losing him to younger women was precisely what had set her on the present course. She had persuaded people to separate from the Skulls in order to keep poor Angelo from the clutches of nymphomaniacs. He was safe among The Terrible Ten, who could not boast a single available young woman (Boo Bang, suffocating under the burgeoning weight of Web, didn't count). The fact of his escape from temptation gave Sag a warm oceanic feeling of contentment, because the horrible truth was that she loved Angelo, a man of no culture almost three decades her junior.

A hot raw wind was blowing through the streets of town, as Sag peered through the eerie gray light in search of Riot's strong stocky figure.

The Skull Caravan, which arrived a quarter of an hour later, was dusty from traveling across a treeless, neatly fenced landscape with low-lying ranch houses in the distance and a solitary windmill (Lil Joint was reminded of *Don Quixote*).

They parked on the *south* side of town, a few discreet blocks from The Terrible Ten, and shuffled panting into the shade of porched stores. With peculiar suddenness the cool air which had accompanied them most of the afternoon had given way to a warm front; it brought sweltering humid air and black shreds of fractostratus clouds from the southwest. The sun went under like a blown-out candle, leaving the dusty street the evil hue of gun-metal.

But Sag was too busy looking for her godlike Italian to notice what was happening. She saw him slouching against the peeling clapboard wall of a hardware store. With both hands he had pinned his tincan against his chest (his mamma had taught him "Cleanliness is next to Godliness" so he was fastidious about spitting and his last distinction on this earth was to be the last of the Skulls to use this outmoded way of expectorating); he was holding the can down to keep it from swinging in the wind.

Sag began crossing to the north side of the street, suddenly fearful of the gusts that had her leaning as if she were walking the deck of a storm-tossed ship. She was thinking of two questions, one important — was her Chanel skirt lifting above her knees? — and one irrelevant — was this terrible wind anything like the typhoons that Payback had experienced at sea?

Riot watched her coming: a thickset woman whose black Chanel suit swept away from her fat knees and whose string of pearls was blowing away from her neck parallel to the ground and whose grosgrained bow had been swept from her white hair.

Riot let go of the tincan; it banged convulsively against his shoulder in the tremendous wind. He cocked his head a moment, listening to a roar like a freight train chugging at open throttle down a steep grade. He couldn't believe it, a train making such time in the middle of this forsaken and level prairie. Then his mouth fell open, the lower lip quivering like a slice of Jell-O, when he saw it coming down the street: a huge black funnel in which debris of all shapes and sizes was whirling counterclockwise, sweeping a clean but narrow path like a briskly wielded broom along the *north* side of the street. He stood there amazed and stricken by the sight of this remorseless thresher, this harvester of objects. It had grown like a twisting root from a towering thunderhead and now approached him at forty miles an hour, a black leg out of his worst nightmare dragging across the town, with rain and hail preceding it, trumpeting doom.

Sag had reached him and was clutching his shoulders, yelling at his face. He couldn't hear a word, not even with her mouth six inches from his own, but he could see her teeth, the gaping red hole of her sudden terror.

He tried to pull free so he could get them both around a corner or across the street where on the *south* side (Adidas still saying S's said south seems safer since stormy squally signs signaling slaughter systematically sidestep southerly sites so some specialists swear) Skulls were wildly gestulating at him, having rushed northward from the caravan, their hair barely rumpled. From where they stood across the street it was like they were viewing him through an impervious glass window, their side comfy, his side perilous.

Riot appreciated the difference, but he couldn't free himself from Sag's grip. Each of her fingers seemed charged with the power of an eagle's talon. In the struggle to get them both out of the tornado's path, Riot lost his balance and fell with her to the ground, feeling the rain and hail lash his eyes and blind him. At the final moment, before the monster reached him, he heard its roar abruptly cease, and Riot felt the queer sensation of being a feather in a vacuum when the low-pressure core of the storm loomed over their flailing bodies. He felt himself lifted by a giant hand of air and hurled like a doll against a wall that was bursting outward to meet his chest and head, while the woman still clung to him, her last breath going out simultaneously with his own, the expelled air of two impossible lovers who were lost together in the dust and the timber and the metal objects blowing out of a disintegrating hardware store.

Minutes later, in the strange new silence, Skulls began to get a look at the devastated town, or more accurately at the *north* side of it, which had been pinpointed by fate for the twister's ultimate destination. Buildings were either leveled or shattered, a maze of wood and steel and glass and furniture and automobiles, glistening wet in the aftermath of the storm. Looking to the northeast, they saw the vortex spin rapidly away and then disappear like Boris Karloff through the dry-ice fog of a horror movie. Some of them, at the outset having run for cover, crawled from under cars and porches to stare at the ruins, among which, surely, lay some of The Terrible Ten.

One of The Ten who peered out at the devastation with the rest of the Skulls was Web, who had left Boo Bang just long enough for a weewee, guess where, on the *south* side of the street.

Minutes later, hard at the grisly task of discovery, Skulls found

Sag naked among the hammers and buckets and chains of the hardware store, plucked clean by air and lacerated by flung debris, so that she looked like a fat white fish thrown up on the shore, pecked at by beach birds.

They didn't find all of Riot, only the torso half a block farther along the street, with a saw blade stuck in his chest.

They found Boo Bang on the exposed second story of the county courthouse. At first they thought she was still alive, because she sat upright, feet dangling over the edge of the floor, her streaked blond head resting against a wall that had been sheared off as if someone with gigantic wire cutters had neatly crunched through office stairway restroom without disturbing the Texas and American flags still fluttering on poles behind a desk no longer there. It took four men to haul away Web and deposit him panting from grief in the back of a supply truck.

Sweet Thing was found inside a gas station. The various tools whirling around in there had managed to make of her slight bony body a remarkable sight, reminiscent of a cadaver after complete dissection in the sort of anatomy class that might have given her a broader knowledge of medicine than that possessed by the red-headed Irish drunk.

Rummaging farther, not a word spoken, the Skulls located Putz and Shadow, both bad-looking Wheezers who for almost two years had spent most of their waking moments in a perpetual diagnosis of their wheezing, which they thought was improving steadily. They were now together in death as they had been in life — two mild-mannered middle-aged white men in the rubble, side by side and nose to nose, which was a miracle in its own right, since nothing else in the path of the twister had managed to maintain such pristine symmetry.

But the Skulls were witnesses to an even greater miracle when to their enduring astonishment they discovered in the midst of flattened houses the scrawny old gentleman Mister Lucky, sitting unharmed on the floor of the house in which he had taken refuge and whose walls from the high pressure inside had exploded outward, stripping the clothes off his lean shanks and leaving him both crosslegged and perplexed, like an infant in a nursery filled with broken toys.

When a cheer went up at his remarkable survival, the old man sniffed and quoted the only OOTHI that he knew, and knew only because someone had teasingly whispered a maxim of La Rochefoucauld's in his ear: " 'Few people know how to be old!' "

50

THEY REMAINED in town a day, cremating what was left of Riot and Helen Detweiler, which was the name Mister Touch called her during the obsequies because she would have hated to have her ashes go up in the name of Sag. No one criticized the main man's disregard of the rule.

When her ashes went up, The Fierce Rabbit smiled, knowing that the OOTHI she had applied to him — "For every inch that is not fool is rogue" — had gone up with her.

At his side Yo Boy was chuckling.

The Rabbit never felt comfortable around laughter; there was always the chance it was at his expense, and even worse, that he might not know it. "Something funny?" he asked coldly.

Yo Boy said yes, in a way. The cut-up bodies reminded him of L.A. jointing. He explained offhandedly that when a gang gunned down a victim, if they were lucky enough to drag the body away, they would take it somewhere, cut it up, throw the parts into a Dempster Dumpster, and send the stamped official number of the Dumpster to the rival gang so they would know where to find their brother. That was called jointing and sending.

The Rabbit stared at him. Yo Boy was having trouble growing a scraggly goatee. He had little eyes set close together, a slim build, and delicate hands. He was nothing. But something came over The Fierce Rabbit. It was not yet identifiable, but it told The Rabbit to keep checking this kid out to keep him in check.

The Skulls did not cremate Boo Bang, not being able to reach where she sat with her feet dangling over the edge forever. Web, who had not touched a bite since her death, sat on the curb and stared up at her streaked blond head resting against the courthouse wall, while people tried to console him. He paid no attention to them or their quotations from OOTHI, even though some people had sat up half the night riffling through books, trying to find appropriate ones: " 'Tis better to have loved and lost than never to have loved at all" — that sort of thing. Or heavy pessimism, as if it could help bring a lover back from the abyss of loss: "Human life is everywhere a state in which much is to be endured and little to be enjoyed." Or stiff-upper-lip stuff: "Nothing happens to anybody which he is not fitted by nature to bear." Or a cool demand for stoic acceptance: "I never saw a wild thing sorry for itself." Web in his grief was deaf to their wisdom, having found the right quote for himself long ago, when the lover before this one, the male one Flash, left him fat and forgotten: "Everyone can master a grief but he that has it."

Nor did the Skulls cremate Putz and Shadow; they seemed much too happy where they lay side by side, nose to nose, in perpetual conversation about the state of their health.

Stunned Skulls wandered through the devastation. The concrete jungle of New York City had not prepared them for the highways of America or for a destiny that seemed to be telling them things they could not understand. It seemed that The Terrible Ten had broken a law of nature by separating from the caravan, and for this transgression they had been punished.

"Hey, homes, see what I see?"

"You know I don't see almost nothing. What is it?"

"That tornado, it drove a straw into this telephone pole here."

"A what?"

"A straw. Like horses eat. Drove it right into the wood, like if you throwed it like a knife."

"Bullshit it did."

"Seen this with my own eyes."

"Don't rub it in, homes. Knowing I can't do like that."

"Yeah, sorry. But I seen it."

"Remember that ad on TV? This chick raise her arms and the wind blow and she say, 'It's not nice to fool Mother Nature'?"

"Yeah?"

"That's what I'm saying. We fooled her and she got us back."

"Fooled her how?"

"By not dying before. She come down on us for fooling her."

"Dig it. I be getting me a rabbit's foot like my uncle had."

"I be staying close to the old man Mister Lucky. He got the power."

It's what a lot of Skulls were thinking. Yesterday he sat on the floor of his nursery as naked as the day he was born and not a hair on his head (what there was of it) out of place. They were going to stay close to him as if he were a living talisman, a little the worse for wear, wrinkled and yellowish, but powerful as hell.

The main man had his Spirit lead him out into the open prairie a quarter mile from town. He told her he wanted to be alone awhile. She had grown accustomed to this quirk of his, still unaware of his real reason for these solitary excursions into woods or prairie or empty motel rooms.

While the smoke of a crematory fire drifted into a distant blue sky, Mister Touch talked the events of yesterday onto tape. He bemoaned the loss of their companions in The North Central Plains Disaster. He recited the casualty list, pausing to consider the miracle of an old man sitting childlike in the midst of all that wreckage. " 'There is something in this more than natural, if philosophy could find it out,' " he recalled from OOTHI. And with the flippancy that often attends joy, he hit the RECORD button and said, "This day will go down in the History of the Skulls as The Day Mister Lucky Got Lucky."

But his well-being was tempered by other recent events. Since Mystique's disappearance, he had felt a strange emptiness, as if someone who had been perpetually looking over his shoulder had vanished. He hoped against hope that she was out there seeking a romantic future with someone else, but within his heart the little throb of emptiness told him she was out of his and any other man's life forever.

He wanted to end this tape with a faithful record of a recent secret talk he had held with Harold. But the main man felt he must withhold that even from Whoever You Are. There was no doubt in his mind that Harold would eventually ascend into Skull Heaven alongside his Jesus Mary Save Souls, who was already enshrined there — rather uncomfortably at present, because the TV repairman's love had rendered her as pregnant as the main man's own Spirit. Once asked to perform his sort of miracle, Harold would locate an oil-driven turbine, wire and transformers, a generator and storage batteries — the ingredients of electric power — for a lighting system. Next, plumbing . . .

But Harold and progress had to wait for Arizona. The main man was going step by step; that was his style, even though within him desire raged to get to the desert as soon as possible.

Next day, when the caravan prepared to leave, No Name was sitting behind the wheel of a car. In six hours he had learned to drive by wearing out eight teachers, not resting until he was confident enough to manage a deserted prairie highway.

So it came to pass, as Mister Touch had hoped, that love had turned a boy into a man. Behind No Name's handsome face was an iron will that the Skulls could surely use.

As the caravan pulled out of the ruined town, one person was very happy because another miracle had occurred and he was part of it. Sluggo, the misnamed Dutch boy who loved jazz-fusion, had found a tape in its plastic box lying on a bed of twisted typewriter keys in the rubble of the post office. Picking it up, he couldn't believe his good-looking eyes. For two years he had searched New York City, risking his life in dog-infested streets to ransack music stores for Azymuth's *Tightrope Walker,* and here, in a tangle of death and destruction, he had found it, a gift from the gods.

Someone else just as happy when the caravan growled into motion was Coco. Her miracle was that every day she got more breath back, enabling her to sing. She held baby Rattler and rocked him to the rhythms of "Amazing Grace," as Aretha Franklin would have sung it.

> *Amazing grace! How sweet the sound*
> *That saved a wretch like me!*
> *I once was lost, but now am found,*
> *Was blind, but now I see.*

They stopped often today because of an outbreak of diarrhea, probably the result of drinking creek water despite Jesus Mary's warnings.

The main man and his Spirit were sitting against a live oak, the moss hanging from it like the long lank hair of an old giantess. Spirit was reading to him from the *Aeneid*. She paused in her reading to catch breath, having noticed that her pregnancy had endangered her status as a Steady Breather. In the silence Mister Touch reached out and touched her arm.

"The Greeks looking for a new land," he said, "reminds me of Arizona."

"Do you need reminding?"

"You know I don't. I've never had a stronger ambition in my life than to get to Arizona."

"Tell me about your other ambitions."

"One was to collect art."

"You never told me you loved art."

"I never did — love art, I mean. I just wanted to collect it. I knew this guy from Goldman, Sachs who was a terror in proxy fights. He collected art. I saw his collection in his town house, and I said to myself, Someday I'm going to have walls filled with de Kooning and Diebenkorn and Dubuffet."

"You're beginning to sound like Adidas on D."

"You're making fun of me."

"Well, I don't quite understand your ambition. Collecting something you don't care about — mechanically, like buying the art of artists whose names begin with D."

Mister Touch laughed. "It wasn't *quite* that bad. But it wasn't good either. You see, I figured I was going to make millions and in desperation was looking around to see what I could do with all that money. But I have a new ambition now."

Now it was her turn to laugh. "I should hope so."

"It's time to become a grandfather."

"Well, you've got a step to go before that."

"What about you, your ambitions in the past?"

"One was a lot like yours is now — to be a grandparent. A married one whose husband was with her when the grandchildren came to visit. My ambition was to have a good steady conventional life."

"And now?"

"Oh, that's obvious. To be a mother."

They were silent awhile. When he spoke again, his sightless eyes were closed and the words came slow, measured in a kind of incantatory revelation. Skull children would have a wonderful and terrifying and challenging future. Someday they would listen to legends of the past, when there had been a ruler as wise as Solomon called IRT.

Spirit interrupted. "And another like Moses who led his people to the Promised Land."

He closed his eyes again and described what the children would hear about. Great warriors who protected a castle in a distant land called New York. Travelers who died in water or drifted away on tides of memory and were lost. A love so strong it made people invisible. Two intrepid hunters who stalked their prey with one riding piggyback on the other. Biblical whirlwinds rushing through prairie towns. Wild beasts roaming a country called Georgia. Kids would listen open-mouthed to the exploits of Olympians: Stitch, god of metalworking; Stay High, god of prophecy; Jesus Mary, goddess of healing; Sphinx, goddess of art. Sister Fate a wandering bard. Kids would wonder at the immortality of Mister Lucky.

The main man opened his eyes. "I think many of us are feeling better, looking better. Am I right? Can you see it?"

"Sometimes I think so. But then I think maybe I'm kidding myself. You know them better."

"But you can see them." After a thoughtful pause he added, "I wish there was a way for me to judge what's happening."

"Maybe there is."

"Well?"

"Listen to them. You might be able to hear how their health is."

"How do I do that?"

"I haven't any idea. You're the Blindie."

That's right, he thought, it was his own affair. Yet his Spirit had confirmed the potential value of his recent interest in listening to things. Not to music but to voices, Skull voices. He found himself cocking his head to listen intently, as if sorting out intonations and their meanings. It was like kicking away cobwebs, searching for something in an attic. And what was that something in the attic? Perhaps an old daguerreotype of stiffly posed ancestors who nevertheless had had the guts to pull up stakes and cross the vast lawless plains of America in search of a new home. Not only did he want to lead the Skulls, Mister Touch felt a burning desire to know them as well as he knew himself.

By squeezing his hand, Spirit loosened him from his thoughts.

"Blue Magic is coming this way. From the look on his face I'd say he's anxious to speak to you." Getting up, she bent down and whispered, "The kid looks plenty worried."

Mister Touch heard the quick steps of her going and then he felt movement between his face and the sun. The space was filled with a sudden chilliness as if Blue Magic had brought winter with him.

The Chinese boy coughed and stammered before getting the truth out.

He had forgotten to mark the dates on the calendar with which he had been entrusted.

In vain Mister Touch tried to discover when this had happened. Blue Magic didn't know. Two days ago, he had abruptly remembered the calendar that he kept in his suitcase and went to put an X on it, but looking at it he realized that he had forgotten to put in X's for numberless days.

"What do you think happened?" the main man asked, appalled.

"I got depressed."

"Why?"

More coughing and stammering. The truth was that he had been depressed ever since Harold had joined the Skulls. Blue Magic had discovered the truth about Harold — that he had been an electronics technician. Even before Blue Magic had worked his way through the basic electricity course, he was facing a rival who knew far more than he himself ever would. He plunged into such a funk that he had completely forgotten the calendar.

So Harold was no longer hidden.

And the main man found himself in a terrible quandary. Should they try to recapture time or ignore it? Perhaps someone among the Skulls knew the date. Not that there was any incentive. Perhaps they could take a vote — is this Tuesday the eighth or Saturday the twelfth? — but that would be upsetting. IRT used to say they had better keep track of time or a stinking wave of despair would seep through their ranks.

Without their calendar, dutifully X'd, the Skulls would be adrift in time, sailing aimlessly through the universe, without hope of anchoring themselves in their own solar system, much less their galaxy.

Stunned and humbled by this possibility, Mister Touch considered the dismal truth: one of the few things to cling to in life is the day, the month, the year. Skulls had dealt cavalierly with these details merely because they felt they had time snug in their grasp. Now it had gotten loose and was sailing away. How could they do without the calendar, a prime symbol of civilization? It provided a space for the human consciousness to reside in. It built confidence by giving a person his very own date of birth. It confronted each individual with the knowledge that others would acknowledge his date of death. The calendar gave people a chance to move in a spirit of hope from one inhospitable square to the next, sustaining a childlike trust in the idea that the new day, duly recorded in earthbound print, would bring solace and good fortune.

If the Skulls knew what had happened, how would they handle the floating days ahead of them? At first, perhaps, they wouldn't care, but as days went by, the loss of precise time might worm into their minds like the insidious virus of V 70, break down their self-confidence, and leave them awash in an oceanic waste of multiplying seconds.

The more he considered the problem the more convinced Mister Touch became of the danger. They might never reach Arizona if it was revealed that they were traveling through unknown days toward a nameless month in a random year.

The main man figured there was only one course of action for him to take.

Making vague but rapid calculations after a blind squint at the sun he couldn't see, Mister Touch said, "It's the tenth of December."

There was a brief silence. Then in a voice lifting toward hope and relief, Blue Magic said, "Ten December?"

"Yes. How does that sound to you?"

"Ten December," the boy mused. "Is that what it is?"

Sighing at the boy's resistance to expediency, the main man declared, "Yes. It's the tenth of December. Now go get that calendar and mark an X in every square until you come to the tenth of December — you hadn't come to it yet, had you?"

"I think the last was twenty-one November."

"Tomorrow you X in the eleventh of December and keep X'ing them in forever and ever and ever after. Do you understand?"

"Yes, sir. I do. I will. Every day forever."

"You will never forget again?"

"Never!"

"Even if we're lucky enough to get more technicians and you feel even more depressed?"

"Never forget again!"

"Blue Magic?"

"Yes, sir?"

"We will never speak of this to anyone. Never."

"Never, sir."

"Take the calendar off somewhere and do the marking *when you are alone.*"

"You aren't punishing me?"

"You've been punished enough. Every moment since you discovered what you'd forgot. Am I correct?"

"Yes, sir."

"So do the marking in private. Then stick the calendar on the wall of a truck for everyone to see. It will give them satisfaction to see it."

Going.

Warm sunshine replaced the cool shadow of Blue Magic and the Skull leader felt that warmth on his bearded face. He called out loudly for his Spirit, anticipating another warmth, her hand in his. What had just happened was something he must never never think of again. Although he might have thrown human history out of mathematical balance for all time, at least he had saved the day.

Coming. A shape blocking out the warm sunshine. Her warm hand in his.

51

THE FIERCE RABBIT could never remember not being angry. His afro seemed to be rigid from electricity, as if he were plugged in to a high-voltage outlet, and in a sense he was — plugged in to his own galvanic fury.

Whenever he thought of the past, which was often, it had a pasty white look to it. He had a vision of white faces in squad cars, behind counters of fancy stores, coming out of elegant restaurants. Every face was washed, primped, and happy. He recalled bitterly the white faces behind the steering wheels of cars racing through Harlem with windows rolled up, doors locked. During hot ghetto nights he used to watch the ads sputtering on the old TV set. Pretty redheads and blond men carrying briefcases were pitching expensive cars, perfumes, fur coats. Loudmouth blacks clowned for the junk-food ads. He remembered his mamma showing him the Christmas card photo of the honky family who paid her a starvation wage for cleaning up their shit. He often saw in memory the fat sweaty pink-cheeked deli manager who hired him to carry boxes and fired him when two hanging Provolones disappeared, because naturally the nigger had done it.

Whenever he saw Mister Touch walking around, images out of the past bombarded him: the cops, the schoolteachers, the social workers. Such memories made his mouth dry and his afro stand out like a halo from hell. V 70 had changed very little for him. He was still taking orders from the enemy or from Hoss, the enemy's Uncle Tom. Anger ran in his veins like old rum, filling him each mile of the journey with the feverish obsessions of a drunk.

Each day in the back seat of a throttled-down car, The Fierce Rabbit would spin out a complicated web of ideas like a spider weaving the truth of its life from its own guts. He became for the first time in his life a philosopher. He developed a theory which placed at the hub of the universe a black man wearing an afro and a dashiki, cradling an automatic rifle in his arms. Once The Fierce Rabbit had securely set this black man at the Universal Center, the rest of his teleological design was easy to create.

For example, from his perspective the ruin caused by V 70 had been the logical outcome of white sinfulness. Black purity must now save mankind from oblivion. It took only a slight leap of the imagination for him to believe that the creator of V 70 had been black, a black scientist; that through this cleansing holocaust mankind would rise again; that it would rise under the domination of black intelligence; that any white survivors would have to view their good fortune in terms of servitude to black rulers; that henceforth the earth would join with other inhabited planets of the cosmos in obeisance to a black God who wore an afro and a dashiki and held as the scepter of his universal rule an automatic rifle.

Not everything would fall into heavenly place, however, until evil elements of the world were removed. Some whites could live — those who recognized black supremacy — but others must die, including Mister Touch and the black Judas in a cowboy hat. So certain was The Fierce Rabbit of his spiritual rectitude that he no longer hated either of them. They must be eliminated but without rancor, being no more than jigsaw pieces illustrative of wickedness that were destined to fit into a moral puzzle which, when completed, would provide the cosmos with a black representation of rectitude and beauty. His hatred for the two leaders was therefore changing to spiritual love as he connived to destroy them. They were, after all, merely images of evil and their function was to emphasize the need for a new purity.

So he waited, and what he waited so patiently for (what his impatient bloods could not foresee) was a heavenly sign from the Universal Center.

And then one afternoon in Texas he received it. He had seen the main man and the Dragon spy go off into a clump of woods together. Something urged him to follow them. If they were going to copulate, he'd get out of there fast, because the sight of a white man humping a black woman would make him sick. Fortunately, he was not subjected to any such humiliating scene that might have forced him to kill the honky before the grand design was completed. What happened was harmless enough — the bitch took the Blindie out there and left him on a log. When he felt he was alone, the white leader spoke into a small tape recorder: "The History of the Skulls, Tape Sixteen." He told somebody called Whoever You Are what had gone down in the past few days. He kept saying this was "history." Whose fucking history was *this*? The Fierce Rabbit asked himself. History of the Skulls? History of the *white* Skulls!

And it occurred to The Rabbit, lying in underbrush, that here was surely a heavenly sign. Until this moment what had been history had been white history. The distortion of things would no longer be tolerated by the Black God at the Universal Center. If The Rabbit could get rid of those tapes, he would eliminate the last white history on earth. And in this final apocalyptic action he would wipe out George Washington with those flabby pink cheeks and General Custer with those girlish blond curls and Lyndon Johnson with those big red ears and fish-pale Marilyn Monroe and all the rest of those honkies — social workers, cops, inner-city bureaucrats, landlords, movie stars, and reporters. He would scrub history clean of the whitewash and expunge those complacent milky faces and blot out the weak blue eyes and erase the thin bloodless lips which spoke of equality and freedom while meaning white hopes, white dreams, white comfort, white success, white salvation. He would rid the world of white lies.

That would leave another history to be written, black history for real, the divine history of the Universal Center. Because God had been waiting patiently since the beginning of time for the appropriate moment to set the record straight. Right now He was waiting for His true agent on earth, Marvin Johnson, to set the apocalyptic events in motion that would click the cosmos into place like a door shut forever — or shut until the Black God in His afro and dashiki decided once again to lift His automatic weapon and blow the door away and stride out among the stars to create the world anew.

Listening to the honky drone on into the tape recorder, The Fierce Rabbit held a knife in his hand, wondering if another heavenly sign would tell him this was the moment fated for the end of white history. The sign didn't come, however, and he understood why — this was only Tape Sixteen, a single tape. *All* the tapes must be destroyed.

The Black God at the Universal Center would have to be patient a while longer before His agent on earth could do His bidding. The Fierce Rabbit felt his heart pounding; looking down, he noticed that his knuckles around the clasped knife handle were nearly white from tension.

Whatever happened to him, he was determined to free the Skulls from their white oppressor and to free them from white history.

The caravan had pulled up on barren land between Midland and Odessa, Texas, above a vast bed of oil that began percolating one quarter of a billion years ago during the Permian period of the Paleozoic era, a fact unknown to Yo Boy, who was holding forth before a group of The Fierce Rabbit's followers. With a stick in his hand, Yo Boy was tracing NUKE BSVG C 187 in the dirt.

"Know what this be?" he asked with a smile.

Nobody did.

In south central L.A., he told them, you could find a message like this on every wall. It was a placa. This one identified the writer as Nuke. In the Blood Stone Villains Gang. Yo Boy completed the placa by X'ing out the *c*. That meant the Blood Stone Villains would do any Crips who invaded their set. This Blood called Nuke had made the *c* small as an insult to the Crips.

"What's that 187?" someone asked.

"The California criminal code for murder." Yo Boy waited for that to sink in before adding, "This Blood Nuke was done by my brother, a Crip in Cuatro Flats."

Snootchy Fingers, the white newcomer from Dallas, pulled down the brim of his fedora to protect his pallor from the sunlight. Then he asked the right question. " 'Doing' means killing?"

Yo Boy nodded with a proud smile.

Later in another town The Fierce Rabbit backed him up against a wall and clutched his doeskin vest from Polo by Ralph Lauren, demanding to know what he'd been telling guys.

Yo Boy looked up at The Rabbit's dark face darkened further by anger, then down at the expanse of black knuckles spread across his vest. Smiling, Yo Boy waited until The Rabbit muttered vaguely and let go. Freed, Yo Boy answered the question. He had been telling them about L.A., which was where they ought to go after Arizona.

"Seem like you be saying a lot these days."

"Yeah?"

"Are you all mouth or what? Don't worry yourself. I give you the chance one of these days to show me which is which. Believe it."

"Yo, I believe it," said Yo Boy, but there was no enthusiasm in his voice.

This angered The Rabbit, who might have grabbed the vest again, but for the memory of Lil Joint slashing Dragon over *Madame Bovary*. Greasers were like snakes, he figured, a simile that encouraged him to drop his hand. He watched Yo Boy swagger off with a nonchalance that must have been learned in the L.A. gang. The Rabbit envied that walk. Although he had acquired an attitude in the ghetto, The Rabbit had no mean-street smarts for real. He was more like Zip, a friend of his brother's, than he cared to admit even to himself. Zip used to swagger around talking about Vietnam, but all he'd ever done (it came out one night under the influence) was cook in the Officers' Mess.

Driving along a monotonous Texas highway, Spirit In The Dark thought of love.

Other occupants of Car One were dozing or lost in their own thoughts. Her husband slept with his bearded face resting against the window. Behind him sat Send Em Back To Africa, whose black-tinted opaque shades never let you know if his eyes were open or not. Snoozing in the back seat were two lovers, although not lovers of each other.

Looking in the rearview mirror, Spirit studied Patch, who had taken Snake from Coco because of Coco's pregnancy and who in turn had lost him to Pearl because of her own pregnancy. Poor Patch had believed in the pencil-thin mustache, the whippet hips, the easy smile. But she had lost all of that machismo charm to Pearl. The Snake had left Pearl pregnant too before wandering elsewhere. Coco, Patch, Pearl. One of these days Snake would wake up to discover that a pack of screaming kids was his and that he was a patriarch.

Love was everywhere, trailing in its wake the debris of infatuations and quick passions and long alliances, the flotsam and jetsam of desire and devotion. Love had reached epidemic proportions among the Skulls, a gentle parody of V 70. It had infected Jesus Mary Save Souls while she nursed Harold back to health. At each day's bivouac they sat tented together and then disappeared into the night as if they had inherited invisibility from Futura and Superstar. Nando was nearly finished nursing Chibo into a bona fide

Wheezer and would doubtless soon be searching for someone else she could lovingly help into the lands of Wheezer or Blindie. Having had his fill of Spat and E.Z., Hoss had managed to take the sacred virginity of the South Indian girl Salt Noody who, having lost it, seemed never to have had it, but flaunted her hips in a sari and exchanged tongue kisses with the ad agency hipster so publicly that generations of Brahmins must have shuddered in their various incarnations. Cougar and Black Pixie, both big powerful people, were shaking the motel beds like joyous elephants. No one doubted that Sweet Walk and No Name could have posed for illustrations of the *Kama Sutra*. The editor Fire burned with lust for the Latin dancer Papo and when they weren't doing it, she read Trollope to him. Anyone except a Blindie could see Stay High following Do You Thing wherever she went. He salivated like a puppy, his inchoate desire rendering him inarticulate, his aching groin making him forget a commitment to "The Mystery of the Universe." Following him with another kind of love was The Boy Who Doesn't Speak Our Language, who in despair for his mentor's attention spoke rapidly a language whose every word ended in a vowel.

Love was indeed everywhere. And the effects of lost love. Mystique had apparently succumbed to the Drive Away Syndrome in Dallas, and Ace had ended up at the bottom of a bay in eternal pursuit of a woman who didn't want him. Riot was dead because in grief over the loss of Bambu he had run straight into a wind that cut him in half. Web couldn't keep food down now that Boo Bang was sitting up there alone forever on the second floor of a Texas courthouse.

Love everywhere, the sound of it and the smell of it. Nights were filled with the muffled moans of lovers. When she arose in the morning Spirit had whiffs of the unforgettable pungency of love that made her think of ponds hidden in woods, thick with vegetation, lactescent from wriggling life.

Until the trip began, Skull women had been using diaphragms, contraceptive jelly, cervical caps, postcoital douches, aerosol foams, and a variety of pills. They had lugged along enough stuff to supply a gynecological drugstore. But the trip seemed to have reawakened maternal instincts. Women had either forgotten or ignored the devices and had just gone for it. Maybe the long drive over neglected roads full of potholes had shaken up the gonads of Skull travelers so that other little travelers got where they wanted to get on time, even if their destination was through the darkest of tunnels. At any rate, sticks were becoming blue, meaning bellies were going to swell. Love was everywhere.

Love was in her own body now, growing. She liked to think it had started to grow in her the first time she lay down with Mark. Their child was curling through her groin like a vine, anchoring its trimester roots where the blind man had sought to solve his own riddle of love.

In this strange world filled with millions of corpses and great cities rotting in weeds, nothing was stranger than what was happening inside her body. There had been a Dragon time when the idea of a penis revolted her. In-and-out and in-and-out, a pounding wounding machine programmed to punish her. At that time there had been no future, only one slimy bolt of daylight and darkness after another. And then Mark had entered her with love so that its penetrating shape became the round one of her own desire. And the future began to grow in her, a vague but satisfying anticipation of a new life breathing crying laughing and eating from the twin conduits of her body.

Unconsciously, she pressed the accelerator and led the caravan toward Arizona at ten miles an hour faster than her strict lover, had he known, would have allowed.

E.Z. liked to live. She liked to eat. Mostly she liked to do it. And the truth was she had never been happier in her life than she was on this trip. She had found stability with the Skulls. She had friends whom she saw every day and didn't have to call to see if they were available. She had lovers who couldn't run out on her, at least not far, and if a guy like Hoss would hit and run, well, there was always someone else. She didn't have to stand on her feet eight hours behind a counter, selling perfume to mean old ladies. Mister Touch was even kind of like the father she had wanted — a guy who told her what to do — because her shiftless pa had skipped before she could walk and her mamma had confronted her with a bewildering variety of temporary daddies. Life had never really been bad, but E.Z. had learned before she could put more than three words together that it was best to take things as they come. Except where men were concerned. After two abortions she had learned to demand things — like "Wear a condom," or "Get me a drink."

E.Z. wiped the sweat from her brow under her floppy hat and squinted into the late afternoon. Something moved across the street. Leaning forward, she strained for a better look, her heart going pitty-pat in her mouth. Something moved again, closer. E.Z. stood rooted to the sidewalk until the thing moved squarely into her vision.

A mangy little dog.

Its tail lifted to wag like a rapid pendulum.

"Look at you," E.Z. said with a chuckle. On the trip she hadn't seen many dogs. They were probably out in the country, foraging among farms and woodland. When the caravan halted near those that didn't flee, they behaved the way dogs used to: barked, growled, crept off — not like those former pets in Washington Square Park who held their ground and dared you to kill them before they killed you.

Bending down, E.Z. said to the dog, "Come here. Come on now. Come here, you lil devil."

The dog wormed his way toward her and turned over, flashing his prominent ribs and tight little balls. E.Z. got down on her knees. With a rush of joy she lifted the dog and felt a warm tongue licking her face. As a child, she had always wanted a dog, but no such luck. Never had anything but a fish (cost her seventy-five cents at a pet store) that she put in a bottle of water and it died the day she brought it home and her mamma threw it into the garbage even though she had wanted to bury it under the rubble of a nearby vacant lot with kind of like a cross over it.

E.Z. hugged the dog, which continued to lick her face. "Lil devil," she murmured with tears in her eyes.

That evening at the campfire in Odessa, the main man made yet another decision that departed from tradition: E.Z. could keep the dog as a pet — and name it too. When she named it Lil Devil, she didn't know that once upon a time the main man had carried a kitten into Washington Square Park, only to have IRT order him to give it up.

The main man passed his hand thoughtfully over Lil Devil's coat, which E.Z. had spent an hour combing out.

Uneasily, the Skulls studied the little mongrel, recalling Dobermans and shepherds and Great Danes in fierce dashes across the park. Was this scruffy little thing a *dog*?

In succeeding days there would be other newcomers — cats, a

ravenous goat, a bitchy parrot — gathered by Skulls exercising their new privilege. The caravan would travel toward Arizona like a moving pet shop. Above the growl of engines could be heard barking, meowing, crowing, and the squawking of that damn parrot, who had been found perched on a corral fence, wearing around its neck a keychain with a plastic insert containing a plaintive message written in the scrawl of someone mortally ill: *Be good to Ralph. Thank you. Mrs. W. S. Geiger, Jr., Lawton, Oklahoma.*

With Lil Devil the sluice gates of affection were thrown open. The caravan would proceed like Noah's Ark, bleating braying clicking trilling yowling howling its way across the open prairie toward the Promised Land of Arizona.

52

"Tornadoes transform time totally."

"Yeah, old butcher boy? Listen to him. Been quiet a few days but starting again."

"Things tilt then toward terrible trouble."

"Do with us, that sure true."

"To tell the truth, thought thrives terrifically through threat tension trepidation tonitrophobia thermophobia traumatophobia tachophobia" — he took a deep breath — "topophobia thixophobia tocophobia and thanatophobia."

"Hear that? He put 'and' in. Spoiled his T that way."

"Shit it do. One 'and' just add a touch, don't it, Adidas?"

"Therefore tremendous tumult triumphs."

"I been saying that all along."

"Don't make fun of him, homes. Old butcher boy doing fine. Outdone himself on T. This T be something. Why not jist stick with T, old butcher boy?"

"Too tiring. Tough talking T."

"See, he really talking now. Something different in old butcher boy. Getting better. You see it, bro?"

"I don't see almost nothing now and you know it."

"But you breathing good."

"Thank you, bro, kindly."

"Ready for this? Rattler, he can see."

"Good news be it true."

"This morning they saw him watching a hand move. His eyes be moving to see it moving."

"Who did?"

"King Super Kool."

"Then I believe it, 'cause he can see."

"Like it could be we gonna be fine."

They had come to the end of a long drive. They had crossed the Pecos River into Reeves County and entered the rough dry land which long ago had been the stamping grounds of Judge Roy Bean.

The caravan halted in early evening at a small tank town consisting of a gas station, a Baptist church, a general store, and a few dozen shacks so weathered by wind and dust that they resembled the land itself, their contours rising from the brown plain like mounds built by prairie dogs. The travelers disembarked and stretched in the warm twilight, then blasted the door off the general store and went inside to rummage for food.

After eating, the Skulls looked for places to sleep. After clearing rooms of any skeletons, they flung themselves wearily on beds or wrapped themselves in blankets and slipped into sleeping bags on the floors. No one stayed outdoors because the wind was blowing range-dust through the streets. By midnight the fagged-out travelers — even the most resolute of lovers — were asleep, although the main man awoke suddenly for a few moments and called out to his Spirit, having seen something terrible in a nightmare, something so fleeting however that he could not remember it a second after waking. But the impact of it still shook his bones, a dream terror rippling through him with the sureness of something about to happen for real, because as William Hazlitt said, "We are not hypocrites in our sleep." Then, mercifully for him (but unfortunately for three other people in the sleeping town), he fell back asleep — leaving only a single consciousness alert, that of a coyote.

The coyote loped down the main thoroughfare to sniff at the burning embers of evening fires before slinking away at a sound that startled it: a sound that humans around here used to make, the crunch of boots on pebbles.

Two men in cowboy hats (for real, not like the one worn by Hoss the hipster), carrying Winchester rifles, approached one of the shacks. They moved with the silent efficient step of hunters stalking game and opened the creaky screen door with care.

Minutes later they emerged, prodding ahead of them three figures swathed in blankets with faces covered. At the edge of town the two shoved their captives into a station wagon and sped eastward at one hundred miles an hour, arriving twenty minutes later at the outskirts of Pecos, where they pushed their blanketed prisoners into a seedy motel.

One of the cowboys lit an oil lamp, casting light on the dazed faces of Soda, Swear To God, and Queen Sexy. They huddled together on one of two beds.

"Now ladies," said the taller cowboy in a West Texas twang, "we gonter have some fun." Grinning, he pushed the Stetson back on a seamed forehead.

Sprawled on chairs, with their Mariposa boots up on tables, the cowboys were soon pulling at fifths of bourbon while boasting of the day's exploit. Queen Sexy pieced together from their comments that they had been returning from a bobcat hunt in the Davis Mountains when something real peculiar had appeared on the windswept road ahead. They had seen a dot, a flicker, the full-blown light of a campfire. Parking outside of town, they had reconnoitered and discovered a bunch of egg-sucking jack-leg no-count piss-ant crazies crazy as a peach-orchard boar just sitting there in the middle of the road eating beans — niggers, Chinee, and whatnot sitting there big as you please like they owned the place.

The watchful cowboys had selected a shanty where women had gone for the night. They hadn't seen live women in more than a year now.

Which meant, Queen Sexy decided, that they had seen women after V 70 Struck. Where were the women now? Dead? Killed by these men? She had a feeling about them. A college summer spent in Texas had prepared Queen Sexy for identifying such cowpokes and imagining the world they lived in. She had seen them lounging against coffee shop walls, toothpicks in their mouths, hats pulled low over their sunburned faces, and she had thanked her lucky stars for a fate that didn't include them. In the pre–V 70 days these two had probably been drifters, just like they were now — scrounging what they could, living at the edge of violence, creating a sad parody of the Old West, until by an unblessed miracle they had been spared death and now controlled much of Southwest Texas. They had even been spared bad eyes, for no one could drive a hundred miles an hour, not even on these straight roads, without good vision; and they had been spared bad lungs too, for they possessed the lean hard bodies of men accustomed to exercise. Moreover, tonight in the shanty they had clamped those bony hands like vises over sleeping mouths and stood three women on their feet with no more effort than it would have taken them to light a match. Of course, they treated fate's twin gifts with the utter indifference of men for whom world disaster meant nothing more than another barroom brawl. To them V 70 was free ammo and supplies for their hunting trips into the hills after white-tailed deer, red wolf, bobcat. Now their playground extended for hundreds of square miles and as long as they had bullets and whiskey and a car they lacked nothing — except women.

Queen Sexy had taken less than a minute to figure out what to expect from them. No pleas would stop them once they were liquored up. She had been reading Shakespeare again since joining the Skulls. Grotesquely ironic that she had been reading *Julius Caesar*, which said, "O! that a man might know the end of this day's business ere it come." All she need do to apply those words to herself was change "man" to "woman" and "day's" to "night's." She had never gotten much pleasure out of irony; she didn't now.

What she had always feared was going to come true. Her mouth was dry from the certainty of it. She had never forgotten that time in high school when a boy had laid a clumsy hand on her leg, groping between her thighs as if trying to locate the gear shift of a truck. And if that hadn't disillusioned her from pursuing heterosexual romance, the truth was she had never found the male organ an object of desire. Far from it. It had always seemed to her an ugly thing, like the defeathered neck of a chicken. And not only that. She disliked the rest of a male body, the hairy chest, the gross definition of arms and thighs, the dollops of fat or muscle at the hips, but most of all she was repelled by masculine hands, which seemed to lack all patience and any trace of music. Not that she hated men; she admired the talent of some of them for being toughest on the verge of defeat, for their tenacity under fire, for their general lack of pettiness when victory seemed near — qualities she often made use of in courts of law to beat them at their own game.

But when it came to love, she had always sought other women, who knew how to stroke her body into myriad tingling cells and to roll her center around with tongue or finger that had been dipped first in the oil of whispered endearments.

A bitter hideous irony. She fled from half-grown boys who might have lacked technique more than sensitivity, only to find herself at the mercy of these two overgrown infants whose idea of pleasure was probably to rip the bowels out of a wounded doe.

They were getting drunker, leering now, their huge boots caked with dusty earth, their funnel-brimmed hats pushed back to expose red remorseless faces. She heard Swear To God whimpering at her side. If the frail girl didn't shut up, they'd take her first. But Queen Sexy couldn't warn her; the terrified kid would probably cry out and instantly set the horror in motion. Queen Sexy felt that as long as the three of them sat motionless on the bed, nothing would happen. They'd be safe in the charmed circle of stillness — like pheasants who die only if they fly. Maybe the cowboys would drink themselves into a stupor first and then . . . and then . . .

She must have had a hopeful look on her face, because one of the cowboys suddenly asked her what was going on. Without awaiting an answer, he turned to stare appraisingly at Swear To God, taking in her pale freckled cheeks, her thin trembling lips, her doe eyes moist with silent pleading, her thick black hair — everyone said her hair was her best feature, a compliment that the shy lass of Scots-Irish heritage always blushed at.

"Drink, miss?" the cowboy asked with a grin, holding up the bottle. Her reply was a whimper.

"We did perty good," he told his partner, "except that nigger."

"At least it's a good-looking nigger." When they both stared at Soda, she edged against the wall, holding the blanket to her chin.

The taller cowpoke took his Stetson off and sailed it like a discus across the room.

When they both giggled, Queen Sexy knew they were sufficiently liquored up.

The taller one then removed his goatskin gloves and threw them on the floor.

His partner, whose name was Rick, asked him if he had an idea.

"Sure do," said the taller one, whose name was Joe Don. "We got real lucky," Joe Don said with a wink. "Like having a bunch of wells coming in."

Rick cocked his head in puzzlement.

"Don't get it, do yer. I'm saying we kin just follow those piss-ant crazies where they go and take what we want. See all them ladies round the fire tonight? We follow where they go like they was a herd. Cut out a few when we need 'em."

Getting it, Rick chortled. Holding a stubby finger to his lower lip, he said thoughtfully, "How we gonter do this?"

Joe Don shook his head. "Always a few bricks shy of a load, ain't yer."

Turning to the women, Rick said with a smile, "What yer say, ladies? Got any ideas how we gonter do this?"

Getting to his feet, Joe Don said, "Entertain our guests while I step outside." He left and returned shortly with a rope. Taking out a hunting knife, he cut off a few lengths. "It ain't we don't trust you ladies, but I reckon yer wouldn't think well of us letting yer run loose like a bunch of barnyard hens. Sure be dumb, wouldn't it."

"Sure would," Rick agreed, taking a drink.

"Come here, nigger."

Soda got to her feet, stumbled, but righted herself and walked over to Joe Don, who stood waiting for her, a length of rope dangling from his hand as if he were ready to throw a couple of hitches on a calf. She did not reach his shoulder. "Put yer hands back." He tied them together with a few deft motions. Then he hobbled her at the ankles with another piece of rope.

"Come here," he said to Queen Sexy, who felt herself rise from the bed like someone else, like someone she was watching in a film. She felt the rough touch of the ropes, and at that moment she hated herself for being a woman.

"I jist bet," Joe Don said, grinning, "yer turn out best." Then he turned to Swear To God, who had begun whimpering louder now that the cowboys had touched the other two women. "What's yer name, honey?"

She said it in a voice so low that the cowboy had to lean forward and ask again.

"Swear To God."

"Swear to God what? What yer swearing to God fer? He ain't gittin nobody out of it. Say yer fucking name."

She had been with the Skulls too long to think of her old one at a time of crisis and anyway, she was too scared to remember it. "Swear To God," she said again.

With the flat of his hand, hard as a board, he struck her across the face, sending her into a sprawl across the floor. "Now get yer ass over here," he demanded, one hand on his belt.

Queen Sexy couldn't bear the doelike despair in the pale girl's eyes as she struggled to get up. Simply couldn't bear it. The tough trial lawyer, in court a vicious self-serving bitch (so rival male lawyers called her), let compassion get the best of her. She heard herself say in an astonishingly coy voice, as if she had practiced coquetry all her life, "Listen, big fella, why not me? Don't you think I'm cute?"

Both men studied her. Joe Don finally smiled. "What's yer name, honey?"

"Queen Sexy."

They both laughed. "Well, honey," Joe Don said with a broad grin, "yer gonter get a chance to prove it. Tie up the kid," he told Rick.

"Don't we get one each?" Rick asked.

"Tie up the kid," Joe Don said, never lifting his eyes from Queen Sexy while Swear To God was trussed and tossed like a sack alongside Soda on the bed.

"We gonter do one at a time," Joe Don said. "Last longer thataway. Nice and easy."

"Nice and easy," repeated Rick.

"Know what yer gonter do first, Queen Sexy?" the tall cowboy said, unbuttoning his jeans.

She knew.

53

AFTER LEAVING the village, the caravan traveled westward, not far from the space-age installations at Fort Bliss, with
Mount Franklin perched above them like a gigantic sleeping eagle.

Even Blindies sensed the vastness of the land surrounding the
silent city. But the landscape was not the reason for the Skulls' so-
lemnity. A pall had fallen over them that morning in the village
when they awakened to find three sisters missing. It was a disheart-
ening mystery. Gone were three women and blankets they had
wrapped themselves in in a shack filled with musty air, two skeletons (shoved into the kitchen area), cobwebs, and a six-pack of Dr.
Pepper still sitting in a fridge along with the desiccated remains of
what had once been some kind of food.

Had something weird whisked the poor women into the night?
On leathery wings? That possibility was scarcely more peculiar
than finding African lions on a Georgia highway or the good luck
of Mister Lucky. Mister Touch vaguely recalled a nightmare that
had awakened him the previous night and it touched him with irrational fear.

He blamed himself for not following the dictates of that fear.
Quite simply, he should have yelled out, waking everybody. His
dream might have saved three people even as an earlier dream
about prairies and rabbits and the sound of breathing might save a
lot more if he got the caravan to Arizona.

The main man decided to remain in the tank town one full day,
hoping the missing women would return from, say, a berry-picking
expedition. Meanwhile, he sent out search parties, but with strict
orders to drive no farther out than ten miles. His job was to get
what people he could to Arizona, come what may.

So he sat in the gas station, struggling with the temptation to
believe in a supernatural cause for the disappearance of Soda,
Swear To God, and Queen Sexy. He also battled an old habit of
requiring a logical explanation for events and wondered gloomily
if ancient men with their superstitions would have been better prepared for life after V 70. He looked back longingly at his recent
reliance on fate, which for a while had turned him into a laid-back

fool who simply enjoyed what came. Now that state of grace was gone.

Perhaps a return to ancient thinking was already in the works. Spirit told him that Skulls were vying these days for seats alongside Mister Lucky in Car Three. Whenever the caravan stopped now, a murmur began. "Where is Mister Lucky, is he safe? Is the old man okay? Does he need anything? Give him a drink." Feed him dress him bathe him stroke him cling to him, because if bogey man gonna come get you, old Mister Lucky he has the power to stare them fuckers down.

Today, while awaiting a miracle that no one believed in — the return of the three sisters — young bloods were crowding around Car Three, where Mister Lucky sat as he usually did even when the caravan had stopped. Usually he said nothing, but chomped his gums and stared ahead. Today, however, he suddenly began talking, and when he did, the crowd became thicker, until people were three deep around the car.

"It is time to be old, to take in sail," he said, borrowing a phrase from the sailor Payback and also unwittingly quoting Emerson. "But first I want pequins."

Thrusting his head into the open window, where the old man sat next to the driver's seat, a young blood asked anxiously, "Pequins, what be them?"

"My brother came out here many years ago and he said he ate chuckwagon chili made with small wild chiles that tasted like nothing else on earth. They were called pequins. I want them." Chomping determinedly, he added, "I want them now."

"You gonna get them," declared a blood. Four of them pushed others away and climbed into Car Three. Before anyone else knew what was happening, Mister Lucky was being whisked out of town by devotees willing to do whatever he desired.

"Where do we get them pequins?" asked a blood.

Mister Lucky shrugged tranquilly and sat back, allowing his followers to worship him by finding the chiles on their own.

They drove about five miles and saw an orchard of stunted-looking trees along the road. "Be that pequins?" a blood asked.

"I wouldn't know," said Mister Lucky calmly, "until I ate one."

"We gonna go see." The bloods climbed out and waited for him, but the old man demurred.

"It is time to be old," he told them. "I'll wait right here. Roll up the windows."

"Gonna get hot in there, Mister Lucky."

"Roll up the windows."

They rolled up the windows and left him there, chomping, looking straight ahead into the vast spaces of extreme age.

"Where we gonna find them pequins?" a blood asked his brothers.

They all shrugged. One suggested that chiles must grow on trees or bushes or something and this looked like an orchard.

"Chiles green, ain't they?"

"Some green, some red."

"Depend maybe on which sort of tree."

"Well, up there in that tree — see that? They be an orange color."

"Like oranges."

The bloods, so busy squinting upward, heard it before seeing it. Airplanes with galumphing old motors; that's what the bees sounded like in approaching flight. Hundreds descended on flesh like a glittering veil of animated agony that had been flung earthward in cosmic malice by a cruel god.

These ferocious African immigrants had come north from Brazil, raping young queen bees and stealing local honey on the way. Looting and ravishing, this hunlike species of Hymenoptera had crossed the Rio Grande without interference from pesky humans who used to trap them by baiting domestic hives with pheromones, enticing them to crawl inside large plastic bags in which they suffocated.

What our Skull bloods didn't know, as they were surrounded by the banzai buzzing of this murderous horde — but what they were soon to learn firsthand — was the fact that whereas ordinary bees can sting ten times in half a minute these sonsabitches can do *eighty fucking five!*

Our Skull bloods were too busy experiencing pain and horror to worry about the stinging capacity of their attackers. They swatted madly, gasped, swelled into crimson lumps, and died.

The swarm moved on, appetite whetted, and found a big black creature near the road. Inside its sleek exoskeleton was a pale morsel of living flesh. They rammed against the Caddy with such propulsive fierceness that their bodies cracked; their mandibles splintered in the attempt to bite through the unyielding chitin of glass; the digestive fluids in their ripped abdomens were flung across the windshield so that Mister Lucky could scarcely see ahead into his age. But they didn't get in. They flung themselves at him in kamikaze fury, but never got to his dry old flesh. Mister Lucky's luck held. He sat there calmly and waited for rescue.

The car covered with bee blood and guts was found around twilight, along with the four bloods so swollen and disfigured by thousands of stings that the Skulls had a hard time deciding who was who. When they were brought back to town and cremated, one of their friends, another blood who shall be nameless, took a bottle of local wine from the general store and poured some on the ground.

"That be for them," he explained, then drank and handed the bottle around. "My brother, he was a player. He gave me two advices in life. One: 'Don't let nobody go sounding on you.' Second he say, 'Goof like you want, do what make you happy, but fucking respect the dead.' When he die in something mean one night, I did what he say, I give my brother respect. I pour wine out then and I pour wine out for him and other dead dudes I know every time I take some fresh. That way I remember. Like I be remembering now," he said, motioning toward the glowing shapes of four bloods within the flame.

Yo Boy guffawed. Later, when he was sitting with Snootchy Fingers and Daddy Rich, the pale faces who had joined up in Dallas, Yo Boy passed judgment on the blood. "Pay no attention to this guy who pour wine out when they should of fucked over who killed a brother."

Sitting in identical postures — chins cradled in hands and elbows on knees — Snootchy Fingers and Daddy Rich both grinned.

"We talking respect," continued Yo Boy. "Know how you get that? You prove. Let me tell you about proving. My cousin out in L.A. and other cholos like him, they had it down. They knew.

"Like they never party with women. They dance by themself and then after they get high they go get women and pop. They earn respect for what they done. They never stop working connections for sales. They work twenty-four, seven, three hundred sixty-five. Night work mostly, not day. Day they spend sniffing coke,

drinking real champagne, all mellowed out with best video and car-
pets and a BMW. They had silk in closets and dressers. My cousin,
he would silk down when he go partying. He silk down and then he
go out. Like my brother he was in the Cuatro Flats out there. They
court him in at sixteen."

"Hey, what was courting in?" asked Daddy Rich, whose buck
teeth dominated his face like a horse whinnying.

"Courting in was how you got membership. They beat the shit
out of you, then you got in. My cousin was no wannabe, he was in,
he was tight partners with the top top cholos. Like my brother." Yo
Boy paused. "Both they die in drivebys."

"Hey," said The Fierce Rabbit. He had come up silently behind
Yo Boy. "What you fronting about now?"

Yo Boy looked up at the tall dark figure blocking out the sunlight in front of him. "Me, I don't front," he said coolly.

"Look, I appreciate what you and Wishbone done back in
Vicksburg or where it was. I know you done that to prove. Like I
appreciate it. But I be the man around my own guys, hear? You
getting to talk like the onliest man in the world was your brother or
your cousin or some other cholo in L.A. gangs. New York was
where most of us come from, and we don't need talk about Crips
and other shit coming out of L.A. You hearing me?"

Yo Boy smiled. "El Viejo talk, we listening. We waiting too," he
added.

"Waiting?"

"For when we move."

"Don't you worry about moving. Let me settle that. When I say
go, we go, we break these motherfuckers apart, we take over, we
do it all but we gonna fucking do it the way *I* say and when. You
hearing me?"

"Yo."

Mister Touch said that night to his Spirit, "Tomorrow, when we go
through El Paso, find an art store."

"An art store."

"And take its sculpting tools."

"Sculpting tools." When he said nothing more, she said, "Okay,
so tell me."

"They're for carving an idol."

That same night The Fierce Rabbit drew Snootchy Fingers aside and ordered him to go use those snootchy fingers for something useful for a change. "Bring me back a couple dozen blank cassette tapes from when you find a music store when we stop in El Paso, you got that?"

"You want tapes, you got them."

The Rabbit was pleased by such blind obedience, which in Snootchy Fingers was unblemished by as much as a questioning glance. It occurred to The Rabbit that although Snootchy Fingers was dumb (but not as dumb as the dumbest nigger in the world, poor dead Wise Guy), to say nothing of being white, he was probably more dependable than that snaky little greaser Yo Boy.

Next day Snootchy Fingers would deliver two dozen tapes to The Rabbit, who would begin to see his plan taking shape like a spider sees its web insinuate the possibility of death into the dark corner of an attic.

The next days were more unreal for Queen Sexy than the days of V 70.

She and her companions were raped, sodomized, degraded in whatever manner the whiskey enabled the cowpokes to imagine. Had she been raped and left to consider those moments, perhaps she might have retained merely the horror and the outrage and lived with their harrowing memory for the rest of her life. Rape was everything she had anticipated and more. Yes, it was. Yes, indeed. In the intervals they left her alone, Queen Sexy had time to worry the idea of rape the way these bastards worried her body. She worked hard to define it. Rape was a struggle between two people to avoid what neither wanted; for it was the burden of a raped woman to remind herself that the physical act was not the consequence of a relationship that she had chosen, while the attacker must strive to keep the physical act free of a relationship he had in fact chosen. She was quite ready to write a treatise on it (and that's when she wondered if she was going mad). But worse than being used like something not quite human was the unreal possibility that she had encouraged such treatment. Well, she hadn't, but she had. She could not escape the reality of sex — that it was a token of some kind of agreed-upon relationship. The ultimate horror: consent to a relationship that even the man didn't want. How possibly had she consented? By being a woman. Proof? His body hard against hers, entering hers.

By remaining with her attackers and watching them with the other women, however, she was forced to leave behind her own misery at times and to meditate on the experience itself as an authentic and indisputable fact of human history. It didn't help, of course, to recognize the repetitive and communal nature of such an event. In fact, it made it worse.

There was leisure for such lugubrious reflections, while the cowboys drank Dr. Pepper laced with bourbon and rested and held rambling conversations and cooked chunks of deer meat over a fire in front of the shabby motel. Time brutally forced her to think. She had the leisure — the abysmally correct word — the *leisure* to contemplate what was happening not only to herself but also to her companions. She felt for them as she had never felt for anyone, not even for the lover who had died of V 70 in her arms.

Their rape became her own. She felt their humiliation and despair and fury as they lay spread-eagled on a bed stinking of sweat and semen. Her own suffering expanded into a sea of feeling for the other women and then for every woman who had suffered in this way and then for anyone, man or woman, who had been forced to endure the worst that human beings can inflict on their own kind.

Tears rolled down her cheeks, her fists clenched, her heart pounded, when one of the other women was called on to perform or be used. Sometimes she lost a sense of her own self and in their mutual suffering felt linked with Soda and Swear To God, as if a white-hot wire threaded them together. She could hardly tell their whimpering from her own, and their pain ballooned within her own body unbearably until she felt she would burst from the pressure of their communal anguish.

Swear To God had thrown up frequently; the odor of sex and vomit filled the hot room as if they were living in a bog, a violent swamp filled with disemboweled and decomposing corpses and mad monsters fornicating. Why didn't the cowpokes move them all to another room? she wondered. There were forty units, goddammit, to choose from. Then she realized that these two fellows were on a journey no one could take with them. They were alone together, wading through a cesspool of degradation that gave them in their madness infinite pleasure. And when she understood how utterly lost she and her companions were, Queen Sexy became ice at the center of her consciousness. She had arrived at the final chill region of Dante's hell.

After that, she saw everything down to the smallest detail without emotion, as if she had turned into a camera constructed of living flesh. She began to study the men as if they were problems in tort law. She listened intently to their jokes and monotonous tales of hunting trips. They boasted to "the ladies" of their bronc-busting skills. They seemed to be developing a kind of primitive regard for the objects they used; it was like a hunter lovingly stroking the barrel of a gun that has just brought him in a brace of pheasant. Sometimes they offered sips of whiskey as young men do in the wimpish ritual of seduction.

But anything could change their mood. She understood that, and she wondered if the other women did too. If these cowpokes heard the call of wide-open spaces or they ran out of stories or got tired of drinking booze and Dr. Pepper in a malodorous motel room or if they simply had enough of three frightened haggard female faces, they would surely revert to what they basically were — two opportunistic predators — and kill what they no longer wanted and go their merry way until the urge for further merriment set them on the trail of the caravan again "to cut a few more from the herd."

Curiosity and the instinct for survival had kept her somewhat sane, Queen Sexy figured. Now she grew saner on the hope that somehow she'd be able to communicate with the other women; when not being used or fed, they were kept well apart and trussed. If she tried something — was she going to try something? — it must be when they were capable of fighting and running.

She waited for the right moment without knowing how to recognize the right moment if it came along.

On the third day at sundown, having run out of fresh meat, the cowpokes built their usual fire from motel furniture in front of the motel, opened some cans of spaghetti sauce, and dumped the contents into a pot, flinging the empties into a garbage heap like good ol' boys who remembered that their mammas told them "Cleanliness is next to Godliness."

Without meat to cut, the women would not be given knives.

Queen Sexy had hoped for knives; now she felt discouraged and might have simply waited for the next day had she not been certain there wouldn't be a next day. These gentlemen would probably kill them before sunup. Since noon they hadn't touched a woman. They were bored and getting restless now that their sexual desire was dwindling. They sat beside the fire in ominous silence and avoided looking at their captives, as if the flesh they had enjoyed was now a burden to get rid of.

When the sauce was hot and the spaghetti cooked, the tall cowboy Joe Don untied the women's hands and shoved plates (unwashed these three days) in front of them, where they sat on the ground around the fire. The eating began in silence. Moodily the shorter cowpoke, Rick, asked his partner for the jar of jalapeño peppers. That was the only sound anyone made, save for the slurping of tasteless pasta and watery tomato sauce two years old. Swear To God ate nothing; she had thrown up bile for the last twenty-four hours. She now sat with the plate gripped in both hands as if holding on to dear life.

Taking a deep breath of decision, sensing this was the moment if there was to be one, Queen Sexy asked the cowboys if they had ever seen two women do it.

Joe Don looked up from his plate, red sauce ringing his upper lip like a mustache.

"Sure," Queen Sexy told him. "Can we show you what I mean? You've had us every way possible, but there's more we can offer."

"Reckon God never meant that kind of thing," Rick claimed with a righteous frown, but his companion waved him off and said shrewdly, "What's in it, blondie, fer yer?"

"If you like it, maybe you'll let us go."

That seemed to satisfy him, so Queen Sexy put her plate down and flung the blanket away that she was wrapped in, exposing her naked body, bruised from neck to knee. She began untying the rope from her ankles.

"Don't do that," Rick said.

"We can't show you all tied up," she said matter-of-factly, picking up the plate and eating again, as if his objection had brought the exhibition to an end.

"Wait a minute," said Joe Don. "What the fuck yer eatin fer? Thought yer was gonter show us."

"Can't show you tied up." She went on eating.

Joe Don sat between the other two women. Looking from one to the other, as if wondering which of them would perform, he said, "Show us, blondie."

"I was going to finish eating and then we'd show you."

"Don't get me mad. I get madder'n a banty rooster."

"He sure do," confirmed Rick with a grin.

Joe Don said, "Show us now, yer fucking bitch!"

With a shrug she stopped eating, but continued to hold the plate while scuttling over to Soda. Their eyes met knowingly. Then for a short but rapturous moment she wished this was for real, that she was approaching Soda with love, the soft lips and skin with a mahogany sheen to it.

"Don't go for French stuff myself," grumbled Rick.

"Shut up," said Joe Don. "Yer elevator didn't go all the way to the top."

"Got my ashes hauled nuff now. Don't need no sexin up."

"Shut up."

"Least have 'em do a pump-handle two-step first," Rick suggested, putting his plate down. "I got some country tapes in yonder. They kin do some dancing. Sure would like to see some."

Joe Don didn't even bother to shut him up. The tall cowpoke sat quietly and watched as the naked blonde, holding a plate in one hand, reached with the other and stroked the black woman's breast through the blanket.

"Don't go in for it."

"Shut up."

Queen Sexy was conscious of the plate and especially of the fork held against it by her thumb and forefinger, even while her lips met Soda's in a trembling kiss. Not even then was she certain of how to do it but she did it anyway — hurled the spaghetti-filled plate into Joe Don's leering face without losing her grip on the fork. She lunged for him and jabbed the fork above his fingers, which were clawing tomato sauce from nose and cheeks. She jabbed at his right eye so hard that she felt the prongs nick the bone, bend, shiver, go deeper in. Not even then was she certain what to do next, but she did it anyway — scuttled to the fire and grabbed hold of the flaming brand of a chair leg. She swung it around and caught Rick in the face with it as he lurched toward her with a drawn knife. He screamed. She gripped the brand though it was burning into her palms and she beat at him, hearing the flesh of her hands sizzle, feeling herself melting against the club, and yet the pain wasn't great enough to stop her from beating him.

Dropping the club finally, Queen Sexy looked down for an astonished moment at the charred peeling palms of both hands. Rick shook his head like a punch-drunk fighter and was trying to get up from the ground. Welts with ashes stuck to them extended from jaw to cheek. His hair was smoking around a wound oozing blood. "Don't," he murmured in a voice that sounded lazy, "don' . . ." as he got to his knees and groped for the knife.

Then there was a loud report. It boomed through the frontier town that had heard its share of them a hundred years ago. And the cowboy never got farther than his knees but fell forward without a sound. A rosette of blood began to soak through the back of his Levi's shirt.

Lying on her side, not three feet from the fallen cowboy, Soda held one of the Winchesters. She was so shaky that it waved around like a hypnotized cobra.

Queen Sexy whirled and saw Joe Don staggering toward a Texas sunset, both hands clutching his face. A terrible moan came from him. It seemed to rise from his scimitar boots, curling out of his tomato-stained mouth like a noise neither animal nor human, like the teeth-on-edge screech of rock grating against rock.

Though hobbled, Soda had managed to shift around in his direction. She tried to steady the rifle, then dropped it. "Let her do it." She motioned toward Swear To God, who was huddled up on the ground like a fetus.

"No," said Queen Sexy. "She can't do it." Stepping forward, she reached for the gun. When she touched the metal, Queen Sexy howled from the pain that shot from hand to shoulder. But she held on. She willed her burned hands to hold on. She stared down at her left hand on the barrel, at her right hand on the trigger guard — two blackened misshapen objects like a pair of rats clinging to a basement pipe in her childhood home in a nightmare she'd had maybe a week ago. It seemed as if she were holding a live wire crackling with voltage.

The cowboy was wobbling, but he kept going forward, his feet stepping jerkily like a toy winding down. Queen Sexy did not shoot from where she stood. She approached by willing each foot to move in front of the other and held the Winchester out in her ruined hands like a gift. When she had come around and stood right in front of him, Joe Don was still shuffling forward. She had the leisure to wait a few moments, to savor the situation and listen keenly to the unbelievable sounds coming for real out of his throat. Behind her staring eyes was a brain frozen in a region of hell; it recorded an auspicious sight: a protruding fork handle between Joe Don's fingers, the prongs sunk deeply into his right eye. Satisfied that she had heard and seen exactly what this moment of leisure had been given to her for, Queen Sexy stood two feet away, aimed for his groin, and pulled the trigger.

54

IN LATE AFTERNOON they camped in the town of Canutillo near the border of New Mexico.

Mister Lucky clicked his dentures and sat stolidly in Car Three, while young bloods gathered around like bees around their queen, hovering and grinning, asking him did he want a soda a candy bar a wet cloth to cool his forehead. Glaring, he waved them away like so many flies.

Mister Touch wanted to walk among the Skulls and listen to them. So with his Spirit leading the way, he strolled through the unseen dusty streets, hearing the Brazilian jazz of Sluggo's new Azymuth tape, *Tightrope Walker,* at pumped-up volume on the Dutch boy's beat box in a town that had never had no truck with music like that. And from a side street he heard the rocking rhythms of Prince's *Lovesexy* — "Grand Slam thank U ma'am, U really made my day!" — from another sound box, doubtless carried by one of any number of young women who were out of birth control.

Another easily identifiable sound was Rattler crying while Coco cooed soothingly. And then there was a metallic bang accompanied by the pungent smell of motor oil, which signified that Stitch was hard at work with wrenches and things somewhere along the line of parked vehicles.

But there were other sounds less obvious. As he strolled with his wife down the main street of Canutillo, the main man heard a pop . . . pop . . . pop . . . , which he soon identified as coming from Salsa Sal, the wizened little Cantonese peasant, popping bubble gum. In her traditional blue jacket and the black trousers of her ancestors she could snap crackle and pop gum as loudly as teenage New Yorkers on the after-school subway.

The main man stopped. "What's that swishing sound?"

"Venus Girl," Spirit said, "sweeping a porch so people can sit down."

He could see Venus Girl in his eye's memory: a stocky Japanese who cleaned things when she had breath for it — bending over to squint at what might be dirt that she could whisk up with a broom and dustpan. Sometimes the main man worried that Venus Girl was so quiet and unobtrusive they might lose her through a faulty buddy check.

A dog barked.

"Is that Lil Devil?" he asked.

"It is."

"What's he barking at?"

"That's what everyone wonders. He'll look at nothing and start barking."

"Like he sees something?"

"Yes, exactly."

"Ghosts," declared the main man. He imagined the little dog trotting along at E.Z.'s heels, barking at unseen presences hovering at the edge of villages and behind gas stations. They weren't there, of course, but how could you explain that to a dog who had seen nothing but death for most of its young life and then finally a caravan of living humans? Into the simplicity of a doggy life had rattled a parade of gaily decked-out automobiles of the shape and size that he must have seen humans drive in his puppyhood — these, however, decorated with images of those little red things that trundled back and forth near his paws while he snoozed and that sometimes gave his nose a sting.

"Stay High's coming," Spirit said. "You wanted to see . . . talk to him, didn't you?"

Coming.

"Stay High," said the main man, "you haven't reported lately on your projects."

A long silence followed. It was rare for Stay High to let such a thing happen; usually he filled in conversational spaces with Trivial Pursuit information. "What was that again?" he asked after a while.

"I'm asking about your projects. How is 'The Mystery of the Universe' going?"

"Well," Stay High said and fell silent, as if a single word were his entire report.

"Let me level with you. At times I've paid little attention to your fine work on the poem. I'll admit other things got in the way. But the poem really is important. The Dream Queen was a damn smart woman and who knows, maybe a visionary. Maybe we need a sign . . . the perspective of someone who knew us but is gone . . . a prediction of some sort . . ." After a long silence, the main man added, "Spirit, is he still here? I don't even hear his breathing."

"Yes," sighed Spirit. "He's right here. And breathing."

"Am I breathing? Is that what you want to know?" Stay High asked indifferently.

"Stay High?" Mister Touch said into the empty air lanes.

"Yes?"

"What about The Boy Who Doesn't Speak Our Language?"

"Oh, he's around."

"Of course he is. He's probably nearby, waiting for you."

"That's true," offered Spirit. "He's right over there, waiting."

"From what I understand," the main man continued, "he's talking a lot these days. He's talking a blue streak in his language."

"Maybe he's polishing it," suggested Stay High without enthusiasm.

"Maybe he's ready to talk *your* language — *our* language. Maybe he wants attention."

"Maybe."

"Stay High?"

"Yes?"

"What the hell's wrong?" After an audible intake of breath directly in front of him, the prez heard going. "What did I do? Frighten him?"

"I think you did," said Spirit.

"Well, what is it? Is it love? Is he sleeping with Do You Thing?"

"You must be kidding. He hasn't even spoken to her. What he does is practice dance steps. When we stop, he gets out of the car and starts dancing."

"Why hasn't he spoken to her?"

"Because he's tongue-tied. As if he's become a disciple of The Boy Who Doesn't Speak Our Language and can't speak his own language anymore. I've seen him when he meets her. His mouth chomps up and down like he's going to say something, but no sound comes out. The girl just stands there staring. Then he takes off his glasses, wipes them desperately, puts them back on, shakes his head as if he's just decided to commit suicide, mutters to himself — who knows, maybe instructions on how to do it — and walks away with that poor neglected boy at his heels, spouting vowels. 'Ain't that man sick or something and that boy too?' Do You Thing asks people, but they just burst out laughing. Are you really interested in the poem?"

"I never have been, but lately, as we get closer to our destination, I wonder. The Dream Queen was dying, yet she worked every day on this thing. She pleaded with IRT to hold on to it. She called it a statement, not a poem. Without a lab to work in, she said, nothing had been left to her but words, so she reverted to a teenage habit of expressing herself in poetry. The Dream Queen meant what she said in this poem. I'm sure of it."

"What do you think the poem means?"

"What Stay High and Doctor Leo say it means. And probably more. I'm convinced The Dream Queen was a visionary scientist who wrote doggerel about the fate of the world."

"Ambitious for someone who wasn't even a poet."

"At least she understood the way poetry can pull people in by not telling them everything they want to know. She didn't write her thoughts down in a scientific way because she knew her audience. She wrote to tempt some of the Skulls into thinking. I believe she was trying to tell us about the future and what will be important to get back to."

"In the future."

"In the distant future."

There was nothing more to say about "The Mystery of the Universe," so they said nothing.

Then Spirit leaned over and kissed his cheek. "Can I bring up Daryll again?"

"Oh God."

"Just to say when I was with him I used to fantasize about being close to the seat of power. In that case, the mayor. Now here I am with the leader of the Skulls."

"Not as powerful as the mayor of New York."

"Yeah? Think about it." She kissed him again, this time full on the lips. "You just might be the guy who decides the future of this planet. I'm fucking impressed, Mark."

He turned and they kissed deeply.

Not a minute later the main man and his Spirit heard the metallic growl of a motor car approaching. People in the streets of Canutillo turned like a flock of sheep toward the sound of possible danger.

A mud-smeared red station wagon with a little flag of Texas rippling from the radio antenna pulled up alongside the lead car and stopped. The dried blood of white-tailed deer and bobcat stained the doors, which remained closed. Skulls walked up cautiously and peered through the bug-besmirched windows at haggard faces inside.

Then the main man heard gasping and murmuring all around him. "What is it?" he asked, pawing the air for Spirit's hand.

When her hand went into his hand, her words went into his ear: "They've come back." Her voice rose shrilly. "The three sisters! They've come back!"

55

WHAT THE SKULLS SAW through the smeared window of the car was this: Soda slumped behind the wheel; Swear To God, mouth slackly open, staring straight ahead; Queen Sexy, head lolling against the back seat, with bandaged hands crossed in arm slings. Jesus Mary Save Souls warned everyone to stand back until she could judge the condition of the three sisters. Gingerly she opened the driver's door and bent down to look at Soda.

Opening her eyes, Soda lifted her head from the wheel and through an act of will managed to tell their story. She told it with reportorial accuracy and a commitment to detail that expressed the horror of memory. She estimated the height and weight of Rick and Joe Don, fussed over the precise color of their eyes, attempted to render their speech patterns. While Skulls paced anxiously beyond the bug-stained car, Jesus Mary leaned through the window and listened to a patient account of agony and murder. After the death of the cowpokes, Soda reported, Queen Sexy lay moaning on the ground, her charred hands smoking like barbecued meat. Locating a doctor's office from a phone book, they drove there in the cowboys' station wagon, shot the office door open, and rummaged around for medicine. Soda had then put into practice some things learned in the Club House dispensary. She cleaned Queen Sexy's burns with hexachlorophene solution, rinsed them in isotonic saline, and wrapped the hands in fine-meshed absorbent gauze. Then she gave Queen Sexy codeine for pain and procaine penicillin to prevent infection. "Did I do right?"

Jesus Mary nodded proudly.

That night, continued Soda, they had remained in Pecos and next day had driven until exhausted, had dozed fitfully in the station wagon, and had pushed hard the following day until they caught up with the caravan here in Canutillo.

After this explanation, satisfied that the three sisters could be moved, Jesus Mary waved people in and they gathered up the trio of haggard, tomato-sauce-and-blood-stained women like fragile bouquets of flowers. There was bunk space for them in the Motorhome, since all but one of the twister victims had been released from hospital.

When someone helped Soda from the car, she pulled free and glanced frantically around for Queen Sexy. "I don't leave her," Soda stammered. "I don't leave her for anything!" She lurched forward to put one hand on the staggering blonde's elbow, so that people had to guide them as one toward the big camper.

Pain had prevented Queen Sexy from adding to Soda's account. Swear To God added nothing either. For that matter, she had nothing to say at all, because at the very instant the sauce-stained fork had entered the tall cowboy's eye, Swear To God entered a dark country in her mind from which she did not emerge.

They slept the rest of that day and all of the next, while the Skulls awaited a signal from Jesus Mary that they were up to traveling again.

The following morning Mister Touch left his Spirit's side and wandered alone into a dry wind blowing along the streets of Canutillo. Bumping into a car, he opened the door and got in, aware instantly that it did not belong to their caravan. Unused for two years, the empty car smelled of dust and leather and the scent of the dead owner — the prez would swear to it — the particular odor of the man or woman who had last slid behind the wheel. The main man had no idea why he was sitting in the car until hearing the sound that he'd been waiting to hear: three metallic taps.

Every morning now there were Skulls who for good luck rapped three times against the side of the vehicle they would ride in. The ritual demanded that they tap a particular spot — the painted emblem of one of the ants that dotted every car, van, truck, and trailer. Mister Touch heard this knock-knock-knock in the cool air of Canutillo like the sound of woodpeckers. Spirit had told him that many people were wearing necklaces with little pendants in the shape of ants that Sphinx had shown them how to twist from wire. Like Saint Christopher medals or mandalas or voodoo charms.

Mister Touch knew what was happening, even without Sag around to remind him of it: the Skulls were creating their own rituals. He heard the door open and felt his Spirit's presence as if he could vividly see each feature a handbreadth away.

"Are you all right?" she asked.

"I'm listening to the tapping."

"Since the sisters came back, there's a lot more of it."

"How are they?"

"Keeping to themselves."

"Someone should talk to them."

"You can't talk brutalization away. It has to go away on its own. Drain off like sewage."

"Yes, you do know about that." Sometimes when they lay together in the night, after moments of deep tenderness, she allowed the metal gates of memory to open and let him partway into the horror, but only just beyond the gates. She would shoo him out then, as she did now. It was like hearing the gates clang shut when she lied to him as she always did, "I never think about it anymore."

After a moment she asked him, "Do you want me to talk to them?"

"Someone has to. We owe them."

"I'll give it a try."

Spirit In The Dark waited. Then on the third day in Canutillo two of the sisters emerged together from the Motorhome dispensary. The slim black girl was holding by an elbow the blonde with the bandaged hands, although Queen Sexy looked strong enough now to navigate by herself. As Spirit approached them, she had the feeling of approaching one person, so evenly did their four eyes study her.

Spirit nearly turned and walked away. It was as if she were interfering with the privacy of their mutual space. Yet she had her husband's plea to respect and another message to deliver, so she went on with it. She told them that something not unlike what had happened to them had happened to her. Spirit heard in her voice the anxious tone of someone already defeated in an attempt to persuade the unpersuadable. She gave flat testimony to her own degrading life among the Dragons and ended with a rather forced observation about people not understanding something unless they had also gone through it.

The two women listened politely, both the black afro and the blond pageboy being ruffled in the main street of Canutillo by gusts of dry wind. The four eyes stared at Spirit, however, as if they were looking through a one-way mirror at the antics of someone observed in a psycho ward.

"I didn't think it would help," Spirit finished, shaking her head sadly.

"You're kind," Queen Sexy said courteously.

Spirit was looking at Soda's black hand firmly holding the white elbow, as if this sisterly gesture of unneeded help would get them both through an unwanted interview. Spirit's mission was not completed, however, so she continued. "Do you know Salsa Sal?" she asked Soda. "Wears Chinese clothes."

"Yes. From Hong Kong," Soda acknowledged listlessly.

"Chews gum," added Queen Sexy.

"That's Salsa Sal. Not everyone knows who she is. This morning she had Nando translate a Chinese proverb for her," Spirit explained. "It's a message for you. 'Keep a green tree in your heart and perhaps the singing bird will come.'" Not sure the sisters heard her in the whirling wind — there was no visible reaction — Spirit repeated it. "'Keep a green tree in your heart and perhaps the singing bird will come.' She wanted you to know."

Queen Sexy turned and walked stiffly away. With Soda holding her elbow, she headed down a side street of the dusty town and halted to lean against a wall.

Following at a discreet distance, Spirit watched the blond lawyer from Cleveland suddenly slump forward and sob with Soda hunched alongside her, one hand on her elbow as if guiding a Blindie through a crowded street. Spirit halted, watching as the sisters held each other and cried.

When Spirit returned to her husband, she said, "I told them about myself, but it didn't work. Then I gave them a message from Salsa Sal. The words seemed to move them off dead center, but I really don't know. They went down this street together and cried. Maybe that helped."

"But you don't know."

"I don't know."

He heard gates closing in her mind just as they must have closed in the minds of the sisters — clanging shut, allowing no one in.

Tall shambling emaciated Web, lover of man and woman, died in Las Cruces, New Mexico, where they had stopped for supplies and at Jesus Mary's insistence for some Cutter snakebite kits. Web had starved himself after his beloved Boo Bang had joined his beloved Flash somewhere over the rainbow. In a town not far from the White Sands Missile Range, Web had taken three dainty sips of a Coke in the midday heat, gripped his grieving heart, gasped twice, and keeled over dead. His body had been unable to withstand so many rapid and severe weight changes, for love and grief had made a yo-yo of his metabolism, sending his poundage either sky-rocketing or crashing, so that according to Jesus Mary he must have died of heart trouble, a not so unreasonable end for a com-mitted lover. A Latino summed him up: "Revento de dolor" — he died of sorrow. Someone else quoted OOTHI: " 'Men have died from time to time, and worms have eaten them, but not for love.' But Web, he did."

Now that Web was gone, the Skulls needed a driver for Truck B. To everyone's astonishment, King Super Kool volunteered to take over, although earlier in the trip he had given up driving Car Six because of his bad lungs. People studied him and saw why he was now ready. He was still a poor-breathing little Hispanic, but looked like a steady-breathing huntsman. He stood straight. He coughed without buckling. He never complained of wheezing when he wheezed. As Hoss explained to the main man, King Super Kool had regained some of his health and all of his confidence by riding the broad shoulders of Chico. He got behind the wheel of that damn truck, coughed, shoved the big fucker into gear, and as steadily as a Swiss watch ticks he drove through New Mexico, the Land of Enchantment, with its roadrunners and coyotes and jave-linas, its yuccas and ocotillos, its greasewood and soapweed, its thousand-foot canyons and three-foot anthills on which the Yaqui and Apache had once spread-eagled their enemies.

That night the main man drew Hoss aside. Here they were at last, he told the second-in-command, near the gates of Arizona, having left twenty brothers and sisters behind. Tomorrow they would cross the border in seventeen of the twenty-seven original vehicles serviced by their Chief Automotive Engineer, Stitch, and they had eight new Skulls, even if one would not or could not speak English and another went wild whenever he heard the word "base." All in all they were ahead of the game. "Feel that air?" he said to Hoss. "Dry as a bone."

"Are we the people who huddled in a building near a park

crawling with dogs?" Hoss asked, having by his amazed tone answered his own question.

"Sag used to call us tyrants. So will other people."

"Even after they breathe the bone-dry air?"

"I once read that the history of mankind is nothing more than a series of escapes from tyranny."

"We're tyrants?"

"We are until we hold general elections."

Hoss laughed. "Are you crazy enough to turn these Looney Tunes over to themselves?"

"It's almost time, Hoss. If they got across this country, they're old enough to vote."

"I have a quirky idea. One of these days Sag might be remembered as a martyred champion of political freedom."

"You think that's quirky? I think it's probable."

"Assuming, of course, we survive long enough to forget what actually happened, long enough to dream up interpretations."

"Assuming we survive that long. It would mean long enough for us to create another generation. Rattler and other kids."

"There will be other kids. Yours, for example."

"Will I live long enough to hold my kid?" Now it was the main man's turn to feel the ratfeet of fear scoot up his spine.

"Can't believe we gonna be in Arizona before we stops again."

"Say in this book I been reading: ten minutes of midday sun could kill a leopard lizard."

"Do it have spots? A leopard have spots, right?"

"How the fuck do I know do it have spots."

"I wanna see the Grand Canyon."

"Say in this book Phoenix has average annual temperature of seventy degree farraheight. And seven inches rainfall."

"That's plenty, ain't it? Nah, can't be. Too much rain ain't good for the lungs. Seven inches gotta be jist a little bit of rainfall or we might of fucked up coming out here in the first place. Right?"

"Might of fucked up anyway."

"Sure do like your uptempo kind of style, nigger. I wanna see the Grand Canyon."

"You couldn't see it was you standing right at the edge. Say in this book the annual relative humidity be like fairly constant at thirty percent."

"That good?"

"Gotta be."

"What is that, relative humidity?"

"You don't know fuck, do you? How dry it is."

"Hey, back there! Shut up and look! See that sign going by? 'Apache State'? You ain't dreaming, homeboys. You got yourself all the way to Arizona!"

THREE

IN THE PROMISED LAND

56

IT WAS a weird-looking caravan that sputtered into this alkaline land of compacted mountain ranges and desert plains gashed by canyons and scarred by washes, this hot bright vastness of bold buttes, mesas, and arroyos. Battered by flying debris from a tornado, carrying dusty Day-Glo images of creatures from the phylum Arthropoda on their mud-caked chassis, the rattling vehicles had proved beyond a shadow of a doubt that Chief Engineer Stitch loved them.

The caravan halted on Route 10 at a fancy motel with sun patios, cabanas, and a spiderwebbed swimming pool. Out poured the Skulls, most of whom had long since discarded their rumpled New York finery for velveteen Navaho blouses, Stetsons, scuffed wrangler boots, beaded headbands, buckskin leggings, squaw dresses, three-tiered pueblo shirts decorated with calico rickrack, and chunky turquoise necklaces. Out poured animals too, a menagerie of dogs and cats, a hungry goat, and Ralph the arrogant parrot.

A Blindie, hearing the crunch of stones underfoot, called out to a passing Looker, "Tell me what you see."

"Well, you got rocks. Mountains like, you know, flat on top like they got a haircut. No trees. Plenty of rocks. Can't see too good cause the sun sure be bright. Rocks and bushes. Lotta rocks."

"Don't sound like much."

"Yeah. But you know, it's def, it's dope, it's fresh, you can groove to it."

Another Blindie, Mister Touch, was consulting with his second-in-command. Their heads were together and Hoss's Stetson wagged in disapproval until finally he declared, "Every time you dream, I worry."

"Maybe it sounds like a dream, but it comes from OOTHI."

"I don't care where it comes from," Hoss said, "I can't see the good sense of it."

"Good sense doesn't apply."

A short distance away from this argument, Stitch was checking the oil in his beloved vehicles; his assistants were siphoning gas from a few trucks parked in the motel lot. Other people broke into the restaurant and emerged with hot Cokes and stale potato chips. Not far away a ground squirrel made sounds like an electronic bleep which startled Harold (secretly into electronics). Two lizards squared off and bobbed aggressively as if proving what tough dudes they were. A turkey vulture soared overhead on buoyant thermals, its eye on a kitten who might slip out of human arms and be left behind and crawl into the sunshine and warm itself into a tasty meal. A Gila monster moved sluggishly from one rock pile to another, its work done for the day.

Visitors from New York City strolled through the motel grounds, unaware that a few yards away a sidewinder was stitching the pattern of its scales into the sand. Nor did the Skulls realize what was up when Mister Touch proclaimed a need to commemorate their arrival in the Promised Land. He didn't give them time to think that through. He just gave them fifteen minutes to get ready. They dragged out canned goods and bottled beverages from the restaurant, clean (but dusty) sheets and pillows from the rooms, and tourist brochures from the office. Having corralled and packed aboard their vehicles the last dog, cat, tasty kitten, the insatiable goat with something indescribable hanging from its goateed mouth, and Ralph, who had been perching in the cool shade of the office porch — for, although spoiled rotten and evil-tempered, he was no fool — the Skulls got under way. They drove off with enough noise to disturb a cactus wren in its cholla nest, causing it to whisk its tail in saucy farewell, having suspected such creatures had departed for good a bird's age ago.

A mile east of Bowie, following the main man's blind hunch, the caravan turned south onto a spur which led past the crumbled ruins of an old fort and through majestic Apache Pass, where more than one Indian and soldier had bitten the dust. After a few minutes Spirit halted — the main man had instructed her to stop at the first junction.

He got out of the car; so did she. He heard under their shoes the grinding surge of little stones.

"Are you really going through with this?" she asked.

"That's what Hoss asks too. Yes, I am. 'If you have two loaves of bread, sell one and buy a hyacinth.' OOTHI."

"Meaning?"

"First of all we got here. Arizona is ours."

"I hadn't thought of it that way."

"Let's say the land is worth two loaves of bread, but we only need one of them. So what else do we need?"

"A hyacinth?"

"Something for the soul."

"They won't all agree with your choice."

He answered this objection by getting back in the car. "Take the fork that way —" Mister Touch threw out his arm cavalierly toward the southeast, so Spirit honked ··— —·· and the caravan proceeded.

They plowed through dusty flatland flanked by the Chiricahua mountain range. At the next junction (after making a pit stop in Galeyville where bad boys like Curley Bill and Johnny Ringo used to chill out after a spell of cattle rustling), the main man pointed southeast again. The sun was getting low, but he didn't know that. Jive Turkey, Official Photographer, rode with them these days (Soda had left for Station Wagon D in order to maintain a firm comforting hold on Queen Sexy's elbow), and at the main man's insistence Sphinx had moved into their car today.

"Do you see anything interesting?" Mister Touch asked them.

"Tall peaks to the left," Sphinx said and turned to the swarthy Korean boy. "Does it look like a good place to you?"

"We can get close to those rocks," he pointed out.

"I think this place will do," Sphinx told the prez, adding carefully, "if you really want to do it."

For an answer the main man told Spirit to leave the road and drive in as far as she could safely go.

A quarter hour later, on parched flatland among barrel cacti where javelinas grunted through the brush like piggies going to market, where wolf spiders and elf owls waited to play Dracula at sundown, the Skull caravan rattled to a dust-whirling halt.

No one could believe the main man had stopped in such a desolate place. Grumbling from heat and fatigue, the travelers piled out of their cars to stare at scraggly brush and looming peaks and rocks haphazardly piled up as if this were the playpen of a gigantic, willful child. Grumpily, they gathered ironwood and tinder from beneath an emaciated paloverde tree that might have taken root in this soil about the time Shakespeare was being uprooted from his mother's womb in Stratford-on-Avon. They built fires and ate beans and spent their first Arizonian night here in rugged country, hoping they'd be spared ambush and the bite of scorpions. Slowly but surely they nestled down singly or in shared bedrolls, hearing from a distant mesa the lonely howl of a coyote.

Mister Touch laid his hand gently on Spirit's belly and asked again if the baby had kicked yet. For the umpteenth time she told him it wouldn't kick for a while yet and in a voice of apprehension warned him not to say too much about that or something bad might happen. Even so, he scrambled around in the bedroll and put his ear against her belly like an Indian listening for the approach of buffalo. He had done this every night for a week.

When the main man awoke, he was deluded by sadness into thinking this was fetid swampland. Something had ended; it was like the morning after graduation. Then he realized where they were and as the depression faded away, so did the swamp. He breathed dry air and reached for his Spirit, but she had already left the bedroll. He thought about her carrying their child. When her gait became awkward, he wouldn't know. If only he could see her for just a moment, say, in the seventh month. His father used to tell him never to stare at pregnant women, but he peeked anyway, fascinated by the translucent skin and limpid eyes. He had been young enough then to harbor a secret wish: that his mother would become pregnant again so he could cuddle up to the mysterious flesh and touch the softness and look into immortal eyes.

Mister Touch got up and raised his arms toward a glowing desert sun he could feel but not see. Blackness stretched ahead of him, yet suddenly he was filled with joy. "Out of the shadows of night the world rolls into light." Then he did something that the Skulls would never forget.

He opened his mouth and bellowed into the morning air of Arizona, yelled mindlessly again and again. People stopped what they were doing, turned, and gawked. "Never did hear a man so *happy!*" remarked E.Z., standing with one hand unconsciously resting on a belly filled with new life, though she didn't know it yet.

Not five minutes later, something else memorable happened.

" 'When will we win what we want?' was what weak weary Web, who witnessed wondrous weeping, whispered. Why worry when wishing won't work? When wicked wayward warriors waged war, we were without caring if they did or not. That's life. We have to take the good with the bad. Take me, a butcher. I took plenty from customers. Like the time this woman came into the store for two pounds of veal for scallopini —"

"Hey!"

"That be *Adidas* talking? Straight on to W and then, bang, he get *normal!*"

"And she said," said Adidas, " 'I'll have a roast chicken too.' 'No chicken,' I told her."

They stared at the square-faced butcher, whose beetling brows partially obscured two widely spaced eyes as blue as Paul Newman's. He had been a quiet pensive man for months after joining the Skulls, until one day he began to repeat, "The quick brown fox jumps over the lazy dog." Many Skulls believed he would soon become OOTLO. It was Stay High, naturally, who figured out what the phrase meant after Adidas had filled the corridors with it for a week. "It contains all the letters of the alphabet," Stay High explained and predicted, accurately, that more tricks with the alphabet were in the offing. The truth was that Stay High had been trading on insider information — Adidas, vulnerable in his first days, had confessed to someone who shall be nameless that a boyhood of writing poetry had turned into a manhood of writing his history in beef blood every day with a bone saw and a cleaver. In the despair of post–V 70 he had turned for solace to a boyhood love of words.

Skulls stared at him intently for the first time in months, because by talking normally he made himself easier to see.

"Listen to the dude. Last time he say something normal was at the meet about Spirit. Said cut her throat like a chicken. Must of had chicken on the mind."

"Then I said to this woman," continued Adidas, his face crimson with memory as he paused to savor what was happening to him.

"Welcome back!"

"Made it to Arizona, didn't you, butcher boy!"

"Got his head back too."

"Like my mamma used to say, 'Don't it beat all?' "

Then a few hours later something else memorable happened.

Perched on Chico's broad shoulders, King Super Kool went

hunting for piglike javelinas, which would become as abundant in a few years as they had been during the old uncrowded days of the Hohokam ancestors of the Hopi Indians. No Name, whose moroseness had turned to ambition between the ivory thighs of Sweet Walk, went with the hunting duo to learn hunting because hunting was there to learn. King Super Kool found it tiring to wear two hats at once — truck driver and hunter — so he welcomed a partial respite from one set of duties. Having in no time become a good driver himself, in no time No Name became a skillful hunter. He bagged two javelinas to every one brought down by the more experienced King Super Kool.

It was during that first hunting expedition that No Name saw her.

She was sitting on a rock, watching them. As No Name reported to the prez, "She was wearing jeans and a cotton shirt and looked like an Indian."

"How does an Indian look?"

"Well, from movies I seen they got black hair and high cheeks and that's what she had. She'd look jist right in buckskin and a headband."

"Did she see you?"

"Stared right at me."

"How far away were you?"

"Stone's throw."

"What did she do?"

"Nothing. Jist stared."

"She wasn't afraid?"

"Nope." Recalling civil war in Vicksburg, No Name added with a rueful little laugh, "Reckon I know what scared looks like."

"Tomorrow, if she's there again, say hello and see what happens."

Next day, rifle strapped to his back, No Name went alone into the same area. Sure enough, there was the woman, sitting crosslegged on another rock, head thrust forward. About fifty yards away, aware that she had probably seen him long before he had seen her, No Name called out, "Hello!"

For a moment he thought she would skitter away like a leopard lizard, but instead the young woman got to her feet and called back, "Hello!"

Before meeting the newcomer, Mister Touch had reports about her appearance and demeanor. "She's in her midtwenties," Spirit told him, "not much over five feet, dark from the sun, so about my color. Not pretty, but not plain either. Interesting looking — it's the big eyes and broad face and straight lips, like they were cut into her face with a razor."

"What's she doing out here?"

"She wanted to get away from people."

"What people?"

"That's what we were asking," said Hoss. He described how Skulls had fired questions when she appeared in camp. How many people had she seen? Any electricians, doctors, plumbers, engineers, pilots, drug dealers, cops, social workers, carpenters? Any dentists? (A dentist could make a fortune among the Skulls, who'd give away Tiffany jewels to have an amalgam filling or just a good cleaning.)

Prepped for his interview with the young woman, Mister Touch sat in the shade of an overhanging rock and waited for Hoss to bring her.

Coming.

There was first a long silence from which the main man guessed she was thoughtful, self-confident, and suspicious. So to put her at ease, he said, "What do you want to know?"

"Where do you come from?"

"New York City. We're just a bunch of people who need to breathe dry air. But enough about us," he said genially. "What about yourself?"

"I came out here to find privacy for my work."

"Which is?"

"Physics."

"Don't you need a lab?"

"I need pencil and paper and solitude. Not the kind of solitude I'd find in a city full of skeletons."

"Your specialty?" He hoped it was something practical.

"It's very theoretical. I'm involved with superstrings."

"Superstrings? Are they somehow connected to transformational grammar?"

"What?"

"An inside joke. We have someone here who tried to formulate the rules of a language whose words end in vowels. That's a different kind of string theory." Zap's shadow crossed his mind. Lying at the bottom of a bay now, Zap used to tie knots in a string and release them with a single motion. It was all he remembered of Zap.

"Do I amuse you?" asked the young physicist.

"No, you impress me. Why?"

"I have the feeling you're amused."

"Well, I admit to thinking of something amusing and something sad."

"Do you think twentieth-century Indians sit around drinking the white man's firewater?"

"I miss the point." He heard a sound — perhaps she was sifting sand through her fingers.

"Forget it," she said after a while. "I've always had to defend myself. People won't believe an Indian, much less a female Indian, can know anything about physics. And frankly I just cheated. I'm only one fifth Indian."

"And frankly I don't know enough about physics to judge you one way or another." After a silence, Mister Touch said, "Can you tell me about your specialty? People will ask me. I'd rather not be totally dumb."

So she gave him a short lecture on the Theory Of Everything, or TOE, which was a mathematical model for unifying the basic forces of the universe. Elemental matter was not particles but strings — one dimensional, about one billionth of a trillionth of a trillionth of a centimeter in length. Strings accounted for gravity, electromagnetism, the strong force that binds an atomic nucleus, and the weak force that causes radioactive decay — in short, everything. In her opinion superstring theory rivaled quantum physics and general relativity in importance, although it did involve difficulties, such as working in ten dimensions. But many of the wrinkles in TOE had been ironed out before V 70 Struck.

Mister Touch had become a passionate collector of talent (far more interesting to him than collecting art that he didn't even like). He knew a good thing when he didn't see it. "Would you like to stay with us?" he asked as casually as possible.

"Well . . ."

"At least stay awhile and then let us know."

"All right, I'll do that."

He explained their theory of names, dubbing her Toe. Having studied the Theory Of Everything, she might have learned something the Skulls could use.

That night there were a dozen campfires in the desert. Around one of them crowded a group of young Skulls to listen to Sister Fate.

She was telling them about the Mountain Above Mountains, the most sacred in China, Mount Tai Shan. "Climbing it is ascending to heaven. So I climbed it. I never expected such cold in April, but even in padded jacket and trousers, I was chilled to the bone. At the summit of the Celestial Pillar I slept under half a dozen quilts, my teeth chattering. Next day I visited the temple of the Goddess of the Azure Clouds. Icy winds swept through the halls. Going down the mountain, I saw pinnacles rising from the mist like islands in a winter sea."

"How come you on cold," someone asked, "when we be here in the hot desert?"

"Contrasts make life worth living."

"Huh, seem like we had enough of them," another grumbled, "to last a fucking lifetime."

57

SPHINX HAD BEEN UP since dawn, searching among canyon walls for the right one. She had brought along her assistant, Jive Turkey. The art critic and the Korean grocer's boy squinted into early sunlight, evaluating the upthrust grain of a large cliff with several boulders scattered at its base. The flat stone rose from the canyon with the power and precision of a New York skyscraper. It reminded Sphinx of standing beside the Twin Towers. When she'd looked straight up, she had the sense of falling backward with the tower falling forward, and she'd wondered if the tremendous mass was balancing an instant, like the last on a house of cards, before crashing down. The impermanent if incalculable power that had awed and humbled her in lower Manhattan now surprised her once again. Wiping sweat from her face and pushing back wet tendrils of auburn hair, Sphinx studied the massive cliff. She wondered if she could do it.

Moving a few feet away from her solemn assistant, Sphinx found space enough to think in. Detached from her mission for these moments, she recalled her student days in a sculpture studio: wood shavings on carving tables, potter's wheels, armatures twisted into various shapes, a nude model posed on a pedestal, the brute sound of pneumatic hammers, the chunk chunk of hand-held chisels, the drone of rasps, the smell of shellac and polymer resin, the look of sunlight spilling through large windows, of air thick with motes of marble dust. And there was the tense comradeship of students who hoped they were geniuses and did everything they could to impress the bull-necked professor who smoked malodorous cigars and sarcastically informed his pupils in a heavy Brooklyn accent that they weren't even talented.

Could she, Sphinx wondered, challenge for real that formidable cliff, so deceptively ephemeral in the morning light? Outsmart and attack with authority such raw power? Succeed in doing what, in a feckless moment of overweening pride, she had boldly promised Mister Touch she could do? But her impulse to take on this project was based on more than vanity. The monument would proclaim the wisdom and vision of her dead lover. That was worth any effort she might make. That was worth the risk of failure.

It had been the fear of failure that had encouraged her to give up the chisel for the pen and become a critic of art rather than a maker of it. Sphinx hadn't handled a chisel since her school days. For many years she hadn't made a single cut in wood or stone. But for the last decade she had cut off more than one promising career, helped to build others, and earned for herself a reputation in the art world for critical acumen.

Now she was standing in a place that had been desolate when the planet Earth was overpopulated, looking at a steep cliff and contemplating the commission which she had so blithely accepted — to carve the image of an insect in Colorado granite.

Studying the grainy surface, she recalled the clichés of her school days:

> Sculpture is precontained in the mass and must therefore only be released.

> A work of art in stone must declare it always was and always will be.

She blinked away the intellectual fog and tried to look cleanly at this particular wall of stone. How large should the sculpture be? That was a good question to begin with and relaxed her momentarily. Should it be done in bas or alto relief?
"You can do it."
Sphinx turned to look at her assistant, a head shorter, the official Skull Photographer who should have been helping his father set out tomatoes and cabbages. "What did you say?"
"You can do it."
"How do you know?"
"I don't know. But you can do it. I know that."
"Let's go back to camp for coffee."

Back at camp the main man was having his own troubles. He had explained to the Skulls in detail what they were going to do, and the more he explained the more people backed away. Fire headed a group of religious dissenters, including the beauticians Pretty Puss and Snow with their followers, old Diamond Doll and young Golden Girl. As Sag would have said, they could not in good conscience commit such a sacrilege, because although they had left the past in New York, they still carried with them the faith of their ancestors. Carving a blasphemous icon in the middle of the desert was beyond tolerance, let alone participation. The idea was Babylonian, a kind of malevolent parody of Moses and the Tablet of the Ten Commandments.
Another group of four followers of Islam resisted the idea of carving idols at all. Still another group saw in the main man's project a plot to discredit racial minorities, suggesting that the disadvantaged were being ridiculed by the glorification of insects. The argument was foggy at best, and after a short exchange with Mister Touch most of them walked away, tired of committing themselves

to anything more fatiguing than a familiar feeling of distrust. Individual dissenters drifted like wayward leaves into the main man's presence, voicing confusion and a general fear of cosmic retribution if they tampered with the spiritual balance of the world by introducing another god.

To his critics the prez replied as he had to Hoss, "If you can't stand the heat, get out of the kitchen." More gently he added, "This monument is a symbol of our perseverance in doing what we are meant to do — survive. There are hundreds and hundreds of species of ants. I don't expect us to select one species from the others and install this favorite in glory at the expense of other ants crawling over the earth, and I have no intention of seeing to it that if you don't like a certain ant you'll be thrown into prison, tortured, and executed. I am not personally an ant worshiper and I don't frankly give a fuck who is or who isn't. If you want to think of the ant as a god, cool. If you don't, cool. But I want something lasting put up out here to let history know what we did. I want an image to remember us by, that's all."

When Sphinx returned for coffee, she told the main man, half hoping to discourage him, that the work would take a considerable amount of time. Without hesitation he offered her as much time as she needed.

So at midmorning she returned to the site, a mile away, with her assistant and a score of curious Skulls. They gathered to stare at tools taken on Mister Touch's blind hunch from an El Paso art store ten days ago, before he really knew what he wanted done with the stuff. Sphinx studied the array of instruments spread out on a blanket: point chisels for roughing out, claw tools, flat chisels, frosting tools, bull sets, bush hammers and picks, large rasps, stone mallets, and a dozen pairs of goggles.

What in hell would she do with these tools? Panic seized her. Then she took a deep breath and stepped up to the sheer facing of rock with a piece of chalk in hand. All right, lady, Sphinx told herself, you have just become an artist for a day. To IRT she said, Wherever you are, honey, which is probably down there, look up and send me some of that strength you used to give me in bed.

Across the smooth-looking but rough surface, she drew in chalk the outline of a large ant, letting the swing of her arm calculate its size. Standing back after a while, she judged the result. Not altogether bad. Not so good either. At least the drawing was persuasively insectile. The bead-shaped head was pointed upward, as if the creature were crawling up the steep cliff. From the tip of its antennae to the end of its abdomen the insect measured nearly six feet. Drawn as thick as human arms, each of the six legs spread out sticklike from the body. It was nothing more than a schematic rendering. Yet she decided that the form should remain somewhat abstract. Trying for a realistic approximation, especially of the jointed legs, would assure failure. The sculpture would consist of a single block, a solid unit in alto relief projecting from the cliff. It would be necessary to cut back the stone surface about two feet deep over about a twelve-foot-square area, starting near the base of the cliff.

With a resigned sigh, she turned to Jive Turkey. "It would go faster with pneumatic drills, but since we don't have them, we'll use point chisels until we get the shape roughed out." Sphinx was surprised by how professional she sounded. She had gone from critic to artist, not the conventional progression of someone in the art world of her experience. But little was conventional anymore, and that idea gave her courage. With a length of cold steel in one hand and a mallet in the other, Sphinx again approached the cliff, this time resolutely. She took a deep breath, set the chisel edge at an angle against the chalk line, and sharply tapped with the mallet. The chisel dug a full quarter-inch into rock. She took another breath, set the edge at an opposite angle, tapped briskly, and a wedge-shaped hunk of stone flew out. The gathered Skulls murmured their approval.

By noon the next day, some of them wanted to try out the chisels and claws for themselves. Tools went from blanket to hand. By midafternoon Sphinx had given up her own chisel to teach people how to handle theirs. "Don't use a lot of tooth chisel yet. Use the point chisel instead — it doesn't control form as much. What does that mean? Don't worry. Just do it. If you do it right, something good will appear in front of you." Sphinx had always suspected that her knowledge was no deeper than the pages on which she wrote and now she realized with increasing wonder that her knowledge had always been that of an artist, even if she was not really an artist. She kept imagining a big black cigar in her mouth, which she chomped while explaining technique in a Brooklyn accent.

In Cougar and Tangy she found talent for real. They had a feeling for stone and a zest for chisels. They worked side by side: the Swedish aerobics instructor and the husky blood with a Doberman's teethmarks etched into his leg. Less gifted workers did the relief work with picks and bush hammers. A truck was backed up to the cliff, allowing sculptors to reach the upper portion of the monument by standing on the cab. Skulls labored in relays from dawn to dusk; fortunately, the cliff was submerged in shade most of the afternoon. They debated which was louder, their breathing or their hammering.

Days passed. They shifted from point to tooth chisels, then to frosting tools and bull sets, then to flat carving chisels and bush chisels. Expeditions returned to Route 10 for supplies in Willcox, Bowie, and San Simon. Close to the site a half dozen tents were pitched, so workers could rest in the shade. When Sphinx could do no more than supervise hoarsely and after Jive Turkey collapsed from heat exhaustion, other Skulls who had never bothered to glance at sculpture grabbed tools and went boldly ignorantly enthusiastically fanatically to work. Slowly the rugged form of a huge ant began to emerge from the stone. Two legs seemed broken because of poorly aimed blows that gouged out a bit too much rock, yet taking shape from the cliff was a head, a thorax, an abdomen, all of it carried skyward on six rough-hewn legs.

Skulls who were not working because of principle or delicate health had set up camp in the crumbling village of Portal to which, at evening, the weary laborers returned. To pass the time in Portal (hardly a fun-filled action-packed resort), Stay High gave daily lectures in a dilapidated corral, where the audience sat on ground that cattle had once shit and pissed into a quagmire of stenchy mud. Few Skulls came at first — after all, he lectured on archeology — even though they had little to do until the "mad main man's massive monument mounting monstrously moonward got where it was going," the final five words illustrating why a Skull who tried to emulate and surpass Adidas at artful and abundant alliteration failed at the task most miserably. The word got around that Stay High was doing his thing in the corral and at first people snickered. But they failed to reckon on the oratorical power of love, so that after a couple of sessions Stay High had a popular lecture series going.

A man whom many considered too intellectual to be interesting had started to give life to facts by learning from his passion for Do You Thing how to persuade, entice, and seduce. Although thirty or forty people sat in the corral, he spoke only to the Texas blonde, whom he considered the smartest girl he'd ever met. Like a boy doing flips from a diving board that he wouldn't have even jumped from until *she* came to the pool, Stay High tried desperately to hold the cowgirl's attention; whenever it appeared to drift, he paced up and down waving his hands like a rabble-rouser, discovering in himself a rhetoric to outshine the halting stammering diffident mumbling that had accompanied his initial shock at falling in love. To keep her from yawning, which the girl did frankly when boredom settled over her pretty features, he found ways to flesh out the bone-dry facts of archeology.

For example, he described for his audience the Ventana Caves not far from Tucson. Twenty thousand years ago the first Americans ate deer and badger there. He explained the Sherlock Holmesian character of paleoethnobotanical research. Seeing Do You Thing open her mouth widely and yawn until he could see down her lovely erotic throat, he defined paleoethnobotany in simple terms as the study of ancient cultures through the carbonized remains of what people ate. Leaning forward, lifting his finger as if to hush the crowd (even Sony Boy slid the ubiquitous earphones off so he could hear), Stay High described the detective work that had taken place before V 70 Struck in a cave only a day's ride at average Skull speed from where they sat this very moment. In the lower level of the cave, a grinding stone had been discovered. On its rough surface the seeds of pickleweed and yucca had been ground up thousands of years ago (he looked anxiously her way) and the resultant meal had been formed then into cakes. They were baked in ashes or boiled like gruel in watertight baskets into which hot stones were dropped (she started to yawn). Stay High paced briskly back and forth and dramatically stopped. "Pretend!" he declaimed. "Pretend you're sitting around the campfire and it's, say, fifteen thousand years ago," he said to Do You Thing, who had completed her yawn and was staring lazily at him as if focusing on a distant spot in preparation for falling asleep, "and you smell the bread cakes made of pickleweed and yucca meal. You inhale their warm grainy smell. But just then you hear outside of the cave entrance the high trumpeting of a mastodon! The thundering hooves of giant bison! Or maybe the low growl of a saber-toothed cat! So you reach for your spear thrower, the atlatl, even as you hungrily thrust the warm cakes into your mouth and spill crumbs. Thousands of years later, people will sit at microscopes and by studying a few little spots on a glass side they'll make educated guesses as to what you had for dinner that night."

Under the spell of the desert and this intellectual in love, the Skulls stepped backward into the ancient past, until not even Do You Thing was sure where she was.

Under the spell of the desert but no longer of Stay High, The Boy Who Doesn't Speak Our Language began to speak in complete English sentences, qualifying as a gifted child if not as a linguistic genius. Having at last given up his mentor because of unrequited love, the boy came clean; he revealed a verbal facility through the complicated clauses of long rolling periods that even Stay High could envy, although many of the sentences ended with the phrase "I am sorry." People felt the phrase was a compulsive afterthought meaning he was sorry for having made a fool of transformational grammar.

Naturally he lost the good will of his mentor. Yet Stay High was so absorbed in Do You Thing that all he could muster when he met the traitorous boy was a sarcastic "zudo" or "yudee" in memory of their false relationship.

When word got around that the kid could speak the King's English, the prez asked to see him. "What in hell were you doing?" Mister Touch asked severely.

"Getting used to the world again."

The response was so blunt and unexpected that the main man was left speechless. Recovering, he said, "OOTHI once wrote, 'The music that can deepest reach, and cure all ill, is cordial speech.' Do you know what I'm saying to you?"

"No, sir, I'm sorry."

"You buffaloed us. You fronted and waxed and manipulated not only Stay High but every Skull who traveled with you. Now you owe them. Do you know how you're going to pay that debt?"

"No, sir, I don't. I'm sorry."

"We arrived in Arizona a few days ago. I want you to keep a diary of everything that has happened and will happen since then. Write your very best. Use a dictionary. If you have any trouble with vocabulary, I'm sure Adidas will serve as a thesaurus. You're the Official Diarist of the Skulls, you hear?"

"Yes, sir." Instead of adding "I'm sorry," he smiled.

On the spot Mister Touch renamed the boy Star Three in honor of Star, who had died of pneumonia in New York City, and Star Two, who had not left the Big Apple either, but had chosen to die uptown in the pork store of his Polish ancestors.

After this interview Hoss came in with troubling news of persistent discontent. People were restless in the dusty village that had probably begun to fall apart before the turn of the century. Others resented the cause for this delay. Still others were brooding about the future, and there was an underground swell of disapproval of the leadership that would lead them into that uncertainty. All the way here there had been unity, even in the midst of the discord aroused by Sag and The Fierce Rabbit. Dissension had been more of a game than actual criticism — until now.

The prez merely smiled.

Hoss exploded. "Goddammit, man! You bring us all this way and you get this loony idea of carving a monument to a fucking *ant!* And here I tell you that things in fact are *worse* since we arrived in Arizona and all you can do is sit there with a shit-eating grin on your face! What's going on?"

"What I expected. We aren't the same people who lived in New York City. I don't think we're the same people who traveled across the country. We're going to be different now that we've got our own turf for real. We're going to go through changes. I'm smiling because there's nothing I would do about it even if I could. It's as it should be."

Hoss shook his head sadly, turned, and walked out, figuring that the main man was in the process of losing his marbles.

No sooner was Hoss gone than someone else came into the musty little room once occupied by a barber, scissors and comb, a bottle of Bay Rum, and two customers, one in the chair and one waiting.

"Who is it?" the main man asked.

"Blue Magic."

"Are you keeping the time?" When there was a long silence, Mister Touch asked again in alarm. "I said, are you keeping the calendar? Do you know what day it is?"

"I do. But —"

"Tell me —"

"We got so busy coming here and with the carving and everything going on, I forgot to pay attention. It was Christmas four days ago."

The main man repeated it slowly. "Christmas four days ago. No disrespect intended to your ancestors, Blue Magic, but I always thought of Asians as disciplined and meticulous. When push comes to shove, aren't you about as spacey, unfocused, and chaotic as any airhead in the bunch?"

"Yes, sir."

"Well, let that be. Keep your mouth shut about Christmas. After all, it's past." Recalling the indeterminacy of time according to the Touch Calendar, Mister Touch resolved to use it in a positive way. "On the other hand, let's amend time a bit."

"Sir?"

"Let's say Christmas is the day after the carving is finished."

"When will that be, sir?" Blue Magic asked innocently.

"Whenever the carving is finished." The main man imagined that the boy was frowning in grave perplexity. "Well, let that be. The thing is, we are going to honor Christ and IRT at the same time."

58

ZOE CAME TO THE PREZ with a story about the one who talked all the time. She had been sitting on a curbstone when this person came along, sat down beside her, and recited a strange poem.

The main man wanted to know who the one who talked all the time was, and she described a boy whom Mister Touch had always thought of as The Boy Who Doesn't Speak Our Language. "You mean Star Three, our Official Diarist. I didn't know he talked all the time." Not adding that perhaps he was making up for lost time.

The poem he recited had been "The Mystery of the Universe." The boy had told her of the long search for its meaning and provided her with a detailed explication of theories championed by Stay High. She had come to the main man with a theory of her own.

"Whatever else anyone says," Toe declared, " 'The Mystery of the Universe' is about physics."

"Tell me about that."

"The explanation is in 'nu' and playing dice with God and the Danish hatter and walking the plank and hitching up your trousers with string and dark matter and charm and the hole and blood-red beam and truth too deep and the singular dream and the hubble-bubble." She drew a deep breath.

So did the main man.

"Five lines interest me especially, because of their application to astrophysics:

> *"Then drop like Alice down the hole*
> *On a blood-red unseen beam*
> *Into truth too deep too rude*
> *Or curl forever nude*
> *Inside the singular dream."*

It was no accident, Toe began, that the poet-scientist had mentioned Alice. Many readers of *Alice in Wonderland* had searched through its text for hidden formulae, because it had long been rumored that mathematician Charles Dodgson had placed them there among the adventures of a little girl.

What sort of hole did Alice drop into? A black hole, according to Toe, a collapsed star whose gravity was so powerful that light couldn't escape from its own surface. "Are you with me?" she asked.

"Almost."

The "blood-red beam" was simple enough, claimed Toe. As light climbs up from the dying star's surface, it grows weary in its struggle against gravity just as an old man grows weary climbing a steep hill. Losing energy, the light shifts toward the red end of the spectrum. As the light becomes redder, time on the star slows down until finally it stops. "For the moment, please accept that idea on faith."

He had dealt with time stopping already. "I do accept it," he said. "Believe me, I do."

Toe continued. The Dream Queen had been describing a black hole and a dying star inside it. From the pressure of gravity the star becomes so densely compacted that a portion the size of a Ping-Pong ball weighs more than the planet Earth.

Toe waited for that to sink in before describing the star's final passage "into truth too deep too rude." Gravity grinds its particles into chaos and final conflagration. The implosion sends tremendous jets of energy into space. Nothing can be ruder than this end to the star.

The next lines were more complicated, Toe warned. A *normal* black hole can't harm the rest of the universe because everything outside of it is protected from demonic chaos by the effect of gravity. But if black hole events take place beyond its boundary, a new kind of singularity occurs. That's where "nude" and "singular" come in. The Dream Queen referred to a naked singularity: a point of infinite density outside of a black hole. Not only does this mean the lawlessness of a black hole can be witnessed, but also that its unpredictable forces can assault the whole cosmos and perhaps even annihilate it: " 'And curl forever nude inside the singular dream.' "

"So are we doomed?" asked Mister Touch anxiously.

"That's uncertain. Some cosmologists believed a *naked* singularity will never occur. And others felt either a normal or naked singularity is a source of creation rather than destruction. It depends on seeing the glass half full or half empty."

"How did they see it half full?"

She explained that a residue of nuclear explosions in space could easily migrate into a singularity, be sucked into the maelstrom of a black hole. Inside its depths heavy elements could be recycled into fresh hydrogen.

"Life-enhancing hydrogen," the main man knew enough to say.

"Exactly. Hydrogen makes the world go round. So there you *are!*" Toe clapped her hands down on her knees as if finishing off a fairy tale for kindergartners.

"Recycling," mused Mister Touch. "Renewed life."

"Not only that. Life in our *own* neighborhood, the Milky Way."

"You're giving up on Copernicus? Are we back to thinking of ourselves as the center of the universe?"

"Maybe we should. If creation comes out of a singularity, a hot region, then the only region that can support life must be *opposite* to it, far from the oven. That cooler area fits the conditions of the Milky Way. We're far from singularities that might produce the raw materials for life. But we're in *exactly the right place* to use those materials when they're ready. The Dream Queen suggested we live in an anthropic universe, its structure tailor-made for us. And I would tentatively go further. It may be that living creatures will someday, in the distant future, modify the environment of the universe, just like we modified the environment of the earth."

"We may be important for real." Mister Touch whistled in awe. "I wish IRT could hear this."

The word got around fast. Doctor Leo's reaction was predictable. Flailing his arms, he yelled, "It's a base lie! The poem's got nothing to do with dead stars! It's all about sex! Life on *this* planet!"

Stay High's reaction was less predictable. "There's more to the poem than that," he solemnly observed. "The exegesis has just begun." But he seemed uninterested in pursuing it himself. Adjusting his glasses, he stared up the street at Do You Thing, who was bending over to pet Lil Devil so that her cutoff jeans rode up high on her thighs, exposing twin moon slices of exquisite derrière.

That night, without warning or farewell, Toe left. The main man tried to make light of her loss, but clearly it hurt him. American governments used to tell Indians to move farther off. The last thing the Skull government wanted was for this Indian to go away (even if only twenty percent of her qualified as Indian), because she took with her a knowledge and a will that somehow they could have used.

While the main man wrestled with the mystery of the universe and government policy toward native Americans, The Fierce Rabbit had been following his own agenda. It began with meditation beyond the village limits — close enough for him to keep tabs on what was happening. Under intense sunlight he sat with eyes closed, seeing a second sun glowing inside his skull. He tried to evoke the image of a Black God wearing a dashiki and cradling an automatic rifle. The longer he sat the more convinced he became that the sun inside his head was actually a voice speaking to him. He strained to hear what was coming down. At last, with sweat in pools under his buttocks, he heard from the Universal Center a renewed exhortation to complete the celestial puzzle by leaving the Skulls without a leader and without a history. A voice was telling him, Get the fuck up mothafucker and *do* something! The sun blazed in his brain, expanding until it seemed to fill every cell in his head with terrible light. His mind overflowed with the image of a bulky Wall Street briefcase (not a slimliner like the young white dudes used to carry on Fifth Avenue, trying to look good, getting the eye of white chicks, waxing everybody into thinking they be hot). The Rabbit knew what it contained: the main man's Walkman and tapes. It was lying out for anyone to see. Laid back and mellowed out lately, the main man didn't even bother hiding his secrets anymore. That arrogance infuriated The Rabbit, who got up and drifted back to his set.

Yo Boy was rapping to half a dozen bloods. "You ain't really down for your set without ready to die for it. You get in a set you go down with it. Cholo get killed, you go kill one for him. Like cholos, they take off their head rags and put them in casket with him with bullets they kill the enemy with. That way the dead cholo, like he knew you did it for him. You proved. But you say, 'Lo hicimos por gusto' — we did it for fun. Like it don't matter. But it do matter. You proved."

Along came The Rabbit, whose frown took the starch out of everyone except Yo Boy and Wishbone, who met him with their own stiff smiles.

"Digging the side out of that fucking mountain, putting some insect on it —" Rabbit blew his breath out to emphasize his disbelief. "Whooo. Honkies gone weirder than shit. Putting on some crazy show out there."

"What about us?" asked Yo Boy.

"What about us what?"

"When do we put on a show *we* make?"

"Keep that under your rag," The Rabbit told him sternly. "Don't you get it yet? When *I* say go, we go."

"Yo."

Thoughtfully, The Rabbit added, "No leader worth shit have gone off halfcocked. Know what I mean?"

"Yo," said Yo Boy dutifully.

"We gonna have a name now."

"Yo," said Yo Boy, citing El Hoyo Maravilla, the oldest gang in East L.A. He held his palm out, describing a chola mark they could draw in blue ink.

"None of that stuff," grumbled The Fierce Rabbit. "This be *my* set. The Rabbit's Set."

"Yo," said Yo Boy. "El Viejo say so, it so."

"Get ready for doing some moving."

Yo Boy rubbed his hands with glee. "My brother and his tight partner, like they get dusted and they drive around in this Vega with baseball bats and when something wasn't so cool they jump out and start hitting. Brother used to say, 'Call me Mister Feelgood.' Who we doing first?"

"We gonna move our own fire over there away from what they got."

"What?"

"Moving our own fire away from them."

"You call that *moving?*" Yo Boy shook his head in contemptuous disbelief.

"Boy, you got an attitude?"

"No te enojes, lo dije en broma."

"You saying don't get mad? You jist joking? Okay then."

"But moving a fire somewhere ain't *moving.*"

The Rabbit stood up, more than six feet of heavy wire and cable. "You going up against me?"

"Do I look like that?" Yo Boy, smiling, opened both hands out in a submissive if unconvincing gesture.

But The Rabbit chose to accept it. "Okay then, we got no problem," he said, sitting down again. "What you don't know nothing about is leading. Don't mind saying I be born to lead. But no leader worth shit be jumping in without looking. Step by step. That's what I do. That's my style." He waited for the customary "Yo," and when it didn't come, The Rabbit said harshly, "You hearing me?"

"Yo."

"Gonna set our own fire over there. When Touch and his Tom come over and say why, then I say, Go your way, we go our own."

"Then we do it, we move, we do them right there?"

"Not yet. I got to be with my thoughts, thinking awhile. Then we see what we see." Again he waited. "You hearing me?"

After a long silence, Yo Boy muttered, "Yo."

But later, confiding to Wishbone, he said, "At this speed we gonna be old and cripple before something move."

That evening, when the new fire started burning a few hundred yards away from the Skull encampment in Portal, Mister Touch asked Hoss to check it out, and when he reported back, the prez asked for his opinion.

"Let them have their fire," Hoss suggested. "It makes them feel good. They've got gang blood in their veins and they like to feel it flowing. Makes them think they've got balls. But I can't see them doing anything. Otherwise, why would they put their fire so close that we can just look over there?"

"You're taking it lightly, Hoss."

"I think that's all it deserves, even though I never have felt comfortable with Wishbone and Yo Boy."

"All right," the main man said, "let them have their fun."

59

WHO CAME OUT of the desert one cool morning? Toe. Characteristically, she didn't waste words — simply called out a brisk hello and asked for the main man.

Brought to him while he sat over a plateful of javelina meat, Toe said, "Someone's with me. I never told you about him because I wasn't sure he'd want that. So after checking you out, I went back and described the Skulls to him. He liked what he heard, so here I am again. Julian was my mentor in grad school, and we've survived together. He was what you'd call OOTLO for about a year. He wanted to live in the desert — far from the memory of losing his wife and three children to V 70. I worked on problems, he sat and looked at mesquite. Sometimes he didn't speak for weeks."

"We have one like that. Stifle."

"Recently Julian has changed. He talks about the past and people he knew and his family. I think he wants in again."

"You say you were his student and the two of you survived together? Remarkable. I mean, the odds. They must be astronomical for two friends or colleagues or family members to come out of all that death alive together."

"I have him waiting over there." She pointed to a dingy pool hall, but then realized that pointing wouldn't work for Mister Touch. "In a pool hall."

"Let's go."

"One thing," said Toe, taking the main man's arm and leading him. "Julian was at one time an important theorist. His field was the grand unified theories. They tried to unite the electroweak with the strong force. Proton decay was an essential feature of these theories, but despite experiments lasting right up to V 70, not a single proton had yet decayed. It almost broke Julian's heart. Well, here we are."

The pool hall was dim inside, which didn't bother Mister Touch, who couldn't see the paunchy middle-aged man sitting next to the pool rack, wearing a muffler around his neck in the musty room, and smoking a pipe.

Mister Touch hadn't taken two steps into the pool hall before sniffing the air doggy-style and calling out, "What in hell is that? Tobacco smoke? I haven't smelled it for so long I forgot what it smells like."

"My pipe," said the heavyset man nervously, knocking ashes into the palm of his hand.

Toe introduced the two and then discreetly left. They sat side by side on the bench beside the pool rack where Ben Fermi and Hal Richter used to sit by the hour, smoking unfiltered Lucky Strikes during Roosevelt's reign and then mentholates and filters right through the reigns of those other guys they didn't consider good enough to shine FDR's shoes until politics didn't matter anymore because V 70 struck, at which time the two old men lugged their ancient bodies down to the pool hall every day for soda pop and a smoke while men half their age were expiring at home so that finally the old friends brought blankets in and waited out the inevitable effects of V 70 together, dying side by side in the left rear corner of the hall, where they were now.

"Tell me about yourself," Mister Touch said to Julian. "How's your health?"

"Good, though I'm still overweight. Digestion's good though we exist on canned goods and maybe a rabbit that Maxine — I think you call her Toe — shoots now and then. No arthritis, perhaps because I live in the desert. Kidneys, lungs, just about perfect."

"After V 70 and all that smoking? Your lungs are still perfect?"

"Still perfect. But my eyes are poor and getting poorer. I'd like to take a shot at that strange poem of yours she tells me about."

"We'd appreciate your looking at it. Will you stay?"

"I think so."

"Toe too?"

"Not for long. She'll go back to the desert. She's got excellent vision, notepads, slide rules, pencils. All she needs. She's in the heyday of her career."

"And you?"

"I'm ready for something new. Practical application of physical principles sounds good."

"Do you know," Mister Touch asked hopefully, "how to build machines?"

Julian laughed. "I don't know a damn thing about what you call the real world. There's a wonderful story about Werner Heisenberg, the Nobel laureate. At his Ph.D. orals he was asked how a battery works and since he didn't have the slightest idea, they gave him a gentleman's C, not having the nerve to flunk the best physics student they ever had. Truth is, my knowledge of practical engineering and related fields is probably about equal to that of a professor of English literature. But from what I do know I can extrapolate to things practical. I'd have to go over basic manuals, of course."

"We have around-the-clock readers."

"Then . . . it's settled."

"Not quite." Mister Touch cleared his throat in embarrassment; even so, in the firmest of voices he announced that smoking among the Skulls was forbidden.

"I see." Julian regarded his pipe with the sad intensity of a pet owner bidding farewell to an old hound dog being put to sleep. "I guess the time has come." He snapped the pipe stem and sighed.

Moved, Mister Touch reached out and touched his arm comfortingly. "The other thing is your name." And in a moment of inspiration, Mister Touch said, "You are Guts."

"Guts?" Julian repeated, looking down at his own.

"Yes, from your field — grand unified theories."

Guts chuckled. "I love it," he said and patted his paunch affectionately.

"Are you ready to enter the world again?"

"I am."

"Let's go."

After a fortnight at the site, on a late afternoon, Sphinx stepped back from the cliff, fluttered her sweaty blouse to get a gust of air against her skin, and mused out loud, "Well, it's not Giacometti or Lipchitz or David Smith or Caesar. It's no Henry Moore or Alexander Calder or Barbara Hepworth. It's medium to poor student work, but it's the best we can do." She herself chiseled the letters under it: SKULLS OF NEW YORK CITY. IRT'S VISION.

Guided to the stone relief, Mister Touch ran his fingertips across the surface. Behind him the Skulls cheered, and under her breath Sphinx quoted OOTHI: " 'We carry with us the wonders we seek without us: There is all Africa and her prodigies in us.' " Sphinx had carved the monument to project a vision outward and had found what had always been within herself.

"We'll celebrate tomorrow night," declared the main man. "And incidentally, tomorrow is Christmas. So we can hold a double celebration."

A casual passerby, motoring along the east-west spur road leading to Portal, might have seen very little from his windshield — a few distant scratchings against the side of an immense cliff — but if he had left his car and strolled toward the sheer wall of stone, on closer inspection he would have discerned the highly stylized shape of an ant, its legs powerfully set in rock as it climbed forever in cold immobility upward to illustrate the noble cliché that a work of art in stone should declare it always was and always will be.

Meanwhile, armed with the blank tapes obtained by Snootchy Fingers and pressed by Yo Boy's insistence on moving, The Fierce

Rabbit decided to put his plan into action, sort of, at least some of it, because the idea of setting it into full motion boggled his mind with unforeseen consequences.

He began by commandeering two of the Skull cars: fast, sleek, like big-time runners' cars. His set merely walked through Portal, took what they wanted, and snatched the keys from the drivers. "We taking this now." Then they parked the BMW 750iL and the Mercedes-Benz 560 SEC close to their campfire of rebellion.

Turning to Yo Boy, The Rabbit grinned. "You gonna see some moving now."

"Yo."

When the main man heard about this misappropriation of public property, he decided to go see The Fierce Rabbit.

But he was waylaid by Guts, who showed up with a report on "The Mystery of the Universe."

As a collaborator, Toe read it aloud to the main man.

> "Although even a lay person can see that the biochemist's poem often lapses into doggerel, it is also an appraisal of modern physics, and as such is not without interest.
>
> "Although Stay High seems to have more pressing matters on his mind than the place of physics in the world's future, he did provide us with his own notes on the poem, which have proved somewhat helpful, and we acknowledge the debt.
>
> "We have proceeded in our exegesis by referring to those lines in the poem which seem especially relevant to our discipline, convinced as we are that the ultimate subject of The Dream Queen's poem is physics.
>
> "A. 'When the moon is nu': When a neutron decays spontaneously into a proton, two other particles are created, one being a neutrino — assigned the Greek letter 'nu.' "

Toe paused and studied the blind man. "How are you doing?"
"So far not bad."

> "This sort of decay in the atomic nucleus is commonplace. On the other hand, the decay of *protons* is so rare that it has not yet been observed."

The main man heard a rush of expelled air. That had to be Guts sighing because, of course, Guts's inability to prove proton decay had almost broken his heart.

"As the chief building block of the nucleus," Toe continued, "the proton has always been considered stable. There is nothing lighter for it to become if it decays. There is nowhere for matter to go. Most of the material in the universe is hydrogen and the nucleus of hydrogen is a proton. The implication is clear."

"Not to me," the prez admitted.

"Let me say a word," Guts put in, unable to stay out. "If the proton is capable of decaying, hydrogen will eventually decompose. That means the end of stars and galaxies. The cosmos will rot and die."

"Like people did when V 70 Struck," the prez noted grimly. "Is proton decay likely?"

"The chances are slim. First it must transform itself into a neutral pion and a positron. A superheavy gluon would also have to change one proton quark into a lepton."

"What are the odds?" asked the former Wall Street gambler.

"About a thousand billion billion to one."

"My God, bigger than the odds against winning the lottery three times."

"In cosmic terms not that big. It would be an achievement of Nobel proportions if an experiment proved the proton finally does decay."

"And mean the end of the universe?"

"Well, yes," Guts admitted casually. "But it would restore a sense of symmetry."

Mister Touch sighed. "So according to you, The Dream Queen may have predicted the end of the world in the very first line. The 'nu' does it."

"Shall I continue?" Toe asked.

He shrugged. "Yes, even if the rest is anticlimactic."

"B. 'Or dice with God': Einstein once wrote, " 'I am convinced that God does not play dice.' Here The Dream Queen is reminding us of Einstein's belief in an orderly universe.

"C. 'Or walk the plank' is a deliberate misspelling of Planck, the German scientist. At the turn of the century he invented quantum theory by calculating that light is emitted in packets of discrete energy — quanta. Planck Time is the time it takes for a photon traveling 186,000 miles per second to move the distance of the Planck Length — about 10^{-36} centimeters. A short time, indeed, often employed in describing the Big Bang.

"D. 'Be mad as a Danish hatter' refers to the Danish physicist Niels Bohr, who once said to Wolfgang Pauli, 'We all agree that your theory is crazy. The question is whether it's crazy enough.' When Bohr developed his Principle of Complementarity, many physicists thought it was crazy to imagine a thing behaving like both a particle and a wave.

"E. 'Hitch up your trousers with string': Called 'spacetime trousers' in superstring theory. When two string loops merge, visually they look like a pair of trousers. In string theory no force or particle is more fundamental than any other."

Toe paused. "Are you with us?"
"I can still see you in the distance."
She read again.

"F. 'In the world of dark matter': This is a complicated concept involving the distribution of unobserved matter in the universe. According to this theory, hidden mass is out there in a form unlike the matter of our observable world. The fate of the cosmos depends on dark matter. The universe can be open, in which case it will expand forever, or it can be closed, in which case it will collapse back on itself, or it can be perfectly in balance, each part of space ending up empty and motionless, a flat universe. If there is sufficient dark matter, then gravity will draw the universe back into itself, until it collapses and possibly recreates the conditions for another Big Bang and rebirth, somewhat like the Indian girl suggests in her interpretation of 'Mea Kalpa.'

"G. 'Until the charm's wound up' refers to 'charm,' one of the six flavors of quark, a fundamental particle. In twos and threes the quark combines to make up protons, neutrons, and mesons. The Dream Queen is alluding here to basic processes that make whatever is be.

"H. An exegesis of 'Then drop like Alice' through 'the singular dream' has already been made. The cosmic consequences of black holes may well be anthropic, but the entire question is still speculative."

Mister Touch figured that Guts must see the glass half empty, Toe half full.

"One more comment on that section of the poem. 'Into truth too deep too rude' carries the additional allusion to 'Deep Truth' as described by John Schwarz, a founder of string theory. Deep Truth leads back to general relativity and by implication to Newtonian gravity. The ultimate formula may well go backward in time to Newton and Einstein. An astonishing idea."

Toe paused again. "You're still there?"

"I'm in the ballpark, I think, although in college I got a C in physics."

"It's best to go on. After you have a total picture, you can backtrack."

"Or stay where I am. Yes, go on."

"I. 'When the hubble-bubble's done': This refers to *Macbeth*, I, i. One of the witches says, 'When the hurly-burly's done, / When the battle's lost and won.' Hurly-burly has become hubble-bubble to conjure up Hubble's Law, which states that distant galaxies recede at a velocity proportional to their distance. A bubble is often used to illustrate the idea that everything is rushing away from everything else. Stars and galaxies are thought of as dots on an expanding surface like a bubble.

"To quote again that scene from Macbeth:

1. WITCH: 'When shall we three meet again
           In thunder, lightning, or in rain?'
2. WITCH: 'When the hurly-burly's done,
           When the battle's lost and won.'
3. WITCH: 'That will be ere the set of sun.'

The three witches imply the three forces of the universe whose symmetry was broken approximately one ten-billionth of a second after the Big Bang (the fourth force, gravity, had split off much earlier at 1/10, 000, 000, 000, 000, 000, 000,-000, 000, 000, 000, 000 000, 000, 000th of a second after the birth of the universe).

"It seems inappropriate to conjecture further about the significance of those lines, but they do suggest a concern with cosmic fate. It is quite possible that the victory alluded to — 'when the battle's lost and won' — refers to the immortality of time and space. Moreover, The Dream Queen probably believed that sufficient dark matter would allow the cosmos to contract back into itself and crunch out everything but the energy to begin again. God says 'Mea Kalpa' or in essence 'My Creation' forever and ever, et cetera. The poem seems to conclude by merging ancient Indian philosophy and modern physics. Aside from her reference to proton decay, she views the world in positive terms. For her it seems immortal, changeless in change, forever renewing itself."

Toe stopped reading, folded the paper, and left the room, leaving the two men alone together.

After a long silence, Mister Touch said, "I'm moved. From your report, as I understand it, the universe is still mysterious but very beautiful."

"Remember, The Dream Queen wrote it, not I."

"Don't you think the world is beautiful?"

"Oh, I do. But until proton decay is settled, I withhold judgment on the world's fate. However, I don't intend to sit around and wait for a verification of proton decay. I have better things to do. This morning that pleasant Chinese boy Blue Magic taught me the basic principles of the battery. When we get to a decent library, I want to start on applications of mechanical engineering. I understand Harold is willing to help me out too."

"Thank you," Mister Touch said with a sigh of relief, "for both theory and application."

"Thank you too."

"For what?"

"For making me do what I could never do before. Frankly, I tried to quit smoking many times, but failed. I'm succeeding now because of the Skulls. They all know I'm trying to quit. They pat me on the shoulder and say, 'Come on, bro, you can do it.'" He paused. "It's very beautiful."

60

THE NEXT DAY music-minded Skulls were rigging the canyon with loudspeakers.

Spirit In The Dark was putting the finishing touches on her main man — gussied up in buckskins, boots, and a Stetson broader-brimmed than Hoss's — when Hoss came to the shack with news.

"Toe took off. Someone saw her with a backpack walking out of town."

"Did she say anything?"

"I'm going now," Spirit said and kissed her husband.

When she had gone, Hoss whistled low. "I've been kissed by women, but none ever kissed me like that."

"It was only a goodbye-for-the-evening kiss," Mister Touch pointed out with a touch of pride. Spirit was giving up the celebration to help Coco with Rattler, who had a stomach upset. Pregnant Spirit wanted a feeling of closeness to a child already on the outside.

Hoss said, "Whatever you call it, that was still the best kiss I ever saw. Now. What was I saying?"

"Toe."

"She had a pencil behind her ear, a notebook in her hand, packets of Ramen and a pot in the knapsack. She waved goodbye to Guts and left without looking back. You seem worried. What's wrong?"

"I had a bad dream last night."

"You put too much stock in dreams."

"The night before learning the SEC was on my case and I might go to jail, I dreamt my apartment building was on fire. Let's celebrate."

After dinner in the torchlit canyon and before the dancing began, Mister Touch made a short speech. He thanked the sculptors for commemorating the Skulls' arrival in Arizona by carving a monument to IRT's vision of survival. As prez, he welcomed back the three sisters. Then the main man confessed to taping a History of the Skulls. Begun in the Club House and continued on the journey, it was a record of their lives, just as the carved ant was a testament to their achievement. At first there was no reaction, then a faint clap, then louder clapping until it told him what a damn fool he'd been to think of his secret project as anything but kind of nice. He stood there tall, red-bearded, smiling, and happy. "Now that's off my chest, let's dance!"

Even the religious dissenters joined the festivities, as if reluctantly awed by the resourcefulness of ant-loving heathens who had hung Christmas decorations on cacti. Light shone from a mesquite bonfire which threw the shadows of dancing Skulls against canyon walls. The hip-hop stereo flooded the desert with the rhythm of zouk. Zouking, they were all zouking, man, were they ever, in Navaho blouses and buckskin leggings and beaded headbands.

Paunchy Guts was there. People stared at him in awe, like he was the guy who had solved that crazy poem the chemistry woman had written. Not that everyone agreed with his interpretation.

Doctor Leo said, "Based on what I hear, Guts pays more attention to the size of atoms than he does to amino acids." Having delivered that criticism, he revealed a new interpretation of his own. Calling The Dream Queen a moonstruck woman who dreamed of being a sex kitten like Cleopatra, he accused her of applying her sensual restlessness to gambling and games, to robbing banks and courting danger by walking the plank. His new analysis focused on sex. The poem needed only a slight adjustment for this purpose. The word "expect" had to be changed to "suspect." That is, "when they least suspect it." This was necessary to remove the letter x from the text. You also needed to remove the word "universal," because it had a v in it. This required a change from "universal goal" to "urinary goal." The two changes altered the poem so that *twenty-three* letters of the alphabet were used in it — minus v and x along with z (which never appeared in the original version). That left *twenty-three* chromosomes supplied by the man and the same number by the woman, when they procreate!

Cupping one hand at the side of his mouth as if saying something conspiratorial, Doctor Leo shouted over the music, "Do the ladies mind if I tell it like it is?"

A few girls giggled.

" 'The urinary goal' is a circumlocution for 'vagina.' I got 'circumlocution' from Adidas, who used it in his C period." He went on to prove that "Hitch up your trousers with string" was a circumlocution for condom, something drawn on and hopefully made to stay put. Alice was not a circumlocution but an anagram for "Cilea," a misspelling of cilia, the hairlike processes that serve as the means of locomotion for free-swimming organisms. Doctor Leo chuckled happily, claiming that what dropped down the hole was not Alice but countless molecules of love on their wriggling way to the center of reproductive activity, a caldron of genetic turbulence. "Let's drop Toe's foolish idea about singularities. What's singular is her failure to realize The Dream Queen is describing the human womb! The 'blood-red beam' is the menstrual tunnel which will soon be closed to traffic and 'the truth too deep too rude' means the ovaries, where push comes to shove, and the fetus curls up naked to sleep until the hubble-bubble of nine months is complete and — it is born!" Again Doctor Leo chortled and went on to agree with Stay High that "Mea Kalpa" was a misspelling of the Latin for "my fault," which is what the man admits to the woman. He had failed to take precautions. But the man ends on a positive note by promising to work hard, establish a home, provide for the child, "et cetera."

His cheeks puffing like bellows from excitement, Doctor Leo continued. "But the poem is also a gene map. I'm searching for enzymes based on each letter of the alphabet. I am confident my research will prove The Dream Queen was a Right To Lifer who wrote about the Genetic Code, the whole Genetic Code, and nothing but the Genetic Code — *so help you God?*" Raising his right hand, he slapped down his left on an invisible Bible and swore, *"I do!"*

But Stay High was not impressed. Shaking his head, the scholar from Columbia declared, "This is not the final solution to 'The Mystery of the Universe.' The poem needs more work, though I can't find time for it myself." Indeed he could not. His mind and heart had slipped like avalanche debris straight down into his genital area, where everything lay steaming and bubbling like volcanic magma. With his customary thoroughness he had learned the mechanics of zouking, but tonight, inspired by Do You Thing, whose shirt was buttoned with only one button, he caught the true kinetic spirit of the dance. His skinny white body looked positively black as he did laid-back limber-jointed New York City footwork. Do You

Thing fell in love. By God if she didn't, and before the dawn came up in Portal on Christmas morning, she figured to reveal to her suitor a few skills of her own. Do You Thing would convince him beyond a reasonable doubt that she was indeed the most intelligent girl he had ever met and erase from his mind forever the seven-inch clay goddess whose breasts, like his mother's, were enormous.

The dancing continued. To a plainsman from the past century it might have looked and sounded like the heathen rituals of red Indians. The prez jumped to his feet and yelled, "I hear it! I hear people getting better! I hear it in their feet! They're on the beat! I hear them getting their health back! I hear it! I hear it!"

The Fierce Rabbit lay in the mesquite all evening, one ear against the ground, feeling the pulse of music. He was ready. He had been chosen the agent of black justice as it was known at the Universal Center. "Marvin Johnson," he said aloud, "it be time!"

Stalking through mesquite along the black border of Portal, he came to the main man's little house. Listening for sound and hearing none, he crept onto the porch and turned the doorknob. Once inside he flicked on his flashlight and searched for the briefcase Mister Touch usually carried but had probably left behind for the party.

The Rabbit guessed right. He found it shoved under the bed. Opening the briefcase he took from it eighteen recorded tapes, replacing them with eighteen blanks. Because Mister Touch had recorded them secretly, he alone had access to them, but being blind he couldn't see the labels; he must identify them by counting along the orderly rows stacked in the briefcase.

Unless he replayed them, which was unlikely in the Skulls' crowded schedule, the main man wouldn't miss them for a long time. By then The Rabbit and The Rabbit's Set would be gone, laughing all the way, convulsed by the idea of Mister Touch declaring that the Skulls had a history when all they had were blank tapes.

Gleefully The Rabbit put his treasure in a tote bag, adding a few of Jive Turkey's photos — processed poorly in a small-town shop along the way. Then he rushed back to his camp and deposited history in the trunk of the BMW, designated as "El Viejo's Limo."

Then he strolled over to his nine followers hunched over their own campfire and told them, "That partying they doing, we going over there and look."

Yo Boy, smoking a joint provided by Snootchy Fingers from a Dallas stash, sat up with a broad smile. "Yeah? What then?"

"We look."

"Yeah? So what then?"

"We stare them down," The Rabbit explained impatiently. "We let them know our set be looking at them."

"So what then?"

"Do what I say do."

"Yo. Meaning move on them? Take a few out?"

"Wait till you see," The Rabbit declared and strode majestically away.

When The Rabbit's Set appeared at the circle of light illuminating the canyon, they were happily welcomed. "Hey! Brothers! Come on in and party hearty! Good you tipping in tonight!"

With his set surrounding him in a tight bunch, like aphids around honeydew, The Fierce Rabbit muttered, "Don't say nothing."

From the zoukers came another shouted welcome. "Come on, brothers! Get down! Tomorrow we be rapping like old times!"

"Don't say nothing," The Rabbit told his gang.

"Hey," someone yelled out angrily, "you got no behavior! Go back where you come from then!"

"Let me do him," Yo Boy said under his breath, sticking his hand in his pocket.

"Don't say nothing." Turning briskly, The Rabbit tramped away and his gang followed into the desert — Wishbone and Yo Boy with obvious reluctance.

"So what now?" asked Yo Boy when they were out of sight of the celebration (but not out of earshot, because zouk was turned up high enough to wake up Sleeping Beauty and the gods on Olympus, Kailasa, Valhalla, and Sister Fate's Mount Tai Shan).

"Don't you know nothing?" The Fierce Rabbit demanded of Yo Boy. "We done what we did. Now we see what they do."

"Yo. We done what?"

"You listening to me?"

The Rabbit waited for "Yo," and when it didn't come, he yelled irritably, "You don't know nothing! Dumber than the dumbest nigger I ever saw!"

Yo Boy maintained a smoldering Latin silence as The Rabbit's Set strode back across a moonlit desert. Later he would say to Wishbone, "Estoy harto de esto."

"I'm fed up too," Wishbone declared, then added thoughtfully, "Perro que ladra no muerde."

"You got it right. Barking dog no problem. Dog you don't see coming out of the night, *that* one get you."

61

SITTING AROUND their own fire were The Rabbit and the other nine of his set, all minorities except Snootchy Fingers and Daddy Rich, the two blanquitos, as Yo Boy contemptuously called them, who lolled around bragging about getting dusted in Dallas and doing rhymes that didn't belong to them, like "Hey little dude, wanna make some bread? Just run these rocks and do what's said."

They were paid a sudden visit.

Mister Touch led by Africa emerged from the darkness. Both tall men, one slim, one broad, approached the firelight. The main man's beard had a coppery color, his eyes a milky-gray opaqueness. A shadow formed like a dark pool beneath his prominent cheekbones, making his face seem stony, obdurate.

Even The Rabbit knew the earned look of authority when he saw it. That only infuriated him. "What the fuck *you* here for?"

"To see why you won't come back over."

"None of your business."

"If we have differences, let's work them out. It's no good for Skulls to split up."

"Yeah? Okay when they be honkies, right? The old white-haired old white bitch wanted out and you said go."

"My mistake. Because see what happened. We'll all do better if we go together."

"We do just fine alone."

"Look at it this way — bad things are going to happen. Most of the medicines in drugstores will expire. All the gas will evaporate out of tanks. Machines are going to rust, gadgets fall apart. What we take for granted now, what we can just shoot a door off for and go inside and take, is not going to last. We've got to work out medicine and transportation and agriculture and industry for ourselves all over again. We can do that. It won't take long to make things happen again, once we settle down. Not like in the distant past when people stumbled from one little advance to the next. It took centuries to get from the wheel to the motor, right? But we have both already. We know what technology can do. We just might get the whole wild thing together again before Rattler becomes a teenager. We've already fine-tuned our memories by learning stuff from OOTHI. We're equipped to absorb massive amounts of information, do you realize that? Instead of reciting Shakespeare, we can use muscle-bound minds to lift equations right out of textbooks. We can create a world better than the old one because we know their mistakes. I'm saying we can do it better, but to do it at all we have to be united and use for all of us what skills we have. I'm afraid of what happened to The Terrible Ten. It was like fate or nature or God or something was warning us to stick together. So I'm asking you not to go. I'm asking you for a meet. I'm asking for talk."

The Fierce Rabbit had listened impassively to this long impassioned speech, almost as if he were attending a fundraiser in someone's living room and a local politician was giving last year's speech again. He was thinking victoriously of the tapes hidden in the trunk of El Viejo's car. When the blind man, who had stood throughout his appeal for negotiation, stopped jawing, The Rabbit guffawed as if he had just heard a backroom joke. Because in a way he had — the joke was on the main man, the dumb whitey, who didn't know where his tapes were. "Just like you honkies," he said with a sneer. "Suspicious. Believe any fucking thing. Believe the old white-haired old bitch be killed by something beside a big wind.

Huh! You call that street smart?" He turned to regard Snootchy Fingers, a honky, who sat across the fire. "Right? Do I know or what?" He jerked a long black finger at the main man. "This honky dude got no street smarts."

"You got it," Snootchy Fingers, another honky dude, enthusiastically agreed.

"What do you want?" Mister Touch asked The Fierce Rabbit.

"What do you give a *fuck* what I want!"

"If we don't talk, neither of us knows what to ask for."

"Don't ask nothing from *you*, dude."

"If you've got nothing to ask of me, I take that to mean we're straight with each other."

"Who gonna say *that*? Never be straight with *you*. You never be straight in your honky life."

"All I hear is anger — blind, straight-out self-indulgent anger."

"Yeah?"

"Yeah! I can understand frustration or a sense of injustice or contempt for something maybe stupid I did — any of that. I can try dealing with what is tied to something, to a thing, an attitude, because then we have that thing to deal with between us. You say A, I say B, maybe we get to C. But if you just scream and shout, man, then forget it, we don't have anything going, nothing to work on."

"Meaning?"

"Meaning, I guess, leave. Go on, take off, do your own thing, live the impossible dream. How do I know? Go play with your anger." The prez balled his fists in front of his chest. "Or stay and work with us to build something."

The Fierce Rabbit arched his head back and roared out some theatrical laughter. "Hear that bullshit? Heard it all my life! Do this, do that, land of the free, we gonna march side by side bullshit coming out of honky mouth. Don't need it no more. Right?" he asked Snootchy Fingers.

"You got it."

"Then go," said Mister Touch, letting his fists open up. "Move! Go on and go and take anyone with you who wants to go too."

The Rabbit stood up. Send Em Back To Africa stepped in front of the blind man. The Rabbit sat down. "Get out of my face," he muttered.

"You want to reconsider," said Mister Touch evenly, "you know where to find me."

Watching huge Africa lead the tall Blindie beyond firelight into the desert evening, The Rabbit snickered in triumph. "Find himself in the fucking grave do that honky dude keep on that way. Fuck."

"Yo," said Yo Boy. "Blanquito. We gonna do them now?"

"Who you talking to, boy?" The Rabbit said. "We go when *I* say go."

"Yo."

But an hour later, having smoked some reefer that Daddy Rich had produced, Yo Boy drew his friend Wishbone away from the set and squatted with him in the darkness out of earshot. "Listen. This Rabbit. Not so fierce like his name make him. Hear me?"

"Yeah. Mouth. But nothing doing in the street."

"Listen to me. He say wait, we wait, but we wait long enough. This motherfucker still doing nothing but talking. A wannabe, no roller."

"No gangbanger," Wishbone agreed.

"So you know now? *We* gonna make it happen, *we* gonna move. You and me make our own set."

"We jump him out?"

"First, we get this blanquito Touch and do him because he fucking insult the set we been in and we have his woman and cut her throat too and then we come back here and jump out The Rabbit from our own set. Do them all three with this." He patted the pocket he kept his knife in. "Could I get some garlic, I rub it on a bullet and shoot that fucking Rabbit, hijo de la gran puta, lambestaca, right in the fucking mouth with it."

"Fucking cool. Lambestaca," said Wishbone.

"That stash of gun he put in El Viejo car. Go get a couple for us right now and put this others in Mercedes, got it?"

Without hesitation Wishbone crept over to the BMW where he vamped the stash of weapons and lugged them over to the Mercedes, while the rest of The Rabbit's Set sat around the fire drinking warm beer and arguing about where to go if they went at all. Wishbone kept a couple of handguns for himself and Yo Boy, like he'd been told, and tossed the rest of the weapons in the back seat of the Mercedes.

When Wishbone returned, Yo Boy was sitting quietly, moonlight streaming over his hunched shoulders.

"We gonna do like that?" asked Wishbone.

"Why not? Sure," Yo Boy said with a shrug. "No cholo who got cojones be going too long with some El Viejo who ain't nothing but some wind in a big mouth. We give him time to prove, right?"

"Right."

"But he don't prove. Sus promesas son puras palabras."

"Right, nothing but talk."

"He don't show nothing but teeth."

"Sí. Se le va demasiado la lengua."

"Saying 'wait' all the time. No tiene sentido."

"Not to me either. Su actitud es, 'Ya lo vermos.' "

"You got it — wait and see, wait and fucking see." He shook his head as if Guts had just explained Planck's Constant to him. "No tiene sentido."

"Es un poco estúpido."

Yo Boy grinned at the thought of The Rabbit being stupid. "About time," he said, "we go looking for dope for our own self, not taking it from this blanquitos he got with him, and we have some fun our style and take along some of this women and one guy for driving us —"

"Like big-time runners."

"Let the rest of this motherfuckers around here die from heat or snake or whatever be under the rock or if they don't die here, let them get up to L.A. and we do them right there in our own barrio, man. Let me see one of this pieces."

Wishbone handed over a gun.

Yo Boy squinted in the moonlight, turning the piece like hot jewelry he was trying to fence. "Walther PPK 9-millimeter. Get off fifteen shot in five second. I know this gun. Like my brother, he had one of this."

"What do we do now?" said Wishbone.

"Go stick the blanquito." He patted his knife.

"Stick him . . . for real?" Wishbone asked with an awed guffaw.

"When I get in I gonna give it some twist." Yo Boy illustrated by turning his hand one hundred eighty degrees through the night air.

They started out right then, across the flat windy desert, with

Yo Boy, flushed by anticipation, telling Wishbone how they were going to wear sharkskin suits and lizard shoes worth seven hundred bucks and blue Izod Lacoste shirts. They were going to be the man, smoke chiba chiba, and have any woman who caught their eye.

They walked through mesquite along the back border of Portal until coming into sight of the main man's shack. It was dark, but that didn't mean anything when a blind man lived in it, although it could mean the woman was out helping with Rattler, that baby like the one she thought she was going to have but didn't know was going to die with her tonight.

They approached cautiously, looking for the bodyguard, Africa. Most nights he sat on the porch, his eyes hidden behind sunglasses that he wore both day and night, so that it was impossible to tell whether Africa was asleep or awake. But tonight he was gone.

"We go in," Yo Boy explained to Wishbone, "I go for him, you go get the woman if she be in there. Don't do her till we have her first."

"Knock her out?"

"Yeah, only not so good she don't feel. My name's Mister Feelgood."

Wishbone giggled.

"Tenga cuidado," Yo Boy warned. Testing the porch boards, he crept up and reached for the doorknob, turning and pulling it in one motion. Then they were inside, each holding a flashlight and a knife. The main man, lying half asleep on a moth-eaten couch, still a bit dopey on wine, sat upright, smiling at the coming.

"Spirit?"

Yo Boy crossed the room and with an inspired arc of rapid motion brought the knife down until he felt the blade go in, catch slightly as he jerked it upward the way a man hoists his belted pants, and then continued as if it were sliding through warm butter.

Wishbone, having gone into the back room, returned in time to hear a whispering sound. "Done him?"

"Get the woman," hissed Yo Boy.

"Gone."

Bending over the fallen prez, Yo Boy said almost soothingly,

"Don't worry, big man, we gonna have some fun. Too bad we can't do some jointing and sending. That be fun — send your Dumpster number to this dumb fucks around here. I am gonna cut your throat and we gonna go get your woman and have her first and cut hers too." But before he could make good on his promise, a noise at the entrance had Wishbone and Yo Boy turning.

What was there in the doorway filled it.

Send Em Back To Africa grunted once before hurtling into the room and grabbing Wishbone before the little fellow could free himself of fear long enough to run. Africa had him hugged to his chest and what Yo Boy heard while fumbling for the Walthers jammed in its holster was Wishbone's spine cracking like a wishbone.

Freeing the gun, Yo Boy shot wildly at the massive shape that had turned toward him, spinning through the eerie glow of the fallen flashlight. Irresistible force met immovable object: three jolts from the Walther sent Africa back, and a fourth lifted all of his three hundred pounds and threw them against the wall.

Satisfied, Yo Boy turned again to the main man waiting for death. "Here it come," he purred, bending over.

But what came instead was a shot from Africa, who had gone down but not out and had managed with his last breath to raise his own pistol.

Yo Boy straightened up, feeling a curious warmth in his side, and in the next microsecond a searing hot pain that nearly crumpled him.

Staggering past Wishbone and the huge bulk of Africa, he lurched through the open doorway into the desert night. If only La Bruja had blessed his gun, this would never have happened, Yo Boy thought bitterly, as he shuffled across the dark flats.

By the time he got to the campfire, blood was bubbling between his fingers. They clutched the wound as if preventing what was inside from spilling out. Half the rebels took one look at him and slunk instantly away as if caught in the glare of a squad car's spotlight. They were heading back to Portal almost before The Rabbit leapt to his feet and yelled at the bleeding boy, "Hey, I told you and *told* you! Didn't I say stay put!"

Following The Rabbit's example, Snootchy Fingers and Daddy

Rich got up too. They had just done some crack and had reached the euphoric possibility of tweaking.

"Done him," panted Yo Boy.

"Done who? What happened to you, boy?" asked The Rabbit.

"Done the main man. Fin. Wishbone dead too, and Africa."

"Holy shit." The Rabbit just stood there, but the two blanquitos, Snootchy Fingers and Daddy Rich, jumped gleefully up and down, ready for tweaking good fun and games. "Gonna have some fun. Let's have some fun, have some fun, have some fun!" they chanted, dancing around the fire like the phony savages in King Kong. *"Have some fun! Have some fun! Have some fun!"*

"Gotta get out of here," muttered The Rabbit.

"Help me. Estoy sin aliento."

"You be more than out of breath, boy." The Rabbit impatiently grabbed hold of Yo Boy and started him toward the cars. The two white boys had already rushed over there, whooping it up, crazed with blood lust and the base (not Doctor Leo's kind) brought from Dallas.

"Crack Attack!" shouted Snootchy Fingers. "Here comes the Crack Attack!"

The two white boys climbed into the Mercedes, revved it up, and were off in a screech of tires before The Rabbit and his wounded companion even got to El Viejo's Limo.

"What they up to?" asked the scared Rabbit.

"Follow them," panted Yo Boy, getting into the passenger's side. "Dese prisa!" So The Fierce Rabbit did as he was told — hurried up and got the car started and followed the Crack Attack. With Daddy Rich driving, the car ahead of them was careening back and forth; from the passenger side Snootchy Fingers had got his snootchy fingers on the trigger of an Uzi and was already firing at will. He stitched the desert night with red-hot rivets of cracked emotion, so that rabbits in their burrows ten feet underground shook from confusion and fear.

"Motherfucking Snootchy Fingers shooting that Uzi," cried The Rabbit, appalled.

The two cars, one spurting bullets, sped down the main street of Portal. From its houses came a burst of gunfire.

"Shooting at us!" yelled The Rabbit.

"Keep going!"

The Rabbit did as he was told, while in the Mercedes ahead of them a Skull bullet flew like an insectile projectile through the open window of the driver's side and stung Daddy Rich full in the left temple, taking him out instantly and sending the car into a store-front where Snootchy Fingers blew through the window, spectacularly dead.

The Rabbit swerved and took off down a side street with bullets thudding against the car, like in the movies. "See what that honky *done?*" he screamed. "Now we gotta go fast!"

Yo Boy, feeling enough pain to be cautious, just stared at The Rabbit without saying what he was thinking: Don't blame this two blanquitos who least was out there proving. We leaving, moving out of here because *you* scared shitless. You got no cojones, no principle, man. All you got is mouth. But the streets had taught Yo Boy to go with the flow, especially if you were hurt, because that was when people came down on you hardest of all. So he said nothing and fought against losing consciousness. If he went out, The Rabbit might dump him.

62

As THEY DROVE ALONG, The Fierce Rabbit glanced anxiously at his wounded companion. Yo Boy was holding his gut with both hands; they were glistening from blood oozing like bog water through his shirt. A fetid smell filled the car. Was that the smell of guts or had the kid shit his pants?

To change his mood, he said, "You got the main man for real?"

"Yeah. Wow. Hurt pretty good now."

"Cut his throat?"

"Yo," lied Yo Boy. "Me causó gracia."

"Made you laugh?" The Rabbit took his eyes off the busy road for a moment to study his companion. "Cut myself a throat oncet. When Dragons come into the Club House. I went —" The Fierce Rabbit lifted one big hand from the wheel and slid it dramatically through thin air.

"Was he down already?" asked Yo Boy.

"Huh?"

"Nothing. No importa."

They drove north awhile before The Rabbit, glancing at him again, whistled low. "You bleeding like hell."

"Nah, not bad. No es para quejarse."

"Yeah? I complain do I have a hole like that."

Yo Boy tried to sit up straight, but the pain bent him over and he squeaked like a small animal.

Minutes later, The Rabbit looked again. "Hey, you slipping?"

"Not me. You get me to L.A. and my set, we be okay."

"Nobody alive there now."

"Could be. Or we make our own set. Hey," he tried to sound jolly, "this cholos in my barrio like prove." Yo Boy was breathing like a Steady Breather, but he felt himself slipping now and then. He worked to keep his eyes open, though the pain hammered to shut them. "My brother, he was top cholo. People offer to wash his car, they ask him how things go. Fancy dinner every night." Yo Boy went on talking, afraid The Rabbit would think he was slipping if he didn't keep saying things. "Once some guys held him up with a gun against his head in this bodega, but he kept back most of money and drugs. Even when they say they cut off his cojones and stuff them up his ass, which guys like this has done. My brother, he just look and say he got nothing more. Then they go, buying it, because no man gonna hold out money for his balls, right? Then he front his boss, saying they got everything. Pocket the difference, my brother. Oh shit."

"What?"

"No importa."

The Fierce Rabbit slowed down to take a better look. "You slipping?"

"Get me to L.A. Be glad you did." Then in the exercise of remarkable will power, Yo Boy inflamed his own mind, if not The Rabbit's, with the memory of past violence, based on the woozy need for revenge heightened by hits of speedball and dust. His nostalgic recall of brutality, added to the buildup of pain, got him not only narrow-eyed but misty-eyed, as if memory itself was a high roller of consequence. You could buy a kilo of coke for ten thousand, he explained, and sell it in bags of crack for quarter million. "He have flashy cars, women to use all the time, white powder, jewelry, man, but it don't matter when you laid out in a coffin less you got cholos to prove who you was, like my brother."

"You sure run off at the mouth," complained The Rabbit, just as a rim of blue appeared on the flat horizon. "Got a fever or what?"

"Get me to L.A. My brother take care of us."

"Your *dead* brother? What happening, boy? You slipping?"

"Fuck this guys with their Rolex and five-liter Mustang and the white Mercedes with car phone. Que lo pase bien . . . me causó gracia . . . lo hicimos por gusto."

The Rabbit tried to follow this meandering Spanish: Enjoy yourself, it made me laugh, we did it for fun. The kid was slipping.

"La caridad bien entendida empieza pro uno mismo."

"Hey, cut the Spanish. I be too fucking tired to fool with it. Talk American."

"Charity begins at home. My brother, he say it when he get all silk down and go out and do something."

"Slipping," declared The Fierce Rabbit glumly. "Now you got blood coming outta your mouth."

"Get me to barrio. My brother do everything. He was no wannabe, no big mouth. Tight partner with top cholos, with top top. Ah, estoy sin aliento."

"Talk all the time," The Rabbit grumbled, "you gonna get out of breath."

"Cada cual se las arregle como pueda."

The Rabbit thought the panted words meant every man for himself or something and it sure made sense. Along with Yo Boy's breath came little gusts of exclamation, "Ah, Jesucristo . . . Jesucristo . . . Jesucristo . . ."

Then by an act of will, he sat up straight and began talking forcefully. "My brother, he die in a drive-by. Wow, like that! Hit him eight times with Uzi and my other cousin, he say one of my brother arms come off, just blown off like that and laying in the street like a baseball bat or something. Oh shit. Oh Mother of Jesus."

The Rabbit stopped.

"Good. No hagamos nada por un rato."

"Sit tight? For what? What we gonna sit tight for in the middle of this fucking desert?"

"Get me home. Ah, Jesucristo . . . . Tengo vergüenza . . ."

The Fierce Rabbit, gripping the wheel tightly as if caught in heavy traffic, looked down the hot dusty road a moment, then turned to Yo Boy, who had scrunched down in the seat, gripping his gut tightly. "What you shamed of, huh?"

"Nothing. No problem."

"Better not be no problem the way things going. Way things going I be thinking what you done got me on a new track."

"Estamos en un aprieto."

"Can't talk American no more? Sure we got trouble. I know that. I be thinking of it."

"Get me home," moaned Yo Boy, adding Spanish that bubbled out of his mouth like blood.

"You gonna get there by yourself, José," said The Rabbit, calling the boy by his old name. "Sorry about it, but I can't take you along no more. Spooking me this way."

"Get me home."

"Can't afford it, bro." Getting out and going around to the passenger side, The Rabbit peered in at Yo Boy, whose sweaty face was ashen, whose fingers, slick from blood and gut fat, seemed frozen like ice against the pulsing hole. Whistling low, The Rabbit opened the car door and gripped Yo Boy's arm.

"Nah," panted the boy. "Brother say, 'El tiempo todo lo cura.'"

"Maybe time heal you, I sure can't." The Rabbit tightened his hold on the boy's arm.

"Nah," Yo Boy declared, grimacing, "nothing I can't live with."

"If you live with it, you gonna do it by your own self. I can't afford it." Yanking on Yo Boy's arm, he dragged the wounded boy into the road. "Just business, nothing personal," he said, recalling words from a gangster movie. Then he mustered up his best Spanish to say, "Ya es la hora." Having announced "Time is up" and without glancing once at the stricken boy, The Fierce Rabbit walked around the car, climbed back in, gunned the motor, and took off so noisily that he couldn't hear one decibel of the sound issuing from Yo Boy's open and straining mouth, calling out in wordless rage at the world.

*   *   *

Five miles after dumping Yo Boy, The Rabbit pulled the car off the side of the road. He blew his breath out wearily. A half moon of sun was appearing over the distant hills; soon it would be broad daylight. Getting out of the car, he opened the trunk, just to make certain of the tapes that lay in there in the black tote bag. Then The Rabbit opened the bag, removed a couple of tapes, and took them back to the car, where he inserted one in the cassette deck. As The Rabbit leapt north again, he filled El Viejo's Limo with the baritone musings of a dead blind man. The Rabbit hooted at things that seemed particularly wack or racist in this white man's History. He almost lost control of the car on an uncrowded highway when the dead dude admitted that Jesus Mary Save Souls wasn't even a registered nurse. He almost regretted that the Skulls would never know what a fraud Touch was. Fraud and fronting — that was their history. He felt more justified than ever in his resolve to erase their lies from time. He would take the tapes out somewhere into the desert and unwind them, one by one, from their plastic spools and toss them into the air where they would wiggle like black snakes before falling into the dust. Jive Turkey's photos would go too. He'd tear up each one into pieces as small as the nail on his little finger and fling them across the desert. Then he'd drive to Tucson and search for a black queen with whom he would create a new Garden of Eden of his own descendants. It was a grand scheme. He could not have devised it alone. He had help from the Universal Center.

Feeling a heavy wave of fatigue roll over him, he slowed down, parked carefully on the side of the road, climbed into the back seat for a quick snooze, and fell instantly asleep.

The Fierce Rabbit was awakened by an insistent rapping against the window of the car. Sitting upright and looking through bright sunlight into a smiling plump white face, he realized instantly and with considerable annoyance that he was unarmed.

The face inched farther through the open window; blue eyes took in every object, including The Rabbit. A high, thin voice came cheerfully out of the plump face. "Hello there! How are you?"

The Rabbit leaned over, hoisting one long leg over the front seat and reaching for the ignition key, just as the door on the driver's side opened and a very large pistol was thrust forward, level to his chest.

"No," warned a voice belonging to a muscular man whose hand held the gun.

From the other side, the fat white face was still smiling. "You don't want to say goodbye, do you? When we've only just met?" Another smiling face, belonging to a mustachioed young man, appeared next to the fat one. Chicano, thought The Rabbit. The young man thrust his head into the car. Black eyes darted, searching.

"How about joining us out here?" suggested the fat man pleasantly.

The Rabbit got out. He confronted three of them: the fat man, the mustachioed Chicano, the muscular fellow with the pistol. Sensing someone behind him, The Rabbit glanced over his shoulder at a short man of middle age who wore a battered fedora and looked like a Mexican.

"We've come from San Diego on a little outing," said Fatty, a tight smile on his sweaty face. "Where are you from?"

When The Rabbit told him New York, the fat man and the Chicano laughed. The other two just stared at the dried blood on the front seat of the car.

"San Diego has fallen on hard times," Fatty said. "You can't find rock there anymore."

The Chicano said, "Maybe he don't know rock. Being he's from the East, maybe he got crack."

"Got any crack?"

"No," said The Rabbit, eyeing the pistol.

"You see," Fatty continued, "we heard a rumor there was business going on out in the desert these days."

"I don't know nothing about it," said The Rabbit sullenly.

The Chicano fingered his bushy mustache a moment and chuckled. "Listen to the speech he just make. Sound like somebody with the San Joaquin County Inter-Agency Task Force on Youth Gang Violence. Hard dude, huh? A masterwork. The kind wore beepers in old days."

"I don't get it," said The Rabbit.

"Sure you do, sweetheart," Fatty claimed. "You wore beepers. Had clients beep you when they had a need."

"Are you a big shot, Mister Feelgood?" asked the Chicano with a thin smile.

The Rabbit thought of Yo Boy's brother calling himself Mister Feelgood — the memory went down his legs, weakening them.

"Let us introduce ourselves." Fatty pointed first to the Chicano. "Jaime and I have been together — how long is it now?"

"Maybe a year," said Jaime.

"Jaime was a Crip with the 103rd Street West Coasters. See that? His color is blue."

Jaime smiled under a blue baseball cap.

The memory of Yo Boy's gangland tales had The Rabbit's legs so weak he could hardly stand.

"That," Fatty pointed to the scowling muscular man, "is Sailor. We met up with him in San Diego. Would you believe he owned all of Coronado? Only person on the island. Had both the NCO and Officers' Clubs to himself. The Mexican came up from Ensenada a few months ago. Doesn't speak much English, I'm afraid. And I came from a facility. You know what that is?"

"Correctional institution," said The Rabbit.

Jaime and Fatty laughed. "Correctional institution! So in the big city of New York that's what they call where they put you when you've been a bad boy? You're educated, Mister Feelgood," said Fatty. "Fuck, we don't care. We can live with that. We're on the sweet side, friend. But we ran out of everything, and I mean everything, even weed, a day ago. So give us a break."

"A break?"

"A look at what you've got."

"A look at what?"

"Are you being difficult? A look at what you're holding, friend."

"Hey," The Rabbit said with a smile, opening his hands out, "I don't do body drug. Seen plenty but don't do none myself."

"Funny. From the look of that front seat, I'd say someone ran into hard times, and it wasn't you, sweetie."

"Car be like that when I got it," mumbled The Rabbit, feeling a mouse of fear run up his spine when Fatty and Jaime guffawed at his explanation.

"Is it just possible you did someone bodily harm over the possession of a controlled substance?" asked Fatty.

When Sailor, who had been searching the car during this exchange of pleasantries, found the tote bag in the trunk, he let out a whoop.

Jaime gave him a high five. "We got it!"

Throwing the bag down on the road in their excitement, they fumbled desperately with the string knotted around it. The Rabbit's heart sank. He knew how people acted when they were in need; he remembered from his childhood the mounting panic of a deep user.

Sure enough, when they finally got the bag open, found the tapes, and proceeded to unwind them, one by one, they became angrier and angrier. "What the fuck! Nothing but tape!"

"Told you I wasn't holding," The Rabbit pointed out.

"Shut the fuck up!"

It was then The Rabbit felt something hovering behind his left ear — a soft animal with big liquid eyes and a quivering nose. Having seen it in recent dreams he recognized it instantly: the shape of his own cowardice.

"A very hyped sight," muttered the Chicano in a tone of bitter irony, as he flung the tapes into the air. "Where's what you have?"

What did The Rabbit have? He had the lives of the Skulls right there on little coiled pieces of ribbon. He had that and more to tell his strung-out captors, but looking hard at them he knew they would just laugh at him and *he would not have them laugh at him*. He would rather spoil the universal plan than be laughed at. So he answered, "I got nothing but what you got there."

"And pictures," the sailor said, flipping with thick fingers through Jive Turkey's Club House photos.

Jaime stared at them. "What a goony load of fuckers. They around here?"

Here was a chance to do harm to the Skulls for real. He could sic these mean motherfuckers on them. But there was still his pride; it surrounded his heart like armor. He wouldn't let these sonsabitches have the satisfaction of using his information against anybody. He wouldn't play snitch for pissers like these.

"I don't know where they gone," he said. "I split a long time ago."

They hadn't abused him, but he knew by now it was the fat man's style. He couldn't imagine how bad the dude was for real, but guessed that one of the worst things to happen since V 70 was the escape of people like him when guards got too sick to control them. The four had huddled together by the side of the road for a confab, with the fat man doing most of the talking. Then the Chicano had driven their pickup truck back to what Fatty called "our motel."

Now they were waiting for the Chicano to return. Pacing restlessly, the fat man stopped now and then to wipe his face with a dirty cloth. He wore a sombrero, which the Mexican should have been wearing instead of the battered fedora, which the fat man should have been wearing. The husky sailor paced too, waving the pistol around nervously. The Mexican squatted and squinted in the sun, a match between his lips.

They're in need, thought The Rabbit, and they be fucking mad. They think I be holding, but I never held in my life. I saw guys drop pieces of shit in my neighborhood, saw them sniffle and shuffle and cry like babies for the stuff and drive Caddies for selling it and look good on the street. But I never used, never sold, never had nothing to do with drugs. And here I being accused of holding out my holdings from these motherfuckers. Being that gun wasn't on me, I'd show them what a black man can do.

It was almost as if Fatty could read thoughts, because suddenly he stopped pacing and with a smile turned to The Rabbit. "You think a black buck like you can do white people like us harm, providing you don't have a gun trained on you? Is that it? Do you feel strong, Mister Feelgood? Do you feel very tough and real bad and just know if you had equality and freedom you could put us all away? Is that it? I think it is. I can see it in your jigaboo face."

The Rabbit took a step forward, enraged, but halted when the sailor pulled back the hammer of his pistol.

"Come on over here," said Fatty in a genial voice. "Come on." He walked off the road into the mesquite, the Mexican following. So did The Rabbit when the sailor waved his pistol.

"Now this sailor here," said Fatty when they reached a small clearing in the mesquite, "was in the navy, and you know what they did to him? He got into a righteous fight with a black nigger like you, sweetheart, and the court decided the nigger was right and he was wrong and they tossed him into the brig for an indecently long time. Ever since then this sailor has had a chip on his shoulder. Can you relate to that? Would you like a go at him? I'm sure he'd like a go at you."

The Rabbit turned to study the sailor, who had already given the pistol to the fat man and was now unbuttoning his colorful Hawaiian shirt. "If that be what turn him on," said The Rabbit, scared but chilled out — he was a lot bigger than the honky sailor.

"Good of you to care what turns him on," said the fat man.

Stripped to his waist, the sailor displayed a formidable torso. He was one of those people who look bigger and stronger without clothes. His chest was a series of moving plates, but even more startling was his gut. Rarely had The Rabbit seen such prominent muscle definition.

Even so, The Rabbit had at least five inches and thirty pounds on him. He had black pride, too, and in his veins a feeling that must be courage because it felt like a great sheet of ice pushing the fear aside.

Fatty eased himself down to the sandy earth, his belly overflowing, one chubby hand holding the pistol against a groin clearly defined by tight pants. "Commence, gentlemen, when ready," he called out.

The Rabbit figured on a street brawl from the brutal look of the sailor and braced himself for a shambling rush. Instead, the stocky half-naked man stood with feet about shoulder width apart. Then slowly he came forward, showing Nihon Nukite, the two-fingered spear, with his right hand.

Holy shit, The Rabbit said under his breath before the first kick, front-snap, reached him. A knife-foot side kick beginning in the Sokuto position pitched him backward and buckled him. But the sonofabitch didn't come in to take advantage. He backed away, terrifying The Rabbit, who realized this honky sailor was going to work carefully and thoroughly. The Rabbit appreciated what this meant, as he rolled his own fists in front of his face, trying not to think of the blood leaking into his left eye. The sailor then executed a series of fore-fist thrusts in a perfect come-and-go Hikite motion, ending with a back-fist strike to the kidney and a knife-hand strike to the collarbone that took The Rabbit down. He was dizzy, nauseous, and just wanted the sailor to knock him out. But the sailor stepped aside and waited calmly until The Rabbit, once again trying to follow his pride to the end of a dark road, got back on his feet and pulled his long lean body to its full height, towering over the sailor.

Closing, unopposed, the sailor had the leisure to perform with special grace a Mawashi Geri, a roundhouse kick applying the swinging motion of his whole body to the right foot. At the end of this arcing trajectory he snapped his instep flush into The Rabbit's mouth, relieving it of three front teeth and putting his lights out for a while, an act of mercy for which the sailor should not take credit.

63

THE BLIND MAN was not dead.

What amazed him was the need to hold on to something. Maybe this was how women in labor felt — the need to hold on with both hands, to keep whatever it was from running out between the fingers like water. He was pushing something like a baby out between his legs, only what it really was was his guts, and he knew it.

He heard his Spirit say *do something, do something*. It frightened him to hear her voice spiral up so thinly. He opened his mouth to tell her he loved her, only all that came out was something sticky. He tried again. "Hoss," he heard himself say. "Hoss."

"Here," he heard.

What he had to say was not about life or death or his love for Spirit, but about the Skulls.

He heard himself say, "It's you. And Queen Sexy." He remembered IRT reaching out from the bed, taking his hand, and whispering, "It be you. And Hoss."

Then he said, "Past."

"Past?"

"Let them have it again." He was saying more, he thought.

"I can't hear you."

"They . . . can . . . handle it."

"They can handle the past again?"

"Old names too." He thought he put his hand out and maybe he did, because the next thing he felt was fingers gripping his, fingers as familiar to him as the scar on his left thigh that he got from climbing a tree when he was ten years old. "Spirit." Her presence was close to his lips. ". . . love you." He felt the words going out.

"Don't talk, don't say anything, just hold on, keep trying," she told him rapidly. He could hardly recognize her voice — so high, thin.

Something below his heart was pulsing. Hot contractions driving the baby out. His own guts sliding through the wound, slithering into view like huge gray worms. Humiliation worse than pain. Everyone would see it, if he didn't hold his breath, hold the tide back, keep it from breaking through. He had talked to Hoss, hadn't he? Said the necessary? He felt tired. God, it hurt. An enormous object, like an iron box, was sliding to and fro below decks. He was in a storm and felt seasick. Parts of him had torn loose from their moorings and were sliding around. Ask Payback what to do. Everything going to slide away. He felt her hand in his and heard her strange voice saying *do something*. Can't I see her once? Now someone was trying to do something. He heard a voice, Jesus Mary. Sounded — scared. Ah that hurt! If he could just tell her, Jesus Christ, Jesus Mary, don't do what you're doing, it hurts!

A weakness was filling him like sludge. He felt something important leaving him. He heard a noise that didn't sound quite human and realized he was trying to say something. He heard Spirit saying *do something* but he hoped nobody would. It hurt too much. It was better just holding her hand. He tried to squeeze back when she squeezed, because the labor down there was unbearable. It wasn't even pain but a terrific weight shifting around below his heart. Jesus, it was his life moving around down there. He felt pure panic and tried to breathe the dry air of his new home. Heard Hoss saying best friend I ever had why did it have to happen why this in a strange a broken a scared voice too.

He gripped his Spirit's hand with all his might, feeling life retreat below his heart, then from his heart. He felt each minute of every day of his life rush into the fingers that gripped hers. He tried holding on, because it wasn't time. He held on by focusing his whole life on the hand in hers, and for a moment he felt immense joy and hope because in front of his eyes he thought he saw a shape emerging — his Spirit's face. He tried holding on and holding on and holding on so he could see it, finally see it, and tried so hard to hold on and kept trying and kept trying . . . and kept trying . . .

"Don't," Spirit sobbed, losing the pressure of his hand. "Don't!" Then his hand gripped tighter. She had a moment of hope before the strength of that grip ebbed away. She held something that yielded, did not press back. "Don't." She bent to kiss his fingers, though they held nothing of him anymore. "Don't," she told him. She turned to Hoss. "Tell him to keep trying. He'll listen to you."

Hoss looked at Jesus Mary, then back to Spirit. "He did try."

"He's got to keep trying," Spirit insisted, taking his hand in both of hers, putting it to her cheek.

"He did try," Hoss said.

"Tell him to keep trying."

"He did try."

The Fierce Rabbit awoke feeling confused, not sure where he was, feeling hot needles of pain under his buttocks, his bloody mouth throbbing, his eyes burning from glare. He tried to move but found that he couldn't — his hands and feet were pegged down. Turning his head he saw his left hand lashed to the metal pole of a beach umbrella; the gaily striped umbrella was still attached, but its ribs drooped like a dry flower. Fuckers, he thought. They had staked him out under the desert sun. Pulling his chin in, so he could look down along the length of his body, he saw that they had stripped him. He saw a few ants crawling along his thighs and up his stomach.

"Hey there, homeboy!" The cheerful voice belonged to Jaime, the Chicano, who bent over The Rabbit and grinned. "Back with us? We didn't know was you gone for good you been out so long. Sailor's a mean fucker, right? Look at you. Look at him," Jaime said to the fat man whose smiling face came alongside his own, so that both were gazing down at The Rabbit. "It's starting. Look." Jaime said to The Rabbit, "Like you sure fucked up, Mister Feelgood. You come out here without thinking right."

"Yes, boy, you made a mistake and your mistake has made us unhappy," added the fat man, peering down curiously at The Rabbit. "We came to the desert in good faith because we heard beautiful things are happening out here, far away from urban memories, in a world where getting high lets you forget those bugs ever existed or anything else except yourself. Mind-boggling, that's what we hear. But lo and behold, we find ourselves on the proverbial wild goose chase. There's a scenario we're not quite sure of, but it goes something like this. You, friend, pitch drugs and you come out here on a meet with a delivery boy who's supposed to bring payment — probably women because what else besides boys and girls are for sale these days, right? And this guy who's supposed to be reliable and respected in the neighborhood has you figured for a sucker and I don't know — there was a hassle and you got him before he got you. So you have the goods but no pussy. The thing is you stash your goods somewhere in this great big cooking house of a desert for the next time. What I'm saying is, look at it this way, you deal with us and we get you women boys girls whatever you want that's left out there and get them fast because we know where some are. Like the song says, we just wanna have fun. You got connections in San Diego, L.A.? You know what's common knowledge on the survivor circuit? A few depressed scientists are in the business of oblivion. They've got some very pretty experience to offer and they do business with people like you. To show good faith I am willing to entertain the idea you aren't holding. Fine. I can handle that. But the labs where the brains are that do the good thing — I won't accept the proposition you don't know their location. I'm asking just this once just one more time."

The Rabbit said nothing.

"Hey, look at that," Jaime said in a low voice of awe. "It's starting but he don't know it yet. What it mean."

"Had you kept something close that was tasty," continued the fat man as if lecturing The Rabbit, "we'd feel differently about you. Life is funny. You don't know what you didn't do until somebody tells you. At other times what you don't know won't hurt you."

What The Fierce Rabbit didn't know, however, was going to hurt him a lot. All The Rabbit knew was the taste of blood from losing three front teeth and a few nasty little ticks of pain, followed by a burning sensation, around his buttocks.

He didn't know, for example, what *Pogonomyrmex barbatus* was. That it was a species of the genus *Pogonomyrmex* from the tribe of Myrmicii in the subfamily of Myrmicinae that belonged to the family of Formicidae. Nor did he know that harvester ants built nests like craters. Usually the nest was a conical shape, its main opening on a slanting east or south wall; it led down into a maze of corridors traveled by gatherers who stored oats pilfered from stables and grass seedlings and mesquite pods in chambers fifteen feet underground.

What The Rabbit didn't know either was the loving care expended by *Pogonomyrmex barbatus* on their nests. Workers excavated the formicaries by carrying out each grain of sand individually and placing it on the edge of the crater for lazy lizards, debris hanging cavalierly from their mouths, to marvel at, be shamed by.

Nor did he know anything about stridulatory organs. In the case of *Pogonomyrmex barbatus* a file of ridges located on the abdomen was scraped by a hard chitinous projection. This rapid scraping caused a high-pitched sound the vibrations of which other ants received on their legs and antennae. It stirred up the troops.

What The Rabbit didn't know but would soon learn for real was that his captors had staked him out over an anthill where the initial alarm was just making its way through the convoluted tunnels. Soon a hastily conscripted army of *Pogonomyrmex barbatus* was emerging from the slanted entrance of the crater. Irate soldiers, prepared to give their lives in defense of home, were rushing straight at the black balls and buttocks of The Rabbit.

He found out soon enough that these ants were bad dudes whose stinging grew fiercer as their attacking numbers grew larger. The pain increased until he felt his crotch was on fire. His spasmodic shaking rattled the beach umbrella. He groaned but never screamed — he wasn't going to let that fat honky and the other motherfuckers get off on it. He'd die first. But the ants kept coming with mounting fury. Looking down at his naked body he saw them streaming up toward him — big sonsabitches with black heads and middles tapering off to a brownish red color, telling the world where the poison was. They came along like a gang out showboating on its turf, wearing colors, taking down anyone they felt like.

He saw them coming with their mandibles clacking, chomping down on his bare flesh. Once they were locked in, the ends of their abdomens doubled up to inject poison through a grooved and pointed gorgeret on the terminal section of the gaster. Illustrating the link between sex and violence, this modified ovipositor was thrust into the flesh, and formic acid from a gland duct flowed through the sting sheath into the wound. The Rabbit did not understand this mechanism, but he was experiencing its power. Tears filled his eyes and he hoped the sailor would punch his lights out again so he couldn't feel anything. Clenching his teeth, balling his thong-tied fists, The Fierce Rabbit took quick shallow breaths and watched the ants march forward. They were close enough for him to see a long curved beard under each large head. And those black jaws clacking. They were going to reach his eyes.

All his life The Rabbit had harbored a secret fear of something happening to his eyes. He used to think, It don't matter what they do to me long as they let my eyes alone. When his mamma used to tell him about divine punishment, he imagined only one worth fearing — God's flunkies holding him down, directing a red-hot poker at his eye. She used to mumble under her breath, "Through my fault, through my fault, through my most grievous fault," and he'd think with satisfaction it didn't have nothing to do with him.

Now he saw them coming, and he was muttering in his head, "Through my fault, through my fault, through my most grievous fucking fault." One had stopped to pinch his left nipple with its jaws, had doubled up, and was ramming the stinger in. But that was nothing compared to the others who kept coming until they reached his chin, his mouth, were running across his face, scooting for a moment into his nostrils and out and into his ear, through his hair, at the edge of his eye. Fear was greater than the stings that had turned his body into a jumping jack, whipping around in its restraining thongs, shaking the umbrella.

Sailor looked down at the writhing black man and shook his head. "Who wants to look at a thing like that? Let's go."

"Aren't you curious? I mean, the sonofabitch owes us something for coming out here empty-handed," declared Fatty. "I can't believe anyone would be here without locating shit, buying selling doing business in the dry air. I resent someone using these roads who can't accommodate us with a taste. Especially when we're in need. Look at that," he said. "Can you *believe* the way they double over and give it to him? Sort of like a guy socking it to a broad.

Know what I mean, figuratively speaking? Doesn't it have some kind of effect on you, Sailor? Or has life at sea left you jaded. You'd think his heart would give out. Have you ever seen anything like it in your *life?*" asked Fatty, who was lighting a large cigar.

"Come on, Sailor, *look*. See his jigaboo skin getting red? Reminds me of something. We had barbecues in the back yard where I come from. Reminds me of starting a charcoal fire. Just after the lighter fluid burns off and the briquettes start to glow. Before they get an ashy color? Know what I mean? Tiny briquettes? Glowing?" He puffed hard on the stogie.

Then he continued. "The Mexican says they aren't fire ants, they're harvester ants and they're much worse, which I concede. He says in Old Mexico this sort of staking out was common. Called it God's worst punishment. Can you beat that?"

Finally Sailor spoke. "I'm going back to the truck. I don't need this."

"Bye-bye," called the fat man as Sailor stepped briskly through the mesquite. Hovering above the groaning, whimpering body, Fatty inspected his own shoes first to see if the ants were coming at him, then held the burning cigar over The Rabbit's forehead. Fatty held his cigar over the scurrying red mass and for a delicious little kick of gratuitous sadism he tapped the ash off. It fell on Rabbit's right cheek, and the agitation called a flurry of ants to the spot, which they circled and stung, while The Rabbit's mouth widened and formed a huge oval of uncommunicable anguish into which ants scurried and from which they scurried out again. What continued to speak for The Fierce Rabbit, however, was a constant terrible whine that flowed from his throat into the outlying brush and sand like something alive, something wriggling, black, furious.

The fat man turned to Jaime. "What do you think? Should we go now?"

The Chicano chewed his lower lip, glancing at the pulsing mass of insects and humanity. "Yeah, why not. Nothing here." He added thoughtfully, "I wonder was he holding. Like the dude wouldn't say where the stash was."

"What could be in it for him to hold out to such a conclusion? No, he was just a loser in life's little game. Let's find some shit before we go mad." Motioning to the Mexican, the fat man set out across the desert, companions on his heels.

Abruptly the Mexican turned back to the spread-eagled Rabbit. Bending over, his square leathery face only inches from the squirming man, he said quietly, "Que lo pase bien." Then he went away.

The words boomed in The Rabbit's head. Enjoy? *Enjoy?* He wandered through his mind in a wild attempt to find joy. After this weird moment of disorientation, he fully appreciated that his only joy would be to die. This is what the Mexican must have wanted him to know.

Aware, despite the pain, that he was alone, The Fierce Rabbit let himself scream. His release from the constraint of pride was as momently wonderful as an orgasm. He howled, opened his mouth and let the ants scuttle in and roam around his gums, but it didn't matter, because he had the luxury of screaming, of letting every cell of his body holler at the world. He yelled and bellowed until it felt like the veins in his head were strained to the breaking point.

His whole body was on fire, the pain streaming from one synapse to another. Slivers of torment pricked each cell, goading him to heights of sensation where he could do nothing, think nothing, but feel an agony beyond his wildest fear. Yet even that was not enough. The nerve endings in his stung eyelids had gone numb, so that they were locked open, as useless now as his hands. The worst of punishments was only seconds away. Against his will and in complete terror he stared from the slit between his paralyzed lids. He saw an ant stride across his left eyeball. He could not shut out the sight of it halting on the curved wet surface. He could see, hideously magnified, the hard chitinous spurs on the end of its middle legs. The strigil-spurs were fringed with bristles. In a rare moment of surcease from frenetic attack, the ant drew one of its antennae through its strigils with leisurely satisfaction. The cleaning motion was like a samurai wiping blood from his sword.

For The Fierce Rabbit it was an instant of grotesque intimacy with one of his killers. In a final moment of lucidity he wondered if this particular ant had been sent from the Universal Center to give him a message. But he could not imagine what the message might be before the final horror sent him over the edge. Joined by companions who had marched up the slope of the tear duct and across the cornea, the ant gave him its message — tore suddenly with its jaws into the meaty pulp of his left eye. A dozen ants snickered their mandibles deeper into it until they reached the jellylike vitreous humor within. They kept boring in as if they had found fresh soil in which to dig chambers and store their seeds. At last the mercy of inconceivable pain released The Fierce Rabbit from the race of humankind altogether, allowing his body to accept the remaining attacks with nothing more than a few cursory jerks and shivers. The final pieces of the celestial puzzle had fallen into place.

64

AFTER THE MAIN MAN'S cremation at the stone foot of IRT's Vision, Hoss, the new leader, cajoled harangued threatened the dispirited band into packing up and moving on.

On a mesa between the Juachuca and Dragoon Mountains, about thirty miles from the Mexican border, stood Tombstone, home of silver mines and Doc Holliday, site of the gunfight at the OK Corral. A town called too tough to die, it had been as quiet as its namesake until the caravan of Skulls appeared on the horizon.

They sat in front of the Wells Fargo Museum, the Crystal Palace, the Bird Cage Theatre, the Camillas Fly Studio where two years ago tourists had strolled in mild pursuit of the Old Wild West. For three days the glum and bewildered Skulls wandered through this town of memories. No hunters went out. There was no lovemaking. Spirit In The Dark fell into a stony silence. For some of the Skulls, who had never completely trusted the Dragon spy, her grief proved her sincerity. She sat all day with hands folded in her growing lap.

But in the silent town of Tombstone other Skulls began to stir. As OOTHI said, "Life goes on forever like the gnawing of a mouse."

Swear To God emerged from her dark country of silence into

a bright world of anger. Without pausing for a breath of air or a swallow of water, she described the horror of three days in a Pecos motel with the sun beating on the roof of a fanless room and the smell of stale whiskey and the look of men whose arms were copper-colored but whose buttocks were the pasty white of fish belly. She had never done anything to warrant such punishment and degradation. It wasn't fair, just, reasonable, or even logical — and she walked away from her wild soliloquy a solemn young woman determined to root out injustice wherever she found it, even if it was in her own bitter heart.

Listening to her outpouring opened the floodgates for other Skulls, especially now that Hoss had abruptly lifted the ban on speaking of the past so they could compare Mister Touch to other great leaders. Stifle, who had intermittently mumbled about stationery and yoga, now collared passersby, snatched at sleeves, pleading for a few moments of time to describe his beautiful wife, whose bones were falling apart three thousand miles away. He claimed that he and his wife had not only slept and eaten together, but had also played violin and piano duets, backpacked through most of Europe together, studied French and cybernetics and gardening together, contemplated the same Zen koan, shopped for clothes together, jointly run a stationery business, and always sat side by side at dinner parties, but they did not die together. She went alone, although he tried desperately to pull her back across the dividing line. She slipped free, went by herself, leaving him so devastated that language itself had only fitful meaning for him. But when he heard Swear To God, he understood that his wonderful wife was dead for real and that he was still alive. With a sigh he stopped talking. Everyone expected him to lapse back into silence. But the next day Stifle sat in the Full Lotus and later took curious Skulls into the desert where he taught them breathing and stretching exercises and demonstrated asanas which many of them assiduously practiced. He no longer sought the company of Doctor Leo, who claimed to be well rid of such a fellow. "A base person," the doctor declared, "who is slowly going mad."

Yet another event took place in the field of communication. "Zonked zoologists," said Adidas suddenly in the middle of Tombstone, "zestfully zap zany zealots."

"Well, listen to that. The sucker did Z."

"Who would of thought it."

"Adidas, ain't you stretching it with Z? You be back with us now, you be welcome, homes. Why not give up on that old alphabet? Doing it now be just a habit. You don't need nothing to prove you ain't OOTLO. You just ain't."

Pondering a moment, the thickset butcher rolled his tongue around in his ample mouth and said, "Okay." With a powerful forearm that had risen and fallen over many a leg of lamb, he gestured as if to throw something, as if the twenty-six letters of the alphabet were nothing more than gouts of unwanted fat he had just trimmed from his mind.

Other Skulls were going through changes. Head hung low, Pretty Puss confessed that her monthly had changed into nothing at all. As Barber, she had apparently done more for someone than cut his hair. She never identified the seducer. Snake got the blame although it seemed odd to think that a girl with awesome friends at the Dalton School and a pet poodle named Socrates would let herself go with that snake-hipped Latin scumbag who had never spoken one word of truth to a woman in his life (so said at least half a dozen women carrying his children).

All his life Hoss had been cool. Once he realized in childhood that his black skin placed him out of the mainstream, he studied the advantages and disadvantages of his situation. He had learned early that a lot of white people felt guilty for setting him apart. These cats, usually well educated, would do plenty to assuage their guilt. If he played it cool, Hoss figured he just might be the beneficiary of their acts of penance. Every time they felt the need of a Hail Mary, he was there with his hand out, grinning slyly, learning how to mine their white guilt like gold. He won scholarships to a private school, an Ivy League college. He learned that a Billy Dee Williams mustache, dark shades, and a gray business suit turned on white foxes until they practically tripped over their feet in the rush to his sack. He didn't mind their stupidity. He liked the attention while regarding them ultimately with benign indifference, because after all they were out of *his* mainstream, the mainstream of survival. He hobnobbed with their white brothers like an exotic prince from a distant land. He went home during school vacations and sat in a Harlem kitchen at a table with a linoleum tablecloth and pontificated about his cool. This cynicism infuriated his father, a schoolteacher, who had striven mightily in the civil rights war for three decades and with only loan payments to show for it. His middle-class, puritanical father couldn't abide smart-alecky black boys any more than white ones. He had wanted his son to return after college and give something back to the community, but Hoss detached himself — and with his mother's approval. She remembered going to school in Jamaica with white children whom she considered her equals only if they were as smart as she was. She wanted her boy to go places.

And he did. It meant little that he was house nigger in a prestigious advertising firm. The job got him a superpad on the East Side, more black and white foxes than he could handle, a month's vacation on the Cape with the beautiful people, and a Ferrari.

In a world operating on the principle of me myself and I, he didn't waste time on hatred or hope, but skirted conflicts and closed his ears to bad vibes. Until V 70 Struck, he had never questioned life beyond assuming that it dealt exclusively with getting yours.

Then in the strange world of the Skulls he found to his amazement that he did have abilities. And now, today, he was Number One for real, facing the task of leading people whom he had come to love and respect. That led to some very uncool reflections. Why should they care what they did? Why should they keep on keeping on? Had the main man known for sure or had he just faked it? Why couldn't they just settle in somewhere like here and live out their lives eating sleeping drinking fucking, and let it go at that? The whole world had let them down and they owed nothing to no one. Was that copping out? Were they really like ants, trundling in and out of a hole, enduring and building and working because that was their function on this planet? Whatever the truth, he couldn't freak out over philosophy simply because he'd discovered that it applied to his own life. He was supposed to get out there and lead those Looney Tunes.

Removing his shades, Hoss tossed them away. He had always worn them to hide the sly calculation he detected in his eyes. He kept the battered cowboy hat, though. It was a shabby crown, ridiculous enough to remind him of the truth: that he was plain scared of the job ahead; that he didn't know what to do; that he needed help. "Damn you, bro," he told Mister Touch just behind his shoulder, "you're worse than my old man, telling me do this, do that." Having spoken to Mister Touch for the first time since the blind man died, Hoss was startled, but no more than Mister Touch had been after speaking for the first time to dead IRT.

On the fourth day after the funeral, the Skulls returned to the main highway and camped that night in a village about forty miles from Tucson. Next morning the new leader failed to give the order to cast off. He remained alone, brooding in a shack all day. Skulls strolled among clumps of fifty-foot saguaro cacti and silently contemplated a broad hot country that somehow had become their own.

Next morning Hoss again failed to give the order. People began gathering outside his adobe hut. Squatting in the dust, they feared that something was wrong with their new leader. Finally his tall figure appeared in the doorway. Without sunglasses he squinted in the glare. The Stetson was pushed back, making him look more like Sidney Poitier than Harry Belafonte. "Find Queen Sexy" was all he said.

While he waited for her, the new prez lit an oil lamp and sat at the rickety table. Someone rapped on the door.

Spirit In The Dark stood in the entrance, holding a yellow plastic shopping bag, a little the worse for wear. TOWER RECORDS was printed on it in red letters. She came in and sat at the table, studying Hoss awhile. Finally she plunked the shopping bag down between them, explaining that here were the history tapes made by her husband.

"I thought they were gone," Hoss said in surprise. "The briefcase was missing."

"I made duplicates."

"I'm glad he thought of that."

"He didn't. He never knew I knew there were any tapes. He thought I learned about them when everyone else did, on Christmas, during the celebration."

"So you did it behind his back."

"I did it behind his back. Loving someone doesn't make you less slippery if you're slippery to begin with. It went this way. At times when we stopped he asked me to leave him alone somewhere — he needed to think things through. Once I came back for him earlier than usual, and as I got closer I heard him talking into a recorder and realized he was taping everything the Skulls did. I also realized he wanted to keep the tapes secret, at least for the time being. I knew his blindness put the tapes in jeopardy — he seemed blind to the fact. They could easily be lost or misplaced or even stolen, though that seemed unlikely. Anyway, I copied each one, replacing it with a blank during the recording, until I had duplicates of them all. It was hard work. I felt like a spy for real."

"Thank God you tricked him," said Hoss, removing a tape from the bag and staring at it. "We'll call them The Touch Tapes. Have you played any?"

"I couldn't bear to."

"We won't play them until" — he scratched his chin — "the right time comes along."

Spirit got up to leave.

"You're looking . . . well . . . good," Hoss said emphatically. "You're looking good."

"I'm fine."

Hoss's father had died shortly before V 70 Struck, and his mother had gone around saying "I'm fine," eyes red, lips trembling, "I'm fine. Don't worry yourself. I'm just fine." Clearing his throat, Hoss said, "Have you got names for the baby?"

"If it's a boy, he'll be Mark."

"If it's a girl?"

"Dorothy — after my mother, who was named Dorothy after Dorothy in *The Wizard of Oz*. Judy Garland was my grandmother's favorite actress. I think this movie was one of the few things that ever gave her pleasure." Spirit turned to leave, then turned back. "Hoss," she said. "Why?"

" 'Show me a hero and I will write you a tragedy.' F. Scott Fitzgerald. He was a white boy whose fiction I could never dig. Maybe because I always felt if I wrote I'd do the same thing — reveal a snobbish longing for upper-class life — from a black boy's point of view, of course."

"Don't just talk to be talking. *Why?*"

"I talk just to be talking because there's nothing to say. I don't know why it happened. He learned not to question fate. He wouldn't have said it's unfair, it's meaningless, it's stupid. He would have said it just happened."

Nodding in reluctant agreement, Spirit started to leave, again turned back. "One more thing. I never liked you. You reminded me of a guy named Daryll — a good-looking middle-class black guy, well educated, slick . . ."

"Thank you for good-looking and well educated. Middle-class I consider neutral. Slick — that's not so nice."

"I saw you as Daryll for a long time. Selfish, slick — but Mark never did. He loved you the way he loved IRT. So after giving up the idea of you being Daryll, I simply got jealous of you because of Mark. Then I tried to work through that foolishness. And I have. What I'm saying is you can lead the Skulls." Without waiting for a reply, wanting none, Spirit turned and left.

He would have wanted me to tell Hoss that, she thought. He would have kissed me for it, squeezed my hand. As she walked down the street, Spirit In The Dark was thinking words she often said these days in the silent hours: " 'Go from me. Yet I feel that I shall stand henceforward in thy shadow.' "

65

A TERRIBLE EVENT having become a terrible memory, the destinies of Queen Sexy and Soda had joined so tightly that neither woman could go anywhere without the other. One night they went off together to place their bedrolls side by side and exorcise the horror by talking it away beneath an audience of stars; in the morning they awoke in each other's arms. The fruity light of an Arizona dawn played across their black and white breasts, as lips touched with a tenderness that words can never match. They were left stunned by the wonder of sharing more than a horrible memory. Their love unhooked them: each could now go somewhere without the other, knowing that the other was already there.

Queen Sexy found Hoss sitting on a dilapidated bunk, his head, hidden by the Stetson, bent over clasped hands. She sat down and waited in silence. Time passed in the hot little room, with a single ray of sunlight trundling across the earthen floor, moving with insectile precision from the far wall across the room, edging closer to his dusty boots. She watched the flame in the oil lamp for so long that it seemed to hypnotize her.

Finally, he spoke. Hoss told her that he *could not move.* They were only thirty miles from Tucson, but he couldn't get them there, he couldn't move an inch from this village. What would they do now? Why go to Tucson? Why go anywhere? Why not hunker down for good in this miserable little village? Wasn't one breathing space as good as another? When you had all the villages, towns, cities, and metropolises of America to choose from? He was entangled in questions like a fly in a web.

"I wonder why you're telling me this," Queen Sexy said.

"You were his choice."

"What?"

"He spoke your name before dying. You were his choice for second-in-command."

"Certainly not yours."

"It was his to make."

"You don't even like me."

"I trust his judgment."

"But you're not convinced. And I know why."

"It's nothing personal. It's just that my sister —"

"Spare me details. Your sister's dead. Leave her and her sexual preferences alone." Queen Sexy rapped the table sharply. "Well?" she said challengingly. "Shall we get on with it?"

"Tell me what you think I should do."

"Go to Tucson."

"Why?"

"Why not? You can't look for the absolute act. You can't be too serious about making decisions. People call you cool but you're acting uncool right now and that's a mistake."

Hoss smiled. "All right, then. Tell me about it."

"You want me to tell you about it?"

"I'm asking."

"You're asking advice from a lesbian?"

"From my deputy."

"All right, then. Listen up. If you start thinking the future of this planet depends on our survival, you'll get so bogged down in worry you'll infect us all and then we might as well crawl around in circles of self-pity like sick dogs and curl up and die. What the hell. Nobody is watching. Nobody's out there looking down from outer space rooting for us. Maybe we live in the best neighborhood in the universe, like Toe said, but she never said we get to meet the land-lord. We're free and clear. We can go to Tucson and if that doesn't work, there's always Phoenix or somewhere else. We're like water. We can flow. Can you imagine what a luxury that would have been in the old world — just to pack up and take off? We don't have rent, bills, taxes to pay. We don't have to compete for jobs or hous-ing or status. We're not weighted down with things. We're as light as air. We don't need to carry thousands of years of law on our backs, if we decide not to. I say that as a former lawyer. We owe nothing to a past that brought us here, right here, to this moment in a desert. We needn't pay homage to gods we never created. We're not only free, we're relatively clean. We're pretty harmless as ecology goes. We do little to increase the greenhouse effect. We're defacing nothing, rearranging nothing, we're not adding things or taking them away. Animals we don't eat we leave alone. We let grassland enrich itself without poisoning it with chemicals. You know what I mean — harmless, forgettable, that's what we are. And as a consequence we can start anew. That's what he was get-ting at, I think, by having us carve an insect on a cliff. And I believe it. We can fool around in the playpen of planet Earth without fear. And come up with something special of our own. Or fail. Or simply go back to the way things were. My God, man, think of the options we have!"

Hoss was staring at his boots. Looking up, unclasping his hands, he said, "Okay." Slowly he got to his feet. "Now I know why he chose you."

"Yeah?"

"Yeah. You're my choice too."

It seemed as though the moment Hoss got off that bunk and stood on his own two feet the entire Skull tribe shuddered into motion too. All afternoon they came to the shack with ideas schemes ru-mors confessions revelations.

Sister Fate, her desire for travel titillated but not satisfied by the trip, wanted to keep going. She wanted to set out in a Lincoln Continental with three other Skulls who shall be nameless — two young women and a middle-aged man. They had Oregon in mind, because Sister Fate had never seen it. Traveling with her would be two potential breeders and an aging stud who just might carry their love of travel into love of one another and populate the future of Oregon.

Then the strapping six-foot-four seventeen-year-old survivor of the Battle of Vicksburg came in with a momentous declaration. In the lamplight No Name's sun-bronzed face, framed by a beaded headband, radiated the quiet confidence of a young Indian chief. On the rickety table he traced with a large forefinger a little map for Hoss to study. Not far from Tucson, out in the desert, were the Ventana Caves, uninhabited for thousands of years. He and a few others — actually ten altogether — wanted to live there.

Hoss was too shocked to say anything. There might be only a dozen survivors roaming a thousand-square-mile area, yet No Name and his followers wanted to hide from them in one of the most inaccessible parts of America. They wanted to walk back through history until there was no history. They wanted to stride through open country that might already have been abandoned when the pharaohs were building temples at Karnak and Memphis.

Hoss wanted to know who would go with him.

Sweet Walk, of course. Stifle. He wanted to practice yoga in the peaceful desert emptiness. The two hunters, King Super Kool and Chico, would follow Stifle because he had become their guru. Stay High also wanted to join the Ventana band — after all, his popular lectures on these caves had fired their imaginations. He harbored a dream of leaving his children an important archeological legacy. Love had given Stay High a new perspective on life, allowing him to appreciate the humor of unburying the dead for the edification of archeologists, all of whom, aside from himself, were dead. If sometimes he proved foolish, it no longer mattered. He was happy and knew it and would stay high as long as Do You Thing shared his bedroll, which she claimed was the thing she wanted to do more than anything in the world.

There was a final member of the group — The Boy Who Doesn't Speak Our Language, now Star Three, wanted to accompany his former teacher to improve his language skills. Someday he wanted to write a history for real and for this purpose needed to warm his genius at the fire of Stay High's intellectual passion.

Hoss walked to the door and again squinted into the afternoon glare. What was it Confucius say? "By nature, men are nearly alike; by practice they grow wide apart."

Then little Sky Hook appeared at the door with his own request. He wanted to get into a Chevy, because that was the Heartbeat of America, and drive all the way to L.A., where the Lakers used to reign as basketball champions of the NBA.

Light was fading, so Hoss went to the door and announced to the gathering, "Tomorrow we go to Tucson. Tonight we vote. Pass the word."

Someone called out, "Vote? You said *vote?* Or what?"

Back inside, Hoss sat in the twilight that was lowering in the doorway like the color of the ocean as you go down into it.

Would they do things differently or would they fail? Hoss wondered. Maybe the insidious process of growing up and older might overtake them and they'd want things that demanded all of their time. If Harold could, as he claimed, patch into motel wiring, they'd have a glowing little village with toasters popping and ovens roasting. Above the office there might be a neon sign flashing welcome to any visiting firemen who happened by the Skull Motel.

And plumbing. Harold could do that too. Toilets gurgling all over the place. Shy Guy could handle the big wrenches for tightening neckline nuts, because thus far the Atlas of the Skulls had been underemployed. Harold could train Blue Magic, who would welcome the chance to learn technology for real.

Then they had their greatest treasure, Guts. His scientific expertise was now fully at the Skulls' service. Giving up theoretical for applied physics, he might accomplish things unheard of.

Free to play with technology and unmindful of consequences, the Skulls might lose all restraint, like weekend drug users. They might want everything at once.

Hoss sought out Queen Sexy. She pursed her lips, but told him to do what he wanted.

After sitting a long time in darkness just like his former boss, Hoss sought out Sister Fate. "I don't want you to go. I don't want anyone to go. IRT held us together in New York. Mister Touch got most of us here. My job, as I see it, is to build. But I can't do that if Skulls leave and take their skills with them. I need you with us. Joining the Skulls is like signing an IOU. So I'm calling it in in the names of IRT and Mister Touch."

"Somehow I can't refuse."

"What do you like besides traveling?"

Sister Fate thought a moment. "Well, in the old days I tried to grow flowers. I wasn't too bad. I could . . . grow tulips."

"And maybe some potatoes, onions, carrots?"

"I can't refuse."

He called in the ten members of the Ventana Caves expedition and asked them to stay. They couldn't refuse either. Stay High volunteered to start a school and even suggested that Doctor Leo might teach chemistry.

Sky Hook also capitulated without a fight. Hoss wondered if his interest in Chevys could extend to all vehicles, so that he and Stitch might eventually open a gas station.

Hoss realized he was going to keep everyone, at least for a while. But opposition was out there. At the moment Fire was challenging the idea of putting a Mad Ave adman in charge of human lives. But the Skulls had lived through too much together to turn their backs on Hoss. He had called in the markers owed to his predecessors. By putting aside their individual plans for a while, the Skulls were giving him his chance. What, though, was he going to do with it?

All that afternoon Skulls came and went, talking of committees: Steering, Ways and Means, Entertainment, Education — someone even mentioned Foreign Relations. They contemplated an ad hoc committee to continue studying "The Mystery of the Universe," because recent exegeses had resulted in heated discussions which, by fanning factious flames, Fire's followers (among them addictive Adidas, at alphabetizing again) figured to create catastrophic conflagrations corresponding to the time that that tornado tore to tatters The Terrible Ten's temper tantrums, terminating them. Hoss decided to make sure that everyone would end up on at least one committee. When he finally walked down the main street of town, Skulls looked at him in wonder and admiration.

That evening after a stew dinner, they were spitting buckshot into campfire flames fed by slow-burning ironwood.

"Hope we see Indians."

"What you figuring on, sucker — dudes on horseback, shooting bows and arrows?"

"Why not? Nothing wrong in it."

"Except Indians ain't like in the movies."

"I know that."

"They got oil wells and drive Caddies."

"You mean *did*. Figure since I be here, I get me a wild pony and ride the fucking range, bro. See if I don't."

Getting to his feet, Hoss called the assembly to order. Rattler could be heard crying in the distance. Soon the Skull tot would have playmates. The kids would probably have nightmares about cruel rabbits and killer bees as large as the ant of IRT's Vision.

The Skulls were going to vote on an issue of primary importance: their names — whether to return to their old ones or keep what they'd come this far with.

"Shit, man," Hoss heard from the crowd, "can you beat that? We gonna *vote*."

I am opening a can of worms, thought Hoss. It's a can that IRT would have left unopened. Mister Touch would have opened it but cautiously, just a crack, to see if voting would have the same effect as opening Pandora's box. But Hoss figured he'd better emulate not imitate his predecessors and if either or both of them shouted in his ear to do this or do that, he should listen but then make his own decision. Isn't that what a leader for real was supposed to do?

So he was going to pry the lid off this can of worms. He was going to let these Looney Tunes vote on their names and inevitably they'd soon want to hold elections so they could fuck themselves over and call it democracy. And what would Hoss do then? He'd vote too.

"Is a show of hands okay or do you need secret ballots?" he asked the assembly.

There was a long silence as everyone absorbed the reality of being in the midst of parliamentary procedures. Finally a few people shouted, "Show of hands!"

Others yelled, "Yeah, it's quicker! Let's get going!"

"All right then," said Hoss, raising both arms to silence them. "Those in favor of using the old names, raise your right hand!"

When a vast majority of hands went up and cheering began, Hoss muttered silently to Mister Touch, who was at his shoulder,

"You called it, bro. They want their old names. But is it a step back-ward or forward?" When the former main man vanished without answering, Hoss knew he was on his own.

Among the assembled Skulls, elated by voting, there was much laughter and jiving, as if they had just climbed Sister Fate's Mount Tai Shan or flushed a toilet for real.

A Skull who shall be nameless boasted, "We probably the bad-dest dudes on this fucking planet."

"Better be. That way we got a chance, maybe one in ten, of making it."

Standing alone beyond the firelight, letting the darkness of human destiny flow around him like the dark waters that had haunted their journey, Hoss stared at the orange glow of burning ironwood and imagined the look of such a campfire thousands of years ago. People hunkered around it, muttering and perhaps laughing, dimly aware of their chances for survival. The idea stunned Hoss as he strained to hear a distant clang of ancient ham-mers. But that was a waste of time. He had to get these Looney Tunes going. Both Mister Touch and IRT were at his shoulder again, badgering him. "Get into it, man," they urged. "Go for it. Do it!" He listened, then made his own decision.

Hoss took a step toward the roaring fire and announced in a loud firm voice, "I am Steven Parcells."

He looked at Queen Sexy, who got to her feet and said, "I am Jean Simms."

After she sat down, Soda got up. "I am Debbie Banks."

Coco got up and said, "I am Beverly Marshall."

Pretty Puss got up and said, "I am Janet Carthon."

Harold said, "I am Harold Dorsey."

Snake said, "I am Ramon Allegre."

E.Z. said, "I am Leona Collins.

Shy Guy said, "I am Larry Taylor."

Golden Girl said, "I am Alice Reasons."

T.T. said, "I am Sylvia Oates."

Doctor Leo said, "I am Daniel Hampton."

Adidas said, "I am Mario Bavaro."

Sister Fate said, "I am Wendy Meggett."

And so the names rolled on through the mesquite and iron-weed, past owl and coyote, into the Arizona night.

APPENDIXES

APPENDIX ONE

"THE MYSTERY
OF THE UNIVERSE"

When the moon is nu
Tides running in the gat
Act freaky as a cat
And do what you want to
Says Cleo
Fly to Rio
Or jump on a nag
Play tag
Where others plod
Or dice with God
Or rob a bank
Or walk the plank
Or make a base hit
When they least expect it
Be mad as a Danish hatter
Hitch up your trousers with string
And have a last fling
In the world of dark matter

Thus do go about, about
As if you had a universal goal
Until the charm's wound up
Then drop like Alice down the hole
On a blood-red unseen beam
Into truth too deep too rude
Or curl forever nude
Inside the singular dream
At the setting of the sun
When the hubble-bubble's done

Mea Kalpa
Et cetera

APPENDIX TWO

THE SKULLS

ACE. A pimply-faced redheaded former mailroom clerk who was reprimanded by Mister Touch for trying to force girls into sleeping with him because he was a Neat Looker, the best next to Flash (but only a Steady Breather). He took part in dangerous expeditions, for which service he felt poorly rewarded. In order to gain the attention of pretty but snobbish Cola Face and in collusion with Mystique, who also suffered from unrequited love, he precipitated The Chesapeake Bay Toll Bridge And Tunnel Disaster. He saw the sailboat on the bay.

ADIDAS. Assumed to be OOTLO, although an Aristotelian agnostic adept at advising atrocities (witness his pungent suggestion at Spirit's trial: "Kill the bitch, cut her throat like a chicken!"). Afterward as amicable as anyone, always accommodating, an agreeable amigo. Adidas finally struggled out of the twenty-six letters like a man out of a swamp and emerged again to stand on solid ground as he had done back in Little Italy in the butcher shop, before sinking back into the bog of his addiction again, arriving appropriately at A, and advocating an aggressive alliance against amoral authority. *See* Fire.

ALLIGATOR. Kicked out of the Skulls for holding. Went to the Dragons along with Santo. Wore wraparound shades, a mean motherfucker.

BABY JANE. A white woman in her late forties who had been happily married and talked often about her husband, a car salesman. When they won at Lotto, they moved into the city, drove a Mercedes, and lived in a condo on Park Avenue. A Steady Breather, but a Bad Looker. Couldn't adjust, so became OOTLO. Died to make destiny get what it wanted in The Dorcheat Bayou Disaster.

BAMBU. Black girl Barber of the Skulls, though scarcely a Good Looker. According to Ace (but he said this about all the women who wouldn't sleep with him and therefore about most women), she was dumb. Killed in The Dragon Attack when she peered around a doorway to see if her boyfriend Riot was in danger. Informed that hair was getting out of hand, Mister Touch talked Pretty Puss into taking her place. *See* Pretty Puss.

BLACK PIXIE. Huge black bad-looking Breather For Real who loved to eat and drink sodas all day. Wore stockings, hats, and red dresses, waiting "for that big black buck who gonna get me outta all this here fucking mess, girl." Helped serve meals and secretly taught Cancer Two how to cook, especially chicken, and deplored the torrents of paprika he shook down on almost everything they ate.

BLUE MAGIC. The Chinese Thomas Edison of the Skulls whose knowledge of electricity was elementary, yet who discovered the loss of button batteries and fought the light-bulb epidemic in the fight against darkness and who nearly destroyed time on earth. Potential assistant to Harold in the future. Taught Guts the physics of a battery.

BOBBY LOVES IT. A small goateed black who died of a bronchial infection of unknown etiology.

BONES. A few miles out of Gaffney, South Carolina, someone in Car Seven noticed the old man was dead, sitting upright, withered like a raisin in the sun.

BOO BANG. A streaked blonde from the Bronx who worked as a countergirl at McDonald's. Superstar once said, "Boo Bang is so dumb that if you told her this was just a nightmare, she would stay up all night waiting for it to end." Nearly a Blindie but a Breather For Real, she loved to dance. Responsible for Web's death, since his love for her made him so joyful he ate himself into obesity and his grief at losing her to the second floor of a Texas courthouse made him so forgetful that he forgot about eating and died of malnutrition.

THE BOY WHO DOESN'T SPEAK OUR LANGUAGE. A healthy twelve-year-old called by Stay High "a linguistic genius." Was he? Edzu hoto moo. Later confessed his duplicity, which perhaps surprised only Stay High, his admirer, mentor, and student. To celebrate the boy's entry for real into the Skulls, the main man named him Star Three, and to punish him for putting everyone on, Mister Touch ordered him to write the official Skull Diary. *See* Star One and Star Two.

BROTHER LOVE. Elder brother of Rerun and Rerun. Carried a gun and a machete and drew his blind charges along by a six-foot length of rope tied to his belt like something out of Samuel Beckett (an insight supplied on the trip by Sag, who knew her theater). Joined the Skulls only long enough to get from Atlanta to Birmingham.

CAKE.. Old black woman who was a better looker and stronger breather than many of the Skulls, yet who didn't want to leave home and so was escorted up to East Twenty-eighth Street, where she had a room in the large apartment of her computer-programming "Eldest."

CANCER ONE. Not mentioned in text. A bad-looking poor-breathing Irish racetrack tout and thief who had spent most of his adult life at Aqueduct giving tips and lifting wallets. Could not stop stealing in the Club House. Snitched canes from Blindies and spitcans from Wheezers, neither of which he yet needed. Excused himself by saying it was only a way of keeping in practice — and always returned what he pinched. People liked his racetrack stories and regretted his sudden death by choking on a hastily swallowed piece of stringy meat during a feast that had resulted from a police horse wandering into Washington Square Park and getting potted by a couple of trigger-happy Skulls before the dogs managed to catch up with the poor-winded animal, which must have galloped for its life all the way from an uptown police stable no longer safe. That feast was erased from memory. Because Cancer One died of food, IRT named the Skull Cook Cancer Two.

CANCER TWO. The Skull Cook who because of his Hungarian background was addicted to the excessive use of paprika. Became adept at cooking huge stews filled with shrapnel. A brawny young blond Good Looker and Breather For Real, fanatically devoted to his art. Black Pixie taught him a thing or two about down-home southern cooking.

CHIBO. Small, wheezing, bad-looking Latino whose chief distinction was having a lovely woman like Nando take care of him when his health got bad for real. After he descended to Wheezer, she left him and searched for someone else to help down the path to helplessness.

CHICO. Big Hispanic bad-looking but for-real-breathing hunter of wildlife who liked to eat what he brought back, giving him a paunch. It hung over his pants so far that when he and King Super Kool stopped in the woods for a leak, he couldn't see the lil amigo down there and often peed on his shoes. Prepared to follow Stifle into the desert, because the man released from silence had become his guru. *See* King Super Kool.

COCO. Poor-breathing bad-looking young woman with two front teeth missing, mottled brown skin, and dreadlocks. Gave birth to Snake's first child, a normal boy who was named Rattler in honor of the Latin Romeo. When she could muster the breath, she was the best singer among the Skulls.

COLA FACE. A smashing blond steady-breathing bad-looking hairdresser, sought after by many male Skulls. Passionate for recognition, which made her lack of confidence seem like conceit. Especially harassed by Ace with his red hair and inferiority complex. Unaccustomed to being called "white pussy" by The Fierce Rabbit, she reported the insult to Mister Touch, but the greatest insult was to die with Ace in The Chesapeake Bay Toll Bridge And Tunnel Disaster.

COUGAR. Tall, muscular, for-real-breathing good-to-bad-looking black dude who had worked in the mailroom of the *New York Times*. Accompanied Riot on the reconnaissance mission to locate the Dragons. Lamed by a dog bite, he became morose and bitter until becoming Official Supply Officer for the trip. During the carving of IRT's Vision, he discovered in himself a talent for sculpting.

DADDY RICH. A bad boy, pallid and red-eyed, probably a Good Looker but a Poor Breather, who begged for sanctuary in Dallas along with Snootchy Fingers. Became a devoted member of The Rabbit's Set because it afforded him a chance to have some fun, which meant tweaking on crack brought secretly from Dallas. Died in The Driveby At Portal, having been stung by an insectile projectile, which broke his concentration at the wheel of a careening Mercedes and sent it crashing into a store. *See* Snootchy Fingers.

DEADLEG. A good-looking old white Wheezer who had fond memories of an upper-middle-class life. A few miles out of Anderson, South Carolina, he demanded to be left on the road where he said goodbye to a world he no longer enjoyed while sitting under a tree with a half dozen bottles of Old Bushmill's Irish whiskey for companions.

DEE BOX. Tall, good-looking steady-breathing black chick who worked in the Club House dispensary. Through the journey a number of conscientious Skull males worked assiduously to get her pregnant, explaining patiently to Dee Box that it was their God-given duty to repopulate the world.

DIAMOND DOLL. A short fat aged Jewish lady with bowed legs like a chicken's wishbone. When a man helped her get around, she said, "Thank you, handsome," whatever he looked like. She was a loyal friend to suffering Snow and stood at one end of the spectrum of friendship, preteen Golden Girl at the other. When they carved the ant on the desert cliff, Diamond Doll heartily approved. "My niece, a go-getter, at Columbia she was in spiders, she traveled and did things you wouldn't believe."

DO IT TO IT. He did it to Sugar. A Neat Looker and a Caucasian who was once a whiz at computer games like "Starflight" and "UMS" and the "Ultima" series, he read recipes to Cancer Two. Died in The Dorcheat Bayou Disaster. *See* Sugar.

DO YOU THING. A Good Looker from her sky blue eyes and a Steady Breather from a chest that had Skull males panting in lust. Tall, leggy, copper-skinned beauty of Swedish descent who came out of the West and made of Stay High a scholar and a lover for real.

DOCTOR LEO. An insurance salesman who had convinced himself that his company would be forced to pay enormous claims on policies he had written for victims of V 70. Transferring blame for the holocaust from himself to DNA — that *base* genetic code — he went mad learning about biochemistry. Disliked and yet admired by Stay High for his brilliant work on "The Mystery of the Universe," he was followed around by Stifle until Stifle regained his sanity. Doctor Leo's X-rated reassessment of "The Mystery" on Christmas Eve was considered scandalous by certain Skulls, definitive by others.

DRAGON. One of the Original Seven Skulls. Heavyset black who got slashed across the face by a small Latino, Lil Joint, in an argument over *Madame Bovary*. A steady-breathing Good Looker, he would have been valuable on the trip, but he was killed by a burst of gunfire in the attack of a West Side gang that had misappropriated his name.

THE DREAM QUEEN. Lanky long-jawed sallow-faced woman

with light green eyes and a long fierce nose and lank brown hair and a Ph.D. in biochemistry. Taught at NYU. Their "treasure of the mind" is what IRT called her. She wrote "The Mystery of the Universe," which Mister Touch ignored at first but eventually came to believe contained a universe of mysterious meaning.

EAGLE. Wearing a tattered yarmulke, the good-looking poor-breathing tailor spent most of his days praying. Defended Spirit In The Dark at her trial. Used Talmudic logic, did Eagle. He discovered Harold in Pelahatchie and at first thought the sick TV repairman was a dybbuk.

EVIL EYE. A neat-looking steady-breathing not really evil black queen who made the big mistake of publicly telling The Fierce Rabbit to get lost, thereby enabling Wishbone and Yo Boy to prove their loyalty to El Viejo by beating and raping and murdering her in a Civil War town. A complicated story and a tragic one, since all that Evil Eye had ever wanted was to stay out of toll booths and away from crowds and live sensually with whoever for the moment caught her naughty (but not evil) eye.

E.Z. Not as "easy" as male Skulls always hoped. Helped in kitchen. For a time was Hoss's girl and wore a floppy felt hat, earrings dangling on six-inch platinum strands, wowee, man. When dinner was ready, this good-looking pretty Breather For Real went around purring, "Dinnah comin up, kiddies." Took in the first pet, the dog Lil Devil, whom she loved more than any man, although one of the latter breed finally bred her, in spite of her oft repeated public announcement: "I don't want to visit no more with none of them."

THE FIERCE RABBIT. Tall, slim-waisted, broad-shouldered, he wore an old-style afro that looked like an iron corona. His health was problematical — no one knew what kind of breather and looker he was because no one dared to ask him. Could never recall not having been angry. He believed that the Black Man at the Universal Center had chosen him for prophet, judge, and executioner. In league with Evil Eye until she vanished like Thomas Becket. The Fierce (not everyone would agree) Rabbit created The Rabbit's Set: five wimps, two druggies, two cholos, and himself. Died on an anthill, bravely. Would have been unmourned by the Skulls had they known what happened to him.

FIRE. Thin, with long hair and a passion for jumpsuits, gold chains, and pixie shoes. A cautious, critical, restrained former editor in a publishing house. Her name was ironic if you equate "fire" with "hot" and "passion" and "impulse," because Fire was cerebral and cold and felt inflamed only when the friction of boredom rubbed her sticks together — typical of mischievous IRT to misname someone when not assigning a name to grow into. The Touch Tapes suggest, however, that Fire was not so cerebral as to pass up opportunities for passionate quickies, let alone more lasting relationships, so perhaps in this instance it was IRT who had been suckered and Fire was one of those who became her name. She became leader of the Opposition Party after the tornado effectively ended the political career of The Terrible Ten. This uptight gal of forty-something became for real a flirtatious frenzied factious femme fatale who, as a former editor of books, grew enamored of a man of letters, adorable (although alphabetically addicted) Adidas, with whom her name was linked not only romantically but politically as well, because the heat they generated together was enough to start more than one kind of conflagration.

FLASH. Web's slim lover, who disliked fat guys and really liked slim guys like Spic, who didn't like him. A Neat Looker, best in the Skulls. Fancy dude too who sported a bushy blond mustache and long sideburns. With pendant ruby earrings asway on his elfin ears, he drove off on a Honda to reconnoiter and never returned, taking the Celtic Turok on a ride into forever.

FUNKADELIC. A Neat Looker but also a confirmed illiterate. Played the part of Polonius in the Skull production of *Hamlet,* which is one reason why it flopped. Had himself dreadlocks and a leather jacket and silver chains and one earring, bro, so he should have been like some kind of bold stud but was for real a well-meaning harmless wimp and a sitting duck for someone as remorseless as Mystique, who miscalculated his ability to drive a guided missile, especially after being stung by a winged insect.

FUTURA. A plain-looking but good-looking secretary from Queens with a receding chin but pretty brown hair. In spite of being a Wheezer, she caught the eye of Superstar and became his white queen for real. Later they entered the Garden of Eden together in Chewacla State Park, Alabama.

GATOR. Not to be confused with Alligator. Tall skinny fisherman discovered by the Skulls one day happily doing his only thing, fishing, in a Louisiana stream. V 70 for him meant an eternal vacation during which he could fish to his heart's content. Probably a Breather For Real and a Good Looker, but only the fish would know for sure. Treated the Skulls to a gourmet feast, then left for better streams.

GOLDEN GIRL. An undersized malnourished poor-breathing bad-looking white preteen who had mysteriously survived on her own for nearly a year before coming out of the park mists one day, frail, haggard, uncommunicative, so uptight that she could never talk about fear. She often sat with The Ladies as if conjuring a mother she could never mention. Befriended Snow when push came to shove, and her courage, loyalty, and endurance suggested why she had made it on her own for almost a year in a city that had forgotten how to nurture anything except fierce puppies.

GUTS. Middle-aged paunchy mentor of Toe who had survived the grief of V 70 by accompanying his student into the desert. Joined the Skulls in an attempt to live again. In exchange for an interpretation of "The Mystery of the Universe," the Skulls helped him to stop smoking. It should be noted that Guts wanted another go at "The Mystery," hoping to incorporate into its meaning the theory of GUM (the grand unified monopole), yet another attempt at unification in which GUM is an inevitable consequence of GUTS and involves a monopole mass that is about 10^{16} times heavier than a proton, making this particle as heavy as an amoeba, a comparison from biology that Doctor Leo grudgingly admired. GUM was a concept so theoretical that Hoss feared it might detach Guts from reality again like a charmed quark from a proton in accelerator collisions, and the Skulls would lose a potential engineer to the study of something no thinking survivor would deem practical.

HAROLD. A gruff, neat-looking, poor-breathing TV repairman who also knew plumbing and whose life was saved by Jesus Mary and whose crankiness was mellowed by her love until someday he would become, along with her, one of "the Skull treasures."

HITLER. Never worried about the name. Probably never thought about it. A Neat Looker and Steady Breather who had a dream in which he rode a stick of dynamite through the sky. His friendly and exhilarating dream came true in a Georgia town. A slightly built boy who wore a mustache that looked like Charlie Chaplin's in *The Great Dictator* — modeled after the mustache of his self-effacing father, an accountant for Maybelline Cosmetics.

HOSS. Steady-breathing neat-looking good-looking black dude with a mellifluous voice, a degree in economics, and jive enough to lay many of the Skull females end to end before they knew what was • happening. Second-in-command of the Skulls at the outset of the journey because of his skill at surviving in a white man's world. Fate and Queen Sexy were going to force him into "being all that he could be" — to paraphrase an ad he worked on for an ad agency before V 70 Struck.

IRT. A short stocky poor-breathing good-looking black bongo player who began the post–V 70 period by looting his way down Fifth Avenue and ended by saving a host of survivors from themselves. Jivy patriarch of the Skulls. Probably a genius who certainly understood ants and people.

JESUS MARY SAVE SOULS. A tall redheaded Irish student nurse who specialized in geriatrics. Had a capacity for undertaking any medical emergency whatsoever. Just ask the wounded survivors of The Dragon Attack. Also see entry for Snow. It was said that "like a kilo of uncut heroin, she was worth killing for." She shone brightly in the Skull Heaven, awaiting the ascendancy of Harold, who would join her there after working his electronic miracles; maybe someday their child would help them form a constellation.

JIVE TURKEY. Wiry son of a Korean greengrocer. Official Photographer of the Skulls. By red flashlight glow in a small-town photo shop he developed group portraits that had the grainy look of old daguerreotypes. Assistant to Sphinx on the IRT's Vision project.

KING RAT. A small Hispanic who was on guard duty in the Club House during The Dragon Attack. His neck was broken while he was ogling a pretty woman with his good-looking cyes.

KING SUPER KOOL. A neat-looking little black Wheezer. Indispensable on pharmaceutical expeditions. Later became a great hunter in combination with Chico. Gunned down countless dinners for the Skulls. As his prowess improved so did his lungs, until he was steady enough to drive a truck. He would have followed his guru Stifle into the desert or anywhere. *See* Chico.

LIL DEVIL. A mutt. Found and befriended by E.Z., whose acquisition of him led to other pets being gathered in by the traveling Skulls, until the caravan, bedecked by garish paintings of insects, roared gaily through the Southwest like Noah's Ark. (Ralph the Parrot would have been listed too had he not been so arrogant and abysmally mean-spirited that people ignored him and somehow left him behind in a village; whenever his name was mentioned, people pretended they had never heard of him.)

LIL GUY. Steady-breathing neat-looking shit who spied for the West Side Dragon gang and scarcely carried the Skull name long enough to die with it.

LIL JOINT. Appointed Official Exterminator for the trip. He wielded an insect-repellent spraycan instead of the knife that he had cut Dragon with during an argument over the meaning of *Madame Bovary* (Lil Joint defended the book). A tiny good-looking steady-breathing Latino who ultimately refused to be seduced by Mystique into declaring that all men were dumbbells and cads.

MELODY. An advantaged white woman in her late forties, but a poor-breathing Blindie who often played bridge (someone, usually preteen Golden Girl, whispered the cards to her) and drank tea with the other Ladies. She stayed behind in the Club House to enjoy the solitude by herself.

MISTER LUCKY. His miraculous escape from death made him a reluctant legend in his time. A scrawny old bad-looking Wheezer, he returned for a few magical moments to a state of infancy during The North Central Plains Disaster. Superstitious Skulls claimed that he "got the power," and therefore fussed over his needs to his profound disgust, illustrating the proposition that you cannot make a saint out of a cranky old party whose only luck in life was staying alive.

MISTER TOUCH. Tall, red-bearded, blind, good-looking former Wall Street crook who inherited the Skull leadership from his idol, IRT. One morning in Arizona, thinking of his pregnant Spirit, he threw his head back and bellowed for joy, and for this act alone, to say nothing of leading them across America, he would always be revered by the Skulls.

MYSTIQUE. A Good, almost a Neat, Looker, and a Breather For Real, she was a medical assistant to Jesus Mary in the Club House and a mistress to Mister Touch until his Spirit appeared on the scene. A beautiful woman, tall, with honey-colored hair and complicated emotions. Unaccustomed to rejection, she became wildly promiscuous (her ardor for vengeance even frightening Snake). After destiny had caught up with some of Mystique's accomplices, it finally caught up with her too in the Texas Schoolbook Depository in Dallas, the details of which are amply available in the text.

NANDO. A steady-breathing good-looking tall and attractive Chinese girl, a liberal arts student at Hunter College and the girlfriend of Mister Touch when he took the path from Bad Looker to Blindie. She then became the lover of Chibo when he descended from Poor Breather to Wheezer. Make of this psychological pattern what you will.

NO NAME. Looker and breather of unlimited potential for real. Six feet four inches of adolescent power and innocence and depression when he was found shell-shocked in the Magnolia Motel after the Second Battle of Vicksburg. The drowned look of his young face nearly sank the Skulls, lowering them into a quagmire of morbidity until Sweet Walk sweetwalked into his life and made of him the Hope of Tomorrow.

OOTHI. Not a character but the collected presence of writers and thinkers down the ages, so that when the Skulls quoted One Of The Hip Immortals they were acknowledging the historical present of all past literature in a way that perhaps even T. S. Eliot might not object to.

OOTLO. One Of The Lost Ones: the designation for approximately ten percent of the Skulls. Guilt for having survived robbed some of them of the best reason for surviving: to go on with their lives. Others struggled weakly in the sticky spiderweb of bad memory. Obsessed by unspoken fears, displaying a compendium of symptoms, they lived on the periphery of the Skull world, squinting their way from place to place, tolerated and loved for still being able to breathe. Sometimes, in a fit of miraculous joy, they pushed back the darkness as if it were an iron door, emerging for a while to smile and laugh and talk until the black hand of depression cupped itself around them again, drawing them back inside, where they simply held on, clutching their waning lives and memories, existing without distinction, except at night when their wheezing and sobbing disturbed the sleep of others.

PAPO. Bad-looking but steady-breathing Hispanic who used to win prizes in dance contests. V 70 cut down the length of his performances but not their quality.

PATCH. Almost a Breather For Real, but on the other hand a Bad Looker with "fantastic boobs," according to some Skull males who shall be nameless. Took Snake from Coco who had got pregnant and in turn lost Snake to Pearl because she herself got caught. She wanted to raise her child as a Spanish Catholic and often tried to enlist sympathy for her cause, but few listened. One of the few Skulls who out of religious principle refused to participate in the fiesta honoring IRT's Vision, which she felt was blatantly pagan. Patch would hate ants until the end of her days.

PAYBACK. A crusty poor-breathing seafaring Bad Looker who made a single contribution to the Skulls: the Morse Code. Thirteen tattoos, a mean temper, a foul mouth, and great tales of the sea for anyone who cared to listen.

PEARL. Good-looking vacant-eyed sweet-faced Poor Breather on the verge of becoming a Wheezer. In spite of limited lung capacity, she was a girlfriend of The Fierce Rabbit and then of Snake, having taken that Latin scumbag (as described by certain women) from Patch, who had taken him from Coco. Pearl proved the adage that where there's a will there's a way.

PRETTY PUSS. A white bad-looking teenage Breather For Real from the Dalton School. Summered in the Hamptons, said things were "fresh" and "awesome." Mourned her parents, her dog Socrates, her tennis, and doing Bloomingdale's. Became the Skull Barber, tagged along, got plump and healthy and somehow pregnant.

PUTZ. A middle-aged bad-looking Wheezer who died as he had lived — in close and intimate conversation with Shadow over the progress of their recovery from the effects of V 70. Died in The North Central Plains Disaster. Wore conservative ties. *See* Shadow.

QUEEN SEXY. Having trailed the Skulls for days on her motorbike, this attractive blond lawyer from Cleveland with good lungs and eyes no worse than 42/20 finally confronted the Skulls in the Texas town of Crow. Heroine of The Two Terrible Texans Incident. Became the lover of Soda after discovering there was more to share with her than a terrible memory. Became second-in-command to Hoss. *See* her commentary on the Skulls in Chapter 65.

RATTLER. Child of Coco and Snake. A Neat Looker and a Breather For Very Real, as can be attested by his squawling, which was music to the ears of hopeful Skulls.

RERUN. The blind, steady-breathing brother of Rerun, both of whom left the Skulls in company with their older brother when they reached Birmingham, Alabama, their home town. *See* Brother Love and Rerun.

RERUN. The blind, steady-breathing brother of Rerun, both of whom left the Skulls in company with their older brother when they reached Birmingham, Alabama, their home town. See Brother Love and Rerun.

RIOT. Neat-looking poor-breathing Eyetalian lover of black Bambu, who used to gasp "O Honey O Honey" in his arms. Accompanied by Cougar on a dangerous mission to New York City's West Side. Never recovered emotionally from Bambu's death in The Dragon Attack. Plotted against Mister Touch, egged on by Sag, until both conspirators met their end together in a Texas town on The Day Mister Lucky Got Lucky. Riot might have become a lover again rather than a plotter had he lived, because his nature was essentially romantic.

SAG. Wore classic black Chanel suits with brass buttons, knew a great deal about outdoor gardening, needlepoint, and the theater, and often recalled her solid Republican background, her husband, and their three grown children lost to V 70. A Poor Breather but a Good Looker. Possessed the temperament of a martyr, the intellect of a debater, the fury of a rebel. Swore vengeance against Mister Touch when he refused to change the name that IRT had maliciously (for what other adverb can apply?) christened her with when she entered the Skulls. Openly used her old name, Helen, as a protest after The Dragon Attack and Spirit's probation. Along with The Fierce Rabbit and Riot, she was a principal critic of the Skull world, until high winds blew her out of it. Shanti Shanti. Being in Riot's arms was her secret desire. It was granted finally — an embrace of death.

SALSA SAL. A wizened featherweight little bad-looking steady breather of a Chinese woman recently over from Hong Kong when V 70 Struck. Her English was so rudimentary that some people suggested if anyone could decipher the jargon of The Boy Who Doesn't Speak Our Language, Salsa Sal could do it as further proof, if needed, of the perversity of cosmic logic. What she had learned in the United States was the joy of chewing gum. Her gray hair pulled back in a bun, her frail body clothed in the blue jacket and black trousers of a Cantonese peasant, she was self-contained, placid, indifferent to the universe except for those gifts of gum

she accepted gratefully from any Skull nice enough and thoughtful enough to get them for her in supermarkets across the land.
She contributed a maxim to Queen Sexy's rehabilitation.

SALT NOODY. A visitor from South India, she had entered the
United States only a few weeks before V 70 Struck. Soon afterward it was rumored that she had become one of Hoss's girls.
Baseless (Doctor Leo had not been a Skull when this word was spoken by someone who shall be nameless and so its utterance had not
therefore started an incident), inaccurate, felonious charge. She
remained, in her sari, a virgin and didn't give up her Indian intactness to Skull lust until, having been convinced by time and association with her companions that a sensible Brahmin marriage
was out of the question, she surrendered to opportunity and passion and did the nasty with Hoss. Even so, she was the Skulls' favorite visitor from overseas, self-effacing and gentle, and every
day with some of Cancer Two's paprika she put on her forehead a
tilaki dot for good luck and protection from the evil eye (but not
from Evil Eye). To do penance for her short-lived romance with
Hoss, she thought about joining the Ventana band and going into
the desert, where she could meditate under the disciplined eye
of her guru, Stifle, and regain contact with the thousand gods of
her ancestors. She would beg their forgiveness for her sexual
transgressions. When that didn't pan out, Salt Noody crawled
back into Hoss's bed and became the third president's mistress
again.

SANTO. West Side raider killed in The Dragon Attack. Former
Skull who had been thrown out for holding.

SATAN. A white wheezing but good-looking former toy salesman
who lived on his memories of combat in Korea. Killed by Dragons while remembering how he had once climbed Heartbreak
Ridge.

SEND EM BACK TO AFRICA. Six and a half feet of coal-black
and barrel-chested good-looking steady-breathing bodyguard.
On duty twenty-four hours a day every day. Fancy dresser, partial
to white silk suits, white ties, white shoes, black opaque shades,
and a one-button jacket with rolled lapel. Louis Farrakhan style
but without the politics. Breathtakingly loyal. Died on the job.

SHADOW. A bad-looking middle-aged Wheezer who died in The
North Central Plains Disaster, facing his friend Putz across the

rubble. It was always Putz and Shadow. Or Shadow and Putz. Like a vaudeville team or a play by Samuel Beckett (which is what Sag, who knew her theater, used to suggest, for although she hated her own name she was not above making fun of the names of others). What had Shadow done in life before coming to the Skulls? Probably what he had done after coming to them — not much.

SHAG. Small Latino doper. Good-looking and for-real-breathing operator who split in Dallas where the grass was greener.

SHITHEAD. Big black poor-breathing but good-looking dispensary guard. Died defending it during The Dragon Attack and took Marty, a chief raider and one mean motherfucker, with him.

SHY GUY. Poor-breathing Shy Guy passed over to Blindie on the trip. Once he accepted this loss of status, the timid black kid, powerful from the waist up, would earn his way by lifting what others could not. Atlas of the Skulls.

SISTER FATE. Inveterate traveler in her girlhood dreams, she became one for real as a woman. Stately, aristocratic, haunted by memories of places, she found happiness again when the caravan set sail from New York. Through her stories of travel she earned the title of Bard of the Skulls.

SISTER LOVE. Superstar's girlfriend who died of an undiagnosed bronchial infection. Her death released Superstar to follow his Futura.

SKY HOOK. A Lakers fan who had only seen them play on television. Loved Chevy cars because between breaks in games they were touted as the Heartbeat of America. A disadvantaged kid out of the Bushwick section of Brooklyn, he had an eager grin and never said anything worse than "shit," except when referring to the Celtics, his beloved Lakers' chief opponents in the golden days, whom he called "no-good motherfuckers from Boston." His test flight with Mystique aborted.

SLUGGO. Played Latin music as a Skull deejay, but his heart wasn't in it. Wanted to be a jazz-fusion pianist like the Brazilian Jose Bertrami. Worshiped the trio Azymuth. This misnamed Dutch boy became one of Mystique's designated hitters.

SNAKE. Snake-hipped Latin scumbag lover whose thick mustache drove the ladies wild. Believed utterly in the maxim "En la variedad está el gusto." This love of variety extended not from something like spicy food to women but only from woman to woman, because for Snake there was only one sort of appetite that counted. He worked hard at only one activity — repopulating the world. A bad-looking Breather For Real, which he had to be, considering his profession. Carried a backpack filled with hundred-dollar bills taken from a bank he broke into (no alarm went off). During the trip he ran to the main man with the terrible news that someone (surely a vengeful woman) had ripped open his pack and taken the money. "Don't worry," Mister Touch assured him, "we'll get you another backpack and load it up with thousand-dollar bills." Even so, Snake ran to more than one woman for solace, slithering toward the rendezvous, his long sideburns and glittering eyes giving him the sleek portentous look of a cobra rising from its coils.

SNOOKY. A steady-breathing but bad-looking woman without luck. Always considered OOTLO by everyone. Her baby was born dead. Her only enthusiasm was for Jamaica, land of her childhood, which she would describe dreamily as "da good ol' place." Killed by a knife thrust during The Dragon Attack.

SNOOTCHY FINGERS. A bad-news white boy from Dallas who, along with Daddy Rich, joined the Skulls by appealing to the main man's generosity of spirit, because as Spirit observed, he would never turn his back on a stray. Snootchy Fingers agreed with The Fierce Rabbit's assessment of honkies, perhaps because the cowardice, depravity, and intemperance of nature attributed by The Rabbit to all white people were profoundly present in himself — a no-good white trash from Dallas. *See* Daddy Rich.

SNOW. A white-haired poor-breathing bad-looking fat cat from Park Avenue whose dentist wasn't available when a lower right cuspid went bad. Her suffering energized two people, one young and one old, into showing her the path to freedom from the past. Became a manicurist for the Skulls.

SODA. Wore an afro and worked as a nurse because of her good-looking eyes, which in the pre–V 70 world she had used as a clerk in a discount pharmacy. One of the three kidnapped women whose travail made them sisters. Offered the gun to Queen Sexy so she could have the honor of finishing off the tall cowboy. Linked by memory to the blonde from Cleveland, Soda learned to share a bedroll with her as well.

SONY BOY. Distinguished by his earphones, which were large and round and as black as his skin. He was never without them. They were clamped to his ears or the metal arms were draped around his neck like a stethoscope or a pair of lobster claws. He was into disco and rap and a little heavy metal like Def Leppard and Vixen. His conversation was usually limited to "Let's boogie," although he did give one prophetic lecture on zouk at the end of the party that celebrated Rattler's birth.

SPAT. A former go-go dancer who was so depressed by being a Wheezer that she effectively became a Blindie as well, although she was a Good Looker For Real. One of Hoss's numerous girlfriends. Because of her diminished vital capacity, she proved an easier lover for him than did E.Z. Her problem was dancing while asleep; it made her perpetually tired.

SPHINX. A fortyish good-looking attractive auburn-haired Steady Breather who taught art classes in the Club House and later conceived and carried out the construction of the memorial to her dead lover's wisdom in the Arizona desert.

SPIC. Loved by Flash, who was loved by Web before Web loved Boo Bang. Spic loved no one, but complained of body odor in the Club House corridors, even though Skulls doused themselves often and liberally with cologne. A touchy bad-looking steady-breathing boy of German heritage — his hair like silver, his lips compressed into a perpetual red knot of No. Named strangely by IRT, don't you think? Died of wounds sustained in The Dragon Attack.

SPIRIT IN THE DARK. Neat-looking steady-breathing spy who drove the lead car of the Skull caravan and would someday give birth to a Mark or a Dorothy — take your pick.

SPOON. There is little to say about Spoon — and little known about her — except that she was always around. Mentioned often in The Touch Tapes as the witness to a scene, a member of a crowd, seated here or standing there. Spoon was apparently so filled with curiosity that there was no space left within her for other traits. Imagine someone elbowing and shouldering perpetually forward — not aggressively but sliding in between until finally making it to the front rank. If the center of activity shifted from one place to another, she'd be there somehow to watch almost before the participants arrived. I came, I saw, but never conquered. That was Spoon.

STAR ONE. Died of pneumonia or something like it long before the

Skulls left the Club House. So young that someone said, "Hell-bells, he probably never even had a hard-on yet," but died anyway, because whoever said life was fair? In his honor a quiet Polish kid was named after him. *See* Star Two.

STAR TWO. Deserted the Skulls for a Polish butcher shop uptown. As someone suggested, "To die among the hanging sausages of his ancestors."

STAR THREE. See The Boy Who Doesn't Speak Our Language.

STAY HIGH. Why IRT persisted in glorifying drugs by naming Skulls after drugs or after activities associated with them is hard to fathom, since he did everything else to discourage their use. But no one ever asked consistency of IRT's hobgoblin mind. At any rate, Stay High was a thin ascetic young Jew who wore glasses mostly from habit, since they badly needed correction and did little for his bad-looking eyes. A Breather For Real, he learned Harlem dance steps for anthropological reasons but his talent for getting down on the dance floor would ultimately win him his Texas sweetie when lectures failed. Ph.D., Columbia. Linguist who failed with The Boy Who Doesn't Speak Our Language. A literary critic, who did valuable work on the "The Mystery of the Universe." Spent one summer at the Çatal Hüyük digs, where he excavated a clay goddess who reminded him incestuously of his mother. Love for Do You Thing steadied his intellect and gave him the determination to become a bona fide archeologist in the ancient caves of Arizona, although his first task was to start a school and thereby honor markers held by Hoss in the names of IRT and Mister Touch.

STIFLE. Breather For Real but a Bad Looker, he suffered from alternate bouts of garrulity and silence. Knew a great deal about stationery and yoga. Galvanized by the moving speech of a brutalized woman into describing his own lovely wife whom he could not bear to lose even when he had lost her two years ago. He gave up a no-win friendship with loony Doctor Leo, started to practice yoga again, and became an overnight sensation as practicing Guru of the Skulls.

STITCH. Chief Automotive Engineer of the Skulls who had learned what he knew in a gas station. Responsibility turned this gangling good-looking young fellow into a creative, energetic leader. Indeed, a stitch in time saves nine.

SUGAR. Energetic, cute, bad-looking steady-breathing mistress of Do It To It. Otherwise quiet, retiring — well, lazy. A newcomer who was killed in The Dragon Attack on the Skull dispensary. Mister Touch said of her, "A together girl who didn't beg to stay with us, didn't expect something for nothing, just went to work," which she actually didn't do at all; the reports about her industriousness were utterly falsified. The thing was she was liked so much that people did her work for her. Do It To It never had another girl-friend, but spent all his time after her death in the Skull kitchen until he died in The Dorcheat Bayou Disaster.

SUGAR HEAD. Another drug-related christening. At any rate, he was a short, wheezing, good-looking Latino. Friend of Zap's, which is one fact that distinguished him from everyone else. Died in The Chesapeake Bay Toll Bridge And Tunnel Disaster. *See* Zap.

SUNOCO. A jivy bad-looking Chinese Breather For Real who was, like, very into music. Friend of Sony Boy even though their tastes were different. He couldn't stand disco, but was mad for progres-sive jazz. Burned candles like a good Buddhist while meditating to Bird and Trane and Sun Ra. Refused to speak to Sluggo, the Azy-muth freak, who refused to speak to him either. Died in The Dor-cheat Bayou Disaster.

SUPERSTAR. A womanizing aggressive handsome black poor-looking Steady Breather who found his queen in Futura from Queens and became a superstar for real in the wilds of an Ala-bama forest.

SWEAR TO GOD. Assistant chef in Cancer Two's kitchen. It was not stated in the text, but in fact Swear To God made frequent if unsuccessful attempts to tone down the amount of paprika in the stews. Kidnapped, raped, and sodomized by the Texas cowpokes. Became mute until the death of Mister Touch, after which this small thin pale poor-breathing bad-looking Irish girl burst into a bitter diatribe against injustice and would continue to harangue about the injustice of life until her own ended. In fantasy she often appealed to the pope, but he never helped even there, proving her fear of complete injustice in the world was well founded.

SWEET THING. A cold tense gray-haired good-looking Poor Breather who caught Spirit In The Dark reading medical labels. Her snitching was her only claim to fame in the History of the Skulls. A committee went to Mister Touch during the trip and

with malicious intent requested him to change Sweet Thing's
name to Snitch, which was what she was, but the main man felt it
might be confused with Stitch or Bitch and in any case would not
do Sweet Thing or anyone else any good. Died in The North Central Plains Disaster, having become one of The Terrible Ten.

SWEET WALK. Good-looking gorgeous-looking hip-swinging
steady-breathing Chinese gal who was mundanely businesslike
about life and sex until she and No Name got it on for real. There-
after she was the soulmate of a leader of the future.

TAKI. Died of a bronchial infection of unknown etiology.

TANGY. A big rawboned Scandinavian aerobics instructor who
breathed like a Breather For Real. Her sea-blue eyes saw better
than almost any other pair in the Skulls. When she was on guard
duty, people breathed easier. Turned out to be a lifeguard too,
enabling Mystique to be born again before dying twice. Tangy
drove a truck on the journey. In the Arizona desert she revealed a
considerable talent for chiseling stone.

TIMBALES. Small-boned goateed Latino who couldn't see stairs as
well as he could climb three flights up into an empty apartment
where he brooded over his loneliness and his common cold among
skeletons and the possibility of ghosts until he braved the terrors
of the park and met a canine destiny.

TITO. Glutton whose capacity for looking and breathing was insig-
nificant compared to his capacity for consuming anything edible
that got in his way. Died in the midst of acute indigestion in The
Chesapeake Bay Toll Bridge And Tunnel Disaster.

TOE. Contributed to the study of the "The Mystery of the Universe," then took both the twenty percent of her that was Indian
and the eighty percent that was not and backpacked with all one
hundred percent into the desert where, apparently, she hobnobbed with the ghosts of Apaches and Navahos who might well
inspire her to contemplate the fractal geometry of clouds or a
black hole which conceivably might suck into itself piles of nuclear
debris like a vacuum sweeper and spit them out again on the other
side of the world in an effort to stimulate the growth of places
where E.T. or E.Z. or T.T. could dwell almost forever and fishes
and ants and anything like you that breathes.

TRIX. Thrown out of the Skulls by IRT for being a black racist even
though she was a neat-looking Breather For Real. Took with her
an old news clipping of a rabble-rousing minister from New York

and kept it in her wallet: a wrinkled, worn, worshiped image of a walruslike fat man with a luxuriant mustache and a fixed expression of inexpressible arrogance. But she was missed for her salty vivid language that could make the halls crackle as if electricity was leaping from one pole to the other.

T.T. No one ever knew for real what the initials stood for, although most people figured they stood for Tina Turner, whom IRT often played on his cassette player. T.T. was a big-butted finger-snapping neat-looking good-looking Steady Breather who seemed always on the verge of breaking out of her existence as a certified airhead among the Skulls and doing something for real with those axle-greased hips and broad shoulders and those long chocolate-colored hands instead of just using them to fit another tape into a cassette player. She was always around, somewhat like Spoon — grinning, expectant, doing nothing.

TUROK. A shaggy blond giant from Minnesota and frequent lover of E.Z., though he had no exclusive rights there in spite of his steady breathing. A Good Looker who liked to shoot dogs. Had an infantryman's heart, but pleaded at Spirit In The Dark's trial for the Skulls to show mercy. Went with Flash on a reconnaissance mission from which neither returned.

VENUS GIRL. A stocky Japanese Wheezer who helped when she could (could be seen bending over a held whisk broom and dustpan, trying with her bad-looking eyes to find dirt somewhere), and throughout the entire trip never once complained.

WEB. Physically strong. A good-to-bad-looking Russian-born Breather For Real who grew fat when in love, so that his disgusted lovers rejected him. Grew fat for a man and then thin for a woman and thin again when she was left on the second floor of a courthouse. *See* Flash and Boo Bang. Web's heart gave out finally because his weight fluctuated wildly — like the stock market during rumors of a change in interest rates. Died in Las Cruces, New Mexico, while sipping a Coke.

WIGGY OF EVERYWHERE. Petite pale poor-breathing bad-looking Staten Island girl who loved pretty clothes and jewelry but who couldn't distinguish between the costume stuff and the stuff people got in Harry Winston's. Died of wounds sustained in The Dragon Attack and was cremated in a spectacular outfit, selected with loving care by her friends.

WISE ASS. Called by The Fierce Rabbit "the dumbest nigger I ever seen." But an excellent driver. For some reason never revealed to anyone, one fateful day he was riding in Car Four, driven by wheezing Wizard Brown, instead of driving Car Ten as he usually did. Perhaps he changed cars because fate had whispered seductively in his ear, "Come on, Wise Ass, for oncet take a chance on some other dude driving," and so did he perish in The Dorcheat Bayou Disaster.

WISHBONE. Aptly named, because when this cholo follower of Yo Boy finally died, it was by having his backbone snapped like a wishbone when people make a wish after the sort of grandiose Thanksgiving meal a disadvantaged kid like Wishbone had never enjoyed.

WIZARD BROWN. Although a Poor Breather and only a Good-to-Bad Looker, he took over Car Four after Hitler went up in a dream of dynamite. Wizard Brown was not brown but pallid white and no wizard, as the text emphatically asserts. Still a virgin at twenty-four years of age, a cross-clutcher and a Bible-beater who liked to get people in a corner and tell them how sinful and how lost and how vicious and how unredeemable and how satanic they were, the critical diatribe ending only with a complete loss of breath, he coughed himself into a Louisiana bayou and took four others with him. *See* Mystique, Do It To It, Sunoco, and Wise Ass.

YO BOY. First appeared with Wishbone under the arch at Washington Square Park, the closest he ever got to the principles of that soldier, statesman, and founding father of the republic. Yo Boy's brother was a bad gangbanger who haunted him until the day he died.

ZAP. Remembered for tying intricate knots in a string that he could hardly see but that would have reminded Toe of superstring theory in a unified concept of the universe, had she known him. Good-looking in the sense of attractiveness, but bad-looking in the sense of seeing, Zap was the white friend of Hispanic Sugar Head. Killed in The Chesapeake Bay Toll Bridge And Tunnel Disaster because he and his friend didn't want to ride in the same car with a nut like Doctor Leo and so died instead in a car driven by a nut like Ace. *See* Sugar Head.

The
Skull

Los Angeles

Phoenix

Tucson

Tombstone   Las Cruces
Portal   El Paso

IRT's Vision

The Skulls Vote

The Three Sisters Reappear

The Day Mr. Lucky Got Lucky Again

The Three Sisters Disappear

The Day [...] Touch Saved the Day

The Day Mr. Lucky Got Lucky
(North Central Plains Disaster)

Do You Thing

Minus Two and Plus Two Equals Zero

d'Art